Louis L'Amour

FOUR COMPLETE NOVELS

Louis L'Amour

FOUR COMPLETE NOVELS

The Tall Stranger

Kilkenny

Hondo

Showdown at Yellow Butte

AVENEL BOOKS · NEW YORK

This edition is published by Avenel Books,
distributed by Crown Publishers, Inc.,
by arrangement with Fawcett Books Group, CBS Publications, The Consumer
Publishing Division of CBS, Inc.
a b c d e f g h
AVENEL 1980 EDITION

Manufactured in the United States of America

Library of Congress Cataloging in Publication Data

L'Amour, Louis, 1908–
Four complete novels.

CONTENTS: The tall stranger.—Kilkenny.—Hondo.—
Showdown at Yellow Butte.
I. Title.
PZ3.L1937Fo [PS3523.A446] 813'.52 80-17734
ISBN: 0-517-324598

CONTENTS

The Tall Stranger

CHAPTER ONE

WITH SLOW, PONDEROUSLY rhythmical steps the oxen moved, each step a pause and an effort, each movement a deadening drag. Fine white dust hung in a sifting cloud above the wagon train, caking the nostrils of animals and men, blanketing the sides of oxen and horses, dusting a thin film over men and women. And the miles stretched on before them, endless and timeless.

Red-rimmed and bloodshot eyes stared with dazed weariness into that limitless distance before them, seeing nothing to grip the eye or hold the attention. Long since all had been forgotten but the heat, the dust and the aching muscles. Each step lifted a powdery dust, stifling and irritating. It lay a foot deep on the plain, drowning the sparse grass and sage.

Rock Bannon, riding away from the train alone, drew in his steel-dust stallion and turned in the saddle, glancing back at the covered wagons, sixteen of them in the long line with some led horses and a few outriders, yet none who rode so far as himself, and none who appreciated their problems as thoroughly as he did himself.

From where he sat he could not see their faces, but in the days just past he had seen them many itmes, and the expression of each was engraved in his mind. Haggard, worn, hungry for rest and cool water, he knew that in the heart of each there was a longing to stop.

The vision was in them yet, the golden promise of the distant hills, offering a land of milk and honey, the fair and flowering land sought by all wandering peoples of whatever time or place. No hardship could seem too great, no trail too long, no mountain impassable when the vision was upon them.

It was always and forever the same when men saw the future

opening beyond the hills where the sun slept, yet this time the vision must hold meaning; this time the end of the trail must bring realization—for they had brought their women and children along.

All but Rock Bannon. He had neither woman nor child, nor anyone anywhere. He had a horse and a saddle, a ready gun and a mind filled with lore of the trail, and eyes ever fixed on something he wanted, something faint and indistinct in outline, ever distant, yet ever real. Only of late, as he rode alone on the far flank of the wagon train, had that something begun to take shape and outline, and the shape was that of Sharon Crockett.

His somber green eyes slanted back now to the last wagon but one, where the red-gold hair of Sharon on the driver's seat was a flame no dust could dim. In the back of that heavily loaded wagon was Tom Crockett, her father, restless with fever and hurt, nursing a bullet wound in his thigh, a memento of the battle with Buffalo Hide's warriors.

From the head of the train came a long, melodious halloo. Cap Mulholland swung his arm in a great circle, and the lead oxen turned ponderously to swing in the beginning of the circle. Rock touched the gray with his heels and rode slowly toward the wagon train. He was never sure these days as to his reception.

Cap's beard was white with dust as he looked up. Weariness and worry showed in his face. "Rock," he said, "we could sure use a little fresh meat. We're all a mite short on rations, and you seem to be the best hunter among us."

"All right," Rock said. "I'll see what I can do after I get Crockett's wagon in place."

Mulholland's head turned sharply, "Bannon, I'd let that girl alone if I were you. No offense intended, but she ain't your kind. I ain't denyin' you've been a sight of help to us. In fact, I don't know what we'd have done without you, and we're glad you came along. But Sharon Crockett's another story. Her pa's bedded down now, and in no shape to speak."

Bannon turned the steel dust sharply. His face was grim and his jaw hard. "Did he ask you to speak to me? Or did she?"

"Well, no—not exactly," Mulholland said uncomfortably. "But I'm headin' this train."

"Then I'll thank you to mind your own business. Headin' this wagon is job enough for any man. Any time the Crocketts ask me to stay away, I'll stay, but that's their affair."

Mulholland's face flushed and his eyes darkened with anger.

"She ain't your kind," he persisted, "you bein' a killer, and all."

Rock Bannon stared at him. "You didn't seem to mind my killing Indians!" he said sarcastically. "In fact, you killed a few yourself!"

"Don't get me wrong!" Cap persisted. "I ain't denyin' you helped us! Without you I don't know whether we could have beat off those Indians or not, but killin' Indians and killin' white men's a different thing!"

"You're new to the West, Cap." Bannon's voice was rough. "In a short time you'll find there's white men out here that need killin' a sight worse than Indians. In fact, I'm not so sure those Indians jumped us without help!"

"What do you mean?" Mulholland demanded.

"I mean," Bannon said, "that Morton Harper told you there'd be no hostile Indians on this route! I warned you of Buffalo Hide then, but he told you he ranged further north. You took his advice on this trail, not mine!"

Pagones and Pike Purcell were coming up to join them. Pike heard the last remark and his lean, lantern-jawed face flushed with anger.

"You ridin' Harper again?" he harshly demanded of Bannon. "He said this was a better trail, and it is. We ain't had no high passes, and we had six days of the best travel we've had since we left Council Bluffs, with plenty of water and plenty of grass. Now we get a few bad days and a brush with Indians, but that ain't too much!" He glared at Rock. "I'm sick of your whinin' about this trail and Harper! I figure he's a darned good man. He was sure a help to me when I needed it. Out of supplies and no medicine for the wife, and he staked me."

"I wasn't talking to you," Rock replied shortly, "and I don't like your tone. As far as your loan from Harper, remember that you haven't heard from him on it yet. I've a hunch he'll collect, and plenty!"

"I don't need no killer to tell me my business!" Pike snapped, reining his horse around to face Rock. "And I ain't afraid of a reputation for killin', neither. You don't bluff me none."

"Here, here!" Cap protested. "We can't afford to have trouble in camp. You'll have to admit, Pike, that we'd have been in bad shape a couple of times in that fight, if it hadn't been for Bannon. He's been a help. I don't agree with him on Mort Harper, either, but every man to his own idea."

Rock swung the gray and cantered off toward the hills. Inwardly, he was seething. He was a fool to stay on with the wagon train—he understood that perfectly well. Not a man here liked him, not a man here talked to him except on business. He was not even a member of their train, except by accident.

They had found him at the crossing of the Platte. Riding, half dead, with two bullet wounds in his body, his horse ready to drop with fatigue, he had run upon the wagon train. Sharon Crockett had bedded him down in her wagon and cared for him, and he had ridden on in the same place where her father rode now.

He had offered no explanation of his wounds, and had talked but little. A grim and lonely man, gentle words came hard and he could only look up into Sharon's face and wonder at her beauty, tongue-tied and helpless. Yet his hard, tough, trail-battered body was too used to pain to remain helpless for long. He recovered rapidly, and after that he had ridden along with wagons, hunting for fresh meat and helping when he could.

He was not a man who made friends easily, yet gradually the ice was melting, and the clannishness of the wagon train was breaking down. Twice he had even talked with Sharon, riding beside her wagon, speaking of the mountains and his own wild and lonely life. All that ended abruptly that night beside the campfire at the fort.

They had been seated around the fire eating supper, listening to the bustle of life around the fort, when a tall, handsome man rode up on a beautiful black mare.

Perfectly groomed, his wide white hat topping coal-black hair that hung to his shoulders, a drooping black mustache and a black broadcloth suit, the trousers tucked into hand-tooled boots, Morton Harper had been a picture to take any eye.

Swinging down, he had walked up to the fire. "Howdy, folks!" His voice was genial, his manner warm and pleasant. In an instant his personality and voice had done what Rock Bannon's could not do in two weeks. He had broken down their reserve and become one of the group. "Headin' for California?"

"Reckon we are," Mulholland had agreed. "We ain't rightly decided whether to stay on the Humboldt Trail or to swing north and go to Oregon."

"Why go either way?" Harper asked. "There's a southern route I could recommend that would be much easier going for your womenfolks." His alert eyes had already found and appraised

Sharon Crockett. "More water, plenty of grass, and no high mountain passes."

Cap Mulholland looked up with interest. "We ain't heard of no such pass, nor no such trail," he admitted. "How does she go?"

"Man named Hastings scouted some of it, and I scouted the rest myself. It is a more southerly route, and within another few months all the travel will be going that way. Right now," he winked, "the trains that go that way are going to have a mighty fine trip of it. Very little dust except in one stretch, fine grass, lots of water. Also, the hostile Indians are all raiding far north of there along the traveled routes.

"But," he added, "I can see you're well led, and you'll no doubt learn about this trail yourselves. From the look of your teams I'd say you were lucky in your choice of a leader."

Leaning against the hub of a wagon wheel, Rock Bannon ate in silence. The even, smooth flow of the stranger's language had an enchanting quality, but his own hard-grained, cynical character was impervious to mere talk.

As the hours flowed by, Harper sat among them, pleasing the men with subtle flattery, the women with smiles. The reserve of the group thawed under his easy manner, and before long they began to discuss his trail and its possibilities, considering themselves fortunate to know of it first.

There was some talk of putting it to a vote, but it was morning before it came to that. Until then Rock was silent. "You'd do better," he interposed suddenly, "to stick to the regular trail."

Harper's head came up sharply and his eyes leveled at Bannon. "Have you ever been over the trail I suggest, my friend?"

"Part way," Rock replied. "Only part of it."

"And was that part easy going for oxen and horses? Was there a good trail? Grass? Water?"

"Yes, I reckon it has all that, but I still wouldn't advise it."

"You say it is a better trail but you wouldn't advise it." Harper glanced around at the others, smiling tolerantly. "That doesn't make much sense, does it? I've been over the entire trail and found it very good going. Moreover, I can give you a map of the trail showing the water holes, everything. Of course, it's nothing to me what route you take, but if you want to avoid Indians—" He shrugged.

"What about Buffalo Hide?"

Morton Harper's face tightened and his eyes strained to pry

Rock Bannon's face from the shadows in which he sat. "He's a Blackfoot. He ranges further north."

Harper's eyes shifted to Mulholland. "Who is this man? I'm surprised he should ask about Buffalo Hide, as he isn't known to most white men, other than renegades. I can't understand why he should try to persuade you to neglect an easier route for a more dangerous one. Is he one of your regular train?"

Pike Purcell was abrupt. From the first day he had disliked and been suspicious of Bannon. "No, he ain't none of our crowd, just a man who tied up with us back yonder a ways. He ain't got no wagon, nothin' but the horse he's ridin'."

"I see." Morton Harper's face became grave with implied doubt. "No offense, friend, but would you mind telling me your name? I know most of the men along this trail, and Colonel Warren was asking about some of them only tonight. You'll admit it is safer to be careful, for there are so many renegades who work with the Indians."

"My name's Rock Bannon."

Morton Harper's lips tightened and his eyes grew wary. For a moment he seemed taken aback. Then, as he perceived where his own interests lay, his eyes lighted with triumph.

"Ah? Bannon, eh? I've heard of you. Killed a man in Laramie a month or so back didn't you?"

"He drew on me."

Rock was acutely conscious of the sudden chill in the atmosphere, and he could see Sharon's shocked gaze directed at him. The people of the wagon train were fresh from the East. Only Cap had been as far West as the Platte before, and he only once. They were peace-loving men, quiet, and asking no trouble.

Morton Harper was quick to sense his advantage. "Sorry to have brought it up, Bannon," he said smoothly, "but when a man advises a wagon train against their best interests, it is well to inquire the source of the advice."

Bannon got up. He was a tall man, lean-hipped and broad-shouldered, his flat-brimmed hat shadowing his face, his eyes glowing with piercing light as he spoke.

"I still say that route's a fool way to go. This ain't no country to go wanderin' around in, and that route lies through Hardy Bishop's country. You spoke of Hastings. He was the man who advised the Donner Party."

As his footsteps died away in the darkness, the members of the wagon train sat very still, their enthusiasm suddenly dampened by that ill-fated name. They all knew the story. The horror of it still blanketed the trail with its bloody shadow of the party caught by snows in the high passes and starving until they resorted to cannibalism as a way out.

Morton Harper shrugged. "Of course they started on Hasting's trail, but left it too soon, and the route I suggest avoids all the higher passes." His eyes swung around the group, gathering their attention like the reins of a six-horse team, and he led them on with promises and suggestions, an easy flow of calm, quiet talk, stilling their fears, quieting their doubts, offering them grass and water instead of dust and desert.

In the morning, when they moved out, they took the trail Harper had advised, turning off an hour after they left the fort. He glanced back, and smiled when he saw that he was unobserved. Then he wished them luck, promised to overtake them when a message came for which he waited, and galloped back to the fort.

Rock Bannon was with them. He rode close to Sharon's wagon, and after a time she looked up. He had watched her the night before, had seen her fascinated eyes on Harper's face.

"You don't approve, do you?"

He shook his head. Then he smiled, somewhat grimly. He was a dark, good-looking man with a tinge of recklessness in his green eyes.

"My views aren't important," he said, "I don't belong."

"Pike shouldn't have said that," she said. "He's a strange man. A good man, but stubborn and suspicious."

"Not suspicious of the right folks, maybe."

Her eyes flashed. "You mean Mr. Harper? Why should we be suspicious of him? He was only trying to help."

"I wonder."

"I think," Sharon said sharply, "you'd do better to be a little less suspicious yourself! You admitted this was a good trail!"

"You haven't met Hardy Bishop yet. Nor Buffalo Hide."

"Mr. Harper said that Indian was farther north." She looked at him. "Who is Hardy Bishop? You mentioned him before."

"He's a man who is trying to run cattle at Indian Writing. They say he's insane to try it, but he's claimed seventy miles of range, and he has cattle there. We have to cross his range."

"What's wrong with that?"

"If you cross it, maybe nothing, but Bishop's a funny man. He doesn't like strangers very much. He's going to wonder why you're so far south. He's going to be suspicious."

"Well, let him be suspicious, then!" Sharon said, her eyes bright and her chin lifting. "We don't care, and we won't bother him any. Does he think he owns the whole country?"

"Uh-huh," Rock said, "I'm afraid he does—with some reason, as far as that valley goes. He made it what it is today."

"How could any man make a valley?" Sharon protested. "This is all free country. Anyway, we're just going through."

The conversation had dwindled and died and after a while he rode off to the far flank of the wagon train. Sharon's manner was distinctly stiff, and he could see she was remembering the story of the killing in Laramie. After a few rebuffs he avoided her. Nobody talked to him. He rode alone and camped alone.

CHAPTER TWO

IT HAD REMAINED like that for six days. They were six days during which Morton Harper's name became one to conjure with. The long green valley down which they moved was unrutted by wagon trains, the grass was green and waving, and water was plentiful. Harper's map showed an accurate knowledge of the country, and was a great help. On the sixth day after leaving the fort, the Indians hit them.

The attack came at daybreak. Rock Bannon, camping near a spring half a mile from the wagons, awoke with a start. It was scarcely light, yet he felt uneasy. Getting to his knees, he saw the steel-dust staring, ears pricked, at a distant pile of rocks. Then he noticed the movement.

Swiftly and silently he saddled the stallion, bridled it and stowed his gear in the saddlebags. Then, rifle in hand, he skirted the trees along the tiny stream and headed back for the wagons. He rode up, and the man on guard got up, stretching. It was the short, heavy-set Pagones. A good man, and a sharp one. He smiled at Bannon.

"Guess Harper had it more right than you when he said there were no hostiles here," he said. "Ain't that right?"

"No," Bannon said sharply. "Get everybody up and ready. We'll be attacked within a few minutes!"

Pagones stared. "Are you crazy?"

"Get busy, man!" Bannon snapped at Pagones. He wheeled and, running from wagon to wagon, slapped the canvas and said, "On your feet! Indians!"

Men boiled from the wagons, crawling into their clothes and grabbing at rifles. "Get around the whole circle!" he told them. "They're in those rocks and a draw that runs along south of us."

Mulholland rushed out and halted, glaring around. The sky was gray in the east and everything lay in a vague, indistinct light. Not a movement showed in the dark width of the prairie. He started for Bannon to protest, when he heard a startled exclamation. Wheeling, he saw a long line of red horsemen not over two hundred yards away and coming at a dead run.

Even as his eyes touched them, the nearest Indian broke into a wild, shrill whoop. Then the whole charging line broke into yells.

Rock Bannon, leaning against the Crockett wagon, lifted his Henry rifle and fired. A horse stumbled and went down. He fired again, and an Indian threw up his arms and vanished in the turmoil of oncoming horses and men, and then the men of the wagon train opened up.

Firing steadily, Bannon emptied his rifle before the Indians reached the edge of the circle. One brave, his wild-eyed horse at a dead run, leaned low and shot a blazing arrow into the canvas of the Crockett wagon. Rock fired his right hand pistol and the Indian hit the dirt in a tumbling heap, just as a second arrow knocked off Rock's hat. Reaching up with his left hand, Rock jerked the burning arrow from the canvas. The fire had not yet caught. Then he opened up, firing his pistol, shifting guns, and firing again. The attack broke as suddenly as it had begun.

Tom Crockett was kneeling behind a water barrel, his face gray. A good shot, he was not accustomed to killing. He glanced up at Rock, a sickened expression on his face.

"I never killed nothing human before!" he said weakly.

"You'll get used to it out here," Rock said coldly. His eyes lifted to Sharon.

"You saved our wagon!" she said.

"It might have been anyone's wagon," he said bluntly, and turned away. He counted seven dead Indians on the prairie. There were probably one or two more hidden in the tall grass. He could see several dead ponies. The Indian who had shot the flaming arrow lay not more than a dozen feet away. The bullet had gone through his stomach and had broken his spine.

Rock walked around. He had eyes only for the men. Cap looked frightened, but determined. Pagones had fired steadily and with skill. Bannon nodded at the short man.

"You'll do," he said grimly.

Pagones started to speak, stared after him, and scowled a little. He was ashamed of himself when he realized he was pleased at the compliment.

They were good men, Rock decided. Purcell was reloading his rifle, and he looked up as Bannon passed, but said nothing. Rock walked back to the Crockett wagon. Cap was standing there, his rifle in the hollow of his arm.

"Will they come again?" he asked.

Bannon nodded. "Prob'ly several times. This is Buffalo Hide. Those were his warriors."

"But Morton said—" Crockett started to protest.

Bannon looked around, then he pointed at the dead Indian. "You goin' to believe Morton Harper, or that?" he demanded. "That Indian's a Blackfoot. I know by the moccasins."

The next time they came in a circle, going around and around the wagon train. A volley of flaming arrows set two wagon tops afire. Rock stood at the end of the wagon and fired steadily, carefully, making every shot count.

Dawn came with a red, weird light flaming in the east and turning the wagon colors to flame. Guns crashed and the air was filled with wild Indian yells and the acrid smell of gunpowder and burned canvas. Three times more they attacked, and Bannon was everywhere, firing, firing, firing. Crockett went down with a bullet through his thigh. Bjornsen was shot through the head, and a warrior leaped from a horse into Greaves's wagon and the two men fought there until the Indian thrust a knife into Greaves's side. Bannon shot the brave with a snapped pistol shot, almost from the hip.

The last attack broke, and the sun lifted into the sky. As if by magic the Indians were gone. Rock Bannon wiped the sweat from his forehead and stared out over the plain. Buffalo Hide had lost men in this fight. At least twenty of his braves were dead; there would be wailing and the death chant in Blackfoot villages tonight.

Two horses and an ox had been killed. They gathered around, buried the two dead men and butchered the ox. Rock sat on a wagon tongue alone. Cap walked over to him. The man's face was round and uncomfortable.

"Reckon you saved us, Rock," he said. "Don't rightly know how to thank you!"

Bannon got up. He had been cleaning his rifle and reloading it while the men were buried. "Don't try," he said.

Bob Sprague walked over and held out his hand. "Guess we haven't been very friendly," he said, "but you were right about the Indians."

Suddenly, boyishly, Bannon grinned. "Forget it, Bob! You did a good job with that rifle of yours!"

They were the only two who mentioned it. Rock helped lift Crockett into the back of the wagon, then harnessed the oxen. He had already gone, riding flank on the steel-dust, when Sharon came to thank him. She looked after him, and her heart felt strangely lost and alone.

It was late that day when they reached the dry country. The settlers did not realize the change until the dust began to rise, for in the distance it had looked much the same, only the grass was darker and there was less of it. Within a mile they were suffused in a cloud of powdery, sifting dust, stifling and irritating in the heat.

This was no desert, but merely long miles of plain where the hills receded, and there was no sub-irrigation to keep the grass green and rich. All the following day the dust cloud hung over the wagon train, and from Mulholland's place in the van the last wagons could not even be distinguished.

Mulholland looked up at Bannon, who was riding beside him. "Harper said there was one bad stretch," he said, almost apologetically.

Bannon did not reply. He alone of all the party knew what lay ahead. He alone knew how brutal the passage would be. Let them find out. . . .

Days later, when Cap asked him to go for game, they all knew. They were still in that desert of dust and dirty brown brush. They had camped in it for five days now. Their water barrels were empty, the wagons so hard to pull in the thick dust that they made only a few miles each day. It was the worst kind of tough going.

When he had killed two antelope in the hills, Rock rode back to join the party. Pagones, hunting on the other side, had killed one. Rock turned toward Sharon's wagon and swung down from the saddle. She looked up at him from over a fire of greasewood.

"Hello," she said. "We haven't seen much of you."

He took off his black, flat-brimmed hat. His dark curly hair was plastered to his brow with sweat.

"There are some here who don't want me talking to you," he said dryly. "Figure I'm a bad influence, I guess."

"I haven't said that!" she protested. She brushed a strand of hair from her eyes. "I like to have you riding close. It—it makes me feel safer."

He looked at her for an instant, then looked away. "How's your dad?"

"Better, I think. But this heat is so awful. How long before we get out of this dust?"

"Tomorrow night, at this rate. This bad stretch is about over."

"Then we're free of that. Morton said there was only one."

He noticed that she had called Harper by his first name. "He was wrong. You'll strike another near Salt Lake that's much worse than this. You'll never get across unless you swing back and take the old trail for Pilot Peak."

"But he said—" Sharon protested.

Rock Bannon looked up at her from where he squatted on his haunches. "I know he did. I heard everything he said, and I'm still wondering what he has to gain by it. Nobody takes this route. Crossing the Salt Desert this way is suicide—with wagons, at least. You've all placed a lot of faith in a stranger!"

"He was right, Rock. Those first six days were heaven, and from now on it should be good."

"From now on it will be good until you hit the desert," he admitted, "unless you stop."

"Unless we stop?" Sharon dished up a plate and handed it to him, then poured the coffee. "Why?"

"Tomorrow we get into Hardy Bishop's country." Rock Bannon's face was somber.

"You always refer to him as if he were an outlaw, or something awful!"

"No," he said. "Bishop isn't that. If you are his friend, or a guest, he's one of the finest men alive. If you are an enemy or try to take something that's his, he is absolutely ruthless."

When she returned from feeding her father, she sat down beside him on the wagon tongue. The sun was down, and the dust settled. Near a fire on the far side of the circle Dud Kitchen was singing softly over his mandolin.

The air was cool now, and the soft music mingled in the air with the scent of woodsmoke and the low champing of the horses or the mumbling of the oxen. In the distance they could see the hills, purple with last shadows before darkness, and shadowed with a promise of coolness after the long days of heat and dust and bitterness.

He stared away at the hills, remembering so much, worried, uncertain, wondering again about Morton Harper. What did the man have in mind? Who was he? Purcell had said he had lent him money. It was not like a man to lend money and not follow it up to get back what was his. Behind all of this was a reason, and in the back of his mind Rock was afraid he knew that reason.

Sharon spoke suddenly. "What are you thinking of, Rock? You're always so silent. You seem so bitter sometimes, and I can never understand what you have on your mind."

"It isn't anything." He had no desire to mention Harper again. "I was just thinking about this country."

"You like it, don't you?"

"Like it?" He looked up suddenly, and his eyes changed. He smiled suddenly and with warmth. "Like it? I love it! This is a man's country! And that ahead? Wait until you see Bishop's Valley! Miles upon miles of tumbling streams, and waving green grass dotted with cattle!

"You should see Bishop's Valley! You go down through a deep gorge along a roaring mountain stream, and you can look up at cliffs that rise for three thousand feet, and then suddenly the gorge widens and you look down a long valley that's six or seven miles wide and all of fifty miles long.

"On each side high mountain ridges shut it in, and here and there deep gorges and ravines cut back into those ridges and there are green meadows and tumbling waterfalls. And all the hills around are timbered to their crests. It's a beautiful country!"

Sharon stared at him, enchanted. Rock had never talked like this before, and as she listened to him tell of the hills and the wild game, of deer, elk, bear and mountain goats, of the catbirds calling in the willows and the hillsides white with groves of silver-columned birch, she suddenly forgot where she was, or who was talking.

"You seem to love it so much!" she said. "Why did you ever leave?"

"It belongs to one man—to Hardy Bishop," Rock said. "He's carving a little empire here. He went there long before any other white man dreamed of anything but going to California, before they thought of anything but getting rich from gold mines. They came through the country like a pack of vultures, taking everything, building nothing. They want only to get rich and get out.

"He was different. Once, when only a boy, he went into that valley on a trapping venture, and he was never content until he came back. He drove a herd of cattle west when there were no cattle in this country, and he got them into that valley and turned them loose. He fought Indians and outlaws, he built a dam, built a home, built irrigation ditches where he wanted them and planted trees.

"He made the valley, and you can't blame him if he wants to keep it his way now."

Long after Sharon lay in her blankets she thought of that, and of Rock Bannon. How tall he was! And how strange! He had risen suddenly, and with scarcely a word had walked into the night, and then she heard him mount his horse and ride away. Yet even as she heard the dwindling hoofbeats, she heard something else. The sound of other horses, drawing near. Still wondering who they could be, she fell asleep. . . .

Scarcely were they moving in the morning before a black mare wheeled alongside her wagon. Flushing suddenly, she saw Morton Harper, hat in hand, bowing to her.

"Good morning!" he said. "I hoped to catch up with you before this, but by tomorrow you'll be in green country again!"

"Yes, I know."

He looked at her quickly. "You know? Who told you?"

"Rock Bannon."

His face sharpened, and she could sense the irritation in the man. "Oh? Then he's still with you? I was hoping he had left you alone. I'm afraid he's not a good man."

"Why do you say that? He's been very helpful."

Harper shrugged. "I'd rather not say. You know of that killing in Laramie, and if that were the only one, it would not matter. There are others. He has killed five or six men. He's a troublemaker wherever he goes. I'm glad Purcell and your men understand that, for it will save a lot of trouble."

He smiled at her. "You look so lovely this morning that it's unbelievable that you have come so far across the prairie. It is a pity you have so far to go. I've been thinking some of settling in this country here." He waved ahead. "It is such a beautiful land, and there is nothing in California so desirable."

Rock Bannon had heard the horses the night before, and he reined in long enough to see them come up to the fire. Harper he recognized at once. There were two men with him, one a lean, sharp-faced man with a long nose. The other man was short, chuckleheaded and blunt featured. Bannon's lips tightened when he recognized Pete Zapata. The half-breed killer was notorious, a gunfighter and desperado of the worst stripe, but none of the wagon train would know that.

All that day he stayed away from the train, riding on ahead. He drank at the spring, killed an antelope and a couple of teal, then rode back under a clump of poplars and waited for the wagon train to come up. They were already on Hardy Bishop's V Bar. Only a short distance behind the poplars, the long canyon known as Poplar Canyon ran down into Bishop's Valley.

He got up when he saw the first of the long caravan of wagons. Better than the others, he knew what this would mean, and knew on how bad a trail they had started. He was standing there, close to the stallion, when the wagons moved in.

The fresh water and green grass made everyone happy. Brown-legged children rushed downstream from where the drinking water was obtained, and there was laughter and merrymaking in the camp. Fires sprang up, and in a short time the camp was made and meals were being cooked.

Watchfully, Rock saw Morton Harper seated on a saddle at Cap Mulholland's fire. With them were the sharp-featured stranger, Satterfield, and Lamport and Pagones. They were deep in a conference. In a few minutes Tom Crockett walked over to join them.

Dud Kitchen was tuning his mandolin when he saw Bannon sitting under the willows.

"All alone?" Kitchen said with a grin, and dropped on the grass beside Bannon. "Saw how you handled those guns in that Indian fight. Never saw the like. Made more tune with 'em than me with a mandolin!"

Rock chuckled. "But not so nice to hear." He nodded at the group of men around the fire. "Wonder what's up?"

Dud shrugged. "Harper's got some plan he's talkin' about. Sayin' they are foolish to go on when there's good country right here."

Rock Bannon sprang to his feet, his eyes afire with apprehension. "So that's it?" he said. "I might have known it!"

Kitchen was startled. "What's the matter? I think it would be a good idea, myself. This is beautiful country. I don't know that I've ever seen better. Harper says that down this draw behind us there's a long, beautiful valley, all open for settlement."

But Rock Bannon was no longer listening. Stepping across the branch of the creek, he started for the fire. Morton Harper was talking when Rock walked up.

"Why not?" Harper was saying. "You all want homes. Can you find a more beautiful country than this? That dry plain is behind you. Ahead lies the Salt Lake Desert, but in here—this is a little bit of paradise. Beyond this range of hills—you can reach it through Poplar Canyon—is the most beautiful valley you ever saw. It's just crying for people to come in and settle down! There's game in the hills, the best grazing land in the world, all for the taking!"

"What about Hardy Bishop?" Bannon demanded.

Harper looked up, angered. "You again? Every time these people try to do anything, you interfere! Is it your business where they stop? Is it your business if they remain here or go on to California? Are you trying to dictate to them?"

Pike Purcell was on his feet, and Rock could see all the old dislike in the big Missourian's face. The other men looked at him with disapproval, too. Yet he went on recklessly, heedlessly.

"Hardy Bishop settled that valley, and he's running two thousand head of cattle in there. You try to settle in that valley and you're asking for trouble. He won't stand for it."

"An' we won't stand for you buttin' in!" Purcell said suddenly. He dropped a hand to the big dragoon pistol in his holster. "I've had enough of you interferin' in our affairs. I'm tellin' you now, you shut up an' get out."

"Wait a minute!" Bob Sprague stepped closer. "This man warned us about the Indian attack or we'd all be dead, includin' you, Pike Purcell. He did more fightin' in that attack than any one of us, or any two of us, for that matter. His advice has been good, and I think we should listen to him!"

Dud Kitchen nodded. "Speak up, Rock. I'll listen!"

"There's little to be said," Bannon told them quietly. "Only the land this man is suggesting you settle on was settled on over ten years ago by a man who fought Indians to get it. He fought Indians and outlaws to keep it. He won't see it taken from him now in his old age. I know Hardy Bishop. I know him well enough to be sure that if you move into that valley many of the women in this wagon train will be widows before the year is out.

"What I don't know is Morton Harper's reason for urging you into this. I don't know why he urged you to take this trail, but I think he has a reason, and I think that reason lies in Bishop's Valley. You're coming west to win homes. You have no right to do it by taking what another man fought to win and to keep. There is plenty for all further west."

"That makes sense to me," Sprague said quietly. "I for one am moving west!"

"Well, I'm not!" Purcell said stubbornly. "I like this country, and me and the wife have seen enough dust and sun and Indians! We aim to stay!"

"That valley is fifty miles long, gentlemen," Harper said. "I think there's room enough for us all in Bishop's Valley."

"That seems right to me!" Cap said. He looked around at Tom Crockett, limping near the fire. "How about you, Tom?"

"I'm staying," Crockett said. "I like it here."

Satterfield nodded. "Reckon I'll find me a place to set up a blacksmith shop," he said. "But there's a sight of things we all need. There ain't no stores, no place to get some things we figured to get in California."

"That will be where I come in." The man with the sharp features smiled pleasantly. "I'm John Kies, and I have six wagonloads of goods coming over the trail to open a store in our new town!"

Silently, Rock Bannon turned away. There was no further use in talking. He caught Sharon's eye, but she looked away, her gaze drawn to Mort Harper where he sat now, talking easily, smoothly, planning the new homes, the new town.

Bannon walked back to his blankets and turned in, listening to the whispering of the poplar leaves and the soft murmur of the water in the branch. It was a long time before he fell asleep, long after the last talking had died away in the wagon train, and when the fires had burned low.

CHAPTER THREE

THEN DAYLIGHT CAME. Rock Bannon bathed, and saddled the stallion. Then, carefully, he checked his guns. At a sound, he glanced up to see Sharon Crockett dipping water from the stream.

"Good morning," he said. "Did you finally decide to stay?"

"Yes." She stepped toward him. "Rock, why are you always against everything we do? Why don't you stay, too? I'm sure Morton would be glad to have you. He's planned all this so well, and he says we'll need good men. Why don't you join us?"

"No, not this time. I stayed with the wagon train because I knew what you were going into. I wanted to help you—and I mean you. In what is to come, no one can help you. Besides my heart wouldn't be in it."

"You're afraid of this crabby old man?" she asked scornfully. "Morton says as soon as Bishop sees that we intend to stay, he won't oppose us at all! He's just difficult because he's old, and he has more land than he needs. Are you afraid of him?"

Rock smiled. "You sure set a lot of store by this Harper fellow, don't you? Did he tell you that Bishop's riders were all crabby old men, too? Did Harper tell you why he carries Pete Zapata along with him?"

"Who is he?" Sharon looked up, her eyes curious, yet resentful.

"You've called me a killer," Bannon replied. "I have killed men. I may kill more, although I hope not. But Pete Zapata, that flat-faced, half-breed who rides with Harper, is a murderer. He's a killer of the most vicious type, and the kind of man no decent man would have near him!"

Her eyes flared. "You don't think Morton Harper is decent? How dare you say such a thing behind his back?"

"I'll face him with it," Bannon said dryly. "I expect I'll face him with it more than once. But before you get in too deep, ask yourself again what he's getting out of all this. He goes in for talk of brotherly love, but he carries a gunman at his elbow!"

He turned and swung into the saddle as she picked up her bucket. He reined in the horse at a call. It was Bob Sprague.

"Hey, Rock! Want to come on west with us?"

He halted. "You're going on?"

"Uh-huh. Six wagons are going. We decided we liked the sound of what you said. We're pullin' on for Californy, and we'd sure like to have you with us!"

Bannon hesitated. Sharon was walking away, her head held proudly. Did she seem to hesitate for his reply? He shrugged.

"No," he said. "I've got other plans."

Sharon Crockett, making frying-pan bread over the fire beside her wagon, stood up to watch Bob Sprague lead off the six wagons, the owners of which had decided not to stay. All farewells had been said the night before, yet now that time for the leavetaking had come, she watched uneasily.

For years she had known Bob Sprague, ever since she was a tiny girl. He had been her father's friend, a steady, reliable man, and now he was going. With him went five other families, and among them some of the steadiest, soberest men in the lot.

Were they wrong to take Morton Harper's advice? Her father, limping with the aid of a cane cut from the willows, walked back and stood beside her, his face somber. He was a tall man, almost as tall as Harper or Bannon, his hair silvery around the temples, his face gray with a slight stubble of beard. He was a fearless, independent man, given to going his own way, and thinking his own thoughts.

Pagones walked over to them. "Did Bannon go along? I ain't seen him."

"I don't think he went," Crockett replied. "Sprague wanted him to go."

"No, he didn't go," said Satterfield, who had walked up to join them. Satterfield had been a frontier lawyer back in Illinois. "I saw him riding off down the canyon, maybe an hour ago."

"You think there will be trouble?" Pagones asked.

Satterfield shrugged. "Probably not. I know how some of these old frontiersmen are. They hate to see civilization catch up with them, but given time, they come around. Where's Harper?"

"He went off somewhere with that dark-lookin' feller who trails with him," Pagones said. "Say, I'm glad Dud Kitchen didn't go. I'd sure miss that music he makes. He was goin', then at the last minute changed his mind. He's goin' down with Harper and Cap to survey that townsite."

"Seem good to have a town again," Crockett said. "Where's it to be?"

"Down where Poplar Canyon runs into Bishop's Valley. Wide, beautiful spot, they say, with plenty of water and grass. John Kies is puttin' in a store, I'm going to open an office, and Collins is already figurin' on a blacksmith shop."

"Father, did you ever hear of a man named Zapata?" Sharon asked thoughtfully. "Pete Zapata?"

Crockett looked at her curiously. "Why, no. Not that I recall. Why?"

"I was just wondering."

The next morning they hitched up the oxen and moved their ten wagons down Poplar Canyon to the townsite. The high, rocky walls of the canyon widened slowly, and the oxen walked on, knee deep in rich, green grass. Along the stream were willow and poplar, and higher along the canyon sides Sharon saw alder, birch and mountain mahogany with here and there a fine stand of lodgepole pine.

Tom Crockett was driving, so she ranged alongside, riding her sorrel mare.

As they rounded the last bend in the canyon, it spread wide before them and she saw Morton Harper sitting his black mare some distance off. Putting the sorrel to a gallop, she rode down swiftly, hair blowing in the wind. Dud Kitchen was there with Zapata and Cap. They were driving stakes and lining up a street.

Before them the valley dropped into the great open space of Bishop's Valley, and she rode on. Suddenly, rounding a knoll, she stopped and caught her breath.

The long, magnificent sweep of the valley lay before her, green and splendid in the early-morning sun. Here and there over the grassland cattle grazed, belly deep in the tall grass. It was overpowering, it was breathtaking. It was something beyond the grasp of the imagination. High on either side lifted the soaring walls of the canyon, mounting into high ridges, snow-capped peaks, and majestic walls of gray rock.

This was the cattle empire of Hardy Bishop. This was the place Rock Bannon spoke of with such amazing eloquence.

She turned in her saddle at the sound of a horse's hoofs. Mort Harper rode up beside her, his face glowing.

"Look!" he cried. "Magnificent, isn't it? The most beautiful view in the world. Surely that's an empire worth taking!"

Sharon's head turned quickly, sharply. At something in Harper's eyes she caught her breath, and when she looked again at the valley, she was uneasy.

"What—what did you say?" she asked. "An empire worth taking?"

He glanced at her quickly, then laughed. "Don't pay any mind. I was thinking of Bishop, the man who claims all this. He took it. Took it from the Indians by main force." Then he added, "He's an old brute. He'd stop at nothing!"

"Do you think he'll make trouble for us?" she inquired anxiously.

He shrugged. "Probably not. He might, but if he does, we can handle that part of it. Let's go back, shall we?"

She was silent during the return ride, and she kept turning over in her mind her memory of Bannon's question, "What's he going to get out of this?" Somehow, half hypnotized by Harper's eloquence, she had not really thought of that. That she thought of it now gave her a twinge of doubt. It seemed somehow disloyal.

For three days life in the new town went on briskly. They named the town Poplar, and Kies's store was the first building up, and the shelves were heavy with goods and needed things. Kies was smiling and affable. "Don't worry about payment!" he assured them. "We're all in this together! Just get what you need and I'll put it on the books, then when you get money from furs or crops you can pay me!"

It was easy. It was almost too easy. Tom Crockett built a house in a bend of the creek among the trees, and he bought dress goods for Sharon, trousers for himself, bacon and flour. Then he bought some new tools.

Those first three days were hard, unrelenting labor, yet joyful labor, too. They were building homes, and there is always something warming and pleasant in that. At the end of those first three days, Kies's store was up, Collin's blacksmith shop, Satterfield's office, and Hardy's Saloon and Theater. All of them pitched in, and all of them worked.

Then one day, as Sharon was leaving Kies's store, she looked up to see three strange horsemen coming down the street. They were walking their horses, and they were looking around in ill-concealed amazement.

Mulholland had come out behind her, and at the sight of him, one of the horsemen, a big, stern-looking man with a drooping red mustache, reined his horse around.

"You!" he said. "What do you think you're doin' here?"

"Buildin' us a town," Cap said aggressively. "Any objections?"

Red laughed sardonically. "Well, sir," he said, "I reckon I haven't, but I'm afraid the boss is sure goin' to raise hob!"

"Who's the boss?" Cap asked. "And what difference does it make? This is all free land, isn't it?"

"The boss is Hardy Bishop," Red drawled, glancing around. He looked approvingly at Sharon, and there seemed a glint of humor in his eyes. "And you say this is free land. It is, and it ain't. You see, out here a man takes what he can hold. Hardy come in here when all you folks was livin' fat and comfortable back in the States. He settled here, and he worked hard. He trapped and hunted and washed him some color, and then he went back to the States and bought cattle. Drivin' them cattle out here ten years ago was sure a chore, folks, but he done it. Now they've bred into some of the biggest herds in the country. I don't think Hardy's goin' to like you folks movin' in here like this."

"Is he so selfish?" Sharon demanded. "Why there's land here enough for thousands of people!"

Red looked at her. "That's how you see it, ma'am. I reckon to your way of thinkin', back East, that might be true. Here, it ain't true. A man's needs run accordin' to the country he's in and the job he has to do. Hardy Bishop is runnin' cows. He expects to supply beef for thousands of people. To do that he needs a lot of land. You see, ma'am, if thousands of people can't raise their own beef, somebody's got to have land enough to raise beef for them. And Hardy, he come by it honest."

"By murdering Indians, I suppose!"

Red looked at her thoughtfully. "Ma'am, somebody's been tellin' you wrong. Plumb wrong. Hardy never murdered no Indians."

"What's going on here?" Morton Harper stepped into the street. To his right was Pete Zapata, to his left Pike Purcell. Lamport lounged in the door of the store.

"Why nothin', mister," Red said thoughtfully. His gaze had sharpened, and Sharon saw his eyes go from Harper to Zapata. "We was just talkin' about land and the ownership of it. We're ridin' for Bishop, and —"

"And you can ride right out of here!" Harper snapped. "Now!"

Sharon was closer to the Bishop riders, and she heard the second man say softly: "Watch it, Red! That's Zapata!"

Red seemed to stiffen in his saddle and his hand, which had started to slip off the pommel of the saddle, with no aggressive intention, froze in position. Without a word, they turned their horses and rode away.

"That's the beginning," Harper stated positively. "I'm afraid they mean to drive us from our homes!"

"They didn't sound much like trouble," Cap ventured, hesitantly. "Talked mighty nice!"

"Don't be fooled by them!" Harper warned. "Bishop is an outlaw, or the next thing to it. . . ."

Tom Crockett was a man who loved the land. No sooner had he put a plow into the deep, rich soil of the canyon bottom than he felt he had indeed come home. The soil, deep and black, heavy with richness, a land that had never known a plow. Working early and late, he had in the next day managed to plow several acres. The seed he bought from Kies, who seemed to have everything they needed.

There were several hours a day he gave to working on the buildings the others were throwing up, but logs were handy, and all but Zapata and Kies worked on the felling and notching of them. Kies stayed in his store, and Zapata lounged close by.

Morton Harper helped with the work, but Sharon noticed that he was never without a gun, and his rifle was always close by. At night in his saloon he played cards with Purcell and Lamport and anyone else who came around. Yet several times a day he managed to stop by, if only for a minute, to talk to her.

He stopped one day when she was planting a vine near the door. He watched her for a few minutes, and then he stepped closer.

"Sharon," he said gently. "You shouldn't be doing this sort of thing. You're too beautiful. Why don't you let me take care of you?"

She looked at him, suddenly serious. "Is this a proposal?"

His eyes flashed, then he smiled. "What else? I suppose I'm pretty clumsy at it."

"No," she returned thoughtfully, "you're not clumsy at it, but let's wait. Let's not talk about it until everyone has a home and is settled in a place of their own."

"All right," he agreed reluctantly. "But that won't be very long, you know."

It was not until they were eating supper that night that her thoughts suddenly offered her a question. What about Morton's home? He had not even started to build. He was sleeping in a room behind the saloon, such in name only as yet, for there was no liquor to be had.

The thought had not occurred to her before, but it puzzled and disturbed her. Tom Crockett was full of plans, talking of crops and the rich soil.

The next day Morton Harper was gone. Where he had gone Sharon did not know, but suddenly, in the middle of the morning she realized he was not among them, and the black mare was gone, too. Shortly after noon she saw him riding into town, and behind him came six wagons, loaded with boxes and barrels. They drew up before the store and the saloon.

He saw her watching and loped the mare over to her door.

"See?" he said, waving a hand. "The supplies! Everything we need for the coming year, but if we need more, I can send a rider back to the fort."

"Then you had them coming from the fort?" she asked. "You were far-sighted."

He laughed, glancing at her quickly. "Well, I thought these things would sell in the mining camps out in California, but this is much, much better."

In spite of herself, Sharon was disturbed. All day as she went about her work the thought kept recurring that those supplies offerred a clue to something, yet she could find nothing on which to fasten her suspicions. Why should their arrival disturb her so much? Was it unusual that a man should start several wagonloads of supplies to California?

Pagones stopped by the spring to get a drink. He smiled at her, pushing back his hat from a sweating brow.

"Lots of work, ma'am. Your pa's sure getting in his plowing in a hurry. He'll have his seed in before the rest of us have started."

"Pag, how do the supplies reach the gold fields in California?" Sharon said suddenly.

He looked up over his second dipper of water. "Why, by sea, of course! Much cheaper that way. Why do you ask? Something botherin' you?"

"Not exactly. Only ever since those wagons came in this morning, I've been wondering about them. Morton said he had started them for California, but thought they would sell better here. Why would he send them to California to sell when they can get supplies easier by sea?"

"Might mean a little ready money," Pagones suggested. He hung the dipper on a shrub. "Now that you mention it, it does seem kind of strange."

The expected trouble from Hardy Bishop did not materialize as soon as she expected. No other riders came near, although several times she noticed men, far out in the valley. All Morton Harper's promises seemed to be coming true. He had said Bishop would not bother them.

Yet all was not going too smoothly. The last wagons had brought a load of liquor, and several of the men hung around the saloon most of the time. Purcell was there every evening, although by day he worked on his place. Pete Zapata was always there when not off on one of his lonely rides, and the teamsters who had brought the wagons to Kies's store had remained, loitering about, doing nothing at all, but always armed. One of them had become the bartender.

During all this time her work had kept Sharon close to the house, and there had been no time for riding. Time and again she found herself going to the door and looking down toward the cluster of buildings that was fast becoming a thriving little village. And just as often she looked back up the trail they had followed when first coming into Poplar Canyon.

Not even to herself would she admit what she was looking for. She refused to admit that she longed to see the steel-dust stallion and its somber, lonely rider. She had overheard him say he would not leave, yet where was he?

The sound of horse's hoofs in the trail outside brought her to the cabin door. It was Mary Pagones, daughter of George Pagones, who had long since proved himself one of the most stable men in the wagon train.

"Come on, Sharon—let's ride! I'm beginning to feel cramped with staying down here all the time."

Sharon needed no urging, and in a few minutes they were riding out of the settlement toward the upper reaches of the canyon.

"Have you seen that Pete Zapata staring at the women the way he does?" Mary asked. "He fairly gives me the creeps!"

"Somebody said he was a gunman," Sharon ventured.

"I wouldn't doubt it!" Mary was an attractive girl, always gay and full of laughter. The freckles over her nose were an added attraction rather than otherwise. "Dud doesn't like him at all. Says he can't see why Harper keeps him around."

As they rode out of Poplar Canyon, an idea suddenly occurred to Sharon, and without voicing it she turned her mare toward their old encampment, but as they burst through the last line of trees, disappointment flooded over her. There was no sign of Rock Bannon.

They had gone almost a mile further, when suddenly Mary reined in sharply.

"Why, look at that!" She pointed. "Wagon tracks coming out of that canyon! Who in the world would ever take a wagon in there?"

Sharon looked at them, then at the canyon. It was narrow-mouthed, the only entrance into a wild, rugged region of crags and ravines, heavily forested and forbidding. Riding closer, she looked down. The wagon tracks were coming from the canyon, not going into it. She studied the mountains thoughtfully, then wheeling her horse, with Mary following, she rode out on their own trail. All the tracks she had observed were old.

She looked at Mary, and Mary returned the glance, a puzzled frown gathering around her eyes. "What's the matter?" Mary asked. "Is something wrong?"

"I don't know," Sharon said. "There are no tracks here since we came over the trail, but there are tracks coming out of that canyon!"

Mary's eyes widened. "You mean those wagons of Harper's? Then they must have come over a different trail."

That wasn't what Sharon was thinking, but she just shook her head. "Don't say anything about it," she said. They rode in. That wall of mountain would not offer a trail through, and if it did, where would it go? If it joined the Overland Trail to the north, it would still be almost twice as far as by the trail they had come, and through one of the most rugged sections she had ever seen. Suddenly, she knew. Those wagons had been here before. They had been back there, in some remote canyon, waiting.

Waiting for what? For a town to begin? But that was absurd. No one had known the town would begin until a few hours before. No one, unless it had been Morton Harper.

On, through hills of immeasurable beauty, the two girls rode. Great, rocky escarpments that towered to the skies, and mighty crags, breasting their saw-toothed edges against the wind. Long, steep hillsides clad with alder and birch, or rising to great, dark, feathered crests of lodgepole pine mingled here and there with an occasional fir.

Along the lower hillsides and along the mountain draws were quaking aspen, mountain mahogany and hawthorn. They had come to the edge of a grove of poplar when they saw the horseman. They both saw him at once, and something in his surreptitious manner brought them to a halt. They both recognized him at the same instant.

"Sharon," Mary said, "it's that Zapata!"

"S-sh! He'll hear us!" Sharon held her breath. Suddenly, she was frightened at the idea of being found out here, even with Mary along, by the half-breed. But Zapata seemed to have no eyes for them, or even for their direction. He was riding by very slowly, not over fifty yards away, carrying his rifle in his hands, and watching something in the valley below which was beyond their vision.

Yet even as they watched he slid suddenly from the saddle and crouched upon some rocks on the rim. Then he lifted his rifle and fired!

"What's he shooting at?" Mary asked in a whisper.

"I don't know. A deer probably. Let's go home."

Turning their horses they rode back through the trees and hit the trail back to the settlement.

CHAPTER FOUR

ALL THE NEXT day Sharon thought about the wagon trail out of the mountains. Several times she started to speak to her father, but he was preoccupied, lost in plans for his new home, and thinking of nothing but it. Later in the day she saw Dud Kitchen riding over. He reined in and slid from the saddle.

"Howdy, Sharon! Sure glad to see you! We been talkin' home, Mary and I, about gettin' up a sort of party. Seems like Satterfield plays a fiddle, and we thought we might have a dance, sort of. Liven things up a mite."

"That's a good idea, Dud," Sharon agreed. She looked up at him suddenly. "Dud, did Mary tell you anything about that wagon trail we saw?"

His blue eyes sharpened and he ran his fingers back through his corn-colored hair. "Yeah," he said, "she did."

"Dud, it looks to me as if those wagons were out here before we were, just waiting. It begins to look as if somebody planned to have us stop here."

"You mean Mort? But what would he do that for? What could he gain? And even if he did, you got to admit it's a good place."

"Yes, it is, but just the same I don't like it."

Her father was walking toward them with George Pagones and Cap Mulholland.

"What's this you young folks figurin' to do?" Cap said, grinning. "Hear we're havin' us a party?"

Her answer was drowned by a sudden rattle of horses' hoofs and she saw three men swing down the canyon trail. When they saw the group before the house, they reined in. One of the men was Red, the man who had called on them the first day. Another was—her breath caught—Rock Bannon!

"Howdy!" Red said. He looked down at the men, then recognized Cap. "Seen anything of a young fellow, 'bout twenty, or so, ridin' a bay pony?"

"Why no," Cap said. "Can't say as I have. What's the trouble?"

"He's Wes Freeman, who rides for us. He was huntin' strays over this way yesterday and he never came back. We figured maybe he was hurt somehow."

"No, we haven't seen him," Crockett said.

Dud Kitchen was grinning at Rock. "Shucks, man! We figured you had left the country. What you doin'?"

Bannon grinned. "I'm ridin' for Hardy Bishop," he said. "Went over there right after I left you folks."

"What made you think your man might have come over here?" Pagones asked. "Was he ridin' this way?"

"As a matter of fact," Red said, "he was ridin' back northeast of here. Pretty rough country, except for one canyon that's got some good grass in it."

The third man was short, thick-set and tough. "Hurry up, Red!" he said. "Why beat around the bush. Tell 'em!"

"All right," Red said. "I'll do just that, Bat!" He looked down at the little group before the house. "Fact o' the matter is, Wes's horse come in about sundown yesterday, come in with blood on the saddle. We back-trailed the horse and we found Wes. We found him in the open valley we spoke of. He was dead. He'd been shot through the back and knocked off his horse. Then whoever shot him had followed him up and killed him with a hunting knife."

Zapata! Sharon's eyes widened, and she looked around to see Dud staring at her, gray-faced. She had seen Zapata shoot!

In stunned silence the men stared up at the three riders. Rock broke the silence.

"You can see what this means?" he said sternly. "Wes was a mighty nice boy. I hadn't known him as long as these men, but he seemed to be a right fine kid. Now he's been murdered—drygulched. That's going to mean trouble."

"But why come to us?" Cap protested. "You don't believe we—"

"We don't believe!" Bat broke in harshly. "We know! We trailed three riders down out of those hills! Three from here! Wes was my ridin' partner. He was a durned good boy. I'm goin' to see the man who done that."

"Turn around."

The voice was cold and deadly. As one person, they turned. Pete Zapata, his guns low-slung on his hips, was staring at the three riders. Flanking him were two men with shotguns, both of them from the teamsters' crowd. The other two were Lamport and Purcell, of the wagon train. Behind them, and a little to one side, was Morton Harper. He was wearing two guns.

"Get out of here!" Harper snapped harshly. "Don't come around here again, aimin' to make trouble. That's all you came for, and you know it! You've been looking for an excuse to start something so you could get us out of here, take our homes away from us. Now turn your horses and get out!"

His eyes riveted on Rock Bannon. "As for you, Bannon," he said sharply, "You're a traitor! You rode with us, and now you've gone over to them. I think you're the cause of all this trouble. If a man of yours is dead, I think it would be a good idea if these friends of yours back-trailed you. Now get moving, all of you!"

"This is a bad mistake, Harper," Rock said evenly. "I'm speaking of it before all these people." He nodded at the group in front of the house. "Bishop was inclined to let 'em stay, despite the fact that he was afraid they'd bring more after them. He listened to me, and didn't run you off. Now you're asking for it."

"He listened to *you*!" Harper's voice was alive with contempt. "You? A trail-runner?"

Red looked quickly at Rock and started to speak. Bannon silenced him with a gesture. "We'll ride, Harper, but we want the man—or men—who killed Wes. And we want him delivered to us by sundown tomorrow! If not, we'll come and get him."

Turning abruptly, they started away. Wheeling, Zapata grabbed a shotgun from one of the teamsters. "I'll fix him, the bluffer!"

"Hold it!" Pagones had a six-shooter and was staring across it at Zapata. "We don't shoot men in the back."

For an instant, they glared at each other. Then Harper interposed. "Put it down, Pete. Let them go." He looked around. "There'll be a meeting at the saloon tonight. All of you be there."

When they had gone, Tom Crockett shook his head sadly.

''More trouble, and all because of that Bannon. I almost wish we'd let him die on the trail.''

''It wasn't Bannon, Father,'' Sharon said. ''Those men were right, I think. Mary and I saw Zapata yesterday. Two of the horses they trailed back here were ours. The other one was his. We weren't fifty yards away from him when he fired that shot. We didn't see what he shot at, but it must have been that man.''

Crockett's face was gray. ''Are you sure, Sharon? Are you positive?''

''Yes, I am.''

''Then we must give him up,'' he said slowly. ''If he killed, he should suffer for it. Especially if he killed that way.'' He got up and reached for his hat. ''I must go and tell Morton. He'll want to know.''

She put a hand on his arm. ''Father, don't. Don't say anything to him until you've told the others. Pagones, I mean, and Cap. I'm afraid.''

''Afraid of what? Morton Harper is a fine man. When he knows what happened, he'll want something done himself.''

Putting on his hat, he started across the road for the cluster of buildings. Only for an instant did Sharon hesitate; then she swung around and ran to her horse, standing saddled and bridled, as she had planned to ride over to Mary's. Dud Kitchen would be there, and Pagones.

They were sitting at the table when she burst into the room.

''Please come with me!'' she said, when she explained. ''I'm afraid!''

Without a word, they got up and buckled on their guns. It was only a few hundred yards to the saloon, and they arrived just a few minutes after Tom Crockett walked up to Harper.

''Morton, my daughter and Mary Pagones saw Zapata fire that shot yesterday,'' Crockett was saying. ''I think we should surrender him to Bishop. We don't want to have a part in any killings.''

Harper's face hardened and he started to speak. Zapata, overhearing his name, stepped to the door, his hand on a gun. Then Harper's face softened a little, and he shrugged.

''I'm afraid they were mistaken,'' he said carelessly. ''You're being needlessly excited. Probably Pete was up that way, for he rides around a good deal, the same as the girls do. But shoot a man in the back? He wouldn't do it.''

''Oh, but he did,'' Dud Kitchen interrupted. ''What the girls say is true.''

"You call me a liar?" Harper turned on him, his face suddenly flushed with anger.

"No," Kitchen replied stiffly, his face paling. "I ain't callin' a man a liar, especially a man who come over the trail with me. But I know what I seen with my own eyes.

"Mary told me about that, and I'll admit I figured there was something wrong with what she said, so I went up and back-trailed 'em. I didn't have any idea about a killin' then, but I trailed the girls, and then I trailed Pete.

"Pete Zapata stalked that cowhand two miles before he got the shot he wanted. I went over every inch of his trail. He was fixin' to kill him. Then I trailed him down to the body. I seen where he wiped his knife on the grass, and I seen some of them brown sort of cigarettes he smokes. Pete Zapata killed that man, sure as I'm alive!"

Zapata had walked, cat-footed, to the edge of the wide plank porch in front of the saloon. He stood there now, staring at Dud.

"Trailed me, huh?" His hand swept down in a streaking movement before Dud could as much as move. His gun bellowed, and Dud Kitchen turned halfway around and dropped into the dust.

"Why, Mort!" Crockett's face was gray. "What does this mean? I—"

"You'd better all go back to your homes," Harper said sternly. "If Pete Zapata shot that man, and I don't admit for a minute that he did, he had a reason for it. As for this shooting here, Kitchen was wearing a gun, and he accused Zapata of murder."

Pagones' face was hard as stone. Two of the teamsters stood on the porch with shotguns. To have lifted a hand would have been to die.

"That settles it," Pagones said. "You can have your town! I'm leaving!"

"I reckon that goes for me, too," Crockett said sadly.

"I'm afraid you can't go," Harper said smoothly. There was a glint of triumph in his eyes. "My friend, John Kies, has lent you all money and supplies. Unless you can repay him what you owe, you'll have to stay until you have made a crop. California is a long ways off, and he couldn't be sure of collecting there.

"Besides," he added, "Indians have rustled some of our stock. I have been meaning to tell you. Most of your oxen are gone." He shrugged. "But why worry? Stay here. This land is good, and these little difficulties will iron themselves out. There are always troubles when a new community begins. In a few years all this will be over and there will be children born here, a church built, and many homes."

Dud Kitchen was not dead. In the Pagones' house, Mary sat beside his bed. Satterfield had removed the bullet, and now he sat at the kitchen table, drinking coffee.

"He's got a chance," Satterfield said. "A good chance. I'm no doctor, just picked up a mite when I was in that Mexican War, but I think he'll come through."

Pagones, his heavy head thrust forward on his thick neck, stared into the fire, sombre, brooding. He turned and looked at Satterfield and Crockett.

"Well," he said, "it looks bad. Looks like we're in a fight whether we want it or not. Hardy Bishop hasn't bothered us none, even after all of Mort Harper's preaching about him. Now that breed has killed one of his men."

"That Red," Satterfield muttered, half to himself. "He don't look like no man to have trouble with. Nor Bat, either!"

"Where does Rock stand?" Pagones demanded. "That's what I'm wonderin'."

"Said he was ridin' for Bishop," Satterfield replied. "That's plain enough."

"If we'd listened to him, this wouldn't have happened," Mary said.

There was no reply to that. The three men stood quiet, listening to Dud Kitchen's heavy breathing. The rap at the door startled them, and they looked up to see Rock Bannon standing there.

Sharon drew in her breath, and she watched him wide-eyed as he stepped into the room and closed the door after him. Hat in hand, his eyes strayed from them to the wounded man lying in the bed.

How tall he was! And his shoulders had seemed to fill the door when he entered. He wore buckskin trousers tucked into hand-tooled star boots, and checked shirt with a buckskin jacket, Mexican fashion, over it. On his hips were two Dragoon Colts in tied-down holsters.

"He hurt bad?" he asked softly.

"Yes, but Jim Satterfield says he's got a chance," Mary said.

Rock Bannon turned to look at them. "Well," he said, "you saw me ride in here today. You know I'm riding for Bishop. From what's happened, I reckon you know that war's been declared. You've got to make up your mind whose side you're on. I talked Hardy Bishop into lettin' you stay on, against his better judgment. He was all for runnin' you off pronto, not because he had anything against you, but because he could see settlers gettin' a toehold in his domain.

"Now one of our boys has been killed. Even Bishop might have trouble holdin' the boys back after that. I've talked to 'em, and they want the guilty man. They don't care about anybody else. What happens now is up to you."

"Not necessarily," Pagones objected. "We'll call a vote on it."

"You know how that'll go," Bannon objected. "Ten of you came in here with Mort Harper. Then he brought in Kies and Zapata. Now he's got other men. Supposin' you three vote to turn over the guilty man. How many others will vote that way? Cap may think right, but Cap will vote pretty much as Harper says. So will Purcell and Lamport. Any way you look at it, the vote is going to be to fight rather than turn Zapata over."

"No way to be sure of that," Satterfield objected. "Harper may decide to turn him over."

Bannon turned, his temper flaring. "Haven't you learned anything on this trip? Harper's using you. He brought you down here for his own reasons. He's out to steal Bishop's Valley from Hardy—that's what he wants. You're just a bunch of dupes!"

"You got any proof of that?" Crockett demanded.

"Only my eyes," Rock admitted, "but that's enough. He owns every one of you, lock, stock and barrel. I heard about that matter of you being in debt to Kies. Don't you suppose he planned all that?"

The door opened and Cap Mulholland came in, and with him was Collins. Cap's face flushed when he saw Rock.

"You'd better light out. If Pete Zapata sees you, he'll kill you."

"That might not be so easy," Bannon said sharply. "All men don't die easy, nor do they knuckle under to the first smooth talker who sells them a bill of goods."

Mulholland glared at him. "He promised us places, and we got 'em. Who's this Bishop to run us off? If it comes to war, then we'll fight."

"And die for Morton Harper? Do you think he'll let you keep what you have if he gets in control of this valley? He'll run you out of here without a penny. You're his excuse, that's all. If the law ever comes into this, he can always say that Bishop used violence to stop free American citizens from settling on the land."

"That's just what he's doin'," Cap said. "If he wants war he can have it!"

"Then I'd better go," Rock said. "I came here hopin' to make some peace talk. It looks like Zapata declared war for you. Now you've got to fight Mort Harper's war for him."

"You were one of us once," Pagones said. "You helped us on the trail. Why can't you help us now?"

Rock Bannon looked up, and his eyes hesitated on Sharon's face, then swept on. "Because you're on the wrong side," he said simply.

Sharon looked up and her eyes flashed. "But you were one of us," she protested. "You should be with us now. Don't you understand loyalty?"

"I was never one of you after Mort Harper came," he said. Sharon flushed under his gaze. "Whatever I might have been, Harper took away from me. I ain't a smooth-talkin' man; guess I never rightly learned to say all I feel, but sometimes them that say little, feel a sight more."

He put one hand on the latch. "As for loyalty, my first loyalty's to Hardy Bishop," he said.

"But how could that be?" Sharon protested.

"He's my father," Rock said quietly, then he stepped quickly and silently out the door.

"His father!" Pagones stared after him. "Well, I'll be danged!"

"That don't cut any ice with me," Mulholland said. "Nor his talk. I got the place I want, and I aim to keep it. Harper says there ain't any way they can drive us off. He says we've got guns enough to hold our own, and this canyon ain't so easy to attack. I'm glad it's comin' to a showdown. We might as well get it over."

"All I want is to get to work," Collins said stubbornly. "I got a sight of it ahead, so if that Bishop aims to drive me off, I wish he'd come and get it over with."

"All that talk about Harper usin' us," Satterfield said uneasily. "That didn't make sense!"

"Of course not!" Cap said hotly. "Bannon was against

everything we tried to do, right from the start. He just never had no use for Mort Harper, that was all.''

''Maybc there is something to what he says,'' Sharon interposed.

Cap glanced around irritably. ''Beggin' your pardon, Sharon. This is man's talk.''

''I'm not so sure,'' she flashed. ''We women came across the plains with you. If we fight, my father may die; that makes it important to me . And if you think I'm going to stand by and let my home be turned into a shambles, you're wrong.''

Her father started to speak, but she stepped forward. ''Bannon said Harper was using you. Well, maybe he is and maybe he isn't, but there are a few things I'd like you to think about, because I've been thinking about them.

''Did Mort Harper look for this townsite? No, he rode right to it, and to me that means he had planned it. What affair was it of his which trail we took? Yet he persuaded us, and we came down here. Who got us to stay? Harper! I'll admit I wanted to stay, and most of us did, but I'm wondering if he didn't count on that. And what about those wagons of supplies that turned up at just the right time?''

''Why, they just followed him on from the fort,'' Mulholland protested.

''Did they?'' Sharon asked. ''Go up and look at the trail. Mary and I looked at it, and no wagons have come over it since we did. Anyway, would he let those wagons come across that Indian country without more protection than they had? Those wagons were already here, waiting for us. They were back up in a canyon northeast of the trail.''

''I don't believe that!'' Collins said.

''Go look for yourselves then,'' Sharon said.

''You sound as if you're against us,'' Cap said. ''Whose side are you on anyway?''

''I'm on the side of the wagon train people, and you know it,'' she said. ''But a lot of this doesn't look too good to me. The first day we were here I rode down in the valley with Mort, and he said something that had me wondering, something about taking it for himself.''

''Don't make sense,'' Cap said stubbornly. ''Anyway, womenfolks don't know about things like this.''

Sharon was angry. In spite of herself, and knowing her anger only made Cap more stubborn, she said: "You didn't think there were any Indians, either. You took Mort's word for that. If it hadn't been for Bannon, we'd all have been killed."

She turned quickly and went out of the cabin. Swinging into the saddle, she started across toward her own cabin. It was dark, and she could see the light in the saloon, and the lights in Collins's blacksmith shop, where his wife and little Davy would be waiting for him to return.

Angry, she paid little attention where she was going until suddenly a horseman loomed in the dark near her.

"Howdy!" he said, swinging alongside.

From his voice and bulk, she knew him at once as Hy Miller, a big teamster who sometimes served as relief bartender. He had been drinking.

She tried to push on, but he reached out and grabbed her wrist. "Don't be in no such hurry," he said, leering at her in the dimness. "I want to have a bit of palaver with you!"

"Well, I don't want to talk to you!" she said angrily. She tried to jerk her wrist away, but he only tightened his grip. Then he pulled her to him and slid his other arm around her waist. She struggled, and her mare sidestepped, pulling her from the saddle.

Miller dropped her, then slid from his own horse and grabbed her before she could escape. "I'll learn you a thing or two!" he said hoarsely. "It's about time you settlers were learnin' who's runnin' this shebang!"

What happened next, Sharon scarcely knew. She was suddenly wrenched from Miller's arms, and she heard a crack of a blow, and Miller went down into the grass.

"Run for the house!" It was Bannon's voice. "Quick!"

Miller came up with an oath, and she saw him charge. Bannon smashed his left into the big teamster's mouth and staggered him, but the man leaped in, swinging with both hands. There was no chance for science or skill. In the dimness the two men fought like animals, tooth and nail, yet Bannon kept slamming his right to the bigger man's stomach. The teamster coughed and gasped, and then Rock swung a right to his chin that staggered him, and followed it up with a right and a left. Miller went down, and Bannon stooped and grasped his shirt collar in his left hand.

Holding the man at arm's length in a throttling grip, Bannon smashed him in the face again and again, then he struck him in the body and hurled him to the ground. Sharon, wide-eyed and panting, still stood there. "Get to your house," Bannon snapped. "Tell your father to go armed, always. This is only the beginning!"

As she fled, somebody behind her said, "Hey, what's goin' on here?"

Behind her there was a pound of a horse's hoofs, and she knew Rock was gone. Swiftly, when she reached the house, she stripped the saddle from the mare and turned it into the corral. Then she went into the house and lighted the lamp. A few minutes later, her father came in. She told him all that had happened.

He stood there, resting his fists on the table. Then he straightened.

"Honey," he said, "I'm afraid I did wrong to stop here. I wish now I'd gone on with Bob Sprague and the others. They'd be most to Californy by now. I'm afraid—I'm afraid!"

CHAPTER FIVE

ROCK BANNON STOPPED that night in a line cabin six miles west of Poplar and across the valley. When morning came, he was just saddling up when Bat Chavez rode in. With him were Johnny Stark and Lew Murray. All three were armed.

Bat grinned at him. Then his eyes fell on the skinned knuckles, and he chuckled.

"Looks like you had some action."

"A little," Rock said, and then explained briefly. "You watch yourselves," he said, "and stick together. That outfit's out for trouble."

"All I want's a shot at Zapata," Bat said harshly. "I'll kill me a breed if I get it."

Rock mounted and rode north toward the ranch house. No act of his could avert trouble now. He had hoped to convince the settlers who came with the wagon train that they should break away from Mort Harper.

That would draw the lines plainly—the ranch against the land-grabbers. He knew that Mulholland was an honest, if a stupid man. The others of the train were honest, but some of them, like Purcell and Lamport, were firm adherents of Harper, and believed in him. This belief they combined with a dislike of Rock Bannon.

It had been a hard task to persuade Hardy Bishop to let them stay. The old man was a fire-eater, and he knew what it would mean to let settlers get a toehold in his rich valley. Once in, they would encroach more and more on his best range, until he was crowded back to nothing. Only his affection for Rock had convinced him—and the fact that he had gleaned from Rock's talk: among the settlers was a girl.

Rock Bannon knew what the old man was thinking. Lonely, hard-bitten and tough, Bishop was as affectionate as many big bearlike men are. His heart was as big and warm as himself, and from the day he had taken Rock Bannon in, when the boy was orphaned at six when Kaw Indians had killed his parents, Bishop had lived as much for Rock as for his ranch. Now, more than anything, he wanted Rock settled, married, and living on the broad acres of Bishop's Valley.

It had been that as much as anything that brought him around to Rock's way of thinking when Rock planned to go east to Council Bluffs. Secretly, he hoped the boy would come back with a wife, and certainly there were no women around Bishop's Valley but an occasional squaw. He had never seen this girl with the wagon train, but he had gleaned more than a little from Rock's casual comments, and what he heard pleased him.

Hardy Bishop was a big man, weighing, now that he was heavy around the middle, nearly three hundred pounds. Yet in the days of his raw youth he tipped the beam at no less than two hundred and fifty pounds. On his hip even the big Dragoon Colts looked insignificant, but he was scarcely less fast than Rock.

Seated deep in a cowhide-covered chair, he looked up when Rock came in, and grinned. He was just filling his pipe. There was a skinned place on Bannon's cheekbone, and his knuckles were raw.

"Trouble, you've had," Bishop said, his deep voice filling the room. "Been over to look at them settlers again? Think they killed Wes?"

"Not the settlers," Rock said. "One of the men with them."

Rock sat down on the butt of a log and quietly outlined the whole situation, explaining about Harper, Zapata, and the teamster.

"They had that stuff cached in the hills," Rock went on. "Red Lunney spotted it some time back. There were about a dozen men holed up back there with a lot of supplies, too many for themselves. He kept an eye on them, but they didn't wander around, and made no trouble, so he left them alone.

"Evidently Mort Harper had them planted there. The wagon train, as near as I can figure, he planned to use as a blind in case the government got into this. He could always say they were honest settlers looking for homes, and the government would be inclined to favor them. What he really wants is Bishop's Valley!"

"He'll have a time gettin' it!" Bishop said grimly. "I'll bank on that. I fit Indians all over these hills, but this valley I bought fair and square from old War Cloud. We never had no Indian trouble until lately, when the wagon trains started comin' through. Those Mormons, they had the right idea. Treat Indians good, pay for what you get, and no shootin' Indians for the fun of it, like some folks do!

"Why, Rock, I trapped all over these mountains. Lived with Indians, trapped with them, hunted with them, slept in their tepees. I never had trouble with them. I was through this country with Wilbur Price Hunt's Astorians when I was no more'n sixteen, but a man growed. I was with John Day in this country after that, and he saw more of it than any other man.

"Took me two years to drive these cattle in here. First ever seen in this country! I drove them up from Santa Fe in six or seven of the roughest drives any man ever saw, with Indians doin' most of my drivin' for me. They said I was crazy then, but now my cattle run these hills and they eat this valley grass until their sides are fit to bust. One of these days you'll start drivin' these cattle east. Mark my words, there'll come a day they'll make you rich. . . . And then some whippersnapper like this Harper—why!" He rubbed his jaw irritably, then looked up at Rock. "You see that girl? That Crockett girl?"

"Uh-huh," Rock admitted. "I did."

"Why not stop this here cayusin' around and bring her home, son? Time you took a wife. Ain't no sense in a man runnin' loose too long. I did, and then hadn't my wife very long before she died. Fine girl, too."

"Hardy," Rock said suddenly, calling him by his first name, as he had since Bishop first took him in hand as a child, "I don't want war with those people. They're askin' for it, and that

Mulholland is simple enough to be led by the nose by Harper. Why don't you let me go get Zapata? I'll take him on myself. In fact,'' he added grimly, ''I'd like to! Then we can take some of the boys, get Harper and his teamsters and start them out of here.''

''Separate the sheep from the goats, eh?'' Bishop looked at him quizzically. ''All right, son. I've gone along with you this long. You take the boys, you get that Harper out of there and start him back for Laramie.

''As for Zapata, do what you like. I've seen some men with guns, and you're the fastest thing I ever did see, and the best shot. But don't leave him alive. If I had my way, we'd string every one of 'em to a poplar tree, and right quick.''

The old man grinned briefly at Bannon, leaned back and lighted his pipe. So far as he was concerned, the subject was closed.

Bat Chavez was a man who made his own plans and went his own way. Loyal to the greatest degree, he obeyed Rock Bannon or Hardy Bishop without question. They were his bosses, and he liked and respected them both. However, he had another loyalty, and that was to the memory of Wes Freeman.

He and Wes had ridden together, hunted together, fought Indians together. Wes was younger, and Bat Chavez had always considered himself the other's sponsor as well as friend. Now Wes was dead, and to Bat Chavez that opened a feud that could be settled only by blood. Johnny Stark and Lew Murray were like-minded. Both were young, hardy, and accustomed to live by the gun. They understood men like Zapata. Of the three, perhaps the only one who rated anything like an even break with the half-breed was the half-Mexican, half-Irish Chavez. However, no one of them would have hesitated to draw on sight.

They weren't looking for trouble, but they were ready. In that frame of mind they started down the valley to move some of the cattle away from the mouth of Poplar Canyon. No one of them knew what he was riding into, and had they known, no one of them would have turned back. . . .

Mort Harper, in his living quarters in the back of the saloon, was disturbed. Things had not gone as he'd planned. Secure in his familiarity with men of Hardy Bishop's type, he had been positive that the arrival of the wagon train and the beginning of their settlement would precipitate trouble. He had counted on a sudden attack by Bishop, and perhaps the killing of one or more of the settlers. Nothing more, he knew, would have been required to unite them against the common enemy. Peace-loving they might be, but they were men of courage, and men who believed in independence and equal rights for all. Typically American, they wouldn't take any pushing around.

On his knowledge of their character and that of Bishop he had built his plans. Over a year before, he had seen Bishop's Valley, and the sight had aroused a lust for possession that he had never known could live within him. Since that day he had lived for but one thing: to possess Bishop's Valley, regardless of the cost.

It was beyond the reach of law. Few people in the country had any idea the valley existed or that it had been settled. His first thought was to ride in with a strong band of outlaws recruited from the border towns, and take the place by main force; but times, he knew, were changing.

Morton Harper was shrewd enough to understand that the fight might arouse government inquiry. Fremont and Carson knew this country, and it was possible the Army might soon move into it. It would behoove him to have justice on his side.

The wagon trains offered that chance. From the first he had seen what a good chance it was. At the fort he watched them go through, and he saw the weariness of women and children, the haggard lines of men's faces. The novelty of the trip was over, and miles upon miles remained before they could reach Oregon. If he could get some of them into the valley country, he believed he could persuade them, by some method, to stay on. With that end in view, he watched until he saw the wagon train he wanted. Those which were led by able and positive men he had avoided. When he encountered Cap Mulholland, he was quick to perceive his opportunity.

In his visit to the camp he noted that Tom Crockett was a mild, tolerant man, friendly, and interested mainly in finding a new home and getting a plow into the ground. Pagones was a strong, able man, but not outspoken or likely to push himself into a position of leadership.

Pike Purcell and Lamport were honest, able men, but ignorant and alike in their dislike of Rock Bannon. Lamport, who was unmarried and thoroughly undesirable, had fancied himself for an inside track with Sharon Crockett until Bannon joined the train.

Rock Bannon was constantly with her, first as a wounded man

needing care, and later as a rider. Lamport grew jealous. Purcell, married to a nagging wife, had looked after Sharon with desire. His own dislike of Bannon stemmed from the same source, but grew even more bitter because Pike sensed Bannon was the better man, and Pike hated him for it.

Mort Harper was quick to curry the favor of these two. He talked with them, flattered them subtly, and bought them drinks. He learned that Purcell was desperately hard up, and lent him some money. He gave Lamport a gun he admired.

The only flaw in the picture had been Rock Bannon, and in Rock, Harper was quick to recognize a formidable and dangerous antagonist. He also realized he had an excellent weapon in the veiled enmity of Purcell and Lamport.

His plans had gone ahead very well until the attack by Bishop failed to materialize. Despite himself, he was disturbed. Would the old man really let them settle there? He caused a few cattle to be killed for meat, and left evidence about. That Rock Bannon had found the remains of the slaughtered cattle and buried them, he could not know. The expected attack failed, and he sensed a falling away from him on the part of the settlers.

The only way he could hope to get the valley was by precipitating open warfare, killing off the Bishop forces, and taking possession. Then in due time he could eliminate the settlers themselves and reign supreme, possessor of one of the largest cattle empires in the country.

Pete Zapata was under no orders to kill, but the fact that he had killed Wes Freeman fell in line with Harper's plans. Yet he could sense the disaffection among the settlers. Crockett and Pagones could be a strong force against him, if they became stubborn. Something was needed to align them firmly on his side.

That chance came, as he had hoped it would come. With Pete Zapata, Hy Miller, Pike Purcell, Lamport and Collins, he was riding down into the valley when they saw Bat Chavez and the two Bishop riders approaching. Had Harper led his party along the trail where they had started, the paths of the two groups would not have intersected, but Harper reined in and waited.

Chavez wasn't the man to ride around trouble. In Lew Murray and Johnny Stark he had two companions who had never ridden around anything that even resembled trouble. With guns loosened in holsters, they rode steadily on.

"Howdy!" Bat Chavez said. His eyes swung and fastened on

Pete Zapata. "Where you ridin'?"

"Who's askin'?" Purcell demanded truculently. "We go where we want."

"Not on this range, you don't. You stick to your valley. This here's Bishop range."

"He own everything?" Miller demanded. "We ride where we please!"

"Looks like you been ridin' where somebody else pleased," Johnny Stark said, grinning. "In fact, that face looks like somebody rid all over you with spikes in his boots."

Miller's face flamed. "There was three of 'em!" he snapped. "You couldn't do it. I think it's time we taught you Bishop riders a lesson, anyway."

"You mean," Chavez demanded insolently, "like that murderin' breed that shot Wes Freeman—in the back?"

Zapata's hand flashed for his gun, and Chavez was scarcely slower. Only the jerk of Zapata's horse's head saved him. As it was the horse took the bullet right through the head, and leaped straight up into the air jerking Zapata's gun and spoiling his aim.

There was a sudden flurry of gunshots, and Mort Harper was quick to sense his chance. He drew his six-shooter and calmly shot Collins through the back.

The attack broke as quickly as it began. Zapata's horse had leaped, then hit the ground, stone dead. Thrown from the horse, Zapata lost his gun and sprawled in the grass, showing no desire to get up and join the fight or even hunt for his gun.

Outnumbered, and with Murray shot through the leg, the Bishop riders drew off. Purcell had been burned along the cheek, and Miller's horse was killed, so the battle ended after only a few seconds, with two horses and one man dead. In the excitement, only Mort Harper saw the flare of pained astonishment and accusation in Collins's eyes.

The blacksmith's mouth refused to shape words, and he died there in the grass. Harper looked down at him, a faint smile on his face. Collins had been a popular man, quiet and well liked. This would do what all Harper's other plans had failed to do.

"Collins got it?" Pike stood over him, his hard face saddened. "He was a good man." Of them all, Collins was the only man in the wagon train Pike Purcell had known before the trip began. They had come through the war together.

"Might's well bury him, I guess," Mort said.

Pike looked up. "No, we'll tote him back home. His widow'll want to see him. Reckon it'll go hard with her."

Mort Harper's lips thinned, but there was nothing he could say without arousing suspicion. Silently, the little cavalcade started back. Collins's body was tied to Pike's horse, and he walked alongside, trailed by Zapata and Miller.

For two days ominous quiet hung over the town of Poplar. Collins had been buried, and the faces of the settlers as they gathered about to see his body lowered into the grave proved to Harper how right he had been. No longer was there any doubt or hesitation. Now they were in the fight. He had walked back from that grave filled with triumph. Only a few days longer, and then he would begin the war in earnest.

Tom Crockett was a quiet man, but his face was stern and hard as he walked back home beside Sharon. "Well, we tried to avoid it, but now it's war," he said. "I think the sooner we have some action the better."

Sharon said nothing, but her heart was heavy within her. She no longer thought of Mort Harper. His glamour had faded, and always now, there was but one man in her thoughts, the tall, shy, hesitant, Rock Bannon.

She always marveled that a man so hard, so sure of himself with men, horses or guns could be so quiet and diffident with women. As a matter of fact, Rock Bannon had never seen any woman but an Indian squaw until he was eighteen years old, in Santa Fe.

Rock Bannon had never talked to a woman until he was twenty. Now he was twenty-seven, and he had probably talked to no more than six or seven white women or girls.

With deepening sadness and pain, she realized the killing of Collins had done all they had hoped to avoid. There would be war now, and knowing her father as she did, she knew the unrelenting stubbornness in him once he was resolved upon a course. She had seen him like this before. He always sought to avoid trouble, always saw the best in people, yet when the battle line was laid down, no man would stay there longer than Tom Crockett.

Only one man was silent on the walk back from the grave. Dud Kitchen, weak and pale from his own narrow escape, was out for the first time. He was very tired, and he was glad when he was back in the Pagones' house and could lie down and rest. He was up too soon, he knew, but Collins had been his friend. Now, lying alone in the gathering darkness and hearing the low mutter of men's voices in the other room, he was sorry he had gone.

He had gone over to the Collins house to see his old friend once before he was buried, and he was there when the widow and Scatterfield had dressed him in his Sunday-go-to-meeting clothes. He saw something then that filled the whole inside of him with horror. He saw what none of them seemed to have noticed, that Collins had been shot in the back! Yet he had seen something more than that, and it was that thing that disturbed him.

Dud Kitchen was a friendly, cheerful young man who liked nothing better than to sing and play the mandolin. Yet in his life, from Missouri to Texas, he had more than a little experience with guns. Once, too, he had gone down the river to New Orleans, and he had learned many things on that trip.

Among other things he knew the Dragoon Colt had the impact of an ax and would blow a hole in a man big enough to run a buffalo through, or so it was phrased on the frontier. The hole in Collins had been much smaller at the point of entry; it had been wide and ugly at the point of exit.

Opening the door between the living room-kitchen of the Pagones' house, Pike walked in to look at Dud. "Better get yourself well, Dud," Pike said. "We'll need all hands for this fuss."

"Was it bad, Pike?" Kitchen asked. His voice was faint, and in the dim light Pike could not see what lay in the younger man's eyes.

"No, I figure it wasn't so bad," Pike said. "Only a few shots fired. It was over so quick I scarce got my gun out. That Bat Chavez, him and Zapata were fastest, but Pete's horse swung around and spoiled his aim for him. Guess it saved his life, though, cause Bat's bullet hit the horse right in the head. Between the eyes.

"The horse rared up and throwed Pete, and I jumped my horse away to keep from gettin' in a tangle. Lamport, he scored a shot on one of them other fellows. We seen him jerk and seen the blood on him as they were ridin' off."

Dud Kitchen waited a long moment, then he said carefully: "Who killed Collins?"

Purcell seemed to scowl. "Don't rightly know. There was a sight of shootin' goin' on. Might have been any one of them three. Don't you worry about that. We'll get all three of them, so we won't miss gettin' the right one."

"Have they got good guns?" Dud asked. "I'll bet they have!"

"Same as us. Dragoon Colts. One of 'em had an old Walker, though. Big gun, too. Shoots like a rifle."

After Pike Purcell had gone Dud Kitchen lay alone in the dark room, thinking. His thought frightened him, and yet, he was himself down from a shot by Zapata, who was on their own side. Collins had been shot in the back.

Whatever he had been shot by, Dud Kitchen was willing to take an oath it had been neither a Walker nor a Dragoon Colt. The hole was much smaller. The chest of the man had been frightfully torn. Sometimes men cut their bullets off flat across the nose to make them kill better. Dud had seen that done. It usually tore a man up pretty bad.

CHAPTER SIX

JOHNNY STARK BROUGHT the news of the fight to Rock Bannon. He was with Bishop at the time, and the old man's face hardened.

"Well, there it is, Rock! We can't give them any more time now. They've had their chance, and from now on, she'll be open warfare." Bishop looked up at Stark. "Take six men back with you. Have Monty go with the buckboard and bring Lew here to the ranch house, where he can have proper care. You tell Red I want to see him, but he'll be in charge when he goes back."

Rock got up and paced the floor. He ran his fingers through his shock of black, curly hair. His face was stern and hard. He knew what this meant. One man had gone down, Johnny said. From his description of the man it would be Collins, one of the good men. That would serve to unite the settlers in a compact lot. Despite all his desires to avoid trouble, they were in for it now, and it would be a case of dog eat dog. What would Sharon think of all this?

Hastily, he computed the numbers at the townsite. Their numbers were still slightly inferior to those on the Bishop ranch, but due to expected Indian trouble and the stock, many of the Bishop hands must remain on the far ranges.

"I'm going out," he said at last. "I'm going down to Poplar. Also, I'm going to have a look in that canyon where Harper's stuff was cached."

"You watch yourself, boy!" Bishop said. He heaved himself up in his chair. "You take care! I'm figurin' on you havin' this ranch, and I ain't wantin' to will it to no corpse."

Rock hurried down to thc corral and saw Johnny Stark leading out the steel-dust, all saddled and ready.

"I figured you'd be ridin', Rock," he said grimly. He handed the reins to him and started to turn away, then he stepped back.

"Rock," he said, "somethin' I been goin' to tell somebody. I forgot to mention it back there. Rock, I don't think any of us killed Collins!"

Bannon wheeled and grabbed the cowhand by the arm. His eyes were like steel.

"What do you mean? Give it to me, quick!"

"Hey!" Johnny said. "Ease up on that arm!" He grinned. "You got a grip like a bear trap." He rubbed his arm. "'Why, I been thinkin' about that ever since. Bat was thinkin' only of Zapata. I shot at that Miller, the guy you whipped. I got his horse. Lew, he burned that long lean mountain man along the cheek, tryin' for a head shot. Actually, this here Collins hombre was off to our left. None of us shot that way."

"You're sure of that?" Bannon demanded.

His mind was working swiftly. If one thing would arouse anger against Bishop among the settlers, it would be the killing of one of their own number, and particularly one so well liked as Collins had been.

Bannon stared at the rider. "Did you see anybody near him? Who was over at that side?"

"This here Collins hombre who got shot was in the front rank," Johnny said. "Then there was a heavy-set sort of guy with a beard, and a tall hombre in a white hat with a dark coat."

The bearded man would be Lamport, the man in the white hat was Mort Harper.

Rock Bannon swung a leg over the saddle. "Johnny, you tell Red to sit tight," he said. "I'm riding to Poplar."

"Want me along?" Stark asked eagerly. "You better take some help. Those hombres are killin' now. They're in a sweat, all of them."

Rock shook his head. "No, I'll go alone," he said. "Tell Red to wait at the cabin."

Rock wheeled the gray and cut across the valley. There was still a chance to avoid a battle if he could get to Poplar in time, yet he had a feeling that Harper would not wait. Hostilities had begun, and that was what he had been playing for all the time. Now he had his excuse to wipe out the Bishop forces, and he would be quick to take advantage of it.

Yet before he was halfway down the valley, he reined in on the slope of a low hill. Miles to the south he could see a group of horsemen cutting across toward the line cabin. Bat Chavez was there, alone with the wounded Murray.

Red would be starting soon, but would get there too late to help Bat or Murray. Within a matter of half an hour they would be attacking. From where he was it would take him all of that time and probably more to reach them. There was no time to go back. Wheeling the stallion, he started down the valley, angling away from the group of riders.

In the distance, around the peaks towering against the sky, dark clouds were banking. A jagged streak of lightning ripped the horizon to shreds of flame, then vanished, and there was a distant roll of thunder, muttering among the dark and distant ravines like the echoes of distant battle.

The gray horse ran through the tall grass, sweeping around groves of aspen and alder, keeping to the low ground. He splashed through a swale, crested a long, low hill that cut athwart the valley, and turned at right angles down the draw toward the cover of the far-off trees. The cool wind whipped against his face, and he felt a breath of moist wind as it shifted, feeling for the course of the storm.

The big horse was running smoothly, liking the feel of running, as he always did, letting his powerful muscles out and stretching them. Leaning forward to break the wind and let the weight of his body help the running horse, Rock Bannon talked, speaking softly to the stallion. He knew it loved his voice, for between the horse and man there was that companionship and understanding that come between a man and horse only when they have known many trails together, have shared the water of the same creeks, and run over long swells of prairies as they were running now.

Yet then he heard the distant sound of a rifle, and then a roll of shots.

"Bat, I hope to heaven you're under cover!" he muttered. "I hope they didn't surprise you!"

He eased the horse's running now, because he might rush upon some of them sooner than he expected. He slid his rifle from the scabbard and raced into the trees. The sound of firing was nearer now. He slowed the horse to a walk, letting him take a blow, his eyes searching the brush. There was still some distance to go, but there was firing, and that meant that Bat was under cover. They had not caught him flatfooted, at least.

He swung the horse up into the rocks and slid from the saddle, easing forward to the rim of the shelf overhanging the line cabin. Lying face down among the rocks, he could see puffs of smoke from the brush around the cabin. Waiting until he saw a gleam of light on a rifle, he fired.

Almost instantly, a man some distance away leaped up and started to run for a boulder. Swinging the rifle, Rock snapped a shot at him and the man went to his knees, then started to crawl for shelter.

A rifle bellowed down below and a shot glanced off a rock, kicking splinters into Bannon's face. He eased back and worked down the slope a bit, studying the situation below. One man at least was wounded.

Suddenly, a horseman leaped a horse from behind some trees, and, dragging a flaming mass of brush, raced toward the cabin. It was a foolhardy thing to do, but instantly, Bannon saw his purpose, for the rifle fire had attracted Bat Chavez to the other side of the cabin. Rock lifted his own rifle and steadied it. A flashing instant of aim, then he fired.

The horseman threw up his arms and toppled back off the horse, right into the mass of flaming brush. He screamed once, horribly, then rolled clear, fighting the fire in his garments and dragging himself in the dust. Another man rushed from the brush to aid him, and Rock held his fire.

Suddenly, there was a heavy roll of thunder. Looking around, he saw the clouds had come nearer, and now there was a sprinkle of rain. At the same instant he heard the pounding of horses' hoofs. Snapping a quick shot at the brush, he was in time to hear a startled yell and then the attackers broke from the brush and, scrambling to their saddles, charged away across the valley, and then the rain broke with a thundering roar, a veritable cloudburst.

Rushing to the gray, he swung into the saddle and put the animal around to a steep slide of shale, and rode down to the barn near the corral. Johnny rushed up to him.

"You all right?"

"Yeah. How's Bat?"

"Don't know. Bat went in. You go ahead. I'll fix your horse up."

Rock sprinted for the house and got in, slamming the door after him. Bat looked around, grinning widely.

"Man, was I glad to hear that rifle of yours!" he said. "They had me surrounded. Lew wanted to get into it, but I was afraid his wound would open and start bleedin' again. Well, we drove' em off."

"'You get anybody?"

"Scratched a couple. Maybe got one. You got one that first shot. I seen him fall. That'll be one down and two bad hurt, maybe four. Looks like we come out of that on top."

"I was headed for Poplar and saw them. I was afraid you'd be outside and they'd split up on you."

Chavez spat. "They mighty near did. I'd just been to the spring for water."

Rock stared into the fire. This would mean nothing one way or another. They had been turned back from the first attack, but they would not be convinced. He had killed a man, and who it was would matter a great deal, he knew. Certainly if it was another of the settlers he would have small chance of selling them on quitting.

Yet he was just as resolved now as before the attack. This thing must be stopped. It was never too late to try. The rain was roaring upon the roof, a full-fledged cloudburst. They would never expect him in a flood like that. They would be inside, and expecting everyone else to be there, too. If he circled around and came down the canyon, it would be the best chance. If they were keeping watch at all, it would be from this direction. . . .

Sharon was outside when she saw the rain coming, and she waited for it, liking the cool air. Over the distant mountains across the valley there were vivid streaks of lightning. It was already storming there, and a frightful storm by all appearances.

She was alone, and glad of it. Mary had wanted her to come to the Collins house, where several of the women had gathered, but she knew she could never stand to be cooped up now. She was restless and worried. Her father was out there, and for all his courage and willingness to go, Tom Crockett was no fighting man. He was not like Bannon.

Strangely, now, she was little worried about Rock Bannon. He was hard, seemingly impervious to harm. Even now he might be over there across the valley. He might be killing her father, or her father might be shooting him. Twelve men had ridden away. Eight of them were settlers. Collins was dead and Dud Kitchen still too weak to ride, but the others had gone to a man. Mulholland, Satterfield, Pagones, Lamport, Purcell, Olsen and Greene. And, of course, her father.

Then the rain came. A scattering of big drops, then the rolling wall of it. She turned and went inside. There were a few places where the roof was not too tight. She put pans under them, and lighted a light which she put on the table near the window. Her father's leg was still not too strong, and it worried her to think he was out there in all this.

She caught a glimpse of herself in the mirror, a tall girl with a great mass of red-gold hair done in two thick braids about her head, her face too pale, her eyes too large.

She heard them coming before she saw them, and saw a horseman break away from the others and cross the grass, now worn thin from much travel. When the horse was stabled her father came in, stamping his feet and slipping out of the slicker. His gray hat was black with rain, and she took it close to the fire. The coffee was ready, and she poured a cup, then went for a bowl to get some soup for him.

He sat down at the table—sat down as suddenly as if his legs had been cut off, and she noticed with a sudden qualm that he looked old, tired. His eyes lifted to hers and he smiled wanly.

"Guess I'm no fighting man, Sharon," he said. "I just wasn't cut out for it. When that man fell into the flames today, I nearly wilted."

"Who was it?" she asked quickly. "One of our men?"

"No, it was a teamster. One of the bunch that hangs around the saloon. His name was Osburn. We rushed the house, and one of the men inside opened fire. Wounded one of the men, first shot. We had the house surrounded, though, and would have had them in a few minutes; but then someone opened up on us from the cliff.

"It was Bannon, I'm sure of that. He killed Hy Miller. Got him with his first shot, although how he saw him I can't imagine. Then he wounded Satterfield. Shot him through the leg, about like I was. This Osburn got on a horse, and—" His voice rambled on, and all she could think about was that her father was home, that her father was safe.

When his voice died away and he was eating the hot soup, she said, "And Bannon? Was he hurt?"

"No, he wasn't hurt. He never seems to get hurt. He's a hard man, Sharon."

"But a good man, Father!" she said suddenly. "He's a good man. Oh, I wish things were different!"

"Don't think it, Sharon," her father said, shaking his head. "He's not for you. He's a wild, ruthless man. A man who lives by the gun. Collins is dead, and by one of this man's friends, and they'll never let up now, nor will we. It's a war to the end."

"But why, Father? Why?" Sharon's voice broke. "Oh, when I think that we might have gone by the other trail! We might have been in Oregon now. Sometimes I believe that everything Bannon ever said about Mort Harper was true. All we've done is to come on here into this trap, and now our oxen are gone, all but the two you use to plow, and we're in debt."

"I know." Crockett stirred restlessly. "But it might have been as bad wherever we went . You must understand that. We may be mistaken in Mort. He's done what he could, and he's standing by us in this fight."

The fire flickered and hissed with the falling drops of rain in the chimney, and Sharon crossed and knelt beside the fire, liking the warm feel of it on her knees. She sat there, staring into the flames, hearing the unrelenting thunder of the rain and wondering where he was.

Where would it all end? That boy, Wes Freeman, slain in the hills. Then Collins, and now Miller. Dud Kitchen recovering from a wound. Jim Satterfield down, and the whole affair only beginning and no end in sight. The door opened suddenly and without warning, and she whirled, coming to her feet with her eyes wide.

Disappointment swept over her, and then fear. Pete Zapata was closing the door after him. He was smiling at her, his queer, flat face wet with rain, his narrow rattler's eyes searching the corners of the room.

"Not here?" he whispered hoarsely. "Purty soon, mebbe."

"Who—who do you mean?" she gasped.

Her father was sitting up very straight, his eyes on the half-breed. Zapata glanced at him with thinly veiled contempt, then shrugged.

"Who? That Rock Bannon. A few minutes ago he comes down the canyon on hees horse; now he ees here somewhere. Who knows? But soon he weel come here, and then—'' He smiled, showing his yellow teeth between thick lips. His eyes shifted from her to her father. ''Eeef one speaks to warn heem, I keel the other one, you see? Huh?''

Fear left her lips stiff, her eyes wide. Slowly, she turned back to the fire. Bannon would come here; Zapata was right. If Rock had come again to Poplar he would not leave without seeing her. He might come at any minute. She must think, she must somehow contrive to warn him.

The steel-dust stallion liked the dim, shallow cave in which Rock stopped him, but he didn't like being left alone. He whimpered a little, and snorted with fear as Bannon started to move away, but when Rock spoke, the stallion quieted, resigned to what was to come.

Rock Bannon moved out swiftly, keeping under the trees but working his way closer and closer to the house of Pagones. He didn't know what he was getting into, but Pagones was the most reliable of them all, and the strongest one. If resistance to Harper was to come, it must come from him. Crockett lacked the force of character, even though he might have the will. Besides, Pagones had the knowledge, very close to him, that one of Harper's men had shot down Dud Kitchen.

Pagones hadn't chosen his son-in-law. Mary had done that for herself, but Pagones couldn't have found anyone he liked better. Dud was energetic, tireless, capable and full of good humor. George Pagones, in his heart, had never felt sure of Mort Harper. He had listened with one part of his mind to Bannon's protests, even while the smooth words of Harper beguiled him.

Pagones had returned wet and tired. Like Crockett, he had no love of killing. He had seen Osburn tumble into the flames, he had seen Miller killed. Knowing the trouble Miller had caused, and how he had attacked Sharon while drunk, Pagones was not sorry to see him die. If it had to be someone, it might as well have been Miller. Yet seeing any man die is a shock, and he had been close to the man.

Many men are aggressive and willing enough to fight, but when they see death strike suddenly and horribly their courage oozes away. Pagones had the courage to defend himself, but his heart was not in this fight, and the action of the day had served to make him very thoughtful.

Something was worrying Dud Kitchen. He had been noticing

that for several days, yet there had been no chance to talk to him when the womenfolks were not around. He felt the need of talking to him now, and got up and went into the room. He was there, beside the bed, when a breath of cold air struck him and he heard a startled gasp from his wife.

Gun in hand, he stepped back to the door. Rock Bannon was closing it after him. He turned now, and looked at the gun in Pagones' hand. Bannon smiled grimly.

"Well, you've got the drop on me, Pag. What happens now?"

"What do you want here?" Pagones demanded sternly. "Don't you know that if you keep coming back they'll kill you?"

"Just so it isn't you, Pag," Bannon said. "I always reckoned you a friend."

Pagones holstered his gun. "Come in," he said. "I take it you've come to talk."

Mary and her mother stood facing him, their eyes shining with apprehension. There was a scuffling of feet from the other room, and Dud Kitchen was in the door.

"Howdy," he said. "They'll kill you, Rock. I heard Zapata say he was after you. He said he was going to get you next."

"All right." Rock dropped into a chair, his right-hand holster in his lap, the ivory gun butt near his right hand. His dark-blue shirt was open at the neck, his leather jacket unbuttoned. The candle and firelight flickered on the bright butts of the cartridges in his twin belts.

Dud's face was very pale, but somehow Rock sensed that Dud was glad to see him, and it made him feel better, and made the talk come easier. Pagones' cheekbones glistened in the firelight, and his eyes were steady on Bannon's face as he waited for him to begin. It was very still in the room. A drop of water fell into the fire and hissed itself into extinction.

Mary stooped, her freckles dark against the pallor of her face, and dropped a handful of small sticks on the fire.

"Pag," Bannon began slowly, "I've never wanted this fight. I don't think you have. I don't think Crockett did either, or Dud here. There's no use me tryin' to talk to Tom. He's a good man, and he knows what he wants, but he hasn't force enough to make it stick. He couldn't stand against Harper. There's only one man here can do that, Pagones, and that's you."

"Harper's my friend," Pagones said evenly. "He led us here. This is his fight and ours."

"You don't believe that," Rock said. "Not down inside, you don't. Collins's death brought you into it. That made it your fight and Crockett's fight. The truth is all you men want is homes. That's what your wife wants, and Mary. That's what Sharon wants, too. That's what Cap wants, and the rest of them.

"What Mort Harper wants is land and power. He intends to have them, no matter who dies, or when. I've been here before to try to stop this trouble. I'm here again, now.

"One of our men died first, and he was a good boy. He was murdered, Pagones, murdered as no man in the wagon train would kill any man, not even an Indian. Purcell didn't like me. Neither did Lamport. Cap was your leader, but he listened too readily to that glib tongue of Harper's."

"We all did," Dud said. "I listened, too. I listened for a while, anyway."

Mary moved up behind his chair and put her hand on his shoulder. He looked up quickly, and she smiled.

"Get to the point!" Pagones said. All that Bannon said was true. He knew it as well as Rock. He had listened to Harper, but secretly he had always been afraid that Bannon was right. He had been afraid of this trail. There might be a way out yet, but it had to be a way. They had no oxen now, they had no money. They were here, and they could not escape.

Rock leaned a hand on his knee. "Pagones, my boys say they didn't kill Collins!"

Dud Kitchen drew in his breath, and Mary looked at him in sudden apprehension.

"What's that you say?" Pagones demanded.

"I repeat, I talked to my boys, and they say they didn't kill Collins. Bat Chavez couldn't see anything but Zapata, Stark and Murray weren't even facing toward Collins then. They say they didn't kill him."

"There was a lot of shooting," Pagones said. "Anything might of happened."

"That's right," Bannon agreed. "But my boys don't think they shot Collins, and that leaves a big question."

"It doesn't leave no question for me!" Dud flared suddenly. "I saw that wound of Collins's! He was shot in the back!"

Pagones face hardened. He stared down at the floor, his jaw muscles working. Was nothing ever simple anymore? Was there nothing on which a man could depend? How had he got into this mess, anyway. What should he do?

"Who do you think?" he asked. "You mean Zapata?"

Their eyes were all on Rock Bannon, waiting, tense. "No," he said. "I mean Mort Harper!" He got up and moved restlessly around the room.

"But that's crazy!" Pagones leaped to his feet. "What would be the object? Is there any reason why he would kill a man on his own side?"

"You know the answer to that as well as I," Bannon said. He got up, too. "He wanted you in this fight, and that was the only way he could get you in. Purcell and Lamport were fire-eaters. They were in, but they weren't enough. He wanted the rest of you, the good, sober, industrious citizens, the men whose reputations at home were good, the men who would look honest to the military if they ever came west."

"I saw that wound," Kitchen repeated. "Collins was killed with a small gun, a small gun with flat-nose or split-ended bullets."

"Who has such a gun?" Pagones said. "You all know that Harper carries a Dragoon, like the rest of us."

"In sight, he does," Bannon agreed. "Mort Harper may pack another one."

Rock stopped, feet wide apart. "I've got to get out of here, Pag. I've got to get going, and fast. There's not much chance of anybody being out tonight, but I can't gamble on that. I've got to get away from here, but this is the last time I'll come. I've tried to tell you about Mort Harper for a long time. You've got your last chance to break away, because I'm telling you that if you don't break away there won't be a building standing on this ground within forty-eight hours."

Pagones' head jerked up. "Is that an ultimatum?"

"You bet it is!" Bannon snapped. "If I'd let Bishop have his head, you'd have all been out of here long ago. Wes would be alive now, and Collins, and Murray wouldn't be packin' that slug in his leg, and Dud would be on his feet. If I'd not kept Bishop off you, he would have faced you with forty armed men and ordered you off before you had a stake down or a foundation laid.

"Those boys of ours are spoilin' for a fight. They hate Harper's innards, and they want Zapata. He's a murderin' outlaw, and they all know it."

"I don't know that I can do anything," Pagones protested. "We have to think of Zapata as it is. Harper's the only thing that keeps him and those teamsters off our places and away from our women, anyway!"

Rock Bannon started for the door. With his hand on the latch, he turned, sliding into his slicker.

"You step aside and there won't be any Zapata or his friends!" he declared. "We'll wipe them out so fast they'll be only a memory. We just don't want to kill good people. You can keep your places. We let you come in, and we'll let you stay."

He turned and slipped out the door into the rain. For an instant, he hesitated, letting his eyes grow accustomed to the dark. Rain fell in slanting sheets, striking his face like hailstones and rattling against his oilskin slicker like on a tin roof. Water stood in puddles on the ground and when he stepped down a large drop fell from a tree down the back of his neck.

He hesitated, close against the wet tree trunk, and stared into the night. There was a glow of light from the window of the Crockett place. Somebody was still up. He hesitated, knowing it was dangerous to remain longer, yet longing for a sight of Sharon, for the chance to take her in his arms.

He never had. He had never kissed her, never held her hand. It was all a matter of their eyes, and yet he felt she understood, and perhaps responded to his feeling.

There were lights from the saloon. They would all be down there now, playing cards, drinking. It was a pity he had none of the boys here. They could go in and wipe them out in one final, desperate battle. Lightning flashed, and revealed the stark wet outlines of the buildings, the green of the grass, worn down now, between him and the Crockett cabin.

He stepped out from the tree and started across the open, hearing the far-off thunder muttering among the peaks of the mountains beyond the valley, muttering among the cliffs and boulders like a disgruntled man in his sleep.

He did not fasten his slicker, but held it together with his left hand and kept his right in his pocket, slopping across the wet ground with the rain battering the brim of his hat, beating with angry, skeleton fingers against the slicker.

Under the trees, he hesitated, watching the house. There was no horse around. Suddenly, a column of sparks went up from the chimney as if someone had thrown some sticks on the fire. He started to move, and another cluster of sparks went up. He hesitated, a signal? But who would know he was near?

A third time. Three times was a warning, three smokes, three rifle shots—what could it be? Who could know he was here? It was nonsense, of course, but the sparks made him feel uneasy.

Then again, three times, once very weakly, sparks mounted from the chimney. Somebody was playing with the fire, tapping with a stick on the burning wood, or stirring the fire.

No matter. He was going in. He felt cold, and the warmth of the room would be good again before he began his long ride to the line cabin. A long ride because it would be foolhardy to go down the canyon toward the valley.

He stepped out from under the tree and walked up to the house. His boots made sucking noises in the mud before the door. Lightning flashed and the water glistened on the smooth boards of the door. He should knock, but he stepped up and, keeping to the left of the door, he reached across with his left hand and drew the door wide.

A gun blasted, and he saw the sudden dart of fire from the darkness by the fireplace. The bullet smashed into the door, and then he went in with a rush.

He caught a glimpse of Sharon, her eyes wide with fright, scrambling away from the fire. Zapata lunged from the shadows, his face set in a snarl of bared teeth and gleaming eyes. His gun blasted again, and a bullet snatched at Rock's jacket. Bannon thumbed his gun.

Zapata staggered as though struck by a blow in the stomach. As Rock started for him, he leaped for an inner door. Rock lunged after him, firing again, and there was a crash as he went through the sack-covered window.

Wheeling, Rock leaped for the door and went out. Zapata's gun barked, and something laid a white-hot iron across his leg. Rock brought his gun up and turned his right side to the crouching man, and fired again, fired as though on a target range.

The half-breed coughed, and his pistol dropped into the mud. He clawed with agonized fingers at the other gun, and Rock Bannon could see the front of his shirt darkening with pounding rain and blood, and then Bannon fired again, and the breed went down, clawing at the mud.

A door slammed and there was a yell. Rock wheeled and saw Sharon in the doorway. "I can't stop," he said. "Talk to Pagones." And even as he spoke, he was running across the worn grass toward the trees.

A rifle barked, then another, and then intermittent shots.

Crying with fear for him, Sharon Crockett stood in the door, staring into the darkness. Lightning flared, and through the slanting rain she caught a brief glimpse of him, a rifle flared, and then he was gone into the trees. A moment later they heard the pounding of hoofs.

"They'll never catch him on that horse," Tom Crockett said. "He got away!" Sharon turned, and her father was smiling. "Yes, daughter, I'm glad he got away. I'm glad he killed that murderer."

"Oh, Father!" Then his arms were around her, and as running feet slapped in the mud outside, he pushed the door shut.

The door slammed open, and Mort Harper shoved into the room. Behind him were four men, their faces hard, their guns ready.

"What was he doing here?" Harper demanded. "That man's a killer! He's our enemy. Why should he come here?"

"I don't know why he came!" Crockett said coldly. "He never had a chance to say. Zapata had been waiting for him all evening. He seemed to believe he would be here. When Bannon came in, he fired and missed. He won't miss again."

Harper stared at him, his face livid and angry under the glistening dampness of the rain.

"You seem glad!" he cried.

"I am!" Crockett said. "That Zapata was a killer, and he deserved killing."

"And I'm glad," Sharon said, her chin lifed. "I'm glad Bannon killed him, glad that Bannon got away."

There was an angry mutter from the men behind Harper, but Mort put up a restraining hand. "This sounds like rebellion. Well, we'll have none of that in this camp. I've been patient with you, Sharon, but my patience is wearing thin."

"Who cares about your patience?" Anger rose in Sharon's eyes. "Your soft talk and lies won't convince us any longer. We want our oxen back, tomorrow! We've had enough of this. We'll get out of here tomorrow if we have to walk."

"No, you won't," Harper said. "Come on, boys. We'll go now."

"Let's teach 'em a lesson, boss," one man said angrily. "To blazes with this palaver!"

"Not now," Harper said. His nostrils were flared with anger, and his face was hard. "Later!"

When the door closed after them, Tom Crockett's face was white. "Well, Sharon," he said quietly, "for better or worse, there it is. Tomorrow we may have to fight. Your mother helped me fight Indians once, long ago. Could you?"

Sharon turned, and suddenly she smiled. "Do you need to ask?"

"No," he smiled back, and she could see a new light in his eyes, almost as if the killing of Zapata and the statement to Harper had made him younger, stronger. "No, I don't," he repeated. "You'd better get some sleep. I'm going to clean my rifle."

CHAPTER SEVEN

ROCK BANNON'S STEEL-DUST stallion took the trail up the canyon at a rapid clip. They might follow him, Bannon knew, and he needed all the lead he could get. Some of those men had been in these hills for quite some time, yet if he ever got away into the wilderness around Day's River, they would never find him.

Shooting it out with six or seven killers was no part of his plan, and he knew the teamsters who had come to Poplar were just that, a band of renegades recruited from the scourings of the wagon trains passing through the fort. After the immediate dash, however, he slowed down to give the steel-dust better footing.

He turned northeast when he came out of Poplar Canyon and rode down into a deep draw that ended in a meadow. The bottom of the draw was roaring with water that had run off the mountain, but as yet it was no more than a foot deep. Far below he could hear the thunder of Day's River, roaring at full flood now.

The canyon through the Narrows would be a ghastly sight with its weight of thundering white water. Always a turmoil, now it would be doubled and tripled by the cloudburst. Rain slanted down, pouring unceasingly on the hills.

The trail by which he had come would be useless on his return. By now the water would be too deep in the narrow canyon up which he had ridden. He must find a new trail, a way to cut back from the primitive wilderness into which he was riding, and down through the valley where Freeman had been killed, and then through the mountains.

Briefly, he halted the big stallion in the lee of a jutting shoulder of granite where wind and rain were cast off into the flat of the valley. Knowing his horse would need every ounce of its strength he swung down, and his shoulder against the rock, he studied the situation in his mind's eye.

His first desperate flight had taken him northwest into the wild country. Had he headed south he must soon have come out on the plains beyond the entrance to Bishop's Valley where he would have nothing but the speed of his own horse to assist his escape.

He was needed here, now. Any flight was temporary, so in turning north he had kept himself within striking distance of the enemy. His problem now was to find a way through the rugged mountain barrier, towering thousands of feet above him, into Bishop's Valley, and across the valley to home.

No man knew these mountains well, but Hardy Bishop knew them better than anyone else. Next to him, Rock himself knew them best, but with all his knowledge they presented a weird and unbelievable tangle of ridges, canyons, jagged crests, peaks and chasms. At the upper end of the valley the stream roared down a gorge often three thousand feet deep, and with only the thinnest of trails along the cliffs of the Narrows.

The isolated valley might have been walled for the express purpose of keeping him out, for as he ran over the possible routes into the valley, one by one he had to forget them. Bailey's Creek would be a thundering torrent now, water roaring eight to ten feet deep in the narrow canyon. Trapper's Gulch would be no better, and the only other two routes would be equally impassable.

Rock stared at the dark bulk of the mountain through the slanting rain. He stared at it, but could see nothing but Stygian darkness. Every branch, every rivulet, every stream would be a roaring cataract now. If there were a route into the valley now, it must be over the ridge. The very thought made him swallow and turn chill. He knew what those ridges and peaks were in quiet hours. They could be traveled, and he had traveled them, but only when he could see and feel his way along. Now, with lightning crashing, thunder butting against the cliffs, and clouds gathering around them, it would be an awesome inferno of lightning and granite, a place for no living thing.

But the thought in the back of his mind kept returning. Hardy Bishop was alone, or practically so. He had sent Red to the line cabin nearest Harper with most of the fighting men. Others were in a cabin near the Narrows, and miles away. Only two men would be at home besides the cook.

Rock Bannon did not make the mistake of underestimating his enemy. Mort Harper had planned this foray with care. He would not have begun without a careful study of the forces to be arrayed against him. He would know how many men were at the line cabin, and the result of his fighting must certainly be to convince him that the ranch house was alone, and Hardy Bishop, the heart, soul and brain of the Bishop strength, was there.

There was a route over the mountain. Once, by day, Bannon had traveled it. He must skirt a canyon hundreds of feet deep along a path that clung like an eyebrow to the sheer face of the cliff. He must ride across the long swelling slope of the mountain among trees and boulders, then between two peaks, and angle through the forest down the opposite side.

At best it was a twelve-mile ride, and might stretch that a bit. Even by day it was dangerous and slow going. And he needed only his eyes to convince him that lightning was making a playground of the hillside now.

"All right, boy," he said gently to the horse. "You aren't going to like this, but neither am I." He swung into saddle and moved out into the wind.

As he breasted the shoulder of granite, the wind struck him like a solid wall, and the rain lashed at his garments, plucking at the fastenings of his oilskin. He turned the horse down the canyon that would take them to the cliff face across which he must ride. He preferred not to think of that.

Drawing near, the canyon walls began to close in upon him until it became a giant chute down which the water thundered in a mighty Niagara of sound. Great masses of water churned in an enormous maelstrom below and the steel-dust stallion snorted and shied from its roaring.

Rock spoke to the horse and touched it on the shoulder. Reassured, it felt gingerly for the path, and moved out. A spout of water gushing from some crack in the rock struck him like a blow, drenching him anew and making the stallion jump. He steadied the horse with a tight rein, then relaxed and let the horse have his head. He could see absolutely nothing ahead of him.

Thunder and the rolling of gigantic boulders reverberated down the rock walled canyon, and occasional lightning lit flares that showed him glimpses of a weird nightmare of glistening rock and tumbling white water that caught the flame and hurled it in millions of tiny shafts on down the canyon.

The gray walked steadily, facing the wind but with bowed head, hesitating only occasionally to feel its way around some great rock or sudden, unexpected heap of debris.

The hoarse wind howled down the channel of rock, turning its shouting to a weird scream on corners where the pines feathered down into the passage of the wind. Battered by rain and wind, Rock Bannon bent his head and rode on, beaten, soaked, bedraggled, with no eyes to see, only trusting to the surefooted mountain horse and its blind instinct.

Once, when the lightning lifted the whole scene into stark relief, he glimpsed a sight that would never leave him if he lived to be a hundred. For one brief, all encompassing moment he saw the canyon as he never wanted to see it again.

The stallion had reached a bend, and, for a moment, hesitated to relax straining, careful muscles. In that instant, the lightning flared.

Before them the canyon dropped steeply away like the walls of a gigantic stairway, black, glistening walls slanted by the steel of driving rain, cut by volleys of hail, and accompanied by the roar of the cataract below.

Two hundred feet down the white water roared, and banked in a cul-de-sac in the rock was a piled-up mass of foam, fifteen or twenty feet high, bulging and glistening. At each instant wind or water ripped some of it away and shot it, churning, down the fury of raging water below. Thunder roared a salvo, and the echoes responded, and the wild cliff clinging cedar threshed madly in the wind as if to tear free its roots and blow away to some place of relief from the storm.

Lightning crackled, and thunder drummed against the cliffs, and the scene blacked out suddenly into abysmal darkness. The steel-dust moved on, rounding the point of the rock, and starting to climb. Then, as if by a miracle, they were out of the canyon, but turning up a narrow crevice in the rock with water rushing, inches deep, beneath the stallion's feet. A misstep here and they would tumble down the crevice and pitch off into the awful blackness above the water. But the stallion was steady, and suddenly they came out on the swell of the mountain slope.

The lightning below was nothing compared to this. Here darkness was a series of fleeting intervals shot through with thunderbolts, and each jagged streak lighted the night like a blaze from Hades. Gaunt shoulders of the mountain butted against the bulging weight of cloud, and the skeleton fingers of long-dead pines felt stiffly of the wind.

Stunned by the storm, the stallion plodded on, and Rock swayed in the saddle, buffeted and hammered, as they walked across that bare, dead slope among the boulders, pushing relentlessly against the massive wall of the wind. A flash of lightning and a tree ahead detonated like a shell, and bits of it flew off into space with the wild complaint of a ricocheted bullet. The stub of the tree smoked, sputtered with flame, and went out, leaving a vague smell of charred wood and brimstone.

A long time later, dawn felt its way over the mountains beyond and behind him, and the darkness turned gray, and then rose as flame climbed the peaks. Rock rode on, sodden, beaten, overburdened with weariness. The high cliffs behind him turned their rust-colored heights to jagged bursts of frozen flame, but he did not notice. Weary, the stallion plodded down the last mile of slope and into the rain-flattened grass of the plain.

The valley was empty. Rock lifted his red-rimmed eyes and stared south. He saw no horsemen, no movement. He had beaten them. He would be home before they came. And once he was home and could stand beside the big old man who called him son, they would face their trouble together.

Let Harper come; he would learn what fighting meant. These men were not of the same flesh or the same blood, but the response within them was the same, and the fire that shaped the steel of their natures was the same. They were men bred to the Colt. Bred to the law of strength. Men who knew justice, but could fight to defend what was theirs, and what they believed.

He was not thinking that. He was thinking nothing. He was only moving, and the steel-dust walked on into the ranch yard. Rock fell rather than stepped from the saddle. Springer rushed out to get his horse.

"My stars, man! How'd you get here?"

"Over the mountain," Bannon said, and walked toward the house.

Awed, Springer turned and looked toward the towering, six-thousand-foot range. "Over the mountain," he said. "Over the mountain!" He stripped the saddle from the big horse and turned it into the corral, and then almost ran to the bunkhouse to tell Turner. "Over the mountain!"

Hardy Bishop looked up from his great chair and his eyes sharpened. Rock raised a hand, then walked on through the room, stripping off his soaked clothing as he went. When he reached the bed he pulled off one boot, then rolled over and stretched out, his left spur digging into the blanket.

Bishop followed him to the room and stared down at him grimly; then he walked back and dropped into the chair. Well, he reflected, for that he could be thankful. He had a man for a son. . . .

It had been a long time ago when he first came into this valley with old John Day. They had come down through the Narrows and looked out over the wide, beautiful length of it, and he had seen what he knew he was looking for—he had seen Paradise.

There were men in the West then, men who roamed the streams for beaver or the plains for buffalo, They lived and traded and fought with the Indians, learned their ways and went them one better. They pushed on into new country, country no white man had seen.

There were men like John Coulter, who first looked into the Yellowstone region, old Jim Bridger who knew the West as few men did. There were John Day, Smith, Hoback, Wilbur Price Hunt, Kit Carson and Robert Stuart. Most of them came for gold, but there were a few even then who looked for homes, and of the first was Hardy Bishop.

He had settled here, buying the land from the Indians, and trading with them long before any other white man remained in the region. Once a whole year had passed during which he saw not even one trapper.

The Kaws were usually his friends, but the Crows were not, and occasionally raiding parties of Blackfeet came down from the north. When they were friendly, he talked or traded, and when they wanted to fight, he fought. After a while even the Crows left him alone, learning friendship was more profitable than death, and many had died. . . .

Bad days were coming. From his seat in the hidebound chair, Hardy Bishop could see that. The trouble with Indians would be nothing to the trouble with white men, and he was glad that Rock was a man who put peace first, but who handled a fast gun.

He raised his great head, his eyes twinkling. They were keen eyes that could see far and well. Even the Indians respected them. He could, they said, trail a snake across a flat rock, or a duck downstream through rough water. What he saw now was a horseman, riding toward the ranch. One lone horseman, and there was something odd in the way he rode.

It was not a man. It was a woman—a white woman. Hardy Bishop heaved himself ponderously from the chair. It had been almost ten years since he had seen a white woman! He walked slowly to the door, hitching his guns around just in case.

The sun caught her hair and turned it to living flame. His dark eyes kindled. She rode up to the steps, and he saw Springer and Turner in the bunkhouse door, gaping. She swung down from her black mare and walked over to him. She was wearing trousers and a man's shirt. Her throat was bare in the open neck. He smiled. Here was a woman!

Sharon looked up at Bishop, astonished. Somehow, she had always known he would be big, but not such a monster of a man. Six-four he stood in his socks, and he weighed three hundred pounds. His head was covered with a shock of iron-gray hair, in tight curls. His eyes twinkled, and massive forearms and hands jutted from his sleeves.

"Come in! Come in!" he boomed. "You'll be Sharon Crockett, then. I've heard of you. Heard a sight of you!" He looked around as she hesitated on the steps. "What's the matter? Not afraid of an old man, are you? Come in."

"It isn't that. Only we've come here like this—and it was your land, and—"

"Don't explain." He shook his head. "Come in and sit down. You're the first white woman who ever walked into this house. First one ever saw it, I reckon. Rock, he's asleep. Dead to the world."

"He's safe then?" she asked. "I was afraid. I saw them go after him."

"There was trouble?" he looked at her keenly. "What happened?"

She explained the killing of Pete Zapata, and what happened afterward. "That's why I'm here," she said. "In a way, I'm asking for peace. We didn't know. We were foolish not to have listened to Rock in the beginning, when he told us about Mort. My father and the settlers want peace. I don't know about Pike Purcell and Lamport, but I can speak for the rest of us."

Bishop nodded his head. "Rock told me what he was goin' for. So he killed Zapata? That'll please the boys." He turned his head. "Dave!" he bellowed.

A face covered with a shock of mussed hair and beard shoved into the door. "Bring us some coffee! And some of that cake! We've got a lady here, by—" He flushed. "Excuse me, ma'am. Reckon my manners need a goin' over. We cuss a sight around here. A sight too much, I reckon. I ain't never figured on gettin' into heaven, anyways. I been pretty much of a sinner, and not much of a repenter. Reckon they'd have to widen the gate some, anyway; I'd be a sight of weight to get in. Most likely they'd have to put some cribbin' under the cloud I set on, too."

He chuckled, looking at her. "So you're the girl what's goin' to marry Rock?"

She jumped, and flushed. "Why! Why, I—"

"Don't let it get you down, ma'am! Reckon I'm a blunt old codger. It's true enough, the boy ain't said a word to me about it, but I can see what's in his eyes. I ain't raised the lad for nothin'. When he took off on this rampage, I was hopin' he'd find himself a gal. You like him, ma'am?" He looked at her sharply, his eyes filled with humor. "You goin' to marry him?"

"Why, I don't know," she protested. "I don't know that he wants me."

"Now listen here! Don't you go givin' me any of that demure, folded-hands palaver. That may go for those young bucks, but not for me. You know's well as I do if a woman sets her cap for a man he ain't got a chance. Only if he runs. That's all! Either give up and marry the gal or get clean out of the country and don't leave no address behind. Nor no trail sign, either!

"You might fool some young sprout with that he-hasn't-asked-me business, but not me. I seen many a young buck Indian give twenty head of ponies for some squaw when he could have had better ones for ten. Just because she wanted him like, and caused him to figure the price was cheap. No, sir! I'd rather try to get away from a bear trap on each foot and each hand, than a woman with her head set on marriage."

Flushed with embarrassment, she ignored what he had said. "Then—then, you'll let us have peace, sir? You won't be fighting us if we draw off from Harper?"

"Of course not, ma'am! I reckon it'd be a right nice thing to have a few folks around once in a while!" His eyes flashed. "But no more, you understand. Only this bunch of yours. No more!"

"And we can have our land, then?" she persisted.

"Sure, you can have it. You can have what them other fellows got, too, when they get out. Sure, you can have it. I can't set my hand to paper on it, though, because I never did learn to write. That's true, ma'am! Never learned to write, nor to read. But I can put my name on the side of a house with a six-shooter. I can do that. But them pens! They always figured to be a sight too small for my hands. No, I can't read printin', but I can read sign. I trailed a Blackfoot that stole a horse from me clean to Montany one time. Trailed him six hundred miles, believe me or not. Yes, ma'am, I come back with the horse and an Indian scalp. Took it right in his own village."

A startled yell rang out and Springer burst through the door.

"Boss! Boss! Here they come! Oh, quick, man! Here they—"

His voice died in the report of a gun, and Hardy Bishop lunged from his chair to see men charging the porch.

Turner had started from the bunkhouse, but the rush of the horses rode him down and they heard his wild, agonized screams as he went down under the pounding hoofs. Sharon never saw the old man reach for his guns, but suddenly they were spouting flame and she saw a man stagger back from the door, clutching at his breast, blood pouring over his hand.

Then a wild figure wearing one boot appeared from the other room swinging gunbelts about his hips. Then Rock Bannon, too, was firing.

A sound came at the rear window, and Rock turned and fired from the hip and the dark form looming there vanished. The attack broke, and Rock Bannon rushed to the rifle rack and jerked down a Henry rifle. Then he grabbed another and ran back, thrusting one at Bishop.

The old man dropped to his knees beside a window. "Come up on us fast!" he said. "I was talkin' to this gal."

Rock's eyes swung to her, and then amazement faded to sudden grimness. With horror, she saw suspicion mount in his eyes.

A wild chorus of yells sounded from outside, and then a volley of shots smashed through the windows. The lamp scattered in a thousand pieces, and from the kitchen they heard cursing, then the crash of a buffalo gun.

"How many did you see?" Rock demanded.

"Most like a dozen," Bishop said. "We got two or three that first rush!"

"A dozen?" He wheeled to the girl. "Did the settlers come? Did they? Are they fighting us now?"

"Can't be that," Bishop said, staring out at the ranch yard, his eyes probing the corral. "No chance of that. This girl come with peace talk."

"And while she was talking, they rode in on us!" Rock raged.

Sharon came up, her eyes wide. "Oh, you can't believe that. You can't! I—"

The thud of bullets into the logs of the house drowned her voice, and the crashing of guns. Rock Bannon was slipping from window to window, moving on his feet like an Indian. He had yanked off his other boot now. A shot smashed the water olla that hung near the door. Bannon fired, and a man toppled from behind the corner of the corral and sprawled on the hard-packed ground near the body of Turner.

"They're goin' to rush us," Bannon said suddenly. He began loading his Colts. "Get set, Hardy. They're goin' to rush."

"Let 'em come! The sneak-thievin', pelt-robbin', trap-lootin' scum! Let 'em come! More'll come than'll go back!"

As the outlaws rushed suddenly, charging in a scattered line, the old man burst through the door, his Colt smoking.

A man screamed and grabbed his middle, took three staggering steps, and then sprawled his full length on the ground. Another man went down, and then a gun bellowed and the old man winced, took another step and then toppled back into the room.

Sharon stared at him in horror, and then ran to him. He looked shocked.

"Hit me! They hit me! Give me my gun, ma'am. I'll kill the scum like the wolverines they are!"

"S-sh, be still," she whispered. She began tearing the shirt away from the massive chest to search for the bullet wound.

Steadily, using now one gun, then the other, Rock Bannon fired. He could sense uncertainty among the attackers. They had shot the old man, but four of their own number were down, and probably others wounded. They were beginning to lose all desire for battle.

Watching closely, Rock saw a flicker of movement behind a corral trough. He watched, lifted his rifle, took careful aim, and when the movement came again, he fired, just under the trough.

A yell rang out and he saw a man lift up to his full height, then topple over.

"All right!" Bannon shouted. "Come on and get me! You wanted me! But you'd better come before the boys get in from north camp or they'll spoil my fun."

They wouldn't believe him, but it might make them doubtful. He heard voices raised in argument. Then there was silence. He reloaded all the guns, his own, Bishop's Henry, and the old man's six-guns. It was mid-afternoon, and the sun was hot. If they waited until night, he was going to have a bad time of it.

There was a chance, however, that they would believe his story, or fear that someone from the line cabin might ride far enough this way to hear the shots. If both groups came, they would be caught between two fires and wiped out.

An hour passed, and there was no sound.

"Rock!" Sharon was standing behind him. "We'd better get him on a bed."

He avoided her eyes, but got up and put his rifle down. It was a struggle, but they lifted Bishop off the floor and put him on his homemade four-poster. While Sharon bent over him, bathing the wound and treating it as best she could, Rock walked back to the windows.

Like a caged panther, he prowled from window to window. Outside all was still. Only the bodies of the dead lay on the hard-packed ground of the ranch yard. A dust devil started somewhere on the plain and twisted in the grass of the meadow, then skipped across the ranch yard, stirring around the body of Turner, and blowing in his hair.

Turner was dead. The old man had been with them almost as long as Rock himself. He had been like one of the family. And Bob Springer was gone, blasted from life suddenly, taking away all the young man's enthusiastic plans for a ranch of his own. Well, they would pay. They would pay to the last man.

The steel-dust stallion had come back from the end of the corral near the creek. He seemed curious and approached the body lying near the trough with delicate feet, ready to shy. He snuffed at the body, caught the scent of blood and jerked away, eyes distended and nostrils wide.

There was no one in sight; apparently the attackers had drawn off. They had anticipated no such defense as this. They had no idea that Rock Bannon was home, nor did they realize what a fighter the old man could be. They had to learn what the Crows had learned, long since.

Rock waited another hour, continuing his slow prowl. Within the house he was comparatively safe, and he knew that to go out before he was sure was to tempt fate. From time to time he went into the bedroom where Bishop lay on the four-poster. He was unconscious or asleep, Sharon sitting beside him.

He avoided her eyes, yet the thought kept returning, filling him with bitterness, that she had ridden here with peace talk, and under cover of her talk Harper's men had made their approach. Knowing Bishop, he knew that unless his attention had been diverted, no rider or group of riders could have reached the ranch without being seen.

Had she planned that with Mort Harper? Everything he knew about the girl compelled him to believe she would do nothing of the kind, yet the thought persisted, and it was almost too much of a coincidence.

After all, what reason had he to believe otherwise? Hadn't she admired Harper? Hadn't Pete Zapata been waiting in her cabin for him? Perhaps she had tried to warn him by throwing sticks on the fire, or it could have been an accident. The fact remained that in visiting her he had been almost killed in a trap laid by Zapata, and while she was making peace talk with Bishop, the raiding party had struck. It was not her fault they were not dead, both of them.

He knew she came to the door from time to time, and once she started to speak, then turned away as he avoided her eyes.

Rock was crouching by a window when the sound of horse's hoofs brought him to his feet. It was Bat Chavez, astride a slim, fast buckskin. The horse shied violently at Turner's body, and Bat had a hard time getting him to the door.

Bannon rushed out. "Everything all right at the line cabin?"

"Shucks, man!" Bat exploded. "That's what I was goin' to ask you. What happened here?"

"They hit us. Dave opened up from the kitchen, Hardy and I shot it out up here. Bishop's down, hit pretty bad. They got Springer and Turner, as you can see."

"Saw them cuttin' across the valley for Poplar a few minutes ago. The boys are gettin' restless, Rock. They want to ride over and wind this up."

"No more than I do," Bannon said shortly. "Yes, we're goin'. We'll ride over and wipe that place out."

"Oh, no! You musn't!" Sharon had come to the door behind Rock. "Please, Rock! You musn't. The settlers don't want to fight any more. It's just Harper's crowd."

"Maybe that's true," Bannon said, "but I've seen no sign of them quittin' yet. There were at least twelve men in this bunch. Did Harper have twelve men of his own? Not that I saw, he didn't. And Zapata's dead. So's Miller. Where would he get twelve men?"

He turned back to Chavez. "Get some food into you, Bat, then ride back. I'll be down before long, and when I do, we'll cross that valley. If the settlers get in the way, they'll get what the rest of them got—what they gave Turner and Springer here! We've dallied long enough." Rock Bannon turned and walked back into the house.

Sharon stared at him, her face white. "Then you won't believe me?" she protested. "You'll go over there and kill innocent people?"

"Who killed Springer and Turner?" Rock demanded sharply. "In what way had they offended? I don't know that your settlers are innocent. I tried to tell them what they were going into and they wouldn't believe me. Well, they came, and if they get their tails in a crack they've only themselves to blame.

"I argued with them. I argued with Bishop to give them a break, and now this happens. There were twelve men in that attack on us. At least twelve! Well, some of them died out here, but you and I both know that Harper didn't have twelve men. Perhaps eight, at best. They came in here and killed two of our boys and wounded Bishop. That old man in there has been a father to me. He's been more than most fathers. He's been a guide and a teacher, and all I know I learned from him. He may die. If he does the fault was mine for ever letting this bunch of squatters in here."

The girl clasped her hands in distress, "Please, Rock," she protested, "you can't do this. Most of your men don't know one from the other. The settlers would be killed whether they fought or not. Their homes will be burned."

"If they don't fight they won't be hurt," he insisted stubbornly. "Next time that Harper attacks, he might get us all. Anyway, it looks to me as if they were plenty willing to ride in on Harper's coattails and get all they could while the getting was easy."

"That's not true," she protested hotly. "They wanted to do the right thing. They thought they were doing the right thing. They believed Harper was honest."

Rock slid into his buckskin coat and picked up his hat. His face was grim and hard. He could not look at Sharon, and knew if their eyes met it would tear the heart out of him. Yet he knew he had waited too long now, that if he had resorted to guns long ago so many things might not have happened. Springer might be living, and Turner, and Collins, the settler.

He started for the door, picking up his rifle from where he had left it. "Rock," Sharon said, "if you go back, I will, too. The first one of your men who puts a hand on a settler's home, I'll kill with my own rifle."

For the first time he looked at her, and her eyes were flashing with pain and anger. "Go then!" he said brutally. "But if you're half as smart as I think you are, you'll take your friends and head for the hills. Go! I'll give you a start. Warn Harper, too, if you want. Let him know we're coming. But if you want to save that precious pack of settlers, get them out of Poplar. Take to the hills until this is over—but be out of town before my boys ride in!"

He walked to the door and went out. She saw him stop by the corral and pick up a rope, then go to the corral for the steel-dust. Running from the house, she threw herself into the saddle of her own black mare, tied at the corner of the house, and spurring to top speed, sprang out on the long ride across the valley.

Rock Bannon did not look up, nor turn his head, but in his heart and mind the hard hoofs pounded like the pulse in his veins, pounded harder and harder, then vanished with the dying sound of the running horse.

He saddled the gray, and as Bat Chavez walked from the house, Rock swung into the saddle. "Dave!" he yelled at the cook. "You watch over Hardy. We won't be gone long."

Abruptly, he swung the stallion south. Chavez rode beside him, glancing from time to time at Rock. Finally, he burst out. "Bannon, I think that gal's on the level. I sure do!"

"Yes?" Rock did not turn his head. "You let me worry about that!"

CHAPTER EIGHT

PIKE PURCELL WAS a grim and lonely man. He had been loitering all day around the saloon. Only that morning, before riding away to the attack on the Bishop ranch house in which he and Lamport had taken part, Dud Kitchen had told him about the bullet that killed Collins.

Pike was disturbed. His heart had not been in the fight at the ranch, and he had fired few shots. In fact, he and Lamport had been among the first to turn away from the fight. Purcell was thoroughly disillusioned in Mort Harper. The attack on the ranch had been poorly conceived and even more poorly carried out. Purcell didn't fancy himself as a leader, but he knew he could have done better.

Men had died back there—too many of them. Pike Purcell had a one-track mind and that one track was busy with surmises over the story told him by Dud. He could verify the truth of the supposition. Mort Harper had been behind Collins. It worried him, and his loyalty, already shaken by inadequate leadership, found itself on uncertain ground.

On the ride back, there had been little talk. The party was sullen and angry. Their attack had failed under the straight shooting of Bishop and Bannon. They were leaving six men behind, six men who were stone dead. Maybe they had killed two, but that didn't compensate for six. Bishop was down, but how badly none of them knew.

Cap Mulholland had ridden in the attack as well. Never strongly inclined toward fighting, he had no heart in this fight. He had even less now. Suddenly he was realizing with bitterness that he didn't care if he ever saw Mort Harper again.

"They'll be comin' for us now,'" Cap said.

"Shut up!" Lamport snapped. He was angry and filled with bitterness. He was the only one of the settlers who had thrown in completely with Harper's crowd, and the foolishness of it was now apparent. Defeat and their own doubts were carrying on the rapid disintegration of the Harper forces. "You see what I saw?" he demanded. "That Crockett girl was there. She was the one dragged Bishop's body back. I seen her!"

Harper's head jerked up. "You lie!" he snapped viciously.

Lamport looked across at Harper. "Mort," he said evenly, "don't tell me I lie."

Harper shrugged. "All right, maybe she was there, but I've got to see it to believe it. How could she have beaten us to it?"

"How did Bannon beat us back?" Lamport demanded furiously. "He was supposed to be lost in the hills."

"He must have come back over the mountain," Gettes put in. He was one of the original Harper crowd. "He must have found a way through."

"Bosh!" Harper spat. "Nothing human could have crossed that mountain last night. A man would be insane to try it."

"Well," Pike said grimly, "Bannon got there. I know good and well he never rode none of those canyons last night, so he must've come over the mountain. If any man could, he could."

Harper's eyes were hard. "You seem to think a lot of him," he sneered.

"I hate him," Pike snapped harshly. "I hate every step he takes, but he's all man!"

Mort Harper's face was cruel as he stared at Pike. Purcell had ridden on, unnoticing.

Pike did not return to his cabin after they reached Poplar. Pike Purcell was as just as he was ignorant and opinionated. His one quality was loyalty—that and more than his share of courage. Dud Kitchen's story kept cropping up. Did Harper own a small gun?

Suddenly, he remembered. Shortly after they arrived at Poplar he had seen such a gun. It was a .34 Patterson, and Mort Harper had left it lying on his bed.

Harper was gone somewhere. The saloon was empty. Purcell stepped in, glanced around, then walked back to Harper's quarters. The room was neat, and things were carefully arranged. He glanced around, crossed to a rough wooden box on the far side of the room, and lifted the lid. There were several boxes of .44's, and a smaller box. Opening it, he saw a series of neat rows of .34-caliber cartridges, and across the lead nose of each shell was a deep notch!

He picked up one of the shells and stepped back. His face was gray as he turned toward the door. He was just stepping through when Mort Harper came into the saloon.

Quick suspicion came into Mort's eyes. "What are you doin' in there?" he demanded.

"Huntin' for polecat tracks," Purcell said viciously. "I found 'em!" He took the shell out and tossed it on the table. It was the wrong move, for it left his right hand outstretched and far from his gun.

At such a time things happen instantaneously. Mort Harper's hand flashed for his gun, and Purcell was far too late. He got his hand on the butt when the bullet struck him. He staggered back, hate blazing in his eyes, and sat down hard. He tugged at his gun, and Harper shot him again.

Staring down at the body of the tall old mountaineer, Mort Harper saw the end of everything. So this was how things finished? An end to dreams, an end to ambition. He would never own the greatest cattle empire in the West, a place where he would be a king on his own range with nothing to control his actions but his own will.

He had despised Purcell for his foolishness in following him. He had led the settlers like sheep, but now they would survive and he would die. In a matter of hours, even minutes, perhaps, Bannon would be here, and then nothing would be left but a ruin.

At that moment he heard a pounding of horse's hoofs and looked up to see Sharon go flying past on her black mare.

There was something left. There was Sharon. Rock Bannon wanted her. Sudden resolution flooded him. She was one thing Bannon wouldn't get! Mort Harper ran to his quarters and threw a few things together, then walked out. Hastily, under cover of the pole barn, he saddled a fresh horse, loaded his gear aboard, and swung into the saddle and started up the canyon toward the Crockett home.

Cap Mulholland watched him go, unaware of what was happening. Dud Kitchen had heard the shots, and had returned for his own guns. He watched Harper stop at the Crockett place, unaware of the stuffed saddlebags. When he saw the man swing down, he was not surprised.

Sharon had caught Jim Satterfield in the open and told him they should flee the village at once. At this moment Satterfield was headed for the Pagones house as fast as he could move. Sharon ran into the house, looking for her father, but he was in the fields. There was not a moment to lose. She ran out, and was just swinging into the saddle when Mort Harper dismounted at the front steps. He heard her speak to the horse, and stepped around the house.

"Sharon!" he said. "You're just in time."

She halted. "What do you mean?" she demanded coolly.

He rushed to her excitedly. "We're leaving! We must get away now. Just you and me! The Bishop crowd will be coming soon, and they'll leave nothing here. We still have time to get away."

"I'm going to get my father now," she said. "Then we'll go to the hills."

"There's no time for that—he'll get along. You come with me!" Harper was excited, and he did not see the danger lights in Sharon's eyes.

"Go where?" she inquired.

Mort Harper stared at her impatiently. "Away! Anywhere, for the time being. Later we can go on to California together, and—"

"Aren't you taking too much for granted?" She reached for the black mare's bridle. "I'm not going with you, Mort. I'm not going anywhere with you."

It was a real shock. He stared at her, unbelieving and impatient. "Don't be foolish!" he snapped. "There's nothing for you here. You were practically promised to me. If it's marriage you want, don't worry about that. We can go on to California, and be married there."

"It is marriage I want, Mort, but not to you. Never to you. For a little while I was as bad as the others. I believed in you, and then I saw the kind of men you had around you, how you'd deliberately led us here to use us for your own ends. No, Mort. I'm not marrying you and I'm not going away with you." She made no attempt to veil the contempt in her voice. "If you're afraid, you'd better get started. I'm going for my father."

Suddenly he was calm, dangerously calm. "So? It's that Rock Bannon, is it? I never thought you'd take that ignorant cowhand seriously. Or,'' he sneered, ''is it your way of getting Bishop's Valley?''

''Get out!'' she said. ''Get out now! Dad and Pagones will be here in a moment and when I tell them what you've said, they'll kill you.''

''Kill me? Those two?'' He laughed. Then his face stiffened. ''All right, I'll get out, but you're coming with me!''

He moved so swiftly she had no chance to defend herself. He stepped toward her suddenly, and she saw his fist start. The shock of the blow was scarcely greater than the shock of the fact that he had struck her. Dimly, she realized he had thrown her into the saddle and was lashing her there. She thought she struggled, but she lived those moments only in a half-world of consciousness, a half-world soon pounded into oblivion by the drum of racing horses.

It was Satterfield who finally got Crockett from the fields. The Bishop riders were already in sight when Tom raced into his house, caught up his rifle, and called for Sharon. She was gone, and he noted that her black mare was gone. She was away, that was the main thing. With Jim, he ran out into the field where he was joined by Pagones, his wife, daughter and Dud Kitchen.

The others were coming. It was a flight, and there was no time to prepare or take anything but what lay at hand. Cap Mulholland, his face sullen, went with them, his wife beside him. The Olsens and Greenes joined them, and in a compact group they turned away toward the timber along the hillside.

Lamport did not go. He had no idea that Mort Harper was gone. John Kies was in his store, waiting the uncertain turn of events. Kies had worked with Mort before, and he trusted the younger man's skill and judgment.

It was over. It was finished. Lamport stared cynically at the long buildings of the town. Probably it was just as well, for he would do better in the gold fields. Steady day-to-day work had never appealed to him. Pike Purcell had been an honest but misguided man; Lamport was neither. From the first he had sensed the crooked grain in the timber of Mort Harper, but he didn't care.

Lamport felt that he was self-sufficient. He would stay in as long as the profits looked good, and he would get out when the luck turned against them. He had seen the brilliant conception of theft that had flowered in the brain of Mort Harper. He saw what owning that valley could mean.

It was over. He had lived and worked with Purcell, but he had no regret for the man. Long ago he had sensed that Harper would kill him someday. Of all the settlers, Lamport was the only one who had read Harper right, and perhaps because they were of the same feeling.

Yet there was a difference. Lamport's hate was a tangible, deadly thing. Harper could hate and he could fight, but Harper was completely involved with himself. He could plot, wait, and strike like a rattler. Lamport had courage with his hate, and that was why he was not running now. He was waiting, waiting in the full knowledge of what he faced.

His hate for Rock Bannon had begun when Bannon rode so much with Sharon. It had persisted, developing from something much deeper than any rivalry over a woman. It developed from the innate, basic rivalry of two strong men, two fighting men, each of whom recognizes in the other a worthy and dangerous foe.

Lamport had always understood Harper. Of all those that had surrounded him, Lamport was the only one Mort Harper had feared. Pete Zapata he had always believed he could kill. Lamport was the one man with whom he avoided trouble. He even avoided conversation with him when possible. He knew Lamport was dangerous, and he knew he would face him down if it came to that.

He was a big man, as tall as Rock Bannon, and twenty pounds heavier. When he walked his head thrust forward somewhat and he stared at the world from pale blue eyes beneath projecting shelves of beetling brows. In his great shoulders there was a massive, slumbering power. Lamport's strength had long since made him contemptuous of other men, and his natural skill with a gun had added to that contempt. He was a man as brutal as his heavy jaw, as fierce as the light in his pale eyes.

Surly and sullen, he made friends with no one. In the biting envy and cantankerousness of Pike Purcell he had found companionship, if no more. Lamport was not a loyal man. Purcell's death meant nothing to him. He waited for Rock Bannon, now filled with hatred for the victor in the fight, the man who would win.

Thinking back now, Lamport could see that Rock had always held the winning hand. He had known about Bishop, was a kin to him, had known what awaited here. Also, from the start his assay of Harper's character had been correct.

From the beginning, Lamport had accepted the partnership with Purcell, rode with the wagon train because it was a way west, and threw in with Harper for profit. In it all, he respected but one man, the man he was now waiting to kill.

When, in the deserted bar, he heard the horses coming, he poured another drink. Somewhere, there were three or four more men. The rest had vanished like snow in a desert sun. Hitching his guns into place, he walked to the door and out on the plank porch.

John Kies's white face stared at him from an open window of the store.

"Where's Mort?" Kies asked. "That's them coming now."

Lamport chuckled and spat into the dust. He scratched the stubble on his heavy jaw and grinned sardonically at Kies.

"He's around, I reckon, or maybe he blowed out. The rest of em' have."

Stark fear came into the storekeeper's face. "No! No, they can't have!" he protested. "They'll have an ambush! They'll—"

"You're crazy!" Lamport sneered. "This show is busted. You know that. That's Bannon comin' now, and when that crowd of his gets through, there won't be one stick on another in this town."

"But the settlers!" Kies wailed. "They'll stop him."

Lamport grinned at him. "The settlers have took to the hills. They're gone! Me, I'm waitin' to kill Rock Bannon. Then if I can fight off his boys, I'm goin'."

They came up the street, walking their horses. Rock was in the lead, his rifle across his saddle bows. To his right was Bat Chavez, battle-hungry as always. To his left was Red, riding loosely on a paint pony. Behind them, in a mounted skirmishing line, came a dozen hard-bitten Indian-fighting plainsmen, riders for the first big cow spread north of Texas.

A rifle shot rang out suddenly from a cabin in back of the store. Then another. A horse staggered and went down, and Bat Chavez wheeled his horse, and with four riders, raced toward the cabin. The man who waited there lost his head suddenly and bolted.

A lean blond rider in a Mexican jacket swept down on him, rope twirling. It shot out, and the horse went racing by, and the burly teamster's body was a bounding thing, leaping and tumbling through the cactus after the racing horse. Chavez swung at once, and turned back toward the saloon. The riders fanned out and started going through the town. Where they went, there were gunshots, then smoke.

Rock Bannon saw Lamport standing on the porch. "Don't

shoot!'' he commanded. He walked the steel-dust within twenty feet. Lamport stood on the edge of the porch, wearing two guns, his dark, dirty red wool shirt open at the neck to display a massive, hairy chest.

''Howdy, Rock!'' Lamport said. He spat into the dust. ''Come to take your lickin'?''

''To give you yours,'' Rock said coolly. ''How do you want it?''

''Why, I reckon we're both gun-handy, Rock,'' Lamport said, ''so I expect it'll be guns. I'd have preferred hand-fightin' you, but that would scarcely give you an even break.''

''You reckon not?'' Rock slid from the stallion. ''Well, Lamport, I always figure to give a man what he wants. If you think you can take me with your hands, shed those guns and get started. You've bought yourself a fight.''

Incredulous, Lamport stared at him. ''You mean it?'' he said, his eyes brightening.

''Stack your duds and grease your skids, coyote!'' Rock said. ''It's knuckle and skull now, and free fighting, if you like it!''

''Free, he says!'' A light of unholy joy gleamed in Lamport's eyes. ''Free it is!''

''Watch yourself, boss!'' Red said, low-voiced. ''That hombre looks like blazin' brimstone on wheels!''

''Then we'll take off his wheels and kick the brimstone out!'' Rock said. He hung his guns over the saddlehorn as Bat Chavez rode around the corner.

Lamport faced him in the dust before the saloon, a huge, grizzly of a man with big iron-knuckled hands and a skin that looked like a stretched rawhide.

''Come and get it!'' he sneered, and rushed.

As he rushed, he swung a powerful right. Rock Bannon met him halfway, and lashed out with his own right. His punch was faster, and it caught the big man flush, but Lamport took it on the mouth, spat blood and rushed in swinging with both fists. Suddenly he caught Bannon and hurled him into the dust with such a force that a cloud of dust arose. Rock rolled over like a cat, gasping for breath, and just rolled from under Lamport's driving boots as the big man tried to leap on him to stamp his life out.

Rock scrambled to his feet, and lunged as he picked his hands out of the dust, butting Lamport in the chest. The big renegade jerked up a stiff thumb, trying for Rock's eye, but Bannon rolled his head away and swung a left to the wind, and then a driving right that ripped Lamport's ear, starting a shower of blood.

Lamport now charged again and caught Bannon with two long

swings on the head. His skull roaring with pain and dizziness, Rock braced himself and started to swing in a blind fury, both hands going with every ounce of power he could muster.

Lamport met him and, spraddle-legged, the two started to slug. Lamport was the bigger, and his punches packed terrific power, but were a trifle slower. It was nip and tuck, dog eat dog, and the two battled until the breath gasped in their lungs and whistled through their teeth. Lamport ducked his battered face and started to walk in, stemming the tide of Bannon's blows by sheer physical power.

Rock shifted his attack with lightning speed. He missed a right, and following it in with the weight of his body, slid his arm around Lamport's thick neck, grabbed the wrist with his left hand, and jerked up his feet and sat down hard, trying to break Lamport's neck.

But the big renegade knew all the tricks, and as Rock's feet flew up, Lamport hurled his weight forward and to the left, falling with his body half across Bannon. It broke the hold, and they rolled free. Rock came to his feet, and Lamport, catlike in his speed, lashed out with a wicked kick for his head.

Rock rolled away from it and hurled himself at Lamport's one standing leg in a flying tackle. The big man went down, and as they scrambled up, Rock hit him with a left and right, splitting his right cheek in a bone-deep gash, and pulping his lips.

Lamport was bloody and battered now, yet he kept coming, his breath wheezing. Rock Bannon stabbed a left into his face, set himself and whipped up a right uppercut to the body. Lamport gasped. Bannon circled, then smashed him in the body with another right, then another and another. Lamport's jaw was hanging open now, his face battered and bleeding from a dozen cuts and abrasions. Rock walked in, measured him, then crossed a right to his chin. He followed it up with two thudding, bone-crushing blows, and Lamport reeled, tried to steady himself, and then measured his length in the dust.

Rock Bannon weaved on his feet, then walked to the watering trough and ducked his head into it. He came up spluttering, then splashed water over his face and body, stripping away the remnants of his torn shirt.

"We got 'em all, boss," Red said. "You want we should go after the settlers?"

"No, and leave their homes alone. Where's Kies?"

"The storekeeper? Inside, I guess."

Rock strapped on his guns and strode up the steps of the store with Red and Chavez at his heels. Kies was waiting behind the counter, his face white.

"Kies," Rock said, "have you got the bills for the goods you sold the settlers?"

"The bills?" Kies's frightened eyes showed doubt, then dismay. "Why, yes."

"Get 'em out."

Fumblingly, Kies dug out the bills. Quickly, Bannon scanned through them. Then he took out a match and set fire to the stack as they lay on the counter.

Kies sprang for them. "What are you doing?"

"You're payin' the price of hookin' up with a crooked bunch," Bannon said grimly, as Chavez held the angry storekeeper. "You got a horse?"

"Yes, I have a—horse. But I—"

"Red," Bannon turned. "Give this man some shells, a rifle, a canteen and two days' grub—skimpy rations. Then put him on a horse and start him on his way. If he tries to load that rifle or if he doesn't ride right out of the country, hang him."

"But the Indians!" Kies protested. "And my store!"

"You haven't got a store," Bannon told him harshly. "You'll have to look out for the Indians yourself."

"Boss," Chavez touched him on the shoulder. "Hombres here want to talk."

Rock Bannon wheeled. Tom Crockett, Pagones and Dud Kitchen were standing there.

"Bannon," Crockett said, "Harper took my girl. Kitchen saw him tying her to a horse."

Rock's face went white, then stiffened. "I reckon he was the one she wanted," he said. "She had Zapata waitin' for me, and she led that raid to the ranch."

"No, she didn't do that, Rock," Pagones said. "The raid wasn't even organized when she left. As for Zapata—"

"He forced himself on us," Crockett protested. "And she was tied to the saddle. She didn't want to go with Harper. She loves you."

"That's right, Rock," Pagones assured him. "Mary's known that for weeks."

"All right," Rock said. He jerked a shirt from a stack on the counter and began getting into it. "I'll find 'em."

"Who goes along with you?" Bat asked eagerly.

"Nobody," Bannon said. "This is my job."

CHAPTER NINE

THE STEEL-DUST stallion liked the feel of the trail. He always knew when he was going some place that was beyond the place where distance lost itself against the horizon. He knew it now, knew in the sound of Rock Bannon's voice and the easy way he sat in the saddle.

Rock rode through the poplars where the wagon train had spent its last night on the trail, and as he passed, he glanced down at the ruts, already grown with grass. It seemed such a long time ago, yet it was scarcely more than days since the wagons had waited here. He had observed them from the mountains, looking back for the last time as he rode away from the train.

He turned the stallion up the long, grassy canyon where Freeman had been killed. The trail Mort Harper had left was plain enough. So far he had been running, later he would try to cover it, yet already Bannon was looking ahead, planning, trying to foresee what plan, if any, could be in the man's mind.

The Day's River region was one of the most rugged in all America. No man knew it well, few knew it even passingly well. Unless a man chose carefully of the trails that it offered, he would run into a blind canyon, a trail that ended in a jump-off, or some blind tangle of boulders.

There were trails through; the Indians had used them. Other Indians, ages before, had left picture-writing on the canyon walls, some of them in places almost impossible to reach. No man living knew the history of this region.

There were places here with a history stranger than any written—an old weapon washed from the sands of a creek, a strange date on a canyon wall. There was one place miles from here where the date "1642" was carved on a canyon wall among other dates and names, and no man has yet accounted for that date, nor said who put it there, nor how he came to be in the country.

From Grass Canyon the trail of the two horses led into a narrow draw with very steep sides overgrown with birch, balsam and cottonwood. His rifle ready, although anticipating no trouble at this stage, Rock pushed on.

The draw now opened on a vast region of jagged mountain ridges, gorges, cliffs and mesas. The stallion followed the trail along the edge of a meadow watered by a brawling mountain stream. Some teal flew from the pool of water backed up by a beaver dam, and Rock heard the sharp, warning slap of the beaver's tail on the water.

The trail dipped now down a narrow passage between great rock formations that towered heavenward. On one side was an enormous mass of rock like veined marble, and on the other a rock of brightest orange fading to rust red, shot through with streaks of purple.

Boulders scattered the space between the walls, and at times passage became difficult. At one place great slabs of granite had sloughed off from high above and come crashing down upon the rocks below. Far ahead he could see the trail leaving the lowlands and climbing, threadlike, across the precipitous wall of the mountain.

Studying the trail and the speed of the horses he was following, Rock could see that Mort was trying for distance, and fast. Rock knew, too, that unless Harper was far ahead, he would, if watching his backtrail, soon know he was followed. From the incredible heights ahead the whole series of canyons and gorges would be plainly visible except when shoulders of rock or boulders intervened.

The trail up the face of the cliff had been hewn by nature from the solid rock itself, cutting across the face of an almost vertical cliff, and only emerging at times in bare rock ledges or dipping around some corner of rock into a cool, shadowed gorge.

"He's headin' for Big Track," Rock told himself suddenly. "He sure is. He's headin' for Big Track Hollow."

He knew the place, and certainly if Harper were following a known or planned route, he could choose no better. Big Track Hollow was a basin over six thousand feet above sea level where there was a wealth of grass, and plenty of water and sheltering woods.

This would be the best place in this region to hole up for any length of time. Long ago, somebody had built a cabin there, and there were caves in the basin walls. It took its name from gigantic dinosaur tracks that appeared in the rock all along one side.

For Harper the place had the distinct advantage of offering four separate avenues of escape; each would take him over a trail widely divergent from the others, so once a follower was committed to one trail he would have to retrace his steps and start over to find his quarry. The time consumed would leave him so far behind that it would be impossible to catch up.

Rock Bannon stared thoughtfully at the tracks. It would soon be night, and the two must stop, yet they had sufficient lead on him to make it difficult to overtake them soon, and at night he could easily get off the trail and lose himself in the spiderweb of canyons.

Reluctantly, he realized he must camp soon. The landscape everywhere now was rock, red rock cliffs towering against the sky, cathedral shaped buttes and lofty pinnacles. He rode down the steep trail, dipping into shadowy depths and riding along a canyon that echoed with the stallion's steps. It was like riding down a long hallway carved from solid rock, lonely and empty.

There was no sound but the walking of the horse and the creak of the saddle leather. Dwarfed by the lofty walls, he moved like a ghost in a vast, unreal world, yet he rode warily, for at any point Harper might elect to stop and waylay him.

Now the trail down the long avenue between the walls began to rise, and suddenly he emerged upon a plateau that seemed to hang upon the rim of the world.

Far away and below him stretched miles upon miles of the same broken country, but there were trees and grass in the valleys below, and he turned the horse at right angles, then reined in. Here for a space was gravel and rock. He studied the ground carefully, then moved on.

The trail was difficult now, and in the fading light he was compelled to slip from saddle, rifle in hand, and walk along over the ground. The trail wound around and around, steadily dropping. Then ahead of him he saw a pool, and beside it a place where someone had lain to drink.

Sliding to the ground, he stripped the saddle from the stallion and tethered him on a grassy plot. Then he gathered dry sticks for a fire, which he made, keeping it very small, in the shadow of some boulders. When the fire was going he made coffee, then slipped back from the fire and carefully scouted the surrounding darkness.

Every step of the way was a danger. Mort Harper was on the run now, and he would fight like a cornered rat, where and when and how he could find the means.

Before daylight Rock rolled out, packed his gear and saddled the stallion. Yet when it was light enough to see, there was no trail. The water of the stream offered the best possibility, so he rode into it himself, scanning the narrow banks with attention.

Finally, after being considerably slowed down by the painstaking search, he found where they had left the stream. A short distance further, after seeing no marks, he found a bruised clump of grass where a horse had stepped and slipped.

He had gone no more than four miles when he found where they had camped. There had been two beds, one back in a corner of rocks away from the other, and cut off from the trail by it. Mort Harper was taking no chances. Yet when Rock looked around, he glimpsed something under a bush in the damp earth.

Kneeling, he put his head under the bush. Scratched in the earth with a stick were the words, *Be Careful,* and then, *Big Track.*

He had been right then. Harper was headed for Big Track. If that were so, they were a good day's ride from there. Bannon thought that over while climbing the next ridge. Then he made a sudden decision. From the ridge, he examined the terrain before him, then wheeled his horse. As he did so a shot rang out. Leaping from the horse to a cleft in the rock, he lifted his rifle and waited.

The country on the other side of the ridge was fairly open, but with clumps of brush and boulders. To ride down there after a rifleman—and Harper was an excellent shot—would be suicide. Only his wheeling of the stallion had saved his life at that moment.

Sliding back from the cleft, he retreated down the hillside to the gray. He swung into saddle, and keeping the ridge between him and the unseen marksman, he started riding east. He had made his decision, and he was going to gamble on it.

If he continued to follow, as he was following now, he would fall further and further behind, compelled to caution by Harper's rifle and the difficulty of following the trail. If Harper reached Big Track Hollow first, it would be simple for him to take a trail out of there, and then it would be up to Bannon to find which trail.

Rock Bannon had never heard of a cutoff to Big Track, but he knew where he was, and he knew where Big Track was. Ahead of him a draw opened and he raced the steel-dust into it and started along it, slowing the horse to a canter. Ahead of him and on the skyline, a sharp pinnacle pointed at the sky. That was his landmark.

The country grew rougher, but he shifted from draw to draw, cut across a flat, barren plateau of scattered rocks and rabbit grass, traversed a lava flow, black and ugly, to skirt a towering rust red cliff. A notch in the cliff ahead seemed to indicate a point of entry, so he guided the stallion among the boulders. A lizard darted from under the stallion's hoofs, and overhead a buzzard wheeled in wide, lonely circles.

The sun was blazing-hot now, and the rocks caught and multiplied the heat. He skirted the gray, dirty mud shore of a small alkaline lake, and rode into a narrow cleft in the mountain.

At one point it was so narrow that for thirty yards he had to pull one foot from the stirrup and drag the stirrup up into the saddle. Then the cleft opened into a spacious green valley, its sides lined with a thick growth of quaking aspen. There was water here, and he stopped to give the stallion a brief rest and to drink.

They had been moving at a rapid clip for the distance and the heat, yet the horse looked good. Again he checked his guns. It was nip and tuck now. If he made Big Track before they reached it, or by the same time, he must hurry. If he failed, then there was not one chance in a dozen that he would ever see Sharon again.

Now, every movement, every thought, every inflection of her voice returned to him, filling him with desperation. She was his, and had always been his—not only, he understood now, in his own heart, but in hers. He had always known what Mort Harper was. He should never have doubted the girl. It was amazing to him now that he had doubted her for even an instant.

So on he went, though the sun blazed down on the flaming rocks in a torment and the earth turned to hot brass beneath the stallion's feet. The mountains grew rougher. There was more and more lava, and then when it seemed it could get no worse, he rode out upon a glaring white alkali desert that lasted for eight miles at midday, stifling dust and blazing sun.

Rock Bannon seemed to have been going for hours now, yet it was only because of his early start. It was past one in the afternoon, and he had been riding, with but one break, since four in the morning.

On the far side of the desert there was a spring of water that tasted like rotten eggs—mineral water. He drank a little, rubbed the horse down with a handful of rabbit grass, and let him graze briefly. Then he mounted again and went on, climbing into the hills.

Big Track was nearer, somewhere not far from the great sky-stabbing pinnacle he had seen. Sweat streamed down his face and down his body under his shirt. He squinted his eyes against the sun and the smart of the sweat. He had to skirt a towering peak to get to the vicinity of Big Track.

He was riding now with all thought lost, only his goal in mind, and a burning, driving lust to come face to face with Mort Harper. Somewhere ahead he would be waiting; somewhere ahead they would meet.

The sun brought something like delirium, and he thought again of the long days of riding over the plains, of Sharon's low voice and her cool hands as he wrestled with pain and fever, recovering from the wounds of a lone battle against Indians. He seemed to feel again the rocking roll of the wagon over the rutted, dusty trail, tramped by the thousands heading for the new lands in the West.

Why had he waited so long to speak? Why hadn't he been able to find words to tell the girl he loved her? Words had always left him powerless; to act was easy, but somehow to shape the things he felt into words was beyond him, and women put so much emphasis on words, on the saying of things, and the way they were said.

He swung down from the saddle after a long time and walked on, knowing even the great stallion's strength was not without limit. The wild, strange country through which he was going now was covered with blasted boulders, the rough, slaglike lava, and scattered pines, dwarfish and wind-bedraggled, whipped into agonized shapes by the awful contortions of the wind.

Then he saw the stark pinnacle almost ahead, and he saw, beyond it, the green of the Big Track. He climbed back into the saddle again, and mopped the sweat from his face. The big horse walked wearily now, but the goal was reached. Rock Bannon loosened the guns in their holsters, and, grim-faced, he turned down a natural trail that no man had ridden before him, and into the green lush splendor of Big Track Hollow.

The smell of the grass was rich and almost unbelievable, and he heard a bird singing, and the sudden whir of wings as some game bird took off in sudden flight. Water sounded, and the gray stallion quickened his pace. He skirted a wide-boled aspen and rode through a grass scattered with purple and pink asters, white sego lilies, and red baneberry. Then he saw the water, and rode rapidly toward it.

He dropped from saddle, taking a quick look around. No human sound disturbed the calm, utter serenity of Big Track. He dropped to his chest on the ground and drank, and beside him, the steel-dust drank deep.

Suddenly, the stallion's head came up sharply. Warned, Rock felt his every muscle tense. Then, he forced himself to relax. The horse was looking at something, the calling of birds was stilled. He got slowly to his feet, striving to avoid any sudden movement, knowing in every muscle and fiber of his being that he was being watched. He turned, slowly, striving for a casual, careless manner.

Mort Harper was standing a short distance away, a pistol in his hand. He was thinner, wolfish now, his face darkened by sun and wind, his eyes hard and cruel. Backed in a corner, all the latent evil of the man had come to the fore. Quick fear touched Rock.

''Howdy,'' he said calmly. ''I see you're not takin' any chances, Mort. Got that gun right where it'll do the most good.''

Harper smiled, and with his teeth bared he looked even more vulpine, even more cruel. ''We both know what it means to get the drop,'' Harper said. ''We both know it means you're a dead man.''

''I ain't so sure,'' Bannon said, shrugging. ''I've heard of men who beat it. Maybe I'm one of the lucky ones.''

''You don't beat this one,'' Mort said grimly. ''I'm going to kill you.'' Suddenly his eyes darkened with fury. ''I'd like to know how in blazes you got here!'' he snapped.

''Figured you'd head for this place if you knew the country at all,'' Bannon replied with a shrug. ''So I cut across country.''

''There's no other trail,'' Harper said. ''It can't be done.''

Rock Bannon stared at him coldly. ''Where I want to go, there's always a trail,'' Bannon said. ''I make my own trails, Mort Harper, I don't try to follow and steal the work of other men.''

Harper laughed, ''That doesn't bother me, Rock. I've still got the edge. Maybe I lost on that steal, but I've got your woman. I've got her, and I'll keep her! Oh, she's yours, all right—I know that now. She's yours, and a hellcat with it, but it'll be fun breaking her, and before I take her out of these hills she'll be broken—or dead.

''I've got her, and she's fixed so if anything happens to me, you'll never find her and she'll die there alone. It'll serve both of you right. Only I'm not going to die—you are.''

''All rat,'' Rock said coldly. ''A rat all the way through. I don't imagine you ever had a square, decent thought in your life.

Always out to get something cheap, to beat somebody, to steal somebody else's work, and fancying yourself a smart boy because of it."

Rock Bannon smiled suddenly. "All right, you're going to kill me. Mind if I smoke first?"

"Sure!" Mort sneered. "You can smoke, but keep your hands high, or you'll die quick. Go ahead, have your smoke. I like standing here watching you. I like remembering that you're Rock Bannon and I'm Mort Harper and this is the last hand of the game and I'm holding all winning cards. I've got the girl and I've got the drop."

Carefully, Rock dug papers and tobacco from his breast pocket. Keeping his hands high and away from his guns, he rolled a cigarette.

"Like thinking about it, don't you, Harper? Killing me quick would have spoiled that. If you'd shot me while I was on the ground, it wouldn't have been good. I'd never have known what hit me. Now I do know. Tastes good, doesn't it, Mort?"

He dug for his matches and got them out. He struck one, and it flared up with a big burst. Rock smiled, and holding the match in his fingers, the cigarette between his lips, he grinned at Mort.

"Yes," he said, "it tastes good, doesn't it? And you've got the girl somewhere? Got her hid where I can't find her? Why, Mort, I'll have no trouble. I can read your mind. I can trail you anywhere. I could trail a buzzard flying over a snow field, Mort, so trailing you would be—" The match burned down to his fingers and he gestured with it, then as the flame touched them he let out a startled yelp and dropped the match, jerking his hand from the pain—the hand swept down and up, blasting fire!

Mort Harper, distracted by the gesture and the sudden yelp of pain, was just too late. The two guns boomed together, but Mort twisted with sudden shock, and he took a full step back, his face stricken.

Rock Bannon stepped carefully to one side for a better frontal target, and they both fired again. He felt something slug him and a leg buckled, and he fired again, then again. He shifted guns and fired a fifth shot. Harper was on his knees, his face white and twisted. Rock walked up to him and kicked the smoking gun from his hand.

"Where is she?" he demanded. "Tell me!"

Mort's hate-filled face twisted. "Go to the devil!" he gasped hoarsely. "You go—to the devil!" He coughed, spitting blood.

"Go to the devil!" he said again. Suddenly his mouth opened wide and he seemed gasping wildly for breath that he couldn't get; then he fell forward on his face, his fingers digging into the grass as blood stained the mossy earth beneath him.

Rock walked back to the horse and stood there, gripping the saddlehorn. He felt weak and sick, yet he didn't believe he had been hit hard. There was a dampness on his side, yet when he pulled off his shirt, he saw that only the skin was cut in a shallow groove along his side above the hip bone.

Digging stuff from his saddlebags, he patched the wound as well as he could. It was only then he thought of his leg.

There was nothing wrong with it, and then he saw the wrenched spur. The bullet had struck his spur, twisting and jerking his leg, but doing no harm.

Carefully, he reloaded his guns. Then he called loudly. There was no response. He called again, and there was no answering sound. Slowly, Rock began to circle, studying the ground. Harper had moved carefully through the grass, and had left little trail. Rock returned for his horse, and mounting, began to ride in slow circles.

Somewhere, Mort would have his horses, and the girl would not be far from them. From time to time he called.

Two hours passed. At times, he swung down and walked, leading the stallion. He worked his way through every grove, examined every boulder patch and clump of brush.

Bees hummed in the still, warm air. He walked on, his side smarting viciously, his feet heavy with walking in the high-heeled boots. Suddenly, sharply the stallion's head came up and he whinnied. Almost instantly, there was an answering call. Then Rock Bannon saw a horse, and swinging into the saddle he loped across the narrow glade toward the boulders.

The horse was there, and almost at once he saw Sharon. She was tied to the top of a boulder, out of sight from below except for a toe of her boot. He scrambled up and released her, then unfastened the handkerchief with which she had been gagged.

"Oh, Rock!" Her arms went about him, and for a long moment they sat there, and he held her close. After a long time she looked up. "When I heard your horse, I tried so hard to cry out that I almost strangled. Then when my mare whinnied, I knew you'd find us."

She came to with a start as he helped her down. "Rock! Where's Mort? He meant to kill you."

"He was born to fail," Rock said simply. "He was just a man who had big plans, but couldn't win out with anything. At the wrong time he was too filled with hate to even accomplish a satisfactory killin'."

Briefly, as she bathed her face and hands, he told her of what had happened at Poplar. "Your folks will all be back in their homes by now," he said. "You know, in some ways, Lamport was one of the best of the lot. He was a fighter—a regular bull. I hit him once with everything I had, every bit of strength and power and drive in me, and he only grunted."

They sat there in the grass, liking the shade of the white-trunked aspens.

"Dud and Mary are getting married, Rock," Sharon said suddenly.

He reddened slowly under the tan and tugged at a handful of grass. "Reckon," he said slowly, "that'll be two pairs of us!"

Sharon laughed gaily and turned. "Why, Rock! Are you asking me to marry you?"

"Nope," he said, grinning broadly. "I'm tellin' you! This is one marriage that's goin' to start off right."

The steel-dust stallion stamped his hoofs restlessly. Things were being altogether too quiet. He wasn't used to it.

Kilkenny

CHAPTER ONE

To Clifton House on the Canadian came a lone rider on a long-legged buckskin. He was a green-eyed man wearing a flat-crowned, flat-brimmed black hat, black shirt and chaps. The Barlow & Sanderson Stage had just pulled in when the rider came out of the lava country, skirting the foothills of the Sangre de Cristos.

He was riding easy when they first saw him but his horse was dust-coated and the sweat had dried on him. The man had a tear in his shirt sleeve and a bloody bandage on his side. He rode directly to the stable and dismounted, caring first for his horse.

Only then did he turn and glance toward the House. He wore tied-down guns. Pulling his hat lower he crossed the hard-packed earth and entered the house. "I could use some grub," he said, "a meal now and supplies to go."

"We got anything you need. We're feedin' the stage crowd now. Go on in."

He paused at the door and studied the room before going in. There were six passengers from the stage. Two women and four men, and there were a few riders from the valley roundup and three men from a trail herd crew. Face by face he studied them. Only then did he seat himself.

The tall girl from the stage lifted her eyes and looked across the table at him, her eyes alive with curiosity as she saw the bloody bandage. None of the men appeared to notice anything, and she filled her cup again and tried her coffee. It was hot, black, and strong.

Her eyes went again to the man in black. He had removed his hat when he seated himself and she noticed that his hair was black and curly. He was a lean, powerfully built man, probably larger than he looked while seated. Her eyes trailed again to the bandage.

"You . . . you've hurt yourself!" she exclaimed. "Your shoulder!"

Embarrassed and irritated, he glanced up. "It's a scratch," he said hastily. "It's all right."

"It looks like more than a scratch to me," she persisted. "You had better have it cared for."

"Thanks," he said, his voice a shade grim now, "I shall."

There was silence for a few minutes, and then from down the table somebody said, "Don't yuh wished yuh was scratched, Ike? Mebbe the lady would fix it for yuh."

The tall man flushed slightly but said nothing, but from down the table came a new voice. "Whatever it was scratched him," the voice said, "it looks like it hit him runnin' away!"

The dead silence that followed saw the tall man turn pale and cold. He lifted his head, his green eyes going down the table to the man who had spoken. He was a tough, handsome youngster with a look of eager recklessness about him. "If you were jokin'," the tall man said, "say so."

The man beside the tall man ducked suddenly and rolled off the bench, while others drew back from the blond young man. The youngster got slowly to his feet. "I wasn't jokin'," he said, with a faint sneer. "It looks to me like you was runnin' away."

As he spoke he went for his gun, and what happened then was seen with utter, piercing clarity by all who watched. The tall man seemed deliberately to wait, to hesitate the split second it took for the blond young man's hand to strike the butt of his gun. Then he palmed his own gun and shot.

The blond man staggered, his gun, half-drawn when the shot struck him, slid back into the holster. The man backed up, sat down, and rolled over on his face, coughing blood and death.

For an instant the room was still, broken by the young woman. She stared with horror at the tall man. "You . . . you *murderer!*" she cried, her lips twisting.

The tall man drew back slightly, his gun still in his hand. From one man to the other, he looked. "You saw it. He asked for it. I didn't want to kill him. I wasn't hunting for trouble when I came here. I was just tryin' to eat a quiet meal. What did he want to jump me for?"

Nobody spoke for a few seconds and then an older man said quietly, "Don't blame yourself, stranger. The boy has been huntin' for trouble ever since he killed a man in Texas."

"That won't make no diff'rence for yuh," another man said. "When Tetlow hears yuh've shot his boy, he'll never rest until he nails yore hide on the fence."

The tall man drew back and holstered his gun. "I'm not looking for trouble," he said. "I'll take my supplies and leave. Just you remember that," he added. "I'm not lookin' for trouble."

He sat down at the table and using his left hand he made two sandwiches from meat and bread. Wrapping them in a kerchief, he shoved them into his chaps pocket, backed away from the table, turned and walked into the other room. Tom Stockton was waiting for him. On the counter was a sack filled with supplies. "There it is, son. I seen it, an' it was a fa'r shootin' if there ever was one. Take this stuff, an' welcome."

"Thanks," the tall man hesitated, "but I want to pay."

"I'll take it hard," Stockton said grimly. "Yuh take this an' go along. It's little enough I can do for *Kilkenny!*"

Although he hissed the last name gently, the tall man looked quickly around. "Don't say that name!" he said. "Don't mention it!"

"*I* won't," Stockton replied, "but there's others in there may. Johnson," he nodded toward the dining room, "is from the Live Oak country. He may know yuh."

"Thanks again." Kilkenny turned, then he paused. "This Tetlow—who is he?"

Tom Stockton leaned his big hands on the counter and his face was grave. He had established Clifton House in 1867 to serve the round-up crowds and it had become a stage station. Since then and before he had seen much of the West and he had known most of it before. He knew this young man both by reputation and by intuition, and he liked him, and knowing this man and knowing Tetlow—

"It couldn't be worse. He's from Tennessee, Kilkenny, with all that means. He's the old bull o' the woods, a big, hard old man, but aristocratic, intelligent, smart, and a politician. Worse, he comes of a feuding family. He'll not rest until he gets you, or you him."

Kilkenny nodded. "I see. What's he doing here?"

"He's not here, not yet. But he's comin'. South of here on the flat he's got six thousand head of cattle. That's the second herd. The first one was four thousand head. He's got two more herds comin'."

"He'll need a lot of land for that many cattle," Kilkenny said. "I hope he's got it spotted."

"If he hasn't," Stockton replied, "he'll get it." He jerked his head. "That one, the one you shot. He was tall-talkin' around here. Said if they didn't get the land any other way they knew how they could get it. And he slapped his gun when he spoke."

"It's been done," Kilkenny said.

Stockton nodded gloomily. "Which makes it mighty tough on the little man who can't hire gunmen. Knowin' somethin' about Tetlow, however, I'd say that he wouldn't fall back on guns until politics failed. He's a smooth one, an' like I said—he's a politician."

To the high valleys then, came a lone rider, a man who rode with the caution born of riding long on strange trails in a land untamed and restless with danger.

The Indian Wars were largely of the past, although there were still the Sioux, the Cheyenne, Nez Percé and the Apache with fight left in them, but on the land from which the Indian had been driven or from which he was being driven the white man had not found peace—or at best an uneasy peace when men rode with guns at hand and eyes alert for danger.

Cattle had come to replace the buffalo, and then bolder men had pushed their herds into the mountain valleys, valleys lush with grass that fattened cattle amazingly fast, and as these valleys began to be settled, some men drifted to the high meadows among the peaks.

Lonely, largely overlooked, but excellent grazing in spring, summer and early fall, the valleys were the last land to be taken. It was to one such valley that Kilkenny rode, and when he drew up and looked around him, he made his decision. This was the home he had been seeking, on this land would he stay.

Riding on, he studied the valley. To right and left lay towering ridges that walled the valley in, and to the east other peaks lifted, and west the valley swung hard around and at one corner the wall was broken sharply off to fall sheer away for more than six hundred feet. Kilkenny paused long upon the lip, looking out over that immeasurable distance toward the faraway line of the purple hills. It was then that he first became conscious of the sound, a faint scarcely discernible whispering. Holding himself erect, he listened intently. It was the wind! The whispering wind!

Wind among the tall pines, among the rocks and the erosion-gnawed holes, a sound such as he had never heard, a sound like far off music in which no notes could be detected, a sound so strange that he could not stop listening. He turned then in his saddle and looked back over the valley he had found. At least two thousand acres! Grassy and lush with growth, water aplenty, and that whispering! The valley of the whispering wind!

It was a strange thing to find this place now, this place where he knew he could find happiness, the place from which he would not move again. He had told himself that before he realized what it might mean, and when he did know, he nodded his head as if at last he could be sure.

Yes. Here he would stop. Here he would cease being the restless drifter that he had become, a man fleeing from a reputation, fleeing from the reputation of a killer. But in this place he would stay, and he would find peace—if they let him.

There was always the chance that some stranger from the plains might drift into the country and recognize him as Kilkenny, yet he was fortunate in that few men knew him well, and most descriptions of him were mistaken. There was always the chance of such a killing as the affair at Clifton's. That man had not even known who he was, just a trouble-hunting kid wanting to prove how tough he could be. But that was over, and it was miles away over some of the roughest land in the world. And here he would stay.

His fire was a lonely gleam in the vast darkness of the valley, and in the morning he saw where the cougars had come down from the rocks to investigate, and once he found the tracks of a grizzly. Killing a deer for food, he started in then to work. Living on the ground under the stars, he laid the foundations of his home, choosing flat stones from the talus of the ridges, carefully laying the foundation and the floor. When a space for three rooms was carefully laid, he crushed limestone, and with sand made a crude mortar and began building the walls from selected chunks of rock.

It was slow, bitterly hard work, but he enjoyed it, and during that first month in the high meadow there was no sound or sight of anything man had done but what he did with his own hands. While he worked, he thought carefully of what he would do now.

The house was nearing completion, and he had cleaned the waterholes and walled up the spring near the cabin.

Soon he must go to a settlement for supplies and ammunition. He felt a curious hesitancy about that, for he had no desire to go. Always now he found himself remembering the queer horror on that girl's face after he had shot Tetlow. True, she did not understand what it meant. She was new to the West. Still, it was not pleasant to have one looked at with such horror.

Who was she? She was without doubt beautiful—very beautiful.

As beautiful as . . . ? He shook his head. No. There was no other like Nita, and there would be no other like her.

On the first day of the seventh week in the high meadow, Kilkenny saddled up and started for town. He knew nothing of the place. Horsehead, they called it, and while riding toward it he had heard it mentioned, but no more. He did not even know how to get there, but must find his way through the canyons.

Horsehead sprawled in lazy comfort along both banks of a creek called Westwater, and the town's main street crossed the creek at right angles. The ancient stone stage station, a veteran of Indian fighting and earlier Mormon settlement, stood near the east bank of the creek. It was a low-roofed, single-storied building with an awning that projected eight feet from the roof and offered shelter to a couple of initial-carved benches polished by the seats of many breeches.

Above the doorway was a crude sign lettered *Horsehead: Stage Station. Eat & Drink.* Drinks were occasionally served over the tiny six-foot bar, but no meals had been served for six years. East of the stage station was the two-story Westwater Hotel & Saloon, and it was here the elite usually ate. East of the hotel in lazy comfort were the Harness Shop, Eli Putnam, Prop.; the Barber Shop, the office of Robt. Early, Lawyer, and a scattering of other structures steadily declining in height until they reached the usual Last Chance Saloon.

Opposite the stage station was the sheriff's office and jail. The town marshal had a desk in the same office but no love was lost between the two men. Alongside the sheriff's office and facing the hotel was the assayer's office, and beyond it in a row were the Pinenut Saloon, the Emporium, the real estate office and then the Diamond Palace Saloon & Gambling Hall and a trail of further buildings.

West of the creek was a section of town all by itself, and one largely ignored by the businesses and citizens who lived on the east bank. A grove of trees, mostly cottonwoods but mixed with willows and a scattering of others, occupied the immediate bank and partly shaded the bridge. Beyond the trees were the corrals and wagon yards of the livery stable, and then the huge and sprawling stable itself. Beyond the stable was the bunkhouse, which was a place for casual sleeping, and possessing no rooms, but merely a dozen tiers of bunks, two high, and a few tables.

Alongside the bunkhouse was Savory's Saloon, but it was not considered very savory. This was the "tough" place of the town. A long, narrow building with a long bar and a good many tables, it had been ever since its construction a hangout for the town's tough element as well as for occasional drifting cowhands.

Across the dusty street and beyond the usual line of hitching rails and opposite the corrals was the office of Doc Blaine, tall, undeniably handsome, forty, of mysterious background, but without doubt, gossip had it, the best surgeon west of the Rio Grande. Doc Blaine was usually drunk, but during his occasional periods of lucidity he removed bullets, patched knife-wounds and bottle-cuts, or otherwise administered to the well-being of the town's wrong side. His office was, obviously, strategically located near the scene of most of the shootings, cuttings and beatings, their source being anywhere along the street in front of the bunkhouse or Savory's.

West of the Doc's was Dolan's a resort with one pool table, several card tables, too much cigar and cigarette smoke and drinks served from another tiny bar. Yet Dolan's was not a saloon. Those who frequented the place were an interesting cross-section of the town. Dolan was an ex-soldier, a former sergeant of cavalry and a veteran of the Mexican, Civil and Indian Wars.

Beyond Dolan's to the west were two deserted buildings and then the blacksmith shop, and beyond it, the canyon. This last was a deep slash in the rock of the mesa, deeper than the nearby creek, but waterless except for the brief rushes of water following heavy rains. This was also bridged.

Lance Kilkenny rode down from the hills into the east side of town, riding on until he reached the stage station, where he dismounted and tied the buckskin at the hitch rail. Pausing there, he took out the makings and rolled a smoke, scanning the town with careful eyes, alert to any attention he might be getting and curious about the town itself.

Ducking under the hitch rail he settled his hat back in place and glanced at the loafer standing in front of the stage station. "Nice little town you've got here," he suggested.

The loafer glanced at him out of the corners of his eyes, then at the two low-tied guns. "I reckon," he agreed, wiping the back of his hand across his mouth, "You seen Dolan?"

"Don't know him," Kilkenny said. "Who's he?"

The loafer stretched, then jerked his head toward the west side of town. "A good man to know if yuh figure to stick around." Turning, the man sauntered away.

His brow puckered slightly, Kilkenny watched him go, then turned east toward the hotel. He was a tall man, well over six feet, with wide shoulders, thick and powerfully shaped. His hips were lean and his waist small. When he walked, it was less the rider's walk than the woodsman's. Turning into the Westwater Hotel, he sought out the dining room and dropped to a seat at a table near the back of the room. He glanced curiously at the menu, then looked again, for here in this cow country hotel was a menu that would have favored any cafe in Paris.

He turned the page, then turned it again. One facing page listed the usual cow country meals, but on the other was a French menu listing at least fifty dishes!

"Surprised?"

Kilkenny glanced up to see a square-shouldered man of medium height standing above him. On the man's vest was a sheriff's badge. Kilkenny's eyes went from the badge to the rough-hewn features. The mustache was white, trimmed, and clean. The eyes were a cool blue, now faintly quizzical and amused.

"Yes," he responded, "I sure am. Sit down, Sheriff."

"Thanks." The sheriff dropped into the chair across the table. "My name's Leal Macy. Whenever a stranger wearing two guns comes into town I try to make his acquaintance."

Kilkenny looked at the menu again, and when the waitress approached he said, "I'll have the Paupiettes de Veau Provençal, an' tell your chef I'll have nothing but Madeira in the sauce."

Macy grinned, but his eyes were alert and curious. "Ernleven will like that. The man's a marvel with food and takes it as a personal favor if anyone orders from the French side of the menu. An' yuh'd be surprised how many do. The West," he added, "is made up of a lot of odd characters. I went over the trail from Texas once with two university men in the crowd. One from the Sorbonne and one from Heidelberg.''

''Yeah.'' Kilkenny was alert now. If the sheriff had been over the trail there was scarcely a chance he had not heard of Kilkenny—unless it had been among the earliest trips. ''The promise of a new country attracts men from everywhere.''

''Going to be around long?'' The question was casual.

''Permanent.''

Macy looked at him again, more carefully. ''We need good men. This is good country. Planning on ranching?''

''Uh huh. In a small way.''

''Located yet?''

''Yeah.''

There was a moment of silence, then Macy asked, ''Might I ask where? I haven't seen you around before.''

Kilkenny nodded with his head toward the northwest. ''Over there.'' He turned his green eyes toward the sheriff. ''An' I haven't seen you around before, either. However, Macy, let's get this straight. As sheriff you've seen these guns I pack an' you're probably wonderin' what all I want around here. I want to be let alone. I've picked the loneliest place I can find and I've holed up there. Unless something unusual happens, I'll be in town no more than once a month after I get located. I don't hunt trouble, an' I've never been drunk in my life. Sometimes,'' he added, ''it doesn't pay to get drunk an' forgetful. You'll have no trouble with me. I figure to run a few cattle and to mind my own affairs—but I want to be let alone.''

''Fair enough,'' Macy nodded agreeably. ''Know anybody in town?''

''Not a soul. And I have spoken to only one man before you. He volunteered the information that I should see Dolan.''

Leal Macy felt a little shock of excitement go through him and he looked again at this tall man, measuring him, wondering. Then he said, more carefully, ''If I were you, I'd not see him. Not now, anyway. Let it ride until your next trip. Dolan,'' he added, ''is a tough case, and around that place of his you'll find most of the rag ends and bobtails of the country. Drifters, rustlers, gunmen, outlaws, and just no-goods.''

''Is he on the rustle?''

''If he is, nobody every caught him at it. Dolan's an ex-army sergeant. A good fighting man, shrewd, and very able, He rode with Sheridan."

"So did I," Kilkenny replied quietly.

He looked up suddenly, hearing the door close, and for a long moment he made no move. In the door stood the young woman of Clifton's and her eyes were on him, wide with recognition. He arose quickly. "How do you do, ma'am? I hope you've been well?"

Her eyes held his, filled with uncertainty. Then she nodded and crossed to a table not far away. Macy said nothing but he was obviously interested.

The waitress returned and served Kilkenny's meal and at his suggestion brought Macy a cup of coffee. The waitress hovered by the table and when Kilkenny glanced up, she said. "The chef says the sauce is *always* with genuine Madeira."

Kilkenny grinned. "Macy, I may be in town more than I planned. If the food is going to be this good, I can't stay away. A man gets tired of his own cookin'."

The door opened again and three dusty cowhands came in and dropped into chairs around a table. All three were unshaven and had obviously been riding hard and long for they had that lean, hungry, wild look of men off the trail. One of them was a lumbering big fellow with fat cheeks and a thick neck, another had a scar along his cheekbone and the small finger missing from his right hand. The third man was a man of sandy complexion, almost white eyes and he wore his gun thrust into his waistband.

After seating themselves they let their eyes wander around the room, noting the sheriff and studying him carefully. If Macy was conscious of their attention he gave no evidence of it. Kilkenny came in for a share of their regard and the big man kept looking at him as if trying to recall where he had seen him before.

The food was excellent and the coffee black and strong. It was like paradise after the long days riding west, eating half-cooked meals in the lee of a cliff or near some wayside waterhole. From time to time he glanced up and twice he met the eyes of the girl from Clifton's. What, he wondered, was her name? Was she stopping here?

He hesitated, then put the question to the sheriff. "Thought you knew her," Macy said. "As a matter of fact, she's just out here from the East. She's a niece of Bob Early, the town's best lawyer. Her name is Laurie Webster.

"New to the West," he added, "but a fine horsewoman. The best I've seen except for Nita Riordan."

Kilkenny felt the shock clear to his heels. He held himself a minute, afraid to speak, and then he said carefully, "Who did you say?"

"Nita Riordan. She's got the KR spread, southwest of here. Runs the ranch herself, although she's got a foreman that knows his business. She rides astride like a Western woman. I hear she came from the Live Oak country, down near the Rio Grande."

"That right? The name sounded familiar, but I guess I was mistaken."

Macy chuckled good-humoredly. "Friend," he commented, "if you ever saw this girl you'd never forget her. Spanish and Irish, and beautiful! All woman, too, but one who can take care of herself. She handles a pistol like a man, and a Winchester, too. But no nonsense about her, and nobody makes her any trouble. That foreman of hers is like her shadow. He's a big Mexican, and I've seen him shoot the heads off quail with his six-shooter."

"Been here long?"

"Not very. About seven or eight months. She came in here and bought out old Dan Marable, but since she took over you'd never know the place. She's built a big new house, new stables and has brought some new stock into the country. I'm afraid she'll have trouble now, though, with this new outfit comin' in."

Macy drank his coffee. "She's running cattle on that country south and west of town, clear back to Comb Ridge. It's good graze and she'll do all right if she doesn't have trouble with this new outfit."

When the sheriff had gone, Kilkenny's attention went to the girl at the nearby table. He hesitated, wanting to speak to her, wanting to explain. But the information Macy had given him crowded out all else.

Nita Riordan was here! Her brand was the KR, but he refused to let himself believe what that K might mean. Kilkenny and Riordan . . . but there were so many reasons why a particular brand might be used. Yet she would soon know he was here, and without doubt they would meet.

The big man across the room was watching him and whispering to his companions. Unmindful of what it might mean, he arose and crossed to Laurie Webster's table. "I beg your pardon, Miss Webster," he said, "but I would like to apologize for causing you any discomfort back down the trail. The fight was forced on me."

"I know. And can you ever forgive me? To have it happen right before me . . . it was awful. But I do understand that you had to do it."

"Thanks." He stepped back. "Maybe we'll see each other again."

He walked out, conscious of the eyes of the three men. It was bright and sunny in the street and there was a fresh smell of hay, dust and warm lumber. It was time to get his supplies and go, yet he delayed, unwilling to leave so soon.

Suppose Nita came into town this morning? Suppose, even now, she was in one of the stores? Yet, if they did meet, what could he expect? He had to run away because he was afraid of what his guns might do to their love for each other, how inevitably he would some day be killed. At the time it had seemed the thing to do.

Through the plains country his name had become a legend, a mysterious rider whose gun skill compared with that of Hickok, Thompson and Earp. He was said to be faster than Hardin. colder than Doc Halliday. Yet few knew him well enough to describe him, for he moved often and used many names.

Partly concealed by the awning post and the shade of a huge cottonwood, he saw the three men come from the hotel and mount their horses. All wore the 4T brand. He watched them ride out, then he crossed to the Emporium and bought the supplies he needed. He crossed the bridge to west town and drew up at the livery stable.

"Got a pack horse for sale?"

"See Dolan. He's the man with horses to sell."

Kilkenny hesitated. Dolan might know him. A lot of men had ridden with Sheridan, but the last thing he wanted was to be recognized in this town. Yet to pack the supplies he wanted he needed at least one more horse.

The man indicated he corrals. "He might sell that paint."

The fellow got up, taking his pipe from his mouth. He was a small man with work-hardened hands. "Seen the marshal yet?"

"Macy? Yes, I've seen him."

"He's the sheriff. I mean the marshal, Harry Lott. If you ain't seen him, you will. He aims to get the jump on strangers. Says the way to run a town is to keep it buffaloed."

"How do he and Macy get along?"

"They don't. Macy's a solid citizen."

The man still hesitated. "My name's Hammett. Tell you what I'll do. I'll see if Dolan has a pack horse to sell."

"It'll be a favor."

Kilkenny walked to the corral and studied the horses. They were not the kind to be found on any cattle spread, but chosen animals, the sort preferred by outlaws who needed speed and bottom. He had walked around the corner of the corral when a big, heavy-shouldered man strode down to where he had been standing and looked around. He had a long, hard-jawed face. He wore two guns tied down and was roughly and carelessly dressed. On his vest was a badge.

Lott looked across the street toward Dolan's, then settled down to wait. Kilkenny rolled a smoke. Hammett came out of Dolan's and stopped on the step. Lott called to him and Hammett crossed the street. Kilkenny could hear their voices. "Where's the man who rode this horse?"

"He said something about getting a drink," Hammett said. "Stranger to me."

"What's he look like?"

"Looks all right. But nobody to monkey with. Looks mighty salty."

"He go to Savory's?"

"Didn't see. He ain't in Dolan's."

Lott walked past Hammett and headed for Savory's Saloon. Hammett watched him go, then caught up the buckskin's reins and brought him to Kilkenny. "Dolan said you could have the paint for fifteen bucks, but you'd better ride out of town until Lott gets over his sweat. He's drinkin' and huntin' trouble."

"Thanks." Kilkenny handed fifteen dollars to Hammett, then got into the corral and roped the paint. Putting on a halter and lead rope, he mounted his own horse and with a wave to Hammett, rode through the trees into the creek. He would avoid crossing the bridge in case the sound drew Lott back to the street.

At the Emporium he bought a pack saddle and loaded up, keeping a watchful eye out for Harry Lott. Irritably he realized he was only avoiding an issue that must soon be faced.

At a thunder of hoofs he turned to see a dozen riders charge into the street. A pistol bellowed, then another. They swung down in front of the Diamond Palace and the Pinenut and charged inside, yelling and laughing. The tall man in black who had led them remained in the street. With him was a wiry man, slender and gray-faced. His eyes seemed to be almost white.

The tall man bit the end from a cigar and Harry Lott came up the street. "Who made that racket?" he demanded. "Who was shootin'?"

The reply came, ice-cold and domineering. "Those were my men, Marshal, and the shooting was harmless. They will come to town often, and we will have no trouble. Understand?"

Harry Lott's eyes glowed. This man, Kilkenny saw, was a killer. Yet he saw more than that. The gray-faced man had moved to one side. The movement drew Kilkenny's attention and for the first time he saw the man's face in the sunlight. It was Dee Havalik,

In the Sonora cattle war his ruthless killings had won him the name of Butcher Havalik. Unassuming in appearance, he was deadly as a rattler and blurred lightning with a gun.

Harry Lott had not even noticed him. Lott was watching the older man, and Lott was in a killing mood.

Why he did it, Kilkenny would never know. Perhaps he wanted to see no man murdered. He spoke softly, just loud enough for Lott to hear. "Careful, Lott! The other one's Havalik!"

Lott stiffened at the name, and Kilkenny saw his eyes shift, then return to Tetlow. "And who are you?" Lott demanded of the older man.

"You mark well the name." The old man stood a little straighter. "I'm Jared Tetlow! And I've fifty riders, enough to sweep this town off the map!"

Harry Lott was no fool. And at that moment he saw the third man. It was the big man Kilkenny had seen earlier in the Westwater dining room. He was fifty yards away, only his face was rifle muzzle showing over the back of a horse. That rifle was leveled at Harry Lott.

It was a cold deck, and Lott knew it.

"Keep your men in line," he said, "and we'll have no trouble." Turning on his heels he walked toward the Emporium, slanting his eyes toward Kilkenny.

Tetlow and Havalik went inside. The man with the rifle loafed in front of the barber shop.

Lott studied Kilkenny suspiciously. "You saved my neck," he said. "They had me in a cross fire."

"I don't like to see a man murdered."

"I heard about Havalik." Lott had buck teeth and a heavy body. "Who are you?"

"I've been called Trent. Seems like a good name."

When he had packed his supplies he swung into the saddle and rode out of town, taking the route across the bridge, past Dolan's and turning right into the hills when he passed Savory's.

The tall old man with the autocratic manner was Jared Tetlow, father of the man he had killed at Clifton's! And such a man would be a desperate and implacable enemy. And this man commanded the guns of Dee Havalik!

CHAPTER TWO

KILKENNY RODE WEST from Horsehead. The Valley of the Whispering Wind was almost due north but he had no intention of leaving a trail that could be easily followed.

One sight of Tetlow had indicated the nature of the man who would be his enemy. Once the cattleman knew the man who had killed his son was nearby he would not rest until that man was dead. Nor was Kilkenny unaware of the danger that lay in Harry Lott.

Several times he paused just over ridges to look back along his trail. As he suspected, he was followed. At dusk he turned into the head of Butts Canyon, riding down a switchback trail that was rarely used. He took his time entering and made sure there were visible tracks. Within the canyon it was black as a cavern, yet he trusted his horse, knowing the mountain-bred gelding would take him through safely. It was cool, almost cold at the canyon bottom.

At the first fork he rode into a narrow, cavernous passage that led back into the plateau to the northwest. He had no idea if there was any trail out, but it was a chance he must take.

When they had gone some distance up the branch canyon the buckskin pulled to the right. With carefully shielded matches Kilkenny studied the ground and found the buckskin had started into a trail apparently used by deer and wild horses. Swinging back into the saddle, he let the buckskin have his head. Nearly an hour later they emerged atop the mesa. A notch in the hills to the north promised a pass and he headed toward it.

The night was cool and the stars seemed amazingly close. Several times he paused to rest his horses, and when traveling stuck to rocky ledges whenever possible. Toward daybreak he made dry camp in a clump of juniper, picketing his horses on a small patch of grass.

He made breakfast over a fire of dry and smokeless wood at daybreak, but before he moved out he took his glasses and from a nearby rock devoted fifteen minutes to a careful survey of the country. He saw no sign of life, no trail of smoke.

Mounting, he rode into wilder and even more lonely hills. It was a desolate land, a jumbled heap of uptilted, broken ledges, enormous basins, knife-like, serrated ridges and toppling towers of sandstone. The sun climbed and grew hot, weirdly eroded sandstone danced like demons in the heat-waved air. Dust devils moved mockingly before him, and the distant atmosphere gathered splendid blue lakes in distant bottoms.

Sweat stained his shirt and got into his eyes. The buckskin turned dark with sweat and the red dust that shrouded the junipers began to cover him, but still he rode north, knowing nothing of the waterholes, into a trackless and forbidding land.

For almost ten miles he rode across windswept rock where no trail could be followed, and then suddenly as though weary of the heights it had been following, the plateau ended in a series of vast, gigantic steps that descended for several miles, dropping little by little into a basin. Coming upon a wild horse trail, Kilkenny followed until he came to a small, blue and beautiful lake where grew a few willows and cottonwoods. Here he watered his horses and rested, smoking a cigarette and relaxing.

It was dusk before he moved again, and now he turned east, for the Blues were abreast of him, and he found a wild horse trail that led across a great natural causeway into the Blues. He made camp at dark and only reached his valley in the early light of the following morning.

There was no evidence that anyone had been here in his absence. With coffee on, he went out and removed the saddles from the horses and rubbed both of them down. The buckskin was accustomed to this and stood patiently, but the paint was restive, uncertain of what this new master intended. But the scraping of the dry handful of grass was pleasing, and finally he grew still and waited, enjoying the ministrations.

After breakfast, he sat on the step of the house and cleaned his guns, then went out and set several snares and deadfalls to trap small game. He had the hunted man's hesitancy to shoot unless absolutely essential and the knowledge that much game could be captured without it. Donning moccasins, he walked off down the valley until he was a mile away from the house, well knowing a time might come when he would want game close around him.

Long accustomed to the wild, lonely life, Kilkenny moved like an Indian, and he could live like one. Few men knew the wilderness better, and although he appreciated the towns and the comforts they offered, he had grown accustomed to living in the wilds and could do it. He knew the plants for their nutritional or medicinal value, knew how to make many kinds of shelters and utensils for camp use, and given a hunting knife, or even without one, he could survive anywhere.

He had chosen a quiet life now, away from the centers of action, but even here trouble was building. A less experienced man could see what was about to happen. Despite the ranches and permanent homes, Horsehead was in no sense a settled community. Many were drifters who had come to get away, often capable men, and fiercely independent. Yet most were poor men, running a few cattle, and starting from scratch. Into this country Tetlow had come with his great herds and dozens of hard-bitten riders. Good range was scarce, insufficient to support his huge herds and the cattle they now carried.

Tetlow was arrogant, sure that his success gave him the right to demand and control. The ranchers were stubborn men, resentful of this outsider. The situation could scarcely have been more explosive.

From his own ranch in the Valley of the Whispering Wind, Kilkenny found nothing in the situation to insure hope. Tetlow's manner to Lott showed the sort of man he was and that he would ride roughshod over all who got in his way.

Aside from the presence of Nita Riordan and the fact that he had killed Tetlow's son, Kilkenny's sympathies were with the small ranchers, the men who were building homes rather than empires. For one man to grow so large as Tetlow meant many men must remain small or have nothing. The proper level lay between the two extremes, and this was the American way.

Three years before Lance Kilkenny had taken the trail to the Live Oak country to help a friend. He had met Nita Riordan there, keeping a saloon inherited from her father. On the border and in outlaw country, she had elected to run the saloon herself when she found it impossible to sell. Jaime Brigo, the half-breed Yaqui who had been her father's friend, had been her strong right hand. From the moment their eyes met there had been no doubt in either her mind or that of Kilkenny. And then Kilkenny had drawn back.

There was no place in his established life pattern for a woman. No day could pass when he felt free from danger, and any woman who loved him would go through a thousand private hells, never knowing when he might be killed by some reputation-hunting gunman. Despite her acceptance of this, Kilkenny had gone away.

The following year they met again in the cedar brakes of New Mexico where Kilkenny had been trying to establish a home. Trouble had come again, and Nita in the midst of it. Now she was here, ranching in this wild country.

Had she believed that because of its loneliness it would draw him? Or had she given him up and started her own life? Or was there, the thought brought a chill, another man? For three days he worked, thinking of this, with increasing restlessness. He used his adze to shape a plow for the share he had picked up in Horsehead, and when it was completed he broke ground for a small corn and vegetable garden.

In the evenings he rode and studied the country, becoming more and more familiar with all the canyons and mesas. There was no such cattle country anywhere around Horsehead.

On the fourth day he saddled the buckskin at daybreak and took the trail down Mule Canyon. By the direct route he was nearing Horsehead by noon and he circled to enter town from the west.

A spring wagon was tied in front of the Emporium with a four-horse team hitched to it. The brands were 4T, the Tetlow brand. Down the street he saw three horses wearing the same brand. Beside them was a sorrel horse with three white stockings, branded KR.

He turned quickly to get off the street and went into the dining room of the Westwater Hotel. As he entered, a man with a square-cut face, iron gray hair and cool blue eyes looked up from his meal. His eyes quickened with interest and Kilkenny turned sharply away and seated himself at a table across the room.

The effort was useless, for the man with the gray hair crossed the room and sat down opposite him. Kilkenny liked the cool, self-possessed manner of the man, and the neatness of his clothing.

"My name is Dolan."

"I'm Trent."

"I've good cause to remember you, *Major*—Trent."

Kilkenny's expression did not change. He had ended the War Between the States as Major Kilkenny.

"I heard you were with Sheridan."

"You'd not remember me, but I've cause to remember you. There was a bit of a skirmish in a little Mississippi village and you came in with ten soldiers to drive out some guerrillas who were looting. You were outnumbered five to one and had to pull out."

"It was a rough go."

"There was a Union soldier lying wounded in a barn. He had been trying to fight them off for more than an hour before you rode into town. You heard about him after you had pulled out."

"I remember. Some village girl told me."

"Through heavy fire you rode back, fought off an attack with six guns, and when they broke in, killed three men with a Bowie knife before they broke and ran."

"Makes me sound a desperate character. Actually, it was mostly luck. They came into the darkness from the glare of the sun."

He studied Dolan. "You seem well informed."

"I was the soldier you carried out of there. But for you I'd be dead."

"You owe me nothing. It was the chance of war."

"Naturally, you'd feel that way." Dolan bit the end from a cigar. "This is a new country. We have two large cattle outfits, the KR and the 4T, and they will soon be fighting. The situation could become prosperous for us all."

"The 4T will spend money," Kilkenny said quietly. "That should increase prosperity. It won't make matters easier for the local rustlers. The 4T can take care of itself."

"Possibly."

"Dee Havalik is foreman for Tetlow."

Dolan stiffened and glanced sharply at Kilkenny. "Havalik?" *Here?*"

"Better look at your hole card, Dolan. And"—some change in his voice made Kilkenny meet his eyes—"don't bother the KR."

Dolan studied Kilkenny with careful eyes. "That means you want it left alone? I suppose you wouldn't answer a question about it?"

"None."

"And Tetlow?"

"If he interferes with the KR, I'll see him."

Dolan waved his cigar irritably. "You don't leave me much."

Kilkenny smiled. "'You look prosperous. If you're pushed you could always turn honest."

Dolan chuckled. "It's a desperate resort, but it may come to that." He got up. "Nevertheless, I'm your friend."

The 4T, or as it was called by its own people, the Forty, had established headquarters east of town. Tetlow sat by the wagon with his three sons, Phineas, Andy and Ben. Jared had been talking of his dead son. "I'll find that man!' he promised. "I'll see him die!"

"Dad," Ben said quietly, "why hunt trouble? You know how the kid was. He was always on the prod. I don't blame anybody but the kid himself."

Tetlow's eyes flamed. "He was your brother, wasn't he?"

Dee Havalik squatted across from Tetlow. The older man wasted no time. With a stick he traced a crude map in the dust. "Carson runs cattle in Brushy Basin and east. He's got a small lake that holds through the dry spell. We'll go see him about sellin' out."

He looked up. "Dee, you're to come. Andy will stay with the cattle. We'll take Phin, Ben and two hands. Bring Cruz an' Stilwell. We'll go see this Carson."

Reluctantly, although he knew better than to object, Ben mounted his sorrel and followed the others. They rode swiftly until they drew up before the door of the small adobe house. A man of fifty came from the house wiping his hands on a handkerchief. "Light an' set, folks!" he invited. "Just got grub on, but there's some extry an' I can make more!"

"How much you want for this place?" Tetlow said abruptly.

Carson blinked. "This here?" He shook his head, smiling. "Why, I like it here. I don't aim to sell. This here's the first home I ever had. I got me a few head of cattle an'—"

"How much?" Tetlow repeated brusquely. "Speak up, man! I've no time to waste!"

Carson's face stiffened, then his eyes grew wary as he looked from one to the other. "So that's the way of it? I wondered what yuh figured on doin' with that big herd. Well, I ain't sellin'. That's all there is to it."

"I'll give you a thousand dollars," Tetlow replied shortly.

"Take it an' a horse an' git!"

"You're crazy!" Carson was angry now. "Why, I'm runnin' four hundred head o' fat stock! I got seven thousand acres o' land under my own use an' more to come! A thousand dollars? You're crazy!"

The men said nothing and there was absolute silence for the space of two minutes. Then Carson drew a step back, then another. He was afraid now, seeing the stern faces of these men. "One more chance," Tetlow said, "you get a thousand dollars an' a horse. Then you get clear out of the country."

"Go to hell!" Carson shouted. He wheeled and sprang for the door. A gun bellowed and he sprawled across the doorstep, his fingers grasping at the floor as if trying to drag himself inside.

"You seen it," Havalik's voice was casual, "he reached for a gun."

Ben's face was pale. He looked from his father to his brothers but their faces were blank, approving.

"Phin," Tetlow suggested, "you ride to town. Look up that Macy feller an' tell him what happened. Get on with it, now. We'll ride on over to Carpenter's place."

Phin swung his horse around and went off at a fast trot. With Jared Tetlow and Havalik in the lead, the rest of them took off for the Carpenter place. It was all of an hour's ride, and when they rode up to the door, Carpenter was walking up to the house with a bucket of milk.

Tetlow drew up, waving a hand around him. "What you want for this place? I'm buyin' land today."

Carpenter looked carefully at the riders and something in their eyes warned him. "Why, I don't know," he said cautiously, "I haven't thought about sellin'."

"Think about it then," Tetlow replied, "I need range and lots of it."

Carpenter hesitated. These riders had come from Carson's place and only a few hours ago he had been talking to Carson. The older man had been telling him of what he planned to do with his place, and both men had discussed the big herd of cattle and the rumor that more cattle were coming.

"What did Carson do?" Carpenter asked curiously. "Have you been over there?"

"Just came from there," Havalik offered. "We'll have that place, all right."

"Carson won't sell." Carpenter was positive. "We talked some last night."

"No," Tetlow agreed, "he won't sell. He won't have to. His place has been let go."

"Let go?" Carpenter was stunned. His eyes went from one to the other. Behind him he heard a sound inside the house, and he knew that sound. His wife was taking the scatter gun off the nails on the wall.

"Yeah, Carson won't be around any more. Cantankerous ol' cuss got right mean when we offered to buy him out. He grabbed for a gun. Well, what could we do?"

Carpenter looked at them, from one cold face to the other. "I see," he said slowly. "And if I don't sell? What happens then?"

Tetlow's horse stepped forward. "You'll sell," he said coldly. "What have you got here?" he sneered. "A little one-horse spread! Why, I've got thousands of cattle! I need all this range! You'll just putter along an' waste it! I'll put it to good use. I'll give you a thousand dollars an' you can keep your buckboard an' a team to fetch you an' your wife away from here."

"Free," the woman's voice spoke from the window of the cabin, "don't bother to talk to 'em any more. We got to strain that milk. Come on inside."

"You stay where you are!" Tetlow shouted, growing angry. "I ain't through with you!"

"You're through here," the woman's voice was cold, "this here's a Colt revolvin' scatter gun. She will fire four times. I reckon that's enough for all of you. Now ride off! You lift a hand to my man an' I'll start shootin!"

Jared Tetlow stiffened, his face flooding wth angry blood. "Easy, Dad!" It was Ben who spoke. "She means it."

"That's right," Havalik added, "she ain't foolin' an' at this range she could kill us all."

Tetlow cooled. That was right, of course. Anyway, they had done enough killing for one day. "All right!" he said crisply. "We're ridin'! But you make up your minds! We want this place!"

Wheeling, they rode away from the Carpenter place and back toward their own camp. "Dad," Ben interposed, "we'd better sit quiet until we see how the sheriff takes this Carson affair."

Tetlow snorted. "You saw him in the street! The man's gun-handy, all right, but we can talk to him! I know how to handle that sort!"

"That wasn't the sheriff, though," Ben persisted.

"Wasn't the sheriff?" Tetlow was growing angrier by the minute. Why did this son of his have to—"What do you mean? He wasn't the sheriff? You saw his badge, didn't you?"

"He was the town marshal, Dad. Not the sheriff. I hear the sheriff is a different sort, a very different sort."

Jared Tetlow scowled, but suddenly he was worried. Lott not the sheriff! He had taken for granted once he had seen the man that there was no need to worry. If the man couldn't be frightened he could be bought. Or enlisted.

"Why didn't you tell me?" he demanded. "You talk enough!"

"I started to tell you once, an' you wouldn't listen," Ben replied. "You'd never listen to me, an' it's time you did."

His father stared at him in amazement. "Since when did I take orders from a milk sop?" he demanded. "You keep a still tongue in your head! I can make up my own mind!"

"All right," Ben replied shortly, "see if you can make up the sheriff's!" Wheeling his horse he rode rapidly off through the junipers. Jared Tetlow stared after him, scowling, his face black with the anger that always mounted quickly at any suggestion of resistance among his own people.

Nobody said anything, and the hands did not look at each other. They pushed on, riding swiftly toward the headquarters wagons.

Ben drew up when he was safely away from the cavalcade and watched them go. Where was all this going to lead? Did his father think everybody would cringe before him? That he could rule everyone with whom he came in contact? And that Dee Havalik! The man gave Ben the creeps.

Turning his sorrel, he rode on into town and left his horse at the hitch rail. He saw no sign of Phin anywhere. Either he had not yet found the sheriff or they had both started for the ranch. Suddenly recalling that the hotel was reported to have an excellent chef, he went up the steps and entered.

There were only two people in the cafe. A slender, attractive girl in a gray suit, and a man.

The man sat alone at a table facing the door. He wore a gray flannel shirt with a black silk neckerchief, black jeans, and he wore two guns tied low down on his thighs. His black, flat-crowned hat was on a hook nearby. As Ben entered, the man looked up, measuring him with careful eyes. Ben Tetlow never forgot that glance. It had in it something wary and unfathomable. It was the expression of a man who knew what it meant to command.

His eyes went again to the tall girl. She was more than attractive, she was really lovely. Suddenly, more than anything else in the world, he wanted to know her.

The man in black got to his feet and picked up his hat. He laid some coins on the table and glanced again at Ben. His glance now was friendly. "Good grub," he said, "you'll never find anything like that in a cow camp!"

Ben's smile was quick. "That's what I hear."

The tall man stopped by the girl's table. "Are you enjoying your stay Miss Webster? I'm afraid there isn't much to do unless you like to ride."

"Oh, but I do! I love to ride!" Then she said quickly, "You have forgiven me, haven't you?"

He nodded, smiling. Then excused himself and started for the door.

Ben Tetlow looked after the tall rider. "Forgive her for what?" he wondered.

He swallowed, then cleared his throat. "Seems like a nice fellow," he ventured.

She looked at him gravely with the expression of a little girl who has been taught not to talk to strangers. "Yes, he is nice, and I'm so ashamed! I said some simply awful things to him! But you see, I had just come out west, and I saw him shoot a man."

"I know what you mean. It is never nice to see a man shot. Not even when he deserves it."

"This one did," Laurie said seriously. "I'm sure of it."

CHAPTER THREE

LANCE KILKENNY HAD seen Ben Tetlow and surmised who he was and, walking outside to the boardwalk that ran along before the buildings, he frowned as he considered the situation.

There would be no avoiding the Tetlows or their riders. In the first place there were too many of them, and in the second the town was too small. What he wanted now was to find out what had been done, if anything. He was standing on the street when he saw Sheriff Macy come from his office in company with a tall, rather stooped young man. That this was Phin Tetlow he did not know, but he did see the 4T brand.

Why were the Tetlows calling on the sheriff? And Macy's face was stern. Kilkenny watched them pass, then turned and crossed the street to the sheriff's office and jail. An oldster with a handlebar mustache sat with his feet on the desk. He nodded at Kilkenny, "Howdy! What can I do fer yuh?"

Kilkenny shrugged and smiled deprecatingly. "Nothing, really. Sort of loafin'." He jerked his head to the east. "Macy looked some upset."

The old jailer spat at the spittoon and scored dead center. "Ain't missed in ten year," he said, wiping the back of his hand across his mouth. "He should be upset. Carson had him an argyment an' tried to drag iron on Dee Havalik. The man must have been crazy!"

"Carson?" Kilkenny shook his head. "Don't know him."

"He's been batchin' out east o' here, got him a little two by four spread, few cows, good water. That young Tetlow said they went there to try to buy the place off him an' he ordered 'em off. When they tried to argy with him, he dragged iron an' Havalik shot him."

So it had started already! Kilkenny sat down and pushed his hat back on his head, stretching out his long legs. Wryly, he shook his head. "That Havalik," he said quietly, "I hear he's pretty slick with a gun."

"One o' the best," the jailer shook his head. "Carson must've been crazy."

"Anybody else see it?" Kilkenny asked innocently. "I mean anybody but the Tetlow outfit?"

"Now that you mention it, I don't reckon there was, but it sure don't make much diff'rence. Hombre like Tetlow wouldn't be startin' trouble with small fry like Carson. What would he want from him? Other way around, I wouldn't be s'prised."

Kilkenny shrugged, then he said ironically, "Yes, Carson might have tried to take Tetlow's herd away from him. He might have figured that fifty to one was about the right odds. Tetlow," Kilkenny added, "wouldn't think o' tryin' to steal Carson's land, or force him off it."

He got to his feet, noticing out of the corners of his eyes that the jailer was scowling thoughtfully. "Reckon I'll look around a mite. See you."

The sun lay lazily upon the town. A red hen pecked at some refuse lying in the dust, and a black and white shepherd dog flicked a casual tail at flies. Kilkenny strolled up to the Pinenut Saloon and rolled a smoke, leaing against the awning stanchion.

It was coming now and there would be no getting away from it. What would Leal Macy do? How much support would he get from this town? The jailer had seemed disposed to accept Tetlow's story without question, although Kilkenny's remarks might have planted doubt in his mind. Yet so many were willing to accept without question the word of any man who seemed to have money and power. Macy was not such a man, but could he get the local support necessary? Jared Tetlow had overnight altered the entire economic situation at Horsehead, becoming the largest single buyer to be found, and buying more than any three outfits in the area. Some of the local tradesmen would be afraid of running him out.

He heard the rattle of a buckboard and glanced up to see Doc Blaine come rolling down the street. He recognized the man from the black medical bag he carried and his manner. It could have been nobody but the town doctor. He pulled up in front of the Pinenut and got down, tying his team. "This isn't really necessary," he commented, faintly humorous, "these horses will stand in front of any saloon in the country. They know their master."

Kilkenny grinned, shifting his feet. "Have you been out to Carson's place?"

Blaine shook his head and looked curious. "What's the matter with him? That hard-bitten old coot isn't sick, is he?"

"He's dead. Dee Havalik shot him." Casually, Kilkenny repeated the story, watching Blaine's reaction. The doctor's eyes sharpened with attention and he nodded as though it followed some secret thought of his own.

"It begins to look," he said, "as if I may get a lot of unwelcome business."

"Could be." Kilkenny waited a minute, then asked, "Who lives near Carson's place?"

"Chap named Carpenter is his closest neighbor. Has a nice little place and a wife. They are good people—and they wouldn't take any nonsense."

"Any others?"

"Old Dan Marable. He sold out to this KR outfit, but kept a few acres for his own use, and then there's a family named Root.

Man and wife and two young boys. They have about three or four hundred head down there, and the KR, of course."

"There may be more trouble."

Doc Blaine studied Kilkenny with alert, interested eyes. "You're looking ahead, my friend. What's your part in all this?"

"That," Kilkenny replied, "will be left to time. But I'm curious about Carson. You think he would draw a gun on a party of armed men?"

Blaine considered that. "No," he said finally, "he's no fool. He wouldn't put a hand near a gun with Dee Havalik around. And so far as I know, he never carried a six shooter. Only a rifle when out for game."

Blaine went into the saloon and Kilkenny walked out to his horse and swung into the saddle. He would be better off at home minding his own business, but if trouble was coming to the KR and to Nita, he wanted to know it.

He took the east road out of town and lifted the buckskin into a space-eating canter. When he found a trail leading off south, he took it, and finally found a crude sign painted with the one word *Carpenter's* and an arrow. He followed along into the late dusk, and came up to the house, riding carefully.

A man's voice called out. "Hold it, stranger! Don't come no further!"

Kilkenny drew up and replied, "I'm friendly, Carpenter. Friendly, and curious."

"Don't get you."

"Had any visitors lately?"

"What's that to you?"

"Like I said, I'm curious. I'd sort of like to talk a little."

"I've got nothin' to say. Nothin' at all. And," he added dryly, "I never seen you before."

"I'm Trent. Just a loose-footed hombre who has a curious mind. I'm sort of wonderin' where a man would put ten or fifteen thousand head of cattle in this country without crowdin' a lot of other folks."

There was a silence and then low conversation within the house. Finally, Carpenter spoke again. "Get down and come in, but don't try nothin' fancy. We folks got faith in shotguns."

Kilkenny swung down and trailing the reins, walked up to the house, keeping his hands wide. A bar was removed from the door and he entered.

Carpenter was a solid looking citizen, and his wife had the firm, quiet face of a woman who knew how to build a home and had courage enough to build it anywhere. Carpenter on his side measured the tall man in the black jeans and gray shirt with a thoughtful eye. "What's on your mind?" he said at last.

"Why nothin' much." Kilkenny dropped astride a chair. "Heard Carson got killed an' I was wonderin' whether you'd had visitors.

"I had 'em, all right." Carpenter told his story briefly and without decoration. "I reckon," he finished, "it was only my woman saved me, an' her only becaue they didn't like the looks o' the shotgun. Maybe," he added, "because they'd already had trouble with Carson."

Kilkenny told them what he knew of Tetlow and the thousands of cattle they were bringing over the trail, and he hinted that he had an interest, purely personal, in the KR. Carpenter chuckled and his wife smiled. "I reckon," he said, "it don't take no wizard to figure out why. That Nita Riordan is a wonderful girl."

"Don't mention me to them," Kilkenny requested, "that will come in good time. But I know Brigo an' you can count on him to stick. You should have a talk with her."

"Good advice," Carpenter agreed. "'Talkin' with old Dan an' some others wouldn't be a bad idea, either."

Kilkenny returned to his horse and drew it back into the trees. For several minutes he watched and listened with care natural to him after the years of his life. Then he mounted and took another route homeward. It was customary for him to do that, also. It could have been merest chance that the trail he took skirted the holdings of the KR and neared the house at one place.

He drew up when he saw the lights and he sat there a long time, looking at them. There, where those lights glowed softly in the evening, was the only girl he had ever loved. There, no more than two hundred yards away, with all her warmth, her beauty, her tenderness and her humor. A girl to walk beside a man, and walk with him, not behind him. He rolled a smoke and lighted up, and spoke softly to Buck. "She's there, Buck, old boy, there in that house. Remember her, Buck? Remember how she looked the first time we saw her? Remember the light in her eyes and the way her lips parted a little? Remember her, Buck?"

The horse stirred under him, and he spoke to it softly, then rode on, and riding on, he did not look back. Had he looked back he would have seen a big man, broad and powerful, step from the darker shadows and stare after him. A man who carried a rifle, and who after a moment of waiting. lighted his own cigarette revealing a strongly handsome, yet savage face. And when he walked away with the cigarette cupped in his palm, his feet made no sound, but moved silently through the brush and grass, silently even over the gravel.

He walked up toward the house, and nearing it, saw another man seated in the black opening of the bunkhouse door. "It's me, Cain." The man's voice was low, a soft, fluid tone. "*He* was out there tonight, Cain."

Casin Brockman came to his feet, a huge man, bulking an easy two forty in jeans and a hickory shirt. Twin guns were belted to his hips. "You mean . . . *Kilkenny?*"

"Si, amigo." Jaime Brigo drew deep on his cupped cigarette. "And I am glad."

"Are you going to tell *her?*"

Brigo shrugged. "Who knows? I have not thought. Maybe he does not wish it."

"Yeah, although he's crazy not to. What man in his right mind would run away from such a woman as that?"

Brigo did not answer, taking another deep drag on the cigarette and then crushing it out in the earth at his feet. "Perhaps, amigo, he does well. Who knows when such a man may die? He thinks of that."

"Anybody who kills him," Cain said gruffly, "will have to shoot him in the back! Nobody ever lived could drag a gun like him."

"They shot Wild Bill so. Have you forgotten? Be sure that *he* has not. But I am glad he is here, for there will be trouble with the Forty."

Brockman agreed to that. "When wasn't there trouble with the Tetlows? Don't I know? I was in Uvalde when they started that fight with the McCann outfit."

He sat down again, then he wondered aloud, "Where's he livin'? Suppose, he's got him a place?"

Brigo did not reply, and Brockman turned to repeat the question and saw the big Yaqui was gone. He had slippped away with no more sound than a ghost.

Jaime Brigo tapped softly on the door of the ranch house and he heard the reply. Opening the door, he stepped in, a huge man, big-chested and yet moving like a cat.

Nita Riordan smiled quickly, a tall girl with long green eyes and very black lashes. "Come in, Jaime! It's good to see you. What has been happening?"

Briefly, the big Yaqui explained to her about the shooting of Carson and the threatening of Carpenter, of which he had heard almost at once. They had talked of this before, and he had been working for the family long before her father's death and knew how this girl felt about such things. He told her what he had been able to find out about the Tetlows and how they had come into the country with their immense herds, many wagons, and Tetlow's fours sons—of whom but three were left.

"The other?"

"He was killed at Clifton's." Brigo hesitated and Nita looked up quickly, her face suddenly white.

"Jaime! Was it . . . was it *Lance?*"

The Yaqui shrugged. "I do not know, senorita. It was a tall man in black. He was riding through. It was young Tetlow who began it. He forced the fight on the other man, who was already wounded.'"

"Do you think we'll ever see him again, Jaime?"

Brigo hesitated, tempted to tell her of what he had seen this night, yet he was torn between two loyalties, that to his employer and friend, and that to the man she loved—who was also his friend. And whom he understood as few men could. "I think—yes, I think so," he said at last. "He will come back one day, when you need him he will come."

"You sound so sure."

"And you?" Jaime asked shrewdly. "Are you not sure?"

"Yes, I guess I am." She got up quickly. "Jaime, is Cain out there on watch? If he is, why don't you have him come in? I'll make some coffee for both of you. Marie has gone to bed."

Brigo nodded and turned to the door. He was gone almost without a sound. Nita walked through the short hallway to the kitchen. Had she been imagining it, or had Jaime seemed *too* sure? Had he seen Kilkenny? She shook her head, dismissing the thought. No, he would not be here, of all places. Yet deep within her she knew it was not only possible but probable, for Kilkenny moved in the loneliest places, and the newest countries, and this one was new.

Then her mind turned to the threat implied by the coming of Tetlow. Accustomed to border warring, she understood what that threat meant as well as any cowhand or rancher in the country. She knew much of men such as he, and knew that he must have not a little land, not a little range, but lots of it. All there was here would not be too much. Realistic as she was, she also foresaw the influence the buying power would have on the businessmen of Horsehead. They would be reluctant to make any move that would in any way displease so big a potential customer, never foreseeing what he could mean to them with his grasping and autocratic way.

What should she do? That alone she did not know. Within a few days she would be faced with the problem and it was not one that pleased her. Better able to resist than the others, because she not only had made friends in town but she had several very able men who were not only excellent hands but who were gun handlers as well. As far as Cain Brockman and Brigo were concerned, she knew that with the possible exception of Havalik the Forty outfit had nobody who could equal them, let alone top them. The Forty had many more, but remembering the lessons learned from her own experiences and those learned from Kilkenny, she had built here with the realization that a time might come when the place would have to be defended, and it coud be. Moreover, behind her was the towering wall of Comb Ridge, practically shutting off all advance from that direction.

The fours hands that she now employed other than Brigo, who acted as foreman, were all good men and personally known to her. Cain Brockman was not only a good fighting man and cunning, but he was loyal to the death. It was strange the influence that Kilkenny had had upon the former outlaw. That Brockman had been a killer she knew. How many men lay behind him she did not know, but it was generally estimated that he had killed over a dozen before meeting Kilkenny.

Pacing the floor nervously, she waited for them to come in, and when the door opened, she looked up, smiling. Cain came in first, a burly, clumsy-looking man with huge fists, a thick, muscular neck and a hairy chest visible through his opened shirt. His nose had been flattened and he had heavy cheekbones and a heavy jaw, one of the toughest-looking men she had ever seen.

"Evenin', ma'am," he said, "sure is nice o' you to have us in for coffee. You make the best coffee I ever did drink."

"Thanks, Cain. Are the rest of the boys asleep?"

"Yeah, they had a hard day of it. That Comb Ridge sure is a

help though. Like a fence, only it never needs to be fixed. No post holes to dig. Reckon yuh got about a thousand head scattered between Westwater an' Comb."

"In the morning, Jaime," Nita Riordan turned suddenly to the Yaqui, "have my horse saddled. I'm riding into town."

"Si." Jaime Brigo dropped into a chair wondering if the tall rider from the shadow to the trees would be in town. Cain had asked a good question: where was he living? It would be wise to find out in case they needed him.

"Also," she added, "I want none of the men riding the range alone from now on. I want them to ride two by two, and keep their eyes open. If they killed one man, they will not hesitate to kill others. However, I'm going to see Leal Macy."

Dawn broke over the hills and Kilkenny rolled out of his bed in the Westwater Hotel and began to dress. He had been rising at daybreak for so long that he could no longer sleep even if he wanted to. This morning he was anxious to be up and around. He wanted to judge the town's reaction to the killing of Carson.

He went down the stairs and turned into the dining room. Doc Blaine was the only man there, but a few minutes later the young man he had spotted as Tetlow came into the room. He glanced at Doc and then at Kilkenny with friendly, questioning eyes. Neither appeared to notice him, and flushing, he seated himself alone.

The waitress came in and took their orders and Blaine ate in silence. "Trouble?" Kilkenny asked at last.

"Usual. Root's wife is ailing. She's worked all her life to help her husband build a home and she's killing herself. She needs a rest more than anything else. She don't want me to examine her, but I'm going to. Nice family. Poor," he added, "but energetic. The kind of people who do half the work of the world but never succeed in profiting from it. Stubborn, sincere, hard-working, but not acquisitive."

"You find them all over the West," Kilkenny said He grinned suddenly. "Maybe, I'm one of them."

Blaine looked up briefly, looking right into Kilkenny's eyes direct and with faint humor. "You're a Western type, as familiar as they are," he said, "but different."

"You've got me pegged?"

"Of course. You're a cut above the average of your type, but still one of them. You're not even strictly a Western product.

Your type has drifted up and down the world since it began. The lone hunter, the man on the prowl, the fighter for lost causes, the man who understands women quite well. Yes, I know your type. They sailed with Drake, they built the Hudson Bay Company. They were the backbone of the free companies of the Middle Ages.''

''You're flattering.''

''Am I?'' Blaine looked up quickly. ''Well, it depends on how you take it. Flattering, perhaps, but not reassuring. Your type fights the wars of the world and gets nothing from it but a lonely grave somewhere and the memory in the minds of a few men who die and then there is nothing.''

Kilkenny laughed softly, his green eyes lighting up. ''Yes, maybe you're right.'' As the doctor got to his feet, he added, ''Give my regards to the Roots. Tell them a man named Trent will call on them some day.''

When Blaine had gone, Kilkenny turned to his meal with interest and a hunger he had not realized he possessed. He was aware of the presence of Ben Tetlow but he said nothing and made no move to speak. The door opened and another man entered. Both looked up. This was a tall, fine appearing man with a trimmed gray mustache, gray hair and a fine, aristocratic face and the bearing to match. ''Good morning, gentlemen,'' he said. ''I don't believe we've met. I'm Robert Early.''

''Trent, here.''

The lawyer looked at him keenly. ''Heard about you. My niece tells me you gave her quite a shock at Clifton's.''

Ben Tetlow was scarcely listening, but at that name he stiffened. Kilkenny threw him a quick glance, but Ben Tetlow did not look up. Sensing something wrong, Early glanced quickly from one to the other, puzzled by their reaction.

Tetlow was thinking swiftly. Yesterday Laurie Webster, this man's niece, had mentioned seeing Trent kill a man. Now Early said it happened at Clifton's. Of course, other men had been killed there, but this could only mean one man. Trent had killed his brother!

Ben glanced sharply around, staring at this man. He recalled what they had said. The flashing draw, the one shot, the gun only half-drawn from his brother's holster. And his brother had been considered fast, had bragged that he was faster than Billy the Kid.

"Your niece is a very lovely girl," Kilkenny was saying, "and I'm truly sorry for what happened. One can't always choose the course of one's actions. I wanted no trouble."

"So I heard." Early ordered and looked back at him. "Staying with us?"

"Yes." Kilkenny was acutely aware of the presence of Tetlow. Inwardly he was wondering what Ben's course of action would be. This was the only Tetlow he had actually talked to except for the dead brother, but he seemed agreeable and anxious to be friendly. "Yes, I like it here and I think I'll stay."

He finished his meal and got to his feet. Outside the street was crowded with Tetlow riders. A dozen horses were tied in front of the sheriff's office and he glanced over that way. What had Macy done about the death of Carson?

He strolled across the street, walking around a knot of armed men. They were typical cowhands in dress, but there was that about them that told him they were something more. He knew the breed. These were fighting men, drawing warriors' wages.

Behind his desk stood Leal Macy. The jailer lounged in the corner. Macy was speaking, and the man to whom he talked was Havalik. Beside the latter was Phin Tetlow.

"The inquest," Macy said sternly, "will be at ten o'clock. You be there, Havalik. We'll get this matter settled right now."

Havalik shrugged. "Oh, all right, but it's a lot of fuss over nothin'. The hombre asked for it."

"That will be established at the inquest," Macy replied coolly.

"Supposin'," Havalik jeered, "that you decide I'm guilty. What happens then?"

"You'll be arrested, put in jail and held for trial," Macy replied quietly.

Havalik laughed, a laugh echoed by several of the Forty riders. "Arrest *me?*" he laughed. "Why, you ain't man enough to arrest me in the first place, an' no Forty hand ever did a day in jail in the second place. The outfit would pull this jail down around your ears."

"They might," Macy replied, "but if they did the law would hunt down every man jack of them. It may have escaped your notice, Havalik, but times are changing. You fellows are on short notice everywhere now. The day when killing could go unpunished in the West is over."

"Yeah?" Havalik laughed. "That's right interestin' to know. I sure would admire to see you ride onto any range held by the Forty to take one o' their men."

Leal Macy was not cowed. Calmly, he replied, "If that becomes necessary, that is exactly what I shall do. We will hold the inquest in the Diamond Palace at ten. Be there." Deliberately, he turned his back and walked into the jail behind the desk. The others turned and trooped out and there was a rush for the Pinenut Saloon. Kilkenny stood out of the way and watched them go, and then he stepped into the office. Macy reappeared from the jail, his face cold.

He nodded to Kilkenny. "That bunch is riding for a fall," he said.

"Uh huh." Kilkenny dropped in the chair in which he had sat on the previous day. "How much help can you get here in town?"

Macy looked at him quickly, then he smiled without humor. "Very little, I'm afraid. A few good men. The rest will be looking at the buttered side of their bread."

"What I figured." Kilkenny ran his fingers through his hair and looked down at his boots. "I like a man with nerve, Macy. Count me in if you need help."

Macy studied him carefully. "All right," he replied, "but no obligations, understand? Wherever my duty takes me, I'll go."

"Sure," Kilkenny got to his feet. "I'm asking no favors nor giving any. This fight if it comes will be everybody's fight, only most of them won't know it until it's too late."

Leal Macy nodded shortly and as Kilkenny reached the door, Macy glanced up. "Thanks, Trent. I appreciate this."

"Sure." Kilkenny stepped out into the street. If there was going to be trouble there was little sense in delaying action and allowing the Tetlows to get too firmly situated. He wanted no trouble, but he knew now there would be no avoiding it. If Ben had been the boss—that fellow could be talked to. Maybe it would be worth attempting.

Three men were standing in front of the stage station. They were the same men he had seen in the hotel dining room. The big man with the lumbering gait was staring at him truculently. Suddenly, he yelled, "Hey, you!"

Kilkenny ignored him and the man yelled again, then wheeled and started for Kilkenny, who came along and stepped up on the walk in front of the Westwater. There the big man reached him. "When I call, yuh stop!'" he bellowed, thrusting his face at Kilkenny.

Suddenly, Lance Kilkenny was coldly, bitterly furious. The attitude of the man, his bullying voice, the attitude of the Forty outfit toward the sheriff, all of it had culminated in this. His right jerked up, not in a close fist, but striking up with the butt of his palm. The movement was so swift the big man had no chance to avoid it and the hard butt of that palm smashed under his jaw, slamming his head back on his neck. The man tottered, and Kilkenny stepped in and struck him a slashing blow across the side of the face with the edge of his palm. The blow laid the man's cheek open for four inches, showering him with blood. Then Kilkenny looked up, facing the other two men.

The man with the white eyes and the gun tucked in his waistband and the man with the missing finger and scarred face. Both stared down at the big fellow on the ground and then looked at Kilkenny unbelieving. "Never even closed his fist!" Somebody said from the gathering crowd.

"This gent's hunting trouble, Grat," the scar-faced man said softly. "He's askin' for it,"

"Then we'll give it to him, Red." Grat started to move, but he was too late. Kilkenny had seen the situation developing and preferred it to be settled with fists rather than guns. Infinitely more experienced at this sort of thing than the average cowhand, he struck swiftly. The blow caught Grat high on the face, and as his hands came up to protect his face, he whipped an underhand blow to the wind. Grat's knee caved and he pitched forward into the cracking left hook that Kilkenny had ready for him.

When he stepped in to meet Grat he had turned in such a way as to put Grat between himself and Red. It gave him just time enough to put Grat out of the running, and as Red rushed him, Kilkenny vaulted over the hitch rail into the street. Red brought up short and in the split second of hesitation, Kilkenny grabbed his outstretched arm and threw his back under him jerking him over the rail and off his back with a flying mare. Stunned, Red stared up, gasping for breath at the man who stood over him.

"I'm not hunting trouble," Kilkenny said, "but it's time somebody showed you where to head in. If you've picked me for the job, I'm the man who can do it."

Jared Tetlow shoved through the crowd, his face flushed and angry. "Here! What goes on here?"

Kilkenny turned sharply at the authority in the voice. His head dropped a little, his hands went wide. "Tetlow!" His voice rang in the narrow street. "You came into this country hunting trouble and you brought a bunch of no-good trouble-hunters with you! These hands of yours jumped me!"

A devil was driving him now and he was cold with fury. He stepped toward the older man, his hands ready to his guns. He felt it building inside him but he was helpless to stop it. He was berserk with fury and ready for anything, heedless of anything. He could not have stopped had he faced the whole Forty outfit.

"Take em and get out of the country! Move 'em out! You've come looking for trouble and here it is! And if you don't like what I say—*fill your hand!*"

Jared Tetlow was appalled. Accustomed to command, surrounded by tough gunhands who protected him from every danger, it had been years since he had personally faced a gun. In company with his men he faced up to them readily, but now, suddenly, he felt lost, alone. He fought for words and none would come. Suddenly, he knew with cold certainty that if he reached for his gun he would die.

Never had he been so aware of the imminence of death. This man would kill him. That realization shook him to the depths of his being. Normally courageous, he had been so protected in the past years that now, naked and alone, he was helpless to move.

Slowly, Kilkenny relaxed. "So that's how it is?" he said contemptuously. "Nerve enough to order a man killed but not nerve enough to face it yourself!"

Deliberately, he turned his back and walked across the street and into the hotel, leaving behind him a blanket of silence.

Jared Tetlow stared around him as if coming out of a trance. Realization came to him. He had been challenged, had been dared to draw and he had made no move. There were thinly veiled smiles on some of the faces, worry on others. Around him the crowd was melting away.

His definite, known world seemed suddenly shaky. He had grown to manhood in a family that fought as a unit. He had trained his sons and his riders the same way. It was always the Forty against everything and everybody, but one man had thrown a challenge into their teeth and he himself had backed down.

Grat got to his feet, sullenly beating the dust from his clothing. The wide cut on Jess Baker's face seeped blood. Red, at the hitch rail, was being violently sick. Tetlow glanced around and saw Ben standing in front of the harness shop. His emptiness filled with fury. "You!" he roared. "Where were you? Why didn't you do something?"

"What could I do? If I had made a move he would have killed you—just like *he* killed Bud."

Jared Tetlow went stiff with shock. "That . . . it was . . . *he* killed Bud?"

"That's the man," Ben said quietly. "And if anyone had made a wrong move he would have killed you!"

CHAPTER FOUR

KILKENNY ENTERED THE hotel to find Leal Macy waiting for him. The sheriff seemed unusually quiet. "That took nerve," he commented, "what if he had tried it?"

"He wouldn't," Kilkenny said, "He's a cinch killer. I saw them work against Lott the other day."

"But he might have."

"Yes, I thought he would, to be honest. Or maybe I just didn't think. Their kind gets in my craw."

"Mine, too. But you'd better get out of town for a few days at least. They'll never rest now until they get you."

"What about the hearing?"

"We'll have it." Macy spoke flatly. "We'll have it and we'll see what a local jury does. The fact is, your stand here in the street may make all the difference. They may not hesitate to bring in a bill against them. Or against Havalik."

"You'll have a fight if you try to arrest him."

"Then I'll have it." Macy was grim and quiet. "There are a few good men in town. Early is one of them, Doc Blaine is another."

"Doc?" Kilkenny was surprised.

Macy nodded. "Oddly enough, he's a fighter. Plenty of sand and a fine rifle shot."

"You can count on Dolan."

"Dolan?" Macy stared, half angry. "You think I'd call on him for help?"

"Why not? It doesn't look to me like you have much choice. I'd say call on him. Dolan,'' he added, ''is a former Army man. He was a soldier for quite some years. Despite the fact that he's on the edge of the law now, such a man is deeply marked with his former experience, and against mob action. Dolan will stand hitched, and keep his boys so. Also, he considers the Forty as fair game.''

Macy considered that. It went against the grain to ask help or even accept offered help from a man of Dolan's stamp, yet Macy had been a soldier himself, and he knew how deeply the years of training were imbedded in a man's nature. And Dolan had not been a citizen soldier, but a Regular Army man, a sergeant of long experience, accustomed to order and discipline. He still bore the mark of it in his neat dress, his square shoulders and his walk, and the sharpness of his actions. It was possible that Kilkenny was right.

''I'll stay if you want,'' Kilkenny volunteered. He admired the stand this man was taking. It was such men whom the West needed if ever there was to be peace and order.

''No, you'd only be another bone of contention. They'll be out to get you now, and your presence might make all the difference. You better leave town—and watch your back trail.''

''That,'' Kilkenny said wryly, ''is something I always do.''

When he was gone, Leal Macy looked after him, a faint frown between his eyes. He had not quite decided what to think about this man. Kilkenny talked right and sized up as all man, yet out there in the street he had been a man driven by the urge to kill, a man literally aching for the fight he expected. That could be a bad thing unless regulated by a stern will. Macy turned that last thought over in his mind, and shook his head. He was not sure.

Kilkenny got his horse and started out of town. The streets were deserted now, but he rode west, his horse's hoofs pounding briefly on the bridge. In front of Dolan's he drew up and called. Dolan came to the door, his hands thrust in his coat pockets, a cigar clamped in his teeth. Kilkenny had an urge to shout ''Attention!'' but stifled it. He had no doubt Dolan would snap to, and might enjoy it. No matter which side of the law this man now stood upon, he would stand under fire, a cool disciplined mind and hand.

''Leaving town,'' Kilkenny commented. ''Macy may need help. I told him he could count on you.''

Dolan was startled. He took the cigar from his teeth and spat, then stared at the end of it before he looked up. ''What the devil inspired that?''

"I know the breed, Dolan." He turned his horse and rode off down the street.

Dolan swore, threw his cigar into the street, then walked into the club and dropped into the chair behind his desk. Without being aware of it he lighted a fresh cigar and stared into the blue smoke of it.

He picked up a week-old San Francisco paper and straightened it with a jerk that almost tore it. Then he looked up at a square-built man who sat against the wall. "Pete, round up Clyde and Shorty. Maybe two or three others who'll stand hitched. We're going to that inquest. We," he added, "are going to side with the sheriff."

"The sheriff?" Pete blinked.

"Yes." Dolan had never explained his actions before. "We've a choice. If they bust Macy we'll have to fight the Forty alone. We want to keep Macy in action."

"That makes sense. The Forty stacks up to be mighty mean."

West of town Kilkenny took a trail into some scattered junipers. The background was desert and sandrock, dotted with greasewood. Against such a background his horse would merge into the landscape. From long practice he avoided metal on his clothing or horse. No man would wear glittering ornaments who was not a braggart or a fool. A chance reflection on a bright buckle or spangle had guided more than one bullet.

He worked to leave little trail, then emerged on a vast table land and, swinging at right angles, rode east. He bedded down for the night on high ground among some rocks where he could overlook miles of country.

Just before dusk he saw two groups of men riding trails out of town, five in each group, at a rough guess. When it was completely dark he rolled in his blankets and was soon asleep.

At the camp of the Forty all was silent. Men ate quietly and slipped away to their bedrolls. All avoided the eyes of Jared Tetlow. Deeply shaken, the old man stared long into the fire.

The realization of failure lay heavy upon him but he had been too long in command not to know what he must do now. Anything less than prompt action would end his hold upon the men who followed him, and he knew that reprisal must be swift, sure, and bitter. They had always known he was not a gunman, but they also knew that whoever this man Trent was, he was gun-slick. Now that Ben's account of how he knew that Trent was the man who killed Bud was around camp, all knew that Trent was a gunfighter.

Under the circumstances they would not blame him, but if he held back now they would lose faith in his courage. Moreover, the inquest on this day had not gone well. He had planned to strike there, to carry it off with a high hand and deny the right of Macy or anyone to question his actions. Then the man Dolan had arrived with several hardcase riders, all armed. They had said nothing, but Dolan was obviously with the sheriff, which was surprising.

Moreover, despite the number of businessmen who had remained away, Bob Early had been there, and Doc Blaine as well, and their position had left no doubt. Autocratic as he might be, there was that something deep within Tetlow that made him respect the authority of leading citizens. They were his kind of men, he felt, and their prestige counted for more than the threat of Dolan's guns.

Early himself had conducted the inquest. It had been sharp and direct. There were no witnesses except those for Havalik, but several witnesses were put on the stand who testified that Carson had never carried a gun. The possibility that he might have had one on that day remained and there was insufficient evidence to warrant holding Dee Havalik. Nevertheless, the weight of public opinion had made itself felt, and Tetlow was irritated by it.

Viewing the matter from the distance, he regretted the shooting of Carson not one whit. He regretted only that they had hesitated to ride roughshod over Carpenter, Marable and the lot of them. There was little that public opinion or anyone could do against the accomplished fact.

The first thing had been to find Kilkenny and wipe him out, and realizing that at once, two groups of Forty riders had been sent out to track him down and kill him. Moreover, Tetlow had been shrewd enough to let it be known that Kilkenny, or Trent as he knew him, had killed his son at Clifton's.

So far the riders sent after him had not been heard from, but they were covering all trails and should find him without trouble. That they would kill on sight, or hang him if they caught him alive, had been their orders as well as their conviction. Bud had been the most popular of his sons with the rougher element.

Ben walked up to the fire and seated himself close to his father. For awhile he smoked in silence. "Dad, let's drive on west. Let's leave this place."

When there was no answer, he steeled himself to go on. It took courage, for Ben Tetlow knew how his father hated weakness, and he also knew what must be going through his father's mind tonight after the facing down he had taken in the streets of Horsehead.

"We're buckin' a stacked deck. There isn't enough range here unless we take it all, and if we start fighting women and other settlers, we're out of luck. They'll band together against us."

"If you ain't got the guts for it, Ben," Tetlow replied stiffly, "get out!"

"No," Ben said quietly, "I'm staying. You're my father and this is our outfit. I'm stickin' even if I think you're wrong, and I do think you are. That's the trouble, Dad, you're committing others to your policy. If you go down you take a lot of men down with you. Some of them mighty good men."

"Leave him alone," Phin spoke from the darkness. "Like he says, if you don't like it, get out while the gettin's good."

Ben was silent, despair mounting in him. He had always entertained doubts of this business of riding roughshod over others, of insisting that their larger herd held inherent rights over all smaller herds and less powerful outfits. Yet there was no give in Leal Macy. The man would stand his ground until death, and for one, Ben was sure that Macy held the right stand.

Dolan was another. He knew how surprised he had been when Dolan showed, and how surprised his father had been. They had heard he was a leader or directing brain behind rustling and rustlers. They heard his place was a resort of the hardcase element, but the way the man stood and his looks belied that. Dolan was a fitting partner for Macy, and the two made a dangerous combination.

Ben had not thought much about Kilkenny. The fact that the man had killed his brother remained in his mind and for that reason he felt he should hate him, yet he could not bring himself to do so. He had the story from one of the older hands who had seen it all, and Bud had deliberately picked the fight, forced it when the man was ready to let it pass. And there had been no quarrel to precede it. Moreover, he felt drawn to the tall, quiet man with the brown face and the easy smile. He was, he appeared, a friendly man.

And then today in the street when he had called Ben's father, he had seen a different personality. In a land where fighting men were the rule rather than the exception, where courage was admired and strength and agility to be looked up to, Kilkenny was a commanding figure. The man had stepped out into that street heedless of all the Forty riders and their threat of power. He had slashed his way through three of them with his bare hands and then faced down his father in such a way as Ben had never seen a man faced. Ben had the courage of his convictions and his convictions were strong enough, but he saw something indomitable in that single-handed stand against the whole Forty outfit.

He had seen something else that none of the others seemed to see. It had not been superior strength that won that fight of one against three. Nor had it even been the violence, shocking in itself, of his onslaught. It had been superior skill and strategy. Kilkenny had never wasted a move. He had known exactly what to do and how to do it. Such skill was no accident. This man was a trained, experienced fighting man.

Jared Tetlow got to his feet. "Phin?" he questioned his son's wakefulness. At the grunted reply, he said, "Carpenter's got range enough for maybe six hundred head. We've got six thousand here now and more comin'. Crowd that range with four thousand head come daylight. Understand? We'll show this town how a Tetlow fights!"

Ben stared at the cold line of his father's jaw. There was no yielding there. Quietly he retreated to his blankets where he lay long awake.

At daylight the cattle were started. Deliberately, they hazed the cattle onto Carpenter's range while the rancher stood helplessly watching from beside his wife. At this rate within a few days they would have him ruined; what grass they had not eaten would be trampled underfoot.

Sitting his big chestnut, Tetlow watched grimly. Then he called to Ben. "You!" he said. "You've no stomach for this, so ride back down the trail an' tell them to push those cattle through fast! We'll show 'em who's going to run this here range!"

Havalik rode up beside him, his small face tightlipped with satisfaction.

"When those herds get here, an' they should make it by the day after tomorrow, push them on the KR range," he said, "we'll have them out of there within the week!"

Riding east, Ben stared grimly at the skyline. Trust his father to think of the one way he could beat them. Nobody had legal authority to make him move his cattle. This was open range, and belonged to the government. No laws regulated it as yet, and even if they had, they could not operate fast enough to save these smaller men. His father could stand a loss if need be, these men could not. Even if his father was forced to move—which he would not be—the range would be ruined for most of the season. The grass would come back, but much of it would be so trampled and overgrazed that the range would be destroyed or injured. His father, with his great holdings and armed riders, could move on or take a loss. These small ranchers could not. Jared Tetlow would ride to power and victory behind a wall of thousands of cattle.

Carpenter stared gloomily at the thousands of cattle on his range. Desperate fury consumed him and his big fists knotted and balled iron hard. He wanted to fight, to strike out at something, at anything. But what could he do?

"We'd better leave the place," his wife said quietly. "Let's go up to the KR like that man said. Let's go up there and get Marable an' the Roots. Together maybe we can do something."

"I'll be damned if I will!" Carpenter flared. "Leave my place? Be driven off what's rightfully mine? I will not!"

The story of the cattle drive reached the KR with the story of the challenge to Tetlow issued in the streets of Horsehead. It was no garbled account, but was given concisely and definitely by Doc Blaine over lunch at the ranch house. Aside from Nita, only Jaime Brigo was there.

Blaine's story started casually enough. "Lots of excitement in town. Fellow whipped three of the Forty hands in less than that many minutes and then called old Jared Tetlow to his face. Dared him at point blank range. I never saw such a thing."

Brigo's eyes were steady on Blaine's face. The big Yaqui sensed what was coming.

Nita called Maria to pour some coffee. "He moved cattle on the Carpenter place this morning. He'll ruin the man."

"That seems to be the idea," Blaine agreed. "Have you thought about yourself?"

"Of course. He can't run as many cattle as he wants without my place." Doc Blaine watched her as she talked. She seemed scarcely more than a girl, yet there was an assurance about her that puzzled him. He knew nothing of her beyond the fact that she had bought out a previous rancher for cash, had built here a ranch home that was far superior in every way to anything around, and she lived in the saddle, worked cattle herself and yet supervised a home that was the most perfect thing he had seen this side of a French chateau. "If he tries that, he will have trouble."

"He has a lot of men."

"And I have Jaime. And Cain Brockman and some others."

"Is Brockman as tough as he looks?"

"Far tougher. I only knew one man who could handle him. Jaime might, I don't know."

"That fellow who faced down Tetlow," Blaine mused, "he's a drifting cowhand, and I think a gunfighter. There are rumors around that he was the man who killed young Bud Tetlow, but he seems like a good man. Why don't you hire him?"

"I don't think we'll need anybody else," Nita smiled, "but thanks just the same."

"You'd better think it over," Blaine insisted, "this man Trent—"

Her head came up sharply. "Who? Who did you say?"

Doc Blaine was surprised. "Why, Trent. At least, that's the name he uses. You can't tell about names, especially with drifters. They might use any name."

Nita was looking accusingly at Brigo. "Is it . . . ?" There was no need to repeat the question for she could see the answer in the Yaqui's eyes and her heart began to pound. Unable to control herself, she came quickly to her feet, then, not wanting them to see her face, she turned quickly and walked to the window. "You . . . how long have you known?"

"The night before last. He came by here, and stopped outside."

"You . . . you talked to him?"

"No. He did not see me. I don't think he saw me."

Blaine looked from one to the other. Too wise in the way of the world and women to be fooled, he could see that Nita Riordan was upset. This surprised and intrigued him, for he had never seen anything startle her before. She was annoyingly self-possessed, and Blaine had been puzzled and disturbed by that self-possession. It was something he was not accustomed to in women, and it disconcerted him.

"You know this man called Trent?"

"I . . . I don't know. I think perhaps I do. I . . . we knew a man once who used that name."

"What was his real name?"

She turned on him. "That, Doctor, is something he would have to tell you himself." Then she remembered what the doctor had been saying, that this man had faced down. Tetlow. Yes, she told herself, her heart pounding, that would be like Lance. He could never stand tyranny of any kind, and he would not hesitate because of numbers.

Lance . . . !

The thought of him disturbed her, and she stood staring out the window, remembering every line of his face. The way he smiled, the way the laugh wrinkles came faintly at the corners of his eyes, eyes long accustomed to squinting against desert suns. She remembered the quick way he walked, the strong brown hands, the way his green eyes could grow cold—although they had never grown cold when they looked at her.

She remembered the first day in the Live Oak country, the day she had first seen him. She had looked across that room at him and suddenly they had seemed alone, as if only they remained in life and nothing else could or did exist. She had looked into his eyes and known this man wanted her, and had known that she wanted him, and they were right for each other and nothing else in the world would ever matter but him.

And now he was here again, close to her. He had been outside in the darkness, nearby. Had he known she was there? Had he been thinking of her? What had been his thoughts as he stood out there in the shadows, watching the lights? What time had it been? Had she been reading? Or getting ready for bed? Or already with her head upon the pillow?

"Jaime," she turned swiftly, "I want to see him."

The Yaqui looked at her and nodded, "Si, but to find him, who knows how? He is like the wind, and he leaves no trail."

"Think, Jaime! Where would he be? Remember what he said? That you did not follow a trail on the ground unless you could also trail with the mind? You have to think as the man you follow thinks, then you know where to go. You know him, Jaime. Where would he be?"

The big Yaqui shrugged, but he was thinking. That was the way, of course. To follow him with the mind. It was like the deer—once you knew where he watered it was not hard to find where he slept and where he fed. It was the same with all game, and with men. They established patterns. Kilkenny had said that, and he had never forgotten, for Kilkenny could follow a trail where even an Apache would fail.

But to follow the trail of Lance Kilkenny was something else again, for he was one who knew how to think, and knowing that he followed men by their patterns of thought as well as by their tracks upon the sand, he would think in different ways at different times. That, too, he had told Brigo.

One possibility there was. He would want a place that was far off and lonely, difficult to find and easy to defend. A place where he might stand off his enemies if need be. Especially would he want such a place with the Tetlows to consider.

''I think—maybe I could find him,'' he ventured. ''I could try, but to be away from here now? It is not good.''

''Find him!'' Nita insisted. ''Tell him I must see him.''

''Perhaps there is another way,'' Blaine ventured. ''Wait until he comes back into town. He will come, you know, and I know from what Leal Macy said that he has offered to back him if he needs help. Dolan knows him also.'' Blaine scowled thoughtfully. ''Dolan might even know where he is. He would know if anybody does.''

''Jaime. Ride to town with the doctor. Find out if Dolan does know.''

Despite her anxiety it almost frightened her to think of seeing him again. She understood well enough his motives for leaving her as he had, and respected him for it even while she regretted it. That she was quite prepared to accept him despite what might happen he well knew. Yet the thought of seeing him again and the chance of losing him again frightened her. After his disappearance she had adjusted herself only after a long time, and doubted if she could go through it again.

Her childhood training, her father, all her background conditioned her to love one man only. Moreover there was something inwardly fastidious about her that avoided the thought of any other man but this one.

''Let me go to Dolan,'' Blaine suggested. ''I know him. I'll explain, and then you'll have Brigo if trouble starts.''

Brigo waited, liking this idea better. He had cared for Nita since she was a child and resented the thought of leaving her at such a time. Kilkenny was the only man who came near her of whom he approved. More than fifty years of age, the Yaqui possessed the strength of a gorilla, the devotion of a dog, and the cunning of a wolf.

''All right,'' Nita decided. ''Tell him I need to see him.''

Doc Blaine got up from the table. Curiously he wondered how she had met the man who called himself Trent. Obviously the man had used the name before, but who was he?

As he started back toward town in his buckboard he could see cattle darkening the range where once Carpenter's few cattle had grazed. How could a woman with so few hands hope to stand against Tetlow's vast herds? There was no way to fight masses of cattle, for now Jared Tetlow had found the method that seemingly could not be stopped. He himself need attack nobody, for those cattle, bunched upon range too small to feed them, would break any man.

Nearing Whisker Draw a man got up from the rocks. He had a field glass and a rifle. It was Cain Brockman.

''Howdy,'' he grinned, slouching down to the trail. ''Reckon we got a fight comin'.''

''You may get help.'' Brockman had been with Nita a long time and might know. ''Miss Riordan has asked me to get in touch with a man named Trent.''

Excitement broke over Brockman's face. ''You mean—'' He broke off sharply. ''Trent? Nobody I'd rather see right now.''

Blaine had gone no more than two miles further when another movement stopped him. A woman, bloody and half her clothing torn, stumbled down the draw, then fell. She was struggling to rise as he reached her side. She was not a young woman and she was obviously exhausted as well as badly hurt. It was Mrs. Carpenter.

''My God! What's happened? Where's Free?''

''Dead.'' She was half dazed with grief and weariness. ''Killed.''

''Shot?''

''They stampeded cattle through the yard. He'd gone for water to the well. He broke for the house but he didn't get halfway before they ran him down.''

''And you?''

''Tried to help him. Steer knocked me down. I . . . I was going for the sheriff.''

He helped her into the buckboard and gave her a drink from his canteen. He wiped her face clean and gave her the best first aid treatment he could manage. "He was all I had," she mumbled, only half-conscious. "Without him it ain't . . . it ain't . . ."

He put a hand on her shoulder. "Think what Free would have done. He was a brave, good man."

After that she sat quietly until they reached town. He turned off at the outskirts and drove to Bob Early's home.

Laurie Webster was watering flowers and when she saw the woman she hurried to help. Blaine explained quickly.

"Is Bob home?"

"He's at the Diamond. He was to meet Leal Macy there."

There would be action now. They would not take this.

Yet even as the thought came to him, he began to doubt. Some would think only of the added profit they were making from the big, new outfit. They would remember the painfully few dollars spent by Carpenter and Carson, and would not allow themselves to think of what might happen when the Forty was in complete control.

There was Macy, however, and Bob Early. And there was Dolan and his men, perhaps a few others. His spirits sagged as he realized how few they were. Yet it had been always so. The many are afraid to act, hoping for the best until it is too late.

A dozen men sat at the table when he entered. Briefly, he explained. Macy leaned on the table, looking around at the faces of the others. "What did I tell you? Carson first, now Carpenter. Nobody is safe."

"We don't know what happened." Woolrich owned the Emporium. "We don't know Carpenter was run down a-purpose. We only got a hysterical woman's word for it."

Happy Jack Harrow of the Pinenut Saloon agreed. "My sentiments. Tetlow's bringing prosperity. My take's doubled since he came. This here's hard country. If a man ain't fit, he can't last."

"Who are we to fight a rancher's battles?" Savory agreed. "There's always been range wars. Far as that goes, what d'you suppose they'd do to the town if we started something? They'd wipe us out."

"So you'll stand by and see men murdered, robbed of their homes, and women driven into the desert?" Macy was disgusted. "Now we know the brand you wear, anyway."

"Easy with that, Sheriff." Savory's face was angry. "Because you're the law doesn't give you license to make free with your tongue. A bullet'll stop you soon as any man."

"Forget that," Early broke in. "Let's not fight among ourselves." He looked around. "I take it then that you're not in favor of taking action?"

"That's right," Savory said. Woolrich, Harrow, and a half dozen others nodded agreement.

Early turned to Macy. "Well, Leal, that shakes out the deck a little but the right cards can still win. I want you to deputize me."

"And me," Doc Blaine replied shortly.

A big man with a shock of black curly hair stepped up from the back of the room. His face was heavy-jawed and sullen. "I want to make me ziss deputy, too."

Pierre Ernleven was rarely seen away from his kitchen. He liked nothing so much as preparing food and seeing it eaten, and he took no part in the affairs of Horsehead. If he did not like a man's conversation or his attitude he would refuse to serve him. He was not above throwing a man bodily from the premises.

"Thanks, Pierre," Macy said. "There's no man I'd sooner have."

Ernleven looked around, his eyes bitter with contempt. "The rest of you don't come to my dining room. That goes for you, Harrow. Stay out."

Harrow got up, flushed and angry. "Cut your throats if you want. You don't know where your bread is buttered."

"That's probably right, Jack." Early spoke quietly. "We're thinking about a little word that has meant an awful lot to this country. A word called Justice. We're thinking of a country where there will be no feudal power, where no man can control the destinies of others. It was little men who built this country, and little men who have been its backbone. You should read Jefferson, Harrow. Had you lived in '76 you'd have been a Tory."

"You call me a traitor?" Harrow's face went white.

"Examine your conduct," Early replied, "then judge for yourself. As for me," he got to his feet, "my Winchester needs oiling. Call on me, Leal, when you're ready." He turned away, then glanced back. "See you later, *gentlemen!*"

Harrow glared around him, then stamped out and slammed the door. Woolrich walked after him. He was gloomy. HIs wife would give him the devil for this. She thought anything Bob Early did was all right.

Macy smiled with wry humor. "There it is, Doctor. If you ever wanted a lost cause, you've got it."

Blaine refused to admit it. "The cause of right is never lost, Leal. I've often thought the biggest damned fool in the world could go down in history as a great man if he would just consistently vote for the greatest good of the greatest number.

"Take Andy Johnson. They hated him, called him a little man, reviled him, tried to impeach him to get the presidency in the hands of a man they could control. He voted as he believed right and acted as he believed. Now the reaction is setting in and most people believe he was right. This is a good cause, not a lost one."

"What about Dolan?"

"He's a seasoned fighter who'll take no back talk from any man. Also," Blaine smiled, "Dolan's Irish and the Irish have an inborn resentment against power and privilege. They imbibe it with their mother's milk."

They were silent, then Blaine looked up. "Who is this man Trent?"

Leal Macy hesitated. This question he had known would come. "I think," he said quietly, "that Trent is probably the fastest man with a gun in the West. I think Trent is Kilkenny."

"Kilkenny?" Blaine was shocked.

"I'm sure of it."

"Kilkenny . . . " Blaine muttered. "Kilkenny . . . here!"

CHAPTER FIVE

DEE HAVALIK HAD his order. They were to hunt down and kill Lance Kilkenny.

Macy's identification of Trent had swept the town. The dramatic scene when he challenged Tetlow and manhandled three of Tetlow's tough riders took on a new glow.

Dee Havalik heard the name with satisfaction. His gun speed was his great pride, and to hear another man named as fast aroused irritation in him. Small, slender-boned and pinched of face, he was a man compact of nervous energy and drive. Far from pleasant at any time, with a gun in his hand he became ice cold and passionless.

By choice three of those riding with him were the men Kilkenny had whipped in the street, and there were four others. One of these was an Apache trailer.

Within a few hours after they took the trail Kilkenny was aware of it. He studied them through his carefully shielded field glass. The make-up of the crew was evidence of its intention. The saddle packs and pack horses meant it was a hunt to the death. The issue was clearcut now. They must die or he would.

At once he struck north into the wildest and loneliest country. If they wanted a hunt, he would give it to them. This was the life he knew best, and there was no trick of white man or savage that he did not know. He rode north and the sun blazed down from a hot and copper sky. He struck out across the sage brush levels where no cattle grazed and where the rattler buzzed and the buzzard soared. He struck north and west and he left a trail they could read without trouble, and deep in his chest something violent and frightening began to grow, the desire to turn on his pursuers and mow them down, to ride with the red lust of battle in him, ride right into their midst with guns blazing. But the time was not ripe for that, first he would show them what hell was like, he would show them what they had started!

The horizon danced and was lost in a haze of heat, the buzzards were the only spot of movement and the sun baked down upon the desert and the sand threw back the heat in his face like the top of a redhot stove. Their faces grew dusty, their throats parched, and riding on and on, he looked back upon his trail and saw the distant rising dust and chuckled. "Let 'em come!" he whispered. "Let 'em come!"

The surface of the desert broke into a maze of canyons, but he rode on. At waterholes he hesitated and waited, then pushed on when dark came. The days marched past and still he led them on, weaving among the canyons and taking them deeper and deeper into one of the most awful lands on the face of God's sometimes green earth. It was a land raw from the furnace of creation, a land without soil, rock shaped like flame and a sky that held no clouds but only a vast and blazing sun. Behind him his pursuers sweated and cursed, their lips parched and they nursed their canteens like mothers over a newborn child. They snarled at each other and grew vicious, and only Dee Havalik did not change except to grow thinner, leaner and more vicious.

Tempers grew short and the men began to hate the land, the sun, each other. And then suddenly the chase changed, and it changed on one bright and awful morning when suddenly from a ridge ahead of them, a shot rang out!

Half asleep in their saddles, the men cursed and slapped spurs to their horses to race for shelter. And there was none.

They were caught on an open flat and the shots came from a ridge all of four hundred yards ahead, but they were accurate shots. The first burned Red Swilling's arm. The second dropped a horse, the third carried away the pommel of Lee Jaeger's saddle. The riders scattered and ran and bullets followed them in their flight.

Remounting the hard-fleshed buckskin, Kilkenny circled swiftly toward a canyon where one of the riders was headed. When he reached it he slid to the ground.

The air was still. Heat waves rippled and then gravel rattled. Then the rider came into view. "Drop the rifle!" Kilkenny held his own in his hands. "Let go your gun belt. A wrong move and I'll gut shoot you!"

The rider's unshaven face was red from the sun. His hesitation was momentary. The rifle left no room for argument. He complied with the order, careful to make no mistakes.

Taking the man's rifle, Kilkenny shattered the stock over a boulder, and jammed the action. The rider stared bitterly as his rifle was ruined.

"That rifle cost two months' wages!" he protested.

"Tough," Kilkenny said wickedly. "You'd have killed me with it, wouldn't you?"

"What d'you want with me? Dee will kill you for this! He'll never quit until he kills you!"

"Dee? That white-bellied weasel? Tell him when I'm ready for him I'll come an' get him. First I want him done brown by the sun. I don't like that pasty hide in front o' me."

The man stared back at him. "What you aim doin' with me?" he demanded.

Kilkenny smiled then. "Why, what do you think? Want a gun in your hand and an even break?"

The fellow touched a tongue to his dry lips. "That wouldn't be no break. I ain't got your speed an' you know it."

Kilkenny smiled and picked up the man's guns and cartridge belts. "All right then," he said, "You want to manhunt. I'll let you, but it won't be comfortable without a saddle."

"Huh?" the man stared, puzzled and suddenly worried.

Coolly, Kilkenny moved toward the man's horse, his eyes faintly humorous.

An hour later, several miles to the south, Spade Woolley joined Havalik and the others. He was dark-faced from cussing and was astride a horse with only a bridle, his saddle gone and his guns gone. Also his canteen was gone.

"What happened to you?" Swilling demanded.

"He headed me off an' laid for me." Woolley was sullen and bitter. "Told me I could go on huntin' but I'd be damn sick of it. He was right, I am sick of it, an' I hope somebody shoots me if I ever throw leather on another razor-backed hoss!"

Havalik stared at him, red-eyed and furious. "What are you? A baby?" he sneered. "Lettin' him sneak up on you? What are we s'posed to do now? Wetnurse you? No canteen, an' you'll want to drink our water, no guns, no saddle. Start for the outfit, Woolley, an' start now."

"Huh?" Woolley's face was ludicrous in its amazement. "Without a canteen? I'd die afore I got anywheres!"

"Tough, ain't it?" Havalik sneered. "That'll learn you a lesson. Get goin'!"

Red Swilling stared at Havalik. "Dee, you don't mean that! Hell, the man wouldn't have a chance!"

Havalik turned like a poised rattler. "Want to make somthin' of it? You want to go with him an' leave your canteen? Or you want to go for your gun? You got a choice o' that or shuttin' your trap an' obeyin' orders."

Red Swilling swallowed and moved his hands carefully away from his guns. Havalik was trembling with eagerness and ready to kill. Swilling was shocked and frightened. "Hell, you're the boss, Dee," he protested, "I only—" His voice trailed off.

Havalik's eyes were on Woolley. "You startin'?" he demanded. "Or do I cut you down? I got no use for a damn fool!"

Spade Woolley stared back at the man and suddenly all the years of his life came up in him to curse him. He looked into those red-rimmed eyes, and suddenly he said, "I'll go, Dee," his voice was low, "an' I hope I get through. I want to get through now just for one reason. I want to be there when Lance Kilkenny shoots your rotten heart out!"

Woolley was beyond caring what happened. He knew the nature of the man before him, could see that flat, ugly mouth, the cold chill of that still gray face, the viciousness of the man's eyes, but deep within him was the courage he had been born with. "You know what he told me to tell you? He named you for a white-bellied weasel and said when he wanted you he'd come for you. He said he wanted your pasty hide done brown before he came for you, but he was wrong, Dee, that dirty white hide o' yours won't brown. It's the hide of a dead man!" Spade leaned forward. "A dead man, d'you hear? You're dead an' you're rotten before you lie down!"

Dee Havalik's flat lips writhed suddenly and his hand was a blur of movement. The gun came up and flame stabbed, and Spade Woolley folded up and slid from the back of his horse, hitting the sand on his side, then rolling over. For an instant, his eyes flared wide. "You saved me, Dee. Saved me from dyin' o' thirst out there! But . . . but you . . . you're dead! *Dead!*" Blood frothed at his lips and only his eys were alive, brilliantly, horribly alive. "Dead! Kilkenny will kill you! He's faster than you! He's . . . he's my kind o' man! I . . . I wish . . . "

"Mount up!" Havalik's voice was shrill. "Hit the leather! We're goin' on!"

Red Swilling stared for a moment at Havalik, his face somber with brooding realization. His eyes flicked to Baker and Grat. They were staring unseeingly at the sand. Slowly Red moved to his horse and the others followed. Nobody spoke of the dead man lying on the sand, but none of them was forgetting. And that ended the seventh day of the chase.

Kilkenny took a narrow wild horse trail that led up to North Point and then turned down the plateau. Far below him he could see the pursuers. He had heard the shot and wondered at it, but supposed a horse had broken a leg. He pushed on into the afternoon, and at night he doubled back again, locating their camp by the firelight.

From a safe distance he watched through his glass. The men's lips were not moving. They were not talking or looking at one another. Havalik sat alone, and nowhere among them was the rider he had seen this morning. Finally, one by one they crept to their blankets. Havalik was the last to go. One man remained, a guard.

For an hour, Kilkenny rested. Then, leaving his horse, he crept forward, flat on his stomach. It was a slow and painstaking progress, but soon he was at the edge of a camp.

The fire was dying. Straight before him was the guard, his back to Kilkenny. Beyond the fire was a low bank, some eight to ten feet high, and between it and the fire were the horses, cropping grass within plain view of the guard. East and west of the fire the men were rolled in their blankets, sleeping.

A stick fell and sparks leaped up. The guard got to his feet and gathered a few more sticks to lay on the blaze. The flames eagerly embraced the sticks with glowing arms and thin tendrils of flame and smoke crept along the length of the sticks. The guard yawned and scratched, staring around into the darkness, but Kilkenny lay among the clumps of bunch grass and was not worried. The guard had been watching the fire and would be almost blind to the outer darkness. No Indian would do that.

Finally the guard seated himself again and began to roll a smoke. Kilkenny studied the situation with care and then found what he wanted. Not far from the nearest sleeper were his saddlebags and canteen. With infinite care, Kilkenny slid forward the stick he had brought with him and, sliding it into the canteen carrying strap, he turned it round and round, winding up the strap. Then he lifed the canteen with care and drew it back to him.

Easing back deeper into the darkness he put the canteen beside a whitish, water-worn boulder and then circled the camp. It took him more than an hour of painstaking effort and waiting, but at the end of that time he had gathered four of the seven canteens. One of those was Dee Havalik's.

When he was a good two hundred yards off, he paused. His horse was close by and he had the four canteens fastened to the saddle. Lifting his Winchester .44-40 he shot three times into the flames as fast as he could lever a rifle.

The guard dove for the outer darkness and men scrambled to get out of sight. Kilkenny reloaded his rifle and walked back to his horse and mounted up. "Come on, Havalik!" he yelled. "What's the matter with you? Can't you read signs any more?"

Behind him there was a yell of rage but he cantered off into the darkness and now he turned west and then south. At daybreak he was camped on an eminence where he could overlook his back trail. He had deliberately avoided all waterholes, having plenty of water himself, and knowing they would be splitting the water of three canteens among seven men.

Riding into a maze of canyons, he deliberately rode and rerode over his trail, confusing it purposely, then he headed out straight east and was on the outskirts of Horsehead by sundown. After two hours of rest he left the buckskin picketed on rich grass and slipped into town, making his way toward the light he saw in Doc Blaine's.

Doc was reading in his study when Kilkenny opened the door, and he glanced up sharply. "Just me, Doc." Kilkenny sat down on the settee in the shadow. "What's been happenin'?"

Blaine put his book down. He could see the fine drawn lines of Kilkenny's face, for the trials of the last few days, the sleeplessness, that heat, shortage of water and all the rest of it were plainly etched there.

"Quiet enough right now," he said, "everybody knows who you are now. Dolan told me, I don't know who told the others."

"Any trouble at the KR?"

"Some. The Forty started to push cattle on the place two days ago and ran into something they didn't like. The KR outfit had tied up with old Dan Marable and the Roots and they opened fire at long range. Knocked one rider out of his saddle, killed a horse and about forty head of cattle, laying them in a line right along the boundary. I hear Tetlow was fit to be tied. He ranted and raved for hours, but none of his boys were very anxious to try to push cattle into that straight shooting. Since then things have been hanging fire, waiting for Havalik to get back I suppose."

"He was following me."

"So I heard. What happened?"

Kilkenny shrugged. "Not much. I made them chase me, shot their camp up, stole most of their canteens an' generally raised a hob just to make 'em miserable. They've had a mighty dry ride."

"We had a meeting in town and the place split right down the middle. Macy has Dolan, Early, myself and a few others on his side. Most of the town are against him, but not all."

"Has he done anything yet?"

"He hasn't tried. He wants to avoid an all-out gun battle if he can. There was an inquiry into the killing of Carpenter, but no proof. Eight witnesses testified that Carpenter deliberately ran in front of the stampeding cattle. Mrs. Carpenter said they drove them into him. That was the way it ended, and the Forty outfit walked out laughing."

Kilkenny turned his hat in his hand. "Make up your mind to this. When Havalik comes back, he'll be killin' mad. The first man to cross his path will die. I mean it, I think he killed one of his own men out there. At least, he disappeared."

"What are you going to do?"

"What I've been doing. I'm going to move against the Forty tonight. Tomorrow night, I should say."

"Nita Riordan wants to see you. She asked me to tell you."

Kilkenny looked up quickly, then he shook his head. "Not yet. I've my own reasons." He got to his feet, then looked quickly at Doc. "How does she look? Is she all right?"

"Yes, she's looking fine, In fact, she's the most beautiful girl I ever saw."

Kilkenny nodded. "She is that. And one of the finest."

Doc Blaine had the quick perception of one long geared to the study of human reactions. It was here, too. This man was in love with Nita. As much, he decided, as she was in love with him. He felt a quick start of pain at the thought. It had been a long time since he had seen a woman who excited more than a passing interest, and Nita Riordan had—there was something about her that stayed with you after you had seen her once.

The man before him was the same sort, Blaine admitted that. Having once seen Kilkenny to know him, one was not likely to forget. He was like an edged blade, sharp, clean, and strong, yet resilient. Yes, that was it, he was resilient.

Yet he was more, too. The man had character. Curiously, he wondered about his background. This man a killer—what had started that? Badmen looking for trouble and a naturally quick hand and eye? Probably.

Kilkenny turned restlessly. He was never very comfortable inside a house. That might come, but not now. "All right," he said, as though just responding to the message from Nita, "I will go see her, but not right away. I've too much to do and," he added quietly, "I know this thing too well. Take your mind off it for an instant and you're shot full of holes. These boys are playing for keeps."

"I'd like to know what Jared Tetlow is hatching right now. You can make up your mind it's something."

"I agree."

Kilkenny picked up his hat and turned swiftly to the door. "Someone coming. I'm going."

Almost before Doc Blaine could adjust himself, Kilkenny was gone. And Doc had not even heard the door close. Or seen it open.

There was a sound of voices, then boot steps and a spur rattled. An authoritative fist pounded on the door and Blaine went to it.

Three roughly dressed men pushed their way into the room. Doc knew them instantly. They were the pursuers of Kilkenny. Havalik was in the lead. "Got a wounded man, Doc. Take care of him."

He turned swiftly and surveyed the room, then walked through into the kitchen. "You alone?"

"Yes," Doc's voice was sharp, "and stay the hell out of my kitchen, Havalik! You're here with a man for treatment, not making an inspection of the furniture!"

Havalik whirled, white hot on the instant. "Yuh talk to me that way?"

"To you or any man. You've a wounded man here and that wound's in bad shape.You stay in here and mind your own business and I'll tend to mine. I won't lift a hand until you do."

Havalik was ugly an he took a quick step forward. Calmly, Doc picked up a scalpel. "This is my business, Havalik. I could cut you open as quick as you could shoot me at this range. And I'd cut where you'd bleed to death mighty fast."

Havalik stopped, staring at the doctor. There was conviction in Blaine's voice, and it surprised Havalik to see that he meant it. He drew back.

"Furthermore," Blaine continued, "this community values my hide. They need me here. There's not another doctor anywhere within two hundred miles. If anything happens to me they'd lynch you, Forty or no Forty. And before this is over, you may need me yourself."

"What's that mean?" Havalik demanded angrily.

"It means—" Doc was working swiftly and surely. It was a nasty wound. "It means," he repeated, "that you're carrying a gun and hunting trouble. It's a combination that gets every man in the end. It will get you. I doubt if you live out the month."

Dee Havalik turned away with a snarl. The driving urge to kill was riding him, but deep inside the doctor's words rang a bell. Was it because he perceived the truth? Or because he had been accustomed since childhood to take a doctor's word for things? It made him surly, and he walked out and slammed the door, starting up the street toward the Pinenut.

Dolan stood on the steps of his place and watched him go, then he stepped off into the darkness and went down the path to the rear of his establishment. He walked swiftly to the edge of the trees, then stopped and said carefully, yet aloud, "I could furnish a good horse if a man needed a rest for his own mount, a good horse with bottom and speed."

"I could use a horse like that." Kilkenny stepped to the very edge of the woods. "Busy place around here, Dolan."

"Yeah," Dolan said dryly, "too busy. One of that outfit that was chasin' you looked in on me. What have you been doin' to that crowd?"

"They wanted to go for a ride," Kilkenny smiled, "so I took 'em for one."

"The man that hit my place was half dead. He must have drunk a gallon of water. He said he hadn't had a decent drink, not more than enough to wet his lips in two days."

"Dolan, how many boys can you muster? I mean boys with sand?"

"Enough. What do you want to do?"

"Stampede the Forty herd."

Dolan was silent, but his eyes glinted. That would be hitting them where it hurt, and right at home.

"When?" he asked then.

"Tomorrow night. They are bunching them for another push toward the KR. I'd like to run them right back over their own camp."

"That might be tough. They've too many hands."

"I've got a plan. It calls for roping a half dozen of their steers." Kilkenny suddenly was tired, more tired than he had believed possible. "I'd need about four good, solid men."

"You'll get them. Where?"

"That lightning struck cottonwood in Whiskers Draw. Nine tomorrow night."

"They'll be there." Dolan stepped closer to him. "Man, you're all in. You'd better get some sleep. You'd better sleep until then." Without awaiting a reply, he turned and walked to a narrow gate in the corral, a very convenient gate for getting a horse into the trees without it being seen. "I saddled this gray when I first saw you. He's cornfed. He'll go all day and all night and was mountainbred."

"Good, and thanks."

"Don't thank me. Get some rest."

When he was gone, Dolan walked around to the steps again and lighted a cigar. Havalik was just leaving with his men. One man wore the white of a bandage. "What yuh mean?" this man was saying. "Yuh think Kilkenny was in that house before us?"

"I know he was!" That was Havalik.

"Think he was hurt?"

Havalik turned and his voice was low and fierce, yet clearly heard by Dolan in the desert air. "How could he be hurt? Who would hurt him? Did you see him? Did I? Are you crazy?"

"What about the Doc?'

"Leave him to me." There was icy promise in Havalik's voice. "Not now, but wait. All of this town that works against me or Forty. I'll take care of them once Forty's in the saddle."

"Dolan's place is right back there. Let's go back and bust it up and get Dolan."

Dolan took the cigar from his mouth and looked at the end of it.

"Later. He's got men with him. We'll get him when he's alone and nobody will care. Who cares about a crook?"

Dolan put the cigar in his teeth. "That's right," he muttered. "Who does?"

He was the vulnerable one. Early and Blaine were respected citizens. Kilkenny was elusive. Only Dolan could be hit without fear of retaliation. He could always, he reflected, go to Tetlow and make a deal.

He chuckled with wry humor. That was the one thing impossible for him. He could rustle cattle, plan a bank or stage robbery or hide a wanted man, but it was not in him to betray a friend or sell out a cause.

The dappled gray Dolan had given him was all horse. Kilkenny rode southwest out of town, dipped into a tangle of washes and then turned south until he finally camped with the battlements of Comb Ridge towering above him. He rolled into his blankets nearer dead than alive.

His tight muscles let go their hold, and clogged with weariness. He slept. The long hours of riding, the constant alertness, all left him and he sank deeper and deeper into a sleep of utter exhaustion. Over the hills men rode and horses moved and cattle lowed gently in the night air. Stars faded and a faint gray crept up the east, barred from him by the gigantic wall of the Ridge, a bulwark that lay across his path to the KR.

He stirred in his sleep, then relaxed. Some faint stimulus made him stir again and a violent need within him culminated suddenly in his eyes. They snapped open and for a time he lay still, unable to bring his thoughts into focus. It was a voice that did it for him. A girl's voice.

"You must have been very tired, Lance."

Unbelieving, he sat up. Nita sat a dozen feet away, her rifle across her knees, her lips widening in the quick, amused smile he knew so well.

"Where . . . where did you come from?"

"Should I be poetic, Lance? Should I say that I'm your past returned to haunt you? No, I'll tell the truth. I was restless last night. I could not stay in the house any longer so I gave them all the slip. I caught Glory—remember my black filly? I saddled her and rode west. Ever since I've been here I've been worried by this Ridge—I wanted to see what lay over here, so I came over just before daybreak and what do I find—you."

"And I didn't hear you."

"You wouldn't have heard if the Ridge had collapsed. If the moon ran into the world and they burst, you wouldn't have heard it. I never knew a man could sleep like that."

"It's lucky it wasn't Tetlow—or Havalik."

She was suddenly serious. "Lance, you're the same. You haven't changed."

"Are you saying that, or asking?"

"Both. You're the same as I see you. I don't know what you're thinking."

He got to his feet, running his fingers through his black hair which was all awry. He must look like hell. Needing a shave, tired, red-eyed and hair all on end. How could a woman ever—or maybe she didn't. Maybe she had changed. He looked at her, trying to guess.

"You—you're so beautiful it hurts."

"Hurts who? Not you surely. You ran off and left me. I can hardly believe that. You're the only man who ever ran away from me, Lance—and the only one I ever wanted to stay."

He looked at her quickly. "You still mean that?"

"I said it, didn't I?"

She got to her feet, tall, lissome, her skin a beautiful olive, her eyes—"It's been a long time." Her eyes widened a little, and her lips parted, he could see the sudden hunger in her eyes, and he stepped toward her, half-frightened by the feeling that shook him. Roughly, he took her arms and pulled her to him and she reached hungrily for his lips and they melted together and deep within him something seemed to well up and the cold dams across his feelings were gone.

He pushed her away, her breath coming quickly, his own ragged with emotion. "It's no good," he said hoarsely, "no good at all. You've too much to waste on me. I'm a drifter, Nita, a saddle-bum, a man with a gun and a few days, weeks or months to live. It might come tomorrow."

"It might," she agreed, "but don't you think I've thought of that? Don't you think I know?" Her voice rose. "Lance, look at the time we've lost. Yesterday, and all the days before that, the long days after you left the border country, and the days after we were together in Cedar—you know and I know we've wasted that time. I know it may not be long, and yet it may be forever. Who knows how long it is for anyone? All of us, all over the world, all of us walk along a thin edge between life and death and it takes so little for us to fall.

"It isn't tomorrow I want unless it comes. It's today, Lance! We women, we don't have so much imagination about some things. We're realistic. You think about what it may mean to me tomorrow, if I lose you. I think about what it means today, if I don't have you.

"It doesn't matter! None of it does. I know how you live, I know what drives you, and I know that maybe the Tetlows, maybe Dee Havalik, maybe someone else will kill you. Or you may kill them and have long years ahead. After all, I've known some of your like who died in bed, and you may. You think about it too much."

"I live with it," he said somberly. "What kind of life is if for a woman when her man never leaves the house walking but she'll fear his body may be carried back? If there's enough of him to carry? Sure, I've stayed away from you and I've hated it, but only because I wanted to spare you pain."

"By causing me pain? It won't work, Kilkenny. Yes, I often call you that. Everyone does. The mysterious Kilkenny, the unknown Kilkenny. Sometimes I wonder if I ever knew you myself, and if you weren't just a dream I had, and then I try to go to sleep again and I remember how your arms felt, and your kisses, I remember how you stood in the center of that room and spoke to me first. Remember what you said, Lance? You don't remember—trust a man to forget, but I remember. I remember every word you've said to me, at any time. Even the foolish little things you've said."

He looked at her and tried to find words and there were none. He watched her lips, the rise of her breasts as she spoke, the wetness of her lips. He turned sharply away, stabbed by sudden pain. Maybe he was a fool. "I'd better get saddled," he said, "we can't stay here."

She smiled at him, laughing a little. "Tough, aren't you? Big and tough! But I know you. Under all that you're sentimental as a kid. And you love me. I've known that from the start, and that's what irritates me about you. Walking away from me!"

Nita dropped to her knees and began to roll his bed. "Get your horse. I'll fix this bedroll."

When he had the gray saddled he strapped the bedroll behind the saddle and helped her with the black mare. They both mounted and he grinned at her. "All right, you tyrant! Wake a man up looking so gorgeous it hurts! Now take me to breakfast!"

"You think I won't? And if Maria doesn't have it ready, I'll fix it for you." She led off, starting for the switchback trail over the Comb. "You know, I'm almost as glad for Cain as I am for myself. Without you he's like a big dog with no master. He needs you, Lance."

"How is he?"

"Fine, and as big and ugly as ever. You should never have broken his nose, Lance. It was probably his one good feature."

"If I hadn't, he'd have killed me. That big lug can fight!"

"I've seen him."

"Does he ever mention Abel?"

"Rarely. What was he like, Lance? I never knew him well."

"Vicious. A killer. Completely and entirely criminal, and very dominating. Cain was never bad, it was just that he followed Abel's lead. That was a good job I did, killing him. A good job for Cain if for no one else."

"He thinks so, too. And he says you were the only person who ever treated him decently, and the only one who could ever handle him."

They rode in silence for a distance and then Nita looked around at him, pausing to breathe her mare. "What's going to happen, Lance?"

"We're going to hit Forty. Tonight. And hit 'em hard."

"And then?"

"Every man for himself. Tetlow will turn loose his dogs then and it'll be kill or be killed all along the line."

"That Dee Havalik—I've seen him, Lance. He's mean, cruel."

Kilkenny shrugged. They topped the ridge and the sun burst bright in their faces. Far below them lay the ranch house and along the distant line of the two ranches was a line of sprawled dark figures, dead cattle.

Beyond them was a dark mass of gathering weight. Suddenly, he was worried. "Let's get down here! They may start something before we can!"

Suddenly the dark herd began to move and behind them, far behind them came a wave of riders firing into the air, starting the cattle. They gathered themselves and lunged, plunging across the line at breakneck speed.

Kilkenny drew up, appalled. "My God! I hope the boys aren't down there! If they are, they're dead!"

CHAPTER SIX

NITA CAUGHT HIS arm. Her face was pale. "Oh, Lance! Jaime! And Cain! The rest of them! What could have happened to them?"

"I wish I knew," he said soberly, "but we can't find out now. If Tetlow's gone this far it means he's ready to go all the way. I've got to get you out of here, Nita. Some place where it's safe."

"In town?"

"No." His mind was leaping ahead. It would not be safe in town now, not even with Early and Blaine. Tetlow had started to move and if he had wiped out the KR hands there would be no end to his killing. "No." He repeated the word. "There's another place, but we've got to move fast.Turn around and we'll go back down the trail."

"But maybe they are down there, Lance. They might be lying injured!"

He had been thinking of that very thing and the thought tortured him. He was torn between te desire to go down there and find out for himself and the need to get Nita to some safe place. She read his thoughts.

"Don't think of me. I'd be safe down where your camp was. You go ahead."

Still he hesitated, worried. "No, I couldn't go down this way now. They'd see me long before I reached bottom. We've got to circle around, and you can be sure they'll have men in Horsehead, watching for me.

"Tell you what," the thought came to him suddenly, "you take that canyon"—he pointed it out from the height of the Ridge—"and follow it up to the second branch. There will be a Y there, but take the left hand canyon. You'll find a switchback trail at the end and when you come out—" Swiftly he detailed the directions of how to get to the small blue lake he had found. "Wait there for me. I've got a place in the mountains east of there."

"All right." It was like her not to question his judgment. "Don't worry about me, and be careful."

They parted with a quick clasp of the hand and he turned north, riding up Comb Wash. When he reached Whiskers Draw he swung into it and followed along, carrying his Winchester in his hands and riding with eyes and ears alert. He had no plan, nor could he make one until he could view the situation that awaited him.

There was every chance that the KR hands had been caught in the rush of cattle or shot down by the Forty riders. There was a slim chance they had escaped, but one scarcely worth mentioning for they were fighting men, not running men. Their only hope in that way, Lance understood, was that Jaime Brigo was uncommonly cunning. He might have done something—on the other hand the men might be lying helpless and injured. He had to know and there was no time to be lost.

He had covered the miles at a space-eating gait but the gray seemed in no whit disturbed by it. In fact, when he slowed down the gray tugged irritably at the bit, wanting to run. At the cottonwoods he paused. Here, tonight, he was to have met the crowd for their attack on the Forty. Too late now—or was it?

Considering that, he shook his head to clear his mind and returned to the thoughts of the present. This was going to be touch and go. Without doubt the country was crawling with Forty riders and they would be hunting Nita as well as himself. With men on the KR, at the camp of the Forty and in Horsehead, he would be in a bottleneck that offered but one escape, retreat the way he had come. Dismounting, Kilkenny crept up to the side of the draw and surveyed the country before him.

The herd had scattered, spreading over the KR range, and they were feeding on the rich grass of the new range. Among them a few riders rode, but they seemed to be congregating at a particular point. That point was near the KR ranch house. A few minutes later the wagons from the Forty headquarters came into sight, headed for the KR. Obviously Tetlow was taking up headquarters at the latter house.

Returning to his horse, Kilkenny advanced with extreme caution, pausing every few yards to listen. He heard no sound, but presently Whiskers Draw gave into Cottonwood Wash, which had been the edge of the KR range, and it was along this wash that the KR hands had been holding their ground.

No sound disturbed the clear air of the afternoon. There was a faint smell of dust in the air remaining from the stampede, and the smell of sun-warmed grass. Keeping away from any stones that might make a sound under his horse's hoofs, he rode forward. When he was over a mile from the opening of Whiskers Draw he drew up. Here the wash was partly overgrown with low cottonwoods and willows, and there were some larger boulders scattered about. Dismounting again, Kilkenny spoke reassuringly to the gray, then walked ahead on cat feet, his rifle at the ready.

The first sound he heard was faint, a rustling. He paused, the rifle coming up. Then he heard a low moan, and he wheeled. The bank on the east side had been broken by the rush of cattle and had caved into the wash. Moving toward it, he saw a bloody hand projecting from under the earth.

Dropping a hand to a boulder top, he vaulted over it and landed beside that hand, and then he could see the face of a man lying on his stomach, his head turned sidewise, also projecting from under the caved-in earth.

It was Cain, and the big man was conscious. Swiftly Kilkenny attacked the pile of earth with his hands, pulling it away from the fallen man's body. Working desperately, he stopped suddenly to hear the sound of a walking horse!

Straightening up, he stared at the bank, panic sweeping him.

There was no way to get Cain quickly uncovered nor to move him. A shot would bring a dozen riders, in a matter of minutes, and—he heard the horse stop, and then the creak of a saddle. Crouching among the boulders, Kilkenny lifted a finger and saw that Cain understood.

The man showed above the edge of the bank, then dropped over. It was Phin Tetlow.

A big, wide-shouldered man, he walked with easy step and he looked curiously around. Obviously he had seen something here that he felt warranted investigation, and he had returned alone for that purpose. He looked around, then walked to a clump of willows and peered into it, then cautiously approached a bunch of boulders.

Kilkenny crouched lower, cursing his luck. He could not shoot it out with Phin and then run for it to leave Cain helpless in this position. His horse was out of sight, but further search might show it to Phin. Kilkenny drew back, easing away from Cain, and the big man watched him go, his eyes wide and trusting as those of a big dog from whose paw one extracts a thorn.

Phin was working nearer and nearer, and now he straightened and looked toward the fallen earth. Quickly, as if having an idea, he strode toward it. He paused when he came in sight of Cain. Kilkenny could see the expression of Phin Tetlow's face, and was puzzled by it.

Phin moved closer. "The big one, huh? I figured the herd must have got somebody here. I seen you a minue or so afore they hit this bank. It would have been a miracle if you was safe."

He sat down on a boulder and calmly lit a cigarette. "Can't move, huh? Well, I reckon you're my meat then. Funny thing. I never kilt a man. Andy has. He kilt eight or nine. Andy's good, maybe better than Havalik. Even Ben kilt an outlaw down in the Big Bend, and a couple of Indians. Me, I never kilt nobody."

He chuckled. "Well, I won't have to say that tomorrow. Because I'm fixin' to kill you.

"Makes a man," he said, "feel mighty small when he ain't blooded. Even Ben, an' he don't like to fight. He thinks too much." He drew deep on the cigarette. "Pap figured you for the tough one. Now here you are, caught like a rabbit in a trap. I don't even need to waste a shot. I'm going to bash your head in with a rock."

He got to his feet and stretched, and Kilkenny, close behind him now, reached out and grabbed him by the gun belt. He gave a tremendous jerk and Phin Tetlow's heels flew up and he hit the boulder hard and turned heels over head to the ground behind it. Kilkenny swung a wicked backhand blow that smashed Tetlow's nose, stifling his yell to a squealing grunt. Then he slugged him on the chin. A full, powerful swing. Phin's head snapped back and he lay still. Swiftly Kilkenny tied his hands and feet, then went to work to free Cain.

A quick examination showed no bones broken but the man was frightfully bruised and skinned. Moreover, he seemed to have lost blood from a scratch or cut in his side. Stopping, Kilkenny lifted the big man on his shoulders and started for the gray. The load was almost too much for the gray, for between them they made a weight of over four hundred pounds, but there was no hope for it.

Returning the way he had come, the gray stayed with it beautifully, but when they reached, Whiskers Draw, Kilkenny swung down and walked ahead, leading the horse. He might have made the attempt to get Phin's horse but had been afraid somebody from the ranch would see him up on the bank, and had not dared to take a chance as Phin had been wearing a brilliantly red shirt that could not have been mistaken.

It was slow going and hot, but he made it back to the cottonwoods. Cain Brockman lolled in the saddle, his huge body swaying to the moves of the horse. His face was gray and his eyes glazed over. Worriedly, Kilkenny spoke to him and there was no answer. The big man was sitting there by sheer will and animal strength. He might be injured internally—Kilkenny crept to the top of the bank and looked around. Far away, several miles off now, he could see the lone horse standing where Phin had left it. How long before that horse would attract attention and investigation? Or how long before Phin would get free?

It was almost noon, of course, and the hands might be eating. There was no more than another hour before the pursuit would begin, for they would notice Phin's absence and if they saw his horse, it would immediately draw them to it. What Cain needed was a doctor, but it was all of five miles to Horsehead from their present position and the last two miles would be across open country.

There was no hope for it but to conceal him here and hope for the best. Alone, he could run for it, but the gray could never carry that weight over a fast run nor could Kilkenny keep the dead weight of the now unconscious man in the saddle before him.

Dismounting the wounded man, he carried him back under the cottonwoods. Here there was a place where the willows hung low, leaving a deep shade. Here, with Kilkenny's slicker for a pillow, he made the big man as comfortable as possible. With water from his canteen he bathed the man's forehead and washed his wounds, leaving him from time to time to take a look around for approaching riders. Then, drawing one of Cain's pistols, he left it close beside the big man, and with him Kilkenny left his canteen.

Then swiftly he wiped out with a willow branch the cracks in the sand, and scattered free handfuls of sand over that, then mounted up and rode swiftly out of the draw and across country keeping to the cover of the cedars. When he was far enough away, he rode swiftly on and followed a dim trail that led through various draws until he was almost on the outskirts of Horsehead. Here he worked his way into Cottonwood Creek and started toward town.

This was the creek that divided east from west Horsehead, the social line of demarcation in the cowtown. It was also the draw that led through the trees past Doc Blaine's.

From the creek bed, he climbed out into the trees and then worked his way up through the brush until he was within a few feet of Blaine's house.

The first person he saw was Laurie Webster. Her eyes widened and he motioned her to silence. When she came to the fence near the trees he spoke softly. Briefly he explained what he had done, where he had found Cain and how he had left him, and told the girl to explain the change in plans to Dolan, although to keep riders on call. "Better not try to get Brockman before dark," he warned, "that country's alive with riders and they'd be sure to take him away from you and kill him, if not anybody who went after him."

"All right." Laurie was quiet. Her eyes searched his. "You . . . you're all right?"

"Sure. How are thing here?"

"Bad." Doc Blaine had told her of what Havalik had said and now she repeated this. "It's going to come to a fight in town. I'm staying down here with Doc and Mrs. Carpenter. My sister is coming down soon, and I think Bob and a couple of others may move to this side of the creek. We want to be together in case of trouble."

"How's Macy?"

"All right, but he's worried. The Tetlows are in town in force now, and Harry Lott is drinking."

Lott? Kilkenny had forgotten the big marshal. A hard, cruel man. Where did he stand, Kilkenny wondered. And he knew there was no answer to that. Probably Lott himself did not know.

"I'll be back." He explained about Nita Riordan and saw the quick frown on the girl's face.

Without thinking of that, he returned to his horse and mounted. Geting around town was going to take him far out of his way. Suddenly a daring plan came to mind.

Why not ride right up the creek bed through town? Except right at the bridge it was tree-shaded and there was small chance of anyone being close unless they were crossing the small bridge. The cut was deep enough to keep him out of sight. He would be in view from the bridge for all of fifty yards before he reached it, but for only about ten yards beyond, for then the creek curved slightly to the west, then made an easy swing back toward the north and then slightly west again. In fact, the trend of the creek bed was in the exact direction he wished to go to reach the lake where he had told Nita to meet him.

Kilkenny was not a man who puzzled about a course of action. The danger of the creek bed was enormous for that sixty yards or so, and to be seen there would probably mean being trapped, yet there was less danger, although extended over several hours by a roundabout route that also entailed loss of time.

Without hesitation he put the gray down the bank once more and turned north. He walked the horse in the sand, taking his time, one hand resting on his thigh within inches of his gun butt. He paused before turning the last bend into that fifty yards of open creek and listened. He heard no sound of approaching horses, nor any voices that sounded close. Taking a quick look and seeing the bridge empty, he rode out into the creek.

They would hear his horse if anyone was close to the creek, but there were horses grazing about the town, owned by the townspeople, so that it might not attract attention. They would know it was not a cow they heard for the difference in the sound of their walk is great. He had to gamble, and he accepted the gamble.

The sun was very hot in the bottom and he was sheltered from the breeze. The sweat trickled down his face and down his sides under his arms. He dried his palms on his chaps and rode steadily forward, his eyes roving. To the right he could see several trees and beyond them the roof of the jail. To the left there was only the thick clump of trees that divided the creek bed from the home of Doc Blaine.

When no more than ten yards from the bridge, he heard footsteps of an approaching man, and the slight jingle of spurs. There was nothing for it now but to continue on, and he did so, his hand ready to grab for a gun butt if it became necessary.

The walking man hove into sight and, despite himself, glanced up. It was Leal Macy.

Macy's face did not change, nor did he pause in his stride until he reached the bridge. Then he stopped and leaned on the rail, looking back the way Kilkenny had come. "Rider coming. Stay under the bridge!" he said.

Kilkenny halted and heard the horses approaching, and then their hoofs on the bridge. They drew up and stopped, and the voice was that of Jared Tetlow!

"Howdy!" Tetlow's voice was cool. "Seen that Kilkenny? We're huntin' him."

"Taking a lot on yourself, aren't you?" Macy demanded. "I'm sheriff here."

"We ain't askin' no law's advice," Tetlow replied shortly. There was a harshness in his voice that grated, yet there was indifference too. "Keep out of the way an' you won't get hurt."

"Tetlow," Leal Macy replied quietly, "I am ordering you to withdraw your cattle from the range you have forcibly occupied. If you do not do that, you will be arrested and brought before the courts."

Tetlow chuckled without humor. "What courts? In this town?" He waved a hand. "I already know your judge is back an' he favors me. So do most of the folks here."

Macy ignored him. "I'm preparing charges against you," he replied, "for manslaughter. I refer to the killings of Carson and Carpenter. You will be arrested, as will all those who participated, and you will be tried in the courts of the land. Withdraw your cattle, pay the damages we will agree upon, and I will allow you to go free on my own initiative. Otherwise, you will be prosecuted."

"Don't be a fool!" Tetlow was impatient. "What do you take me for, man? An idiot? What witnesses do you have? Who will testify against me? I had no reason to dislike Carson and Carpenter. Carson made the mistake of trying for a gun while Carpenter got caught in front of a stampede. As for my cattle, why shouldn't they move on empty range? There's no one on the KR."

"There was until you drove them off."

"Prove it."

Tetlow had spoken his last word. Clapping spurs to his horse, he rode on across the bridge into the east side of town. Dust from the disturbed planking fell down Kilkenny's neck. He started to move when another voice interrupted. He recognized the hoarse voice of Harry Lott, thickened now by liquor.

"How long you puttin' up with this, Macy? You standin' by while they run the town right out from under you? I thought you was a tough sheriff?"

"I'm waiting, Harry." Macy's voice was patient. "I want to avoid a pitched battle if I can. I've seen a cow outfit hit a town like this before. I know what happens. I know how the innocent suffer. You're right, and something should be done, and it's up to us, but the time is not yet. When I can muster enough support, I'll arrest Tetlow and Havalik both, and I'll hold them for trial."

Harry Lott laughed. "Yeah? Well, you won't arrest Havalik! I got him figured! He's their backbone! Git him an' they'd blow up higher'n them clouds! An' that's what I aim to do—*git Havalik!*"

Macy did not reply and Kilkenny heard the drunken marshal's footsteps as he moved off toward the east side of town.

"Be seein' you!" Kilkenny said softly, and rode on up the creek. Rounding the bend in the creek bed, he walked his horse faster and when the last buildings were behind he pushed him into a trot.

There was far to go and it was midafternoon. He would never reach the lake now before dark. There was not a chance of it. Not a chance.

Near a lone waterhole high on Black Mesa, south of the KR ranch house, a big man crouched alone in the darkness, cleaning his rifle. That man was Jaime Brigo.

Hunted like an animal, he had contrived to escape. To the best of his knowledge, all on the ranch had been killed except Nita Riordan and Maria. The former had gone ridding in the early dawn and so had missed the attack. Where she was he did not know, but he had infinite respect for her judgment, and she had been mounted on a good horse and had been armed. Further, he was sure he had later seen Kilkenny atop the ridge overlooking the ranch. As for Maria, she was an old woman and would not be harmed. They would need her services to care for the house.

Of Cain Brockman, Ed, and the other three men, he thought only with a dumb pain. He had known these men and worked with them. Ed he had seen go down shooting, trying to stem that awful mass of cattle. One of the other men had been roped and dragged to death by Andy Tetlow. So far as he knew, he alone was left of the KR outfit. He was an educated man, but beneath the knowledge he possessed he was first, last and always an Indian, a Yaqui. He was basically still a savage, and his home and his friends had been attacked. Now he was moving out on his own private war.

He had no horse. He had discarded his boots and made of his saddle bags a pair of crude moccasins. Now he was starting out and he was not thinking of prisoners. He was thinking of death. Huge, powerful and cleanly muscled, he was not disturbed by what lay ahead. In the darkness he moved out, and in the darkness he struck.

Carl Hadley was a tough young Missouri rider of the old Bald Knob breeding. He had killed three men in his time, robbed a bank and rustled a good many cows. The first job he had held had been with the Forty, and he had helped them to take over range before this. He was enjoying the power of the brand he rode for. He was happy to see the herd take over the KR. He had been one of those who looked upon the murder of Carson with satisfaction.

On this night he was riding along a dim trail north of Black Mesa. Ahead of him, a stone fell, then rolled. He rode forward, gun in hand. Above him loomed a boulder, and as he rode past it he had a sensation as of something huge and black dropping upon him. He was wrenched from the saddle and hurled to the ground.

Stunned, he started to stagger to his feet and was struck and knocked rolling. He came up and grabbed for the knife he always carried, but his knife wrist was seized by a big hand that shut down hard and the bones in his wrist crunched under that power and a scream of agony rang from his lips, and then another huge hand seized his throat and there was a brief instant of blind struggling before a darkness washed over him and he went limp and helpless.

Brigo dropped the body of Carl Hadley and walked to the horse. It shied slightly, then hearing the easy voice of the big man, it thrust out a nose at him. Brigo had a way with animals. They understood him and he them. He swung into the saddle and felt the scabbard. There was a rifle here.

Jaime Brigo started toward the KR. Somewhere his hat had been lost. The wind ruffled his straight black hair, his big jaws moved ponderously over the chew of tobacco. Enemies had moved against his beloved employer, the girl he had seen grow from childhood, whose father had meant more to him than any living being. He was counterattacking with all that was in him.

He struck again, later, with that knife, killing one of them and injuring the other. The injured man told a wild and incoherent story. Cowhands of the Forty listened uneasily and avoided each other's eyes. They were superstitious men, but sometimes things happened, and . . . two men left the Forty that night. They just rode off.

Phin was found, still bound. He could give no good account of what had happened except that the man who struck him down had been Kilkenny. Jared Tetlow knew men too well not to realize what he must do if he was to keep his hands in line. The time had come to move.

The moon was high before Kilkenny reached the tiny lake. An hour before, Brigo had killed his first man. Fifteen minutes earlier, Phin Tetlow had been found and released. News had not yet come in of the attacks by Brigo.

In town the lines were being harshly drawn . Bob Early with his family had moved across the creek to Doc Blaine's older but sturdier home, a home moreover that was backed by Dolan's. Ernleven had deserted his beloved stove and come across the creek bringing with him two finely engraved pistols and a twin-barrel shotgun. He also brought a burlap sack of shotgun shells.

In his saloon, Happy Jack sat staring at the cards he was riffling. Harry Lott had stopped drinking and was staring sullenly up the street. Aside from Macy, he had been king in this town. He was no longer. He wore both guns and he was thinking of his own express gun upstairs in his room.

The streets were empty and still. Few men loitered around the bars and as the evening drew on, these grew fewer. Somehow the news that Kilkenny had been in town filtered through and was whispered around the bars and tables. Dee Havalik rode through in the afternoon accompanied by several men, but he had taken the road west and had not stopped in the streets.

Doc Blaine went with Dolan and Shorty to pick up Cain Brockman. They found him conscious and wary, and they got safely back to town. All he could tell them was that Nita had been away from the ranch when the Forty struck, and that he thought Brigo had escaped. He remembered Kilkenny coming for him, remembered his fight with Phin, and the beginning of the ride on the horse. He had passed out and recalled little else. He had awakened in darkness under the willows and found the gun and canteen. The rest he surmised and waited.

Elsewhere in the town people talked and there was much disputing about the rights and wrongs of the fight. And very little about the impending result. Agreement was unanimous that Forty could not lose. As the night drew on, the east side of town waited, breathless. On the west side, the people in Doc Blaine's house went to sleep with their clothing on, ready to rise at a moment's notice.

Shorty was on watch in the trees alongside the bridge. Pete was watching westward from Dolan's roof.

Kilkenny approached the lake carefully, but found no campfire, no one. Carefully he searched the place from a wide circle, but saw no hint that anyone was there. Twice he risked being shot to call out, but there was neither a shot nor a reply.

Daylight broke under lowering skies, and in the first light, Lance made a hasty search. He was tired and stiff from sleeping on the ground. It looked like rain and he had no slicker, but then, on the far side of the lake he found the kicked-out remains of a campfire. And he found where a horse had been picketed. Searching around, he found a place where a struggle had taken place, and then where Nita had walked away with three men. One of those men had very small feet.

Backtracking, he found their tracks. Four riders had come here, and three had dismounted and approached Nita's camp while one remained with the horses.

Kilkenny paused and lighted a cigarette, carefully shielding the glow of the match. The logical place for them to have awaited him was right here. They might have ambushed him here when he came to meet Nita. However, Havalik was no fool, and having lived as a hunted man himself, he would guess that any camp Kilkenny approached would be approached too warily. Moreover, they had several times lost his trail before this and knew he was a skilled frontiersman, adept at woodcraft and with all the tricks of the trail.

So they had taken Nita and gone. To return to Tetlow? That was their best bet, but would that be the bet Havalik would make? He would be thinking more of Kilkenny and killing him than of anything else. And he had no doubt those small boot-tracks belonged to the gunman.

Mounting the gray, Kilkenny turned to trailing the party. The trail led east into the worst of the mountains, toward his own cabin and the Valley of Whispering Wind!

Dolan had not been mistaken about the gray, for the horse had a willingness for the trail equaled only by Kilkenny's own buckskin. The tracks led plainly off toward the east and after crossing the plateau, dipped into a narrow gap between gigantic cliffs. Here the sand was hard-packed and the hoof scars were plain as print. Kilkenny gave some time to studying each hoof print, knowing that upon his memory of their characteristics might depend success or failure.

Kilkenny looked at the sky. He had left his slicker under Cain's head and had no protection against the rain. He rode on, and the trail became increasingly bad. He was not worried about Nita, for she had been born to the saddle, nor much worried about these men as long as Havalik was along, for the gunman was not eager after women. He was a man who lived to kill, and Kilkenny doubted that he even thought of Nita as anything but a pawn in the game. That might not be true of the others, but in the West few men would risk bothering a woman. It was the one thing the frontier would not accept.

A few spattering drops of rain fell, and Kilkenny dug into his bedroll and got out his ground sheets and wrapped it about him as best he could. It was cumbersome and did not help around his neck, for it kept slipping down. It did, however, keep off the worst of the rain, and it was now raining hard.

He hurried the gray, lifting the horse to a canter. If the rain continued the tracks would be washed out.

And within a half dozen miles, they were.

But not before they had told their story to Kilkenny. Havalik was hunting a place where there was shelter from the wind and rain. It showed in every deviation of the trail. He was hunting such a place, and he would not go much further. The rain eased a little, and lowering black clouds crowded down around the mountains, drifting in gray tendrils through the passes and between the cliff tops. The wind stirred and on the breath of the wind came a faint smell of woodsmoke!

It was late evening now, for the trail had been long. Kilkenny stripped off his ground sheet and rolled it, returning it to the place behind the saddle, and then he slipped into a worn buckskin jacket, but one that left his gun butts free. His mind was utterly cold, his eyes like those of a searching hawk. He walked his horse, keeping to the sand or soft earth, careful to strike no stone.

Again he paused. The smell of woodsmoke was stronger now. A gleam caught his eyes, and looking through the junipers he saw the fire. It was built in a cut back under a bulging cliff and several men stood about the fire. Their horses were picketed just beyond, and Nita Riordan stood alone on the outside of the fire.

Kilkenny hesitated for the wink of an eyelash, and then he slapped the spurs to the startled gray and palmed his Colt. The first shot rang out and he charged into the camp, yelling and shooting. A man spun and dropped, others dove for shelter, and Nita, her eyes suddenly alive, sprang quickly left. His gun exploding, Kilkenny hit the camp at a dead run, bending swiftly to sweep his arm around Nita's waist. Instantly, her foot sought the stirrup and then the gray was past the camp and running while the frightened horses lunged and plunged. One jerked free a picket pin and stampeded out of camp.

Behind them a savage yell rang out, then a shot, but the shot was wild. Kilkenny did not halt the gray and Nita crawled quickly behind him despite his demand that she get in front. The gray loved to run and despite the added burden, he ran now, plunging through the wet junipers that slashed at their faces and drenched them with water. Looping the reins about the pommel, Kilkenny fed cartridges into the now empty Colt.

Then he slowed the racing horse and turned swiftly right. He descended into a canyon, and rode south at a trot, then coming to a branch, he turned north again. They had been riding for not more than ten minutes when Kilkenny drew up sharply. Far off, distant in the mountains, came a muffled roar!

His face went white and he felt his breath go out of him. Swiftly he glanced right and left. On either side were the broken but unscalable walls of the canyon, and behind him for more than a mile were the same canyon walls!

He did not hesitate, but spurred the frightened horse forward. The roar grew and behind him he felt Nita's clasp tighten with fear. Nobody needed to speak, they all knew it was a huge wall of water roaring down the canyon toward them at express train speed!

A wall of water running off the rocks of the mountains into the canyon. And behind them, there was no escape. Before them was the water.

Nevertheless, flight was useless. Their only hope lay ahead. Rounding a bend in the canyon, Kilkenny's heart sank, for nowhere in sight was there anything that looked like escape.

Nita's arms tightened. "Lance! On the right there! Isn't that a ledge?"

It was. Swinging the gray, Lance cut across to it. The path was unbelievably narrow. Dropping to the ground beside the girl who had instantly realized the necessity, Kilkenny took thc bridle. "Go ahead," he said, "and hurry!"

Up she went and Kilkenny followed. It clung to the face of the cliff like an eyebrow of crumbling rock. Several times rocks fell away from under the feet of the horse and fell into the canyon, and now they were only six feet off the bottom. Yet the path switched back and led to a higher ledge, at least fifteen feet above the canyon floor. Nita turned and went up and Kilkenny got the gray to the switchback. It was close, but the horse made it, ears pricked at the trail, nostrils wide with fear at the now thunderous roar behind them. They climbed to the ledge, and Nita was already crawling into what was almost a crack that ran back in the direction from which they had come, but a crack floored with talus and wide enough for the horse. It might be a trap, but it did lead up.

Nita scrambled into the crack and mounted swiftly as an Indian, and Kilkenny followed. Nothing loath, and frightened by the roar behind it, the gray scrambled after them, fighting for hoof surface, slipping and scrambling. They gained another ten feet and then came out on a ledge that was forty feet above the canyon floor, and here they seemed to be stopped. Hastily Nita went searching about among the rocks for some means of escape, and then the roar mounted until the very mountains seemed crumbling and crashing about them. Turning, Kilkenny glanced back.

A huge, rolling wall of water, bearing great logs on its crest and tumbling them like chips, was sweeping down from the higher mountains. It was high, higher than their present ledge, and he saw at a glance they would be engulfed. Swinging his eyes to Nita, he saw her mouth wide. She must have been screaming but he heard no sound, but she was beckoning. Dragging the horse, he raced to her. She was pointing into a black opening whose floor slanted upward into the rock itself!

She instantly scrambled into it and then the wave hit. Kilkenny felt the tug on the reins as the water caught the gray. Off on one side, the full force of the blow broken by the rocks about them, Kilkenny managed to keep his hold on the bridle even as the water washed over him.

Water roared about him and he fought his way forward. Nita had disappeared somewhere in the darkness ahead but he managed to keep a hold on the bridle. His feet were on the sand and the horse was struggling to follow.

"Lance!"

The cry was a faint sound from the darkness, lost in the thunderous roar that filled the cavern. His thrust-out hand, feeling into the darkness before him, suddenly struck wet cloth and excited fingers grasped his arm. Cowering together in the darkness, they listened to the sound of the water, the gray horse trembling beside them.

Then slowly the sound began to die and the water receded suddenly as it had come. Clinging together, soaked to the skin, they waited in the cave's darkness.

They were free. They were safe. The water was gone.

CHAPTER SEVEN

"LANCE?" NITA STIRRED in the wet darkness. "Do you think they were killed?"

"No telling." He got up and, holding her hand, led the way down the slanting floor into the gray light of outer day. Wet and bedraggled, they looked down the canyon, unchanged except that now the sand was hard-packed and the walls were wet and dripping. Painstakingly they made their way to the canyon's bottom.

They walked on, anxious to keep moving. Slowly warmth returned to their flesh and watching ahead, Kilkenny could see they were bearing directly into the heart of the Blues.

"Where are we going, Lance?"

"Home. We're going home."

Mounting an alluvial fan, they found their way through a shattered opening in the canyon's upper wall and came out on the plateau.

Before them was the towering rampart of the Blue Mountains. Three mighty peaks loomed against the sky, and forward of their position, three more peaks. The sky was heavily overcast, the peaks shrouded in black masses of cumulus. About them the desert was gray, tufted with midnight blue clumps of shrubbery. The scene was shocking in its majesty, breathtaking in its power. The great shoulders of the mountain vanished into the clouds, the gray earth was streaked with the white trails of runoff water.

Turning, they looked over a vast panorama of foothills and valley. Despite the clouds the rainwashed air was piercingly clear, and miles to the south a few faint trails of smoke marked the town of Horsehead. Nearer the terrain was slashed with ragged canyons, ripped deep into the rocky terrain and tufted here and there with juniper.

''We're going up and through those mountains.'' Lance indicated the vast jumble of peaks, black under the clouds.

''Now? In this storm?''

''Now,'' he said grimly, ''right now!''

They mounted the gray, who switched his tail at the added burden. There was no trail, for they followed along a mountainside with the vast sweep of forty miles lying below and beyond them. In the distance gray rain drew a veil across the valley. Twice they passed the paths of small slides, and once worked their way through a great gully ripped from the mountain by a rush of water.

There was nothing to be gained by worrying of what might happen in Horsehead. The men were seasoned in frontier warfare and he had first to get Nita to a safe place, and the only one that might be secure was the Valley of Whispering Wind.

Despite the lateness of the hour the sky retained a strange afterglow as of distant fire, but now that had gone and they were left in utter darkness broken only by far-off lightning and the mutter of thunder among the canyons. They could go no further in the unknown darkness.

''We'll make camp,'' he told her. ''There's some cliff dwellings near here.''

He had seen the dwellings from afar, days ago. A white gash of the cliff marked the canyon.

A flare of distant lightning showed them a steep path and they stumbled up and into one of the dwellings. Obviously, the place had been used for shelter at some distant date for a few dry sticks lay near the remnants of a fire. Drawing them together, Kilkenny soon had a fire going. Roaming through the other rooms, Kilkenny found a pack rat's nest, a mine of fuel. Nita started to make coffee.

"Ruined?" He looked at the soggy mass.

"We can use it."

He dropped to a seat near the fire. Cold and wet they might be, but her very presence changed everything for him. She caught his glance and smiled. "I never imagined I'd start housekeeping in a ruin! And both of us soaked to the skin!"

Twice he went into the darkness and listened, every sense alert to the sounds of night. And he heard nothing but the wind, the rumble of distant thunder, and the occasional stirring of some small animal. He found grass and rubbed down the gray horse.

Nita was waiting with coffee when he returned, and they sat beside the fire and sipped the coffee in silence, listening to the faint hiss of the fire as the flame drained the strength from the dry wood.

Long after she was asleep on the blankets, he sat feeding the flames. Once he thought he heard horses, but after a long time of listening believed he was mistaken. Sometime after that he slept, awakening suddenly in the first light of coming day. He awakened Nita, threw sticks on the fire and went outside. When he looked into the overhang where it had left the gray, two more horses stood beside it!

Both were saddled, and one was Nita's mare, Glory. Searching for their tracks, he realized the horses had not been ridden but had found their own way here, evidently following some scent left by his own horse.

After a quick cup of scalding black coffee, Kilkenny stripped the extra horse of saddlebags, rifle and canteen and took them to his own horse. He had just hung the canteen to the pommel when Nita spoke. "On your left. You're covered."

Kilkenny turned carefully and found himself facing Jess Baker. The cut on the big man's face was an ugly red scar. He held a .44 Colt and he was grinning.

"Never figured on no such luck. I was a-trailin' them horses. Havalik figured we might need 'em."

"Where is he?"

"Maybe eight miles back." The big man was vastly pleased. "Means I get to kill you and keep your woman."

Kilkenny turned and walked away from Nita. He knew Baker would do just what he said.

"Stand still!" Baker yelled.

Kilkenny halted abruptly. "Why, sure, Jess. Look, can't we talk this over? I mean—" He drew and fired.

That draw was incredibly, unbelievably fast. Baker had not dreamed any man would attempt a draw when covered at thirty paces. One instant Kilkenny's voice had been pleading, a salve to the big man's wounded pride, and the next that hand blurred and flame spouted. Something struck Baker hard in the stomach and he took a step back, his eyes blinking. The gun slid from his fingers and he went to his knees, then simply rolled over and curled up dead.

All day they pushed on, higher and higher into the stormswept peaks. He had taken the slicker from the spare horse, probably belonging to the man killed when he rushed their camp.

Rain fell intermittently, washing out any trail. They topped the pass among heavy clouds and Kilkenny had to bend low from the saddle to study the earth. The way dipped down and they entered a forest rich with pine smell and the sound of rushing water. At last Twin Peaks loomed on their right and Kilkenny turned, weaving a pattern among the trees, then skirted a great rock slab and drew rein on a ledge.

Nita rode up beside him and sat for the first time overlooking the Valley of the Whispering Wind.

Walled upon two sides and almost upon the third, the valley lay between, a rolling expanse of lush green grass dotted with clumps of trees and bounded by the ridges covered with green forest. Even under the lowering clouds the valley was indescribably lovely.

"It's home," he said, his heart suddenly full. "I call it the Valley of the Whispering Wind."

"How did you come to name it?"

"Wait . . . you'll see."

A mile further into the valley he drew up and waited. Nita paused beside him.

A minute passed, and then another, and slowly she became conscious of a nameless stirring, a faint rustling through the grass and leaves. It was a sound not unlike the rushing of a fast train, sometimes heard in big timber, but something fainter, as though from wind singing in the strings of a far-off violin. A whispering wind, a singing wind.

"Hear it?" he asked gently. "When you hear that sound it means you're home."

On the day of Kilkenny's arrival in the valley, Dee Havalik returned to Horsehead.

He was in a savage mood. Kilkenny's sudden charge from darkness had caught him flat-footed. Despite their pursuit they had found nothing, and only precipitate flight saved them from death under the torrent of water. Returning to confess failure did not sit well with the gumman, nor did he like to think of Kilkenny outsmarting him. Yet rain had washed out all tracks, and the canyons were a maze.

The street of Horsehead was deserted. Nobody was in the Westwater dining room, and the stove was cold. Havalik walked out on the street with his two remaining men. No horses lined the hitch rails. The Emporium was closed and the shutters were up. Crossing to the Pinenut, Havalik shoved through the swinging doors. A bartender read a week-old newspaper and the saloon was empty.

"Where's everybody?"

"Hidin' out. A few holed up across the creek."

"Who's over there?"

The bartender shrugged. "Maybe Macy can tell you. He's in the office."

The KR, he found, had been taken. Several KR hands had been killed, but it was believed that Kilkenny had somehow saved Cain Brockman.

The news gave Havalik no pleasure. Already there was an uncertainty among the Forty riders. The strange night attacks were having their effect, and a few of them were wondering if Jared Tetlow had not overreached himself. Yet Tetlow believed the situation in hand.

Within an hour after Havalik's arrival in Horsehead, Jared rode into town sided by his two sons, Ben being with the big herd on the trail. They went at once to the Diamond Palace where they joined Havalik. A few minutes later four of the 4T riders appeared on the edge of town and rode along back streets and into the patch of woods that concealed a narrow bridge. Two more drifted into the Pinenut Saloon. Within an hour there were twenty-five men disposed about the town, filtering in so gradually that all remained unaware of any concerted movement.

All but Harry Lott. Big, unkempt and surly, he prowled continually, and he saw things. Lott had nothing against Tetlow, but Horsehead was, he fancied, his town. His authority was being scorned.

Kill Havalik, he reasoned, and the backbone of Tetlow's power would be broken. He was seated at a table in the Pinenut Saloon when he reached this decision. He shoved the bottle away from him and began to think.

The scattered groups of 4T riders broke up and vanished and the town lay still. Harry Lott went up to his bed and turned in, resting before what was sure to come.

Dawn broke bright and lovely, but a few clouds hung over the mountains. The first riders in the street were Jared and Andy Tetlow and they rode straight down the street and across the bridge, drawing up before Blaine's.

Blaine, accompanied by Leal Macy, appeared on the porch.

"I want to see that Riordan girl," Tetlow said abruptly. "I want to make her an offer."

"She's not here, and I'm sure she will consider no suggestion of selling."

"I'll have her word for that!"

Cain Brockman limped into the doorway. He was wearing two guns. "She won't be forced into no sale, Tetlow!"

The older man's lips tightened with impatience. "No occasion for trouble. I'll buy her place."

"Like you did Carson's and Carpenter's?" Macy asked.

"What happened to them was their own fault."

"You're like a lot of others, Tetlow. You believe anything that is good for you is good for the country. You're guided entirely by selfish motives."

Macy stepped to the edge of the porch. "Now let me tell you something. If you haven't moved your cattle off the KR range within twenty-four hours, and if you haven't made restitution to Mrs. Carpenter for damage to her property, I intend to telegraph the Territorial Governor as well as the United States Marshal."

Andy Tetlow pushed his horse forward. "Dad, we're wastin' time. Let's burn the place around their ears."

Jared Tetlow swung his horse and the two men rode back up the street and across the bridge. Phin sat his horse near the bridge, and as they passed he rode into the trees and started back.

Four riders waited in the trees back of the livery stable, and with these around him, Phin circled to the back door of Savory's. Dismounting, they trooped in through the back door and took stations near the front windows. Savory's was west of and catercorner across the street from Dolan's and Doc Blaine's.

Six Tetlow riders moved down the main street toward the bridge, and took station in the trees nearby. Dolan and Blaine were now covered from every approach.

Harry Lott came down the stairs of the Westwater Hotel and stopped in the lobby. He had seen Dee Havalik standing on the boardwalk in front of the Diamond Palace. Lott eased his guns in their holsters and stepped out, closing the door behind him. He was cold sober and ready to make his play. He saw himself as no hero. He was the town marshal and trouble was breaking in his bailiwick and he was going to stop it.

He walked into the street and faced about. He was a hundred yards from Havalik when he started toward him, and he had covered thirty yards before Andy Tetlow saw him. At some word from Andy, Havalik turned. His face seemed to grow tighter and grayer. "Lott," he said, "and he wants me."

Facing Lott he walked ten paces toward him. "Lookin' for something, Harry?"

"Call in your boys, Dee! There'll be no fighting today. I'm the law!"

"You were the law." Havalik shifted his position to put a big plate glass window behind him. The morning sun shone into that window. "Now you're a dead man."

As he spoke he stepped off the walk, still keeping the window behind him. As he stepped down, he drew.

Harry Lott was fast and game, but he knew with immediate awareness that he was going to die. As his hands grasped the gun butts, the guns for Dee Havalik were coming into line.

Lott squinted against the glare. He heard the concussion of Havalik's guns and something struck him a blow in the midsection. There was no pain. His draw completed, his gun lifted and blasted sound. The window behind Havalik crashed, but the gunman took a step nearer and fired again. His third shot crossed Lott's second. Lott felt himself struck again and his eyes blurred.

Desperately, he knew he had missed. Havalik's figure seemed to waver before him, and Lott braced himself, trying to steady his aim.

Phin Tetlow leaped his horse from behind the barber shop, gun up, ready to chop down with a shot. Lott faced squarely around and shot Phin twice in the stomach, then swung back and took his last shot at Havalik and missed again.

Still standing, he used the border shift to exchange guns and peered through the blurring haze toward Havalik. "You killed the wrong man!" Havalik yelled. "You crazy?"

"Couldn't see you, saw him." The voice seemed to issue from a great distance. "One rat's as good as another."

Havalik shot again and Lott tottered forward, his gun blasting into the earth. He hit the street on his face, rolled over and tried to get to his feet, shooting as fast as he could trigger his shots. All went wild. One broke a window in the Diamond Palace, one buried in the wall within inches of Jared Tetlow, and then Harry Lott sprawled in the street, his buck teeth biting the dust of Horsehead, his guns empty.

Shaken by his near escape and the shooting of Phin, Jared Tetlow crossed the street. Phin was dead.

Suddenly, Tetlow felt old and lost. Four tall sons and now two of them killed. A bad luck country. Two dead and one disloyal. It was like him not to consider that Ben had his own intelligence, his own loyalties. Harry Lott, dying, had struck out. Unable to kill the man he wanted, he chose the next best.

At Blaine's the shooting held them still and listening. Yet news passes all boundaries and within a few minutes they knew.

South of town a rider rode up Butler's Wash and with a shielded field glass studied the cattle on the KR. A big steer with wide horns was not far from him, and only a few yards away was another. Kilkenny rode from his shelter and hazed the steers back into a cul de sac among the boulders. The grass was rich there and they would stay. He studied the other steers, and sometime later captured another.

At the Blaine house Shorty stuck his head into the kitchen and grinned at Laurie. "How's for some coffee?"

"You'll have to get wood. The doctor keeps it in that shed near the stable."

"Huh!" Shorty was disgusted. "Every time you open your mouth to a woman she puts you to work!"

He opened the door and a bullett slammed the door jamb within inches of his face. Shorty hit the steps on his belly, then scrambled back into the room. He got to his feet and glanced sheepishly at Laurie. "Looks like I won't get my coffee," he said.

Dee and Macy had been drawn by the shot. "Looks like we're bottled up," Shorty told them. "Two of 'em out in the trees. Maybe more."

Dolan came into the kitchen. "From upstairs I could see a rider skirting Comb Ridge, high up. Might have been Kilkenny."

"Havalik went after Kilkenny and Nita with four men, and he came back with two . . . looks like he found them."

"Tetlow thought they were here so they must have gotten away," Laurie said. "I know Kilkenny has a place in the mountains. He bought supplies and a pack horse."

"I sold him the horse," Dolan said. "If anybody could make it, he could. I know the man."

Tentatively Blaine tried the door, standing well to the side. Instantly a bullet smashed the wall within inches. Shorty, crouched near an open window, fired three shots as fast as he could lever the rifle. Another shot spattered glass and he ducked flat. "Think I nicked somebody," he said. "He dropped his rifle."

For a few minutes the air was punctured with the staccato bark of guns. Then silence fell. The shooting did no damage in the strongly made house.

Doc Blaine had stationed himself in his office with Cain Brockman at the other window. Brockman was far from recovered from his injuries but his huge body was amazingly tough and he refused to be coddled.

Dolan's place was guarded by his own men, who welcomed the chance for action.

From the edge of Black Mesa, Kilkenny watched the Forty riders heading toward the KR ranch house and supper. Two riders remained on guard. The cattle moved toward the waterhole, bunching as night drew on. He listened to the distant firing, to imagine what was happening. The sound was reassuring. It meant that his friends were holding out. And he knew the caliber of Dolan, Brockman and Blaine.

As dusk closed around he moved back to the gray horse and began to tighten the cinch. Suddenly he knew he was not alone. He could not have explained how he knew, for there had been no sound.

He dropped the stirrup into place, and let his eyes search the terrain. His head still lowered, he fooled with the saddle while watching the rocks.

There was no cover behind him. Yet to move from the side of the horse would leave him in the open and, considering the situation, Kilkenny liked no part of it. Only two places beside him offered cover, and one of these was far more likely than the other.

Turning his horse on a three-quarter angle, he started walking on the oblique toward the rocks, keeping on the far side of the horse. Quite near, he suddenly slapped the gray, vaulted to the saddle and shucked a gun in the same instant. The startled horse leaped past the rocks, and Kilkenny, gun poised, looked into the face of Jaime Brigo.

Brigo grinned up at him. "I knew it was you, señor, but there might have been someone else near."

"You nearly got shot, compadre. Want to help me?"

"Si." The Yaqui looked curiously at the now hog-tied steers. "But I do not understand what it is you do."

"It's like this—" Kilkenny explained his plan as briefly as possible.

"Good!" Jaime said. "We will do it."

He caught Kilkenny's sleeve. "Senor? The señorita? She is safe?"

"Safe. But let's get busy. It will soon be time."

CHAPTER EIGHT

SWEDE CARLSON OF the Forty walked his horse slowly across the range toward the herd. The night had clouded over and the distant rumble of thunder hinted at the possibility of more rain. A hundred yards away he could see the dark outline of Slim's angular figure slouching in the saddle.

Slim rode toward him. "I got the creeps!" he said, looking around. "It's mighty dark, all of a sudden."

Swede told him about the killing of Harry Lott and of Phin. "The old man's turned mighty mean. Losin' his second boy."

"Yeah." Slim glanced over the herd. They were restless over

the imminent storm. "Ben's coming up the trail with ten thousand head."

An electric current seemed to run through the cattle and as if on signal they came suddenly to their feet. One instant the night was still and then the herd was up and running. Horns clashed and somebody shouted vainly. Swede swung his head as he fought his horse around. Rushing down upon the herd was a row of dancing, leaping lights!

With one mind the herd was gone. Swede caught a glimpse of Slim trying to swing his horse, saw a charging steer hit them broadside and saw Slim and his horse go down under the charging cattle, and then he was fighting blindly, instinctively, for his own life.

Under him the pony stretched out, running desperately while Swede tried to edge him over and escape from sure death under the pounding hoofs.

Far behind, Kilkenny drew the gray to a halt. Brigo drew up beside him and they watched the herd go. "They asked for it," Kilkenny said, "now they've got it."

Away in the darkness, Swede Carlson finally saw an opening and lunged his horse toward it. They got out of the herd and into the brush. He stopped there, his heart pounding. A steer ran past him, fire still blazing around one horn. Old sacking and grass had been rolled together and tied between the steer's spreading horns, then set afire. Such a fire would not burn long and would blow or burn itself free before it could harm the cow. The flames had been all that was needed with the skittish herd.

Slim was dead and there was no telling how many more. It was not going to be a one-sided fight this time, Swede decided. From the town a rifle shot sounded, lost in the vast silence left behind after the rushing hoofs of the cattle. Dismally Swede turned back and began to search for the other riders. Far off, very far off, he could hear the running herd.

Ben Tetlow was riding the point of his trail herd nearing Westwater. He was tired from the long ride and was about to bed down the herd when he heard a distant thunder. He drew up, listening. A rider cantered up. "Boss," he said, "that sounds like—" He broke off, rising in his stirrups.

The sound was suddenly louder and the skyline was broken by bobbing heads and horns. Fear went through Ben like the shock of cold water. "Ride, damn it! Ride! It's a stampede!"

There was no chance to stop the rush of cattle and they rode for their lives to get to the edge of the herd. The heads of the ten thousand cattle came up, eyes rolled, and then as the shock of charging cattle hit them they wheeled in their tracks and lit out at a dead run.

Ben Tetlow stared after them. All they could hopc now was that weariness from the long march would have left the herd too tired to run far.

"What started 'em?" he asked a rider who trotted up.

"Somebody tied burnin' rags between their horns."

"Kilkenny." Ben started off to the north. "I wish Dad had never started this fuss."

The rider was Swede Carlson. "The Old Man's too high-handed, Ben."

"Phin and Andy like it that way. Otherwise he might have slowed down a little."

"You . . . you ain't heard about Phin?"

Ben turned on him. "What about him?"

Swede explained, telling what he had heard of the gun battle in the street.

Phin dead! Ben was thinking more of his father than of Phin. He himself had always been closer to Andy but Phin had been a silent, hard working man. His father had told Ben that he took after his mother, and Ben had not been sorry. The Old Man had always been proud of his big sons, and now two were dead because of the path down which he had guided them.

"Where'll it end, Swede?"

Carlson shrugged. "The Old Man's usin' his spurs too much, Ben. These folks have got their backs up. We've lost men. Two killed out on the range by nobody knows who. Killed with a knife."

"I'm going to talk to Dad."

"Won't do you no good, Ben. He's fierce mad now. And you know how Havalik is."

The day dawned hot and still. Strong as was the Blaine house, it was also a trap. Any movement near the windows drew fire. Luckily, there was plenty of food in the house, but the water was outside. During the night they had succeded in drawing three buckets of water, but the third one had spilled, warning the watchers, who opened fire.

Nobody felt like talking. There was no relief in sight and all knew how ruthless Jared Tetlow was.

Kilkenny was hidden between two peaks atop Black Steer Knoll, overlooking the town. With him was Brigo. Vainly he searched his mind for a solution. In the town below no life stirred except around the saloon and then only when drinks were sold to riders from the Forty. Through his glassess Kilkenny could see the location of the surrounding attackers.

"They'll need water inside the house," Brigo said. "The well is in the yard."

Kilkenny could see what the Yaqui meant. The well was thirty feet from the house and surrounded by a stone coping three feet high. Once at the well a man would have shelter, but he could return only at the risk of his life.

Two riders appeared from the east and rode into town. Kilkenny swung his glasses. "Ben Tetlow, bringing news of the stampede."

Below in the town a man moved near the edge of the woods at Blaine's. "Get ready to run," Lance said. "I'm going to show them they have friends outside."

He nestled the rifle stock against his cheek. Heat waves danced in the air, giving it a curiously liquid appearance. Deceptive, but not too much so. The distance was no more than five hundred yards. The stock felt cool against his cheek.

The muzzle wavered slightly and Kilkenny held what he had on the trigger and as the muzzle steadied he squeezed off his shot. The rifle leaped in his hands and the man in the trees leaped forward, hands outflung, then sprawled on his face in the clearing beyond the edge of the trees.

Quickly, before any return fire could be directed, Kilkenny dusted the woods with three more shots, and swinging his rifle he sent a shot into the street that made a walking man dive for shelter. Brigo pulled back and started toward the horses, with Kilkenny following, feeding shells into his gun.

Mounted, they rode swiftly across the plateau, then up Dry Wash to the butte. A glimpse toward the town showed riders fanning out into the hills to begin the pursuit. The shots had at least drawn away the attack on the house. A few minutes later, from behind a ridge, they saw Ben Tetlow ride east with ten or eleven men.

Kilkenny drew rein. "Right now," he said, "would be a good time to get our crowd out of there. Most of the Tetlow outfit are gone."

Holding to low ground, they circled the town and rode back into Horsehead. The body of the man lay where it had fallen at the edge of the woods. "Switch saddles to fresh horses," Kilkenny said. "Buck for me."

Dolan stepped out as they swung down. "You're taking a chance, man! The town's lousy with Forty riders."

Kilkenny explained, then added, "It's time to take to the hills. We can fight from there. Stay here and sooner or later they'll get you."

Dolan took his cigar from his teeth and knocked off the ash. "Of course," he said. He turned and went inside. In a matter of a minute the corral was swarming with men.

Brigo walked to the door of Savory's and pushed it open. Two startled Forty riders leaped to their feet. They turned their heads and their guns. Brigo fired and his first shot knocked a man to the floor, coughing from a chest wound. The second took a bullet through the hand and he dropped his rifle and stepped back, hands lifted.

Brigo gestured to Savory. "Fix his hand. And stay out of this or I'll kill you!"

He walked out the door in time to see Kilkenny move into the center of the bridge. The shooting had drawn Jared Tetlow into the street and what he saw was Lance Kilkenny standing alone in the middle of the bridge. There was no mistaking the tall figure with the flat-crowned black hat.

Jared Tetlow looked down the street and felt a queer chill. Over a hundred and fifty yards separated them but there could be no mistake. The hills were covered with riders searching for this man and here he stood in the middle of the town.

Defeatism was not familiar to Tetlow, yet now he felt its first premonitory wave. With all the armed men at his command he had failed to stop this man or bring him down.

"Tetlow!" Kilkenny's voice sounded like a clarion in the silent clap-boarded street. "Take your cattle and leave the country! You brought this war. Now take it away or we'll break you!"

Tetlow felt the heat on his shoulders. Sweat trickled down his leather-like cheeks. He was strangely alone, and then from deep within him came a welling, over-powering fury. It was loosed in one great cry of fury at his defeat, pain at the loss of his sons, and shock at what was happening to all he had lived by. "You!" he roared. "I'll—"

Only the bridge was empty, and where Kilkenny had stood there were only dancing heat waves and a faint stirring of dust.

Had he imagined it? Or had Kilkenny actually been there?

A red-headed cowhand with blunt features came into the door of the Diamond Palace. "I'll give five hundred dollars to see that man dead!" Tetlow shouted.

The redhead's eyes shifted. He remembered what he had heard about Kilkenny and drew back into the shadows of the saloon. Five hundred was a year's wages, but a dead man couldn't spend a dime.

In a close knot the defenders of the Blaine house began their retreat. Most of the Forty riders were gone from town, and those who remained had no desire to dare the guns of that tight little group. So the Blaine group rode west at an easy trot. Dolan, Blaine and Shorty led the group. Early, Ernleven and Macy brought up the rear. In the middle were Laurie Webster, Mrs. Carpenter, Mrs. Early and two other women surrounded by four men from Dolan's. Kilkenny scouted ahead and Cain Brockman brought up the rear. Brigo scouted on the far flanks.

Kilkenny had chosen the little lake as their first stop with some misgiving. If Havalik returned in time he might easily move across country and intercept them.

As they neared the lake, Kilkenny waited for them to come up to him. "Drink up, water the stock and fill your canteens, We'll push on."

"Tonight?" Early glanced doubtfully at his wife's drawn face. She was not used to riding and they had come long miles since leaving Horsehead.

"Tonight." Kilkenny was positive. "It's better to be dog-tired than dead. They'll come after us and our only hope is my place."

"Do they know this lake?" Dolan asked.

Kilkenny explained about the capture of Nita at this point. He had made his plans. There was doubt that the women would stand the long ride to the valley by the route they must take. His idea was to strike due north into the unknown country, then swing west to the valley. By so doing they might avoid or lose the Forty altogether. Mounting once more, he led them north until they struck a dim, ancient trail.

It would soon be dark and he was in known country. Far off on the skyline were the Blues, but what lay between he had no idea. The night was fresh and cool and there was a faint smell of sage in the air.

When the moon came out its pale yellow light lay upon a

broken land of rock like a frozen sea of gigantic waves. Knowing the restlessness of Havalik, Kilkenny rested but little, pushing on toward the north. Finally, at daybreak they made dry camp. There was a little grass and the horses ate. The women fell asleep at once, and most of the men. Only Dolan seemed sleepless.

"Know where we are?" Macy asked. His own face looked tired and drawn.

"Roughly." He nodded to indicate direction. "My place is over there."

"How far?"

"As the crow flies, maybe ten miles. The way we'll have to go, twice that far."

Macy was worried. "Lance, this doesn't look right to me. We should have stayed in town."

"We couldn't." Dolan's tone brooked no argument. "It was either that or be burned out. That would have come next."

The sky was gray and the morning was cold and sharp due to the altitude. From a small peak Kilkenny studied their backtrail. Once he believed he saw far off dust, but he could not be sure.

All night his thoughts had been of Nita. Yet if she was undisturbed she would get along well. There was food, and there was water and ammunition. She was an uncommonly good shot with a rifle. She would be all right.

He could tell from the way the women got to their feet that they were still stiff and sore form the long ride. Yet there was no escape from it now. It was go on or die here. When all were mounted he led the way up the trail again. By midmorning they had crossed the flat and were headed toward a gap in the range.

There were a few cottonwoods in the bottoms, and the mountain mahogany was everywhere. Greasewood lessened and from time to time they saw a pine. Soon the number of pines increased, and twice he paused to allow the women rest. Before noon they struck an old Indian trail up the bottom of a smaller canyon. Most of the canteens were dry and the horses were suffering from thirst. A turn in the canyon left them looking up a long slope mantled with evergreens. Kilkenny headed up the slope and was overtaken by Macy.

"Mrs. Early's just fainted. We've got to stop."

"Carry her," Kilkenny said. "There's water ahead."

Macy looked doubtfully at the slope and Kilkenny indicated the Indian trail he followed. "An Indian never made a trail without purpose. And look, '' he pointed out a faint thread of game trail down the slope, ''deer have been going the way we're headed.''

Within ten minutes they dismounted beside a clear mountain stream. The water was cold and sweet. All drank and drank again, then filled their canteens.

Bob Early came up to him. ''We can't go on. My wife's all in and Mrs. Carpenter is quite ill.''

''All right. You're close enough and safe enough.''

Picking up an ax, Lance walked into the surrounding pines. Forcing his way into a tight clump of second growth, all ten or twelve feet high, he cut down several close to the ground. Then he drew the tops of the surrounding trees down and tied them together until he stood under a living hut of green. With branches from the cut-down trees he wove a quick thatch over the hut. Cain and Bob lent a hand with the thatch and soon the hut was tight and strong. Then with more boughs they made several beds for the women.

Blaine walked around the hut. ''First time I ever saw that done. I'm minded to stay here myself.''

''You'd better. I'll go on ahead with Brigo and Cain.''

''Shorty and I'll come with you,'' Dolan said. ''One of us can return for these people when they are feeling better.''

The trail was not easy. Crossing the creek, they found themselves facing a mountainside that could not be climbed on horseback. Circling, they were fronted by an even steeper cliff. Only after several hours of searching did they find a shallow creek that could be followed higher into the timbered mountains. When it seemed they had found a way through they were stopped by a ten-foot fall.

Brigo found a way around. Part of a cave had been cut by water. The ledge at the top had proved too hard for the slow-cutting water and as the rock below was softer, the stream had cut under, forming one more arch to add to those in the area. Riding under part of the fall and getting well splashed, they went under the arch and clambered up a steep rock slope and found good going before them.

They emerged suddenly into the valley not fifty yards from the house. Nita was standing on the steps looking toward them, a rifle in her hands.

Her recognition was immediate and she turned at once and went back into the house. When she emerged they were swinging from their saddles. ''I've coffee on, Lance. It will be ready in a few minutes.''

He could see the relief in her eyes and he pressed her arm gently. As the others looked around he quietly explained the situation. Brockman had sat down at once, his face showing the exhaustion of the long trip after his injuries. Only his great strength and iron resistance could have stood up under the punishment.

Shorty remained only to eat and to rest a little. Then he mounted up and started back.

The night came slowly and the dusk seemed to remain over long. Kilkenny had gone to sleep in the bedroom, exhausted after his long ordeal, almost without sleep. Dolan sat with Cain and Brigo on the steps watching the shadows gather under the lodgepole pines. The air was cool at that altitude and hour, but none of them thought of going inside.

The situation was brutally apparent to them all. They had gained a respite, but Jared Tetlow would never stop until they were dead. Not only had he lost a second son but he had been thwarted, and it was galling to a man of his ego and firm belief in his own strength and rightness.

Horsehead lay quiet. In the lobby of the Westwater Hotel, Jared Tetlow sat in a huge leather chair, his face old and bitter. Several heavily armed men loitered on the steps outside.

The town was his. The range was his. He, Jared Tetlow, had taken them and he would hold them. Yet his cattle were scattered, two of his sons were dead, and he had lost men. Jared Tetlow knew nothing of military tactics. He did not know that the end result of all tactics is not only victory but the destruction of the enemy's power to strike back.

Yet, despite his victory, some subconscious realization of his position left him uneasy. Despite his possessions of the range and the town, Kilkenny was alive. Brigo and Cain Brockman were alive. Dolan, Blaine—all of them had gotten safely away. They would not run. He knew fighting men when he saw them and he knew they were not defeated. They would be waiting somewhere for a chance to strike again. And so these men outside guarded him.

Two of his sons remained. Andy, the tough one. The gun slinger. And Ben, the quiet one. Perhaps, the thought came unbidden to his mind, perhaps Ben was right after all? It galled him to think of Ben being right, yet looking back down the years it had always been Ben who talked prudence and peace. And he was the only cattleman of the lot. Phin had never been more than a steady worker. Bud had been a trouble hunter, Andy the fighting man. But it was Ben who had managed the herds, sold the cattle, assured their prosperity.

Jared Tetlow stared at his gnarled hands and a kind of anger welled up within him. No matter. Their cattle were here, on good grass, and no gunfighter could stop him. This would pass. He would win, somehow, and time, like the grass, would cover all scars. If the law did come in he would show them his herds, his ranch, and the quiet countryside where before there had been only these shabby holdings. This was a land for the strong, and he was strong.

He got up from his chair and strode across the room. His own cook was in Ernleven's kitchen, but the food was merely rough ranch fare. Why had the big Frenchman chosen to join Kilkenny?

The waitress had refused to come to work and the stores had not opened. He held the town in the palm of his hand but the town was an empty shell.

Happy Jack Harrow walked into the dining room, looked around, then swore. Tetlow glanced up. "Set down. There'll be grub soon."

"'Yeah? But what kind of grub? I'm no chuckline rider!"

Tetlow did not resent the remark. "Seen times I'd been glad to get it."

"Any news?"

"No."

"They got away?"

"Seems like."

"Why not let 'em go, then? What'll you do if you get 'em?" Harrow had not slept well. He was doing his own worrying now. He had not sided with Early, but he liked the man, and he liked his wife. Doc Blaine was solid, too. Looking around him Harrow found no comfort in the situation. "What about the women? Do you plan to murder them?"

"Hush that talk," Tetlow replied irritably. "What has to be done will be done."

Tetlow shifted irritably in his chair. For the first time he began seriously to think about the women, and they worried him. He had never been able to cope with women. He had never been able to cope with his wife.

"You'll never keep them quiet," Harrow said, "and Mrs. Early comes of good family. If anything happens to her there will be questions asked. And if they talk there will be a United States marshal out here.''

Jared Tetlow was not worried about the marshal. Let him win this fight and there would be no witnesses to accuse him. He did not like troubling women, but Harrow's wandering comments decided him. The women must die.

He had seen a man hung for striking a woman. He had seen Western men hunt down men who molested women. He knew the rage he could incite by any move against the women. But they were in the hills. Who knew where they were now? And if they did not come back, who could say what happened to them?

Yet he did not relish the thought. How had he got into this corner, anyway? ''If they turn Kilkenny over to me I'll bother them no longer,'' he said.

''Fat chance!'' Harrow scoffed. ''And if you had him you'd wish you'd never seen him.'' Harrow leaned toward the older man. ''Tetlow, call off your men and gather your herd. Head west for new country. Then this will all blow over.''

Tetlow turned his head sharply. ''Be damned if I will. This is my country now! Here I'll stay!''

''You'll stay then.'' Harrow accepted the plate and cup from the cook. ''They'll bury you here.''

Tetlow stared at the beef and beans, feeling old and tired. Why had he come out here? What had gotten him into this mess? Would there be no end to killing? Yet now he could not stop. Irritation filled him. He stared at Harrow. The man was nobody. He had swung to his side quickly enough, and at the first intimation of change he would swing again. There was only one answer now that it had begun.

Kill them.

Kill Harrow, too. Once he would have been appalled by the thought. He only killed in battle. Now these were merely insignificant humans who interfered with him. Harrow had succeeded in making him realize what he had subconsciously known all along. There could be no safety for him as long as any of them lived. Bob Early was a strong, capable man. Leal Macy was a duly constituted officer of the law. Their words would carry weight and outside people did not realize the circumstances here.

He got up suddenly and strode to the door. ''Ernie, take this note to Havalik!'' He scratched words on a bit of paper. When the man was in the saddle he returned to the table.

''You're right, of course. They'd talk.''

Something in his tone made Harrow look up quickly.

"You told me so yourself," Tetlow said, watching Harrow almost absently. "I can't leave them alive."

A man stood in the doorway with two guns. Harrow stared at him. If Tetlow would kill those women then his own life wasn't worth a plugged nickel. His appetite gone, he sat over his food trying to think of a way out.

"Well," he tried to keep his tone casual, "I'd better check on my bartender. I can't trust him too much."

Jared Tetlow looked up at Harrow as he got to his feet, and at something in his eyes Harrow felt a faint chill go over him.

Why had he been such a fool as to straddle the fence? You never could, not when the chips were down. He turned on his heel and walked to the door, his spine crawling. Jared Tetlow watched him to the door, then got to his feet again.

"Jack?"

Harrow turned and saw the drawn gun in Tetlow's hand. He grabbed wildly for his own gun, but Tetlow fired, the crashing report louder in the closed room. Happy Jack Harrow's knees folded and he went down, rolling over on the floor, the half-drawn gun spilling from relaxed fingers.

The man with the two guns had stepped inside. "Bury him," Tetlow said. "He was going for the U.S. marshal."

He sat down at the table again and the acrid smell of gunpowder mingled with the smell of fresh coffee.

CHAPTER NINE

THE KILLING OF Jack Harrow did not pass unnoticed. Men who had remained on the sidelines saw it with misgiving. East of Horsehead two Forty hands came together on a little branch that emptied into the Westwater.

"Tetlow killed Harrow."

"Hear he figures to kill them women, too."

"The Old Man's losin' his grip. Killin' in a fight, that's one thing. Massacre, that's another."

The first cowhand wiped his mustache with the back of his hand

and took a sidelong glance at his companion. "Personal, I ain't goin' to have no hand in it."

"Sort of been thinkin' thataway myself."

"I got two months comin'."

"So've I, but we try to draw our time there'll be trouble."

The first man waved a hand at the scattered cattle. "They'll never git 'em all rounded up, an' they'll pay your wages. Cross country, it ain't so far to Sante Fe."

"What are we waitin' for?"

Two cowhands and two hundred head of cattle headed south. Before noon three other riders came upon the trail. Being skilled readers of sign, they recognized the horse tracks and read the story in the dust.

"Not a bad idea," one of them commented casually. It took no more than minutes to reach a meeting of the minds. Cattle and men made a new trail.

In Horsehead Jared Tetlow heard the story from Andy with sullen fury. Had it been Ben who reported the stolen stock and the vanished riders he would have waved him aside and stomped out to begin a chase, but this was Andy, the tough one.

He could see only one way out. Wipe out all opposition and then go after the rustlers and cattle.

"Pick fifteen tough men," Tetlow said, "mount them on the best. Promise each one hundred dollars cash when the job is done and take them to Havalik. Tell him I'll give him forty-eight hours."

Dee Havalik received the reinforcements with satisfaction. With Andy and several others he squatted beside the fire. "Three times now Kilkenny has disappeared from a place due north and a mite east of here. That means he's got him a hideout in the Blues. He's got a good bunch of fighters with him but they've women to worry about. We can use fire to bluff 'em to surrender. But first we've got to find them.

"Andy, you take five men and head up Mule Canyon. Better keep a rider on each wall as you advance, scoutin' the country. Watch for trail sign. Grat, take five more men and ride east until you find a pass. When you do, go over and ride for the nearest bottom. Then wait for us. If we follow true courses we'll meet back in there and by then we should know something."

Havalik led his own group along the western flank of the mountains roughly opposite the trail the searched-for party had left a few days before. When he came to the rough country around Cottonwood Creek, they turned up the Blues into higher mountains. At the point where they turned they were less than three miles from the waterfall under which the party had ridden to find the back door to the Valley of Whispering Wind.

By nightfall the three parties had come together, camping on a branch of Indian Creek. Due north of them towered the Twin Peaks, and beyond the peaks lay the valley.

Grat swung from his dusty horse and crossed to where Havalik and Andy conversed in low tones. "Struck a trail!" he told them triumphantly. "In that pass a little south of here. The rain washed out some of the tracks but two or three were that mare the Riordan woman rides."

Havalik spat with satisfaction. "Good! Good!" He nodded affirmation. "That fits. Must be the trail we lost."

"That ain't all. We found Jess Baker."

"Dead?"

"Uh-huh. Right through the center. He had his chance, too."

"Kilkenny." Havalik paced off a few steps. "I'd have given ten to one that was what happened ot Jess."

"You got any ideas?" Andy asked.

"We know they came this far. From the way they appeared and disappeared it can't be much further. It could be in the mountains right around us. From now on we ride careful."

The wind whipped the fire and blew hard in the treetops. The air was cold and the sky spotted with clouds. Dee Havalik walked to a big log and sat down. What would they say in the Live Oak country when they heard he had killed Kilkenny? He had always known they would meet some day. He only hoped it would be face to face, man to man, and not in a general fight where the killing might be attributed to others.

Cain Brockman rode up to the cabin shortly before midnight. He went to the nest of rocks and trees beyond the spring where Kilkenny had bedded down after his brief rest in the house. "Lance?" he whispered.

"I'm awake."

"Spotted a couple of fires on Injun Crick, looks like Brigo's gone down for a closer look."

"Two fires? Close together?"

"Uh-huh. Means a big bunch."

"Who's on the peaks?"

"Shorty. It took me nigh an hour to get back down."

"All right. You get some sleep."

He lay there, hands clasped under his head, studying the problem. The expected attack would come tomorrow and it would be with all the force Tetlow could muster.

There was movement near him and he caught a faint breath of Nita's perfume. He sat up and she moved down beside him. "What is it, Lance?"

"They are over the peaks. We'll have trouble tomorrow." He ran his fingers through his hair. "I'm tempted to hit them tonight with an ambush."

"Don't do that. Let them start it."

"When this is over, Nita, will you go back to your KR?"

"Not unless you send me."

"It will be cold and lonely up here in winter."

"I don't care! I'd love to see those peaks all covered with snow!" She listened to the wind. "In this valley with you? Riding, working, walking together, I'd want it more than anything, Lance."

"You'll have it, then. I'm through running. This place here in this valley will be my last stand. I made up my mind when I came here."

Nita was suddenly thoughtful. "Lance, I'm afraid."

"Of Tetlow?"

"Only a little of him. Mostly of Dee Havalik."

Kilkenny leaned back and began building a smoke. "Don't let it bother you. I don't."

"That's easy to say."

"Yes," he admitted, "and this is what I've tried to save you from without much luck. But Havalik will get more than he bargains for. He never bucked a combination like this before, and so far we've just defended ourselves."

Her mind shifted. "I think Laurie likes Doctor Blaine."

"She'd be a fool if she didn't. He's a rare sort of man."

"So are you."

"Me?" Kilkenny chuckled, then drew deep on his cigarette. The glow was bright in the darkness and Nita momentarily caught the strong lines of his face, somber and brooding. "Maybe."

The moon was rising above the wind-worried trees. They sat hand in hand, her head against his shoulder. the faint smell of tobacco smoke mingled with that of wood smoke and pines. The peaks were a hard, serrated line across the face of the moon.

Someone stirred, and with a start, Kilkenny realized it must be

Taggart. It would be two o'clock in the morning and he would be going to relieve Shorty.

Kilkenny reached for his moccasins. "Better get some sleep. I'm going to scout around. Brigo isn't back."

"Don't worry. He has a sixth sense, like a wolf."

He buckled on his gun belts and picked up his Winchester. Taggart waited for him. He was a tall man, lean-jawed and haggard of face. "I'll walk along," Kilkenny said. "Brigo's been gone all night."

"That Yaqui never sleeps."

They mounted and rode away together. "Figure the fight will come today?"

"It'll start."

"I want one shot at that Tetlow."

Surprised at the tone, Kilkenny glanced at him. "You sound like you had a personal grudge."

"Knowed Tetlow since we was boys together. Before he owned one cow I had a nice ranch back in Texas. He stole my cows, burned me out, took my range."

"He's been hurt himself, now. Lost two boys, his herds scattered, his men shot up."

"He'll never quit."

They parted at the trail to the peaks. "Tell Shorty to get some sleep and to get the crowd up by five, ready for trouble."

There was a dim trail east of Twin Peaks, winding around the mountain toward the place where the fires had been seen. When he was still some distance away he swung the buckskin to a thicket and left him tied.

He heard their voices before he reached camp. Then a pistol barked, and a louder voice taunted, "Hell, Grat! You never even touched him! Bet I can notch his ears!"

Kilkenny slid through the brush, easing branches aside and moving close to the edge of the firelight. Then he peered into the clearing.

Jaime Brigo was tied to a tree and men were sprawled on the ground eating breakfast. Grat and two others were standing with drawn pistols facing the tree. The big Yaqui watched them, his contempt obvious. Blood from a scalp wound trickled down his face. Havalik sprawled on the ground nearby, looking on without expression.

The man who offered the bet lifted his gun. As he did so,

Kilkenny stepped into the open, his Winchester at his hip. He held the gun on Havalik, but his command was for them all. "If you want Havalik dead, just make a wrong move!"

Caught unawares, all remained without moving and Kilkenny said quickly, "You! With the pistols! Drop them! Untie that man and make it quick or I'll splatter Havalik's skull all over your breakfast!"

Havalik sat very still. He was no fool, and he knew one wrong move would kill him. "You won't get away with this, Kilkenny. I'll have your hide."

"You'll get your chance all in good time."

He saw Brigo step away from the tree, rubbing his arms to restore circulation. Then the Yaqui picked up his rifle and buckled on his pistol belt. He turned his big head toward Grat. "This man shoot at me," he said. "I want him."

"I'd like nothin' better!" Grat challenged.

"All right." Kilkenny knew Brigo. Few could face him in any sort of hand-to-hand combat. "Walk out beyond the fire. Now all of you turn to face them. Your backs will be toward me and anyone who wants to die will have an easy chance."

Grat was a big, strongly built man. He looked from the Yaqui to Kilkenny. "You mean I can fight him?"

"Choose your weapons. Gun, knife or bare hands."

"Knives!" Grat said, smiling with cruel satisfaction. "I always heard Injuns were good with knives but I never saw one yet who was! I go for a Bowie!"

Both men put off their gun belts and with knives held low, cutting edges up, they circled warily. Grat was a powerful, quick moving man and he had stripped off his boots for better footing. Grat moved suddenly, but Brigo caught the darting blade on his own, and deflected it. Grat lost balance and fell forward.

The Yaqui stepped back carelessly, his face hard with contempt. Angered, Grat lunged again. Like a chaparral cock with a rattler, the Yaqui began to bait him. He left openings, he appeared to slip on the grass, he circled and feinted, moving to draw Grat in.

Suddenly, Brigo lunged and the edge of his knife left a thin red line across Grat's cheek. Blood welled to the surface and began to trickle. Grat rushed and the Yaqui sidestepped away and the point of his knife flicked the biceps of Grat's left arm.

"Hah!" the Yaqui grunted as he moved away. "You wish to kill. How does it feel to be living, but upon the edge of death?"

Grat was sweating now. He was frightened, knowing that his knife skill was puny compared to that of the man he faced. The big Yaqui moved gracefully, easily, unwearied. Brigo's knife was like a snake's tongue, darting . . . darting . . .

The point flicked again at the biceps, the edge touched Grat's ear. Where the knife touched there was blood.

Grat threw caution away. His only chance was to rush, to close with the Indian before the loss of blood weakened him. He rushed, and Brigo met the rush, knocking aside the knife arm and thrusting, low and hard into Grat's belly. Eye to eye they stood, then Brigo threw him aside.

Grat landed on his knee, and instantly threw his knife, but Brigo had already moved, and throwing his own knife as Grat tried to turn away, drove it to the haft in Grat's kidney, the point driving up.

Screaming, Grat caught at the haft of the knife and tried to jerk it free. In this position, he could not exert the strength and he staggered like an insect on a pin. Brigo walked to him and, putting a hand on his shoulder, he withdrew the knife. Without looking at the dying man he wiped the blade clean in the sand. Then he belted on his guns once more and picked up his rifle.

''You are fools,'' he said. ''As he dies, so will you all!''

Surprisingly, Macy, Taggart and Dolan stepped from the brush. Worried by Kilkenny's plan, Taggart had started them along his trail.

Supported by their rifles, Kilkenny and Brigo disarmed the Forty riders. Kilkenny took the guns from Havalik's holsters. ''I'm going to unload these,'' he said, ''And give them back. One day we'll meet and you'll want your own guns.''

Taking Havalik's hat, he spun it high in the air. Then, slip-shooting with Havalik's guns, he emptied them into the spinning hat. Then he tossed the guns into the grass at the gunman's feet.

Mumbling, the Forty riders started for their horses, minus guns, ammunition and gunbelts. Then as they rode away the men from the valley walked into the trees toward their horses, taking with them all the guns but the two returned to Havalik.

In the pass, Havalik drew rein. ''We're not goin' back. Dave, you take Joe and get to Horsehead. Get guns and come running. We're not through here.''

Leal Macy stepped into the saddle and then turned. There was resolution in his jaw. "This has gone far enough! We're going into town and I'm going to arrest Tetlow. I'm going to deputize the lot of you right now!"

Dolan glanced at Kilkenny. "What do you say, Lance? This might be the time."

Kilkenny hesitated, weighing their chances. "All right. Brigo can stay here with Doc Blaine, Early and a couple of men, just in case. The rest of us will go."

At the ranch they wasted no time. Leal Macy and Kilkenny would head the group for town, taking with them Dolan, Cain Brockman, Shorty and Taggart. It was a good, hard-fighting crowd.

Kilkenny led off toward town, but he had not gone far when they intercepted the trail of the Havalik men. "Only two men went to town! Havalik and the rest have stayed in the hills!"

Macy's face was a study in uncertainty. "Do we stay or go?"

"We'll go on," Kilkenny said. "We'll trust to Brigo."

"My guess is that those two have gone after guns. If we get along fast we can take them along with Tetlow."

Day was breaking when the party rode into town. They tried no subterfuge, but rode right into the street. The only horse they saw wore the 4T brand. The center was at the Diamond Palace.

"Dolan, you and Brockman go down the street and pick up anybody that's loose. Taggart, you and Shorty cover the street."

Kilkenny turned toward the Palace with Macy. "You think those two beat us here?" Macy asked.

"Doubt it. I know the trails better and we pushed out horses."

Only one Forty hand was in the Palace. He was eating, but when he saw who had come in he dropped his fork. Two guns covered him and he attempted no more. In a matter of minutes he was hog-tied.

"Where's Jared Tetlow?" Macy demanded of the bartender.

"Don't know, but if I was you I'd dust out of here."

"I'm sheriff, in case you've forgotten. You make a move from behind that bar or help in any way and I'll arrest you for complicity."

Leaving their captive with the men on the steps, Macy started for the Pinenut. A shot sounded down the street and Kilkenny ducked across the street and ran into an alleyway between Bob Early's office and the harness shop. Running to the back of the

Westwater Hotel, he opened the door and stepped quickly inside.

Jared Tetlow stood in the front door staring into the street. Beside him was a big man with hair the color of corn.

"You're under arrest, Tetlow! You'll stand trial for murder and theft!"

The old man stiffened, then turned slowly. His face was white and the bones stood out against the skin. "You? Arrestin' *me?*"

"I'm sworn deputy of Leal Macy, county sheriff. Both of you unbuckle your guns."

The big young man was wide-shouldered and strong. He wanted to take a chance, but there was no chance. Carefully he let go his gun belt and, after an instant's hesitation, Tetlow did likewise.

Gathering up the guns, Kilkenny led his prisoners into the street. Macy stood in front of the stage station with a Winchester, looking across the bridge into west town.

"Brockman had trouble," Macy explained. "A man named Harper. He was dead before he hit the floor."

When Tetlow and the light-haired man who proved to be Swede Carlson were jailed, the posse turned to and made a clean sweep of the town. They rounded up but six scattered riders from the Forty. There was no sign of the two men Havalik had sent for guns.

Leal Macy worked swiftly. He sent three wires by the noon stage to be telegraphed from the nearest station informing the governor of what had happened and the steps that had been taken.

He was behind his desk and Kilkenny was loafing in the office when Ben Tetlow came in. "I understand you've arrested my father?"

"That's correct. He'll be held for trial."

"Is there any charge against me?"

"Not so far."

"Do I get to see my father?"

"No reason why not."

Ben Tetlow unbuckled his guns. He glanced at Kilkenny. "What's your part in this?"

"Deputy."

"A killer!"

"Might call me that. I never hunted trouble."

"I suppose," Ben said bitterly, "you'll kill my father now?"

"Don't build trouble where there is none," Lance replied quietly. "Your father tried to ride us down. He'll get what's coming to him . . . legally."

There was a sincerity about the tall rider that convinced him. Without replying he went down the hall.

Jared Tetlow appeared to have aged, but his eyes were hard as marbles. "Son! Ride for Havalik! I want out of here!"

"You mean to have him take you out? By force?"

"Don't be a fool!" Tetlow said irritably. "How else would he get me out?"

"You're to stand trial."

"Me?" The old man's face was bitter. "Jared Tetlow tried like any common criminal? I never figured I'd hear a son of mine say a thing like that! You git out of here and git Havalik!"

"I'm staying out of it, Dad. I'm staying out because when this is over you'll need money and a place to come to. I'll tell Havalik you're here, but I'll have no part in breaking the law."

There was something approaching hate in the eyes of Jared Tetlow as he watched his son walk away. Then he turned angrily and walked to the bunk.

Ben picked up his guns. "Any law against moving my cows?"

"Not at all," Macy said, "but your herds will have to be cut to get out the stock belonging to other ranchers."

Ben nodded seriously. "Fair enough. I'll cut all I can with the few hands I've got. You can cut them again whenever you like."

"There's a place east of Comb Wash called Texas Flat. You could hold your cattle there with the ridge as east fence." Kilkenny gave him directions for moving the herd.

"Thanks." Ben felt uncomfortable with these men. He started to leave, then hesitated in the door. "That Carpenter affair," he said, "I had nothing to do with any of that."

"We know it." Macy looked up from his desk. "We've no trouble with you, Ben."

"That Carlson you have in there," Ben said. "I don't think he was in this."

"We'll see," Macy promised. "If he had no part in it we'll turn him loose."

Suddenly as it had begun the trouble was over. Business in Horsehead resumed, and the arriving and departing stages began to bring in drummers and other passengers. An official arrived from the governor's office to hear the evidence and make report to the governor himself. It was announced that a special court would be convened to sit on the case.

Jared Tetlow remained in jail. Neither Dee Havalik nor Andy Tetlow put in an appearance. The party from the valley returned to town and Nita Riordan retained Bob Early to represent her and Mrs. Carpenter. Smoke rose lazily from the chimneys of the town and the days stared brightly from frosty mornings. The KR range was grazed by its own cows. The big herd had been split and was fattening on range west and south of town.

A lawyer named Jaeger arrived from El Paso to defend Jared Tetlow after it had been recommended that he be held for trial on a dozen charges including the murder of Jack Harrow. Ben Tetlow rarely came to town. Only at the end of the month did he come to see Kilkenny. He found him at the Westwater, dining with Nita.

"You said something about buying cows?"

"That's right. Will you sit down?"

Hesitantly Ben reached for the chair. "How many could you use? We need cash."

"Depends on the price. I'll buy as many as I can afford."

"I'll make the price right." Ben explained, "We'd have to drive at least a hundred and fifty miles to sell. We'd lose beef and we haven't the time."

They talked, straightening out the details of the bargain. Kilkenny contracted to buy one thousand head of the 4T cattle to be delivered on his range in the Valley of Whispering Wind. Ben's stiffness left him slowly. He found nothing but friendliness in either of them.

When he was gone, Lance looked across the table at Nita. "Well, honey, we're back in business."

"Will you go with him on the drive?"

"Sure. I'll take Cain and Shorty along and once the cattle are in the valley they'll make no trouble." He put his hand on her arm. "I'll leave them there and come back to you."

There was a shadow of worry in her eyes. "You're still thinking about Havalik?"

"I guess so. Brigo saw tracks of a dozen riders in Dry Wash two days ago. Ben hasn't said anything but I know he's lost cattle."

"Would they rustle from him?"

"They wouldn't consider it rustling. Andy's with them, and he owns part of the cattle. They still consider themselves part of the Forty, anyway."

"Do you believe Havalik will leave once Tetlow is sentenced?"

"No." Kilkenny knew he must reply honestly. "No, I don't. Havalik will never leave until he faces me. Dee Havalik intends to kill me."

CHAPTER TEN

BEN TETLOW WAS waiting on the edge of Texas Flat when Lance Kilkenny rode the buckskin toward the herd. He looked tired, and his face was shadowed with worry.

"We cut the herd for you," he said. "It's mostly young stuff."

Kilkenny studied the cattle with care. The herd was not so tightly bunched that he could not make a fair estimate of what he was getting. Obviously, Ben had made no attempt to saddle him with a lot of culls. These were good stock.

"They look all right to me," he said. "I'll take your word for the number."

Tetlow turned to instruct his riders, and Brigo rode up to Kilkenny. "A full thousand, señor. Perhaps even more."

"Thanks. See you in a couple of days."

Ben rose in his stirrups and yelled and the riders moved in on the herd. Slowly it began to move. As always, Kilkenny felt a lift at the sight of a great herd in motion. And soon these would be his cattle, on his range. He would, for the first time, be a man of property. He was through running. Here he would make his stand.

"This a good place you've got?" Ben asked as he joined him at the point.

"Best range in the country. I'll have to cut hay for winter feeding, but I've good meadows and the range I have will carry more stock than most Western range. There are some valleys branching off that can be fed off, too."

They rode in silence for several miles. "What will happen to Dad?" Ben asked suddenly.

"I can't guess. Feeling is changing in the cattle country. They want law and order now, and they'll go a long way to have it. Lots of nesters coming into the country and they'll welcome a chance to see the issue decided in the courts."

"This change you speak of. Won't that make a difference to men like you and Havalik?"

"We're as outmoded as the buffalo. That's why I'm buying cattle. I'm going to work my stock and stay out of trouble."

Kilkenny's eyes went to the narrowing gap between Texas Canyon and North Fork. Cain Brockman, as if sensing his thought, suddenly rode past them, cutting over toward Texas and

Shorty rode into North Fork. Both searched the rocks and brush with drawn guns.

"Nothing stays the same," Kilkenny said. "A man has to go with the times. No man can put a rope on the past and hope to snub it down. The best thing is to learn to ride the new trails."

He glanced at Ben. "You've learned."

Ben shrugged. "Dad says I take after my mother."

"Maybe. You were the first in your generation. You'll have kids and most of them will go the way you do."

From Texas Flat the trail mounted to Long Point and led over the route taken by Kilkenny on previous occasions. By nightfall they would be at Duck Lake. From there a trail led east into the mountains and thence to the valley. Now that there was no pursuit and no necessity for keeping the valley a secret, they need no longer use the devious routes.

By high noon the drive was passing through the Notch. On the far side they paused for lunch and Cain Brockman rode up to Kilkenny and swung from the saddle. His heavy jaws were unshaven and he looked tough and rugged as always. He moved over to Kilkenny, his huge bulk moving with the ease of a big cat. He dropped on his haunches.

He jerked his head toward the west. "They've spotted us. Fresh tracks over there."

"How many?"

"Five in that bunch. Shorty saw somebody over east, too."

Kilkenny finished his plate and got to his feet. He walked over to where Ben Tetlow sat with his men. "I don't expect any of you to do anything but handle cattle. Havalik is out in the hills with a bunch of riders. You leave it to the three of us."

His eyes swept the group. These men had all been Forty riders, had worked beside those men in the hills. On the other hand, these were the best of the lot, cowhands rather than gunmen. And the drive and day to day work had enabled them to see the kind of man Kilkenny was.

A sour-faced man looked up from his beef and beans.

"Three against twenty-five or thirty?"

Swede Carlson shifted his weight. "I never did cotton to Havalik, and this fight's over. So if you need help, count on me."

"Thanks."

The sour-faced man spat. "I'll herd cattle."

Ben Tetlow had sat silently. Now he spoke up. "A man can get mighty saddle-sore trying to straddle a fence. I've made my play and I'm backing it. So I say this. If there's anybody here who figures to help Havalik or Andy, for that matter, he can ride out now. When trouble starts those who want can herd cattle. If any of you want to, you can lend a hand to Kilkenny. It's every man to his own conscience. I'll herd cattle. I couldn't draw a gun against my brother. One more thing. Anybody who decides to help Kilkenny, don't expect anything from Andy. When he starts shooting he ain't going to mind where his shots go. He's my brother, but I want no man to die because of that."

He walked away from the fire and Cain Brockman went to his bedroll and got out his extra gun. Few men could equal him with a pair of sixguns. Kilkenny had beaten him, but nobody else ever had.

Horns bobbing, the herd moved steadily north. Dust arose and filled the air. The lowing cattle and occaional shrill yells of the cowhands were the only other sounds. Kilkenny rode ahead, scouting the trail.

There was a tenseness in the air, an expectation. Cain rode lazily, but under his battered brim his eyes were ceaselessly moving.

If Havalik planned to hit the herd he would not do it until it was in the valley. If he had not learned the circumstances of Ben Tetlow's deal he would be puzzled by the personnel of the riders. Yet there was no reason why he should hold off any attack on Kilkenny or his own riders.

Until the cattle reached the valley it was a Tetlow herd. Once there it belonged to Kilkenny and was fair game.

As the day drew on, Kilkenny grew increasingly restless and irritable. He rode far ahead of the herd, anxious to meet the issue and face it out. His eyes were never still and his nerves were on a hair trigger.

For the first time there was much at stake besides his own life, for now he had definitely committed himself and had bound, both in his own mind and in words, his future to that of Nita. Yet knowing the danger could not be avoided he wanted it to be now, quickly, and then over and done.

Cain Brockman, who knew his friend, watched him warily. When action came it would be explosive. Lance Kilkenny was a man who could be pushed only so far and Brockman could see that a devil was riding him.

Suddenly Kilkenny smelled dust in the air. He swung wide and saw the tracks of four riders where they had cut across the trail the herd was taking. He wheeled his buckskin and rode down the trail after them.

They were standing in a tight group not sixty yards off the trail, concealed from it by a rocky projection. As the buckskin walked in sand they did not hear his approach.

Kilkenny drew up, his right hand resting on his thigh. "Huntin' trouble or just riding?"

They jerked around, their faces written large with surprise. All four were tough men. "What's it to you?" The speaker was a big, wide-faced man.

Kilkenny's eyes had gone flat and hard. For three long breaths he did not reply. Nor did he think. He had it in him, and he felt something rising strong and hot inside him. He walked his horse nearer.

"You've been ridin' with Forty. This herd will be Forty until it reaches my ranch, but I won't have any saddle bums riding my flanks. If you think this is bluff, suppose you grab iron."

Silence hung heavy in the small canyon. The man who had spoken wanted to act, but he knew he looked into the eyes of death.

Fury mounted within Kilkenny. He stepped his horse nearer and, sensing his master's urgency, the buckskin began to tremble. "Come on, damn you! If you want trouble, start it! Otherwsie start ridin' and don't stop until you're out of the country!"

The man with the wide face possessed his own fighting pride. Something exploded within him. "I'll be damned if I'll run! I'll—" He grabbed at his gun butt and Kilkenny slammed home the spurs.

The buckskin leaped like a startled rabbit and hit the other man's horse a glancing blow. Caught off balance, the horse staggered, then fell. And then Kilkenny was in the circle of horsemen, not shooting, but slashing with his gun barrel.

One man caught a blow across the skull and crumpled from his saddle. Another caught the tip of a raking blow that laid his cheek open. Wheeling his horse, he headed south at a dead run, blood streaming from his ripped face.

The man who had talked was struggling to get out from under his horse. The remaining man backed off, hands in the air. His face was white, for he had never seen such berserk fury. "Lay off!" he yelled. "I ain't huntin' it!"

As suddenly as the fury had come, it was gone. "Get down there, and pull your partner from under that horse."

The fellow reached for his belt buckle. "That isn't necessary," Kilkenny told him. "Keep your guns. You might feel lucky."

Carefully the man got down from the saddle and catching the horse by the bridle he helped it up. The man who had tried for his gun lay on the sand. "You busted my leg!" he complained bitterly. "You busted it!"

"You're playing a rough game, amigo. Any time you draw chips you should figure what you can stand to lose."

Nevertheless, he swung down. "Let's get that leg set. Then you can come on to our camp. You're in no shape to travel."

Together they set the man's broken leg, and as they bound the splints the rider who had been knocked out began to groan. Kilkenny jerked his head toward him. "Get his gun. He might start shooting before he has a chance to think."

The rider hesitated. "You'll trust me to get his gun?" He was incredulous.

"You're tough," Kilkenny said, "but you aren't a damned fool!"

Kilkenny retrieved the fallen man's horse, then his own. The man with the Mexican hat was holding his head in both hands. "We'll start for camp. Listen, sorehead, you can make up your mind whether you want trouble or ride away under your own power."

"Trouble?" The fellow looked up through eyes squinted with pain. "I got trouble!"

"Mount up, then, and start for Horsehead."

It was evening when they reached the valley. The long sweep of country lay before them, dotted now with streamers of mist. Far away the mountains were a deep purple with evening except their higher ridges which caught a hint of fire from the setting sun.

"Lord!" Tetlow breathed. "What a country!"

The herd flowed past them, and the heads of the cattle came up, nostrils distended. After two days of driving they scented the flowers, the grass and the pines. They began to trot and then of their own volition, as if knowing they were home, they began to spread out and sink their muzzles in the grass. And then, faintly, the wind stirred.

The cattle felt it, and the men. As if on signal they began to listen. And the wind seemed to whisper faint words, not quite discernible, and the cows moved on, ears wide, stopping from time to time for a mouthful of grass.

"This is where I stop, Tetlow," Kilkenny said. "This is home."

Together the riders bunched and rode down the valley toward the cabin, and there was silence among them.

At daylight the riders from the Forty rode away down the valley, and only Cain Brockman and Shorty remained with Kilkenny. There had been no sign of Havalik, nor of his men.

Two days later, riding among the cattle near the foot of the range, Nita drew rein beside Lance. "What now, Lance?" she asked. "Us?"

"Not yet. First there's Dee Havalik."

"I see no reason to wait, Lance. I'm not afraid."

"You never were."

They walked their horses back to the ranch. Shorty was sitting on the top step whittling and he looked up as they drew near, then jerked his head at a stranger who stood near a saddled horse. "Tetlow wants to see you. He sent this gent."

Kilkenny studied the man, who was a stranger. "Heard anything from Havalik?"

"Not much," the rider admitted. "Most of the men left him. He's mighty mean. I rode with him myself, but he ain't fit to be around. Only one can get along with him is Andy Tetlow."

"How many men has he got?"

"Maybe six. He killed West. The others just drifted off when the chance offered."

"What's Tetlow want?"

"Never said. That jail's mighty hard on him."

Kilkenny tied the buckskin in front of the livery stable and left instructions for his care. Brockman did likewise, and then the two men crossed the bridge to east town.

Leal Macy got up with a quick smile as they entered. "Glad to see you, boys! Tetlow's been asking for you, Lance."

"How's everything?"

"Couldn't be better! Haven't had a fight in town in two weeks and business couldn't be better."

He opened the door to the cells and Kilkenny walked along until he came to that occupied by Tetlow. There had been no attempt at rescue by either Andy or Havalik, yet the old man was ramrod stiff. Ben had sent him tobacco despite his rebuffs. Now Tetlow came to the bars. "Didn't figure you'd come." There was no warmth in his voice.

Tetlow stood silent at the bars, and searching his face, Kilkenny could see no change in the man. If anything he had grown harder, colder. Yet there was a change. There was something cruel in his eyes, something cruel and somehow triumphant.

"I bought some of your cows from Ben. A nice lot."

"He'd no right to sell. Not to you, leastways."

"He stood his ground, played a man's part."

Kilkenny was puzzled. Jared Tetlow made no move to introduce whatever it was he wanted to discuss. He waited, giving the old man time.

"You'd better take care of that man Brockman," Tetlow said. "Andy figures to kill him along with you."

"He's better leave Cain alone. Jared, you don't know about Cain. Neither does Andy. The man's hell on wheels."

He hesitated a moment longer. "What did you want to see me about?"

Jared Tetlow stared at him. Then he turned away. "Changed my mind," he said abruptly.

Kilkenny felt a little alarm bell ring in his brain. Carefully he turned his head and looked down the hall. At the end there was a small window, but there was no one in sight. And there was no one else around. He drew back from the bars, studying Tetlow.

His black coat was shabby and worn. There was a stubble of beard on his jaws. He looked mean . . . like a cornered, half-starved wolf.

"Then I'll go," Kilkenny said.

He had walked three paces and had a hand on the knob when Jared Tetlow spoke. "Maybe I just wanted to see how a man looks before he dies."

Kilkenny hesitated, his mind working swiftly. Then he stepped out and drew the door to behind him.

Macy looked up, but after a quick glance around the office Kilkenny walked past to the door. He stood there, looking up and down the street.

"What did he want?"

Without replying to the questions, Kilkenny stepped out and then stopped abruptly. A man stood in the center of the bridge staring across the street from Kilkenny.

The man on the bridge was Andy Tetlow and he was staring at Cain Brockman.

Brockman stood in the shadow under the awning, bulking, ominous.

And Tetlow took a step forward, then spoke, his voice ringing with arrogance. "All right, Brockman!"

Cain Brockman stepped from under the awning. Two hundred and forty pounds of him, his big head lowered and thrust slightly forward, his thick hands swinging near his gun butts. He stepped into the street but he said nothing.

Kilkenny, who understood such things, saw that Tetlow was surprised. Obviously, Havalik, who knew about Cain, had told Andy Tetlow nothing about the big man. It was apparent from Andy's attitude that he expected an easy kill, but there was no fear in the big man. He came out like a lion stalking game, easy on his feet, utterly dangerous.

"I'm going to kill you, Brockman!"

Andy Tetlow shouted, staring up the street at the big silent man. The realization that all was not as expected was revealed in that shouted statement when no statement was necessary.

Cain Brockman moved forward on cat feet and for the first time Andy Tetlow got the full weight of the menace that faced him. He saw for the first time that far from being frightened the big man accepted the fight with eagerness.

Instantly, Andy Tetlow took a step back and his hands dropped for his guns.

They dropped and they came up but even as his finger tightened on the trigger Brockman's gun flowered with flame and a bullet struck Andy in the shoulder, knocking him back a step and deflecting his aim. A second bullet smashed him in the chest and two drove through his stomach. He fired again, his bullet smashing into the bridge rail, and then Andy fell against the rail, fought for balance and finally got his feet under him. Dying, he turned blindly to face Cain Brockman, but the big man knew no mercy.

Guns hammering, he walked in. A bullet smashed Tetlow's knee, another ripped into his stomach and Tetlow fell back against the bridge railing, which gave way, and he fell heavily to the creek bed, twenty feet below.

As suddenly as the shooting had begun it was over. Leal Macy came running to stand beside Kilkenny and Brockman, looking down at the bullet-riddled body. Blood stained the small creek and the water washed around the body, turning dark the dead man's clothing.

"This country," a bystander said, "is mighty hard on Tetlows. They'd better find a different climate."

"Watch yourself." Brockman looked around. "He wouldn't have been alone."

Kilkenny had been thinking the same thing. It was all very plain now. Jared Tetlow had sent for him to set him up in the right alley for the guns of Havalik. Dee and Andy had divided the work between them, only Dee had not let Andy know what he was facing. It was just like the man.

"We'll need a couple of pack horses," Kilkenny said. "I want to take more supplies home. I'll get Buck."

Lance turned on his heel and walked across the bridge toward the center of town. Doc Blaine, drawn to his door by the shooting, stood talking to Laurie Webster. About Dolan's there was an air of bustle and business. Men loitered on the steps at Savory's, and Kilkenny gave them a quick glance before he entered the big livery stable.

It was cool inside and there was a pleasant barn-like smell of hay, manure and horses. A horse stomped in a stall and blew contentedly through his nose. Several horses rolled their eyes back at him, showing whites. There was no one about as he led Buck to the trough, then went back through the barn and into the wide corral.

Behind this corral was a wagon yard, and to the left of that, another corral. It was in that corral where Dolan kept his stock.

Trees walled both the corral from which he had come and the wagon yard, and the latter was filled with huge old ore wagons. Two freight wagons stood in the center of the yard, not together, and five others stood, tongues pointing high, in a row. Others lined the sides of the yard.

Men had been greasing the wagons and preparing them for use, but they had gone to eat and the yard was lifeless and still in the hot noonday sun.

Kilkenny closed the gate and was about to cross the yard to the other corral when a boot scraped. Instantly he froze in position, every sense alert.

The air was very still. The dust was warm. Cottonwood leaves brushed their polished palms together. He listened, but there was no other sound. Stepping quickly into the shelter of a huge freight wagon, he dropped to his haunches and studied the yard through the spokes of a high wheel.

At first there was no sound of movement, and then through the myriad of spokes of other lined up wheels, he caught a glint of sunlight on a spur!

He dried his palms on his jeans. His sun-browned face was still and cold, his eyes a deeper green. He pulled his hat brim a little lower and touched his gun butts, loosening them in the holsters. He saw the boots again, and the neat, small feet.

Havalik . . .

Rising swiftly, Kilkenny turned and ran lightly and swiftly to the wagons along the corral fence. Ducking behind them, he could see the wagon where Havalik had been. The gunman was gone.

Kilkenny hesitated, studying the situation. The corral comprised approximately an acre of ground, and in it were at least thirty wagons. Kilkenny decided that Havalik had seen him, had been stalking him, and was now about where Kilkenny had been before. Also, Havalik was not aware the trap had failed.

Kilkenny squatted and peered through the spokes. A bullet smashed within inches of his face, stinging it with tiny splinters, and a shot sounded in the stillness of the corral.

He sprang back, and his spring sent him toppling off-balance to the ground. A second bullet nailed the hub of the big wheel near his face, splattering him with fresh grease. Lunging to his feet, Kilkenny ran around the end of the wagon at the same instant Havalik rounded another wagon thirty yards distant. Both men fired.

Havalik's bullet tugged at Kilkenny's shirt collar and Dee sprang to shelter, apparently unhurt.

Kilkenny called out, "In the open, Dee! Let's settle this now!"

There was no reply. Behind him he heard movement. He turned swiftly and saw Dave, one of Havalik's men, with a shotgun at his shoulder. Lance fired and the shotgun bellowed, but Kilkenny's shot had been fired as a man points a finger. The swing, the point in one unceasing movement. The bullet drilled Dave through the shirt pocket and his knees buckled, throwing the charge of shot harmlessly into the air.

Instantly, Kilkenny sprang and grabbed the wagontop,

swinging over the edge and dropping soundlessly into the wagon. He crouched there, listening. The last report gave Havalik six men.

Andy Tetlow was gone. And now Dave.

He waited, letting them look for him. Through a crack in the side of the wagon he saw nobody, so he swung over to the ground again. Seeing movement, he rounded the wagon.

Dee Havalik was moving across the open, but seeing him Dee stopped and swung to meet him. Under the old gray hat Havalik's eyes seemed to blaze with malignant fire. Kilkenny saw the guns come up, lining on his belt, and then both men fired at once.

A bullet tugged at his shirt, and he saw Havalik flinch.

Kilkenny ran straight at Havalik, his guns ready. Havalik lifted his gun to shoot, but the charging man was too much for him and he broke ground. Instantly Kilkenny skidded to a halt and dropping to one knee he shot three times as fast as he could slip the hammer off his thumb. The bullets slammed into Havalik and he backed up, cursing. His gray face was suddenly livid with a red gash where his lips had been. The red grew and blood trickled from both corners of his mouth. Havalik fired and the bullet burned Kilkenny's ribs and Kilkenny fired again.

He saw Havalik jerk as the bullet struck him in the belt and the gunman seemed to shrink, his face twisting. He fired again, and Kilkenny snapped a shot with his left hand gun at the gun barrel that showed through the spokes of a wheel.

Then he walked around Havalik, forcing the wounded man to turn. When he got around on his left side he fired again and saw the bullet strike dust from the man's ribs in front of his drawn-back arm.

Havalik went down then, cursing bitterly. He tried to get up, failed, and fell face down on the hard-packed earth.

The echoes lost themselves against the hills and Lance Kilkenny stood erect and still in the open yard, looking carefully around him.

It was very hot. A trickle of sweat moved down his cheek. He heard a big fly buzz heavily in the sun. Leaves rustled . . . and then there was movement and he turned swiftly.

Havalik was on his feet, swaying drunkenly, his clothing smeared with blood and dust. Kilkenny fired and the bullet smashed Havalik in the teeth. He fell flat on his face, all sprawled out, and did not move again.

A man sprang from hiding and lunged at the fence. He was too slow, for as he grasped the top of the fence and swung himself over, Kilkenny snapped a quick shot that knocked him loose from his hold and he hit the ground on the far side, leaving a finger behind him.

Cain Brockman came into the wagon yard and with him were Dolan, Early and Macy.

Kilkenny walked to his horse, and mounting, rode up the street to the Pinenut where he went inside for a quick drink. When he came out Cain sat his horse, holding the lead ropes of two packed horses. Kilkenny mounted and the two men rode out of town.

Nita saw them coming and rode to meet them. Cain rode on ahead, but Kilkenny waited for her. When she rode up to him he said, "Honey, there's a minister in Horsehead. I think we should go see him."

Her eyes searched his face. "Then . . . it's over?"

"All over."

"Was . . . was it very bad?"

"Dee was in too much of a hurry."

They rode on in silence, their hands joined. Then he stopped abruptly and pulled her to him. Their bodies came together as their horses stopped side by side, and his lips touched hers and melted into welcoming softness, and he felt a strange fire thread through his veins.

And then the wind came, moving among the pines and then down the long grass levels where the cattle grazed, rippling the tall grass into changing gray and green and silver, and the horses pricked their ears, listening. It was very quiet then, in the Valley of the Whispering Wind.

Only the wind itself, whispering words of endearment to its first people.

Hondo

CHAPTER ONE

HE ROLLED THE cigarette in his lips, liking the taste of the tobacco, squinting his eyes against the sun glare. His buckskin shirt, seasoned by sun, rain, and sweat, smelled stale and old. His jeans had long since faded to a neutral color that lost itself against the desert.

He was a big man, wide-shouldered, with the lean, hard-boned face of the desert rider. There was no softness in him. His toughness was ingrained and deep, without cruelty, yet quick, hard, and dangerous. Whatever wells of gentleness might lie within him were guarded and deep.

An hour passed and there was no more dust, so he knew he was in trouble. He had drawn up short of the crest where his eyes could just see over the ridge, his horse crowded against a dark clump of juniper where he was invisible to any eye not in the immediate vicinity.

The day was still and hot. Sweat trickled down his cheeks and down his body under the shirt. Dust meant a dust devil or riders . . . and this had been no dust devil.

The devil had shown itself, continued briefly, then vanished, and that meant that he also had been seen.

If they were white men fearful of attack, they were now holed up in some arroyo. If they were Apaches, they would be trying to close in.

He studied the terrain with care, a searching study that began in the far distance and worked nearer and nearer, missing no rock, no clump of brush, no upthrust ledge. He saw no further dust, heard no sound, detected no movement.

He did not move. Patience at such a time was more than a virtue, it was the price of survival. Often the first to move was the first to die.

Hondo Lane took out the makings and built another cigarette. When he struck the match he held it well back in the foliage of the juniper, keeping the flare invisible. He drew deep on the cigarette, returning his attention to the terrain.

The rough-looking mongrel dog that followed him had lowered himself into the soft earth beneath another juniper a dozen yards away. The dog was a big brute, gaunt from running.

It was hot. A few lost, cotton-ball bunches of cloud drifted in a brassy sky, leaving rare islands of shadow upon the desert's face.

Nothing moved. It was a far, lost land, a land of beige-gray silences and distance where the eye reached out farther and farther to lose itself finally against the sky, and where the only movement was the lazy swing of a remote buzzard.

His eyes wandered along the ridge. To his right there was a shallow saddle, the logical place to cross a ridge to avoid being skylined. Logical, but obvious. It was the place an Apache would watch.

There were junipers beyond the ridge, and broken boulders upon the ridge itself. In less than a minute he could cross the ridge and be in the shelter of those junipers, and if he took his time and made no sudden moves to attract the eye, he might easily cross the ridge without being seen.

He thought none of this. Rather it was something he knew, something born of years in wild country.

Hondo Lane crossed the ridge into the junipers and hesitated briefly, studying the country. His every instinct told him those riders had been Apaches and that they were somewhere close by. Yet the dog had given no sign.

He eased his weight in the saddle and checked the eagerness of the horse, which smelled the water in the river not far ahead.

Finishing his cigarette, he pinched it out and dropped it to the sand and angled down the slope. He slid his Winchester from its scabbard and rode with it across the saddle, keeping his horse to a walk. Vittoro was off the reservation with his fighting men, and that could mean anything. Council fires burned and there was much coming and going among the lodges. Mescaleros had been hunting with the Mimbreños and the border country was alive with rumors.

Hondo Lane could smell trouble, and he knew it was coming, for others and for himself.

Ahead lay the river, and after the rains it would be running full and part of the crossing would be swimming. Lane liked no part of it. Since the rains he had crossed the trails of four bands of Apaches and they had been riding without their women and children, which meant raiding. Young bucks out to lift some hair or steal horses.

He went down the slope to he river, knowing there was no way of avoiding the crossing. He used every bit of cover and changed direction frequently, heading toward an inviting sand bar that led far out into the stream, yet when he was near it he suddenly switched direction and rode behind a clump of cottonwood and willow, going into the water in the shadow of the trees, and quietly, to make no splash.

The dog went along with him and together they crossed. As the buckskin went up the bank, Hondo heard the twang of a bowstring and felt the buckskin bunch its muscles under the impact of the arrow. As the horse started to fall, Hondo Lane rolled free.

He hit the sand on his shoulder and rolled swiftly behind a drift log. When he stopped rolling he was looking past the butt end of the log with his rifle in position. He saw a movement of brown and his finger tightened and the rifle leaped in his hands. He heard the *whop* of the striking bullet and saw the Apache roll over, eyes wide to the sun.

As he fired, he moved, getting into a new position in coarse grass with almost no cover. And then he waited.

Hondo dried his sweaty palms on his shirt front and blinked to keep the sweat out of his eyes. The sand was hot beneath him, the sun hot upon his back. He smelled the stale sweat of his body, the smells of tobacco, horse, and greasewood smoke that lived with him. He waited, and there was no sound.

A fly lighted on the back of his hand, he heard the sound of water running over stones. Around him were the gray bones of a long dead tree. His shoulder cramped.

There was no movement; only a small bird started to land in a clump of brush, then veered away. It was a small bunch of brush and Hondo took a chance. He fired suddenly into the brush, spacing his shots. He heard a faint, gasping cry and fired again at the same spot.

Rolling back to his former position, he waited, then looked past the butt of the log. He saw a moccasin toe dig spasmodically into the sand, then he saw it slowly relax.

Two Indians, or more? He lay still, ears alert to sound. The moccasin toe remained as it was. A tiny lizard appeared on a branch near him and stared, wide-eyed. Its tiny heart pounded, its mouth gaped wide with heat. He dried a palm, then flicked a stone into the brush twenty feet away. He heard it fall, and no sound followed.

Probably not more than two. His mouth felt dry and he dearly wanted a drink. Yet he waited, wanting to take no chance, and knowing too well the patience of the Apache.

Only after several minutes did he ease away from the log and circle to get a better look. The Apache lay still, his lower back bathed in blood that glistened redly in the hot afternoon sun.

Hondo Lane got to his feet and moved closer. The bullet had struck the Indian in the chest. It had cut through his body from the top of his chest and had come out in the small of his back, breaking his spine.

Lowering the butt of his rifle, Hondo took off his hat and mopped his brow with a handkerchief. He looked again at the sprawled brown body of the Indian, then glanced over at the other. Both are dead . . . and this was not a good place to be.

The dog stopped under a tree and lowered himself to the ground, watching him. Hondo glanced at his dead horse, then stripped it of saddle, bridle, and saddle bags. It was a load, but swinging them together, he shouldered them and started off through the trees, walking with a steady stride. The dog rose from the ground in one easy movement and started after him.

Reaching the stream at a bend, Hondo Lane walked into the water on an angle that pointed upstream. When he was knee-deep he turned and walked back down-stream and stayed with the stream for half a mile, then emerged and kept to rocks along the stream for some distance farther, leaving them finally at a rock ledge. When he left the rock he was again walking upstream. He used every device to hide his trail, changing directions with the skill of an Apache, and finally he reached a ridge, which he followed, just below the crest.

The sun sank and the long shadows crept out from the hills, but Hondo Lane did not rest. He moved on, checking distance by the stars, and continuing along the ridge. When he had walked two hours into the night, he finally lowered his heavy burden to the ground and rubbed his shoulder.

He had come to a halt in a tiny circle of rocks among scattered piñons. The rocks rimmed a cup that sat down at least ten feet lower than the hills around. Unrolling his blankets beneath a tree, he made a quick supper of a piece of hardtack and jerked beef. Then he rolled in his blanket and slept.

At dawn he was awake. He did not awaken gradually, but his eyes opened quickly to consciousness and he listened, then glanced at the dog. It lay some yards away, head resting on paws. Hondo relaxed and swiftly rolled his blankets. After a quick check from the edge of the cup, studying the country, he returned and gathered dry branches from the curl-leaf, a shrub whose branches give off a hot flame and are almost smokeless.

He built a small fire under a piñon so what little smoke there was would be diffused by rising through the branches. He made coffee, ate more jerky and hardtack, then eliminated all evidence of his fire and brushed leaves and sand over the spot. Carefully he removed evidence of his resting place and tracks. Then, shouldering his saddle and saddlebags again, he left the cup and started along the ridge.

The morning air was fresh and cool. He walked with a steady stride, rarely pausing to rest. His lean, wolf-hard body, baked by too many suns and dried by winds, carried no soft flesh to melt away under the sun. At midmorning he heard birds chirping and went toward the sound. A shallow basin in the rock held water. He dropped to his belly and drank, then moved back, and the dog moved in, lapping the water gratefully, but with eyes wary.

Among the rocks near the water Hondo Lane smoked a cigarette and studied the country. There was no movement but an occasional buzzard. Once he saw a lone coyote. He drank again, then shouldered his saddle and moved on.

Once he stopped abruptly. He had found the old track of a shod horse. The track was days old, and from its appearance had been made before the rain. Little was left but the indentations. Thoughtfully he studied the terrain around him. It was an extremely unlikely place for a rider to be. No soldier would be in such a place unless scouting for a larger command.

Shouldering his burden once more. Hondo backtrailed the hoof marks, finding two more tracks, then losing them on lower ground where the rain had washed them out. Finally, making a guess, he quartered on his route and cut across the shallow valley, moving toward a place of vantage from which he could see the country.

He saw a bunch of squaw cabbage and broke off a few stalks and walked on, eating them as he went. Twice more he found isolated tracks of that same shod horse, and then suddenly the dog stiffened.

Hondo eased himself back to the ground. There was sparse grass where he lay, a few scattered chunks of rock. He lowered his saddle among the rocks and lay perfectly still. The dog, a few yards away, lay absolutely immobile. He growled, low and deep.

"Sam!" Hondo's whisper was quick, commanding. The growl subsided.

Several minutes he lay still, and then he heard the movement. There were nine Apaches riding in a loose bunch, heading in a direction roughly parallel to his own. He lay still avoiding looking directly at them for fear of attracting their attention.

Nine. At this distance he wouldn't have a chance. He might get three or four before they hit him, and then that would be all. Nor was there any shelter here. Only his absolute immobility and the neutral color of his clothing kept him from being seen.

He listened to their movement. They did not talk. He heard the rustle of the horses through the coarse growth, an occasional click of hoof on stone. And then they were gone.

He lay still for several minutes, then got up and cut across their trail, still occupied with those shod hoof tracks. They had all been made at the same time. This meant a white rider had spent some time in the area. He might still be here. One horse could mean another.

A few miles farther and suddenly the cliff broke sharply off and he was looking into a deep basin at the bottom of which lay a small ranch. It was green, lovely, and peaceful, and with a sigh he started down the slope, walking more slowly.

Below him, near the worn poles of the corral, a small boy was playing. Suddenly, attracted by some sound, he lifted his head and looked up the slope at the descending man.

"Mommy! Mommy!"

A woman came to the door of the cabin, shading her eyes against the sun. Then she walked out to the child and spoke to him, and together they watched the man on the hillside. He walked still more slowly, the fatigue of the long days and his heavy burden at last catching up with even his iron strength. She hesitated, then turned quickly and walked back to the cabin.

Hanging in a holster from a peg on the cabin wall was a huge

Walker Colt. She lifted the heavy weapon from its holster and walked back to the door, placing it under a dish towel on the table where it would be immediately available.

She put her hand on the child's head. "You let Mommy do the talking," she said quietly. "Remember!"

"Yes, Mommy."

Hondo reached the bottom of the slope and walked slowly toward the cabin. As he drew near his eyes went from the house to the corrals and the open-face shed that sheltered an anvil, a forge, and a few tools. His eyes went beyond, searching, still wary. Not even the presence of the woman and child in the doorway dispelled his suspicion.

"Remember," the woman whispered, "no talking."

Hondo lowered his saddle to the ground under the shed and took off his hat as they walked toward him. He mopped his face. "Morning, ma'am. Howdy, son."

"Good morning. You look like you've had trouble."

"Yep. I lost my horse while I was gettin' away from Indians a few days ago. Made a dry camp above Lano last night." He gestured toward the dog. "Then Sam here smelled Apaches, so I thought I'd make some more miles."

"But why? We're at peace with the Apaches. We have a treaty."

Hondo ignored her comment, looking around at the stables. There were several horses in the corral. "Yes, ma'am, and now I've got to get me a new horse—borrow or buy one. I'll pay you in United States scrip. I'm ridin' dispatch for General Crook. My name's Lane."

"I'm Mrs. Lowe. Angie Lowe."

"Can you sell or hire me a horse, Mrs. Lowe?"

"Of course. But I've only got the plow horses and two that are only half broken. The cowboy that was training them for me got hurt and had to go to town."

They walked toward the corral together. Two of the horses were obviously mustangs, wild and unruly. Hondo Lane moved around, studying them carefully. Both were good animals.

"I'm sorry my husband isn't here to help you. He's up in the hills working some cattle. He *would* pick this day to be away when we have a visitor."

"I'd enjoy meetin' him, ma'am." He glanced toward the boy, who was walking toward Sam. "I wouldn't pet that dog, son. He doesn't take to petting. And now, ma'am, if you'll allow me, I'll give those horses a try."

"Of course. And I'll get you some food. I imagine you're hungry."

Lane grinned. "Thank you. I could eat."

Lane hesitated before going to the corral. There was work that needed to be done around here. The little things that are done by a man constantly living around were undone. The recent rains had run off the barn and started to run back under the foundation timbers, gouging out a hole. Another rain and that hole would be much larger. It should be filled and the water trenched away toward the arroyo.

He rolled a smoke and lighted it, then leaned on the corral bars. The two mustangs moved warily, edging away from the man smell and the strangeness. Both had good lines and showed evidences of speed and power. There was a lineback that he liked, a dusky, powerful horse, still wearing his shaggy winter coat.

Lane went through the bars and into the corral, rope in hand, cigarette dangling from the corner of his mouth. The horses moved away from him, circling against the far side of the small corral. He watched them moving, liking the action of the lineback, and studying the movements of both horses.

He talked quietly to the horses and dropped his cigarette into the dust. He was conscious that the boy was perched on the corral, watching him with excitement. Dust arose from the corral, and he shook out a loop. The lineback dun tossed his head and rolled his eyes, moving away from the threat of the loop.

Hondo smiled, liking the horse's spirit. He spoke softly, then moved in. When he made his throw it was quick, easy, and deft. The loop dropped surely over the bronc's head, and the horse stopped nervously. He knew the feel of a rope, at least. That much he had learned, even if he had not learned the meaning of a saddle.

Leading him to the corral bars, Hondo talked softly to him, stroking his neck and flanks. The mustang shied nervously, then began to quiet down. Finally he nosed at Hondo curiously, but shied when Hondo reached for his nose.

Making no quick movements, Hondo walked to the bars and crawled through. When he had his saddle and bridle he walked back, dropped them near the horse, talked to him a little, and then after rubbing his hand over the dun's back he put the saddle blanket on him. Then the saddle. The horse fought the bit a little, but accepted it finally.

Once, glancing toward the house, he saw Angie Lowe watching from the doorway.

Leaving the saddle and bridle on the horse so the animal could get used to them, Hondo left the corral. He stood beside the boy, letting his eyes trace the line of the hills. It was amazing to find this woman and her child here, in Apache country.

Suddenly curious, he walked toward the stable, then circled around the bank of the stream and back to the house. The only horse tracks entering or leaving since the rain were his own. Thoughtfully he studied the hills again, and, turning, walked back to the house.

There was a tin washbasin on a bench beside the door, a clean towel and a bar of homemade soap beside it. Removing his hat and shirt, he washed, then combed his hair. Donning the shirt again, he stepped inside.

''Smells mighty good, ma'am,'' he said, glancing at the stove. ''Man gets tired of his own fixin'.''

''I'm sorry my husband picked today to go hunting those lost calves. He would have enjoyed having a man to talk to. We welcome company.''

Lane pulled back a chair and sat down opposite the plate and cup. ''Must be right lonely here. Specially for a woman.''

''Oh, I don't mind. I was raised here.''

Sam came up to the door and hesitated, then came inside, moving warily. After a minute he lay down, but he kept his attention on Hondo. He seemed somehow remote and dangerous. There was nothing about the dog to inspire affection, except, perhaps, his very singleness of purpose. There was a curious affinity between man and dog. Both were untamed, both were creatures born and bred to fight, honed and tempered fine by hot winds and long desert stretches, untrusting, dangerous, yet good companions in a hard land.

''What can I feed your dog?''

''Nothin,' thanks. He makes out by himself. He can outrun any rabbit in the territory.''

''Oh, it's no trouble at all.'' She turned back to the stove and picked up a dish, looking around for scraps.

''If you don't mind, ma'm, I'd rather you didn't feed him.''

Curiously she looked around. The more she saw of this man, the more she was impressed by his strangeness. Yet oddly enough, she felt safer with him here. And he was unlike anyone she had ever known, even in this country of strange and dangerous men.

Even when he moved there was a quality of difference about him. Always casually, always lazily, and yet with a conservation of movement and a watchfulness that belied his easy manner. She had the feeling that he was a man that lived in continual expectation of trouble, never reaching for it, yet always and forever prepared. Her eyes dropped to the worn holster and the polished butt of the Colt. Both had seen service, and the service of wear and use, not merely of years.

''Oh, I think I understand. You don't want him to get in the habit of taking food from anyone but you. Well, I'll just fix it and you can hand it to him.''

''No, ma'am. I don't feed him either.''

When her eyes showed their doubt, he said, ''Sam's independent. He doesn't need anybody. I want him to stay that way. It's a good way.''

He helped himself to another piece of meat, to more potatoes and gravy.

''But everyone needs someone.''

''Yes, ma'am.'' Hondo continued eating. ''Too bad, isn't it?''

She moved back to the stove and added a stick of wood. She was puzzled by him, yet there was a curious attraction, too. Was it simply that he was a man? That the woman in her needed his presence here? That the place had been needing a man too long?

She stirred up the fire, turned over a charred stick, and moved back to the table. He ate slowly and quietly, not talking, yet without the heedlessness of manner of so many Western men, accustomed as they were to living in camps and bunkhouses and away from the nearness of women.

His boots were worn and scuffed. And there was a place on his left thigh where the jeans had been polished by the chafing of some object. A place that might have been made by a Holster. Only this man wore his gun on his right side. Had he, then, worn two guns? It was unlikely. Not many men did.

''You're a good cook, ma'am.'' Hondo pushed back from the table and got to his feet.

''Thank you.'' She was pleased, and showed it. She smoothed her one good apron with her hands.

''A woman should be a good cook.''

He walked to the door and hesitated there, looking out over the yard, then at the trees, the arroyo, and finally the hills. As he did this he stood just within the door, partly concealed from the outside by the doorjamb. Then he put on his hat, and turning he said, "I'm a good cook myself."

CHAPTER TWO

IT WAS HOT and still in the afternoon sun. The boy perched on the corral bars and watched Hondo Lane lead the lineback dun through the gate, then replace the bars. From the lean-to he got a sack of grain and put it across the saddle. The dun humped his back and sidled nervously away, but when Hondo walked off, leading him, he hesitated only briefly, then followed along.

The mustang was used to rope, and had probably been saddled before, but not often. Angie Lowe had said that he had never been ridden, and there was little time to waste. Hondo walked around the yard a few times, then removed the grain sack and proceeded to take off and put back the saddle several times.

He glanced at the boy. "Gets him used to it," he said. "He'll learn it's nothin' to be scared of. First thing they've got to know: not to be scared. After that, if they find out the man in the saddle is boss, then they'll do to ride."

He talked to the horse a bit, then stripped off the saddle and bridle, returning him to the corral. As he did so, Hondo stepped back and looked around at the hills, a slow, studying glance.

Angie Lowe came from the house and the boy trotted away and began picking sticks from under the cottonwoods, where a few dried twigs and branches lay.

"It surprises me that you picked the most savage horse," Angie commented. "He's always been a fighter."

"Wouldn't give a plugged nickel for one wouldn't fight. Horse without spunk will let you down when the going's tough."

He glanced toward the woodpile and then at the boy, starting toward the house with an armful of kindling.

"Only fair I should trade kindling for a meal." He picked up the ax and placed a chunk of wood against a log, in position for splitting. Then he glanced at the ax. It had no edge. Obviously it had not been sharpened in some time. It was equally obvious that it had suffered much misuse.

"No edge," he said. "I'll turn the grindstone if you'll hold the ax, Mrs. Lowe."

"I'll be glad to. That ax has been driving me crazy."

The grindstone was a heavy, old-fashioned type and turned heavily. He started the stone turning and the rasping whine of steel against stone cut into the clear, still air of the afternoon. He paused in the turning and poured water in the funnel-shaped can that allowed slow drops to fall on the turning stone. "You were raised here on the ranch, Mrs. Lowe?"

"Yes, I was born here. My husband was raised here on the ranch, too."

He glanced at her, starting the wheel turning again. Watching her intent eyes as she moved the ax against the turning stone, he found himself liking the stillness of her face. She was, he suddenly realized, a beautiful woman. Even the hardness of desert wind and sun had not taken the beauty from her skin. But there was a shadowing worry around her eyes that disturbed him.

It made no sense, a woman living like this. Not this woman, anyway. Maybe she had been born to it, maybe she was doing a better job here than almost any woman could be expected to do. It still was not right.

He straightened from the wheel and glanced around briefly at the hills, then bent to the turning again. The woman was skillful with the sharpening ax, he had to admit that.

When he straightened again she returned to the subject of her husband. "He was an orphan. His parents died in a wagon-train massacre. My father took him in and raised him here."

"Handy," he said.

The wheel turned again and the ax showed an edge, carefully honed down now.

He straightened, taking the ax from her hands. She looked at him, not understanding his use of the word. She said as much.

"Figures are against it. Only young fellow in a thousand square miles, only young girl in a thousand square miles, and they get in a whirl about each other. That's what I mean. Handy."

"I guess it was a coincidence. But they say the right two people are going to meet by an arrangement of destiny."

He held the ax in his hands. He looked at her thoughtfully. "You believe that, Mrs. Lowe?"

"Yes, I do."

He studied her for a minute, and she met his eyes frankly, a little puzzled, and faintly excited. He turned away. "Interesting," he said.

He walked slowly to the woodpile. There were several logs and a number of large trimmed branches. There were also some stumps that had been grubbed out, and some chunks of ironwood. These last were all their name implied, hard as iron, but they burned with a bright and beautiful flame.

His first swing of the ax split the chunk he had chosen. Methodically he went to work, and for a few minutes she stood watching him. There was a beautiful and easy rhythm in his movements. He handled his body as if it were all one beautifully oiled and coordinated machine. Nor was he awkward on his feet, as are so many riding men. He moved, she thought, like an Indian.

He did not look up, moving easily from stick to stick. He cut through the log, then cut through it again, handling the ax with the skill of long use. Several times he paused, each time his eyes circled the hills rimming the basin.

Keeping clear of the ax, the boy gathered the big chips into a neat pile, watching as Hondo swung the blade. Sinking it into a log for the last time, Hondo straightened. "Son, always sink the blade into a log when you've finished cutting wood. The edge stays clean of rust."

Angie walked from the house, watching him repile the wood to keep too much of it from becoming rain-soaked at any one time. As he piled it, the boy looked toward Sam, who watched from close by.

The child hesitated, looked longingly toward the dog, then at Hondo. "Pet?"

"You do what you want to, young one."

Hesitantly the boy reached his hand toward the dog. Sam bristled, then snapped. The boy drew back quickly, frightened and half ready to cry.

Angrily Angie turned on Hondo. "Really, Mr. Lane, if you knew the dog bites, why would you—"

"Mrs. Lowe," Hondo said patiently, "I told the boy earlier not to touch the dog, but still he wanted to pet him. People learn by gettin' bit. The youngster learned."

To cover her confusion, she turned sharply on the boy. "Johnny, don't ever touch that dog again!"

Johnny looked up at Hondo, and Hondo grinned, dropping a hand to the child's head. "Don't let it get you, old-timer. You'll get snapped at a lot in this life. Might as well get used to it. Don't trust nothin' too much."

He wiped his hands on his shirt front. "And now I'll get back to that horse."

The lineback had been thinking it over. He was losing his fear of the saddle and bridle, for already he had discovered they did him no harm, but he did not like the bit, and he did not like being led around. Yet he had learned the folly of fighting a strangling noose.

He stood quietly, trembling a little, as Lane came down the rope toward him. He submitted to being tied, and although he jerked his head back several times, he finally took the bit. He worked it in his jaws, not liking it. He jumped a little and tightened when the blanket was thrown over his back, and then the saddle.

Later he would learn to blow himself up against the girth, but that he had not discovered as yet. He felt it tightened and tensed again. The man's voice was soothing, and he was so sure of himself that the horse almost unconsciously relaxed. Then he was led outside and the man gathered the reins.

Angie, half frightened, had come to the door to watch. Johnny clutched her hand, wide-eyed and excited. Hondo Lane stepped into the saddle.

Instantly the horse bunched his muscles and bucked. The man remained in the saddle. Angrily the dun tried to get his head down so he could really go to bucking, but the man in the saddle kept his head up. Then suddenly the reins slacked a little and the lineback began to pitch. He buck-jumped across the yard, swapped ends swiftly, and tried to throw himself over backward. Yet the man stayed with him.

There was a certain brutal beauty in the struggle between man and horse. The mustang, given his chance, decided to make a fight for it. Infuriated by the thing clinging to his back, the powerful horse bucked wildly, but the man remained in the saddle. Seeming to anticipate the horse's every move, he swayed and bobbed with the maddened plunging of the horse, but stuck to the saddle and even seemed to urge the lineback on to do his worst.

And the lineback liked a fight. He put his heart and his powerful muscles into the battle, and with it all the fiendish ingenuity he had acquired in his years on the range and inherited from his bronco ancestors. It was a good battle.

Dust arose, lather flew from the plunging horse, but Hondo Lane stayed in the saddle, and suddenly the horse lunged into a run. He raced down the trail, went under a low branch, and tried to charge into the brush, but Lane was ready for him and swung him into the trail and they went up and over the hill with no obvious slackening of pace.

Behind them the dust settled. The yard was empty of turmoil, the trail dust settled, the skyline of the hill remained empty. Angie waited while the slow minutes passed. Johnny tugged at her hand. "Mommy, will he come back? Will the man come back?"

"Yes, Johnny," she replied quietly. "He'll come back. I'm sure of it."

Yet as the slow minutes dragged by, she began to wonder if he might be lying up there with a broken leg, or if the horse was still pounding off into the desert on that furious run. She watched the skyline, and the skyline was empty.

Nervously she bit her lip, then shaded her eyes to look again, circling the hills as she had seen him do, and as she often did herself.

For the first time she found it impossible to understand her own feelings. There was an element of strangeness about the visitor that disturbed her, but was it only that? Was it his strangeness? Was it the fact that she had been so long alone? Or was there something else?

He kept her excited and upset as she had never been around any man. Why should that be? Moreover, and what was far worse, she was sure he knew how she felt. Yet he did not look like a man who would have seen much of women. He was remote, and—the woman in her told her this—he was lonely.

Yet he was a man who shielded his loneliness as he did all his feelings. He was ruthless, as ruthless with himself as he would be with others. Oddly, despite his strangeness, she felt more at home with him than she ever had with anyone else. When he had as much as called her a liar she had not been offended.

The horizon was still empty. She walked back inside and glanced in the mirror, straightening her hair. Her heart was beating strangely, and it was no way for a married woman to feel, no way for any respectable woman to feel.

That might be it . . . that might be the thing that disturbed her so. He made her feel like a woman. He made her feel . . . yes, that was it. She blushed into the mirror. He made her feel like a female.

She turned quickly away from the glass, a little shocked at herself. That was no way to be thinking. He would be back soon, and she must not even allow such thoughts to enter her mind.

When he came back over the hill the dun was lathered but moving smartly. Lane glanced at the woman in the door and was surprised by the relief in her eyes. Had she been worried about him or the horse?

And this was a lot of horse. The dun had fight. He also had speed and bottom. Lane had not allowed him to run himself out, just enough to let the horse know that the rider could handle that, too. Then he circled and rode back to the ranch.

A lot of horse, all right. Hondo Lane glanced up at the door and at the woman standing there. And that was a lot of woman, too. Slim, but graceful and with a lot of spirit and heart.

"Ready to shoe now, ma'am. And while I'm at it, I'll shoe that pair of plow horses of yours. Their hoofs are clean grown over the front plate."

"Thank you very much. They do need shoeing, I guess."

He led the dun to the stable, stripped off bridle and saddle, and he took a handful of hay and gave the mustang a brisk rubdown. It was new treatment for the horse and he took it nervously, needing time to decide whether he liked it. But again the calm sureness of the man prevailed. There was simply nothing the dun could do about it. He was wary to kick, but he got no chance with this man, who seemed to understand just how he felt.

Lane stoked the forge and heated the shoe. Angie watched, impressed. "You'll find everything there." Then she turned to Johnny, who stood watching with excited attention. "You'd better go to the house and get ready for your nap."

Johnny was hurt. "Oh, Mommy, can't I stay?"

"You'll do as you're told!" Her voice was firm. "Run along now."

With a backward glance, Johnny trudged off toward the house, hating to leave the glowing forge and the ringing hammer, hating also to leave this man who treated him so matter-of-factly, almost as if he were a man himself.

Angie Lowe looked at Hondo's face from time to time, uncertain as to the best words. There was a point she wanted to get across to him, but everything she could think of to say seemed somehow flat and foolish.

Finally, shading her eyes toward the hills, she said, "I don't see any dust coming down from above. I guess my husband's having a hard time finding those strayed calves. Perhaps he won't be home until late tonight."

Lane made no comment, continuing with his work. She watched him, noting the deft, sure movements and the easy way he had with the horse. He seemed almost not to have heard her.

"He might even camp out in the hills and come in tomorrow after you've gone. He'll be so sorry to have missed one of our very occasional visitors."

She looked at his face, but there was no indication of feeling or hint of what he was thinking. Suddenly she was confused and wanted only to get away.

She drew her hands down her apron. "I'd better go look after Johnny."

"Mrs. Lowe?"

His tone stopped her as she turned away, and, half frightened, she looked around at him. He was turning a shoe in the forge, not looking at her. She noted the breadth of his shoulders and the narrow hips. He must be awfully strong.

"You're a liar," he said.

His voice was so calm, so matter of fact that it was impossible to take offense.

"An almighty poor liar," he added.

"I don't understand." She faced him, drawing herself up a little, a picture of dignity and reserve.

There was, he thought, a good deal of queenliness about her at such moments. She had breeding, that was obvious. Not even this ranch and the simple clothing could deprive her of that. It was like seeing a thoroughbred horse in his winter coat. The blood lines were there, despite season or situation.

He nodded toward the horses in the corral. "Those horses haven't been shod in months. Your ax hasn't had an edge on it in just as long, and no man has been using it. The five-pound tea can in your house is empty. Your husband's been gone a long time."

Angie Lowe's face was pale. "Now, see here, Mr. Lane, I don't think you have any right to—"

"Not talking about rights. I'm talking about lies. Why'd you lie to me, Mrs. Lowe? You were scared that you wouldn't be safe with me here and your husband away. That it?"

"That's part of it."

Hondo took the shoe to the anvil and hammered it out. The sparks flew and the ring of the hammer precluded any conversation.

"Women always think every man that comes along wants 'em."

She turned swiftly, chin high, and walked toward the cabin. Her heart was pounding and she had difficulty breathing.

"Besides," she heard him say. "I looked around when I first came. Nobody has been out of here ahorseback since the rain. Maybe not for a long time before."

When he had finished shoeing his own horse, he turned it back into the corral and led out the plow horses. It was growing late but he trimmed down their hoofs and went to work with the shoeing.

He stopped when he had finished with the first of the big horses and rolled a smoke. He stepped away from the stable and inspected the rim of the valley again.

This was a nice little place. The right man could do a lot with it. Of course, it was no place for a woman to be alone, and no right kind of man would ever leave such a woman alone in this country . . . unless he was dead.

He read more into the place than she would have believed. There had been a lot of work done here, good solid work that a man could be proud of, and it had been done by a man with pride in the work. But that had been a long time ago.

Since then the place had been slowly running into the ground, and here and there were the fixings of a man who was shiftless, a rawhider if he ever saw one.

Her father must have built the cabin. It was carefully done by a man who knew his business. It was built of stone, and the stones were fitted carefully. It was logically located both for use and for defense and for shelter from northers. A good man with a rifle could stand off almost any attack from this place, situated as it was.

And the corrals had been well built. They needed work now. The whole place needed work. The roof of the shed needed thatching. The water hole should be cleaned out, too. And once there had been a small dam to catch water in a pool to irrigate a small kitchen garden. The dam had been washed out by some cloudburst and never repaired.

A man could look around and draw his own conclusions. Her father had died, and her husband, whoever he was, had let the place run down. She had been trying to keep it up, but it was a man's job, and she had her woman's work and that child. He was a well-behaved child, and you could always tell what the parents were by the child.

She was a woman, all right. Scarcely more than a girl in years, but all woman. And mighty pretty. He took the cigarette from his lips and looked at it, took one more drag, and dropped it to the earth, where he automatically rubbed it out with his toe. He'd best get on with his shoeing. It was growing late. It was sundown, and in this cup it would grow dark sooner than it would up there on the level country. If you could call it level.

He heard the door close and saw her coming, carrying a water pail. He did not turn or speak as she walked by behind him, but heard her footsteps hesitate a little as if she had thought to speak, then went on. Returning she stopped and shifted her pail to the other hand.

"Mr. Lane?"

"Yes, ma'am?"

"You're right. I was lying. My husband is overdue. In fact, he should have been home long ago."

Hondo nodded. "Figure Apaches killed him?"

She stiffened, shocked at his acceptance of the idea that had occurred to her many times. "Of course not. There are a hundred possible explanations."

She knew of several that she never allowed herself to consider. She had known Ed Lowe enough to understand him.

"Indians are one of them."

"But we're at peace with the Apaches, except for a few renegades who—"

"Mrs. Lowe." Hondo straightened from his job. "If you've got good sense you'll pack up you and that child and come out with me. There's a lot of trouble cookin' in the Apache lodges. The main chief, Vittoro, has called a council. A full report of it is in the dispatches I'm carryin'."

"Oh, no." She shook her head with decision. "We've always got along splendidly with the Apaches. They drink and water their horses at our spring. I haven't seen the great Vittoro, but there've been plenty of Apaches here."

"I've seen Vittoro," Hondo's tone was grim. "Before the

treaty. He had forty scalps hung in his horse's mane."

"But that was before the treaty."

"We broke that treaty," Hondo persisted patiently. "There's no word in the Apache language for 'lie,' and they've been lied to. If they rise there won't be a live white in the territory."

Angie was not convinced. "They wouldn't bother me. Us, I mean. We've always got along well."

Hondo returned to his work. There was little to do now, and he was tired. The hammer drove home the nails, straight and sure. She watched him, noting the way the horses trusted him. Even that wild mustang he had broken had seemed to trust him. And there was Sam, that curious dog. She looked at Hondo's face, wondering what was behind it.

What was he thinking? What, above all, did he think of *her*? Woman-like, she wanted to know. What kind of man was he? What had his home been like? What sort of woman would he want? A queer little shock of something almost like fear went through her. Suppose he was married?

Well, then. Suppose he was? It was no business of hers. What could it possibly matter? Nevertheless, the thought disturbed her, and she looked at him keenly, trying to find the marks of a woman on him, but she could find none. But you could not tell with his sort. A woman made her impression, but it was inside of the man. A woman could change a weak man, but not such a man as this. Yet to be loved by him would be . . . would be . . .

"People I know," Hondo commented on her last remark, "man and wife, got along real well for twenty years. Then she blew a hole in him a stagecoach could drive through. She got mad. The Apaches are mad."

"I have nothing to worry about, I'm sure."

"Nice to be sure."

Sam trotted up as they were talking. The big dog had been away on some business of his own. From the tuft of fur at the corner of his jaw, the business had concerned rabbits. He seated himself several yards away and watched Hondo. Both were somehow remote, untouchable, unreachable. She studied the dog as if hoping to learn more of the man.

"That's a strange dog you have."

"I don't have him."

She was puzzled. "But the two of you are together!"

"He stays with me. He can smell an Indian at half a mile."

He returned the last of the horses to the corral and racked up the old shoes on the corral fence. He looked at Angie as he spoke, and, fighting the desire to look away, she met his eyes.

"He smells Indians? I don't believe it."

"Lots of dogs smell Indians. You can teach them."

"Teach them? How?"

He leaned on the rail, shoving his hat back from his brow. The hair curled damply against his forehead. She repressed an urge to reach up and push it back.

The sun was down but it was still light, and the air was turning cool with the desert night. Long streaks of red remained in the sky, and on the western edge of a cloud there was a blush of old rose. Pale yellow light lingered on the topmost leaves of the cottonwoods, and their leaves whispered in the dry way they have.

Shadows gathered beneath the trees and beneath the western shoulder of the mountain, reaching out in long fingers toward the cabin and toward the man and woman who stood by the corral, talking.

"You get a puppy and hire a tame Indian. Then cut a willow switch and four or five times a day you have the Indian beat the puppy with the switch, and all the rest of his life he'll signal when he smells an Indian."

"Beat a puppy?" She was shocked. "How cruel!"

He shrugged. "That's the way you do it."

"And anyway," she scoffed, "I don't believe a dog can smell Indians. I mean as different from anyone else. You or me, for instance."

He gathered the tools and returned them to the bench beneath the lean-to. "They can, Mrs. Lowe. Matter of fact, Indians can smell white people."

"I don't believe that."

He smiled, and the smile lightened his features with a whimsical, almost boyish expression. "It's true, ma'am. I'm part Indian, and I can smell you if I'm downwind of you."

She was uneasy, but to cover it, she laughed, then shook her head. "Why, that's impossible!"

"No, Mrs. Lowe. It's not impossible."

He stepped around so that he was facing her and downwind of her. She felt a strange tenseness come over her, and fought it, with sudden desperation. He stood close, his nostrils widening, narrowing. For a moment she thought he was going to . . .

"You baked this morning." His voice was matter of fact. "I can smell fresh bread on you. Sometime today you cooked salt pork. I can smell that on you. And I can smell soap all over you. You took a bath. On top of that, you smell all over like a woman. A woman's got a different smell from a man. Not salty and sharp, but kinda soft and rich and warm. I could find you in the dark, Mrs. Lowe, and I'm only *part* Indian."

He was standing close to her and they were both aware of a sudden tension. She started to speak but would not trust her voice. There was something about him . . . It was impossible. It was ridiculous, but there it was.

She drew back a little. She smoothed her apron. "I think I'll go back to the cabin," she said hastily.

She turned swiftly, fighting down an overwhelming urge to run, to escape to the familar surroundings of her own house. To get away somewhere, anywhere, away from him, away from this feeling.

It was wrong. It was all wrong. She should not feel like this about any man.

She told herself it was wicked, but deep within her she did not believe it.

And what sort of man was he? What did she know about him? What could she know? He had said nothing of himself, just nothing at all.

There was something big and hard and sure about him, something in the way he moved, or something from inside of him.

She had the feeling that there was nothing anywhere that could frighten or disturb him. That he was a man who knew himself, knew his strength and his weakness, who had measured himself against the hard land of his living, against the men of that land, and against its wilderness. Whatever he had discovered, he was no longer afraid.

It was dark now, and the wind stirred among the leaves and moaned softly around the roof. She knew that sound. It was a lonely sound, a sound that always frightened her, because it made her know her aloneness. But not tonight. Tonight even the wind had a comforting sound. And why was that?

She avoided the thought, turning swiftly to work, busying herself with preparations for supper, trying not to think of that big, easy-moving man out there in the gathering dusk.

She had known other men. There had been many visitors to the ranch while her father was alive, and some of them had courted her, yet none of them had ever disturbed her as she was now disturbed.

He was moving around out there. She could hear the murmur of his voice, talking to the horses. She heard the twang of a pitchfork prong striking some object. He was feeding the horses. Soon he would be through. Her throat felt tight. Soon he would be coming to the house.

She heard his footsteps on the hard-baked earth. He was coming now. He was coming to the house. She looked blankly around, biting her lower lip as if she had forgotten something. He was coming to the house, and it was night, it was dark. . . .

CHAPTER THREE

SHE PUT HER hand to her hair, looked around, and went to the door as she heard him stop. There was a moment of silence, then a knock.

Angie put out her hand to the door, then took it quickly away. "What do you want?"

"I've fed and grained your horses."

"Thank you."

"I'll bed somewhere near till morning."

She heard him turn away. She hesitated, then she opened the door. He stopped and turned, clearly revealed in the light from the doorway.

"You can't sleep outside. There's a wind rising. I'll fix a pallet for you in the corner."

Hondo hitched his saddle higher on his hip and followed her into the house. Behind him Sam slipped through the door and sat down near it, looking at the room with bright, interested eyes.

Angie turned up the kerosene lamp and Hondo took in the room with a glance. Her bed and Johnny's were in a small alcove, curtained by an Indian blanket. He removed his hat and hung it on a peg, then dropped his saddle in a corner out of the way.

She took blankets from an old trunk and carried them to a corner. She indicated a buffalo robe to him and he spread it on the floor, then covered it with the blankets. She started to bring a pillow, but he shook his head.

"Never use a pillow. Only sometimes my saddle. Too soft. A man can't hear good with a pillow around his ears."

"But you'll be asleep."

"Yes, ma'am, but I wake up easy. This country a man had better."

She straightened the blankets with a few quick feminine, and totally unnecessary movements, then straightened. Without looking at him, she explained, "It would be uncivilized to let anyone sleep outside. And after all, we are civilized, aren't we?"

"Speaking for you, of course. Speaking for me?" He considered it for a minute, then agreed. "I guess you could call me that."

"I have to set some batter for morning. I hope the noise won't bother you."

"It won't." He sat down on his pallet and pulled off his boots, "Good night, Mrs. Lowe."

He drew his pistol from its holster and with the gun in his hand he rolled over on the pallet and pulled a blanket around him. Almost at once his breathing was even and regular. Glancing at him, Angie saw that he was actually asleep.

He must be very tired. How far had he walked that morning? It had been just past daylight when he lost his horse, and it had been a long, very hot day. Yet he moved little in his sleep, and she worked, only dimly conscious of his presence. It had been a long time since there had been a man in the house, and it was a comforting thing.

As she mixed the batter her thoughts returned to Ed. Where was he? Had he been killed by the Apaches? No, he was simply gone, and he might not come back at all. Nor could she wish for him to come back, for these past few months they had grown further and further apart, and he had worked less and less. Most of the time he was gone, finding some excuse to be away in town.

He gambled, she knew that, and returned home only when he was broke. What had seemed to be love she realized now had been merely the natural result of proximity. It was not so amazing a coincidence as Lane had made it seem, for there were no other girls around, and few men. They had been together, and it had been a natural thing for them to talk of marriage. And Ed Lowe had got along well with her father.

In fact, he usually got along well with people when it was to his advantage. He had deliberately set himself to cultivate her father, for in those days the ranch looked good, and it was growing. After her father died, Ed came to realize that a ranch grows only by the work that is put into it, and he gradually let it go, selling a few cattle, breaking wild horses for the Army, and sometimes she suspected, stealing them from the Indians whenever he could.

She had tried. Not even Ed Lowe could deny that. She had tried hard, because she was his wife and because he was Johnny's father. But it had not worked, and now he had gone off and it had been a longtime since she had seen him. Now considering the matter, she knew she hoped he would not come back.

He wanted no responsibility. The chores of the ranch nagged at him and irritated him, and the problem of buying cattle and tending them on the range was not for him. Her father had got along well with the Indians. Even old Vittoro knew him, and they had done business together. Several times he had given the Apaches sugar and tobacco, always sure they understood that it was as a gift to friends and not tribute.

There was none of this feeling in Ed Lowe. He despised the Apaches and feared them.

She put the pan aside and went to the lamp to turn it down. As she did so her eyes fell upon a brass plate set in the cantle of his saddle. She bent closer, suddenly curious.

FIRST PRIZE
Bronc Riding
Hondo Lane

She drew back quickly, startled by the name. Her sudden movement caused a stirrup to fall to the floor, and Hondo Lane was on his feet in one swift movement, gun in hand.

With almost the same movement, she had dropped back to where she had put the Walker Colt earlier. Instantly she lifted it. "You're *Hondo* Lane! The gunman!"

"I carry a gun."

Slowly the muzzle of his gun lowered and he blinked in the light.

"Only last year you killed three men in a gun fight. We heard about it. *Three men!*"

"Yes, ma'am."

He smiled and stepped toward her, reaching for the gun, and in a panic of some sudden emotion, she knew not what, her finger shut down on the trigger. The hammer fell with an empty click and he stood with the muzzle of the gun against his chest, looking down at her.

Frightened by what she had done, she stood helpless while he gently took the gun from her hand. "Shouldn't point a gun at anybody when there's an empty chamber under the firing pin. It can be seen mighty plain. Specially with the light behind it."

He armed the Colt, then dropped it in the empty holster.

"I keep it that way because of Johnny."

"Keep it out of reach, and with a load in the chamber."

He ran his fingers through his hair. "Empty gun's no use to anybody, ma'am. If you need that, you'll need it fast."

"I might have shot you."

"Yes, ma'am."

He turned toward his pallet. "Guess I sort of scared you. Usual noises don't bother me. It's those unusual ones that wake a man. Sorry, ma'am."

He sat down on the pallet and once more he rolled over and drew up the blanket. He was once more asleep. He still held the gun.

Lane . . . Somehow the thought of his being Hondo Lane had not entered her mind. She should have realized who he was, for she had heard he had become a dispatch rider and scout for General Crook.

Crook valued such men, and made every effort to recruit them. She had seen the General when he first arrived on the Arizona station. He had not been in uniform. In fact, he rarely was, and he was traveling without fuss or ceremony. She had heard it said that no man alive knew more about pack trains than General Crook, and he got on well with the Apaches.

She stretched out in her bed, tired but wakeful. She had almost shot Hondo Lane. She had not intended to. So why had it happened? What had she been afraid of? She felt her face grow warm in the darkness and she turned her back on the room, trying to forget his even breathing. Yet she could not forget. And it was a friendly, comforting sound. For the first time in months she slept without fear, without worry.

Outside the wind moaned around the eaves and the cottonwood leaves rustled with their dry, companionable whispering.

She awakened once during the night and lay awake for several minutes. She had been worried about fuel, and now she need no longer worry. And the horses were shod. He had accomplished so much in so little time, and cutting through the big log . . . It would have taken her days.

If she had to leave, the payment for the horse would help. But she could not think of leaving. This was her home, and here she could eke out a living whether Ed returned or not. She could shoot, and she had been able to kill an occasional rabbit or antelope. Johnny was getting older and in a few more years he could take over the hunting and she would at least have the land to leave him. And she could trade with the Indians.

Shortly before daylight Hondo awakened quickly. He sat up, listening, placing the sounds of the predawn hour. Then he got to his feet and slung on his gun belt, dropping the Colt into its holster.

From the window he scanned the ranch yard. There was a faint gray-yellow light in the east. The yard was empty and still. The horses were standing relaxed and lazy. Returning to his pallet, he folded the blankets, then the buffalo robe and placed them in a neat pile upon a chair.

With a glance at the curtained alcove he picked up his hat and boots and eased open the door, stepping out into the brisk chill of morning. Lowering himself to the step, he put on his hat, then his boots.

The horses came to meet him and he forked hay for them. The lineback let his hand touch it before it shied away, and then he went to the creek.

The water gurgled darkly over the stones with little places of bubbling water where it ran around a branch or other obstruction. He removed his hat and, squatting, bathed his face in the cold water. The creek water was miraculously soft and very cold. He bathed his eyes, spluttering a little, and then combed his hair and straightened away from the creek.

The trees were dark and mysterious, and the cold of the morning was bracing and good. A few stars lingered, reluctant to abandon the clear sky to the coming sun. He took his time, skirting around the ranch, looking for fresh tracks, finding none but those of deer that had come down to graze on the greener grass around the edges of the corral.

The garden her father had irrigated was growing, but the few rows were painfully small, and obviously irrigated by hand now.

Across the creek he saw a clump of squaw cabbage and there were no broken stalks. He must tell her about it, for apparently she knew nothing of the desert plants on which the Indians survived.

There was food in the desert if a man knew where to find it, and the Apaches knew. That was the item that defeated the Army. The Apaches lived off the country they passed through, and they knew all the water holes, and could if necessary go for several days without water, just carrying a pebble in their mouths. But the Apaches knew the plants that conserved water too.

Hondo rolled a smoke and glanced around the rim of the hills as his tongue touched the paper. Of course, the food the Apaches loved was mule meat—and that meant Army mules. An Apache preferred it to any other, with horse meat second, and only after that would he consider beef or mutton. Pork he would not eat at all.

Yet there was plenty to eat in the desert if a man knew where to look. Lane crossed the stream and gathered a double handful of squaw cabbage. He was walking back toward the house when the door opened and Angie Lowe stepped out.

"Squaw cabbage," he said. "Lots of it across the creek. Mighty good stew when you boil it with meat. Some folks like it raw."

She accepted the whitish stalks and put them down on the table inside. "Breadroot out there, too," he said, "an' you can grind mesquite beans into flour an' bake them into a loaf."

"You must have learned a lot from the Indians."

"Some," he said. "They've lived here a long time."

He walked on to the corral and roped the lineback. When he led it out of the corral he bridled and saddled it, then went to the house for his saddlebags and rifle.

"You're leaving?"

"Yes, ma'am. Got to go on." His eyes met hers. "Sure you won't come along?"

"No. This is all I have."

"Dam ought to be rebuilt," he said. "Hard to get water in the garden."

"If you're going, I ought to wake Johnny to say good-by to you."

"Was it me," Lane coiled his rope, "I'd let him sleep. Youngsters grow sleeping. But you do what you want to."

"He's delighted with the whistle you gave him. It's more like a flute than a whistle."

Lane felt uncomfortable. He liked to avoid good-bys, and this was leading to one. He fiddled with the girth, rearranged the saddlebags.

"Learned to make them when I lived with the Mescaleros. My squaw used to make them for all the youngsters in the camp."

"You lived with the Apaches?"

"Five years."

She hesitated, but her curiosity overcame her reluctance to pry. "You had an Indian wife?"

"Wife . . . squaw. Took the liberty of borrowing a few feet of rope off that roll in the lean-to. Mine was 'most worn out. I'll be glad to pay you for it if you'll let me."

"Of course, not."

He tied the rope to the corral post, then to the pommel of the saddle, and moved the horse back to stretch the newness out of the rope. She fidgeted, wanting to know more but hesitant to ask. There was no sound from the house. The air was still fresh and cool but carried the promise of a hot day. As he worked, she watched him, reluctant to see him go.

"It must have been interesting, living with the Apaches."

"I liked it."

"This Indian wife you have—"

"Had. She's dead." He spoke quietly, without emotion.

"I'm sorry. I didn't mean to bring up an unhappy memory."

He turned, letting the horse stand. He pushed his hat back on his head and considered her remark. "I don't remember anything unhappy about Destarte."

"Destarte! How musical! What does it mean?"

"You can't say it except in Mescalero. It means Morning, but that isn't what it means, either. Indian words are more than just that. They also mean the feel and the sound of the name. It means like Crack of Dawn, the first bronze light that makes the buttes stand out against the gray desert. It means the first sound you hear of a brook curling over some rocks—some trout jumping and a beaver crooning. It means the sound a stallion makes when he whistles at some mares just as the first puff of wind kicks up at daybreak.

"It means like you get up in the first light and you and her go out of the wickiup, where it smells smoky and private and just you and her, and kind of safe with just the two of you there, and you stand outside and smell the first bite of the wind coming down from the high divide and promising the first snowfall. Well, you just can't say what it means in English. Anyway, that was her name. Destarte."

Rather amazed, Angie stared at him. "Why, that's poetry!"

"Huh? Didn't mean to go gabbing." He looked around at Angie. "You remind me of her. Some."

He untied the rope and began to coil it again without looking at Angie. "Good rope," he commented. "Sure I can't pay you for it?"

"I remind you of an Indian girl? Was she fair?"

He turned and looked at her without emotion. He inspected her hair, her coloring and her face. She flushed as his eyes went over her figure.

"Her hair was black as ten feet down. It shined black like those plums you find up on the Powder. You know how the wing of a crow is shiny? Black and gleaming." He tied the rope to the saddle horn. "That's the way her hair shined." He tightened the knot. "I'd like to pay you for this rope. Dispatch riding I've got the right to give you United States Army scrip."

"You loved her?"

He hesitated thinking about it, his eyes wandering toward the hills. He hitched his belt a little and took out the makings. "I don't know. I needed her."

"But if she was dark and I'm fair?"

"Why you remind me?"

"Yes."

"I dunno. It's hard to figure. I thought about it. You walk like her with your head up."

He put the cigarette in his lips. "You walk like an Indian. You don't toe out like a white woman."

He looked at her and their eyes met. He took the cigarette from his lips and took the front of her dress in his left hand and drew her to him and their lips met. There was nothing forceful about it, and she neither resisted nor helped, yet she was far from merely acquiescent. And when they parted her face was a little pale. She stepped back, not frightened, but not sure of what it meant.

"I'm surprised at you, Mr. Lane."

"No, you're not surprised, Mrs. Lowe. You knew."

"I'm a married woman."

"I thought about that, too. I thought about it a long time. Last night."

She touched her lips with the back of her hand and took another step back. Nothing about it had seemed wrong. It had seemed natural, right. Angie was puzzled at her own feelings and trying to find a meaning for them.

"Maybe I kissed you because you make me think of Destarte. Or maybe because I hate to think of your hair drying, slung from the center pole of an Apache wickiup. But a long time ago I made me a rule: I let people do what they want to do.

"I got it figured now. Handsome woman like you, walks with her head up, ought to kiss a man before she dies."

"You're very strange. Mr. Lane."

He swung into the saddle and the lineback humped its back, then settled down, restless, but aware of the man in the saddle and remembering the fight of yesterday. "I don't know about that," he said thoughtfully. Then he looked away. "Good-by, Mrs. Lowe."

She waited, standing very still in the center of the yard until he went over the hill, and even then she did not move, but stood there, silent and alone in the middle of the bare yard. The dust settled into the trail and the rim of the hills showed nothing but the morning sky, brightening. It would be very hot.

She turned, picked up her pail and walked to the spring.

CHAPTER FOUR

NO MAN KNOWS the hour of his ending, nor can he choose the place or the manner of his going. To each it is given to die proudly, to die well, and this is, indeed, the final measure of the man.

The forty-seven men of Company C rode with an awareness of death, for there were no recruits in their twin files. All were seasoned, desert-wise fighting men who knew the character and ability of their enemy.

The mission allotted to Company C was a wide sweep of the basin to warn, and to bring to the camp if possible, all ranchers, prospectors, trappers, and pioneer home-builders who might still be at large and unaware of the impending outbreak of fresh hostilities. Their commanding officer was Lieutenant Creyton C. Davis.

At thirty-two, Creyton Davis was a case-hardened veteran. Graduated from the Point in time to serve the last year of the War between the States, he had transferred west following the war in time to ride with Carpenter to the relief of Forsyth at Beacher's Island. Later he was at the destruction of Tall Bull's villages in '69.

In the five succeeding years he had campaigned in the desert, working from a series of bleak, wind-swept sun-baked posts against the Apache, that fiercest and wiliest of guerrilla fighters.

Squinting his eyes against the sun glare, he tried to penetrate the shimmering heat waves. Beyond the heat waves were the mountains, and from the liquid movement before them arose the sentinel spires of the saguaro, those weird exclamation points of the desert.

No sound disturbed the fading afternoon, no sound but the creak of saddle leather, the rattle of accouterments, the click of hoofs on stone—and these were always with them.

Sweat trickled through the dust on his face, and alkali had made his uniform stiff and gray. His neck itched from the heat and dust, and his skin was raw from the baking sun. Nowhere, in all that vast expanse, was there movement. Yet out there somewhere was the Apache.

When he saw the solitary rider sitting motionless against the background of the hill, he almost drew rein.

Cotton Lyndon was a square-built man of forty, his face so seamed and lined wih desert years that he looked twenty years older. The nickname was born of his hair, once corn yellow, now pure white, and his one apparent vanity.

He swung his horse alongside the Lieutenant's. He indicated the direction in which they rode. "Water yonder."

"What do you think?"

"They're around. I don't know where."

"See anything of Lane?"

"Won't—not until he wants you to."

"The General expects him. He's overdue."

Lyndon tilted his hat against the sun. "He'll make out." There was a slight change in his voice. "Hope you an' me do as well."

Davis glanced aside at Lyndon, a quick frown shadowing his eyes. Coming from Lyndon, it sounded ominous. Davis knew enough of such men to realize they often knew things without being able to explain why they knew them. It was, he supposed, a result of some subconscious perception.

As if in answer to his thoughts, Lyndon added, "That's Vittoro out there."

Davis let his horse walk on a dozen steps, then turned in his saddle. "Sergeant Breen? There's water ahead. We'll make camp."

Breen involuntarily glanced at the sun. Two good hours of riding left, and Davis was not a man to waste time on a trail.

"We may not find more water and I want the men to rest," Davis said. "A bad day tomorrow."

He felt an immediate satisfaction with the spot. The water was a small stream, clear and cold, that flowed from the mouth of an arroyo scarcely fifty yards deep. At the head of the arroyo the spring flowed down from a dozen cracks in the rock.

The spot selected for the camp was in a basin under shelving rock, and about twenty yards out from the face the ground sloped away, offering a fine field of fire. The camp was masked from the wide plain by a ridge of volcanic rock several hundred yards off.

It was a sudden relief from the saddle and the men relaxed quickly, getting their horses out and mounting guard at once. Old Pete Britton, who had just joined as a scout, went atop the cliff for a look around. There was little talking, the men bathing, filling canteens, and taking the unexpected rest.

The sun declined, the shadows reached out from the cliff, faint smoke lifted from the few fires. Lieutenant Davis walked alone to the edge of the hill and with his glass studied the volcanic ridge, then the plain. He saw nothing.

He had the feeling now himself. Despite that, there was a solid confidence within him. If they had to face serious trouble, he could not face it with a better company of men. Sergeant Breen had a record of twenty years of service, and he had been in the Southwest when Mangus Colorado was active, and Cochise. After that he had seen service at Bull Run, Shiloh, and the Wilderness.

Corporal Owen Patton had ridden with Nathan Bedford Forrest, and had been a lieutenant himself. He was a tall, rangy young man with blond hair that waved back from his brow. He was the best shot in the company, and one of the finest horsemen. O'Brien had been a freighter before he joined up, veteran of many Indian battles. Silvers and Shoemaker had been buffalo hunters.

The faint, smoky haze of evening lay over the desert, and the clouds were tinged with the rose of the setting sun. Davis stopped by the spring, drank of the cold water, then walked back to where his bedroll was dumped against the cliff's face. He threw his campaign hat aside and sat down, digging writing materials from his saddlebags.

Lyndon opened his eyes and watched him. It was the first time he had ever seen Davis writing on patrol. Sergeant Breen noticed it, too, and looked quickly at Lyndon. No courier was being sent back. The command would return in just two days . . . if it returned.

Breen checked the guards and added a word of warning, then returned to camp. Lyndon was lighting his pipe.

"Too quiet out there," Lyndon said. "I wish Pete woud get back."

"Comin' now."

Pete Britton had lived fifty hard years, forty of them in Indian country. He did not stop, nor did he look toward Lyndon and Breen, but walked on by to where Davis sat.

Davis glanced up. "Yes?"

"No use to ride by the MacLaughlins'."

Davis felt something inside him go sick and empty. He had liked the MacLaughlins, had sat at meals with them more than a dozen times. Three stalwart men and two women, four youngsters.

"You sure?"

Pete Britton's irritation sounded in his reply. "Sure? Ah'm almighty sure." He jerked his head to the north. "Smoke. Too much for a small fire. That barn an' house, most like, sometime this afternoon."

Lieutenant Creyton C. Davis sat very still, the trial of command before him. If he moved out now, one or more might still be alive. He might affect a rescue. On the other hand, he would be riding off into darkness with tired men against a relentless and ruthless enemy that would know he was coming. And if they were gone, the tracks could not be followed before daybreak.

If he led out his command and men were lost, he would be asked why. If he did not lead them out and some of the family could be saved, he would also be asked why. He sat very still, then said quickly, "Thanks, Pete. Anything more you can tell me?"

Pete Britton shook his head. "Daylight, mebbe."

The old man turned and walked away to join Breen and Lyndon, who had listened. Britton jerked his head. "Ain't no fool. Afeerd he'd want to go traipsin' after them in the dark."

Breen shook out his bed and pulled off his boots. He sat for a minute, looking off toward the first faint stars, then he rolled in his blankets. When he finally dropped off to sleep he could still hear the faint scratching of the Lieutenant's pen.

In the first clear light of dawn Davis stood over the campfire with a cup of coffee. He glanced around for Britton.

"Pulled out before sunup," Lyndon said.

Horses were led out and saddled and mounted, and the company moved out. Dust lifted, sun glinted on rifles. Davis swung his horse into the trail toward the MacLaughlins'.

Lieutenant Davis did not doubt that Britton had been correct, but it was his duty to check, and to bury the bodies if they were to be found. It was, he reflected, no pleasant task for such an early morning.

With a lift of his hand, Cotton Lyndon moved out to the flank and angled up the slope. Davis watched him, frowning slightly then turned in his saddle. "Sergeant?"

"Yes, sir?"

"We're riding into trouble. I don't know where it will come from or when. Pass, the word along. No lounging in the saddle, no carelessness. I want every man alert. This is no routine patrol."

Breen dropped back, and Davis let his eyes go again to Lyndon. The man was riding quietly, keeping his mount to the crest of the ridge and in such a position that he could see over without exposing more than his hat and eyes.

Dust climbed, the sun grew warm. Through a notch in the trees Davis saw a fleck of bright green. That would be the cottonwoods at the MacLaughlin ranch.

As they came out of the draw into the wide valley, all was still in the morning sun. Where the ranch house had stood they could see blackened ruins and a slow lift of smoke. Davis tightened his lips. His eyes swung around the valley.

"Sergeant?"

When Breen moved up, he said quickly, "As we move in I want a perimeter defense. Detail a burial party. There'll be bodies down there. Have Corporal Patton take six men and sweep those woods."

"You think they're still here, sir?" Breen was dubious. "It ain't like them, sir."

"They're Apaches, Breen."

"Yes, sir. Of course, sir."

Breen dropped back. The Lieutenant was right, of course. There was no telling what an Apache might do, except that it would be the most unexpected thing. Breen had heard it said that Davis was too careful. With Apaches a man could not be too careful.

The company moved into the ranch yard and swung down. The bodies were there. After a quick glance, Lieutenant Davis turned aside. MacLaughlin, his two sons, and the women. They had all died here. It was better than being prisoners, except, perhaps, for the children. The Apache, a cruel and vicious fighter, was kind to children, often adopted them into the tribes and treated them gently. With women it was otherwise.

He glanced around. Patton was moving out with six men toward the small grove of trees, the burial party was working, other men had moved out, and the perimeter defense was set up. Suddenly Davis glanced around. There was no sign of Lyndon.

Anxiously he walked to the edge of the yard and glanced around the hills. No rider, no dust.

Breen walked toward him, hat in hand, mopping his face. "Nasty job sir. They're hacked up mighty bad."

"How many do you think?"

"Maybe a dozen. Not more'n twenty." Breen put on his hat. "Nothing we could have done, sir. It was earlier than Britton thought. Yesterday morning, I reckon." He indicated the corral. "Horses didn't eat all the hay they were fed."

Davis nodded. It fitted what he himself had observed. The Indians must have been waiting out there at daybreak, lying perfectly still, probably scattered around the ranch.

MacLaughlin had died at the corral, struck down by three arrows. Jim MacLaughlin, the older of the boys, had evidently received some warning, for he had rushed to the door, gun in hand. There was a spot of blood at the barn that could mean a dead or wounded Indian. And Alex MacLaughlin lay sprawled and dead with an overturned bucket beside him.

"Must've been comin' from the spring," Sergeant Breen said, "an' he saw something and yelled. Then they got him. Jim rushed to the door, an' he stood 'em off a spell. One of the women had her hands blackened like she'd been firin' that old muzzle-loader."

Davis tightened his lips. Corporal Patton stopped before him and saluted sharply. "Woods clear, sir. Found where several Indians had bedded down, sir. Looks like they'd remained some time."

The burial party was returning, their faces gray and sick.

"All right, Sergeant. Mount up."

They were in their saddles and moving up when they saw the rider. A horse was coming down toward them at a dead run and on the back was the bobbing figure of a man. It was Cotton Lyndon.

But it was such a Cotton Lyndon as they had never seen. The proud white mane of hair was stained red with blood. Strips had been peeled from his hide. Blood streamed from his wounds and stained the sides of the paint pony on which he was tied.

Patton raced out and caught up the horse and men surrounded the dying man. For an instant, as his body was lowered to the ground, Lyndon's eyes rolled up to Davis.

"Vittoro. Must have seventy . . . men." Lyndon caught at Davis' sleeve. "Get out! Get out, Davis, while you can!" He choked, but clung with agonized grip to the sleeve. "Stalkin' you! Mescaleros, Mimbreños, Chiricahuas, an' Tontos . . . all up! More comin'! Get to . . . fort."

The scout's body saggged back to the grass. Lieutenant Davis straightened. "All right, Sergeant. Bury him here, where he lies."

He swung back into the saddle. No sign of Pete Britton. No sign of an Indian. And he had not met Hondo Lane.

Lane was out there somewhere, and his dispatches were important. His thoughts leaped ahead, placing the few outlying homes. The decision was his, and it might mean life or death for the poor unwarned devils who were at their ranches or in camp. It might also mean the end to his command.

He glanced around at them, his face expressionless. He knew every man of the company. Knew something of their troubles, trials and tribulations. Clanahan, who drank too much, Nabors, who was surly and hard to get along with, and Sandoval, who wore a knife scar he had picked up from a *señorita* in Tucson.

They moved on into the desert and the morning. Lieutenant Creyton C. Davis rode beside the guidon now. His eyes reached out to the hills, and he thought of Vittoro.

Cunning as a wolf, the old chief was a fierce and vindictive fighter. His treatment of Lyndon had been a warning of what he intended for them all, if they were caught alive. And how had he caught Lyndon alive? Cotton Lyndon, who knew so well all the Apache tricks? And where was old Pete?

The command moved on, trotting now, and swung around a group of low hills. They passed another burned-out ranch, and buried the dead. Davis hesitated, then made his decision. "Sergeant, have the men refill their canteens here. We'll swing south toward Mescal Springs. When we reach the open country we'll dismount and walk the horses."

"Dismount?"

"Yes, Sergeant." Davis hesitated, then said quietly, "We're going back, Sergeant. These ranches are answer enough. There's no reason to go on. If anyone is alive up ahead, they know more about the Indians than we do." He paused. "We'll dismount in the open country where they can't ambush us. That will rest the horses. We'll make camp early, as we did last night. When the men have rested we'll mount up and move out slowly. I dislike to leave a good fight, but if the tribes are out, the General should be informed.

"Moreover," he smiled, "we may get a chance to trap the old boy himself. He's waiting for something, you can bank on that. For more warriors, possibly. I think he's waiting to get us in rougher country, where he can use an ambush. If he thinks we'll go on south of Mescal, he'll probably wait. There isn't better ambush country in the world."

Breen nodded, waiting. Lieutenant Davis had always let him know just what he was thinking. There was nothing of the martinet in the man and he believed that if the men knew the score, each could carry on in better fashion.

"Once he knows we've started back, we'll have a fight."

"Does the Lieutenant hope to lead him back?"

Davis hesitated. "If we can, Sergeant. If we can."

The plain opened before them, and once they were well into it, he slowed the column and dismounted the men to save their horses. Apparently they were moving into rugged country where by tomorrow every mile would offer a new trap. Would Vittoro wait? Or would he attack at the first opportunity?

Vittoro might be waiting for a contingent of Apaches from another tribe. A successful battle and much loot would do much to cement the allegiance of his allies. Nobody would realize this better than Vittoro.

They walked slowly. It was very hot. Dust arose. A road runner darted away ahead of them, a streak of dull brown against the desert. A rattler buzzed from under a mesquite bush. They walked on.

A mile, three miles. The hills were dawning nearer now. No sign of Pete Britton.

The Lieutenant mounted the column and they moved out at a walk, and they came up to Mescal Springs at four in the afternoon. Under doubled guards, they bedded down for a rest.

The sun dropped behind the hills, long shadows reached out, the mesquite clumps turned to blobs of blackness against the gray of the desert. Horses had been rubbed down and watered, a few fires were lighted, coffee was made.

Against the boulder where he sat, Lieutenant Davis waited. He was a slender young man with a face darkened by desert suns, a pleasant face, composed and still now.

He signaled Breen and Patton. They drew near and then dropped to their knees as he motioned to them. "We'll move out at midnight," he told them, "keeping downslope in the sand. If we get away, when we're a mile out we'll mount up. Then we'll move at a trot."

When they had gone, he turned to his blankets and stretched out. He would not sleep, he knew. He might rest a little. . . .

A hand was shaking him. It was Breen. "Time, Lieutenant. Midnight."

Davis sat up, amazed. He had slept for hours. Quickly he was on his feet, straightening his uniform, checking his gun. His horse was saddled and waiting.

All was dark and silent. Taking the lead, he moved out. The slope was soft sand and stoneless, as was much of the valley bottom. The small column moved without sound.

For ten minutes they walked. Corporal Patton moved up from the rear. "Seems quiet, sir."

"All right." He turned. "Sergeant, pass the word along. Mount up. Walk the horses another ten minutes."

After ten minutes he lifed the column into a trot. Holding the pace, they held on down the valley. If they had escaped the Indians, there would be no following them until morning. It would give them a safe lead. He was already thinking ahead, checking over the country in his mind, and he knew the place.

It was not a good place for an ambush, hence was sure to be unexpected by Vittoro. There was a place among low hills. . . . He rode on, heading directly for the fort, yet his plan was made. It was a chance to trap Vittoro and he meant to take it. The defeat of the Apache war chief might easily end the outbreak. Certainly it would end the trouble for a time. Until another chief was selected.

He held the horses to a trot for an hour, then slowed to a walk. All night they moved steadily, taking only two short breaks. At daybreak the country was opening out and by noon they would be less than forty miles from the post.

Suddenly he saw the hills. It would be here. . . . He halted the column and quickly gave his orders. On the spot, the situation looked even better than he had remembered.

The valley down which they had been riding had ended, leaving them in a country of rolling hills. Two low hills lay on each side of the meadow, and he rode down this meadow, then moved to the right and concealed his horses in a draw. On the far slope of the hill there were several hollows ideal for concealment.

"Corporal," Davis looked at Patton, "Take Silvers and Shoemaker and get behind that hill opposite. When the enemy are well into the meadow, fire on them. I want three Indians down with those three first shots. Then fire again, get into your saddles, and swing wide and get back here. Understand?"

"Yes, sir." Patton hesitated. You're going to be here, sir?"

Davis nodded. "When you fire, I think they'll run to this hill for shelter."

"Yes, sir."

Silence fell, the little dust settled. The sun rose well into the sky, the earth smelled faintly. A few flies buzzed. An hour passed slowly. Men drank from their filled canteens.They waited.

Clanahan saw them first. Davis felt his scalp tighten. They had been strengthened. There were more than seventy. There were ninety or more.

No matter.

They seemed to have no fear, no realization of what lay ahead. They rode steadily down the meadow. Two Indians were well ahead, and suddenly one of them drew up sharply. Instantly Davis knew the man had seen the bent grass where the horses had turned. The Indian wheeled his pony and yelled sharply.

From across the meadow there was a crash of shots. The Indian fell headfirst off his racing pony and turned head over heels in the grass. Two more fell, the other lead warrior and one man in the column.

It worked perfectly. Instantly the Indians broke for shelter, charging the hill behind which lay Davis and the company.

They came on a dead run, and Davis let them come. At point-blank range he fired. A crashing volley hit the charging Indians and those in the lead went down in a wild melee of screaming, wounded horses and yelling Indians. Firing coolly, Company C poured lead into the mass below. And then the Indians were out and running.

Scattered shots, then silence. Corporal Patton came up at a dead run and swung down. He saluted swiftly. "Silvers gone, sir. Tangled with a 'Pache and both of 'em gone, sir."

"Thanks, Corporal. Get set. They'll be back."

There was sporadic firing, and Davis studied the shadow and the slope. The ambush had taken seventeen Indians and half again that many horses. A number of wounded had been carried away.

He studied the grassy plain where the Indians had disappeared. There was a faint stirring of the grass. He fired into the grass and saw an Indian half rise, then sink back.

He studied the situation. Nothing more to be gained here by sniping fire. In any event, they had taught Vittoro a lesson.

"Sergeant?"

"Yes, sir?"

"Get the horses. We'll move on."

Clanahan's voice boomed. "Lieutenant! *Look!*"

Davis wheeled and saw the rider. At first he thought it was an Apache, and then he knew no Indian ever rode like that. The man was hunkered down low and riding hard, but he had stirrups and there was a flash of sunlight on polished leather, and then he recognized the horse.

The rider was coming at a dead run and he did not slow up until he had plunged into the very circle of soldiers. Then he drew up sharply, his horse rearing high, and he slid to the ground. It was Pete Britton.

His hard old face was gray and there was blood on his shirt. "Lieutenant," his voice was calm, "you got more'n a hundred Mimbreños comin' up behind you."

Lieutenant Creyton C. Davis stood very still. He had his hat in his hand and he felt the wind stirring his hair. "What chance of getting through to the fort, Pete?"

"Not none a-tall." Pete Britton hesitated, then he said quietly, "I caught me a brave. He wasn't so brave an' he talked. He said forty Mescaleros left the reservation last night. There's more Mimbreños comin', too. You're boxed in, Lieutenant. My guess is what we know ain't but part of it. I figure half the Apache nation is betwixt us an' the fort."

"Could you get through?"

"Might."

"I want a message taken."

Old Pete spat into the dust, then he grinned slowly. "Lieutenant, git yo'self another boy. I got a crease in my hide back yonder. I ain't fixed for ridin'. Anyway, I've took a lot of 'Pache hair in my time. I'll give 'em a chance at mine."

Davis put on his hat. "All right, Pete. Glad to have you."

"They'll know soon enough," Pete said dryly. "Anyways, I'm agittin' rheumatic these days. Figure I'd like it better thisaway."

Lieutenant Davis turned to Breen. "All right, Sergeant. Have the boys dig in and get settled. We'll wait for them."

Wind stirred the grass. Sweat trickled down his face. He shook his canteen. It was over half full. They moved back to the rim of the hills around the tiny basin where the horses were held.

There was dust to the south, and away there to the east there was dust. He mopped his brow and waited. He took the letter to his wife from his pocket and thrust it conspicuously over a spear of bear grass.

He settled down and lighted a smoke. Clanahan was squatted on his heels and he grinned at the Lieutenant. "Wished I had a drink," he said. "I could get drunk without makin' the guardhouse."

Davis turned and reached into his saddlebag. He drew out a flat bottle and tossed it to the burly Irishman.

Clanahan grinned and caught the bottle in his big palm. The pulled cork made a comfortable sound. He tilted back his head and drank.

There was no sound but the wind, no movement but the bending grass.

CHAPTER FIVE

HONDO LANE WALKED the lineback into the willows and let the horse plunge his dark muzzle into the cold, clear water of the stream.

Day had come but the sun was obscured behind towering masses of thunderheads. The morning was cool. There was no wind.

Two days out of Angie Lowe's ranch and he had just reached the bank of Little Dutch Creek. At this rate he would be four days getting to the post. If he got there at all.

Twice on the first day he had cut the trail sign of small Apache bands. Yesterday, after swinging wide to try to avoid further meetings, he had narrowly escaped being seen on a grassy hillside.

Luckily he had left the lineback in an arroyo over the ridge, so he flattened out in the grass and lay unmoving, and so unseen.

Thunder rumbled like the booming of far-off guns. The cumulus had darkened. Hondo flattened beside the stream, drank, then filled his canteen. Sam had crossed the stream and was drinking there. His head came up sharply, muzzle dripping water.

Hondo caught the lineback's nostrils and held them.

Two Mescaleros came up the creek, one of them riding a big chestnut horse with a U.S. brand. The other wore a lieutenant's blue coat, now dusty and darkly stained.

Not twelve feet away they stopped. Hondo slid his bowie knife into his hand. A gun would be more certain, but how far away were other Indians? He took a quick, sure step.

The Mescaleros turned like cats and he lunged. The nearest Indian struck down barehanded at the knife blade . . . too late. The blade went in hard and Lane jerked it across and free. The Mescalero grabbed his wrist and pulled Hondo down, dying under him.

Jerking free, Hondo rolled over, and then he saw that the other Indian was down. Over him, humped in awful fury, was Sam. The big dog had sprung from close up, and the startled Apache had no chance with ninety pounds of snarling, driving fury on top of him.

Lane scrambled to his feet and put a hand on the dog. "All right, Sam."

Reluctantly the dog let go. There was a long scratch on his ribs. Ears pricked, still growling, he walked stiff-legged around the dying Indian, then at another word from Hondo he turned and went into the cold water, lying down.

Lane peeled bridle and blanket from the horse with the Army brand and turned it loose. There was a bloody scratch on the flank not yet a day old.

The Mescalero with the officer's coat had something else. Hondo stopped and pulled it from the pocket. The guidon of Company C, trampled, dusty, and bloody.

He stepped into the leather and moved off, riding with caution. there was a faint stirring in the grass now, and there was a smell of dampness in the air. Sam moved far out on the flank, trotting with his head up, knowing the danger.

Then he saw the buzzards. They were low down over a distant hill. He put the lineback into a trot, and then, turning in the saddle, he looked back. Only the long grass moved, only the distant hills lined the horizon.

He inhaled deeply, liking the cool, fresh air. He rode down into the long valley down which the Apaches had come.

At least eighty warriors, likely more. Davis had been outnumbered two to one. He puckered his brow. The Indians had been moving right along, not like men going into battle.

The first thing he saw was a dead pony. He drew up, scanning the ground. He counted nine more, moved ahead, and saw too many to count. There was blood on the grass where men had fallen. He saw a spot of white. It was a dead trooper, stripped and mutilated.

Swinging right into the hills, he saw several brass cartridge cases. Two, three men here. He saw it then. Ambush. Not by the Indians, but by Lieutenant Davis and Company C. And they had hit hard at the moving Apaches.

On the opposite hill, toward which the Apaches had fled for shelter, he saw more horses and several spots of white.

Atop the hill he drew up, looking around. He saw all that remained of Company C, the naked bodies of the dead, fallen in their blood and their glory as fighting men should. Some were scalped, many were not.

Lieutenant Davis had been shot three times, twice through the body, then a finishing shot throught the head. His body was not mutilated. Neither was that of big Clanahan, lying close by.

They had died together, the Lieutenant and the malcontent.

Nearby lay a broken whisky bottle. Hondo Lane rolled a smoke and lit it, knowing what had happened here. That bottle had belonged to Davis, and at the end he must have given it to Clanahan. Hondo could picture the scene . . . the Lieutenant giving the bottle to the man he had several times sent to the guardhouse for drunken brawling, but a man who died well beside an officer he understood.

He drew deep on the cigarette. This was no place to stop. Yet he hesitated, looking for the one man who should be here. He saw him then, some thirty yards away.

Old Pete Britton had outlasted them all. That was evident from the scattered shells around his body. Despite the Apache's need for weapons, the two rifles he had used were not taken. His body was unmutilated. These were signs of respect paid by the Apaches to a fighting man.

Judging by the signs, the old man must have held out at least an hour longer than the others. On his hard old face there was a taunting, wolfish grin. He had defeated his ancient fears of loneliness, sickness, and poverty.

Only when he was once more in the saddle did he see the fleck of white on the blade of bear grass. It was a thick letter, addressed to Mrs. Martha Davis.

Turning down the valley, he saw the rest of the story. The ambush had worked, a decisive blow if not a conclusive victory. And then the Mimbreños had come up from behind. The unknown factor. . . .

Briefly he scouted around, reading the last grim details of the story, written plainly here. Then he started the lineback down the long valley at a steady trot. So it had started, then, and with a crashing victory for the Apaches. Yet a victory that had cost them much. The Apaches carried off their dead and wounded, but there were bloodstains on the grass and many of them marked where men had died.

He rubbed the scrabble of beard on his jaws, staring bleakly into the west. He felt the stir of wind upon his neck, the grass bent around him, and the lineback's mane streamed away, and with the wind came a few large, scattered drops of rain.

Turning, the slap of rain against his hard cheeks, he dug into the bedroll for his slicker. When he had it on, he kept to low ground, off the hills where lightning would strike. And then came the rain and the wind. It struck with a solid blow. There was an instant of pause, then the downpour. Thunder roared in the distance, then lightning snapped at the ridge to his right and there was a smell of brimstone and charred grass.

The lineback moved out, wanting to run, and he let it go. The rain roared down and the wind swept it along the grass. In a matter of minutes there was a trickle of brown water down the valley, then a widening rush. He moved the horse to ground a few feet higher and pushed on.

Suddenly an arroyo cut the ground across before him. Already the sand was damp and there was a trickle of water. He hesitated, hearing the roar of the water coming downstream, knowing that wall of rolling water would be upon him in seconds. Then he gambled.

He put the lineback down the bank and slapped him hard on the hip. The startled animal leaped from under him, and, snorting in terror, was running, belly down, across the arroyo. Almost in the middle he saw the wall of water upstream, bearing great logs on its crest. Bank to bank the rolling wall of brown water rushed at him, and he slapped spurs to the lineback and the horse gave a pain-maddened lunge and reached the bank. Its hoofs slipped in the clay, then caught, and with two great bounds the horse was up and away from the water.

"Good boy." Hondo patted the horse's shoulder. "You'll do to take along."

The horse tossed his head impatiently and they pushed on. Rain pelted them, the sod turned soggy underfoot, waves of wind washed over them, and great whips of lightning lashed the darkened hills. Stones glistened like gems, and the gray veil of the rain strained out the distance and left nothing but the wet and roaring world through which they moved, man and horse, joined now before the common terror of the storm.

A dozen times he turned aside, working away from torrents of white water roaring down arroyos. Once he saw a great cottonwood uprooted and lying upon its side. He saw tall grass flattened to the ground, and hail beat upon them, then passed.

There was no stopping, for there was no place to stop. He rode on, half stunned by the driving fury of the storm, remembering the house in the basin and wondering how Angie fared. She should have a man. It was not good for a woman to live alone. Nor a man.

And that boy . . . The lad needed a father.

From a low place in the hills his eye caught a glistening something, and he reined over and rode nearer. It was a low roof, a stone-faced dugout in the side of a hill. He rode the horse down and, swinging down, opened the door. It was roomy and dry within.

It was a struggle to get the horse through he door, but he made it. At the back of the dugout there was a dirt-floored cave where there was a hitch rail and a trough. He shucked out of his slicker and took wood from a pile of mesquite roots and built a fire in the crude fireplace. There was a little grain left in the bag brought from Angie's, and he hung a feed bag on the horse, then wiped him as dry as possible.

The fire blazed up, the room grew warm. Hondo barred the

door and fixed a meal, then lay down on the boards of the bunk and dozed. The firelight played on his face, the rain roared and pounded on the roof overhead.

What kind of man could leave a woman like that in Apache country? His eyes were suddenly wide open and he was angry, thinking about it. She was all woman, that one. And a person . . . a real person.

Somewhere along the tangled trail of his thoughts he dropped off and slept, and while he slept the rain roared on, tracks were washed out, and the bodies of the silent men of Company C lay wide-eyed to the rain and bare-chested to the wind, but the blood and the dust washed away, and the stark features of Lieutenant Davis stared at the sky, where the lightning played and the fury of the storm worried its way out. Lieutenant Creyton C. Davis, graduate of West Point, veteran of the Civil War and the Indian wars, darling of Richmond dance floors, hero of a Washington romance, dead now in the long grass on a lonely hill, west of everything.

The fire smoldered and blinked its light away, finding no fuel, and in the cold sundown Hondo Lane opened his eyes and looked up at the roof, and then swung his feet down.

The rain was gone. There was no wind. Out there all was silent. He opened the door and stepped out. Broken clouds floated above, and in the far-off west the storm rolled and grumbled like a drunken sergeant in his sleep.

Lane led his horse and tightened the cinch, then stepped into the saddle again and followed westward, after the storm.

And the storm clouds were topped with fire, spears of crimson shot out, piercing the tall sky, and a star appeared. It was cool now, and still.

The miles fell behind. In the distance there was faint smoke, then came the rain-washed walls of the village and the rain-darkened parade ground, the sutler's store and the home of the Army west of the Rio Grande.

Hondo Lane pulled his hat brim lower and started the lineback down the slope. At least, he thought, this is still here.

But behind this thought there was the memory of a quiet-faced woman and a child, of a house beside a stream, and of a woman moving in the house while he slept. He shifted restlessly in the saddle and swore at the horse to cover his feelings and his wonder at it.

CHAPTER SIX

THE STORM, SWEEPING westward across the vast reach of desert and mountain, had crossed the little ranch in the basin before it reached Hondo Lane and the bodies of Company C's fallen veterans. It had come roaring out of the sky, driving before it a barrage of rain that pelted the dry soil, lifting dust as it struck, and bringing to the air that peculiar odor that comes when rain first strikes dry ground.

Not even the cliff protected the cabin from the force of the storm, or from the roar of thunder but it was filled with warmth, comfort, and the smell of coffee. But it was a house empty, for the man was gone.

The sound of rushing water in the usually dry wash frightened her a little, for she had seen those torrents move all before them, and had seen them come when the sky was clear above, and rain only over the distant mountains. Yet now the rain was general, and the parched earth of her garden drank it eagerly.

Some water would remain in the hollow behind the washed-out dam, too. It would last a few weeks, enough so she could irrigate several times, and so it might be the difference between a good crop and none at all.

Johnny was unusually quiet, watching her, his face serious. "Will the man come back, Mommy?"

"I don't know, Johnny. He's very busy."

The same question was haunting her own thoughts. Would he return? And why should he? But if he did, what would she do?

The thought disturbed her. Why should she think of doing anything? What was there to do?

Worried by her own feelings, she sorted clothes for washing, then dusted and mopped, doing work she had not planned to do, merely to keep her thoughts occupied. Yet she kept wondering about him. Had he found shelter?

Remembering the incidents of his visit, she tried to tell herself that he was hard, cruel. His attitude toward the dog, toward Johnny . . . all of it. Yet in her heart she knew he was not cruel. Hard,yes. But how else could he be? And how deep did the hardness go?

What lessons he had learned had come to him in a bitter school. It was the way he knew of learning, a hard way but a fast way that taught its lessons well. She remembered the way he had come off the pallet, gun in hand. What life had a man lived who could be so alert, even in sleep?

It was nearly sundown when the rain ended at the basin, and she went outside. The air was miraculously cool and washed clean and clear. To breathe it was like drinking cold water. The sky was still a broken mass of cloud, and thunder rumbled off in the canyon of the faraway western hills. Lowering masses of cloud filled the hollows of the hills and nestled in the saddles where the ridge dipped low. Occasionally the bulging domes of cloud flared incandescent with distant lightning.

Leaves dripped, water whispered against the banks of the wash, brown and swirling. She fed the horses and stood silent in the yard, looking around at the hills. He was gone. Even his tracks were gone. What kind of woman was she, a married woman and a mother, to be thinking like this of any man.

A man who had gone as if he had never been. But that was not true. His footprints were gone from the yard, yet something remained, something intangible, yet present. A something that set her heart yearning toward the way his horse had gone, that made her remember the way he walked, the strange, somber, almost lonely expression of his eyes. The hunger in them when she had looked up suddenly and met his gaze . . . She flushed, remembering it. And the way he had kissed her, and what he had said.

"A woman walks with her head up ought to kiss a man before she dies."

She repeated the words, feeling the heavy beat of her heart. What a strange thing to say to a woman! And the way he had kissed her . . . not fierce, not possessive, not demanding, and yet so much much more.

Slow drops from the eaves fell into the barrel placed to catch the runoff. In the late dusk the hills were unnaturally green and lovely after the rain. She would take the horses out to the hills in the morning and picket them on the grass where she could keep watch on them from the garden. She walked to the corral and put her hand on the wet top rail and looked again at the hills. The hills etched themselves against the sky darkening and gray. It would be lonely now, lonely as never before.

She turned quickly from the thought, gathering her skirt in a quick gesture and biting her lip against sudden tears. She brushed them away hastily and, squaring her shoulders, walked to the house. Yet in the door, as if reluctant to close it finally against the night where he had gone, she turned again to look toward the hills. And the silent hills lay still. Even in the moments of her walking their green had gone, and the dark wings of night shadowed the basin.

She closed the door and dropped the bar in place. It was no use to think. He was a man with his life to live, a man who had stopped for a night, bought a horse, and ridden away. Other men had come and gone. He was no different . . . yet he was.

This was her home. She had no time for pilgrim thoughts to go wandering away over the hills after a strange rider. She had a home and a son. It was like her that she no longer thought of Ed. She did not believe him killed, but he would not come back, not unless he were hurt and running. He was out of her life . . . a boy who had taken vows it took a man to keep.

And a woman.

And keep them she had. Only now he was gone, and their marriage was a shadow thing that had left only Johnny behind it. And even here Ed seemed to have failed; he was a man who left his mark upon nothing, not even upon his son.

It was enough to think of her son, enough to see that he grew tall and strong, that he became a citizen of his land, a father of children in his time, that he learned to build instead of destroy, that he learned to use the land and protect it, not waste the wealth it gave. This was her mission, her problem.

There was something her father had said. "We do not own the land, Angie. We hold it in trust for tomorrow. We take our living from it, but we must leave it rich for your son and for his sons and for all of those who shall follow."

Yet as she put supper on the table her thoughts were not upon the land. They were hearing the creak of a saddle and a big man's slow voice, quiet in the room.

And when she lay in bed, and drew the blankets high, she looked up into the darkness and remembered Johnny's question. "Will the man come back, Mommy?"

The morning was nearly gone when Angie took the two buckets and walked to the well. The sun was high, and only a few lost tufts of cottony cloud floated in the wide sky. All morning she had worked steadily around the house, only going out to feed the horses and to check the amount of water behind the dam. There was not so much as she had hoped, but enough to irrigate her garden several times. She had cleared mud away from the gate her father had built so the water would be free to flow when it was opened. Her decision to take the horses to the hills had been changed in favor of discretion. She did not believe the Apaches would ever bother her, but horses were a temptation she did not intend to make too inviting.

She filled the first bucket, then the second. She heard no sound, and was standing looking toward the hills when something made her turn.

An Indian had come from the trees and sat the back of his rough-looking paint pony, staring at her. She had heard no sound, no movement.

Another appeared, and then another. And then they began to materialize from the trees as though by magic until there were a dozen.

She had seen them ride by, from time to time she had seen them at the spring, yet this was the first time she had seen so many at such close range.

They were men of medium height who seemed shorter than their height because of wide shoulders and deep chests. Most of ther faces were flat-lipped and cruel, but all were sinewy and powerful in build, dark-skinned and dusty now, their lanky black hair hanging to their shoulders, bound only with headbands.

One of these men sat a very striking pony, and by his looks, Angie knew him for their leader. Her eyes looked past him at a tall, evil-looking Apache who whispered something to the older man, who seemed to be a chief. From the mane of the tall Indian hung several strips of bloody flesh and hair. Scalps, and none of them more than a day old.

She felt herself turn faint and sick, but she forced herself to stand straight. Pale and frightened, she nevertheless managed to keep her voice strong as she spoke to the older man.

"You are Vittoro."

"I am the one who is called Vittoro."

"Your horses have watered here."

His flat black eyes made no change. His face might have been hewn from mahogany.

"You were warned."

"I could not leave. My husband is away. And this is my home."

Vittoro looked at her, and the Indians waited. A vagrant breeze caught at the drying dust of the yard and it swirled briefly, then died. The cottonwoods rustled among themselves.

"This is an Apache spring."

"The Apaches live in the mountains," Angie replied. "They do not need this spring. I have a son. I do need it."

"But when the Apache comes this way, where shall he drink? His throat is dry. You would keep him from water."

"There is water yonder." She pointed to the hills. "But if the people of Vittoro come in peace, they may drink. When have I denied them?"

Vittoro's voice was shaded with impatience, and with a stab of fear she knew that talking was over.

"It is sworn there will be no whites in Apache territory." He turned on the tall Indian. "Silva!" He spoke rapidly in the Apache tongue, and Angie saw the quick grin on Silva's face. The tall Indian slid from his pony. He touched the mane of Vittoro's palomino and said something, evidently comparing it with the color of Angie's hair. Then he drew his knife and started toward her.

She did not scream. She could not. Nor would she let them see her fear. She stood straighter, putting contempt in her face. And then Johnny came out of the door.

He had the Walker Colt. He was holding the big pistol up and pointing it at Silva.

Silva stopped, and one of the Indians chuckled. Even Silva grinned at the ludicrous sight of the boy holding a pistol nearly as large as himself, and so obviously determined.

Angie wheeled and started for the rifle on the porch, but an Indian grabbed her from behind. As he did so the gun bellowed.

The gun was tipped high, and when it went off the bullet creased Silva's scalp, knocking him down. Johnny, knocked backward by the kick of the huge pistol, also fell.

Jerking loose from the Indian who held her, Angie ran to Johnny. Silva lay still on the ground, unconscious.

Vittoro sat his pony his face showing no expression. He looked at the boy. "You are the mother of a strong son," he said quietly. "It is well you have no man. You might raise an army of warriors to fight my people."

"I have no wish to fight your people." Angie spoke with dignity. "Your people have your ways, I have mine. I live in peace when I am left in peace. I did not think," her chin lifted, "that the great Vittoro made war upon women!"

Vittoro slid from his horse and drew his knife. Angie clutched her son, wishing she had picked up the pistol, knowing now it would do no good. There was nothing anyone could do now.

He walked toward them, a bigger man than she had believed, and every inch the chief. The Indians behind him sat their horses in silence.

Vittoro picked up Johnny's hand and knicked his thumb with the point of the knife, then his own. He pressed them together, their blood mingling.

"He is my blood brother. I name him Small Warrior, of the Moon Dog Lodge of the Chiricahua Apache." He looked at Angie, a flicker of something that might have been kindness in his eyes. "You will care for him well. As mother of a Chiricahua warrior, you may live here in safety."

Silva came swiftly to his feet, staring around. He put a hand to his head. It came away bloody. Knife in hand, he started forward, but Vittoro spoke sharply. Sulking, Silva turned and strode to his pony.

Angie clutched Johnny. Vittoro swung to the back of the palomino. "I knew you were a great warrior," she said. "I hope someday someone befriends your sons."

The iron face turned bleakly savage. "My sons are dead—in a white man's prison."

They rode swiftly off. Only Silva looked back, and Angie caught that look. From that day on she knew only Vittoro stood between her and the shame and anger of Silva. And she knew the story of Silva's defeat would be told in the villages, and his hate would harden to an evil thing.

She lifted the pistol from the ground. It had been loaded. Even when he was not with them, Hondo Lane had been the reason of their security. It was he that had advised her, and had loaded the pistol.

CHAPTER SEVEN

BEYOND THE SPRAWLING villages of adobes and jacales were the neatly ranged tents of the cavalry unit, and beside them and forming two sides of the square were the sutler's store, the quartermaster's storehouse, the bakery, the headquarters building, the blacksmith shop, and the stables. None of these were imposing structures. All looked squalid and dismal even after the bathing of rain.

A few scouts and frontier drifters lounged in the area near the sutler's store, or sat on the steps before it. They watched the lone rider come down the slope and ventured guesses as to who he was and where he came from. It was not a time to be riding alone, and not many were willing to chance it. Not even the hardy souls who loitered around the sutler's store.

A man came to the door of a jacal, a structure of upright logs set in holes in the ground and plastered with mud, roofed with smaller branches and more mud. He stared at the rider. He said something over his shoulder and another face appeared in the door of the jacal, and then both men walked out.

It took little to get men out of the jacales, places more suited to the residence of scattered and indifferent centipedes, scorpions, or occasional tarantulas than of human beings.

"Him, all right." Dick spat tobacco juice at an unoffending lizard and chuckled. "Knowed it."

Hondo walked the lineback to the hitch rail and swung down. Sam stopped a few feet away looking at the scouts without pleasure. He did not even pant. He just sat and stared glumly.

"Well," said Buffalo, a huge, whiskered man in a greasy buckskin shirt, "I owe you a jug of redeye. Settle come payday." He walked around the dog. "That dog's as friendly as a puma."

He looked carefully at the lineback, noting the strangeness of the horse. His eyes were sharp and attentive and as quick to see and catalogue as the eyes of an Apache. Hondo Lane had been places and none of it had been easy. It showed where the scout could see it.

"Figured your hair would be hanging in some Apache wickiup. Bet Dick on it. You're sure a disappointment to me, Hondo."

"You like to won. I wore out some horses."

"You wore out you, while you was at it," Dick said. "Lemme get that war bag."

Headquarters building was a structure of adobe and rough planks identified by the flagpole. A sergeant sat behind a box that did duty for a desk. An enlisted cavalryman and a scout sat on a bench against the wall.

A tall, rather handsome young man with a petulant, irritable expression was addressing the sergeant. He was a lean-bodied man with a low-tied gun and something of the dress of a frontier dandy, limited only by his cash outlay.

"I say I got a right to talk to this here bowneck major." His voice was casually insolent. "I don't talk to no underlings."

"The Major's sleeping." The sergeant spoke in a careful, noncommittal tone. His manner betrayed all too clearly that he spoke to a civilian, to a man he disliked, and to a man he would cheerfully throw out of the office if it were permitted. At the same time, he spoke with the exasperated patience of a man who knows he must keep peace with citizens.

"That's too bad about him. I'm a citizen and I want to see him."

"Major Sherry ain't slept for three days. I can tell you everything just as well as him. We ain't heard nothin' from up north."

The lean-hipped rider stared at him with contempt. "If you ask me, the Cavalry's scared of Vittoto. And I think the U.S. Cavalry . . . "

Major Sherry came in from the room behind the sergeant. He was a tall man, wire-taut and strong, but his face was lined and exhausted. The speaker, suddenly aware of his presence, let his voice die away.

"I am greatly interested in your opinion of the United States Cavalry," Major Sherry said dryly. "Continue, Mr. Whatever-your-name-is."

"I'm Ed Lowe," the lean-hipped man said. His voice lost its irritation before the sharpness of the Major's and became complaining. "The Cavalry's supposed to support the settlers. I've got some cattle up north and I—"

"Company C is making a sweep to the north to escort out any settlers they may find. Company C is over a week late in returning. That is all I am able to tell you."

Hondo came through the door behind Lowe, followed by Sam. The big dog sank to the floor just inside the door. Hondo crossed and hung his saddle on the wall beside several other saddles. When the saddle was hung he looked back over his shoulder.

"C Company won't be back."

He turned slowly, as if reluctant to give them the news, and on the desktop before the sergeant he dropped the crumpled, blood-stained guidon of C Company.

Major Sherry stared at the guidon, his face growing stiff and old. Crey Davis. . . . He would have to tell his wife. Why the hell did he ever volunteer for the Arizona command?

The story was there. Hondo would provide the details, but actually, none were needed except for the reports. Suddenly, wearily, Major Sherry knew he would rather not hear them. Good friends gone . . . good soldiers, good fighting men. C Company had been his best, his toughest outfit.

Looking up, he saw Ed Lowe. A flicker of disgust showed, and he said irritably, "You may leave. I have business to attend to."

Major Sherry's head came around. "Sergeant!"

The implication was plain and the sergeant came to his feet abruptly. He started around the desk. "Git!" he said. "An' don't come botherin' around no more!"

Lowe turned angrily and started to the door. Hondo had moved back to the wall to hang up his pistol belt. Lowe found himself facing the big dog, and although there was plenty of room to pass, his anger flamed sudenly. "Get out of the way, you mangy cur!" He drew his foot back.

Sam came to his feet with a swift, almost catlike move, crouched, his muscles bunched to leap. His lips curled back from his teeth but he neither growled nor snarled, only looked up at Lowe, his face ugly with readiness.

Taken aback by the sudden reaction, Ed Lowe stepped back. Then he reached for his gun.

Hondo's gun belt was on the hook but his Winchester was in his hand. He tipped the barrel forward with his left hand slapping the butt into his hand. The butt struck his hand and at almost the same instant his thumb cocked the hammer back. Lowe froze at the sharp click, turning his head.

There was no mistaking the rifle. It was hip-high and the muzzle was aimed at his stomach and not eight feet away. Ed Lowe looked at the rifle and his eyes lifted to the bleak, wind-raw face of Hondo Lane. Something in Ed Lowe seemed to back up and sit down.

"If that's your cur, get him out of the way."

Hondo neither advised nor threatened. "Walk around him."

"I'll be hanged if I ever go out of my way for a cur dog!"

Lane's face did not change. His voice was matter of fact. "Man should always do what he thinks he should."

A fly buzzed in the room. Outside somewhere a horse stamped

and there was a clang of iron on iron. Ed Lowe stood very still.

He did not know this man. He might be anybody. Yet there was something in his manner that was too calm, too casual. Ed Lowe was a good man with a gun and had found occasions to demonstrate it. He figured there were few better. Yet suddenly he was examining his hole card and he did not like what he saw.

There was that in the attitude of the stranger that implied all too much familiarity with such situations. Ed Lowe's thoughts probed his memory for the face, for something that would be a clue. He liked to know what he was going up against.

Nor did he like the obvious satisfaction in the sergeant's face. The sergeant would not be unhappy to see him dead, and the sergeant seemed all too sure that he was about to see just that. And Ed Lowe did not have the kind of guts it would take to find out.

The blue fly buzzed. Somebody laughed in the outer air, and the flickering instant of hesitation was ended. Ed Lowe had been fairly called and he knew it. All he had to do was gamble. . . . Suddenly sick and empty inside, Ed Lowe stepped around the dog and went blindly through the door.

For an instant there was silence and the sergeant sighed briefly, with genuine regret. "Thought maybe we'd be rid of him," he said to nobody in particular. "He's got it coming."

Hondo pushed the dog aside with his foot. "Don't block the door," he said quietly.

Major Sherry gestured to the guidon. "Where did you get this?"

"About half a day's ride south of Twin Buttes."

"How?"

"Off two Indians. Running Dog Lodge of the Mescaleros."

"So the Mescaleros are up, too. That makes all the Apache lodges."

Hondo shoved his hat back and began to build a smoke.

"Went up there," he said, "and backtrailed them Mescaleros. Davis ambushed Vittoro. Figure he got twenty or more. He was pullin' out of the ambush when they hit him from behind. 'Nother outfit, maybe a hundred strong. He never had a chance."

"All there?"

"Yes. They got no prisoners, if that's what you mean." Hondo hesitated, and then said quietly, "Clanahan fought 'em off Davis' body at the end. They went out together, him an' the Lieutenant."

"Clanahan?" The Major's eyes brightened a little. He remembered the man, a big, black-haired Irishman with a brutal face. A drunk, a brawler, a troublemaker, but a fighter. And he was Army. "He was a good man."

Hondo described the action briefly as he had seen the sign on the ground. It was a clear, accurate picture and had its value. Every battle was a lesson; in each there was something to be learned. Major Sherry never ceased to marvel at what these men would read from the ground, yet he had seen their facts proved too many times to doubt them.

"They won," Hondo said, "but it hurt. They got hit hard."

He took a long drag on his cigarette and turned to the door, then paused. "Any settlers out of the north basin since I been away? Lately?"

"A few."

"Handsome woman? Fair? With a small boy, maybe six years old?"

"No. All middle-aged or elderly people."

Hondo Lane walked to the door and found Buffalo waiting with his war bag. He reached for it but Buffalo pushed his hand away. "I'll tote it."

Hondo walked out into the cool of the evening. They had not come out, then. He had hoped that after he had gone Angie would change her mind. She could have made it through while he rode north to follow through on the story of Company C. But there was nothing.

Buffalo walked along beside Hondo, shifting the war bag to his other hand. "Old Pete Britton was scoutin' with C Company. Wintered with Pete oncet up on the Divide. Ornery cuss."

"Last of them," Hondo said. "Maybe an hour, alone on a hilltop."

They walked on in silence. At the door of the jacal where Hondo stopped, Buffalo put down the bag.

"Old Pete, he worried himself a lot. That winter on the Divide he was laid up lot of the time. Rheumatic, he was. Skeered of being crippled."

They stood together and smoked quietly. Hondo explained about the body. Buffalo dropped his cigarette, then walked away, saying no more. Hondo stood alone then, looking into the night.

He was no man to be thinking about a woman. He had never lived with a woman . . . wouldn't know how to. He wouldn't know how to handle a kid, either. And women . . . It was one thing with a squaw. After a while you knew them. But a girl like Angie, now, that would be different. He was a fool to even think about it. What did he have to offer a woman?

He sat down in the doorway and took off his boots. He saw a soldier coming down the line of tents. It was the same trooper that had been in the headquarters building.

"That fellow, complaining to the Major. Who was he?"

The trooper hesitated, liking the big man and ready to talk. "Don't know his name."

"Why doesn't he go in?"

"Same reason he walked around your dog when you told him." He waited, wanting to talk, hesitating. "Them Indians you took that C pennant off'n. Dead Indians?"

"Finally."

He got up and turned inside. The trooper stood outside in the dark, a faint shadow in the greater darkness of the night.

The cot creaked. Almost at once there were snores. The soldier stood alone, looking into the night, thinking of a night in his own little New England village. A night like this, cool, quiet . . . .

There had been a girl there. He could not even remember her name, just a quiet, pretty girl. He wished he could remember. He would like to write her a letter.

He thought of Company C, lying under the rain, and under the stars.

A man needed somebody to think about, he needed somebody somewhere. . . .

CHAPTER EIGHT

It was after ten when Hondo awakened. Accustomed to sleeping in short snatches, when and where it was possible, his body could not attune itself to long, unrestricted rest. To oversleep was dangerous, and despite his weariness, he awakened suddenly and with a start.

He stared up into the dark, not moving until his mind knew where he was and the countless tiny sounds began to sort and adjust themselves. Slowly his muscles relaxed. He was at the post.

Groggily he sat up and ran his fingers through his hair. His body felt heavy and his mouth tasted bad. He swore, walked to the bucket on the table, and lifted it to drink, then he spat into the street.

It was very dark but there were stars. A coolness left by the rain still pervaded the desert night. He bathed his face, combed his hair, and then picked up his hat. From up the company street he heard the sound of an out-of-tune piano, and with it a clear Irish tenor singing "Brennan on the Moor," an old Irish folk song of a highwayman and his love.

Hondo Lane stepped out into the night and looked around, sensing the darkness, taking his feel of it before moving on. Far out over the hills a coyote yapped his loneliness to the listening stars. A faint breeze stirred the tent flaps. A tent not far away showed the dull glow of a lamp and he heard a murmur of voices and a slap of cards.

Hondo Lane walked up the street toward the sutler's store, his boots grating on the gravel and clay of the parade ground. Two men sat outside the store, smoking. One of them murmured a greeting, and Hondo replied with a short "Howdy," not knowing the man.

Inside the room was crowded. It was a long and dingy room without color, without light, without women. Several men leaned against the homemade bar at one end. At the other there was a counter where trade goods were dispensed, with shelves behind it.

The Irish tenor leaned on the battered upright piano, wearing a rumpled but once fashionable gray suit and a derby hat with a dent and a badly scuffed brim. He was a young man with a dashing mustache, and he needed a shave. The man at the piano was a cow hand, bearing out the fact that in the melting pot of the West there was no estimating the hidden talents of a drifting man.

All were roughly dressed but the soldiers. A few were still around, although most had turned in by now. The men of the crowd were cow hands, cattlemen, gamblers, prospectors, drifters, and scouts. There was a tension in the group, and nobody was talking of what they were all thinking. In the morning a burial party would go out to inter the bodies of Company C—a party that must in itself be strong. Not a man here but might be called upon to go, and not a man here who had not lost a friend or drinking companion in the massacre of Company C.

Hondo walked to the bar and the sutler reached underneath for a bottle of Irish whisky. He winked at Hondo, filled his glass, and said quietly, "On the house." Then the bottle vanished again, unseen by the habitués of the saloon and store.

Hondo looked around slowly. A card game was going at the other end of the room. Buffalo was sitting in, and Hondo recognized the man with whom he had had trouble at headquarters. There was another character of whom he had seen a good deal, not only here but at the Pass, over in Texas. A sour-faced man with a snaky look to his eyes and a habit of winning in poker games, no matter how. The last of them was Pete Summervel.

Pete was seventeen, a hard-riding youngster, cocky, overconfident. Now he was not quite drunk, but nearing it. Obviously he was in no condition to play poker, and obviously the gambler was encouraging him to drink. Hondo tossed off his own drink and watched the game. The man with whom he had had trouble earlier seemed adept with the cards. Hondo put down his glass, drew the back of his hand across his mouth, and walked over to the table.

Ed Lowe looked up when Hondo stopped by the table, and something in him tightened. "Three sixes and two pretty fours," he said, spreading his cards. "I win. Let's go again."

Pete looked up and grinned. "Hi, Hondo! Broke my heart when I heard you made it."

"Your pa know when you started going against that so-called whisky, Pete?"

Pete grinned. The whisky was already having its effect. "Ain't seen him for a month."

Hondo dropped his hand to his shoulder. "I know you haven't, an' I've got a message from him for you. Come on."

Pete got to his feet, staggering a little. "Sure, Hondo."

"Come down to the bar where we can talk. These gents'll excuse you."

"I won't."

The words were low-spoken, but Hondo heard them clearly. He turned. It was the man with whom he had had trouble earlier.

"I'm out almost a hundred simoleans."

"That I can figure," Hondo replied mildly, "with Buffalo in the game. Come along, Pete."

Lowe came to his feet quickly and caught Hondo by the shirt front. "*Wait* a minute!"

Hondo looked at the hand gripping his shirt, then lifted his cold eyes to Lowe's. "I just bought that shirt," he said mildly. The other men were on their feet, too.

Hondo pushed Pete out of range as Lowe started a punch. It was the wrong thing for Lowe to do. As the punch started, Hondo's left hand came up and knocked the grip loose from his shirt and he stepped inside of the looping left with a lifting right uppercut to the chin.

Lowe staggered, and instantly Hondo swung a right that knocked Buffalo into a corner. Lowe had gone down hard, but as Buffalo sat up, Lowe gathered himself.

"What did you hit me for?" Buffalo demanded in pained surprise.

"Because you're the most dangerous."

Hondo had started to turn away when Lowe went for his gun. "Not in the back!" Buffalo shouted. "Leather it!"

Turning swiftly, Hondo kicked the gun from Lowe's hand, then he grabbed him by the shirt front and jerked him to his feet. Hondo smashed a right into Lowe's stomach, then shoved him away and hit him in the face with both hands. Lowe lunged, swinging, but Hondo knocked down Lowe's right and crossed over his left. Lowe staggered and Hondo walked in, his face expressionless. He hit Lowe with a left to the body, then a right.

Lowe backed up, not liking it, and Hondo slapped him. It was a powerful, brutal slap that jarred Lowe to his heels and turned him half around. Then Hondo dropped him with a straight right.

Lowe sprawled on the floor and Hondo picked him up by the scruff of the neck and the seat of the pants, and when somebody opened the door, he heaved him out into the dirt. Lowe landed on his face in the gravel and Hondo waited an instant in the door.

Ed Lowe rolled over. His body was alive with vindictive hatred and he stared up at Hondo. "You ain't heard the last of this!" he said thickly.

"Then I'll keep listenin'," Hondo said, turning back into the saloon. The door closed and Ed Lowe remained on the ground, staring at the blackness.

The two men seated outside had not moved. One's cigarette glowed red.

Lowe gathered himself and got shakily to his feet. He spat blood from a cut lip. His head felt foggy and there was a raw pain in his side. "I'll kill him!" he said into the night. "I'll kill him for this!"

The cigarette glowed briefly. "I was you," the voice said mildly, "I'd figure I was lucky he wasn't packin' a gun. That's Hondo Lane."

Inside, Hondo walked over to Buffalo. He put his hand on the big man's shoulder. "Sorry, friend. I didn't know who all was in that shindig an' I figured I wanted no part of you in a brawl."

Buffalo chuckled. "All right. I was wishin' the kid was out of it. Ed an' that sidewinder from the Pass roped him in."

Hondo jerked his head toward the door. "This is the second time I've tangled with that mouthy no-good. Who is he, anyhow?"

"Calls himself Lowe. Ed Lowe."

Ed Lowe. . . . Hondo looked at the glass on the bar. Angie's husband, and alive.

What kind of man would leave a woman and child alone at such a time as this? And he had been lifting the roof at headquarters about his cattle. Nothing said about his wife and child.

When F Company rode out of the post at daylight Hondo Lane was standing by to watch them go. With them was riding a company of scouts commanded by Lieutenant Crawford. These were a mixture of Apaches, Yaquis, Opatas, and Mexicans, with a scattering of Americans. All were skilled Indian fighters. It was a strong force for a burial detachment, but their orders were explicit. They were under no concern to attempt to follow Vittoro or to engage in any battle unless first attacked.

Hondo watched them go, his face somber. There was small chance they would encounter Vittoro, although the company of scouts carried enough wild-country brains to have found him no matter where he fled, if they had been permitted. The orders of Major Sherry had been definite, however, and he did not intend to overstep them unless the situation was drastic. To send good men after those who had died with Company C would be worse than foolish. When Crook was present in force, it would be a different story.

Hondo watched them ride out, then walked back to the jacal and began mending gear. He was thinking of Angie. It was no business of his. She had a husband. But she should not be out there alone.

Restlessly he went to the corral and curried the surprised lineback, then fed him a couple of carrots he found in a garden patch near the end of the village.

Buffalo wandered over and joined him. "Don't you be careless, Hondo," he advised. "That Lowe ain't liable to forget what you handed him last night."

"I won't forget."

He worked over the horse a little longer, then released him with a slap on the shoulder. As he watched the lineback cross the corral, he asked, "Lowe been around long?"

"Month, maybe more. Plays a little poker." Buffalo bit off a chew of tobacco. "Hangs out with that rattler Phalinger."

All day reports came in of moving Indians. Twenty Chiricahuas had left the reservation, all young bucks. Some Tontos had been seen crossing the Francisco River heading south. There was a gathering of the tribes.

Twice groups of settlers came into the post, worn and tired from travel, and found shelter in the abandoned tents of a departed Army unit. Each time Hondo made inquiries among them, but they had come in from farther south and there was no report of anyone in the Basin country. Restlessly he awaited return of the burial detail. They had no orders to go beyond the scene of the massacre, but the scouts would be riding over more country, and they might have some information.

It was unnaturally quiet at the post. There was no roistering or loud talk around the bar in the sutler's store. Men came and went hurriedly, and the mounted patrols that left the post moved in and out like clockwork. The last patrol in before dark reported a running battle with a handful of Indians in which one Indian was slain and a trooper wounded.

As the hours passed, tension grew. It was noon a day later before the burial detail rode in. No Indians had been seen, although they had cut the trails of several small groups.

Shortly after the burial detail returned, Hondo Lane walked into the headquarters building. The sergeant looked up as he entered.

"Major Sherry in?"

"He's in. Just a minute."

The sergeant returned. "Go on in. He said he wanted to see you, anyway."

Sherry was leaned back in his chair looking out the window at the heat-baked parade ground. He was a grim-faced, clean-cut man of forty-four, a professional soldier who knew the frontier and liked it. He knew the country, the Indians, and the men he commanded. Years of duty in face of the enemy had burned away all the spit and polish. He was a fighting man, and wanted to be nothing else. He had been close to the top of his class at the Point, but had never cared for Eastern duty. He knew the book on combat tactics, but most of what he knew had been learned by applying it in battle against enemies that could be counted the greatest guerrilla tacticians the world had ever known.

''What's on your mind, Lane?''

''I want to go out there.'' Lane jerked his head toward the hills. ''Personal business.''

Sherry turned to his desk and shuffled his papers. ''Sorry, Lane. It can't be done. The General wants you here for the time being.'' He stacked the papers. ''Personal business, you said?''

''Yes, sir. There's a woman out there, with a child. They wouldn't come in then. They might come now.''

The Major took out his pipe and stoked it with tobacco. ''You lived with the Apaches, that right?''

''Yes, sir.''

Major Sherry touched a match to the pipe. ''I've been ordered to hold all scouts in. The General has something in mind. Nevertheless, I'd like—and I know he'd like—some information on Vittoro. If anybody could get it, you could.''

Hondo Lane shifted in his chair, waiting. The Major's face did not change.

''It's mighty dangerous out there. Any man who went out alone would be a fool. And we've orders to stop anyone—anyone at all.''

Hondo Lane got to his feet and turned to the door. ''That all, sir?''

''Yes.'' Major Sherry drew on his pipe and looked out the window. As Hondo pulled on his hat and opened the door, Sherry turned his face toward him. ''Lane,'' he said quietly, ''be careful.''

CHAPTER NINE

ANGIE CAME TO the door to shake out her broom. She glanced around the yard, but Johnny was not in sight. A thrill of fright went through her, and she stepped out into the yard. "Johnny! Johnny!"

There was no sound. Shading her eyes, she scanned the hills. Johnny was an obedient child. He had been told not to go to the hills, and so far he had always obeyed, going only when they went together.

Frightened, she walked quickly around the house. He was nowhere in sight.

"Johnny!"

Her call sounded, and the empty hills threw back her voice. Her heart pounded heavily. She walked toward the corral. "Johnny! Johnny!"

And then from the trees walked two horses. On one of them was Vittoro, and Johnny rode the other.

Relief went over her like a cold shower, yet she looked uncertainly at the hard-faced old Indian.

"Oh, I thought . . . I didn't know . . . I heard nothing."

"The Apache does not make noise."

The old Indian lifted Johnny to the ground, and his hands were gentle, almost fatherly. A hand lingered on the boy's shoulder.

"Mommy, Vittoro says I'll make a good warrior."

The Apache nodded, starting the child toward his mother. "He will ride well and he does not fear."

"Look, Mommy. I have a headband."

Proudly he showed her the headband. There was an opal of exceptional beauty in the center.

She knelt to look at it. "How beautiful! And it has an opal!"

"It is the emblem of his lodge." Vittoro glanced at Johnny. "I speak with your mother. Go inside the house."

"Yes, Vittoro."

Obediently Johnny turned and ran into the house. Angie watched him, a little catch at her heart.

Vittoro looked at her and his eyes were serious. Mentally she stiffened, for instinctively she knew what was coming, and she knew that she must use every word with care. She had seen several parties of Indians pass, and she had seen the fresh scalps they carried. That she was alive only at the sufferance of Vittoro she knew. Whatever came, he must not be offended.

"A lodge should have a man. Small Warrior should have a father to instruct him."

"My husband will be home any day."

Vittoro considered this. Then he shook his head. "I do not think so. I think your man is dead. I will deliberate on this."

She hesitated, then said quietly, "It is the way of my people for a woman to choose her own man. If my man is dead, there will be another."

"Many braves ride with me."

"They follow a strong leader," she said, "but an Apache woman for an Apache man—a white woman for a white man."

Vittoro considered this. He said, "Small Warrior is blood brother to Vittoro. He must grow strong in the ways of Vittoro."

Her eyes looked frankly into those of the proud old man. "I would have it so. My son could have no better model than Vittoro. I had heard his greatness. Now I have known it—and he is also kind.

"My son," she continued slowly, "is born to this land. I would have him know it as the Apache knows it. The man I choose will teach him to know the ways of the Apache."

There was nothing to read in his face. He merely turned to his horse. "Of this I shall think," he said, and he walked his horse away into the trees.

For a long time after he was gone she stood perfectly still, forgetful of the hot sun, forgetful of the work that remained to be done.

An issue was before her, and she knew she walked a narrow way between life for herself and her son and death for them both. Yet she had not lied. She would like her son to know how to live off the country as the Apache did, yet he must remain true to his blood, true to his God, and true to his people and his country.

How long would Vittoro allow her to wait? Not long, that she knew. And then what remained for her? Unless the Army came, unless she escaped and abandoned her home, all she had in the world, then she must take a husband from among Vittoro's braves.

Yet what had she said? "The man I choose will teach him to know the ways of the Apache."

And who, of the men she knew, could do that? She blushed and bit her lip, unwilling to frame his name in her mind. Yet when she had taken up her broom again, she faced the fact of it. She had never been one to dodge issues. If she knew nothing else, she had learned in these lonely months to know herself, and she knew there was only one man of whom she could think in that way.

She was a woman still married, and she was thinking of Hondo Lane.

But what was it that made a woman married? Had her husband acted the part of a husband? Had he remained with her? Where was he now, in her time of trial?

He had never been her husband, not as her father had been to her mother. He had been a young man whom she married and with whom, for a time, she lived. And he had left no impresssion here, not even in his son.

Mentally she stood him before Vittoro, and she saw the old chieftain's decision, understood his scorn. And then she saw Hondo Lane, and he stood squarely before Vittoro, a man.

She worked steadily, yet her thoughts would not remain still. Her problem was with her, and she was a woman born to a Christian life, reared to a moral life, yet always an honest life. Her father had always been a man with whom she could talk, and those talks had reached into her present life with their clear-cut wisdom, their simple truth.

To each of us is given a life. To live with honor and to pass on having left our mark, it is only essential that we do our part, that we leave our children strong. Nothing exists long when its time is past. Wealth is important only to the small of mind. The important thing is to do the best one can with what one has.

These things her father had taught her, these things she believed. A woman's task was to keep a home, to rear her children well, to give them as good a start as possible before moving on. That was why she had stayed. That was why she had dared to remain in the face of Indian trouble. This was her home. This was her fireside. Here was all she could give her son aside from the feeling that he was loved, the training she could give, the education. And she could give him this early belief in stability, in the rightness of belonging somewhere.

Now it was threatened. The very thing that had saved their lives might turn her son from the life that should be his. He was excited by the attentions of the old chief, and he hungered for the company of a man. How else was a boy to learn how to become a man?

Was she a fool to think always of Hondo Lane? The man was a killer.

But this also her father had given her: reserve of judgment, and to judge no man or woman by a grouping, but each on his own character, his own ground.

In Hondo Lane she had recognized some of the same virtues she had known in her father. The singleness of purpose, the honesty, the steadfastness, and the industry. A killer he might be, but a man must live as he must. There were things a man must face and things a man must do that no woman could understand, just as the reverse was true.

Tonight the hills were lonely. A coyote yapped at the moon, and in the silence a quail called.

How long did she have? How long before Vittoro came again and demanded a decision of her? But Indians did not permit women to make decisions . . . or did they? She had heard not, and yet, knowing women, she was not altogether sure of this. She smiled into the night.

Johnny came out and sat on the steps beside her. "Mommy? Do you think the man will like my headband? Do you think he will?"

"I'm sure of it, Johnny."

Then carefully, thinking of the future, she said, "You're a white boy, Johnny, and although someday you may live with the Indians, you will always be a white boy. Mr. Lane lived with the Indians, and he remained a white man."

Darkness crept in and crouched around the stable, and in the darkness she smelled the sage and heard the stirring and the stamping of the horses in the corral. In the east there was a bright star low above the mountains.

Would he come back again? Would he come in time?

"Mommy!" Johnny pulled at her hand. "What will I have to learn to be a warrior?"

"Oh, you'll have to learn to track wild animals, to ride, to hunt, to find food in the desert . . . many things."

"Will I learn to ride like the man did?"

The man . . . "Yes, I think so." She hesitated just a little. "Maybe he'll come back and teach you. He's a good man, Johnny."

"I liked him." Johnny watched the quiet star. "I liked the dog, too."

"But he snapped at you!"

"But he didn't know me!" Johnny said. "He didn't know I was his friend! If a dog let anybody touch him before they were friends, somebody might hurt him."

A faint sound caught her ears. She held her breath, listening.

It was the sound of a horse . . . of many horses.

And then she saw them, a dozen Indians, filing by toward the spring, just beyond the reach of her light. An Indian's horse's eyes caught the light and reflected it.

An Indian left the group and started toward them. She got to her feet, recognizing Silva.

He stood looking at her, and there was a pride in his bearing, and contempt, too. He gestured at her head, then lifted a scalp at his belt. It was fresh, red-haired.

Another Indian came up behind him and said something. Silva hesitated, looking from her to the child. The other Indian spoke again, more urgently. The only word she knew was "Vittoro." The second Indian used the name several times. Silva turned away, finally, and walked back to the horses.

She stood very still, holding Johnny tightly to her until she heard their horses moving away.

For a long time after they were gone, she was uneasy. Inside she checked the pistol again. Since Hondo had loaded it, and since Johnny had nearly killed Silva, she always kept it loaded.

Silva would come back. He would come alone. Afterward he could always blame some other Indians for what was done. He had forgotten nothing, and he would not forget. Her only hope was to have a man of her own. But who could stand against Silva if anything happened to Vittoro?

She asked the question into the night, and her heart gave her the answer.

CHAPTER TEN

BEHIND THE STABLES the lineback was saddled and ready. Hondo Lane came around the corner carrying his rifle. He slid the Winchester into the boot and began tying his bedroll behind the cantle.

He looked over his shoulder when he heard the approaching feet, his fingers continuing to work. It was Ed Lowe, and with him was Sergeant Young.

"See?" Lowe said angrily. "It's my horse. That's my brand."

He indicated the E L on the horse's shoulder. Sergeant Mike Young examined the brand as if hoping to find it a mistake.

He looked up at Hondo. "What he says true?"

"Yes, this is his horse."

"Where did you get it from?"

Hondo looked at Lowe with casual contempt. "From his place. That's where I'm takin' it back. That's where he can find it."

Young hesitated. He liked no part of this. He had no use for Ed Lowe. He knew he was a fourflusher, although a dangerous one. By the same token, he liked Hondo Lane and had ridden in several long patrols guided by Lane. He knew the man and knew him well.

He also knew he had inadvertently walked into something of which he would have preferred to know nothing. There was a standing order that no one was to leave the camp, but at the same time Lane was very close to Major Sherry, and had talked with Sherry on the previous day. The order had gone around that no one was to leave, but at the same time the whisper had followed that no one was to pay any attention to the activities of Hondo Lane. And this had come from the sergeant major.

Major Sherry disciplined his men with strictness, and he had company punishment and the court-martial to enforce it. The sergeant major had only two large fists, but a way of being convincing with them.

Carefully, and merely for the record, Sergeant Young said, "But that's in Injun territory now—strict orders against any white goin' in."

Hondo pulled at his ear. "Know somethin'? I got a bad ear. Can't hear what you're sayin'."

Coolly he stepped in the leather, and then he swung the horse and, keeping the stable between himself and the parade ground, he rode off.

Lowe grabbed the Sergeant's arm. "You can't let him steal my horse!"

Young jerked his arm free. "He may be an ornery son-of-a-anything-you-want-to-call-him, but I'm not calling him a horse thief either to his face or behind his back."

Abruptly Young turned and walked away, glad to be out of it.

Behind him he heard Lowe swearing. As Young crossed to his quarters he saw Phalinger come out of the sutler's store, and Young paused at the door of his tent, waiting. A moment later, Ed Lowe crossed the area and joined Phalinger. The two men talked, then walked away together.

Sergeant Major Joe O'Bierne came out of the tent and glanced sharply at Mike Young. "What's the matter?"

O'Bierne nodded. "You did right, boy. 'Twas none of our affair."

"They'll follow him, I'm thinkin'."

O'Bierne shrugged. "Then on their own shoulders it'll be." He chuckled. "If the Injuns don't get 'em, Lane will, an' good riddance."

Hondo Lane was moving swiftly, with no idea of those who came behind. He knew exactly what situation he faced. Between the post and its relative security and the basin where lay Lowe's ranch, lay miles of country, wild and desolate, crossed and recrossed by hostile Indians. Rarely did they move in as large parties as those encountered by C Company on that fatal day of the massacre. Rather they traveled in smaller groups of eight to a dozen warriors, and were the most dangerous because of this.

An Apache might be anywhere. This was his country, this heat-baked nightmare of waterless, treeless land, cut by no streams and with few water holes. Dotted with clumps of greasewood and cut by savage arroyos or uplifted ledges of black volcanic rock or sandstone, it was a weird and dangerous country rock over which to travel.

No man knew better the art of concealment than the Apache. His own hide, his instinctive feeling for terrain, and his ability to live for days with little water and less food made him a fearful antagonist always. Hondo Lane rode into that heat-baked wilderness knowing exactly what lay before him. He had lived with the Apache. He knew his ways and much of his thinking, and he knew better than anyone how small was the chance that Angie Lowe and her Johnny were still alive.

Yet he knew also that the Indian was a creature of whim, and although cruel to his enemies or those he believed were enemies, he could be kind to children. No Apache had ever been known to strike his child. He might beat his wife, but never his child. And the very fact that Angie Lowe was alive this long proved she had been fortunate. She might continue to be so.

He moved now as he had before. He scouted the terrain before him, and only then did he move. He knew much of it, but he did not rely on that knowledge. He kept out of low places, held to the concealment just below ridges, studied every fresh track. He wore nothing that gleamed. The lineback's dun color shaded into the desert as did his own clothing.

With no weapons but his bow and arrows, his lance and war club or knife, the Apache had ruled over this vast area for generations, and when the rifle was introduced, he quickly learned its use and became an adept. Although always lacking ammunition, the Apache became a marksman in many cases second to none.

At noon Hondo rode the lineback into an arroyo and swung down, leading the horse back into the shade of an overhang. Some dead curl-leaf lay in the canyon bottom and he collected it, then a few more sticks, all dry. He ate jerky with hardtack, and drank two cups of coffee hastily made over the fire.

The dry wood made no smoke, and when the coffee was hot, Hondo extinguished the fire and carefully buried the coals, brushing over the surface with a loose branch. He squatted there, finishing his coffee and smoking, letting the heat of the day slip by while the lineback ate of the grass close under the cliff's edge.

Sam lay panting in the shade a few yards off. Hondo leaned back against the wall and dozed. Not until two hours had passed did he move, and then he tightened the cinch on the lineback and stepped into the saddle.

Taking his time, he worked his way out of the arroyo, careful to study the country before moving into the open. All afternoon he traveled on, keeping a steady gait but frequently shifting his trail. Several times he paused, studying his backtrail. A faint dust was visible once. A dust devil? Or was it someone on his trail?

At dusk he was approaching Deadman Water Hole, and he took his time. A mile from the water he crossed the trail of four unshod ponies. The trail was scarcely an hour old. A word to Sam and the dog moved out warily, scouting ahead. Hondo moved up to a place among some rocks where he looked over the approaches to the water hole. There was nothing in sight. And then he saw Sam.

The big mongrel was moving closer, belly down among the rocks. Only the faintest of movements rendered him visible. Hondo waited, his rifle ready to cover the dog if need be, but suddenly the dog lifted himself to his legs, seemed to hesitate, sniffing the wind, and then trotted toward the hole. Relieved, Hondo Lane got a foot into the stirrup and swung his leg over. The lineback, sensing the water, walked eagerly forward.

Deadman was a seep. The water was still but fresh, and Hondo drank, then allowed the horse to drink. Sam's muzzle was already wet. The Apaches had been here, but had not remained long. Hondo mounted again and they moved on. Twice he paused before darkness to study his backtrail. He saw nothing.

Far behind him two horsemen rode out of a gully. Ed Lowe was in the lead, Phalinger close behind. Phalinger was a lean, dark man. He stared at the darkening hills.

"I don't like it, Ed."

Lowe said nothing. He had already come farther than he had intended, but turning back was not part of his plan. He was a good man on a trail, but Phalinger was better. It had taken all their skill to follow Hondo Lane, although the big rider was making no undue effort to conceal his passing.

"He's gettin' deep in Injun territory, and so are we," Phalinger added.

"What you squawkin' for? He's carryin' plenty, and you know it. Besides, he ain't goin' much farther without makin' camp."

Phalinger shrugged. "We never found his camp last night."

"We'll find it this time."

They pushed on, finding an occasional track of the shod horse. Lowe had the added advantage of knowing where Lane was headed. He had said he was returning to the ranch, and Lowe believed him. It was an added reason for continuing. No one at the post must ever learn he had abandoned Angie and his child at the ranch. He would not be allowed to stay around for one minute.

That had been one advantage. At the Pass they knew he was married. At the post they knew nothing of him except that he had a ranch and cattle. He had never mentioned Angie.

At first he had intended to return. It was not Indians that worried him, but the long days at the ranch without company. Nor did he want to work. No sense in that. It was easier to play cards and win money from those that did work. So why be a fool? Besides, he had the ranch and cattle. When the Apaches settled down he'd hire a couple of men to round up the steers and sell them to the Army. The rest he would let run, and in time there would be more cattle. Not being there, he'd lose a few, but longhorns knew how to get along. A longhorn bull would tackle anything that walked. They had been known to whip grizzlies.

He tried to avoid thinking of Angie. The thought of her accusing eyes made him uncomfortable. She was all right, only she had such notions about staying with the ranch. As if they wouldn't be better off in town. And she didn't want him to gamble. He won, didn't he? He grinned a little, thinking of how he won. But she didn't know that, and it was none of her business. Besides, he had worked hard enough for two men while her old man was alive.

"Lots of 'Paches movin'," Phalinger said. "If we don't come up with him tonight, I'm goin' back."

Ed Lowe felt rising anger, but stifled it. Phalinger was no man to fool with, and besides, he wanted his company and his help. Ed Lowe was shrewd enough to know that he would get nowhere tackling Hondo Lane alone. The man's reputation had been acquired the hard way.

"Must be packin' a thousand dollars," Lowe said, urging Phalinger's greed. "Where else we goin' to get that much? Take us to Frisco."

"If we live."

They moved on as evening gathered, more slowly now. They were only a few miles behind Hondo at Deadman. They found the tracks of his horse there overlying those of the Indians.

"All right," Lowe agreed, "it's tonight or we both go back."

They pushed on. Lowe mopped sweat from his face. He had the feeling they were close, and now that they were drawing near his mouth was growing dry, and he was tense.

Long shadows stretched from the hills, the sun died beyond the mountains behind them, and the air grew cool. Lowe's shirt felt sticky and uncomfortable. Phalinger moved closer. From time to time they paused, listening.

"Ed."

Lowe turned to Phalinger. The gambler's face was white and set.

"I got a hunch, Ed. I got a gambler's hunch. We've had it."

Irritation mounted within Lowe, stifling his own doubt. "Don't be a damn fool!" He kept his voice down. "Hour from now we'll have him right where we want him. It's him ain't goin' to get back."

Their horses walked in sand. Ahead leaves rustled. Leaves meant a cottonwood, and a cottonwood meant water. Ed Lowe's hatred mounted within him. He loosened his gun, urged his horse forward, then stopped.

A faint sound reached him: a hoof on stone, the creak of saddle leather.

Lowe drew back, triumph choking him. "We got him!" he breathed. "Let's move back a bit. We got him right where we want him!"

CHAPTER ELEVEN

WHEN ANGIE HAD collected a double handful of the tender stalks of the squaw cabbage she put them in a basket and straightened to look at the hills. They were brown now, the grass fading under the blazing summer heat.

The days had passed slowly, each filled with its quota of work, but days that found her going more and more often to look from her doorstep at the surrounding hills. Hondo had said nothing of returning, and yet within her she was sure he had intended to come back.

Had she really read that intention in him, or was it only that the wish was father to the thought?

And her time was growing short. At any time Vittoro might return and say that she must choose now. Perhaps she should have gone with Hondo when he wanted to take her. She might be with him now. Yet she could not bear to leave all this, this place to which she had given the labor of her hands, and where she had seen her father rebuild the house, and lay the poles for the corral.

A man might drift, but a woman must belong somewhere, if it was no more than a hovel on a hillside. A woman must have a home, and this belonged to her. To herself and to Johnny.

There had been a great battle fought. That she knew from the scalps she had seen and the cavalry horses ridden by the Apaches. They had slaughtered one and eaten it not a half mile down the arroyo. Why the Apaches preferred horse and mule meat to good beef she did not know, but so they did, preferring mule meat to all else.

Her father had told her once that the early-day mountain men had liked the meat of the panther best, preferring it to the most tender venison. And they had their choice of game in a country where only Indians had hunted and there was much game.

Picking up her basket, she walked back, going a little out of her way to look at the bushes along the creek. There would be berries later in the season. Maybe enough to preserve some for the winter. This year would be the first when Johnny could help, and anxious as he was to appear a man, she knew he would do more than his share.

She had reached the house and was washing the cabbage stalks when she heard the rush of hoofs. At one moment the ranch was silent and the next it was a circle of rushing horses, a half-dozen hard-riding Indians sweeping by at a dead run, picking objects from the ground, leaping on and off their horses, performing like a circus gone mad.

Rifle in hand, she stopped at the door, staring in consternation at the yelling. charging Indians. Then she saw Vittoro, standing calmly beside the door.

"I thought the Apache were always silent."

"Except during the squaw-seeking ceremony."

Angie felt her heart miss a beat. For an instant she held herself still. "The what?"

"Ceremony of seeking new squaw. Then the braves show off their skill that the squaw may choose."

He took a step forward and lifted a hand. "Hola!"

The Indians swung into a charging line and rode up, rearing their horses, then quieting them to sit waiting.

"You will pick one. It is not good for Small Warrior to grow up without a father to teach him how to perform a man's duty."

Fascinated, she stared at Vittoro, and then at the Indians. Physically, they were magnificent specimens. Two were tall, the others the barrel-chested men of medium height typical of the Apaches. All were dressed in their fanciest regalia, but at least two wore parts of uniforms taken from dead soldiers.

Vittoro gestured at the one on the left. "This is the one called Emiliano. Very brave, and has six horses. Two squaws, but one is old and will soon be gone. He is a good hunter. It is never hungry where he sits.

"This one is Kloori. Ten horses, only one squaw. He is . . ."

Turning swiftly, Angie ran into the house, her heart throbbing painfully, too frightened almost to breathe. As she fought to regain control, tears came into her eyes. She heard Vittoro come into the house behind her, and turned quickly to face him.

Turning to Johnny, he said, "Go stand by my horse."

"Yes, Vittoro."

When the boy had gone the old Indian said sternly, "Small Warrior is never to see tears. The Apache does not weep."

Angie drew herself up. Desperation gave her strength. "Chief, you can't make me . . . I'm married."

"Married? Oh, the white man's word for it. You are a fool. Your man is dead."

"No. I do not know he is dead. Among my people it is not so easy. I . . . I must be sure. But even if it were true, I don't know . . . I . . . "

Vittoro did not seem to be listening. He gestured toward the waiting braves. "Sachito. Brave warrior. Many horses, does not beat squaws much. Sings very loud."

Desperately she searched for an argument that might move him, some common ground. Suddenly she believed she had it. "You don't understand. It would be against my religion. You Apaches have your own religion, and live up to it. I know that. Can't you understand? Can't you see that if mine tells me—"

Vittoro was impatient. He spoke quickly now, and more sharply. He was not accustomed to arguing with women, and the warriors who waited outside were the pride of his people, not to be lightly disdained by any woman.

"When religion makes you act like a fool, it is a wrong religion." He hesitated, then said brusquely, "Very well I have decided. We will wait." He pointed toward the mountains. "Soon will come the planting rain. If your man comes by then, good. If not, you take Apache brave. It is spoken."

He walked out of the house without a backward glance, mounted his pony, and, followed by the braves, rode from the basin. Angie, her heart pounding, watched them go.

Again, for a little while, she was safe. And after that there would be no choice. For a few minutes she thought of flight, suddenly, and in the night. Then she knew the absurdity of the idea, for by daylight they would be upon her trail and then there would be no more waiting . . . if they did not kill her out of hand. And one among them, at least, would do just that. She remembered the hatred in the eyes of Silva.

There would be no chance to get away, for she knew what an

Apache on a trail was like, and she knew nothing of hiding a trail, and with Johnny they could not travel fast. She was not even sure exactly where the Army post lay. And even there she might not find security. Who knew if there was even an Army post left? Many soldiers had been killed, perhaps all of them.

Yet from that moment she began to plan. There was no definite knowledge of what Hondo planned to do. She was foolish to think he might return, and the chance that Ed might return was even smaller. She must now, as always, rely upon herself.

The thing to do was to remain quiet, yet to plan and make preparations. She would need two horses, she would need food and ammunition. She did not know exactly where the post lay, yet she did not know where the Pass was, and the Pass was large enough to be safe from any Indian attack. There was an Army post there, also, and there were rangers here.

Somewhere among her father's things there was a map—she remembered seeing him make it—and if she could find it, she might be able to plan a way out. And he had taught her, while she was only a little girl, to use the stars to guide her travel. There would be a time when the braves of Vittoro would be far away at battle, raiding in Mexico or elsewhere. She had learned to know those times, and often the parties went through her basin on their way out.

The next time they went, she would take her horses and go at once, within the hour.

That night, after Johnny was asleep, she packed the saddlebags with ammunition and filled two canteens. If she had to wait she could always refill them. She prepared some jerky, placed it and some hardtack where they could be reached and packed in an instant.

Searching through her father's trunk, she found the map. It was a square of some twenty inches of hide, the lines drawn and notations made in his painstaking hand. The map itself was not crude, but a small work of art. She located the ranch, then searched out a way among the buttes and canyons by which they could travel.

Only one of the horses was fit to ride, so she must break the other. Fortunately, she believed there would be time. If there was not, she could always take Johnny on the same horse. Yet she went at once to the corral and remained beside the horses until it was completely dark, talking to them and feeding them.

She could not conquer them as Hondo had done, but the horse

she needed was a much less dangerous animal, and she had seen both her father and Hondo make friends with a horse until the battle was half won. Those were the tactics she would use; they were all that remained to her.

Once her decision was made, she planned every move with it in mind. There was an old lock. . . . Perhaps the Indians would break it, but she could at least try to protect her house until she returned.

She would wait until every other chance was gone. Perhaps she might escape during the rain. With the rain to wipe out her tracks, their chances would be greater. Yet that meant exposing Johnny to the fury of the storm . . . for storm it would be when the planting rain came.

It was almost midnight before Angie finally retired. During most of that time she had tried to plan her course of action. At the last moment she might have to act entirely opposite to her decided course, but she would have a plan. What to do would depend upon the events of the moment, but the very fact that she had a plan gave her confidence and a feeling of greater security.

Yet even as her eyes closed, her last conscious thought was that Hondo Lane might return. And the question remained in her mind: What had happened between them that she should feel so sure of how he felt? So little had been said, so little done. Yet the knowledge was there, and a deep inner realization that this was the man with whom she could be happy, this was the man with whom she wanted to live out her years.

And it could never be. Even if she escaped the Indians, if she survived all the fighting, and if Hondo felt about her as she felt about him, there was still no chance for happiness for either of them. There was always Ed Lowe. He might be dead, but Angie was not prepared to believe that. And he was her husband, the father of her child.

At daybreak an idea came to her. The Apaches would know how many horses were in the corral, and when two were missing they would immediately know she had fled. But for that she could plan. That very morning she led out two of the horses and picketed them on the grass in the trees and out of sight of any passing Indians. She would do this occasionally, while still remaining in sight herself. In that way the Indians would not be suspicious when they noticed the missing horses. There were several places they could be picketed out of sight, and where they could not be found without a search. Thus their disappearance would not be sudden, and not a cause for investigation.

Yet even as she worked and planned, Angie knew that her chances of escape were small. Only one thing made her decision to make the attempt one from which she could not retreat. There was no other way.

She was hanging out her wash when she heard approaching horses. Turning quickly, she saw that three Indians had ridden their ponies into the ranch yard. Scarcely two hours after the horses had been moved, and the Indians were here!

One of them was Silva.

They rode around the corral, noting the tracks. One of them rode in the direction the horses had gone, then returned, saying something to Silva. He shrugged, then walked his pony toward Angie.

She faced him, standing very straight, her face composed. To show terror could mean death, and she knew that of them all, Silva feared Vittoro less than the rest. He was, she knew, some sort of subchief.

"What do you want?"

He looked at her insolently. "Maybe soon you be my squaw."

"You?" Her contempt was plain. "Of all the braves in the lodges of the Apache, you would be the last, Fighter of Women!"

Silva's nostrils flared and temper quickened his eyes. It would not do to tempt the man too far, she realized. His was a hair-trigger temper, and he was naturally vindictive. Nor had he forgotten his defeat by her child. The story must have aroused many a chuckle in the wickiups.

One of the two braves riding with him was Emiliano. She remembered him instantly as one of those who had come with Vittoro to the squaw-seeking ceremony. He was a lean and powerful Indian, not the sort to be intimidated.

"I no fight women!" Silva's temper lashed at her. "I kill soldier! I count plenty coups!"

Sensing sympathy from the other Indians, she answered him. "And my child counted coup over you, Brave Warrior! And he is but six summers! Think, Brave Warrior!" Her contempt was thick, "What if he had been twelve?"

Silva started forward as if prodded with a lance, but Emiliano's voice rang sharply.

Silva whirled his horse and the two Indians faced each other, tempers flaring. The third Apache looked at her and she thought she detected a faint smile on his face. Whatever was said between Silva and Emiliano, the former suddenly wheeled his horse, and moved away.

The others hesitated a moment and then Angie said quietly, "Thank you, Emiliano. I shall speak of this to Vittoro."

His eyes held her briefly, then the two wheeled their ponies and followed after Silva. It was only then that reaction set in. What if Emiliano had not been there? What if Silva had with him some braves more of his own nature?

He would never, she knew instinctively, make this mistake again.

Suddenly her knees began to tremble, and the muscles in her legs shook uncontrollably. She got to the house and sat down on the steps, and it was a long time before she could move.

She had been a fool to stay on. She had been a silly fool. What good would she be to her son if they were taken to an Indian village? What good would the ranch be to either of them.

She would think no more of Hondo Lane. She would not think of Ed. Neither of them would come. The latter was faithless and vacillating, the former had no reason to return. No real reason. She was a lonely woman and her loneliness had magnified his respect and a chance kiss into something that was not there.

She would think of one thing only: escape. When the planting rain came, she would go. And if the rains were hard, they would wash out her tracks, and she would take a direction where they would never expect her. Then she might escape.

In the night she was awakened suddenly. A waiting moment of silence, then a sudden rush of hoofs across the hard-packed yard, then a hoarse cry. A long moment when there was no sound, then a shot and after it a long-drawn, wailing scream as of a mortal soul in pain.

Crouching by the window, rifle in hand, she peered out, and she could see nothing, only the moonlight on the cottonwood leaves, only the white-seeming roof of the stable, only the empty hills.

A dream? No. Johnny was crouching beside her, trembling, partly from cold and partly fear. He tugged at her arm. "Mommy! Mommy, what was that? What happened? Did the man come back?"

Did the man come back?

She felt something like horror mounting within her. Had he come back and been killed at her door?

There was no more sleep. When Johnny was safely in bed she wrapped a blanket about her and sat by the window, the rifle at her hand.

Slowly, with a quiet chill, the night passed. A faint yellow faded the eastern sky, the tips of the cottonwoods turned gold, like the sun-tipped lances of a moving army. The shadows in the yard drew back, hiding in the barn and under the brush along the stream, crouching there. A quail sent out an inquiring call, and somewhere across the basin another quail responded.

It was morning.

CHAPTER TWELVE

WHEN PHALINGER AND Ed Lowe had ridden back a quarter of a mile from Hondo's place of stopping, Lowe drew up. "Look," he said quietly. "We've got him. Right now he's makin' camp. He'll be mighty cautious. So we let him be. Come daylight, either before he's up or when he's gettin' up, we'll take him."

The gambler shrugged. "Your party." He studied the hills.

"His fingers will be stiff then."

Phalinger looked at Lowe with a faint shadowing of contempt. "Don't take many chances, do you?"

"Why be a sucker?"

From the position Lowe had chosen, the arroyo was in view. They could not see Hondo Lane, nor could he see them, but escape from his camp was impossible without alerting them.

Phalinger was quiet. The farther he had gone, the less he liked any part of it. He was a man without qualms. Lowe knew little about him aside from his utter lack of scruples and the fact that he was a slick second dealer who knew cards and who worked well with a partner. Phalinger had done murder in Missouri, drifted west into Kansas, then south into Texas. He was wanted in both places.

Yet he had an admiration for a brave man, and Hondo Lane was such a man. Despite the fact that he worked with Lowe, he despised him. Yet not even Phalinger knew that Lowe had deserted a woman in Indian country. Had he known, he might have killed him out of hand.

Phalinger was restless. Their camp was good. They needed no fire. They had food and whisky. Nevertheless, the premonition he had felt earlier now returned. Hondo Lane was carrying several months' wages from the Army and a small poke of gold of his own. It would make a rich haul, and gambling had not been profitable. Too many had lost to them and the word had gone around. It was time to drift, and without money drifting was impossible.

Broodingly he watched Lowe. What drove the man? What was there in him aside from greed and hatred? Yet no man was all bad. Phalinger, who was bad in most ways, knew that he himself was not all bad. Lying on his back he looked up at the stars, thinking about Lowe. He decided that Lowe was weak . . . weak and jealous.

He would always, Phalinger decided, strike at what was stronger and better than himself.

The only reason that Lowe had neither left him nor struck at him, the gambler was sure, was because he considered himself smarter or braver. The thought was galling.

"It better be tomorrow." He said the words suddenly. "I'm going back."

"It'll be tomorrow."

Hondo Lane had made dry camp in the gully. It was also a camp without fire. He was drawing too near to his objective now to take any chances. Also, there had been occasional dust along his backtrail, and once his eye had caught a flash of sunlight on some moving object behind him.

He could be mistaken, of course. But somebody seemed to be trailing him—somebody not an Indian.

The bed he had chosen was in a small open space in the middle of a thicket of mountain mahogany and prickly pear. There was a little catclaw, too. In this place he could sleep without fear, for nothing human could approach his bed without making considerable noise.

On the soft sand he hollowed a place for his hips and rolled in his blankets and ground sheet. He slept, as always, gun in hand.

His saddle lay beside him, his rifle in the scabbard, and his horse was picketed a few feet away. Sam crept under the brush on his belly and put his dark muzzle down on his paws and looked at the man he loved.

The man had strange ways, but he was Sam's friend, and they understood each other. And upon this night Sam too was restless. Twice that day his nostrils had caught a vague smell, faintly familiar, but scarcely tangible. Sam was uneasy, no more.

A quarter of a mile apart three men looked at the night sky. One was discontented with his situation, but ready to accept the profits of murder; the second was thinking first of murder and second of profit; and the third, lying on the sand among the thorns and brush, thought of a cabin, of the fireflight on a woman's face, and of her shadow on the wall as he tried to go to sleep.

The moving shadow of a woman on a wall, and the faint sounds of a woman working. It had been a long time, a long, lonely, restless time, since he had heard such sounds.

The lineback had found some grass. He pulled at it, then ate. The sound of his moving jaws was pleasantly relaxing. The man who thought of a woman went to sleep.

Twice in the night the dog awakened and looked at the man, then listened with pricked ears. Had he heard something, far off? He listened and the night listened around him, and there was no sound, and the dark muzzle lowered to the paws against the sand, and the dog's eyes closed, and the horse, too, lay down.

A coyote moved to the arroyo's edge and lifted his nose to the sky, but catching the scent of dog and man, it moved warily away.

Three miles to the south and west a Mescalero walked up a trail, then suddenly stopped. His feet, sensitive through the moccasins, detected something wrong in the path. He knelt, his fingers explored, and he found the indentation made by a horseshoe.

He muttered something to the others, who gathered around him, and the three stood talking in undertones and looking away to the north and east. Then they walked their horses into a hollow hand of hills and prepared to wait until morning.

There was a white man ahead of them, and possibly more than one. These were scalps to be had, coups to be counted, and they would return to their village men made stronger by the death of enemies. Their dark faces relaxed and they did not talk. And then they, too, went to sleep.

And the planet turned slowly in the vast night sky, and the stars looked down, and there was a smell of damp and coolness in the air.

Far over the mountains low clouds gathered. Perhaps the planting rain?

Under a quiet sky the planet turned, and horses ate, and men slept, and death waited for morning.

A bright star hung like a distant lamp in the sky when Hondo opened his eyes. He did not lie still. To awaken was to rise, and he did so now, getting swiftly to his feet, buckling on his gun belt, holstering the gun, and drawing on his boots.

Sam came to his feet with one swift, unnoticed motion as Hondo rolled his bed. The dog growled low, and Hondo looked up at him, watching.

The Indians were near, and their moving disturbed a rattler, which coiled and sent out a short, sharp warning. Hondo relaxed, but Sam growled.

"Cut it out, Sam! I can hear him."

Yet in that instant, his perceptions sharpened by danger, he sensed something else. The dog was disturbed as he had not seen him before, and the dog was not directing his attention toward the sound of the rattler.

There was a frozen instant when Hondo's ears caught at sound, when with the instincts of a wild thing he dropped suddenly and rolled over the bank beneath its added protection, backed by the deeper portion of the brush-choked gully. As he moved, one swift grab slid the Winchester into his hands.

And after that single, violent, animal-like dive for safety, all was still, unmoving. And the movement itself had been relatively soundless.

Now Hondo lay still, listening, scarcely able to breathe. A bee buzzed near, landed on a bush. Hondo could see the texture of the wings, the flexing of the tiny muscles of the body. Sam was quiet. The lineback, seemingly aware of the sudden tension, was still. Not a sound disturbed the clear, bell-like beauty of the morning. There was nothing.

And then there was.

Two riders showed up suddenly on the canyon rim, rifles ready, starkly outlined against the morning.

Lowe and Phalinger had ridden their horses forward through soft sand. At first they considered crawling to the rim, but Lowe was aware of the dog's danger, and had no desire to come upon the big mongrel suddenly. It would be a simple matter to ride right up to the rim, keeping a spacing of about twenty yards, then fire. Hondo Lane would be offered two shots, which was sure to make him hesitate an instant if he saw them at all, and they could cut him down.

The plan was perfect—up to a point. They had not counted on the alertness of Hondo Lane or the hearing of Sam.

Nor did they know about the Apaches.

Phalinger liked no part of it. His heart was pounding and his mouth was dry. He had no breakfast, and he desperately wanted coffee. They had killed their whisky during the long night and his nerves were jumpy. It was too quiet. Moreover, he was moved by the beauty of the morning. Something deep within him seemed urging him to stop, to breathe, to enjoy. This was something one could not buy in bottles. It was bright, clear, all too beautiful.

Phalinger had killed. He had shot men in the back, and he would not hesitate to do so again. Yet he loved life and loved it dearly, and in that awful moment of realization he saw in the clear, sharp beauty of the morning what wasted years he had left behind. He looked over at Lowe, started to speak.

And he hesitated. Lowe was alert, tense. His rifle was ready. Lowe was a killer, as are many cowardly things, and he could not accept that there should live things and persons superior to him. Angie's father had always been a better man, but wanting the ranch, Ed Lowe had played a game, fooling the father more successfully than he could ever fool the daughter.

Their horses walked in the soft earth. They moved forward, step by step. Before them their view of the arroyo widened, the morning grew brighter. The sun lay against the far bank and at their backs, for they had circled for this advantage, so that Hondo would have to fire into the glare of the sun.

Phalinger heard a bird call. He heard the soft fall of his horse's hoofs. A leaf brushed his face, and off across the far hills there were low clouds. The very canyons, moraines, and hanging valleys showed sharply clear in the bright air. He liked the feel of the horse moving under him, liked the smell of it. He liked the smell of sage, and of crushed cedar. . . . Why had he waited so long to realize this?

Lowe caught his eye with a signal. Phalinger's rifle came up. It was live or die now. They brested the slope.

They saw the rolled blankets, the open space in the brush, the linebacked horse . . . and nothing else!

In that single, awful moment of awareness, both men were caught, suspended, in the moment. Both had expected a target, were ready for it . . . and there was nothing.

Then from Phalinger's far right a flash of sunlight on a rifle barrel turned his head. For one swift, stark moment he saw the Apache, saw the dark, slim body, saw the rifle muzzle not forty yards away, and knew he looked upon death.

He lifted his rifle, and heard soft, gasping words torn from him. "Oh, God!" And then the rifle bullet smashed into his jaw, tearing through his throat, and he fell.

His horse sprang from under him. Vaguely he heard other shots, but they were not for him, nor was he for them. He lay flat on his face with the taste of blood and earth in his mouth and he was choking and he was seeing again the bright morning he had left, and with his last muscular effort he rolled over to look at the sky.

There was a white cloud there, so small, so lonely, so white against the vast blue dome of the morning. For day had come. It was here, and Phalinger looked up at the sky and saw the cloud fade and knew he was gone and he tried to speak past the blood and there were no words, there was nothing any more. . . .

One moment there had been nothing and then the two riders appeared on the skyline. Their wide separation rang a bell of warning in Hondo's brain, but at the same time he knew that while it was this that had disturbed Sam, it was not this that had disturbed the rattler. And the crash of shots told him he was right.

He saw the nearer man drop, saw him hit the ground, heard a thin, despairing cry. Then he saw the other man drop also.

The Apaches had been following Hondo Lane. They had not expected two men. They had no reason to believe there could be three.

To count coup upon the body of a dead enemy is not so great a glory as to do it upon a living one. All three Apaches sprang suddenly forward . . . into death.

The nearest Apache was a tall, splendidly built man, and he sprang eagerly, rifle held high. Hondo Lane's bullet took him under the breastbone, striking at an angle, and ripped out of his side below the heart. The splendid leap was the last movement, for when the Apache touched the ground all that amazing wiry strength was dead, a blasted, wasted thing, giving blood to the sand.

Hondo fired swiftly, saw the second man go down, the third vanish.

For an instant Hondo lay still. The second white man to be shot by the Apaches had fallen from his horse into the arroyo. Worming his way through the brush, Hondo made it to his side. It was Ed Lowe.

Even as he reached his side and laid down his rifle, the remaining warrior leaped from the brush into the saddle of Phalinger's horse and was gone from sight.

Hondo checked Lowe, then sat back on his heels. "You're not hurt too bad."

Lowe, badly shaken, sat up. Some color was returning to his face. There was blood on his shirt. He drew a picture from his shirt pocket. "This tintype saved me."

The bullet had struck his chest at a flat angle and, hitting the tintype, had glanced away, tearing the skin beyond it with a burn rather than a wound.

Hondo Lane got to his feet, picking up his rifle. "I wish that Indian hadn't got away. All the Apaches between here and the post will be alerted now."

"You mean we're cut off?"

"What else?" Lane turned to study the terrain carefully. It was time to move. No telling how far away there were other Indians.

As Lane turned away, Ed Lowe realized two things: Here was the man he had come to kill, and there was only one horse left—Lane's horse.

Hondo heard the sudden sharp growl from Sam. He sidestepped quickly as he turned and saw the flash of Lowe's gun. Hondo fired his rifle from the hip and the bullet smashed Ed Lowe back to the sand. His muscles convulsed, bringing him almost erect. Hondo Lane did not fire again.

Lowe came almost up, then fell, and there was no sound in the brightness of the desert morning.

Hondo looked down at what had been Angie's husband, then picked up the tintype. It was a picture of Johnny.

He dropped to the sand, his face gray and ghastly, holding the tintype and his rifle and realization. And Sam came close and nudged against him, whining softly. And this time he was allowed to come close.

CHAPTER THIRTEEN

FOR AN HOUR of lonely riding there had been no life upon the desert. The sun was high, and sweat trickled down Hondo's neck, and the body of the lineback became dark with stain. And before them stretched the vast and rolling plain of sand, rock, and cactus that is the desert of the Southwest.

Here there was no moment of security. Somewhere out there the escaped Apache had joined his friends, and somewhere those hard and tireless desert fighters were moving out, beginning their search for him.

Desert . . . but a desert strangely alive. Not a dead land, but a land where all life is born with a fire, a thorn, a sting. Yet a strong land, a rich land for the man who knows it. One cannot fight the desert and live. One lives with it, or one dies. One learns its way and its life, and moves with care, and never ceases to be wary, for the desert has traps and tricks for the careless.

The lineback walked with dainty feet, knowing this land, knowing its fears and its dangers. And on his back Hondo Lane never ceased to watch, taking in each small shadow, each dark rock, each possible place of cover before moving on. Once, riding along a rocky hillside, he followed the fresh trail of a deer. Suddenly the animal's tracks broke sharply to the left and into the bottom.

Hondo swung the lineback and followed, his hand ready for his rifle. Whatever the deer had seen or heard might now be gone, but he was not gambling. Later he came upon the fresh trail of a mountain lion. Probably not Apaches, then.

He followed down the arroyo until it widened into a small valley where a stream flowed, cottonwood and willow lining its banks. Riding into the brush, he dismounted. Then, slipping off his boots, he walked back, brushing out his trail and leaving the tracks pointed toward the water as if to ride in or cross the stream.

Then he retreated carefully, avoiding branches. Wild game will not step on fallen branches. Neither would an Indian. Only a horse, a cow, or a white man would be so foolish. The weight of the horse or cow or man would break the branch into finer pieces and press it into the ground. Hondo retreated with care, and when he was in the shelter of the trees he loosened the girth on the saddle and sat down with his back against a tree.

It was not yet noon, at least an hour short of it, but the heat was great despite the time of the year, and he must conserve both his horse's strengh and his own. He chewed on some jerky and hard-tack while the horse cropped grass, then went down to the stream through the thick brush and drank. Then he emptied his canteen and refilled it with cold, fresh water.

After an hour's rest he pulled on his boots and tightened the girth. At the edge of the small grove where he had waited, he studied the terrain with care before moving out. Knowing the Apaches, he had no idea they would lose his trail. All he could do would be to delay their pursuit as much as possible. Yet now, when he left the grove, he rode swiftly forward, following down the stream bed, using the concealment of its trees. He left the creek on a shelf of rock and rode straight up the side of the valley. The last few feet was a hard scramble, but they topped the crest and were immediately off the ridge.

A wide, long valley opened before him, dotted with the tall sentinel fingers of saguaro and the serrated ridge of an upthrust ledge that cut down the opposite wall. It was of dark, sun-blackened rock. The lineback was rested and he moved out eagerly.

Suddenly a startled bird flew up some distance off, and instantly Hondo swung the lineback. The Apaches broke into sight scarcely seconds later, but the lineback was already running. With wild, shrill yells the Indians booted their ponies and the chase was on.

The lineback was a fast, powerful animal with fire and a love of running. He took to it now, mane flying, nose into the wind.

Glancing back, Hondo saw he was gaining ground, and suddenly he heard a whining yelp from Sam, and turning back he saw four more Indians coming down off the ridge ahead of him. To turn to avoid them was to lose distance, but there was no help for it. He swung the racing horse into a branching canyon and went up the side on a long angle.

There were at least eight Apaches behind him now, and they had gained ground. He went up the ridge and then suddenly before him there was a long gray slide of shale. There was no stopping. The lineback plunged into it, lost footing and went down. Sam was racing close and he was lost in the swirl of dust. The horse scrambled madly, fighting for a foothold, got it, and Hondo went back into the saddle and then he saw Sam come out of the dust on three legs.

With a quick glance back at the Indians, Hondo bent and

scooped the injured dog into his arms, and then they were racing away again.

The time lost was too much. The Apaches had gained, and even as he cleared the ridge they converged around him. There was no chance to grab a gun with the dog in his arms, and they sprang from their horses and knocked him from the saddle. He struck out viciously, the dog leaped away, snapping at Silva, who was one of the attackers, but then the Indians were all over him.

Hondo Lane was thrown on his face and his hands were jerked behind him and lashed hard with rawhide.

A few yards away Sam stood, growling, waiting the expected command to attack. It was not given. Hondo glanced around. Nine Indians.

Silva's eyes went to Sam, and he turned and barked a request at the nearest warrior for his bow and an arrow.

Hondo jerked his head around. "Sam! Vete, Sam! Vete!"

Instantly, the big dog wheeled and darted into the brush, making fast time even with his bad leg. Once back in the brush he crouched and crawled back, lying in the brush, growling low in his chest, but securely out of sight.

Silva walked to Hondo and struck him across the face. There was cold triumph in his eyes. There would be a big time in the village this night. This man was strong. If he had courage, he might live a long time. . . . But why delay? Why wait until night? He could sing of his deeds when they returned, and the man was here, now.

"The white man speaks our language," he said. "It is good. He will know his treatment in advance."

"Your coup stick shows many scalps."

"Truly."

Hondo spoke slowly, clearly, and with contempt thick upon the words. He knew the Apache, knew the words would lash his fury. "You took them from squaws and papooses and dogs. Your lodge should be proud of you."

Hondo spoke in Spanish, then in the tongue of the Apache. One of the Indians gave a grunt of laughter, but Silva's eyes flared hot and ugly. The insult had not been expected.

"Truly," the Apache said, "you will feel much."

"It is nothing," Hondo sneered, "to torture a captured man. You are a woman of the village, a runner after rabbits. Without the bravery of these others you would be food for coyotes now!"

Hondo Lane spoke with cold calculation. He was a man who

knew his land, and knew the people who held him now. There was always, one thought, a chance of escape. Rarely with the Apache. He bound his captives too brutually, he stayed with them too closely. A prisoner had only to die . . . to die slowly, over a fire, head down, or staked out on an ant hill, or bound in a green hide and laid out in the hot sun. Or one might die quickly. If Silva could be angered enough . . .

But Silva was a patient as well as a vindictive man. There was no desire in him to give the white man quick death instead of the hours of torture he planned. And this one had courage. He was a strong man, with wiry, powerful muscles. He would die slowly, and when at the end he broke, it would be a triumph to be remembered.

Silva's anger at the insults was a white-hot thing that wound through his body like blazing wire. But the man was here, tied, a prisoner. A delayed revenge could be the sweeter for all of that. And when they tied Hondo Lane upon a horse, his hands were bound so tightly that they swelled. And then they moved on, winding across the long hills, a tiny cavalcade of Apaches, bare-backed on their ponies, their flat faces emotionless and still.

And with the afternoon the heat became a living thing. The sun hung in a wide sky and seemed to spread until all the sky was a great reflector pouring its heat upon the desert, which reflected it back. And the vast distance was a space across which moved the tiny figures of the Apaches and their captive, and sitting his horse, Hondo Lane lost himself in a world of pain and heat and movement where there was only feeling and where all was lost in space and there was no time. . . .

The moments became hours and the hours weeks and the days seemed years. His hands had swollen greatly, his shirt was soaked with sweat, and the salt sweat got into his eyes and they smarted, red-rimmed and narrowed against the sun and the glare.

Yet behind the monotony of their travel, behind the blank vacancy of his face where lay a world sodden with pain, behind it all there still prowled the restless desperation of a strong man wanting to live. There was no way now . . . but there might be a way.

Bitter within him was the desire to fight, to die in battle if no more, but to escape, to get away, to live. The bitterness of his capture was through him like a poison. He stared through heat-rimmed eyes at the evil face of Silva, knowing instinctively that here was his enemy. This one was the one he must kill.

The distance shimmered with heat. Sweat trickled down his body under his shirt. He felt the pain in his hands and the wicked bite of the taut rawhide, cutting into the raw flesh.

And he lifted his head and stared at Silva. He spat. "Squaw!" he sneered. His hatred made his speech ugly. "Old woman!"

Silva's head turned, his eyes liquid with ugliness. Then the Indian looked ahead once more.

Hondo Lane was tempted to touch a spur to the lineback, to lunge into the Indian, to make a break for it, hands tied or not. But his good sense told him the futility of that. There would be a time. He must wait. He flexed his stiff, swollen fingers. But he made no sound. He did not groan, he did not curse.

At every step of the horse his hands hurt him, at every move there was new pain.

He hung his head forward and let his body move with the steps of the lineback, and his mind lost itself in remembering. The ranch beside the stream, the clear, cold water, the woman with the clear, expressive eyes, her quiet movements about the house, and the sound of a child's voice . . . A yearning mounted within him and the pain was forgotten. He remembered the dry rustle of the cottonwood leaves, the good taste of coffee, the smell of wood smoke from her fireplace.

Then he smelled smoke, and another, older, more familiar smell. An Apache *rancheria.*

He looked up and saw them. It was familiar, old in his memory, the sights, the smells. He almost looked for the quick movement of Destarte. But she was gone, dead.

He saw the flat, hard faces of the men, the wide cheekbones, the square jaws, the headbands.

How many times had he come here from hunting to such a place? How many months had he lived among such people as these? There might be some here who knew him. There might be those with whom he had hunted, and with whom he had ridden to Mexico to steal horses for their people.

He sat straight in the saddle, holding his head up, looking neither to right nor to left. If he must die, he would show them how a man should go, he would show them with contempt and insults that there burned within him a fire that could not die. He knew the Apache heart, knew the Apache mind.

When they stopped he looked around him at the brown faces, saw the one man who stood apart and knew it.

Hondo Lane said loudly, "It is my shame that I am taken by warriors with whom rides an old woman."

Hondo was taken roughly from the saddle and the rawhide was cut from his hands. He was shoved into position beside the fire. There was a pot of water standing there, and without asking questions he dipped his swollen hands into it, feeling the coolness of the water soothing the pain.

Vittoro, who had stood aside, came to the circle around the fire and looked down at him.

"The white man speaks our language," Silva said. "He has spoken many insults."

CHAPTER FOURTEEN

HONDO GENTLY CHAFED his hands. Nobody had made any move to stop him from administering to his hands. He glanced up to see Vittoro studying him. The old chief acknowledged Silva's remark.

"It is a brave man who insults at such a moment." To Hondo he said suddenly, "Where are the pony soldiers, white man? And how many are they?"

"This I do not know, Vittoro."

"You know how I am called?"

"I saw you at the treaty council at Fort Meade."

"The treaty! The rustle of wind to the white man." His voice grew sharper. "Where are the pony soldiers?"

"This I do not know."

Vittoro gestured toward the saddle on the lineback. "Your saddle bears the mark of the pony soldier."

"Once I was a pony soldier. Now I am not."

Vittoro seated himself and looked across the corner of the fire at Hondo's swollen hands. They looked bad, but already they felt better. The swelling had been caused by the tight binding, and once they were released, much of the swelling had gone down.

"If you are not a spy, what do you seek in our land?"

Hondo Lane hesitated, and then he said more slowly, careful to make his voice sound its respect. "This if for me to know, Chief. What I do does no harm to the people of Vittoro, or to any Apache."

Vittoro got to his feet and walked away across the camp. And then for a time Hondo was left alone. His feet were tied but his hands were free. He flexed their muscles, feeling the swelling going away. His wrists were lacerated by the tight-drawn rawhide, but the blood was flowing normally once more.

He looked around him at the *rancheria* in the shallow valley. It was a scene anciently familiar to him . . . the low wickiups of brush or hides gathered about pyramided sticks, the horses grazing, the children playing about.

Only then he had not been a prisoner. He had been one of them. An alien, yes, but a friend and a hunting companion and the man of Destarte. And he smelled the desert air, the smell of roasting venison and mule meat, the nopal drying and watched the people moving about their tasks.

He sat alone. Knowing the ways of these people, he knew the death that awaited him now, knew what they would do, and knew that he must be strong, to show no fear, to show no pain. He must at all costs die well.

And it was not so easy to die well. He had seen other men die, and he had seen the remains of men who had died well. It had never seemed possible that what they had endured could be endured by any man. Could he do as well?

A squaw brought him food, and he thanked her in her own tongue, and she glanced at him from the corners of her eyes, astonished. Then she went away, but later she returned with a gourd and cool water from the spring.

Was it kindness or because they wanted him strong for dying?

In the woman he decided it was kindness, yet the others did not object, and they missed nothing. The woman was the squaw of one called Emiliano.

It was good to live. How could a man prepare himself for death with the smell of the desert in his nostrils? What he wanted was not to die, but to live, to return again to Angie . . . and to Johnny.

He had always wanted a son. But what man does not want a son? What man wishes to die and leave no man to carry on, to continue the strain, the bloodline? Who wishes to waste what he has learned? Who wishes to see it die with him?

Old as life is the desire for sons. Old as all life upon the planet. It is this that carries on the species, and it is necessary for each man and woman to breed. That was the will of nature. All else came after. The species must continue, it must go on.

So there is deeply seated this desire, this wish. And he, Hondo Lane, what did he have to pass on? His skill with a gun? His ability to kill? To destroy?

No . . . but there were the desert and the mountains and the love of strong things, man things. The creak of saddle leather in the sun, the taste of cold, clear water, the ways of wild game and of horses, the little tricks of working . . . all these were ancient instincts, basic in the blood of man, built upon the ancient drive to carry on the race, the blood, the species.

And he sat here ready to die . . . for what? He left behind him nothing. A few people who would remember for a day or an hour. A man needed something on which to build. A man without a woman, without a home, and without a child was no man at all.

Johnny. If there had been no son of his own, he could at least have given Johnny what he had learned, the way of the desert and mountains, the thousand tiny things he had learned for himself, in bitterness and struggle, and the philosophy, too.

The things he had learned that were right and good, the things that living taught him—must these die?

He stared across the *rancheria* at the lonely squalor of the Apache camp, and knew that he must live. He must go on. He was not ready to die. He had done nothing, nothing at all.

And these people—how could he blame them? They were the People. That was what their name meant. They had believed they were meant to be the People. Yet when the first Americans came they had greeted them with friendship, and had been met with war. Then fiercely they had fought back. Not one but knew he fought in vain. They saw the white men endlessly coming, their many soldiers, their many ponies, their food supply that was endless, and their many cartridges of brass.

The Apache knew his hour was past. He knew the white men would take even his last land, but it was not in him to knuckle under. He would fight, sing his death song, and die. And he, Hondo Lane, was only a small part of the much vaster picture, and it mattered not at all to that picture that he was not through living, that he left things undone, that he wanted a son, that a woman waited for him. Or did she?

Yet there was no doubt even as his mind framed the question.

He had kissed her because a woman should not die unkissed, unloved. Yet after the kiss it had not been the same. He had gone away, yet even as he rode he knew he would return. And here he was, a prisoner beside the fire, awaiting the death by torture of the most fiendishly skillful of all savage torturers.

Vittoro got to his feet, and as upon a signal the others arose also, and then they moved toward him, and he sat quietly upon the ground and watched them come.

Here it was.

They grabbed him then and drew him back upon the sand and staked his arms out. Then with a piece of bark Silva scooped glowing coals from the fire and poured them into Hondo's open palm.

He felt the pain shoot through him, smelled the burning of his own flesh, but he stared at Silva and said bitterly, "Silva is a scalper of children, a runner after rabbits!"

"This only begins. We Apaches are patient." Silva looked his hatred and his triumph.

Beyond Vittoro a couple of braves had found Hondo's saddlebags and were going through them. Suddenly one straightened, grunting. He had found the tintype of Johnny, and he walked swiftly to Vittoro and thrust the picture before him.

Hondo saw the action, his teeth shut tight against the awful pain of his burning flesh.

Vittoro came suddenly to his feet and kicked the embers from Hondo's palm. "Loose him!"

A couple of Indians moved to obey, and Silva sprang between them and the prisoner, his face dark with angry blood. "It shall not be so!"

Vittoro's voice was even, cold. "I have need of this man."

"It shall not be!"

Vittoro glared at him, then snapped at the others, "Obey!"

As they slashed Hondo's bonds and released him, Silva shouted, "I claim the blood right!" He was beside himself with fury. "It is my privilege. It is so written."

Hondo looked down at his charred hand. Huge blisters were already beginning to shape, yet the hand was not so badly burned as he had believed, or so deeply. It was a hard hand, calloused by much work and much handling of guns. Now it was burned and crippled for a time, but a hand still, with fingers to move and to grip.

The medicine man had come forward with knives. Hondo was scarcely aware of what they did. He clutched the wrist of the burned hand and looked down at it, his face twisted with agony.

Then he heard, through his pain, the muttering words of the medicine man, blessing the knives, and he looked up suddenly.

"That life may ebb cleanly."

"That life may ebb cleanly," Vittoro repeated. "It is so written."

Silva stripped off his jacket, a lithe, powerful warrior in the prime of his young manhood. Vittoro stepped to a quickly drawn circle and flipped a knife into the ground on each side.

"White man, do you understand?"

"I lived with the Mimbreños many winters."

He came swiftly to his feet, only to stagger from the clumsiness of his recently released feet. Silva swooped for a knife, and Hondo caught his in his burned palm, then threw it, as one would a gun doing the border shift, to his left hand. He caught the knife deftly, and Silva sprang close, his eyes glowing with eagerness.

Hondo circled , knowing the danger of the man. He was strong, uninjured, and filled with hatred. Under any circumstances, he would be dangerous. Silva extended his left hand, but was bothered by the knife in the wrong hand. It should have been in the right, so he could seize the wrist. Circling to study this, he lunged suddenly. Hondo felt the sharp point of the knife rip his shirt, then he stomped down hard with his boot on Silva's bare foot and slashed with his knife edge. The Indian twisted away but the knife left a red line that rapidly turned red with blood along a shoulder.

They circled, and around them the sweaty faces stared eagerly, Hondo could hear the breathing of the warriors. He could see the glow of firelight, he could see the eagerness in their eyes, for this to them was the great moment, the greatest of sport. Fighting men all, they could know and respect a fighting man, and not one there but knew the odds each man faced.

Silva came in low, his point flicking. Hondo sprang back, then lunged. The knife of Silva stabbed and the blade sank into Hondo's shoulder.

Before it could be withdrawn, Hondo pressed forward against

the haft, holding the knife in the wound to prevent its withdrawal. They went to the ground and Hondo caught Silva's hair and forced his head back, exposing the brown throat, then he put the edge of his knife against the throat of the Indian and looked at Vittoro.

Vittoro stood above them and he said, unhurried, "The white man permits you to choose, Silva."

Silva hesitated, his hatred a living, fighting thing. Yet there was only the one choice, to yield or to die. And he was not ready to die. If he lived he might yet kill the white man and take his hair.

"I choose," he muttered.

Vittoro gestured, and Hondo released Silva and stepped back. But he still held the knife.

Silva stared at Hondo, then turned abruptly and stalked away to his wickiup.

"White man," Vittoro said, "is it in your thoughts you have purchased life?"

"It is my thought that the one called Vittoro is a great chief, and a chief considers all that happens in this world."

"It is possible you may live. Or you may die. We shall see what is written."

CHAPTER FIFTEEN

ACROSS THE VAST sweep of the sky there were clouds, darkening clouds pressing ominously down toward the far hills. Flat upon the earth, skyward they lowered in huge, unbelievable masses.

A low wind caught the breath of their coolness and moved across the desert, moving down the arroyos and canyons, creeping across the face of a land scarred by canyons and ridged by the backbones of ancient ridges. And the cool wind came swiftly and crossed the land and dipped into the basin and the ranch.

The wind stirred the curtain and Angie looked up from her ironing and glanced outside. A few leaves skittered across the hard-baked clay of the yard, the horses' tails streamed past their hocks, and a whisp of hay blew to a corral post, then hung there, still and quiet.

Angie walked to the stove and exchanged her iron for one freshly heated, testing it with a dampened finger. At the window Johnny stared at the towering battlements of cloud, looming now above the basin's edge.

"Mommy, big clouds are coming up."

"It feels like rain." She drew the apron over the end of the board and sprinkled it lightly.

"Why is rain, Mommy?"

"God's way of making the earth green. This is what the Indians call the planting rain."

The planting rain . . . She looked quickly past the trees at the sky.

Black, threatening clouds piled high. Quickly she put down the iron and went to the door, apprehension written large upon her face.

There could be no doubt. There would be rain, the planting rain, and then there was no time. When the storm began it would rain hard, then it might settle down for a long hard rain. They must leave before it ended, while it would still wipe out their tracks.

She folded her clothing and put it away, then went quickly to the cupboard. She packed swiftly, according to plan. She was sure, definite in her movements. There was no choice, no further decision to be made. Before the Indians could come, she must be gone.

Going to the bed, she took blankets and the old ground sheet and wrapped them in a tight roll. Johnny turned from the window. She caught his glance. "Would you like to go on a picnic, Johnny? In the rain?"

He looked doubtful. "In the rain?"

"It would be fun in the rain. We've got to ride a long way, and you'll have to take good care of Mommy."

"You mean I can ride a horse? All my own?"

"Yes, all your own. You can ride Old Gray."

Instantly he was all eagerness. She gave him several small tasks to do, then went to the barn and after some trouble lured the horses to the corral bars and got a rope on them. Leading them to the barn, she turned to the saddles. Hearing Johnny call out, she turned.

It was too late. A small cavalcade of Indians was coming down the slope.

Her heart pounding heavily, she walked to the house. "Johnny, you stay inside. They want to see Mommy."

There were a dozen Indians in the little group, and they had a prisoner. She saw that at once, only seeing the hanging head of a man, the dim shape of a haggard face beneath the hat. Vittoro dismounted and came to her. Behind him the man was dragged from the saddle.

"Is this your man?"

Angie looked beyond him. The man had lifted his head and he stared into her eyes. His own were glazed with suffering and weariness. She could see that something was terribly wrong with his hand. But she noticed nothing, only that it was Hondo Lane, and that he had come back.

"Speak!"

At a gesture from Vittoro, an Indian threw a pail of water into Lane's face. He blinked, then shook his head, straightening a little. Their eyes met and held.

"Is this your man?"

She understood suddenly, and she smiled quickly at Vittoro, coming down from the steps. "Yes. This is my husband."

She went to him quickly, taking his arm. Vittoro stared at her, then at Hondo Lane.

"White man," he said sternly, "you have lived with the Apache. That is good. You know how the Small Warrior should be taught so that he will be the honored son of Vittoro.

"Watch like the hawk, be patient as the beaver and courageous as the puma that he may learn well. Know it, then, or your dying will be long before you welcome death."

He turned away and mounted. Without looking back, the Indians rode from the valley.

Holding tight to his arm, for she sensed his weakness, she led him toward the house. In the distance thunder rumbled and there were scattered drops of rain, large drops striking hard on the baked clay.

She took him to the bed and he sat down, then fell loosely into sleep. She looked down at the blistered and swollen hand, the lacerated wrists, the bloody shirt. Turning quickly, she went outside with the pail to get fresh water.

Sam was coming down the slope, making slow time on three legs. She started to call, then saw Silva. The Apache came over the slope and started for the dog on a gallop. Sam turned, trying to run, but with a shrill yell Silva dropped his lance and ran the dog through the body. In a wild, desperate effort, the dog snapped at the lance, then fell free. Silva rode on over the slope.

Leaving the pail, Angie ran up the slope to the dying dog. His body was horribly torn; blood was flowing from him. Nothing could be done. She touched his head gently. "Good boy, Sam," she said softly. Feebly he tried to lick her hand.

She straightened then and looked in the direction Silva had taken. She knew then how a man could kill.

Rain was falling fast when she reached the house with her bucket. Once inside, she closed and barred the door. Quickly she got water on the fire to heat, got out the bandages she had made for emergencies. She had turned the horses back into the corral, and there was shelter for them under the overhang of the lean-to.

With a needle she ran a bit of colorless yarn previously soaked with antiseptic through each blister to allow it to drain. Then she put grease over the burned hand and wrapped it, not tightly. She was taking off his shirt when he sat up groggily.

"I'm all right."

"You will be when I fix your shoulder. The cut on your chest is only a scratch."

"It's not that. I've other things to keep me awake."

She looked at him quickly, thinking he had seen Silva's killing of Sam. "You saw it, then?"

"Saw what?"

"Silva. He finished Sam. Sam is dead. I'm sorry."

He held himself still, looking down at the clumsy-looking hand and its loose bandage. Sam . . . a man's dog.

"He was gettin' old. . . . Been with me goin' on eleven years. Old for a dog."

She was furious. "That beast Silva killed him. For no reason."

"Silva's scalp lock should be dryin' from a ridgepole."

"I know how you feel. That loyal dog, and . . . and . . ."

Hondo turned the bandage, looking at it. She could not see his expression, only hear his voice. He was keeping his eyes down.

"Wasn't he an ugly cuss, that Sam? Mean as a catamount in the breeding season. I almost ate him once. Up on the Powder. Quick freeze caught us, and after I'd been three days without rations, I took to looking at Sam.

"Lucky for him I found us a snowbound moose. Didn't look forward to eatin' Sam. Probably been tougher than a trail-shiny moccasin."

Angie turned down the light and moved away. She could sense

the man's grief, and she was feeling it herself. That brutal, ugly-looking mongrel . . . and there at the last, dying, he tried to lick her hand.

A fighting dog, so strangely gentle. The thought moved her and she looked quickly at the man who lay face to the wall.

So strangely gentle. . . .

Did the dog take on the qualities of the man? Or under the hard exterior were they much the same?

She turned to her work and saw the rolled-up blankets she had meant to take away. Now she need not go.

But what had she done? Her face turned crimson. She had told Vittoro this man was her husband! And he dared not leave now.

Yet what else could she have done? Had she not accepted him as her husband, he would have been killed, and she would have no choice but to become a squaw to one of Vittoro's braves. Still, what must he think of her?

Outside thunder rumbled and rain was falling, falling steadily, without the fury of the storm that had come those long days ago after he had ridden away before. She added fuel to the fire. A gust of wind sent a little smoke into the room. Then a big drop fell down the chimney and hissed upon the coals.

Johnny had already gone to bed, sleeping contentedly. The man was back.

And outside the rain was no longer a threatening thing, but suddenly it made the house seem even cozy, very warm. She listened to the heavy breathing of Hondo. Was this what she wanted? A man in the house?

No, not a man. *This* man . . . and no other.

He turned, muttering in his sleep, and something fell to the floor with a tinny sound. Glancing down, she saw it was a tintype. She picked it up. Johnny. But the tintype was scarred. Instinctively she knew what that scar meant.

Turning, she went to him and thrust it back into the pocket from which it had fallen.

For a long time she sat at the table, staring at the rain-streaked window. There was nothing to think of now, nothing to wait for. There was only the night and the steady rain falling, and the quiet, good sound of a man breathing heavily in his sleep. She knelt beside the fire, and banked it with a log, and then another, gathering the coals close.

When she got up, she brushed her hands down, straightening

her apron. She looked over at his broad back, at muscles relaxed and sleeping now. She wanted to touch him, to put her hand upon his hair.

She turned quickly to her own bed and began to undress. A large drop hissed on the dying coals, a stick popped loudly. There was rain on the roof, but it was quiet in the house, and there was no fear. The man was back.

CHAPTER SIXTEEN

WHEN SHE AWAKENED it was daylight and the house was silent. Suddenly, and with a start, she realized that Johnny was gone, and so was Hondo.

Glancing through the window, she could see Hondo at the corral, Johnny beside him. They were pitching hay to the horses. Quickly she dressed.

The ground was wet, and rain dropped from the eaves, but the rain had stopped for the moment. There was no break in the clouds. When she had breakfast started she returned to the mirror and fixed her hair more carefully.

When she opened the door, Hondo glanced around. ''Breakfast is ready!'' she called, and he started to the barn with the fork. Together they trudged toward the house, and after Johnny had bathed, Hondo followed.

His hair was freshly combed when he came in, but he was favoring his bandaged hand and his shoulder was stiff. He avoided her eyes, seating himself quickly. They ate in silence, and when his cup was empty she reached for the pot. ''More coffee?''

''Thanks.''

He was silent, brooding. Once he started to speak, then stopped.

''After breakfast, you'd better take off your shirt and let me fix it.''

He gulped his coffee, then said quickly, ''Not before I show you something.''

He took the tintype from his pocket and handed it to her. She looked at it, and then at him.

"Did Ed give it to you?"

"No. I took it off his body."

She had known this. She had felt if from the moment she saw the tintype with the bullet scar. Now she waited, but she felt nothing. There was nothing to feel. Later, she knew she would. But Ed . . . For months now he had seemed like somebody who had never really been. Like someone who had walked across the page of her life and left no tracks.

"He's dead."

When she had spoken the words, tears came to her eyes. There were no sobs, just a welling of tears. She sat silent, and no words came to help.

"I tried to tell you last night. I wanted to."

"I'm not surprised. It's . . . it's like something that happened long ago. I guess I never really expected him to come back."

Hondo tasted his coffee and tried to find the words to tell her the rest of it. But how did you tell a woman you had killed her husband? One of you had to be in the wrong. He was not prepared to accept the blame for trouble he had not wanted. Nor was he sorry for Ed Lowe. He was sorry only because the dead man had been the husband of Angie.

The door burst open and Johnny came charging back into the room. He rushed at Hondo, seizing his arm.

"Look out for his hand, Johnny." She crossed the room to the stove. "It's very noble of you."

"Noble?" Hondo looked at her under his brows. "Me?"

"You came in here to get us out."

"I'm going to give you something," Johnny said. "My Indian emblem. Vittoro gave it to me, didn't he, Mom?"

He started off quickly to get the headband. Hondo shifted his feet under the table and allowed Angie to fill his cup again. He was deeply stirred. Johnny's prize possession, and he wanted him to have it.

Angie hesitated, putting the coffeepot back on the stove. "The Indians," she said at last, "place such a great value on dying well. Did Ed die well?"

"Yes, ma'am. Well."

Angie resumed the ironing halted by the coming of the Indians. Something in Hondo's attitude disturbed her, but she could not explain her feeling. It was unlike him to be so silent.

It was something about Ed. Something was wrong there, very wrong.

Nevertheless, she said, "When Johnny is old enough, and when he has to be told, it will make him proud."

Johnny came in with his emblem. He placed it on the table before Hondo. "Here's the emblem. You're a chief now!"

Hondo Lane turned away from the table and picked up the headband. He turned it in his hands, studying it. After a while he put it back on the table. Talking to a child . . . what did he know of that?

"Johnny," he said slowly, uncertain of what to say, "I'd like to take it, because that's a mighty fine gift. Guess there ain't anything you could give me that would be nicer. But you see, that headband was given to *you,* not to me.

"It was given to you by Vittoro. He meant it for you. Now I'd like to have you give me something, but this is yours: Wouldn't be right, nohow, to give it to me.

"Vittoro, he's a mighty big chief. Not many folks he likes. He must admire you quite some to give you that, so you stick by it.

"You an' me, Johnny, we got a lot of ground to cover together. Vittoro wants you to know how an Apache gets along. Good thing to know, too. You can live in this country, you better know most of it. Man can never tell when he'll be lost in the desert, have to feed himself, find water, maybe. All that you've got to learn."

"Will you teach me?"

Hondo placed his hand clumsily on the boy's shoulder. "I reckon I'd like that, son. I sure would. I guess I've learned so much I'm up to here with it. Need somebody to learn it from me."

When Angie was washing clothes at the edge of a pool in the creek, Hondo rode down the slope with an antelope slung behind his saddle.

Angie looked up with a smile. "More fresh meat. We're living high."

Johnny sat on a round rock some distance above the pool, fishing.

Hondo swung down from the saddle and said quietly, "Don't turn around too fast, but there's an Indian up on the rim right now, just under that stunted pine."

"I can't see him. You must have wonderful eyesight."

"Learned. There was one up there day before yesterday, too."

He ground-hitched the lineback near a patch of grass, then walked back, starting to roll a smoke.

"Why? I don't understand."

"To watch the boy, I think. Vittoro must set store by him."

He left Angie to her washing and strolled upstream to where the boy was fishing. He took off his hat and ran his fingers through his hair. It was cool under the cottonwoods, better than out there on the desert. Was he getting soft? Or had this life got to him?

"If you want my opinion, you won't catch any fish there."

"He never does," Angie said, "but it keeps him amused."

"Might as well catch him a bass while he's at it." He glanced around, his brow furrowing. "Course, I don't mean to interfere."

"Please do."

She dipped a boy's shirt into the water, rinsing it. When she straightened up, she said quietly, "He needs a father. He's getting to that age now. He loves me, but I'm a woman. Sometimes he tolerates me."

Hondo grinned. "Boys are that way. Wait'll he gets older. He'll do mor'n tolerate a pretty woman."

She flushed a little, but she was pleased. "He has lots of time."

"Grow up before you know it."

"I . . . I don't want him to be here. Not when he's older."

"No, ma'am. But right now he's best off here. Boy should know how to hunt. How to get along. He'll learn better here, and you're safe, long as Vittoro lives."

She looked at him quickly. "You don't think I would be if he died?"

"Don't figure to scare you, but what'd you think about Silva?"

She remembered the hatred in the Indian's eyes, the way he started toward them that first day, the way he had killed Sam.

"He'll be the big man when Vittoro dies," Hondo said. "Do to think about."

Johnny trudged downstream to Hondo, who shoved his hat back on his head and looked down at the boy.

"Where's the sun?"

"There." Johnny pointed.

"On the back of your neck." He indicated the shadow the boy threw upon the water. "Shadow. If you can see it, the fish can see it. Always fish with the sun in your face. That's if you want my opinion. And that bank's the place."

"Can I, Mommy?"

Angie hesitated. She was afraid of the creek. There were deep pools, and some old snags that had washed down from upstream. "Some of those pools are deep. I worry about him out here."

"He can't swim?"

"He's so young."

"I've seen Indian boys that age swim the Missouri at flood." He watched the boy lazily as Johnny started across the stream on the stones. At the far bank, Johnny stepped ashore. "Hey, boy!"

Johnny hesitated, looking back, and Hondo said, his voice carrying easily across the small stream, "Hot this time of day. Was I you, I'd walk on the sunny side of that rock. When it's hot the snake will be in the shade, when it's cold he'll be in the sun."

Johnny skirted the rock, then found a good place and seated himself, dropping his hook into the water.

"Funny thing. An Apache won't eat fish."

"What?" Angie was astonished. "I thought all Indians fished."

"What most folks think. Maybe it's because they live mostly in desert country, but no Apache will eat fish."

"I never heard of such a thing!"

"Fact. Down at Camp Grant the 'Pache kids used to hang around, beggin' candy or biscuits. When the pony soldiers got tired of havin' them around, they'd open a can of fish and set it out. They'd all leave." He threw the stub of his cigarette into the water. "Two reasons for that, though. Partly it was the fish, partly the label on the can."

"The label?"

"You know that red devil they have on some brands of fish? Scares Apaches. They call it ghost meat." Hondo squatted on his heels, watching her wash. "That Indian's gone from the rim."

"How do you know? You haven't looked up."

"I looked."

Angie dried her hands. "Do you think Vittoro really means it when he says he'll make an Apache out of Johnny?"

"If I were you I'd believe him. There's a lot of dead men that didn't believe what Vittoro said."

"He seems to love the baby."

"Baby? That kid's no baby. He must be five or maybe six."

"He's six. But he's still a baby."

"Time there was a man around here. Treat him like a baby and he'll be one. Spoils a boy to be protected. How'll he ever learn to care for himself?"

It was cool beside the stream. Hondo put his back against the trunk of a huge old cottonwood and watched the water. The clothes were drying in the sun, and Angie sat on a stone at the water's edge, her hair a little disarranged, lovely in the morning sun. Hondo Lane squinted his eyes at her, seeing her clear, poised beauty, yet uneasy at what lay between them.

The boy sat upstream, watching the line that hung into the water, slow-moving at that point. Before Hondo it rippled over stones, chuckled into hollows, and slid silkily past the weathered trunk of a blown-down cottonwood, long dead.

He glanced at the lineback, lazily cropping grass in the shade, an then past him at the hills. A man could get used to this. He grinned when he thought of Major Sherry. He was probably throwing a fit by now, thinking him dead, his scalp hanging in some Apache wickiup.

"Mommy! Mommy! I caught one!"

Johnny came running across the rocks toward them with a fish flopping at the end of his hook. Hondo was unimpressed. He slashed a thong from his buckskin shirt. "You can gill him on this, if you want to."

"Thanks, Emberato."

Angie turned to Hondo. "He calls you Emberato all the time."

"My Apache name. I told him."

"What does it mean?"

Hondo shrugged, turning his shoulder against the tree. "You can't put Apache words into English. It means Bad Temper."

Angie looked at him again, studying the line of his profile. Bad Temper? How could he get such a name as that? Or had they taken him seriously with his growling? He was as gentle as his ugly brute of a dog had been. All Sam had needed was a chance. And a little petting. The thought made her flush, but it amused her, too, and she looked at him quickly. He was watching the boy with his fish.

Another thought occurred to her. "You cut that thong from your jacket. Aren't you afraid you'll have no ornamentation left if you cut off all that fringe?"

"Isn't for ornament. Not only. The fringe helps the buckskin to shed water. That's why it's there."

Johnny tied his fish to a stick and let it hang in the water, then he came back to Hondo and Angie.

"You say he can't swim?" Hondo sat up. "You do what you want to, but if it was me, I'd see the kid could swim." He reached out suddenly and picked Johnny up by the seat of the pants and threw him into the deepest part of the pool.

Angie sprang to her feet crying out. She started to the pool and Hondo came to his feet quickly and put a hand on her shoulder.

Johnny surfaced, spluttering and floundering. Angie was furious. She struggled to pull away, but he held her, while Johnny, floundering but clumsily swimming, made his way to a rock. Clutching the rock, he turned to Hondo. "Emberato! I did it!"

"Just reach out your hand and grab a handful of water and pull it toward you, not too fast. Keep your fingers together so it won't get away. That's how I learned, if you want to know."

He released Angie, and she looked up at him, her anger dying. "Sometimes you're cruel."

"Am I? The kid can swim, can't he?"

He gathered the reins of his horse and picked the fish from the water. "I'll go clean the fish for him. Right he should eat it tonight, eat his own game himself."

"But how will he get back?"

"Swim."

"He may drown!" she protested, staring anxiously at Johnny, cheerfully kicking at the cool water.

"I don't think so."

He turned and walked off, leading the horse. Johnny yelled after him, then slid into the water and paddled awkwardly to the bank and climbed out. He was swelling with childish pride. "I swam, Mommy!" he said.

Hondo Lane had vanished toward the stable, and Angie took Johnny's hand and started toward the house. She was still not over her anger at his sudden and to her unbelievably brutal action. She mentally told herself he was cruel. He was rough. He was no fit man to be around a child. But the fact remained that now Johnny could swim.

CHAPTER SEVENTEEN

THE WIND TALKED among the junipers and brushed cheeks with the skeleton face of the cactus and along the hills walked two horses and two riders. Hondo Lane, the killer from the Brazos, and a boy of six, riding Old Gray.

They rode in silence through the morning, but Hondo's eyes were careful on the desert. It was a gamble, taking the child out this way, for there were other Apaches than those of Vittoro, yet the boy must learn, and there was no better time than now.

A bird flew up, sailed away for a few yards, then vanished into the brush. "See that bird? We'll ride his way. Want you to get a good look at him."

The bird flew up again several minutes later. "It's a Gambel's quail, Johnny. Drinks a lot, so you never find him too far from water. Thing to remember."

They rode on. The sun was up and hot. They had brought no lunch, deliberately.

As they rode on, Hondo pointed out plants used by the Indians for food, for medicine, or for making fire. He had the boy stop to examine the leaves, to learn how each one grew, and whether on low ground or high mountain slopes. There were other plants that the Indians gathered for making dyes or soap, or for their strong fibers.

"See the other fellow first," Hondo said. "Then you can let him see you or not as you like. Never make a fire with smoke, even in good times."

He turned his horse wide around a boulder. "Best thing is a small fire, maybe under a tree. If there's any smoke at all, the branches and leaves will spread it out. There won't be no column.

"Use dry wood. Curl-leaf is good, never makes smoke. Look out for that rubber brush I showed you. Makes heavy, black smoke."

He drew up. "That there," he pointed at a broomlike shrub about four feet tall, "is *yerba del pasmo.* 'Paches chew the twigs for toothache."

They drew up a moment later at another plant. "Arrowweed. 'Paches make arrows from the straight stems. Use 'em for makin' cages an' baskets, too. Stuff smells good. Night, sometimes you can smell it quite a ways." They rode on, and after a bit he said, "Pimas use that arrowweed for makin' a tea for an eyewash."

On a hillside they saw some bones and part of an old hide. Hondo Lane drew up and rolled a smoke. "Deer," he said, nodding. "Dead a long time. See those tracks near it?"

"Yes." Johnny straightened in his saddle and peered at the tracks. "What are they?"

"Wolf. Bigger than a coyote."

"Maybe it was a dog."

"No. Dog walks right up to something. A wolf is suspicious. He circles around, stops, smells, smells the air. Wolf's more careful."

They rode alongside the dead animal. Only the bone and hide remained. ''Cat now, cougar or *tigre,* you don't see claw tracks. Dog or wolf you do. Cat draws his claws back inside. Puma or cougar, no dif'rence in 'em, sometimes they don't leave tracks. Mighty light on their feet. If they got reason to, they can jump thirty feet.''

They mounted a long slope, and Hondo talked on, forgetting time and distance, yet keeping his eyes always roving, always alert to point out something of interest. ''Nobody but a fool or a tenderfoot wears bright, shiny stuff on his clothes. Only a fool would ride a white horse. See it too far off. That bright, shiny stuff is for sissies, townfolk. You wear it out here an' some Injun see you ten mile off by sun reflectin'. You'd lose your hair mighty quick.''

Suddenly Johnny pointed. ''There's one of those birds! The quail you showed me!''

''Sure is. You got a quick eye, son.'' He drew up. ''Now it's gettin' nigh to noontime. Should be water not far off.''

He studied the country carefully, and finally he turned the lineback down a long slope toward an upthrust of rock. ''Could be down there. Water falls in rain an' sinks down. Sometimes underground water forms a sort of a pool above clay and along a layer of sandstone. If that's busted, there's liable to be a spring. Up ahead there, that ground is faulted. May be water there.''

''I'm hungry,'' Johnny said suddenly.

''Me too.'' Hondo glanced at the boy. ''Noticed any insects lately?''

''Bees. There was a bee on a flower back there. One flew off, too.''

''Which way'd he go?''

Johnny scowled. Finally he pointed. ''Thataway, I think.''

''That's right. But don't have to think. You notice hereafter. Bees can take you to water. Need water, an' they go often. So you watch where they go.''

He stopped his horse suddenly. Johnny drew up, looking at him curiously. Then, aware that something was expected of him, he looked around carefully. Suddenly he saw the rounded, ugly body of a golden and brown lizard lying near a rock. It was fat-tailed and repulsive. The boy instinctively drew his horse away from it.

''Gila monster, son. Mighty poisonous. You leave him alone, he'll leave you alone. No wild animal wants no truck with a man. Up to you to keep away from him, or give him a chance to get away from you. That there lizard, now, you watch out for him. Mostly he don't aim to move. He likes it where he is."

A broken ledge of rock tilted sharply against the sky, a ledge broken off in some bygone upheaval of the earth and thrust up like a broken bone, splintered and ragged on edge. The wind, blown sand, and rain had tapered those edges but little, yet on the underside they found a hollow of water, a few desert willows, and one cottonwood, still young.

Hondo swung down and helped the boy to the ground, then led the horses into the shade to cool off. With Johnny helping, he gathered dry sticks for a fire. A bee buzzed near them, then another.

Hondo caught Johnny's arm and pointed. A small swarm of bees hovered around a crack in the rock above them. "Hive up there. Lots of honey, too."

"Can we get some?" Johnny was eager. "Can we get some away from them?"

Hondo studied the situation. "Hard to get it, but maybe later."

Earlier he had killed a rabbit, skinned and cleaned it, then sprinkled it with salt. Now he broiled the rabbit over the fire, then led the horses to water. He walked out away from the rocks, keeping among the brush, and studied the terrain. Twice that morning he had seen unshod hoofprints. There were Apaches around.

He walked back to the boy and ate his share of the rabbit while Johnny was brushing the spines from a tuna the way he had shown him earlier. As the boy ate the desert fruit, he thought about how fast the morning had gone, how much he had enjoyed it. And this was the son of the man he had killed.

How could a man have left a boy like this alone? To say nothing of Angie. What possessed a man with everything in the world to live for to go to a post and spend his time gambling and cheating passing strangers and soldiers from the post?

"We'll start back," he said suddenly. "Your mother may get worried."

He thought of those unshod ponies. This boy had learned enough for one morning. There was no sense in taking a chance. While Johnny filled his canteen again, he walked back among the rocks to look in the opposite direction. Then he squatted suddenly.

Four Indians had come out of the wash along which they had ridden earlier. Even at this distance he could tell they were mountain Apaches, strange to this area. They were studying the ground, apparently puzzled.

If they had followed him far they would have occasion to be curious, for the horses had wandered from one point of interest to another, studying plants, tracks, and rocks. Now they were looking toward the serrated rock where lay the spring.

Hondo Lane turned and walked swiftly back. There was a hollow among the rocks. "Johnny," he said in a quiet voice, "we're in trouble. Mountain Apaches . . . not from Vittoro."

The boy, he thought suddenly, looked eager rather than frightened. He chuckled a little, and Johnny looked up at him and smiled. "Will we fight?" he said quickly.

"Not if we can help it," Hondo said. "An' don't be so durned eager, youngster. People get hurt fightin'."

He led the horses into the hollow of rock and they waited. Suddenly he heard a hoof strike rock, then he saw the slim brown bodies of the Indians. White Mountain Apaches, by their look. They were studying the tracks at the spring.

Hondo slid the thong from the butt of his six-shooter. "Trouble starts," he said, and his voice was flat and harsh, "get behind the rocks and stay there, you hear me?"

He stood up slowly, and almost at once the Apaches saw him. His rifle was in his hand. The distance was no more than forty yards.

"Hola, brothers!" He spoke clearly. He was aware that Johnny, unable to restrain his curiosity, had appeared beside him.

The Apaches stared, uncertain what to make of the strange pair. Yet soon he was puzzled himself, for they kept staring, and then they walked forward hesitantly. It was not Hondo himself at whom they stared, but at Johnny. Suddenly Hondo realized the boy was wearing Vittoro's headband. The opal had caught the light and reflected into their eyes. A white boy with an Apache headband puzzled them.

"The boy is Apache?"

The Indian sounded doubtful, for despite Johnny's deep tan, he was obviously a white boy.

"Blood brother to Vittoro!" Hondo made the name ring against the crags. "He is Small Warrior!"

Hesitantly, still wary of a trap, the Indians came forward. One of them hung back. His face was narrow and mean, with a cross-grained look about it. Hondo looked at this one, then never let the corners of his eyes stray away from him.

The Apaches stopped a dozen yards off, staring from the boy to Hondo. Rifles were hard to come by, and Hondo's was a new Winchester '73, firing seventeen shots without reloading. He wore a pistol also, and there were horses. Yet the name of Vittoro carried a large sound to Apache ears.

"What do you here?"

"The boy learns the way of the desert."

They accepted this and considered it. The wandering tracks were now explained. "It is the wish of Vittoro," he added. "Small Warrior is to be as an Apache on the desert."

Three of the braves were obviously interested, and as Johnny stood there beside Hondo Lane, he carried a certain indomitable look that amused and interested them.

"The Small Warrior takes scalps?" the nearest Apache asked, grinning.

Only the tall Indian who hung back disturbed Hondo. The others were fascinated by the stalwart youngster. The carriage of Johnny was Apache, and it made them chuckle.

"The Small Warrior takes scalps?" The Indian repeated.

"Not of dogs or women!" Johnny had not listened to Vittoro for nothing. "Go in peace!"

One of the Indians shouted with laughter, and the three started to turn away.

The fourth Indian stood his ground, looking at Hondo. "This one I know," he said suddenly. "He was scout for the pony soldiers."

There was sudden tension, and the other three turned quickly, looking from Hondo to their companion.

"I *was* scout for the pony soldiers," Hondo agreed. "I have lived among the Mimbreños also. This you do not like?"

There was challenge in his tone. It did no good to draw back or show hesitation.

"I have killed pony soldiers," the brave boasted.

"And I have killed Apaches."

They stared at each other. One of the others said something about Vittoro, but the tall Indian merely sneered. It was partly the rifle, partly the horses, but mostly it was that the Indian was a trouble-hunter. Hondo knew white men like him.

"I wear the scalp of a pony soldier on the mane of my horse!"

"An old pony soldier," Hondo said with contempt, "With white in his hair and age in his back."

"You are friend of Vittoro?" The Apache sneered. "I say you lie!"

Hondo ignored him. He spoke to the others. "The Small Warrior is the brother of Vittoro. Harm to him would mean blood feud. He is protected by Vittoro. I protect myself!"

He turned suddenly and struck the tall Indian across the mouth. It was a wicked, powerful blow, and the Indian staggered and fell in a heap.

An instant he lay there, eyes blazing, blood trickling from a smashed lip. Then like a cat he sprang to his feet and the rifle muzzle started to swing up. It was exactly what Hondo had wanted him to do. Deliberately he let the muzzle lift. Then he palmed his Colt and fired.

His rifle had been held by the barrel with his left hand. His right hand was free to grasp its trigger guard as it lifted if he elected to use it. The Colt came as a complete surprise.

The bullet struck the tall Indian over the heart and he grunted. His rifle's bullet dug earth at Hondo's feet, and then he fell face downward upon the ground.

To the unsuspecting Indians, who had never seen a fighter in action, the appearance of the Colt smacked of sheer magic. They stared at him, stared at the gun, and then they turned the Indian over and looked at the wound. Awed, they stared at Hondo.

Suddenly there was a clatter of hoofs and a dozen horsemen raced into the basin near the spring and ringed the small group. First among them was Vittoro. His hard old eyes looked first at Johnny, who stood close beside Hondo, his face white and still, but without tears or fear.

Then he looked at the other Indians, and Hondo spoke quickly. "Only one among them looked for war." he said. "That one is dead. These others are true men."

Vittoro stared at them and one Apache stepped forward. He held himself proudly. "We spoke in admiration of Small Warrior," he said. "This one wanted the scalp of that one." He pointed at Hondo.

Vittoro looked at them, then at Johnny. The Apache who had spoken then repeated what Johnny had said about not taking scalps of dogs and women, and Vittoro's hard old eyes glinted and the others chuckled. Nobody seemed much upset by the death of the tall Indian. Hondo holstered his gun. One of the others said something of that to Vittoro, speaking of the gun of magic. Vittoro looked at Hondo, then nodded. "The watcher of my brother is well chosen," he said. Then he lifted his coup stick and pointed at Johnny.

"Take the stick!" he commanded. "Count coup!"

Johnny hesitated. Hondo was suddenly glad that Angie was not present. "Johnny," he said distinctly, "you must do as Vittoro says. Take the stick he offers you and tap the Indian with it."

The boy's eyes were round and frightened. Yet he walked forward, his steps like those of an automaton, and, taking the stick, he tapped the dead Indian. Then he returned the stick and walked back to Hondo. His face was stiff and white but not a tear showed.

"Good!" Vittoro grunted. "Small Warrior soon be Big Warrior!"

Hondo took the boy and put him into his saddle, then he stepped into the leather. He glanced over at the chief. "It has been a long day. Small Warrior has learned the tracks of the wolf and the *tigre.* He has learned the *yebra del pasmo* and the mescal, and many other things besides. He has caught game and cooked it, and he has counted coup. It is enough."

Vittoro nodded, and the two rode from the hollow of the spring, and scarcely were they on the desert when Johnny's face began to twist. With sudden instinct Hondo lifted him from the saddle, and then Johnny was crying. Startled to find himself holding a crying child, Hondo merely held him and said nothing.

After a long time, Johnny looked up at Hondo, but Hondo appeared not to notice. Then he leaned back against Hondo's arm and watched the desert.

Not until they were almost home did he get back into his own saddle.

"It was a hard thing," Hondo said. "You did well, Johnny."

"Look!" Johnny pointed, there's some arrowweed!"

CHAPTER EIGHTEEN

THE SHOCK OF seeing a man killed and being forced to count coup upon his body was a severe test for Johnny, yet Hondo noticed that he bounced back the next morning. He was a little more quiet, ready to remain at home for a day, but apparently no worse off for his experience. Hondo hesitated, then decided to tell Angie nothing about it for the time being. But she guessed something had happened, and finally he told her.

"Without the headband of Vittoro," Hondo told her, "we might have had a bad time of it."

"Or if you had not killed that man."

That silenced him. The killing of another man was very much in his thoughts. It seemed somehow wrong to have killed a woman's husband and to be here with her, not to have explained. Yet no matter how many times he tried to tell her, the words of explanation would not come. She sensed he was worried about something and it bothered her.

He had returned to the house to replace his coffee cup and left her sitting beside the stream. Johnny was asleep. The tintype was on a shelf above his head. Hondo Lane stood and studied it, gnawing at his lip and thinking.

There was nothing else he could have done. It was a treacherous thing Lowe had attempted, and the man had been no good, not any way you looked at him. Still, he had to explain. He had to tell Angie, and he would tell her now.

It was late evening, not yet dark. The cottonwoods were at their endless whispering and the stream seemed unusually noisy tonight. Not loud, but with no other sound it was more obvious.

All day he had worked around the ranch, finding the little things to do that a handy man with tools can find on any such place. He had worked, always conscious of the woman up there at the house. This was as it should be . . . a man and a woman working toward something, for something. Not apart, but a team.

Leaving the house now, he walked across the yard toward where she sat alone by the stream. She turned to look up at him. In repose her face had a quality of true beauty that disturbed him. He knew she liked him, probably more. . . . But why should she? To him she was a woman, but a rare and wonderful thing, too.

"Angie, I've got something to tell you, and it's not gonna be easy."

"Then don't tell me yet." She lifted her face to the moon. The cottonwood leaves were like tiny silver mirrors, catching the light. "Just look. How odd the moon looks in this quarter! When I was a child my mother used to tell me it was a teeter-totter. You know, the tilted plank a child plays on. Do the Apaches have a name for it?"

"Bermaga, the planting moon . . . like they call the first rain the planting rain. Won't plant their corn until the moon's like that."

"You liked living with the Apaches, didn't you?"

He did not reply. The stream rustled against the banks, chuckled around the rocks as water does, and shimmered in the moonlight farther down. A horse stomped and blew in the corral.

"Don't have locks."

"I don't believe I understand."

"White man locks his cabin. No way to lock a wickiup. But you can be gone a whole season and your gear will still be there. Nobody steals. The old women with no men to provide for them . . . the chiefs drop half their kill at the old women's lodge before they take the rest home to feed their women and kids. Nothing selfish about an Apache. Yeah, I liked living with them."

She liked listening to his voice. It was slow, somehow restful, and underlying his words there was understanding, compassion. There was none of this you-get-along-on-your-own-or-die-feeling. He had seen too much of that. The more people had, the more they felt that way. But this man had known loneliness and hardship.

"I think I would like that part of it, too. The way you speak of it."

"I know you would."

She tried to see his face in the deepening shadows, but outlines were gone, and she could only see where he was, not details or expression.

"Why did you decide that?"

Hondo shifted his boots, searching for the right words. "Because you're a warm woman. Because you can sit and watch a little boy doing something like drawing in the mud at the creek bank and the corners of your mouth wrinkle up and a man can see that what you're looking at makes you happy. Your hands are nice and clean when you put cooked meat down in front of a man, and your face is happy while he eats it.''

Angie was surprised. She had not realized he had noticed these things. She felt a sudden desire to reach out in the darkness and touch him. Instead she said, ''You notice everything. And thank you. Thank you very much.''

A faint, far-off sound caught at his attention. He listened. There was nothing more.

She was close to him now. It was dark. He listened a moment longer.

''Angie, I've got to tell you somethin'. I'm not much for lyin'—or for livin' a lie. Last time I was here, before Vittoro brought me . . .''

''Yes?''

''Rode some dispatch after that. Then there was some trouble. Killed a man.'' The sound came again then, closer. He reached swiftly and drew her off the rock. His gun was in his hand. ''There's someone in the willows.''

''Do not shoot, white man.'' It was Vittoro's voice. He stepped from the trees. ''Small Warrior had a knife. He sleeps with it.''

''You were in the house?'' Angie asked.

''Yes.''

''Tell your brave behind us,'' Hondo said, ''not to walk in the water. I like to killed him a few minutes ago.''

Vittoro chuckled, then he said loudly, ''Kloori, you are very clumsy. Go to the horses.''

''I almost threw a shot at him.''

''He is very young. He will learn.''

''If he lives.''

''You are Apache.'' Vittoro paused a minute after the compliment, then turned to speak to Angie.

''A wickiup is an empty place without sons. Mine is an empty wickiup. I treasure Small Warrior. Now hear me! The pony soldiers are near. Soon will be fought a remembered fight. They will come here first. You will not go with them, white man.''

''I will not go with them.''

''The leader of the pony soldiers will question you. You will say you have seen the Apaches trailing to the west.''

''This I will not do.''

''You will not?''

''I will not.''

There was a long moment of silence while the leaves rustled. Somewhere a fish jumped.

"You have a good man," Vittoro said at last to Angie. "Treasure him."

"I do!"

Vittoro was gone in the darkness. They stared after him, eyes straining in the darkness, and then her arms were around him, her head against his chest.

An arm around her shoulders, he listened. "They're mounting up now."

"I don't hear a thing."

"Going off now. About eight, I'd say. Maybe nine."

She could hear nothing. The night was silent to her . . . and then she did hear something.

"There's something in those trees."

"Squirrel. Talking woke him and he's put out. There are nine Indians."

She drew back from him, looking up. His face was vaguely visible now, for the stars were bright and the moon was low over the trees.

"I love you."

She said the words suddenly, surprising even herself. Her hand went to her mouth. "I didn't mean to say that . . but I did mean it. I *did.* I know it's an unseemly thing—my husband so shortly dead and . . ."

"I don't guess people's hearts got anything to do with calendars."

He kissed her gently, holding her close, and for a moment they were silent.

"You were wonderful, refusing to lie for Vittoro."

"Figure he was testing me. Indians hate a lie. I got to feel the same way. But I guess there's sometimes when a man has got to lie, if it makes it easier for someone."

"I feel strange . . . new. Well, like music. I am being silly, aren't I?"

"No. The Apaches have a word . . . Like I said, I can't explain it. As close as I can come is 'happy breathing.' "

"Kiss me again."

Their lips met in the darkness, clung, and then she leaned against him and for a long time they did not talk. It was growing cooler. The moon was down now, below the line of hills.

Somewhere a coyote sent his lonely cry at the wide sky. An owl called.

"Don't think I'm crazy, but tonight I just couldn't bear to sleep under a roof with the moon and all. I'll go get some blankets."

"I'll get them if you want."

"No, I want to. A squaw would. I want to feel like a squaw woman. Feels good. Real good."

She moved away into the darkness and he listened to the water over the stones. Behind him the squirrel chattered.

Hondo sat up and looked around. "Squirrel, if you bother me some more, I'll eat you in a stew tomorrow."

The squirrel chattered inquiringly, and then there was silence. The water rustled, and at the house a door closed and then there were footfalls. Hondo Lane got up, moving back nearer the trees. "Better here," he said when she was close. "Leaves under the trees. Anybody comes, we'll see them first."

She handed him the blankets and the ground sheet and he shook them out, then put them down under the trees. Angie got down on her knees and spread the ground sheets over the leaves, then the blankets.

"You never forget, do you? I mean about seeing things first."

"Hope I never."

He was oddly uncomfortable, hesitant. "Good way to lose your hair, not noticing things."

He sat down and pulled off his boots. The cottonwoods whispered more softly. The squirrel gave one short, inquiring chatter, then was silent.

The lone coyote spoke to the sky and the stream rustled busily about the stones. A bit of mud fell into the stream with a faint plop.

It was night, and there was no sound. Or anyway, not very much.

CHAPTER NINETEEN

HONDO LANE TURNED from tightening the wheels of Angie Lowe's wagon to watch the column of cavalry file into the basin and past the butte. It was a sight to behold. Glittering, yes, but more than that, for these were part of the force that Lord Wolseley, then commander in chief of the British army, had declared was the finest fighting force in the world—and they looked it.

And, Hondo reflected as he stood beside Angie and Johnny, they had better be!

When the men dismounted outside the ranch yard, the officer in command and the scout rode over to Hondo and Angie. The Lieutenant dismounted, and behind him Buffalo swung down.

The Lieutenant was impeccably garbed. His uniform was perfect in tailoring and perfect in military requirements. He walked to a position in front of Hondo and stopped, shifting his gloves. Heels together, he bowed.

"Madam and sir, may I present myself? Lieutenant McKay, Squadron D, Sixth Cavalry."

Behind him, Buffalo grinned at Lane. "Hi, Hondo, you old cabin-robber! Lieutenant, this is Hondo Lane. He's scouted some and rode dispatch for the cavalry. I don't know this here lady."

"Mrs. Lowe . . . Lieutenant." Hondo grinned at Baker. "Hi, Buff."

"You people are lucky," Lieutenant McKay assured them. "Obviously Vittoro and his renegades just happened not to find this hidden valley."

"Vittoro's been here," Hondo said. "Lots."

"And you live? One lone man stood off Vittoro?"

"No lone man stands off Vittoro. Not for long, anyway. He lets us live here."

"He's our friend," Angie said.

"Friend? Vittoro?" Lieutenant McKay was astonished. "Ma'am, I dislike saying such a gruesome thing in a lady's presence, but there are almost a thousand dead settlers on both sides of the border, scalped by this cowardly criminal."

Hondo lifted an eyebrow. "Vittoro may be a criminal by the book. I don't know. But if he's a coward it never showed up yet."

"Amen!" Buffalo said.

"My men will bivouac here for the night," McKay said, then he turned. "I must disagree with you, Mr. Lane. He has run before us for two hundred miles. My scouts and outriders report his band before us every day, yet each time we start to come to grips to fight an engagement, he runs."

"Indians got a story," Hondo said, "about a hunter who chased a puma until he caught him. Then it was the other way around."

McKay smiled. "That story goes back further than the Indians know. It is originally attributed to the first Roman army to enter Tartary. The soldier caught a Tartar and yelled out. His officer called back to come in and bring his prisoner, and the soldier replied, "The Tartar won't let me."

McKay chuckled at his story, but neither Hondo nor Buffalo was amused.

"It's one of the favorite stories of Colonel Mays, who teaches cavalry tactics at the Point. The story is world-wide."

Hondo rolled a smoke. "How long you been out of West Point, Lieutenant?"

McKay listened, not liking to answer. He was afraid he knew what the question implied, and he did not like to appear a greenhorn. "Graduated class of '69, sir." His ears grew a little red. It was not long ago, and he resented the doubt of his ability the question seemed to imply, yet he was no fool. He had heard Major Sherry and even General Crook speak of Hondo Lane with respect.

"That story you told," Hondo said, "can be almighty true right here. You hear about Fetterman?"

"Lieutenant Colonel Fetterman, sir? You mean the massacre?"

"Well," Hondo said, "call it what you like. Fetterman was a good man, I guess, but he made the mistake of takin' the Sioux too lightly. He said give him eighty men an' he'd ride through the whole Sioux Nation. Remember what happened?" Hondo touched his tongue to his cigarette. "He had eighty-three men, an' he lasted less than twenty minutes."

McKay flushed a little. "I know. Ambush, wasn't it?"

"In a way. Ambush they led him into because he was bigheaded." Hondo smiled. "You ain't that sort, Lieutenant, but don't take Vittoro lightly. Napoleon never knew anything the old 'Pache don't know."

"Oh, come now, sir!" McKay was astonished, half believing he was being led on. "You don't mean that!"

"I do mean it." Hondo was dead serious. "Lieutenant, what

would you say was the main object of a leader facing a superior force?''

McKay's eyes searched Hondo's. He was curious, and suddenly aware there was more to the man to whom he talked than a knowledge of the desert and Indians.

''Why . . . why, offhand, sir, I'd say to harass the enemy, to fight a delaying action until he could get him on ground of his own choosing, but at all costs to preserve his own force intact.''

Hondo nodded. ''I'm no military man, Lieutenant, but I'd say you couldn't go far wrong on that plan. And ain't that what Vittoro's been doing?''

Lieutenant McKay's brow puckered. ''Well . . . yes,'' he admitted, ''after a fashion.''

Buffalo grinned at Hondo after the Lieutenant had moved off to inspect the bivouac area. ''Gave him somethin' to puzzle over, you did.'' He chuckled. ''Got a sight to learn, that one.'' Then he nodded. ''But he's all right, I think. I like him. Only I wish it was the Major out here in command.''

Lieutenant McKay turned toward the house, where Angie had stopped at the door. ''Mrs. Lowe, my orders are to make a clean sweep as far as Twin Buttes. We will go on to Twin Buttes tomorrow and return tomorrow night to escort you and your boy out to safety.''

''We're safe. We have Vittoro's word.''

''The word of an Indian criminal!'' McKay was incredulous. ''Even if Lane is willing to take the risk, I don't think you should.''

''I'll take his word. We'd rather stay.''

''I'm sorry. My orders are to bring out any settlers who have survived.'' He hesitated. She was such a pretty woman, and he did not like to think of leaving her here. He had been on the frontier only a few weeks, but he had already seen the bodies of some of the settlers. It had not been a pretty sight. ''I . . . if you will excuse me, ma'am.''

Hondo and Buffalo had come to the house. ''He's very nice,'' Angie said, ''and very young.''

''Yes, ma'am,'' Buffalo agreed, a shadow of worry in his tone, ''he sure is.''

''You been scouting for this patrol?''

''This is about the twentieth day I had them out, Hondo. Many a scalp's been took.''

Angie looked down at Johnny. ''You watch Lieutenant McKay,

Johnny. That's the kind of manners I want you to have." She turned back to the men. "And he has such handsome eyes. And that beautiful black, curly hair."

"That hair will be hanging from the top pole of an Apache wickiup." He looked over at Buffalo. "This little-boy lieutenant will get you killed."

Buffalo shrugged. McKay was not the first one he had seen come to Indian country. Nor, with luck, would he be the last. Some of them had it, some of them did not. Some were pretty, some were all spit and polish, and some of them sharpened down into first-class fighting men. There had been Major Powell, for instance, up at Kearney. Had he taken the command the day Fetterman went out . . . It was useless to think of that. Fetterman had outranked him, forced the issue, and gone glory-hunting with eighty-odd better men.

"You know how it is," Buffalo said. "Us scouts got to get these young officers educated."

Suddenly he remembered. "Say, you rec'lect how you whupped me at the post? My medicine must have been bad. You busted off a tooth and it went to hurting so bad I had to go to the barber so he could pull out the rest of the tooth. Partner, that *hurt!* Did I catch you that day, I'd have set your sun for you. You'd never have seed another morning."

Angie came to the door, drying her hands. "Hondo, I notice the soldiers are starting their food fires. I naturally can't invite very many to eat with us in the cabin, but if your friend Mr.—uh . . . "

"Yeah, Buffalo will eat with us." He turned to look at the big buffalo hunter. "We've known each other eight or ten years. You got to have a last name. Or have you?"

Buffalo looked up sharply, offended. "Sure I got a last name. What do you think I am?" He tried to emulate the Lieutenant's bow. "Mrs. Lowe, my name is . . . " He hesitated, and his face got red. "Baker. That's what it is, Baker." He sneered at Hondo. "Didn't think I had any last name!"

Buffalo looked around slowly. "Been tryin' to figure what this place reminds me of, Hondo. It's that ranch of your'n in California. Where we stayed before we went to fight with those people up north. Under a bluff just like this, creek and mesa spreading out . . ."

Angie looked up at Hondo. "You have a place that looks like this?"

"East of San Dimas."

"Just like this. Reminds me all to . . . " He hesitated, took a quick look at Angie, and ended weakly, "Reminds me. It sure does."

"You can wash in the basin on the bench. Towel hangin' right there."

"Wash? Towel? Oh, sure."

"It's wonderful, Hondo. About your place, I mean. That our tastes are so similar. You picked a basin with a creek, as I did."

"I guess we could winter in the same lodge without nobody getting their throat cut in the night."

They stopped at the door, watching the camp settling down. There was an Indian up on the bluff again, but that was to be expected and Hondo said nothing until Buffalo walked up, drying his hands. Buffalo mentioned it, and he nodded. "Seen him. No use mentionin' it to the Lieutenant. He'd send out a patrol to catch him, an' these boys need their sleep."

Buffalo hung the towel on a peg near the door. "Don't you peg the Lieutenant too low. He's young, but he's different than some. He'll listen, an' he ain't afraid to ask questions. Most of 'em figure they got to know it all."

Buffalo looked awkwardly at the table. Angie had taken out her red-checkered cloth and there were napkins of the same color by the plates. Buffalo looked around, embarrassed. "I ain't et—ate—at a table like this in a coon's age, ma'am. Reckon I'm some rusty."

She smiled. "We're hoping you'll eat with us often, Buffalo, so don't be afraid."

Buffalo blushed, then as the significance of her remark reached him he looked quickly at Hondo and started to speak, but Hondo scowled at him and he closed his mouth.

When they had finished, Angie got up and took down an apple pie and started to cut it, then she turned. "Hondo, would you like to ask the Lieutenant to join us for pie and coffee? I'm sure he'd like it."

When Hondo was gone, Angie turned quickly and looked at Buffalo. "Mr. Baker," she said quietly. "I want to ask you a question. Did you know Ed Lowe? My husband?"

"That no-a—" As the significance of her last words reached him, he broke off sharply. "Yes," he said after a minute, "I knew him."

She hesitated, then turned back to her pie. That explosive

beginning answered her question in part, at least. Buffalo Baker said no more, and when the Lieutenant came in, she was talking about Indians.

Buffalo excused himself and the Lieutenant sat down. He glanced quickly at Johnny, then smiled.

Lieutenant McKay might know little of Indian fighting, but he understood the things a lonely woman wants to know. He talked briefly of things at the post, then of what women were wearing in Washington, New York, and Richmond. After several minutes he switched the subject. He glanced sharply at Hondo. "What do you think Vittoro will do now? Will he keep running?"

"No. Not far, anyway. He's ready to fight."

"Mr. Lane, my business is to command, but I've been thinking of what you said. I'm not above taking advice. You know the Apaches. What would you advise?"

Hondo looked at his coffee. There was no doubting the earnestness of this man, and he had a sudden hope that whatever happened, this man might live. They needed men on the frontier who could learn.

"Can't advise you, Lieutenant. Only when you come up to him, it'll be because he's ready. If he's ready it'll be because he figures he can beat you or hurt you mighty bad. So when you come up on him, look around, because whatever you don't expect, that's what he'll do."

CHAPTER TWENTY

WHEN BUFFALO HAD finished sharpening his knife, Hondo moved to the grindstone. Lennie Sproul lounged near the barn, and Hondo felt irritation strong within him. Lennie Sproul had been on the frontier for fifteen years, a lean, saturnine man with a cynical eye and a way of showing up with unexpected money.

Hondo Lane possessed no quality of the hypocrite. He was a man whose likes and dislikes were obvious. His distaste for Sproul was especially obvious.

The scout lounged nearer in his greasy buckskins and stood watching the knife edge on the grindstone.

"Mighty fine rifle in your saddle scabbard. Always envied you that there gun. Hard to come by, that new issue."

"Keep your hands off it." Hondo was short.

Lennie Sproul watched the grindstone for sseveral minutes while Hondo Lane's anger mounted. Sproul was not here by accident. There was something on his mind.

"Knowed you ten years," Sproul said. "Never worked a day beside you."

"Don't like you," Hondo replied, testing the edge of the blade.

"Figured you didn't. But now I think you might admire to give me that there rifle."

Too astonished for reply, Hondo looked up, staring at Lennie, who answered with a broken-toothed smile. "Ways out of the post I come across some bodies. One of 'em was this lady's husband. Horse tracks around there, an' one set belonged to your lineback."

Hondo waited, his heart pounding heavily, anger building hard within him. Not the irritation he had felt for a disliked and disagreeable man, but the hard anger of a man.

"Nice setup you got here. Nice ranch, pretty woman."

Hondo took a slow, deep breath. He knew himself and he wanted no violence. Not the kind to which he was impelled.

"You can get yourself killed acting like this." He said the words slowly, taking his time, hoping the words would be a warning, that Lennie Sproul would know when to stop.

There was no stopping in the mind of Lennie Sproul. He had felt Hondo Lane's dislike keenly, but there had been nothing he could do. Now he saw the gun fighter's strength and skill humbled, his proud, easy manner broken. Why, the man had a ranch here. There was no telling what all he might get from him, given time.

Knowing triumph, he felt no discretion. "Could be I could get killed," he said with a smirk, "or I can get that new-fashioned Winchester. You didn't bushwhack that lady's husband, but it could look mighty like it. Did she know what happened, I don't reckon you'd set so well around here."

Hondo Lane dropped the knife and came up in one smooth, perfectly timed flow of motion. Lennie, too late, tried to step back. Hondo Lane's right fist caught the angle of his jaw and knocked him thirty feet into a heap on the ground

The last staggering steps had carried Sproul past the lean-to stable and he had fallen in view of the cow corrral.

Hondo Lane rushed after Lennie, who started to get up. He scarcely reached his feet before Lane struck him. Two hard punches, left and right. He hit the ground hard and Lane lifted a moccasined heel to stomp him when he saw Angie.

She was just rising from the stool beside her cow, the milk pail in one hand, the stool in the other. Nothing was needed beyond her expression. She heard it all.

For a long moment their eyes held, searching, measuring, then she turned to walk away.

Lennie seized his chance, crawled a few feet, then got to his feet and hurried away, a hand to his jaw.

At that instant Lieutenant McKay walked up to them. He looked at Lane. "We are about to leave, Mr. Lane." He faced Angie. "Mrs. Lowe, I hope you will not mind if Hondo accompanies us for half a day. We'd like him to go with us as far as Single Butte. It's rough country, I heard, and none of the other scouts knows that country. He can be back by tonight, so you will not be alone long."

"No, of course not."

McKay bowed, then turned to Hondo. "If you will saddle up, Lane."

"Can't go."

McKay looked at him as if he had not heard aright. A slight frown gathered between his brows. "You said you were not going?"

"That's right."

"But why?" McKay was incredulous.

"Gave my word I wouldn't."

"Your word? To whom?"

"Vittoro."

"Surely," Lieutenant McKay expostulated, "a word given to an Indian desperado can't be—"

"Lieutenant," Angie interrupted, "as an officer and a gentlemen, surely you must agree that one's word given to anyone is binding."

"Of course." McKay flushed a little. "Sorry you must remind me, Mrs. Lowe. I forgot myself. Good day."

"Lieutenant," Hondo called after him, and the officer turned, "you won't have any trouble if you keep north of the butte. See it to the southwest about six miles out of here. You keep north. Country south looks flat, but she's broken into canyons and washes."

"Thanks."

They stood together watching the Lieutenant walk away, carrying his back straight and walking as if on a drill field. The men were in the saddle, waiting. The sun was hot and the horses stamped restlessly, eager to be moving.

Lennie Sproul rode by, moving to his place near the head of the column. His jaw was badly swollen, his right eye closed. An ugly cut had opened his other cheekbone. He did not look at them as he passed, and when Buffalo Baker drew up near them he looked curiously at Hondo Lane.

"Lennie must've run into something," Buffalo commented, biting off a corner of his plug tobacco. "Had it comin', I reckon." He gathered his reins. "Wish you was with us, Hondo."

"Sorry."

Buffalo lifted a hand. "See you." He moved off to join Lieutenant McKay at the head of the column.

Then the column was moving, and the dust rose around them, then settled slowly, and the sun shone brightly on the last of the horses, glinted from the carbines. Neither of them moved.

Johnny walked down the trail of the horses and looked after them, his world suddenly empty with their going. He had never before seen so many soldiers, so many horses. He stood, scuffing his toe in the dirt, liking the smell of the horses, and remembering the easy, rough-handed friendship of the soldiers.

"Should have told you," Hondo said at last. "Tried to . . . didn't. It happened like this, Angie. I—"

She turned sharply away. "I can't talk now. I want to think. I need time. I'll put your war bag outside the cabin."

He watched her go, then walked to the corral. Uncertainly he looked around, trying to recall something he had intended doing, but the thought would not come. There was nothing in him, nothing but a vast impatience and a vast restlessness.

He looked up the trail the way the soldiers had gone, riding into battle. Because that was what it would be. Somewhere out there on some sun-blasted slope the Apaches would be waiting. Somewhere out there men would die.

Buffalo was along. . . . Luck to him, and to McKay and the others. That McKay, now, he was all right. Young, but he would grow into it. Proud, the way a young man should be, but conscious there was much to learn. He was the kind they needed out here. More officers like Crook, who understood the Indian.

Hearing the door open, he looked around. She was putting his war bag outside the door.

There it was, the end of whatever it had been, and all because of a small-caliber coyote who tried to shoot him in the back. He walked to the corral and led out the lineback. Then he went for his saddle.

CHAPTER TWENTY-ONE

THE DOOR SLAMMED and Hondo glanced around. It was Johnny. Hands in pockets, the boy walked slowly toward him, looking big-eyed at the saddled horse.

"Goin' away?"

"Yeah."

"Can I come?"

"You better stay with your mother. She'll need you."

Johnny said nothing, kicking his toe into the dirt. He looked at the saddled horse with fear. Hondo Lane was going away, riding off without him.

"Nobody ever stays," he said.

Hondo glanced at him, packing his saddlebags. He checked the ammunition. Enough, but not too much. He refilled the empty loops in his belt, checked his gun and rifle.

"Pa rode off and never come back. Now you're ridin'." Johnny watched him, fighting back tears.

Hondo turned his back. It was a lonely life for a kid. Only his mother here. The boy should have a father. He felt sick and miserable, thinking about that. This boy had no father, and it was his, Hondo's fault. But he had never had a father, actually.

Carrying his saddlebags to the lineback, he strapped them in place.

"You take care of your mother, you hear?"

"Yes," Johnny watched him, slowly drawing back. "You ain't comin' back." His said the words with sudden realization.

Hondo finished strapping the pack, then turned and, taking his time, began to build a smoke. He knew how the boy felt, because he had felt like that himself. When they were the age of this boy it was an awful thing to see a friend ride off. Later you became used to it. Later you learned that nothing was for long. It was a pity you had to learn that.

Hondo struck the match and lighted his cigarette. "Goin' to the fort. Maybe you'll come along someday. We'll have us a hunt together." He squatted on his heels. "You study sign, son. You remember what I taught you, an' try to learn more. Man walking in tall grass, he kicks the grass away from him in the direction he's travelin'. Horse or cow, their hoofs have a circular, swingin' motion, so they knock the grass down an' back. With them it points in the direction they come from."

Johnny had moved closer, but he did not look at Hondo. He stared at the ground, listening.

"No two animals and no two men leave the same track. Like signin' your name. Every one is different. You study at it, son. Readin' sign comes mighty handy."

He squeezed the boy's shoulder and got to his feet. His throat felt tight and choked up and he walked to his horse and gathered the reins. Then he put a hand on the pommel, and when he looked across the saddle, Angie was standing there, her face showing nothing. A tendril of hair hung down by one ear, stirring a little in the wind.

How white her shoulder was, where the dress pushed back from the tan! He felt himself tighten up inside, and then he said, "Didn't have any choice. He cut loose on me."

"I knew you were lying . . . to make me think well of him. Poor Ed. He wasn't the type of man to die well. I'm sorry now that I hated him so much . . . after I got to know how tawdry and weak he was. I guess he couldn't help being that way. He never saw the beauty of this country. Not the way my father and I saw it. He called it the country God forgot."

Hondo held the pommel, afraid to let go, afraid this little sign of hope would turn the fates against him. It was like keeping his fingers crossed.

"I didn't have a choice."

"I know."

He hesitated, waiting a long minute. "You going to feel different about me?"

"No one has any control about how they feel. I'm not going to change the way I feel about you."

Johnny had walked away, toward the stream. He did not want the man to go, but maybe his mother could do something about that. She always seemed able to do things about things.

"What about him?" Angie asked.

"What about him?" Hondo repeated the words thoughtfully. "Well, he'll make a man. Got a good spread to his shoulders. Head works too. Tell him something, he remembers. Moves good—light on his feet. Other night while you were asleep he climbed on my bunk an' kissed me. Gave me a kind of funny feeling. First time I was ever kissed by a kid." Suddenly he dropped the reins to ground-hitch the lineback. "There's things I'd rather do than this."

Johnny was squatting near the river looking at some tracks, and Hondo walked slowly toward him.

Angie stared after him, feeling sudden panic as she realized what Hondo meant to do.

Johnny looked up from the tiny writing of tracks he had found. "Hondo, what track is that?"

Hondo squatted. "Squirrel there. This one with only four toes is the front foot. Back foot has five toes." He indicated another, larger track. "Badger. Follow him and you'll find holes where he dug out field mice or pack rats. He eats 'em. See the claw marks? Those are his front feet. Never see the claws on his back feet. Always toes in a mite, too."

Hond rubbed his cigarette into the sand. "Want to tell you. While back a man came at me with a gun. Killed him."

"Good! Indian?"

"No. He was a white man. I didn't have any choice. This man I killed—"

"No!" Angie put her hand across his mouth. "Your ranch in California . . . California's far. Too far for gossip to travel."

Hondo got up slowly, relieved. Johnny wandered off, trailing the badger.

"California's far. He needs a father. He likes you, Hondo."

"Easy to say California's far, that he'll not hear. Could happen." He looked at her. "What then?"

"We'll face it then. Nobody lives their life without having to face things from time to time. It will work out, I know."

The cottonwood rustled its leaves and Hondo looked at the

hills. She was right, of course, Face that issue when it came. By that time he would have been a father to the boy, and they would understand each other.

"The Apache don't have a word for love," he said. "Know what they both say at the marriage? The squaw-taking ceremony?"

"Tell me."

"*Varlebena.* It means forever. That's all they say."

Angie put her hand on his sleeve. "Forever," she said quietly.

"Forever."

They stood together in silence, his arm about her waist. The lineback looked around impatiently, stomping a hoof at a fly. Johnny came trudging back from upstream. He looked at Hondo and his mother. "You going to stay?"

"Yes."

"Saw a hole that ol' badger dug."

He wandered off toward the corrals, and Angie looked up suddenly. "I'd hate to leave this place. Can the Lieutenant make us?"

"Guess so." They turned toward the house. "Better, anyway," he said. "No trouble around my place. Vittoro can't live forever."

"I planned to leave once, before you came back."

"Might have to. Anyway," he glanced around, "more grass and trees on my place. When I left they talked some of building a school not far off. We got to think of that."

"All right."

She looked up at him. "Hondo, I . . . It's Father. He's buried back there at the trees. He—he liked the cottonwoods so much, I hate to leave him."

"You won't."

She looked up, and he said. "He left you. He lives in you and Johnny. I reckon no man ever dies who leaves a son or a daughter."

"We'll go, then?"

"We'll wait."

They heard the rush of hoofs and the rattle of wheels over stones before anything came into view, and then Johnny came running, and over the rim of the basin came a racing wagon. The horses lunged down the trail and drew up in a cloud of dust that overtook and settled around and over the wagon. Buffalo Baker was driving, and he sprang down and lifted the unconscious Lieutenant McKay from the wagon. The movement seemed to bring him out of it.

"We caught Vittoro," Buffalo said.

"Can't understand," McKay muttered, only half aware. "They had us surrounded. Could have cut us to pieces. Then they withdrew."

Hondo picked up a headband that had fallen from the wagon when the Lieutenant was lifted clear.

"Vittoro's."

"Killed him," Buffalo said, "on the last charge."

"Then that's it. That's why they pulled out. Any time the leader is killed, that means the medicine is bad."

He turned to Angie. "We'll go out with the squadron. Vittoro's dead."

Buffalo walked past them, carrying the Lieutenant through the door Angie held open.

"Now Silva's the leader. Get your things together."

"Wait. I've some medicines. Maybe I can do something for Lieutenant McKay."

"Thank you, Mrs. Lowe. I'd be grateful if you'd pass among the men and see what you can do for them."

"But you're bleeding, and—"

"Yes, ma'am, and many of the men are bleeding. I dislike to ask a lady to perform such a disagreeable task, but—"

When she had gone, McKay lay back on the bunk, breathing heavily. His eyes rolled toward Hondo. "You were right. Vittoro was just luring us on. Will you see that my troops get out."

He fainted then, and Hondo opened his shirt and went to work. He had that rough skill men acquired on a frontier where doctors were rare, and medicines even rarer.

"He didn't know much," Buffalo said. "He led us into an ambush. But I ain't ashamed of him, nohow. All his bullet holes is in the front of him."

Hondo had taken warm water from the stove and was gently sponging away the blood from the wounds. "All them youngsters from West Point is like that."

"They got to learn."

"Partly they learn, partly they die. I got to float my stick same as you. I never saw one of them I had to be ashamed of."

He worked on, sponging off the wounds, then binding them with Indian remedies. They were methods he had used on himself, and they worked.

Finally he straightened up. "Better get them started out there. Take the wagon here, harness the horses, and load the wounded.

There's a good deal of bedding. We won't have much time."

"You think Silva will come here?"

"Yes." Hondo Lane turned and glanced out the door to Angie, coming toward the house. "It'll be the first on his list."

CHAPTER TWENTY-TWO

WESTWARD THE LAND was bright. The moving column wound like a gray-blue snake across the beige-gray hills. Sweat streaked the faces of the troopers and dust settled on the blue of their uniforms. Many were stained with the blood of their enemies, and not a few with the blood of their own veins. The wagons rolled and rumbled, jolting over the stones, and in one of the wagons a man cursed in a high, hard, monotonous voice.

Saddles creaked; men watched the hills. Sweat darkened the hides of horses. The sun was hot. The uniforms of the men were stiff with ancient sweat and dust, and their lips cracked. Occasionally a low wind moved among them, cooling and fresh like a draught of cold clear water.

Sergeant Young mopped his face and looked over at Hondo. "You think he's coming?"

"I know he is."

"How much time we got?"

"Three—four hours."

"Wished the Lieutenant was up."

Hondo Lane said nothing. He knew how the sergeant felt. They were pitifully short of officers all along the frontier.

Lane dropped back along the column, then swept the hills behind them. No sign of anything yet, but it was too soon. But once the medicine was made, Silva would not wait long. He was dangerous, but too impatient. He would be relentless and ruthless, but less shrewd than old Vittoro had been.

Behind the column the dust settled and there were only the tracks, a plain trail that nothing could remove. Not even a bad storm would wipe out that trail, and behind them would be the Mescaleros and their allies.

He looked around at the parched and lonely country, then

swung the lineback. there was yet time, but to hole up and make a stand would be worse than useless. They must keep going, get near enough for a relief column to reach them.

He rode after the moving train, and they plodded on wearily, pushing toward the afternoon and the rim of distant hills beyond the post, still so far, far away.

There was a brief noon halt near a water hole whose waters swiftly dwindled and died as the horses drank. No man touched any water but that from his canteen, and sparingly. The horses were all-important now, and each horse drank.

Lieutenant McKay was delirious, talking of Richmond, of the Point, and of a girl somewhere who had said no, when she could not have found a better man.

The sun was high and hot. Fifteen minutes of halt, then the column moved out. Men slumped in the saddle, weary after miles, yet knowing what was yet to come. In the wagons the cursing man had lost consciousness, and a man with a broken collarbone and a bandaged skull was singing to a mandolin the good songs, the old songs. . . .

In the hot stillness of the afternoon they came down from the hills, their dark bodies dusty with the trail and the column swung its few wagons into a tight circle and the rifles spoke. The Indians vanished, then came again, swiftly, some on horseback, but more upon foot. The Apache was a daring runner, and he trusted his feet.

Cold eyes looked down the barrels of rifles and then men fired. Dust leaped from the hillside. An Apache stopped in mid-stride as though he had run headlong into some obstruction, and then he fell, his shrill dying cry hanging in the stillness of the afternoon long after the man was dead.

The charge ended, the rush was gone, the hillside was a barrren and empty thing, alive with death.

Like ghosts, somebody said. Vanished, melted into the landscape, as was the Apache way. A rifle spoke. A trooper cried out and died. Hondo rode swiftly around the inner circle. He called his orders in a low, hard voice, Sergeant Young making the other loop. The rush came suddenly, and as it did the column sprang into life and went hurtling forward, wagons three abreast, horses racing, surrounded by cavalry.

It caught the Apaches by surprise. Most of them were dismounted, moving forward among the rocks. It caught them unprepared and the tight knot of wagons and men rolled out and over the crest and down the long sweep of the valley. A mile fell behind . . . two miles. Whooping Indians came up behind, firing and missing, yet racing forward.

Hondo yelled at Young and the Sergeant gave a quick command. Ten troopers swung their horses into line and dropped to the ground, to their knees. An instant they waited as the Apaches charged nearer. The volley was a solid sound, a sound that struck and melted the advancing Indians. Swiftly the kneeling men fired again.

Leaving chaos behind them, they swung into their saddles and were off after the train.

"We'll try that again!" Young yelled.

"Won't work again," Hondo said. "They'll be scattered out now."

But some of the atackers had gone on ahead, cutting across the hills, and now they came down, pouring over the crest like a dark flood, lit by flashes of color and flame. The wagons rounded again into a circle and the troopers swung down from their horses. Hondo put the butt of his Winchester against his shoulder and fired, his shots seeking out the Apaches, firing carefully, squeezing off every shot.

Attacks began and ended. The Apache was never one to trust a wild charge. He was a shrewd and careful fighter, knowing the value of cover, moving with care, never wasting time or shots. They moved in closer, then closer.

They were elusive, targets scarcely seen. A flash of brown against the desert, then no sign of life, no movement. Worming their way closer, they used scant inches of cover for their movements. When they came again it would be from close up, their charge only a few yards. Hondo worked his way around, warning the troopers to be ready. He scattered the few men with pistols in positions to cover every yard of space.

A half hour passed. The sun beat down from a wide and brassy sky. Sweat trickled down the faces and necks of the waiting troopers. Its salt made them blink. Their rifles were hot from the desert sun.

The Apaches knew the value of waiting, and as they waited, they drew nearer. A single rifle shot sounded. A trooper had seen a flashing brown leg and fired. His shot ripped the heel from the vanishing Indian.

Silence lay heavily upon the circle. Heat waves shimmered. A man coughed, a horse stamped at a fly. There was no other sound. Hondo shifed his Colt, drying a sweaty palm. They waited, hugging their sparce cover.

Suddenly fifty horsemen charged over the hill. Eyes lifted to them and rifles . . . and in that instant, the nearer Indians charged also. It was perfect—except for Hondo's pistol men.

There were six of them in all, but their fire was point-blank. It broke the force of the charge, and the Indians that reached the barricades were clubbed down by battering rifle butts. And then the horsemen came.

Some had gone down, but a dozen leaped their horses into the circle. One big brave lunged his horse at Hondo, his lance poised. Hondo's side step saved him and his quick grasp of the lance wrenched the Indian from the saddle. The Indian hit on the small of his neck, and as he tried to roll over, Hondo kicked him under the chin, then shot him.

A horse was down, screaming. The inner circle was a whirl of fighting men. From the outer circle came the heavy bark of rifles to prove that Indians were still coming. Lieutenant McKay was on one elbow, firing his pistol.

Hondo swung his pistol barrel at a head, heard it crunch, saw a lance aimed for him and swung aside. And then in the swirl of dust and smoke he saw Silva.

The big Indian's face was a twisted mask of fury and he leaped his horse at Hondo. The animal's shoulder hit Hondo, and he was knocked rolling. Silva swung down from his horse and sprang, knife in hand. Hondo came up from the ground and his kick caught Silva below the knee. The Indian stopped in mid-stride and another Apache swept by. Hondo struck out at him and saw the man fall, then caught up his broken lance in time to meet Silva's lance. He parried the blow, then gutted the Indian as the Indian had gutted the dog.

Silva went down, the lance ripping him up, and Hondo said, "Like my dog . . . you die!"

As suddenly as it had begun, the attack broke. A swarm of Apaches swept round him, and then they were gone, carrying Silva among them.

And then there was only settling dust and the moans of the wounded and the dying.

Again the wagons rolled, only now there were more wounded,

now there were empty saddles, now there were more bandaged heads.

Sergeant Young dropped back beside the wagon where Hondo rode. "That hurt 'em!" he said. "We hurt 'em bad!"

"They won't bother us."

"You don't think they'll attack again?"

"Another chief's dead. We'll make the fort before they have another leader."

Angie started to bandage a wound on Hondo's arm. He handed the reins to Johnny, who accepted them eagerly.

"He's never learned to drive!" Angie protested.

"By the time we make California, he'll be top teamster." He yelled shrilly at the horses, and they moved out.

Angie finished with the arm, and held it, and all up and down the column there was only the movement of wagons rolling, the sound of horses' hoofs, and an occasional low moan from a wagon.

From far back in the column a mandolin sounded and a rolling bass started the words of "Sweet Betsy from Pike."

A long time later, when the column rolled over the long hill and headed for the parade ground, Hondo looked up from the reins he now held. He could see the flag fluttering in the wind, the troops marching onto the field for retreat, and westward the land was bright with a setting sun, and a dull rose shaded the clouds and faded away against the higher heavens, and from the parade ground he heard a bugle, its notes bright and clear.

He heard Sergeant Young's command, saw the men form up, and saw them, battered and wounded and bloody, riding proudly to the parade ground.

He saw them go, and knew their fierce pride, and their glory. But he was remembering a long meadow fresh with new-cut hay, a house where smoke would soon again rise from the chimney, and where shadows would gather in the darkness under the trees, quiet shadows. And beside him a woman held in her arms a sleeping child . . . a woman who would be there with him, in that house, before that hearth.

Showdown at Yellow Butte

CHAPTER ONE

EVERYTHING WAS QUIET in Mustang. Three whole days had passed without a killing. The townfolk, knowing their community, were not fooled. They had long since resigned themselves to the inevitable. In fact, they would be relieved when the situation was back to normal—a killing a day; more on hot days. Several days without deadly gun play built up a mounting tension that was unbearable. Who would be next?

Moreover, with Clay Allison, who had killed thirty men, playing poker over at the Morrison House, and Black Jack Ketchum, who richly deserved the hanging he was soon to get, sleeping off a drunk at the St. James—trouble could be expected in the very near future.

The walk before the St. James was now cool, and Captain Tom Kedrick, a stranger in town, sat in a well-polished chair and studied the street with interested eyes.

He was a tall young man with rusty brown hair and green eyes, quiet mannered and quick to smile. Women never failed to look twice, and when their eyes met his their hearts pounded, a fact of which Tom Kedrick was totally unaware. He knew women seemed to like him, but it never failed to leave him mildly astonished.

The street he watched was crowded with buckboards, freight wagons, a newly arrived stage and one about to depart. All the hitch-rails were lined with saddled horses wearing a variety of brands.

Kedrick, suddenly aware that a young man stood beside him, glanced up. The fellow was scarcely more than a boy and he had soft brown eyes and hair that needed cutting. "Cap'n Kedrick?" he inquired. "John Gunter sent me. I'm Dornie Shaw."

"Oh, yes!" Kedrick got to his feet, smiling, and thrust out his hand. "Nice to know you, Shaw. Are you working for Gunter?"

Shaw's brown eyes were faintly ironic. "With him," he corrected. "I work for no man."

"I see."

Kedrick did not see at all, but was prepared to wait and find out. There was something oddly disturbing about this young man, something that had Kedrick on edge and queerly alert. "Where's Gunter now?"

"Down the street. He asked me to check an' see if you were here, an' if you were, to ask you to stick around close to the hotel. He'll be along soon."

"All right. Sit down, why don't you?"

Shaw glanced briefly at the chairs. "I'll stand. I never sit in no chair with arms on them. Apt to get in the way."

"In the way?" Kedrick glanced up, and then his eyes fell to the two guns Shaw wore, their butts hanging wide. "Oh, yes! I see." He nodded at the guns. "The town marshal doesn't object?"

Dornie Shaw looked at him, smiling slowly. "Not to me, he don't. Wouldn't do him no good if he did.

"Anyway," he added after a minute, "not in Mustang. Too many hard cases. I never seen a marshal could make it stick in this town."

Kedrick smiled. "Hickok? Earp? Masterson?"

"Maybe," Dornie Shaw was openly skeptical, "but I doubt it. Allison's here. So's Ketchum. Billy the Kid's been around, and some of that crowd. A marshal in this town would have to be mighty fast, an' prove it ever' day."

"Maybe you're right." He studied Shaw surreptitiously. What was it about him that was so disturbing? Not the two guns, for he had seen many men who wore guns, had been reared among them, in fact. No, it was something else, some quality he could not define, but it was a sort of lurking menace, an odd feeling about such a calm-eyed young man.

"We've got some good men," Shaw volunteered, after a minute. "Picked up a couple today. Laredo Shad's goin' to be one of the best, I'm thinkin'. He's a tough hand, an' gun wise as all get-out. Three more come in today. Fessenden, Poinsett an' Goff."

Obviously, from the manner in which he spoke, the names meant much to Shaw, but they meant exactly nothing to Kedrick. Fessenden seemed to strike some sort of a responsive note but he could not put a finger on it. His eyes strayed down the street, studying the crowd. "You think they'll really fight?" he asked, studying the street. "Are there enough of them?"

"That bunch?" Shaw's voice was dry. "They'll fight, all right. You got some tough boys in that outfit. Injun scrappers, an' such like. They won't scare worth a durn." He glanced curiously at Kedrick. "Gunter says you're a fighter."

Was that doubt in Shaw's voice? Kedrick smiled, then shrugged. "I get along. I was in the Army, if that means anything."

"Been West before?"

"Sure! I was born in California, just before the Rush. When the war broke out I was sixteen, but I went in with a bunch from Nevada. Stayed in a couple of years after the war, fighting Apaches!"

Shaw nodded, as if satisfied. "Gunter thinks well of you, but he's only one of them, an' not the most important one."

A short, thick-set man with a square-cut beard, that made him look enough like General Grant to be his twin, was pushing through the crowd toward them. He even smoked a thick black cigar.

The man walking beside him was tall as Kedrick, who stood an easy inch above six feet. He had a sharply cut face and his eyes were cold, but they were the eyes of a man born to command, a man who could be utterly ruthless. That would be Colonel Loren Keith. That meant there was still one left he had to meet—Burwick. The three were partners, and of the three, only Burwick was from the area.

Gunter smiled quickly, his lips parting over clenched white teeth that gripped his cigar. He thrust out his hand. "Good to see you, Kedrick! Colonel, this is our man! If there ever was a man born to ramrod this thing through, this is the one! I told you of that drive he made for Patterson! Took those cattle through without losing a head, rustlers an' Comanches be danged!"

Keith nodded, his cold eyes taking in Kedrick at a glance. "Captain—that was an army title, Kedrick?"

"Army. The War Between the States."

"I see. There was a Thomas Kedrick who was a sergeant in the fighting against the Apaches."

"That was me. All of us went down some in rank after the troops were discharged."

"How much time in the war?" Keith's eyes still studied him.

"Four years, and two campaigning in the Southwest."

"Not bad. You should know what to expect in a fight." His eyes went to Kedrick's, faintly mocking. "I have twelve years, myself. Regular army."

Kedrick found that Keith's attitude irritated him. He meant to say nothing, but suddenly he was speaking. "My American army experience, Colonel, was only part of the story. I was with Bazaine, at the defense of Metz, in the Franco-Prussian War. I escaped, and was with MacMahon at the Battle of Sedan."

Keith's eyes sharpened and his lips thinned. Kedrick could feel the sharp dislike rising in the man.

"Is that all?" he asked coolly.

"Why, no. Since you ask, it was not. I was with Wolseley, in the Second Ashanti War, in Africa. And I was in the two-year campaign against the Tungans of northern T'ien Shan—with the rank of General."

"You seem to get around a good bit," Keith said dryly, "a genuine mercenary!"

Kedrick smiled, undisturbed. "If you like. That's what you want here, isn't it? Men who can fight? Isn't it customary for some men to hire others to do their fighting for them?"

Colonel Keith's face flamed, then went white, but before he could speak, a big, square-faced man thrust himself through the crowd and stopped to face them.

"You, is it, Gunter?" the man cried. "Well, I've heard tell the reason why you're here, an' if you expect to take from hard-workin' men the land they've slaved for, you better come a-shootin'!"

Before anyone could speak, Dornie slid between Keith and Gunter and fronted the man. "You lookin' for trouble? You want to start your shootin' now?"

His voice was low, almost a purr, but Kedrick was startled by the shocked expression on the man's face. He drew back, holding his hands wide. "I wasn't bracin' you, Dornie! Didn't even know you was around!"

"Then get out!" Dornie Shaw snarled, passion suddenly breaking through his calmness, passion, and something else, something Kedrick spotted with a shock—the driving urge to kill!

"Get out!" Shaw repeated. "An' if you want to live, keep goin'!"

Stumblingly, the man turned and ducked into the hastily

assembled crowd, and Tom Kedrick, scanning their faces, found hard indifference there, or hatred. In no face did he see warmth or friendly feeling. He frowned thoughtfully, then turned away.

Gunter caught his arm, eager to take advantage of the break the interruption had made to bring peace between the two. "You see what we're up against?" he began. "Now that was Peters. He's harmless, but there's others would have drawn, and drawn fast! They won't be all like that ! Let's go meet Burwick!"

Kedrick fell in beside Gunter, who carefully interposed himself between the two men. Once, Tom glanced back. What had become of Dornie Shaw he did not know, but he did know that Dornie, who was to be his second in command, was a killer. He knew the type from of old.

Yet he was disturbed more than he cared to admit by the man who had challenged them. Peters had the look of an honest man, even if not an intelligent one. Of course, there might be honest men among them, if they were men of Peters' stripe. But Peters seemed to be a follower, and he might follow where the men led.

Certainly, if this land was going to Gunter, Keith and Burwick through a Government bill, there could be nothing wrong with the deal. If the Government sold the land to them, squatters had no rights on it. Still, if there were many like Peters the job was not going to be all he had expected.

Gunter stopped before a square stone house set back from the street. "This here's headquarters," he said. "We hole up here when in town. Come on in."

A wide veranda skirted the house, and as they stepped upon it they saw a girl in a gray skirt and white blouse sitting a few feet away with an open book in her lap. Gunter halted.

"Cap'n Kedrick, my niece, Consuelo Duane."

Their eyes met—and held. For a breathless moment no voice was lifted. Tom Kedrick felt as though his muscles had gone dead, for he could not move. Her own eyes were wide, startled.

Kedrick recovered himself with a start. He bowed.

"Miss Duane!"

"Captain Kedrick," somehow she was on her feet and moving toward him, "I hope you'll like it here!"

His eyes had not left hers, and now color was coming into her cheeks. "I shall!" he said gently. "Nothing can prevent me now."

"Don't be too sure of that, Captain!" Keith's voice was sharp and cold. "We are late for our visit. Let's be going. Your pardon, Connie. Burwick is waiting."

Kedrick glanced back as he went through the door, and the girl was still standing there, poised, motionless.

Keith's irritation was obvious, but Gunter seemed to have noticed nothing. Dornie Shaw, who had materialized from somewhere, glanced briefly at Kedrick, but said no word. Coolly, he began to roll a smoke.

CHAPTER TWO

BURWICK CROUCHED BEHIND a table. He was an incredibly fat man, and unbelievably dirty. A stubble of graying beard covered his jowls and his several chins, yet the eyes that measured Kedrick from beneath the almost hairless brows were sharp, malignant, and set close alongside a nose too small for his face. His shirt was open, and the edge of the collar was greasy. Rims of black marked each fingernail.

He glanced at the others, then back at Kedrick. "Sit down!" he said. "You're late! Business won't wait!" His bulbous head swung from Kedrick to Gunter. "John, this the man who'll ramrod those skunks off that land? This him?"

"Yes, that's Kedrick," Gunter said hastily. Oddly enough, he seemed almost frightened of Burwick. Keith had said nothing since they entered the room. Quietly, he seemed to have withdrawn, stepped momentarily from the picture. It was, Kedrick was to discover, a faculty he had when Burwick was near. "He'll do the job, all right!"

Burwick turned his eyes on Kedrick after a moment. He nodded. "Know a good deal about you, son!" His voice was almost genial. "You'll do if you don't get soft with them! We've no time to waste, you understand! They've had notice to move. Give 'em one more notice, then get 'em off or bury 'em. That's your business, not mine. I'll ask no questions," he added sharply, "an I'll see nobody else does. What happens here is our business."

He dismissed Kedrick from his mind and turned his attention to Gunter. "You've ordered like I told you? Grub for fifty men for fifty days? Once this situation is cleaned up I want to get busy at once. The sooner we have work started, the sooner we'll be all set. I want no backfiring on this job."

Burwick turned sharply at Tom Kedrick. "Ten days! I give you ten days! If you need more than five I'll be disappointed. If you've not the heart for it, turn Dornie loose. Dornie'll show 'em." He cackled suddenly. "That's right. Dornie'll show 'em!"

He sobered down, glanced at the papers on his desk, then without looking up, "Kedrick, you can go. Dornie, you run along, too!"

Kedrick hesitated, then arose. "How many of these men are there?" he asked suddenly. "Have any of them families?"

Gunter turned on him nervously. "I'll tell you all you need to know, Tom. See you later!"

Kedrick shrugged, and picking up his hat, walked out. Dornie Shaw had already vanished. When he reached the veranda, Connie Duane still sat there. She was staring over the top of her book at the dusty, sun-swept street.

He paused, hat in hand. "Have you been in Mustang long?"

She looked up, studying him for a long minute before she spoke. "Why, no. Not long. Yet long enough to learn to love and hate." She turned her eyes to the hills, then back to him. "I love this country, Captain. Can you understand that?

"I'm a city girl, born and bred in the city, and yet when I first saw those red rock walls, those lonely mesas, the desert, the Indian ponies—why, Captain, I fell in love! This is my country. I could stay here forever."

Surprised, he studied her again, more pleased than he could easily have admitted. "That's the way I feel about it. But you said to love and to hate. You love the country. Now what do you hate?"

"Some of the men who infest it, Captain. Some of the human wolves it breeds, and others, bred elsewhere, who come to it to feed off the ones who came earlier and were more courageous but are less knowing, less tricky."

More and more surprised, he leaned on the rail. "I don't know if I follow you, Miss Duane. I haven't been here long, but I haven't met any of those you speak of."

She looked up at him, her eyes frank and cool. Slowly, she closed her book and turned toward the door. "You haven't, Captain?" Her voice was suddenly cool. "Are you sure? At the moment, I am wondering if you are not one of them!'' She stepped through the door and was gone.

Tom Kedrick stood for a moment, staring after her. When he turned away it was with a puzzled frown on his face. Now what did she mean by that? What did she know about him that could incline her to such a view? Despite himself, he was both irritated and disturbed. Coupled with the anger of the man Peters, it offered a new element to his thinking. Yet, how could Consuelo Duane, John Gunter's niece, have the same opinion owned by Peters? No doubt they stemmed from different sources.

Troubled, he walked on down to the street of the town and stood there, looking around.

He had not yet changed into Western clothes, and wore a flat-crowned, flat-brimmed black hat, which he would retain, a tailored gray suit, and black Western-style boots. Pausing on the corner, he slowly rolled a cigarette and lighted it. He made a dashing, handsome figure as he stood there in his perfectly fitted suit, his lean, bronzed face strong, intelligent, and alert.

Both men and women glanced at him and most of them looked twice. His military erectness, broad shoulders and cool self-possession were enough to mark him in any crowd. His mind had escaped his immediate problem now and was lost in the never-ending excitement of a crowded Western street. All kinds of men and women seemed jammed together without rhyme or reason.

For the West was of all things, a melting pot. Adventurers came to seek gold, new lands, excitement. Gamblers, women of the oldest and most active profession, thugs, gunmen, cow rustlers, horsethieves, miners, cowhands, freighters and just drifters—all crowded the street. That bearded unshaven man in the sun-faded red wool shirt might, if prompted, start to spout Shakespeare. The slender young man talking to the girl in the buckboard might have graduated from Oxford, and the white-faced gambler might be the scion of an old Southern family.

All men wore guns, most of them in plain sight. Few of them would hesitate to use them if need be. The man who fought with his fists, although present, was a rarity.

A big man lurched from the crowd. Tom glanced at him, and their eyes met. Obviously, the man had been drinking and was hunting trouble. In Kedrick, he thought he found it. Sensing a fight, other passers-by became wary and stopped to watch.

''So?'' The big man stood wide legged, his sleeves rolled about thick, hairy forearms. "'Nother one of them durn thieves! Land stealers!" He chuckled suddenly. "Well, your murderer ain't with you now to save your bacon, an' I aim to git my share of you right now! Reach!"

Kedrick's mouth was dry, but his eyes were calm. He held the cigarette in his right hand near his mouth. "Sorry, friend. I'm not packing a gun. If I were, I'd still not kill you. You're mistaken, man, about that land. My people have a rightful claim to it."

"Have they, now?" The big man came a step nearer, his hand on the butt of his gun. "The right to take from a man the land he's sweated over? To tear down his home? To run his kids out on the desert?"

Despite the fact that the man was drunk, Tom Kedrick saw beyond it a sullen and honest fury—and fear. Not fear for him, for this man was not afraid, nor would he be afraid of Dornie Shaw. He was afraid for his family. The realization of that fact struck Kedrick and disturbed him anew. More and more he was questioning the course he had chosen.

The crowd murmured and was ugly. Obviously, their sympathies were with the big man, and against Kedrick.

A low murmur, then a rustling in the crowd, and suddenly: deathly silence. Kedrick saw the big man's face pale, and heard someone whisper hoarsely, "Look out, Burt! It's Dornie Shaw!"

Kedrick was suddenly aware that Shaw had moved up beside him. "Let me have him, Cap'n," Shaw's voice was low. "It's time this here was stopped."

Kedrick's voice was sharp, cold. "No! Move back, Shaw! I'll fight my own battles!"

"But you ain't got a gun!" Shaw's voice was sharper in protest.

Burt showed no desire to retreat. That the appearance of Shaw had shocked him was evident, but this man was not Peters. He was going to stand his ground. His eyes, wary now, but puzzled, shifted from Shaw to Kedrick, and Tom took an easy step forward, putting himself almost within arm's length of Burt.

"Shaw's not in this, Burt," he said quietly. "I've no quarrel with you, man, but no man calls me without getting his chance. If you want what I've got, don't let the fact that I'm not armed stop you. I wanted no quarrel, but you do— so have at it!"

Suspicion was in the big man's eyes. He had seen guns come from nowhere before, and especially from men dressed as this one. He was not prepared to believe that Kedrick would face him unarmed. "You got a gun!" he snapped. "You got a hide-out, you durned coyote!"

He jerked his gun from the holster and in that instant, Tom Kedrick moved. The edge of his left hand chopped down on the rising wrist of the gun hand, and he stepped in, whipping up his right in an uppercut that packed all the power in his lean, whipcord body. The punch was fast and perfectly timed, and the crack of it on the corner of Burt's jaw was like the snap of a teamster's whip. Burt hit the walk just one split second after his gun, and he hit it right on his shoulder blades.

Coolly then, Kedrick stooped and picked up the gun, an old 1851 Model Navy revolver. He stood over the man, his eyes searching the crowd. Wherever he looked there were hard, blank faces. He glanced down at Burt. The big man was slowly sitting up, shaking his big head. He started to lift his right hand, and gave a sudden gasp of pain. He stared at it, then looked up. "You broke my wrist!" he said. "It's busted! An' me with my plowin' to do!"

"Better get up," Kedrick said quietly. "You asked for it, you know."

When the man was on his feet, Kedrick calmly handed him his six-shooter. Their eyes met over the gun and Kedrick smiled. "Take it. Drop it down in your holster an' forget it. I'm not worried. You're not the man to shoot another in the back."

Calmly, he turned his back and walked slowly away down the street. Before the St. James, he paused. His fingers trembled ever so slightly as he took out a paper and shook tobacco into it.

"That was slick." It was Dornie Shaw's soft voice. His brown eyes probed Kedrick's face curiously. "Never seen the like! Just slapped his wrist an' busted it!"

With Keith, John Gunter had also come up, and he was smiling broadly. "Saw it all, son! That'll do more good than a dozen killings! Just like Tom Smith used to do! Old Bear Creek Tom who handled some of the toughest rannies that ever came over the trail with nothin' but his fists!"

"What would you have done if he had jerked that gun back and fired?" Keith asked.

Kedrick shrugged, wanting to forget it. "He hadn't time," he said quietly. "But there are answers to that, too!"

"Some of the boys will be up to see you tonight, Tom," Gunter advised. "I've had Dornie notify Shad, Fessenden and some of the others. Better figure on a ride out there tomorrow. Makin' a start, anyway. Just sort of ride around with some of the boys to let 'em know we ain't foolin'."

Kedrick nodded, and after a brief discussion went inside and to his room. Certainly, he reflected, the West had not changed. Things still happened fast out here.

He pulled off his coat, waistcoat and vest, then his boots. Stripped to the waist, he sat down on the bed and dug into his valise. For a couple of minutes he dug around and then drew out two well-oiled holsters and gun belts. In the holsters were two .44 Russian pistols, a Smith & Wesson gun, manufactured on order for the Russian Army, and one of the most accurate shooting pistols on the market up to that time.

Carefully, he checked the loads, then returned the guns to their holsters and put them aside. Digging around, he drew out a second pair of guns, holsters and belts. Each of these was a Walch twelve-shot Navy pistol, caliber .36, and almost identical in size and weight to the Frontier Colt or the .44 Russian.

Rarely seen in the West, and disliked by some, Kedrick had used the guns on many occasions and found them always satisfactory. There were times when the added fire power was a big help. As for stopping power, the .36 in the hands of a good marksman lacked but little that was offered by the heavier .44 caliber.

Yet, there was a time and a place for everything, and these guns had an added tactical value. Carefully, he wrapped them once more and returned them to the bottom of his valise. Then he belted on the .44 Russians, and digging out his Winchester, carefully cleaned, oiled and loaded it. Then he sat down on the bed and was about to remove his guns again and stretch out, when there was a light tap at the door.

"Come in," said Kedrick, "and if you're an enemy, I'll be pleased to know you!"

The door opened and closed all in a breath. The man that stood with his back to it facing Kedrick was scarcely five-feet-four, yet almost as broad as he was tall. All of him seemed the sheer power of bone and muscle, and not an ounce of fat anywhere. His broad brown face might have been graved from stone, and the bristle of shortcropped hair above it was black as a crow's wing. The man's neck spread to broad, thick shoulders. On his right hip he packed a gun. In his hand he held a narrow-brimmed hard hat.

Kedrick leaped to his feet. "Dai!" The name was an explosion of sound. "Dai Reid! What are you doing in this country?"

"Ah? So it's that you ask, is it? Well, it's trouble there is, much of trouble! An' you that's by way of bringin' it!"

"Me?" Kedrick waved to a chair. "Tell me what you mean."

The Welshman searched his face, then seated himself, his huge palms resting on his knees. His legs were thick muscled and bowed. "It's the man Burwick you're with? An' you've the job taken to run us off the land? There is changed you are, Tom, an' for the worse!"

"You're one of them? You're on the land Burwick, Keith and Gunter claim?"

"I am that. And a sight of work I've done on it, too. An' now the rascals would be puttin' me off. Well, they'll have a fight to move me—an' you, too, Tom Kedrick, if you're to stay one of them."

Kedrick studied the Welshman thoughtfully. All his doubts had come to a head now . . . for this man, he knew. His own father had been Welsh, his mother Irish, and Dai Reid had been friend to them both. Dai had come from the old country with his father, had worked beside him when he courted his mother, and although much younger than Gwilym Kedrick, he had come West with him, too.

"Dai," he said slowly, "I'll admit that today I've been having doubts of all this. You see, I knew John Gunter after the war, and I took a herd of cattle over the trail for a friend of his. There was trouble that year, the Indians holding up every herd and demanding large numbers of cattle for themselves, the rustlers trying to steal whole herds, and others demanding money for passage across land they claimed. I took my herd through without paying anything but a few fat beefs for the Indians, who richly deserved them. But not what they demanded—they got what I wanted to give.

"Gunter remembered me from that, and knew something of my war record, so when he approached me in New Orleans, his proposition sounded good. And this is what he told me.

"His firm, Burwick, Keith and Gunter, had filed application for the survey and purchase of all or parts of nearly three hundred sections of land. They made oath that this land was swampland, or overflowed and came under the General Land Office ruling that it was 'land too wet for irrigation at seeding time, though later requiring irrigation, and therefore subject to sale as swamp.'

"He went on to say that they had arranged to buy the land, but that a bunch of squatters were on it who refused to leave. He wanted to hire me to lead a force to see the land was cleared, and he said that most of them were rustlers, outlaws or renegades of one sort or another. There would be fighting and force would be necessary.''

Dai nodded. ''Right he was as to the fighting, but renegades, no. Well,'' he smiled grimly past his pipe. ''I'd not be saying that now, but there's mighty few. There are bad apples in all barrels, one or two,'' he said. ''But most of us be good people, with homes built and crops in.

''An' did he tell you that their oath was given that the land was unoccupied? Well, it was! And let me tell you. Ninety-four sections have homes on them, some mighty poor, but homes.

''Shrewd they were with the planning. Six months the notices must be posted, but they posted them in fine print and where few men would read, and three months are by before anything is noticed, and by accident only. So now they come to force us off, to be sure the land is unoccupied and ready. As for swamp, 'tis desert now, and always desert. Crops can only be grown where the water is, an' little enough of that.''

Dai shook his head and knocked out his short-stemmed pipe. ''Money we've none to fight them, no lawyers among us, although one who's as likely to help, a newspaper man, he is. But what good without money to send him to Washington?''

The Welshman's face was gloomy. ''They'll beat us, that we know. They've money to fight us with, and tough men. But some of them will die on the ground, and pay for it with their red blood. And those among us there are who plan to see 'tis not only the hired gunners who die, but the high an' mighty. You, too, lad, if among them you stay.''

Kedrick was thoughtful. ''Dai, this story is different from the one I've had. I'll have to think about it, and tomorrow we ride out to look the land over and show ourselves.''

Reid looked up sharply. ''Don't you be one of them, bye! We've plans made to see no man gets off alive if we can help it.''

''Look, man!'' Kedrick leaned forward. ''You've got to change that! I mean, for now. Tomorrow it's mainly a show of force, a threat. There will be no shooting, I promise you. We'll ride out, look around, then ride back. If there's shooting, your men will start it. Now you go back to them and stop it. Let them hold off, and let me look around.''

Dai Reid got slowly to his feet. "Ah, lad! 'tis good to see you again, but under happier circumstances I wish it were! I'd have you to the house for supper and a game, as in the old days! You'd like the wife I have!"

"You? Married?" Kedrick was incredulous. "I'd never believe it!"

Dai grinned sheepishly. "Married it is, all right, and happy, Tom." His face darkened. "Happy if I can keep my ground. But one promise I make! If your bloody riders take my ground, my body will be there when they ride past, and it will not be alone, but with the dead men around!"

Long after the Welshman had gone, Tom Kedrick sat silently and studied the street below the window. Was this what Consuelo Duane had meant? Whose side was she on? First, he must ride over the land, see it for himself, and then he must have another talk with Gunter. Uneasily, he looked again at the faces of the men in his mind. The cold, wolflike face of Keith; the fat, slobby face of Burwick, underlined with harsh, domineering power; and the face of Gunter, friendly, affable, but was it not a little . . . sly?

From outside came the noise of a tinny piano, and a strident female voice, singing. Chips rattled, and there was the constant rustle of movement and of booted feet. Somewhere a spur jingled, and Tom Kedrick got to his feet and slipped into a shirt. When he was dressed again, with his guns belted on, he left his room and walked down the hall to the lobby.

From a room beside him, a man stepped and stared after him. It was Dornie Shaw.

CHAPTER THREE

ONLY THE DWELLER in the deserts can know such mornings, such silences, drowsy with warmth and the song of the cicadas. Nowhere but in the desert do the far miles stand out so clearly, the mesas, towers and cliffs so boldly outlined. Nowhere will the cloud shadows island themselves upon the desert, offering their brief respite from the sun.

Six riders, their saddles creaking, six hard men, each lost in the twisted arroyos of his own thoughts, were emerging upon the broad desert. They were men who rode with guns, men who had used their guns to kill and would use them so again. Some of them were already doomed by the relentless and ruthless tide of events; and to the others their time, too, would come.

Each of them was alone, as men who live by the gun are always alone. To them, each man was a potential enemy, each shadow a danger. They rode jealously, their gestures marked by restraint, their eyes by watchfulness.

A horse blew through his nostrils, a hoof clicked on a stone, someone shifted in his saddle and sighed. These were the only sounds. Tom Kedrick rode an appaloosa gelding, fifteen hands even, with iron-gray forequarters and starkly white hindquarters splashed with tear-shaped spots of black—a clean-limbed horse, strong and fast, with quick, intelligent eyes and interested ears.

When they bunched to start their ride, Laredo Shad stopped to stare at the horse, walking around it admiringly. "You're lucky, friend. That's a horse! Where'd you find him?"

"Navajo remuda. He's a Nez Perce war horse, a long ways off his reservation."

Kedrick noticed the men as they gathered and how they all sized him up carefully, noting his Western garb, and especially, the low-hung, tied-down guns. Yesterday, they had seen him in the store clothes he had worn from New Orleans, but now they could size him up better, judge him with their own kind.

He was tall and straight, and of his yesterday's clothing only the black, flat-crowned hat remained, the hat, and the high-heeled rider's boots. He wore a gray wool shirt now and a black silk kerchief around his neck. His jeans were black, and the two guns rode easily in position, ready for the swing of his hand.

Kedrick saw them bunch, and when they all were there, he said simply, "All right, let's go!"

They mounted up. Kedrick noted slender wiry Dornie Shaw; the great bulk of Si Fessenden; lean, bitter Poinsett and the square blond Lee Goff; sour-faced Clauson, the oldest of the lot, and the lean Texan, Laredo Shad. Moving out, he glanced at them. Whatever else they might be, they were fighting men. Several times Shaw glanced at his guns.

"You ain't wearin' Colts?"

"No, .44 Russians. They are a good gun, one of the most accurate ever built." He indicated the trail ahead with a nod. "You've been out this way before?"

"Yeah, we got quite a ride. We'll noon at a spring I know just over the North Fork. There's some deep canyons to cross, then a big peak. The Indians an' Spanish called it The Orphan. All wild country. Right beyond there we'll begin strikin' a few of 'em." He grinned a little, showing his white even teeth. "They are scattered all over hell's half acre."

"Dornie," Goff asked suddenly, "you figure on ridin' over to the Malpais this trip?"

Clauson chuckled. "Sure, he will! He should've give up long ago, but he's sure hard to whip! That girl has set her sights higher'n any West country gun slinger."

"She's shapely, at that!" Goff was openly admiring. "Right shapely, but playin' no fav'rites."

"Maybe they're playin' each other for what they can git," Poinsett said, wryly. "Maybe that's where he gets all the news he's tellin' Keith. He sure seems to know a sight o' what's goin' around."

Dornie Shaw turned in his saddle, and his thin features had sharpened. "Shut up!" he said coldly.

The older man tightened and his eyes blazed back with genuine hate, yet he held his peace. It was educational to see how quickly he quieted down; for Poinsett, a hard, vicious man with no love for anybody or anything, obviously wanted no part of what Shaw could give him.

As the day drew on, Kedrick studied the men, and noticed they all avoided giving offense to Shaw, even the bulky Fessenden who had killed twenty men, and was the only one of the group Kedrick had ever seen before. He wondered if Fessenden remembered him and decided he would know before the day was out.

Around the noon camp there was less friendly banter than would occur in a cow camp. These men were surly and touchy. Only Shad seemed able to relax, and everything came easily for him. Clauson seemed to take over the cooking job by tacit consent, and the reason was soon obvious: he was an excellent cook.

As he ate, Tom Kedrick studied his situation with care. He had taken this job in New Orleans, and at the time had needed money badly. Gunter had put up the cash to get him out here. If he did back out, he would have to find a way to repay him. Yet the more he looked over this group, the more he believed that he was in something that he wanted out of—but fast.

He had fought as a soldier of fortune in several wars. War had been his profession, and he had been a skilled fighting man almost from the beginning. His father, a one-time soldier, had a love for tactics, and Tom had grown up with an interest in things military. His education had mostly come from his father and from a newspaper man who lived with them for a winter and helped to teach the boy what he could.

Kedrick had grown up with his interest in tactics, and had entered the army and fought through the War Between the States. The subsequent fighting had given him a practical background to accompany his study and theory. But with all his fighting and killing it had entailed, he had not become callous.

To run a bunch of renegades off the land seemed simple enough and it promised action and excitement. It was a job he could do. Now he was no longer sure it was a job for him. His talk with Dai Reid as well as the attitude of so many of the people in Mustang convinced him that all was not as simple as it had first appeared. Now, before taking a final step, he wanted to survey the situation and see just whom he would be fighting, and where. At the same time, he knew the men who rode with him were going to ask few questions. They would do their killing, collect their money, and ride on.

Of them all, only Shad might think as he did, and Kedrick made a mental note to talk with the Texan before the day was over, find out where he stood and what he knew. He was inclined to agree with Shaw's original judgment, that Shad was one of the best of the lot with a gun. The man's easy way was not only natural to him, he was simply confident. He had that hard confidence that comes only from having measured his own ability and knowing what he could do when the chips were down.

After he finished his coffee he got to his feet and strolled over to the spring, had a drink, then arose and walked to his horse, tightening the cinch he had loosened when they stopped. The air was clear. Despite their lowered voices, he could catch most of what he said.

The first question he missed, but Fessenden's reply he heard. "Don't you fret about him. He's a scrapper from way back, Dornie. I found that out. This here ain't our first meetin'."

Even at this distance and with his horse between him and the circle of men, Kedrick could sense their attention.

"Tried to finagle him out of that Patterson herd up in Injun Territory. He didn't finagle worth a durn."

"What happened?" Goff demanded. "Any shootin'?"

"Some. I was ridin' partners wtih Chuck Gibbons, the Llano gunman, an' Chuck was always on the prod, sort of. One, two times I figured I might have to shoot it out with him my own self, but wasn't exactly honin' for trouble. We had too good a thing there to bust it up quarrelin'. But Chuck, he was plumb salty, an' when Kedrick faced him an' wouldn't back down or deliver the cattle, Chuck called him."

Fessenden sipped his coffee, while the men waited impatiently. When they could stand the suspense no longer, Goff demanded. "Well, what happened?"

The big man shrugged. "Kedrick's here, ain't he?"

"I mean—what was the story?"

"Gibbons never cleared leather. None of us even seen Kedrick draw, but you could have put a half dollar over the two holes in Chuck's left shirt pocket."

Nobody spoke after that, and Tom Kedrick took his time over the cinch. Then leaving his horse, he walked away further and circled, scouting the terrain thoughtfully.

He was too experienced a man to fail to appreciate the importance of a knowledge of terrain. All this country from Mustang to the Territory line would become a battleground in the near future, and a man's life might depend on what he knew. He wasted no opportunity to study the country or ask questions.

He had handled tough groups before and he was not disturbed over the problem this one presented. However, in this case he knew the situation was much more serious. In a group the men would be easier to handle than they would separately. These men were all individualists, and were without any group loyalty. In the last analysis, they had faith in only two things: six-gun skill and money. By these they lived and by these they would die.

That Fessenden had talked was pleasing, for it would at least settle the doubts of some of the others. Knowing him for a gunhand, they would more willingly accept orders from him, not because of fear, but rather because they knew him for one of their own, and not some stranger brought in to command.

When once again they all moved out, taking their time, the heat had increased. Nothing stirred on the wide, shallow face of the desert but a far and lonely buzzard that floated high and alone over a far-off messa. Tom Kedrick's eyes roamed the country ceaselessly, and yet from time to time his thoughts kept reverting to the girl on the veranda. Connie Duane was a beautiful girl. Although Gunter's niece, she apparently did not approve all he did.

Why was she here? What was her connection with Keith? Kedrick sensed the latter's animosity and he welcomed it. A quiet man, he was slow to anger; but when he was pushed, a deep-seated anger arose within him in a black tide that made him a driving fury. Knowing this rage that lay dormant within him, he rode carefully, talked carefully, and held his temper and his hand.

Dornie Shaw drew up suddenly. "This here is Canyon Largo," he said, waving his hand down the rift before them. "That peak ahead an' on your right is The Orphan. Injuns won't let no white man up there, but they say there's a spring with a good flow of water on top.

"Yonder begins the country that Burwick, Keith and Gunter bought up. They don't have the land solid to the Arizona border, but they've got a big chunk of it. The center of the squatters is a town called Yellow Butte. There's maybe ten, twelve buildin's there, among 'em a store, a stable, corrals, a saloon, an' a bank."

Kedrick nodded thoughtfully. The country before him was high desert country and could under no circumstances be called swamp. In the area where he stood there was little growth: a few patches of curly mesquite grass or black grama, with prickly pear, soapweed, creosote bush and catclaw scattered through it. In some of the washes he saw the deeper green of pinon or juniper.

They pushed on, entered the canyon and emerged from it, heading due west. He rode warily, and once, far off on his left, he glimpsed a horseman. Later, seeing the same rider, nearer than before, he deduced they were under observation and hoped there would be no attack.

"The country where most of the squatters are is right smack dab in the middle o' the range the company is after. The hombre most likely to head 'em is Bob McLennon. He's got him two right-hand men name of Pete Slagle an' Pit Laine. Now, you asked me the other day if they would fight. Them three are shinnery oak. Slagle's an oldish feller, but McLennon's in his forties an' was once a cowtown marshal. Laine, well, he's a tough one to figure, but he packs two guns an' cuts him a wide swath over there. I hear tell he had him some gun trouble up Durango way an' he didn't need no help to handle it."

From behind him Kedrick heard a low voice mutter, "Most as hard to figure as his sister!"

Dornie's mouth tightened, but he gave no other evidence that he had heard. However, the comment served to add a little to Kedrick's information. Obviously, Dornie Shaw had a friend in the enemy's camp, and the information with which he had been supplying Keith must come from that source. Was the girl betraying her own brother and her friends? It could be, but could Shaw come and go among them without danger? Or did he worry himself about it?

There had been no mention of Dai Reid, yet the powerful little Welshman was sure to be a figure wherever he stood. He was definitely a man to be reckoned with.

Suddenly, a rider appeared from an arroyo not thirty yards off and walked her horse toward them. Dornie Shaw swore softly and drew up. As one man, they all stopped.

The girl was small, well made, her skin as brown as that of an Indian, her hair coal black. She had large, beautiful eyes and small hands. Her eyes flashed from Dornie to the others, then clung to Tom Kedrick, measuring him for a long minute. "Who's your friend, Dornie?" she said. "Introduce me."

Shaw's eyes were dark and hard as he turned slightly. "Cap'n Kedrick, I want yuh to meet Sue Laine."

"Captain?" She studied him anew. "Were you in the army?"

"Yes," he said quietly. Her pinto was not the horse of the rider who had been observing them; therefore, there was another rider out there somewhere. Who was he?

"You're ridin' quite a ways from home, Sue," Shaw interrupted. "You think that's wise?"

"I can take care of myself, Dornie!" Her reply was cool, and Kedrick saw blood rise under Shaw's skin. "However, I came to warn you, or Captain Kedrick, if he is in charge. It won't be safe to ride any further. McLennon called a meeting this morning and they voted to open fire on any party of surveyors or strange riders they see. From now on, this country is closed. A rider is going to Mustang tonight with the news."

"There she is," Goff said dryly. "They are sure enough askin' for it! What if we ride on, anyway?"

Sue glanced at him. "Then there will be fighting," she said quietly.

"Well," Poinsett said impatiently, "what are we talkin' for? We come here to fight, didn't we? Let's ride on an' see how much battle they got in them."

Tom Kedrick studied the girl thoughtfully. She was pretty, all right, very pretty. She lacked the quiet beauty of Connie Duane, but she did have beauty. "Do they have scouts out?" he asked.

She glanced at him. "Not yet, but they will have." She smiled. "If they had I'd never have dared ride to warn you."

"Whose side are you on, Miss Laine?" Kedrick asked.

Dornie's head came around sharply and his eyes blazed. Before he could speak, Sue Laine answered for herself. "That decision I make for myself. My brother does not make it for me, nor any one of them. They are fools! To fight over this desert!" Contemptuously, she waved a hand at it. "There's no more than a bare living on it, anyway! If they lose, maybe we can leave this country!"

She swung her horse abruptly. "Well, you've had your warning. Now I'll go back."

"I'll be ridin' your way, " Shaw interposed.

Her eyes swung back to him. "Don't bother!" Then she turned her attention deliberately to Kedrick and measured him again with her cool eyes, a hint of a smile in them now. "If anybody comes, let Captain Kedrick come. They don't know him!"

Somebody in the group chuckled, and Dornie Shaw, his face white as death, swung his horse. His teeth were bared, his right hand poised. "Who laughed?" he said, his voice almost trembling.

"Miss Laine," Kedrick said quietly, "I think Dornie Shaw could make the trip better than I. He knows the country."

Shaw's eyes glittered. "I asked: who laughed?"

Kedrick turned his head. "Forget it, Shaw." His voice was crisp. "There'll be no fighting with other men in this outfit while I'm in command!"

For an instant, Dornie Shaw held his pose. Then his eyes, suddenly opaque as a rattler's, swung toward Kedrick. "You're tellin' *me?*" Incredulity mixed with sarcasm.

Tom Kedrick knew danger when he saw it, but he only nodded. "You, or anybody, Dornie. We have a job to do. You've hired on for that job as much as any man here. If we begin to fight among ourselves we'll get nothing done, and right now we can't afford to lose a good man.

"I scarcely think," he added, "that either Keith or Burwick would like the idea of a killing among their own men."

Shaw's eyes held Kedrick's and for an instant there was no sound. A cicada hummed in the brush, and Sue Laine's horse stamped at a fly. Tom Kedrick knew in that instant that Dornie Shaw hated him. He had an idea that this was the first time Shaw had ever been thwarted in any purpose he held.

Then Shaw's right hand slowly lowered. "Yuh got me on that one, Cap'n," his voice was empty, dry. "I reckon this is too soon to start shootin'—an' old man Burwick is right touchy."

Sue Laine glanced at Kedrick, genuine surprise and not a little respect in her eyes. "I'll be going. Watch yourselves!"

Before her horse could more than start, Kedrick asked, "Miss Laine, which of your outfit rides a long-legged grulla?"

She turned on him, her face pale. "A—a grulla?"

"Yes," he said, "such a rider has been watching us most of the morning, and such a rider is not over a half mile away now. Also," he added, "he has a field glass!"

Fessenden turned with an oath, and Poinsett glared around. Only Shaw spoke. His voice was strained and queer. "A grulla? Here?"

He refused to say more, but Kedrick studied him, puzzled by the remark. It was almost as if Shaw knew a grulla horse, but had not expected it to be seen here. The same might be true of Sue Laine, who was obviously upset by his comment. Long after they rode on, turning back toward the spring on the North Fork, Kedrick puzzled over it. This was an entirely new element that might mean anything or nothing.

There was little talking on the way back. Poinsett was obviously irritated that they had not ridden into a fight, yet he seemed content enough to settle down into another camp.

CHAPTER FOUR

DORNIE SHAW WAS silent. Only when Tom Kedrick arose after supper and began to saddle his horse did he look up. Kedrick glanced at him. "Shaw, I'm ridin' to Yellow Butte. I'm going to look that setup over at first hand. I don't want trouble an' I'm not huntin' any, but I want to know what we're tacklin'."

Shaw was standing, staring after him, when he rode off. Kedrick rode swiftly, pushing due west at a good pace to take advantage of the remaining light. He had more than one reason for the ride. He wanted to study the town and the terrain, but also he wanted to see what the people were like. Were they family men? Or were they outlaws? He had seen little thus far that tended to prove the outlaw theory.

The town of Yellow Butte lay huddled at the base of the long oval-shaped mesa from which it took its name. There, on a bit of flat land, the stone and frame buildings of the town had gathered together. Most of them backed against the higher land behind them, and faced toward the arroyo. Only three buildings and the corrals were on the arroyo side, but one thing was obvious. The town had never been planned for defense.

A rifleman or two on top of Yellow Butte could cover any movement in the village; and the town was exposed to fire from both the high ground behind the town and the bed of the arroyo, where there was shelter under its banks. The butte itself was scarcely one hundred and fifty feet higher than the town and looked right down the wide street in front of the buildings.

Obviously, however, some move had been made toward defense—or was in the process of being made—for occasional piles of earth near several of the buildings were plainly from recent digging. He studied them, puzzled over their origin and cause. Finally, he gave up and scouted the area.

Thoughtfully, he glanced at the butte. Had the squatters thought of putting their own riflemen up there? It would seem the obvious thing, yet more than one competent commander, at some time during his career, had forgotten the obvious. It might also be true of these men. He noted that the top of the butte not only commanded the town, but most of the country around, and was the highest point within several miles.

Kedrick turned his palouse down the hill toward the town. He rode in the open, his right hand hanging free at his side. If he was seen, nothing was done to disturb him. What if there were more than one rider?

He swung down before the Butte Saloon and tied his horse at the rail. He knew the animal was weary and in no shape for a long ride.

The street was empty. He stepped up on the walk and pushed through the swinging doors into the bright lights of the interior. A man sitting alone at a table saw him, scowled and started to speak, then thought better of it and went on with his solitaire. Tom Kedrick crossed to the bar. "Rye," he said quietly.

The bartender nodded and poured the drink. It was not until Kedrick dropped his coin on the bar that the bartender looked up. Instantly, his face stiffened. "Who're you?" he demanded. "I never saw you before!"

Kedrick was aware that two men had closed in on him. Both of them were strangers. One was a sharp-looking, oldish man, the other an obviously belligerent redhead. "Pour a drink for my friends, too," he said. Then he turned slowly, so they would not mistake his intentions, until his back was to the bar. Carefully, he surveyed the room.

There were a dozen men here, and all eyes were on him. "I'm buying," he said quietly. "Will you gentlemen join me?"

Nobody moved and he shrugged. He turned back to the bar. His drink was gone.

Slowly, his lifted his eyes to the bartender. "I bought a drink," he said quietly.

The man stared back at him, his eyes hard. "Never noticed it," he said.

"I bought a drink, paid my money, and I want what I paid for."

All was still. The men on either side of him leaned on the bar, ignoring him.

"I'm a patient man," he persisted, "I bought a drink, an' I want it—now."

"Mister," the bartender thrust his wide face across the bar, "we don't serve drinks to your kind here. Now get out before we throw you out!"

Kedrick's forearms were resting on the edge of the bar, and what followed was done so swiftly that neither man beside him had a chance to move.

Tom Kedrick's right hand shot out and grabbed the bartender by the shirt collar under his chin, then he turned swiftly, back to the bar, and heaved. The bartender came over the bar as if he were greased and hit the floor with a crash. Instantly, Kedrick spun away from the two men beside him and stood facing the room, gun in hand.

Men had started to their feet, and several had moved toward him. Now they froze where they were. The .44 Russian had appeared as if materialized from thin air.

"Gentlemen," Kedrick said quietly, "I did not come here hunting trouble. I have been hired for a job. I came to see if you were the manner of men you have been represented as being. Evidently your bartender is hard of hearing, or lacking in true hospitality. I ordered a drink.

"You," Kedrick gestured at the man playing solitaire, "look like a man of judgment. You pour my drink and put it on the end of the bar nearest me. Then," his eyes held the room, "pour each of these gentlemen a drink." With his left hand he extracted a gold eagle from his pocket and slapped it on the bar. "That pays."

He took another step back, then coolly, he holstered his gun. Eyes studied him, but nobody moved. The redhead did not like it. He had an urge to show how tough he was and Kedrick could see it building. "You!" Kedrick could see it building. "You!" Kedrick asked quickly. "Are you married? Children?"

The redhead stared at him, then said, his voice surly, "Yeah, I'm married, an' I got two kids. What's it to you?"

"I told you," Kedrick replied evenly, "I came to see what manner of men you are."

The man who was pouring the drinks looked up. "I'll answer your questions. I'm Pete Slagle."

"I've heard of you."

A slight smile came to Slagle's mouth. "Yeah," he said, "an' I've heard of you."

Nobody moved nor spoke while Slagle calmly poured the drinks. Then he straightened and glanced around the room. "Men," he said, "I reckon there's no use goin' off half cocked and gettin' somebody killed. Let's give this man a chance to speak his piece. We sure don't have to buy what he wants to sell us if we don't like his argument."

"Thanks, Slagle." Kedrick studied the room. Two of the faces seemed hard, unrelenting. Another was genuinely interested. But at the door in the rear, loitered a man who had shifty eyes and a sour face. He could have been, in disposition at least, a twin brother to the former outlaw, Clauson.

"The land around here," Kedrick said quietly, "is about to be purchased from the Government by the firm that's employed me. The firm of Burwick, Keith and Gunter. In New Orleans, where I was hired, I was told that there were squatters on the land, a bunch of outlaws, renegades and wasters, that they would resist being put off, and would aim to keep the badlands for themselves. My job was to clean them out, to clear the land for the company. I have come here for that purpose."

There was a low murmur from the back of the room. Kedrick took time to toss off his drink, and then calmly began to roll a smoke. To his right, the door opened and two men came in. One of these was as tall as himself with coal black hair turning gray at the temples. His eyes were gray and cold, his face firmly cut. He glanced sharply around the room, then at Kedrick.

"Cap'n Tom Kedrick, Bob," Slagle said quietly, "speakin' his piece. He's just explained that we've been represented as a bunch of renegades."

"That sounds like Burwick," McLennon said. "Get on with it, Kedrick."

"I've little to say but this. Naturally, like any good fighting man, I wanted to look over the terrain. Moreover, since arriving in Mustang certain rumors and hints have reached me that the picture is not one-sided. I have come out here to look you over, to see exactly what sort of people you are, and if you are the outlaws and wasters you have been represented to be. Also, I would like to have a statement from you."

Red's face was ugly. "We got nothin' to say to you, Kedrick," he said harshly, "nothin' at all! Just you come down here with your killers an' see how many get away alive!"

"Wait a minute, Red!" Slagle interrupted. "Let Bob have his say."

"Aw, why bother?" Red said roughly. "The man is scared or he'd never have come huntin' information!"

Kedrick's eyes held Red's thoughtfully, and he said slowly, "No, Red, I'm not scared. If I decide the company is right and you are to be run off, that is exactly what I'll do. If the men I have are not enough, I'll get more. I'm used to war, Red. I've been at it all my life, and I know how to win. I'm not here because I'm scared. I have come simply because I make a pass at being a just man. If you have a just claim to your places here, and are not as represented, I'll step out of this.

''Naturally,'' he added, ''I can't speak for the others, but I will tell them of my conclusions.''

''Fair enough,'' McLennon agreed. ''All right, I'll state our case. This land is Government land, like all of it. The Navajos an' Utes claim some of it, an' some of us have dickered with them for land. We've moved in an' settled on this land. Four or five of us have been here upwards of ten years, most of us have been here more than three.

''We've barns built, springs cleaned out, some fences. We've stocked some land, lived through a few bad summers and worse winters. Some of us have wives, an' some of us children. We're makin' homes here. The company is tryin' to gyp us.

''The law says we were to have six months' notice. That is, it was to be posted six months before the sale by the Government to the company. This land, as we understand it, is supposed to be unoccupied. Well, it ain't. We live on it. Moreover, that notice was posted five months ago, stuck around in out-of-the-way places, in print so fine a man can scarcely read it without a magnifyin' glass.

''A month ago one of the boys read it, but it took him a few days to sort the meanin' out of the legal phrasin', an' then he high-tailed it to me. We ain't got the money to send a man to the Government. So all we can do is fight. That's what we figure on. If the company runs us off, which I don't figure you or nobody can do, they'll buy ever' inch of it with their blood, believe me.''

A murmur of approbation went through the room, and Kedrick thoughtfully scanned the faces of the men. Dornie Shaw had judged these men correctly. They would fight. Moreover, with men like McLennon and Slagle to lead them, they would be hard to handle.

Legally, the company seemed to be in the best position; also, the squatters were bucking a stacked deck. From here it would take a man all of two weeks, and possibly three, to get to Washington, let alone cut through all the Government red tape to get to the men who could block the sale—if it could be blocked.

''This here's a speculation on their part,'' McLennon stated. ''There's rumors this here land is goin' into an Injun reservation, an' if it does, that means they'll stick the Government a nice price for the land.''

"Or you will," Kedrick replied. "Looks like there's two sides to this question, McLennon. The company has an argument. If the Federal Government does make this a reservation, you'll have to move, anyway."

"We'll face that when it comes," Slagle said. "Right now we're buckin' the company. Our folks aren't speculators. We aren't gunmen, either."

Another man had entered the room, and Kedrick spotted him instantly. It was Burt, the big man he had whipped in the street fight. The man stopped by the wall and surveyed the room.

"None of you?" Kedrick asked gently. "I have heard some stories about Pit Laine."

"Laine's a good man!" Red burst out heatedly. "He'll do to ride any river with!"

Neither McLennon nor Slagle spoke, and the latter shifted his feet uneasily. Evidently, there was a difference of opinion here. He made a note to check on Laine, to find out more about him.

"Well," he said finally, "I reckon I'll study on it a little. In the meantime, let's keep the peace. I'll keep my men off if you will do likewise."

"We aren't huntin' trouble," McLennon said. "As long as there's no shootin' at us, an' as long as the company men stay off our land, there'll be no trouble from us."

"Fact is," Slagle said, "we sent Roberts ridin' in with a message to Burwick to that effect. We ain't huntin' for no trouble."

Kedrick turned toward the door, but the bartender's voice stopped him. "You forgot your change," he said dryly.

Kedrick glanced at him, grinned, then picked the coins up. "Be seein' you," he said and stepped away.

At that instant, the door burst open and a man staggered into the room, his arm about another man, whom he dropped to the floor. "Roberts!" the man said. "He's been murdered!"

All eyes stared at the man on the floor. That he had been shot many times was obvious. He had also been ridden over, for his body was torn and beaten by the hoofs of running horses. Tom Kedrick felt his stomach turn over. Sick with pity and shock, he lifted his eyes.

He looked up into a circle of accusation: McLennon, shocked and unbelieving; Slagle, horrified; Red and the others crowding closer. "Him!" Red pointed a finger that trembled with his anger.

"While he stands an' talks to us, his outfit murders Bob!"

"Git him!" somebody yelled. "Git him! I got a rope!"

Kedrick was standing at the door, and he knew there was no reasoning with these men. Later, they might think and reason that he might have known nothing about the killing of Roberts. Now, they would not listen. As the men yelled, he hurled himself through the swinging doors and jerking loose his reins, hit the saddle of the palouse. The startled horse swung and lined out, not down the street, but between the buildings.

Behind him men shouted and cursed. A shot rang out, and he heard a bullet clip past his head as he swung between the buildings. Then he knew his escape had driven him into a *cul de sac,* for he was now facing—not more than two hundred yards away—the rim around the flat where the town lay. Whether there was a break in that wall he could not guess, but he had an idea both the route up and down along the arroyo would be covered by guards. Swinging his horse, he charged into the darkness toward Yellow Butte itself.

He remembered that coming into town he had noticed a V-shaped opening near its base. Whether there was a cut through the rim there he did not know. It might only be a box canyon, and a worse trap than the one into which he had run on his first break.

He slowed his pace, knowing that silence was the first necessity. If they heard him, he could easily be bottled up. The flat was small, and aside from crossing the arroyo there were but two routes of escape. Both would surely be watched.

The butte towered high above him now, and his horse walked softly forward in the abysmal darkness. Kedrick's safety was a matter of minutes.

The palouse was tired, he knew, for it had been going all day. The riding had been hard and he was a big man. He knew he was in no shape for a hard run against men with fresh horses. The only possible escape lay in some shrewd move that would keep them guessing and give him time. Yet he must be gone before daylight or he was through. By day they would comb this area and surely discover him.

Now the canyon mouth yawned before him. The walls were not high but at least were steep enough to allow no escape on horseback.

The shouts of pursuit had stopped now, but he knew the men were hard at work to find him. By now they would know from the guards on the stream that he was still on the flat, and had not escaped. Those guards might be creatures of his own imagination, but knowing the men with whom he dealt, he felt it was a safe bet that if they had not guarded the openings before his arrival, they certainly would have sent guards out at once.

The canyon was narrow. He rode on, moving with extreme caution, yet when he had gone but a short distance he saw the end of the canyon rising above him, black and somber. His throat tightened and his mouth went dry. The palouse stopped and Tom Kedrick sat silent, feeling the labored breathing of the horse and knowing he faced a stone wall. He was trapped.

Behind him, a light flared briefly, then went out. There was a shout. That had been a struck match—somebody looking for tracks. They had found them. In a few minutes, for they would move cautiously, they would be on him.

There would be no reasoning with them now. They had him. He was trapped!

CHAPTER FIVE

CAPTAIN TOM KEDRICK sat very still, listening. He heard some gravel stir. A stone rattled down the canyon. Every move would count now, and he must take no unnecessary chance. He was cornered, and while he did not want to kill any of these men, he had no intention of being killed.

Carefully, he dismounted. As his boot touched the sand he tested it to make sure no sound would result when his weight settled. Haste now was his greatest danger. There might be nothing he could do, but he was a man of many experiences, and in the past there had always been a way out. Usually there was, if a man took his time and kept his head.

Standing still beside the appaloosa, he studied the situation. His eyes had grown accustomed to the darkness under the bulk of Yellow Butte. He stared around, seeing the faint gray of sand underfoot, the black bulk of boulders and the more ragged stretch of underbrush. Leading his horse, he followed a narrow strip of gray that showed an opening between boulders.

Scarcely wide enough to admit his horse, the opening led back for some twenty feet, then widened. These were low boulders, rising scarcely above his waist, with the brush somewhat higher. The horse seemed to sense the danger, for it, too, walked quietly and almost without sound.

Literally, he was feeling his way in the dark. But he knew that trail of sand must come from somewhere, for water had run here, and that water might spill off the cliff edge, or might come through some opening. Walking steadily, he found himself going deeper into a tangle of boulders, weaving his way along that thin gray trail into he knew not what.

Twice he paused and with his hat, worked back along the path brushing out the tracks. He could not see how good a job he was doing, but the opening was narrow enough to give him a good chance of success. When he had pushed back into the tangle for all of ten minutes, he was brought up sharply by the cliff itself. He had found his way up the slope, through the talus, brush and scattered boulders, to the very face of the rock.

Above him, and apparently out of reach, was a notch in the cliff, and this was probably the source of the sandy trail he had followed. Worried now, he ground-hitched the palouse and moved along the cliff, feeling his way along the fence, searching each crack.

To his left, he found nothing. Several times he paused to listen, but no sound came from down the canyon. If this was a box canyon, with no exit, the men would probably know it and make no attempt to close in until daylight. In the darkness a man could put up quite a fight in here. Yet, because of their eagerness to avenge the dead man, they might push on.

Speaking softly to the horse, he worked his way along the face to the right, but here the pile of talus fell off sharply and he dipped into a hollow. It was cool and the air felt damp. There might even be a spring there, but he heard no water running.

Despite the coolness he was sweating and he paused, mopping his face and listening. As he stood there he felt a faint breath of wind against his cheek!

He stiffened with surprise, then with a sudden surge of hope, he turned and eagerly explored the rocky face. But could find no source for that breeze. He started on, moving more cautiously. Then the talus began to steepen under his feet, so he worked his way up the cliff alone. He carried his rifle with him.

At the top he could turn and glance back down the canyon at the faint grayness in the distance that indicated the way he had come. Here the canyon turned a bit, ending in a sort of blind alley on an angle from the true direction of the canyon. There, breaking the edge of the cliff above him, was a notch. A steep slide led to the top.

It must have been some vague stirring of wind from up there on the rim that had touched his cheek. He noted that the slide was steeper than a stairway and might start sliding underfoot. Certainly, such a sound would give away his attempt, and it would be the matter of only a few minutes before he would be encircled. As far as that went, the men could even now be patrolling the rim above him.

Turning, his foot went from under him and only a frenzied grasp at some brush kept him from falling into whatever hole he had stumbled upon. Scrambling back to good footing, he dropped a pebble and heard it strike some fifteen or twenty feet down. Working his way along the edge, he reached the foot of the slide and knew what he had come upon.

Water, flooding down that slide during heavy rains, had struck a soft stratum of sand or mud and, striking it with force, had gouged out a deep cut that probably ran back into the canyon itself. There was always a chance that deep within this crack there might be some hiding place, some concealment. Turning abruptly, he returned for his horse.

The slide continued steeply to the bottom of the crevasse scooped from the earth, and when they reached bottom he glanced up. The cut had taken him at least fifteen feet below the regular terrain of the area. Above him he saw a swath of dark sky that stretched about seven feet between the sides of the cut. He led the horse deeper along the narrow bed, and after only a short distance he noted that the top of the cut immediately above him was almost covered by a thick growth of brush growing together from the sides near the top.

It was cool and still down here, and he pushed on until he found a spot where the rush of water had made a turn, and had gouged deeply under the bank, making a sort of cave beneath the overhang. Into this he led his horse, and here he stopped. A little water stood at the deepest part of the turn, and he allowed the palouse to drink. When the horse had finished, the shallow pool was gone.

Kedrick tried the water in his canteen, then stripped the saddle from the horse and rubbed him down with a handful of coarse grass. Then he tied the horse, and spreading his blanket, rolled up in it. He was philosophical. He had done what he could. If they found him now there was nothing to do but shoot it out where he was.

Surprisingly, he slept, and when he awakened it was the startled breathing of the palouse that warned him. Instantly, he was on his feet, speaking in a whisper to the horse and resting his hand on its shoulder. Day had come, and somewhere above them, yet some distance, there were voices.

The cave in which he stood was dug in sandstone, no more than fifteen feet in depth, and probably eight feet high at the opening. Kedrick moved to the mouth, studied the crevasse down which he had come. It was as he had supposed, a deep-cut water course from the notch in the cliff. Evidently during heavy rains this bed roared full of water, almost to the brim.

At the place where he now stood the brush on either side almost met over the top, and at one point a fallen slab bridged the crack. Glancing back the way he had come, Kedrick saw that much of it was also covered by brush, and there was a chance that he would not be found. A very, very slim chance. He could ask for no more.

He wanted to smoke, but dared not, for the smell of tobacco might warn them of his presence. Several times he heard voices, some of them quite near. He glanced toward the back of the cave and saw the gelding drinking again. Evidently water had seeped through during the night, even though not much. His canteen was over half full, and as yet water was not a problem.

His rifle across his knees, he waited, from time to time staring down the crevasse in the direction he had been going. Where did this water flow? Probably into the arroyo below, near town, and in that case the townspeople would certainly know of it.

Yet as the morning wore on, although he heard occasionally the sound of voices, nobody approached his place of concealment, nor did anyone seem aware of it. Once, he ventured out into the crevasse itself and pulled a few handfuls of grass growing on a slight mound of earth. This he fed to the horse, who ate gratefully. He dug some jerky from his own pack and chewed on it, wishing for a cup of coffee.

Later, he ventured farther down the crevasse, which seemed to dip steeply from where he was. Hearing no voices, he pushed on, coming to a point where the crevasse turned sharply again. The force of the water had hollowed out a huge cave which looked like a bowl standing on edge. Then the water had turned and shot down an even steeper declivity into the black maw of a cavern.

Having come this far he took a chance on leaving his horse alone and walked on down toward the cave. The entrance was high and wide and the cave extended deep into the mountain with several shelves or ledges that seemed to show no signs of water. There was a pool in the bottom, and apparently the water filled a large basin, but lost itself through some cracks in the bottom of the larger hollow.

Although he penetrated no great distance he could find no evidence of another outlet, nor could he feel any motion of air. Yet, as he looked around him, he realized that with some food a man might well hide in this place for weeks, and unless someone went to the foot of the slide and found the opening into the crevasse, this place might never be discovered.

The run-off from the cliff, then, did not go to the arroyo, but ended here, in this deep cavern.

The day wore on slowly. Twice he walked back down to the cavern to smoke, leaving his horse where it was. In a few hours he would try to make his escape. Yet when dusk came, and he worked his way back up the crevasse slide and crawled out on the edge where he could look toward the entrance, he saw two men squatting there beside a fire. They had rifles. They believed him concealed somewhere near and hoped to starve him out.

Kedrick knew that by this time Dornie Shaw must have returned to Mustang with news of his disappearance, and probably, of their murder of the messenger. For he was sure that it had been his own group who had committed the crime. It was scarcely possible that Gunter or Keith would countenance such open violence near town where it could not fail to be seen and reported upon by unfriendly witnesses.

Returning, he studied the slide to the rim. It was barely possible that a horse might scramble up there. It would be no trick for an active man, and the palouse was probably a mountain horse. It was worth a gamble . . . if there was no one on top to greet him. Pulling an armful of grass from near the brush and boulders, he returned to the horse, and watched it gratefully munch the rich green grass.

Connie Duane was disturbed. She had seen the messenger come to her uncle and the others, and had heard their reply. Then, at almost noon the following day, Dornie Shaw and the other men had come in. Tom Kedrick had not returned with them.

Why that should disturb her she could not have said, but the fact remained that it did. Since he had stepped up on the veranda she had thought of little else, remembering the set of his chin, the way he carried his shoulders, and the startled expression when he saw her. There was something about him that was different, not only from the men around her uncle, but from any man she had known before.

Now, when despite herself she had looked forward to his return, he was missing.

John Gunter came out on the veranda, nervously biting the end from a cigar. "What happened?" she asked. "Is something wrong? Where's Captain Kedrick?"

"Wish I knew!" His voice was sharp with anxiety. "He took a ride to look over those squatters an' never came back. I don't trust Shaw, no matter how much Keith does. He's too bloodthirsty. We could get into a lot of trouble here, Connie. That's why I wanted Kedrick. He has judgment, brains."

"Perhaps he decided he wanted no part of it, Uncle. Maybe he decided your squatters were not outlaws or renegades."

Gunter glanced at her sharply. "Who has been talking to you?" he demanded.

"No one. It hasn't been necessary. I have walked around town, and I've seen that some of these outlaws, as you call them, have wives and children, that they buy supplies and look like nice, likeable people. I don't like it, Uncle John, and I don't like to think that my money may be financing a part of it."

"Now, now! Don't bother your head over it. You may be sure that Loren and I will do everything we can for your best interests."

"Then drop this whole thing!" she pleaded. "There's no need for it. I've money enough, and I don't want money that comes from depriving others of their homes. They all have a right to live, a chance."

"Of course!" Gunter was impatient. "We've gone over all this before. But I tell you most of those people are trash, and no matter about that, they all will be put off that land, anyway. The Government is going to buy out whoever has control. That will mean us, and that means we'll get a nice, juicy profit."

"From the Government? Your own Government, Uncle?" Connie studied him coolly. "I fail to understand the sort of man who will attempt to defraud his own Government. There are people like that, I suppose, but somehow I never thought I'd find one in my own family."

"Don't be silly, child. You know nothing of business, you aren't practical."

"I suppose not. Only I seem to remember that a lot of worth-while things don't seem practical at the moment. No," she got to her feet, "I believe I'll withdraw my investment in this deal and buy a small ranch somewhere nearby. I will have no part in it."

"You can't do that!" Gunter exploded impatiently. "Your money is already in, and there's no way of getting it out until this business is closed. Now, why don't you trust me like a good girl? You always have before!"

"Yes, I have, Uncle John, but I never believed you could be dishonest." She studied him frankly. "You aren't very happy about this yourself. You know," she persisted, "those people aren't going to move without a fight. You believed they could be frightened. Well, they can't. I've seen Bob McLennon, and he's not the kind of man who can be frightened. Even by that choice bunch of murderers Loren has gathered together."

"They aren't that. Not murderers," Gunter protested uneasily, but refused to meet her eyes. "Reckless, yes. And temperamental. Not murderers."

"Not even Dornie Shaw? The nice-looking boyish one who has killed a dozen men and is so cold blooded and fiendish at times that others are afraid of him? No, Uncle, there is no way you can sidestep this. If you continue, you are going to countenance murder and the killing of innocent people.

"Loren doesn't care. He has always been cold blooded. You've wondered why I wouldn't marry him. That's why. He has the disposition of a tiger. He would kill anything or anyone that stood in his way. Even you, Uncle John."

He started and looked at her uneasily. "Why do you say that?"

"Because it's true. I know our tall and handsome man. He will allow nothing to come between him and what he desires. You've chosen some choice companions." She got to her feet. "If you hear anything of Captain Kedrick, let me know, will you?"

Gunter stood still for a long time after she left. He swore bitterly. Connie was like her mother. She always had the faculty for putting her finger on the truth, and certainly, she was right about this. It was beginning to look ugly, but away down deep in his heart, he was upset less over Keith than over Burwick. That strange, fat, and dirty man was a thing of evil, of corruption. There was some foul thing within him, something cold and vicious as a striking snake.

Connie Duane was not the only person who was disturbed over the strange disappearance of Tom Kedrick.

Bob McLennon, unofficial commander of the forces for defense, sat in his rambling ranch house on the edge of Yellow Butte. Pete Slagle, Burt Williams, Dai Reid and Pit Laine were all gathered there. With them was Sue Laine, keeping to the background. Her dark, lovely eyes were alert for every word.

"Blazes, man!" McLennon said irritably. "Where could he have gone? I'd have sworn he went into that box canyon. There was no other place for him to go—unless he took wings and flew. He had to go in there."

"You looked yourself," Slagle said dryly. "Did you see him? He just ain't there, that's all! He got plumb away."

"He probably did that," Dai Reid commented. "A quick man, that Tom Kedrick. Hand or mind, he's quick." He drew out his pipe and stoked it slowly. "You shouldn't have jumped him," he continued. "I know the lad, an' he's honest. If he said that was what he come for, it was the truth he told. I'd take my oath he'd no knowledge of the killin'!"

"I'd like to believe that," McLennon agreed. "The man impressed me. We could use an honest man on the other side, one who would temper the wind a bit, or get this thing stopped."

"It won't be that Shaw who stops. He's a murderin' little devil," Slagle said. "He'll kill like a weasel in a chicken pen until there's nought left to kill."

"Kedrick fought me fair," Williams said. "I'll give him that."

"He's a fair man," Dai persisted. "Since a lad I've known him. I'd not be wrong. I'd give fifty acres of my holdin' for the chance to talk to him."

Daylight brought the first attack. It came swiftly, a tight bunch of riders who exploded from the mouth of the arroyo, hit the dusty street of Yellow Butte on a dead run, pistols firing, and then there followed the deep, heavy concussion of dynamite. As suddenly as they had come, they were gone. Two men sprawled in the street.

Peters, the man Shaw had faced down in the streets of Mustang, was one of them. He had taken three .44 slugs through the chest and died before he hit the ground. He had made one fine effort to win back his self-respect. He had seen Dornie Shaw in the van of the charging riders and rushed into the street to get him. He failed to get off a single shot.

The second man down was shot through the thigh and arm. He was a Swede who had just put in his second crop.

The riders had planned their attack well and had worked near enough to the guards at the mouth of the arroyo, and had come at a time when no attack was expected. The one guard awake was knocked down by a charging horse but, miraculously, suffered only bruises. Two bundles of dynamite had been thrown. One had exploded against the door of the general store, smashing it off its hinges and tearing up the porch. The second exploded harmlessly between the buildings.

The first rattle of rifle fire brought Tom Kedrick to an observation point. He had saddled his horse, hoping for a break, and instantly he saw it. The two guards had rushed to the scene of action. Quickly, he led his horse out of the crevasse, rode at a canter to the canyon's mouth. Seeing dust over the town, he swung right and skirting close to the butte, slipped out into the open—a free man once more.

CHAPTER SIX

KEDRICK DID NOT return toward Mustang. He had come this far for a purpose, and he meant to achieve it. Turning west and north, he rode upstream away from Yellow Butte and Mustang. He wanted actually to see some of the homes of which so much had been said. By the way these people lived he could tell the sort they were. It was still morning and all was motionless and warm. Soon he slowed his horse to a walk and studied the terrain.

Certainly, nothing could be farther from swampland. In that, at least, the company had misrepresented. Obviously, they had lied in maintaining that the land was vacant. But if the squatters were a shiftless lot, Kedrick knew he would continue his job. Already he was heartily sick of the whole mess, yet he owed Gunter money, and how to pay it back was a real problem. And then, although the idea lurked almost unthought in the back of his consciousness, there was Connie Duane.

In his fast-moving and active life he had met many women, and a few had interested him, but none so much as this tall girl with the quiet, alert eyes. His desire to get back to Mustang had nothing to do with the company, but only with her. At the same time, Dornie Shaw had acted without his orders, had slain the messenger and attacked the town. For all he knew, Dornie and the others might think him dead.

Turning due north, he rode through the sagebrush and catclaw toward two towering blue mountains. They stood alone this side of the rim that bordered the country to the north. On his left, he saw broken land, and what was evidently a deep arroyo. He swung the appaloosa over and headed it toward the canyon. Suddenly, he reined in.

On the ground before him were the tracks of a trotting horse, and he recognized them. They were the same tracks left by the strange rider on the grulla mustang who had scouted their approach to Yellow Butte. The tracks were fresh.

Riding more slowly, he came to the edge of the canyon and looked down at a long green meadow, fenced and watered by a small stream. At the far side, tucked in a corner, was a stone cottage. It was more attractive and better built than any other he had seen in this section. Ahead of him he saw a trail. Without delay, he rode down it and walked his horse across the meadow toward the house.

It was a pleasant place of sandstone blocks and a thatched roof. Shade trees sheltered the yard, and there were a half-dozen hens pecking about. In the corral there were several horses. His heart jumped as he saw the grulla, saddled and waiting.

He drew up in the dooryard and swung down, trailing his reins. The door opened and a girl came out with a pan of water. She started as she saw him, and he recognized her instantly. It was Sue Laine, the girl of the trail, the girl in whom Dornie was reputed to be interested.

"You!" she gasped as she stared at him. "They told me you were dead!"

He shrugged. "Not dead, just hungry. Could you feed a man?"

She studied him a minute, then nodded. "Come in. Better tie your horse, though. He'll head for that meadow if you don't. And," her voice was dry, "you may need him. This isn't exactly friendly country."

He tied his horse near the grulla and followed her inside. "Isn't it?" he said. "Somehow I gathered you weren't exactly an enemy to the company."

"Don't say that!" she flared. "Don't ever say that!" Her voice lowered. "Not around here, anyway. If my brother ever heard . . ."

So Pit Laine and his sister did not see alike? That was an interesting point. He washed his hands and face, then combed his hair.

Ruefully, he rubbed his chin. "Your brother got a razor? I hate to go unshaven."

She brought a razor without comment. He shaved, then dried his face and hands and walked into the house. It was amazingly neat. On a side table there were several books. Flowered curtains hung at the windows, and several copper dishes were burnished to brightness. He sat down and she brought him food: beef, eggs, and homemade bread with honey.

"Everybody's looking for you," she said. "Where have you been?"

He accepted the statement and ignored the question. "After that messenger was killed, I had to get out of Yellow Butte. I did. What's been happening?"

"Keith served a final ultimatum. We either move, or they run us out. McLennon refused."

"He did right."

She turned on him, her eyes questioning. "You think that? I thought you were their man?"

He looked up from his food and shook his head. "I don't know where I stand, but I don't go for murder, not for running people out of their homes."

"They can't stay anyway. If this land becomes a reservation they will all be moved off. We will, too. They are foolish to fight."

"At least, the Government will buy their land and pay for their investment. In any event, the company has misrepresented things."

"Does it matter?" She sat down opposite him. "They will win.

They have money, influence, and power. The settlers here have nothing.'' She looked around her bitterly. ''Perhaps you think I am going against my own people, but that's not true. These aren't my people. Pit and I don't belong here and we never have, although Pit won't see it. Do you think I want to slave my life away on this desert?''

She leaned toward him. ''Look, Captain Kedrick, you're one of them, not just working for them, not just a hired gunman like Dornie Shaw. You can lead the men you have, and I wouldn't be surprised but what you could even handle Keith. You could be a big man in this country, or any country.

''Why be foolish and start thinking like you are? These farmers and ranchers can do nothing for you . They can't even help themselves. The company will win, and if you are one of them, you will have a share in the winning. Don't be foolish, Captain. Stay with them. Do what you have to do.''

''There are things more important than money. There's self-respect.''

She stared at him, her eyes widening. ''You don't really believe that? Try buying supplies with it, sometime. You won't get any place. But that isn't the point. You'll do what you want, but I want a man who will take me out of this desert.'' She got up quickly and came around the table. ''You could do it, Captain. You could become rich, right here.''

He smiled at her. ''Ambitious, aren't you?''

''Why not? Being a rancher's wife doesn't appeal to me. I want to get away from here, go someplace, be something and enjoy life.'' She hesitated, studying him. ''You could edge Gunter out of it, and Keith—maybe even Burwick. But the first two would be easy, and I know how.''

''You do?'' He looked up at her. She stood very close to him, and she was smiling down at him. She was, he had to admit, a lovely girl. And an exciting one. Too exciting for comfort right now, and that was a fact she understood completely. ''How?''

She shook her head. ''Oh, no! That I'd tell you only if you threw in with me, joined me. But this much I'll tell you—John Gunter is small potatoes. They needed money, and he had that girl's money so they roped him in. Keith is dangerous because he is ambitious and unscrupulous, but the man to reckon with is Burwick. He will be top man when this thing is over, and you can bank on it. He has a way figured, all the time.''

"You seem to know a great deal."

"I do. Men like me and men talk. They don't have any idea how much I lead them to say, or how much I remember."

"Why tell me all this?"

"Because you're the man who can do what has to be done. You could whip that bunch into line. All of them would listen to you, even Dornie Shaw—and he's suspicious of you."

"Of me? Why?"

"He saw Dai Reid come from your room. He was watching you."

So that was it? He had suspected that Shaw had something on his mind. But why had Shaw been watching? What was the gunman thinking of? And had he reported that conference to Keith?

Kedrick finished his meal and lighted a cigarette. Ever since their first meeting in the desert this girl had puzzled him. He was inclined to doubt if any girl, reared as she must have been, could be so sincerely disdaining of all loyalty, and so plainly self-seeking. She seemed scarcely more than a child, slim, brown and lovely, with her quick, measuring eyes and soft lips.

Now, apparently she had selected him as the man who was to take her away from the desert. But how many others held the same idea? However, he had no idea of leaving the desert.

"Your brother around?" he asked.

Her glance was a quick flash of alarm. "You don't want to see him, or talk to him. You'd better get out of here."

"On the contrary, Sue, I'd like to talk to Pit. I've heard about him and I'd like to know him."

"You'd better go," she warned. "He'll be back soon, and some of that Yellow Butte crowd may be with him."

"You mean he's not here? Then whose horse is that out there. That grulla?"

Her face was strange as she shook her head. "You'll think I'm a liar, but I don't know. I never saw the rider."

His eyes searched hers. He could see nothing but sincerity there, sincerity and a little fear. "You mean that horse showed up there, tied like that? And you never saw the rider?"

"That's right. I looked out this morning, shortly after Pit left, and he was tied right there. This isn't the first time! He has been here twice before, when Pit was gone, and some others have seen him, most of them women when their husbands are away. Mrs. Burt Williams has said he was tied to her corral for three or four hours one day."

"But surely someone sees the rider come and mount up?"

"Never. He'll be out there like he is now—he's gone!"

Kedrick came to his feet with a start and stared out the door. Sue was right. The mouse-colored horse was gone. His own palouse stood where he had left it, but the grulla had disappeared.

Walking out into the yard, he looked around very carefully. But there was nothing in sight on the plain or the hills. The horse was gone! He looked at her and saw the strained expression on her face. Then he walked out to the appaloosa. Pinned to his saddle was a note. He grabbed it up and glanced at it, then passed it to Sue who had come up beside him.

"Stay away."

Kedrick shrugged. "Your brother do this?"

"Oh, no! I told him about the horse and he knew no more about it than I. Besides, he didn't print that. He couldn't. Pit never learned to either read or write."

Long after he left the malpais arroyo behind, he was puzzling over the strange horse. Somebody was seriously trying to puzzle or frighten the squatters. Yet it was an action unlike the company. Moreover, it must be somebody who had a lot of time to spend.

Kedrick rode north toward Blue Hill, then swung east, crossing the Old Mormon Trail and skirting the rim.

This was good grazing land. There was an abundance of rough forage here and a good herd of cattle could fatten on this range without trouble. Moreover, the herding problem was solved in part by the rim, which provided a natural drift fence beyond which the cattle could not go.

When he reached Salt Creek he turned down the creek toward the river. Swinging east again and passing near Chimney Rock, he rode southwest until he struck the Hogback Trail. Once over that ridge, he headed due east for Mustang.

Yet as always, his eyes were alive and alert. He loved this land, harsh though it might be at some times. He loved the dim purples and blues, the far-flung mists and morning and night, the gray-green of the sagebrush, and the rust-red of the sandstone. It was a good country, and there was room for all if it were left open for settlement.

His own mind was not yet resolved. The problem of his debt to Gunter weighed heavily upon him, and there were other considerations. He wanted no trouble, and to withdraw now might mean plenty of it. This was especially so if he remained in the country, which he had every reason to do. He would try to talk the company out of withdrawing, but he knew that would fail.

Just where, in all this, did Connie Duane actually stand? Was she involved more deeply than he believed? Or was it only what had been implied, that her uncle had invested her money in the land speculation? If such was the case, it might be difficult or impossible to get out at this stage—even if they would allow it.

Burwick puzzled him. Obviously the controlling power, he gave no evidence of where that power came from aside from some native shrewdness. There might be much more to the man, and evidently there was. That Keith and Gunter deferred to him was obvious.

Purposely, Kedrick had said nothing of his hide-away near Yellow Butte when talking to Sue. That young lady already knew more than was good for her, and that spot might again become useful. It was something to know.

Mustang was asleep when he rode into the town and headed for the stable. He put his horse up and rubbed it thoroughly, gave it a good bait of corn and forked down some hay. Then he made his way quietly to the St. James. As he neared the hotel a tall, lean figure arose from the chair where he himself had been sitting a few days before. The build and the broad hat, the very hang of the guns left no mistake. It was Laredo Shad.

"Cap'n?" The voice was low. "You all right?"

"Yes, and you?"

Shad chuckled. "Don't worry none about Shad! I stay healthy." He motioned to a chair. "You better sit down. I've been hopin' you'd show up."

"What's the talk? Did they think I was dead, or skipped the country?"

"Some o' both, I reckon. Keith was fit to be tied. He wants to see you as soon as you show—no matter when."

"He'll wait. I'm tired."

Shad nodded, then lighted his cigarette, which had gone out. "You know, I ain't right sure about this business."

Kedrick nodded. "I know what you mean. I'm not the man to run folks out of their homes."

"You quittin'?"

"Not yet. I'll talk to 'em first."

"Won't do no good. They are mighty bloodthirsty. It was Poinsett shot that messenger. Dornie put him up to it. Poinsett killed him, an' then four, five of those rannies shot up the body. I don't think Fessenden shot any, an' maybe Goff didn't. You can lay your last peso I didn't shoot none. It was mighty raw, Cap'n mighty raw!''

''They'll pay for it. Were you on the Yellow Butte raid?''

''Uh huh, but I didn't shoot nobody. I'm no Bible packer, Cap'n, but I do figure a fightin' man shouldn't tackle folks who cain't fight back, an' I ain't the man to be firin' on no women or kids.''

''What are they talkin' up now? Any plans you know of?''

Shad hesitated, then shrugged. ''Reckon you'd better talk that out with them, Cap'n. I may know somethin' but I ain't tellin,' not yet.''

The Texan sat silent for a few minutes while both men smoked, and then he waved an impatient hand. ''Cap'n, I hired on as a gunhand, an' such I am, but I didn't figure on this sort o' thing. Some of those hombres on the other side o' this shindig look a durned sight more human than some on our own side. I'm gettin' shut o' the whole shebang.''

''Uh huh—'' surprisingly, Kedrick found resolution coming to him—''I know how you feel, but my own way will be different. I think if I can't talk Gunter an' the rest of them out of that I'll change sides.''

Shad nodded. ''I've thought of it. I sure have.''

Kedrick turned suddenly and found Dornie Shaw standing not twenty feet behind them. Slowly, he got to his feet, and Laredo Shad did likewise. Shaw's eyes avoided Kedrick. ''If you figure on leavin' us, Shad, you better figure on killin' me first.''

''If I have to,'' Laredo said quietly, ''then I reckon you can die as simple as any other man. Want to try it now?''

''That's enough, Shad!'' Kedrick's voice was sharp. ''I've said there would be no more fighting! Not in this outfit!''

Dornie Shaw turned his head slowly and smiled at Kedrick. ''Still like to give orders, do you? Maybe that'll be changed.''

''Maybe.'' Tom Kedrick shrugged. ''There will be time enough for me to stop giving orders. I'm turning in.''

''Keith wants to see you.''

''He can wait. I've had a rough time. There's nothing he wants won't wait.''

''Shall I tell him that?''

"If you like."

Shaw smiled again. "You must carry a lot o' weight where you come from, Kedrick, but don't forget it ain't here. Keith is a bad man to buck. So's Burwick."

Kedrick shrugged again. "I've bucked worse. But at the moment, I'm bucking nobody. I need sleep, and by the Lord Harry, sleep is what I'll get. Whatever Keith has on his mind can wait until daylight. I'll be up then."

Shaw started to go, then hesitated, unable to restrain his curiosity. "What happened to you? We figured you were dead or taken prisoner when you didn't come back."

For the first time Kedrick began to wonder. Had Shaw wanted the messenger killed for that very reason. Had he deliberately moved that way hoping the enraged settlers would kill Kedrick? It was most likely. "It doesn't matter," he said, passing off the remark casually. "I found a way to keep out of sight."

Shaw turned away, and when he had gone only a few steps, Tom Kedrick spoke up suddenly. "By the way, Dornie. Know anybody who rides a grulla mustang?"

Shaw stopped abruptly, but he did not turn. His whole body had seemed to stiffen. Then he started on. "No," he said gruffly, "I sure don't."

Laredo Shad stared after him. "You know, pardner, you'll either kill that hombre someday or you'll be killed."

"Uh huh," Kedrick said quietly, "I've the same feeling."

CHAPTER SEVEN

KEITH WAS PACING the floor in the office at the gray stone building when Kedrick walked in. He stopped and turned swiftly. "Shaw tells me you came in after midnight. Why didn't you come to me according to my orders?"

"Frankly, I was tired. Furthermore," Kedrick returned Keith's look, "I'd nothing to report that wouldn't keep."

"You were hired to do a job, and you haven't done it." Keith stood with his hands on his hips. "Where've you been?"

Briefly and clearly, Kedrick explained, omitting only the visit to

Laine's and the story of the hideout. "Frankly," he said, "having looked the situation over, I'd say you had small chance of driving those people off. Also, you and Gunter misrepresented things to me and the Government. That land is occupied not by renegades and outlaws, but by good, solid people. You can't get away with running them off."

Keith smiled contemptuously. "Gettin' scared? You were supposed to be a fighting man! As for what we can do or can't do, let me tell you this, Kedrick: we've started to run those people off, and we'll do it! With or without you! Hiring you was Gunter's idea, anyway."

"That's right, it was." Gunter, followed by Burwick, walked into the room, and he glanced swiftly from Kedrick to Keith. "If you're complainin' about his going to look over that country, you can stop. I sent him."

"Did you tell him to come back scared to death? Saying we can't swing it?"

Burwick had been silent, but now he moved to the big chair behind the desk and dropped into it. He sighed heavily and wiped the back of his hand across his mouth, then glanced at Kedrick keenly. "What did you find out?"

"That they are determined to fight. I talked to Bob McLennon and to Slagle. There's no quit in those men. They'll fight at the drop of a hat, and to the last ditch. Right now, at this minute, they are ready for anything. Your raid killed one man, wounded another. The dynamite blasted a door loose and blew a hole in the porch."

Burwick turned swiftly and glared at Keith. "You told me three men dead and a building destroyed! Hereafter you be sure reports to me are accurate." He swung back to Kedrick. "Go on, what happened to you? You got away?"

"I'm here."

Their eyes met and held for a long time. Burwick's stone cold and hard, examining, probing.

"What do you think of the deal?" he asked finally.

"The fight," Kedrick replied carefully, "will raise a stink clear to Washington. Remember the Lincoln County War? We'll have us another general down here, and you know how much profit you'll make out of that place then!"

Burwick nodded his huge head. "Sensible, that's sensible!

Have to think our way around that. At least,'' he glared again at Keith and Gunter, ''this man can bring in some sensible ideas and make a coherent report. You two could learn from him.''

He looked up at Kedrick. ''Anything else?''

''A couple of things. There's a mysterious rider out on those plains. Rides a mouse-colored horse, and he's got those folks more jittery than all your threats.''

''Hah?'' Burwick was uninterested. He shuffled papers on his desk. ''What's this I hear about you quittin'?''

''I won't be a party to murder. These people aren't outlaws, but good, substantial folks. I'd say: buy them out or leave them alone.''

''You aren't running this fair!'' Keith replied coldly. ''We will decide what is to be done.''

''Nobody quits,'' Burwick said quietly, his eyes on Kedrick's, ''unless I say so.''

Tom Kedrick smiled suddenly. ''Then you'd better say so, because I've quit, as of now!''

''Tom!'' Gunter protested. ''Let's talk this over.''

''What of the money you owe the firm?'' Keith demanded, unpleasantly. ''You can repay that, I suppose?''

''There's no need.''

They all turned at the voice. Connie Duane stood in the door. ''You have money of mine in this project. When Uncle John got it from me he told me it was a real-estate speculation. His other activities have been honest and practical, so I did not investigate. Now, I have. I shall withdraw my money, and you can pay me less the sum advanced to Captain Kedrick. He may repay me when circumstances permit it.''

All in the room were still. Gunter's face was pale, and Keith looked startled, then angry. He started to protest, but he was too slow. Burwick turned on Gunter. ''You—'' he snorted angrily. ''You told me that was your money. You fool! What do you mean, bringing a woman into a deal like this? Well, you brought her in. Now you manage her or I shall.''

''Nobody,'' Connie replied, ''is managing me or my affairs from now on. I'll handle them myself!'' She turned to Kedrick. ''I'm glad, Captain, that you've made this decision. I am sure you'll not be sorry for it.''

Kedrick turned to follow her from the room, but Burwick's voice stopped him. ''Captain!''

He turned. Keith's eyes were ugly and Gunter's face was haunted by doubt and fear. "Captain Kedrick," Burwick said, "I believe we are all being too hasty. I like your caution in this matter. Your suggestion that cleaning out those people might make trouble and cause talk in Washington is probable. I had considered that, but not knowing McLennon, had considered the chance negligible.

"Slagle," he added, "I know. McLennon I do not know. Your suggestion eliminates a frontal attack. We must try some other means. Also," he added, "I believe that your presence has some claim on that of Miss Duane. Consequently, as we can brook no failure now, I have a proposition for you. How would you like to come into this firm? As a silent partner?"

Keith's face flushed angrily, but Gunter looked up, his eyes suddenly hopeful. Burwick continued. "We could give you a fifteen per cent interest, which, believe me, will be adequate. I believe you could keep Miss Duane in line, and with you at the helm we might straighten this whole thing out—without bloodshed."

Kedrick hesitated. The money was a temptation, for he had no desire to be indebted to Connie, yet the money alone would mean nothing. It was that last phrase that gripped his attention and made him incautious. "Without bloodshed," he repeated. "On those terms, I accept. However, let's discuss this matter a bit further."

Keith spun on his heel. "Burwick, this doesn't make sense! You know the only way we'll get those people off is by driving them off. We agreed on that before. Also this man is not reliable. I happen to know that he has friends on the other side and has actually been in communication with them."

"So much the better." Burwick pursed his fat lips and mopped perspiration from his face. "He'll have a contact he can use to make a deal." He chuckled. "Suppose you two run along and let me talk to Captain Kedrick?"

Hours later, Tom Kedrick paused on the street and studied it with care. Burwick had been more than reasonable. Little as he was able to trust him, he thought it possible that Burwick was sincere in his agreement to buy off a few of them, and to try to convince others. Certainly, if the Government moved in they would have to move, anyway. With McLennon and Slagle out of the picture the chances were there would be no fight, for the others lacked leadership. No fighting meant no deaths, and the settlers at least would come out of it with a little money.

He paced the street irritably, avoiding company. Burwick stank of deceit, but the man was a practical man. He realized that a sudden mess of killings preceding the sale of the land would create a furor that might cause them to lose out all around. At least, trouble had been avoided for the time and even Connie was hopeful that something might be done. Tomorrow Kedrick intended returning again to try to make some deal with McLennon and Slagle. A neutral messenger was leaving tonight.

"They won't come to town," Burwick had agreed, "so why not pick some intermediate point? Meet them, say, at Largo Canyon or Chimney Rock? Have your talk there, and I'll come with you. Just you and me, McLennon and Slagle. We can talk there and maybe make peace. Ain't it worth a try?"

It was only that chance for peace that had persuaded him and helped him to persuade Connie. She had listened in silence as he explained the situation. Then she had turned to him frankly. "Captain, you don't trust them, and neither do I. Uncle John has never been this way before, and I believe somehow he has fallen under the domination of those other men. However, I think that if Burwick is willing to talk, we should at least agree. I'll stand by you in this and we'll hope something can come of it that will prevent trouble."

Kedrick was less hopeful than he had let it appear, and now he was studying the situation from every angle. As things stood, it was a stalemate. He was confident that with McLennon and Slagle to lead them, the settlers could manage a stiff defense of their town and their homes. Certainly, they could prevent the survey being completed and prevent any use being made of their lands.

Yet there were fiery elements on both sides, and Keith did not like the turn things had taken. Colonel Loren Keith had from the beginning planned on striking fast and wiping out the opposition. It would be merely another unsolved mystery of the West. Kedrick resolved to keep an eye on the man and be prepared for anything.

He returned to the St. James and to bed, yet he awakened early and was surprised to see Keith mounted and riding out of town at daybreak.

With a bound he was out of bed and dressing. Whatever Keith

had in mind, he meant to know. Swiftly, he descended the stairs and went to the livery stable. Mounted, he headed out of town, found Keith's tracks with ease, and followed them. Keith turned off the trail and headed west and slightly north. But after a few miles, Kedrick lost the trail and took a wide swing to try and cut it again. He was unable to. Keith had vanished somewhere in the vicinity of Largo Canyon.

Returning to the hotel he found a message from Bob McLennon. He and Slagle would meet with Burwick and Kedrick at Chimney Rock at three in the afternoon on Wednesday. It was now Monday, and a whole day lay between. Yet during the remainder of Monday he saw nothing of Dornie Shaw, although Laredo Shad appeared a couple of times, then vanished into one of the saloons.

At midnight the door of his room opened slowly and Tom Kedrick, gun in hand, sat up. It was Laredo Shad.

"Somethin's up," he said, dropping on the bed, "an' she looks mighty peculiar. Couple of hours ago Poinsett an' Goff showed up an' said they had quit. No fightin' here, so they were pullin' out for Durango. About a half hour later they mounted up an' took out."

"What's peculiar about that?" Kedrick inquired, building a smoke. "That's in line with Burwick's talk with me."

"Yeah," Shad replied dryly, "but both of them came in here with a good deal of gear. They lost their pack horses somewheres and went out only with what they could carry on the one horse, and durned little o' that."

"What about Fessenden?"

"Ain't seen him."

"Any of the others gone?"

"Clauson is. At least, he ain't around in sight. I ain't seen him since morning."

That left Shaw, who had been around little himself, and Fessenden, if he was still in town. Despite himself, Kedrick was disturbed. But if Burwick was getting rid of his gunfighters it was a good sign, and probably he, Tom Kedrick, was getting too suspicious. Nothing, Shad said, had been said to him about quitting. "In fact," he said dryly, "the Mixus boys pulled in this morning, an' they went right to Burwick."

"Who are they?"

"Killers. Drygulchers, mostly. Bean an' Abe Mixus. They were in that Sandoval affair. Couple of men died awful opportune in that affair, an' come to think of it, Burwick was around. Fact is, that was where I met him."

"Were you in that?"

"Uh uh. I was in town, though, an' had me a run-in with Roy Gangle. Roy was a mighty tough ranny who'd been ramroddin' a big spread down thataway, an' when he got into the war he went bad, plumb bad. We'd had trouble over a steer, an' he braced me. He was a mite slow."

It made no sense—gunmen leaving, but others arriving. Of course, the Mixus boys could have been spoken to before the change of plans. That must be it. He suggested as much to Laredo and the Texan nodded dubiously.

"Maybe. I don't trust that hombre none. Your man Gunter is in over his head. Keith, well, he's all around bad when it comes to that, but neither of them can hold a candle to that Burwick."

Study the situation as he would, Tom Kedrick could see no answer to it, and the fact remained that they were to meet Slagle and McLennon for a peace conference. Out of that anything might come and he had no real cause to distrust Burwick.

The morning was bright and clear with the sun promising a hot day. It was still cool when Kedrick appeared on the street and crossed to the little restaurant where he ate in silence. He was on his second cup of coffee when Connie came in.

Her face brightened with a smile as she saw him, and she came over to his table. "You know, you're the one bright spot in this place. I'm so tired of that old stone house and seeing that dirty old man around that I can scarcely stand it. I'll be glad when this is all over."

He studied her. "What will you do then?"

"You know, I've not really thought of that. What I want to do is to get a ranch somewhere, a place with trees, grass, and some running water. It doesn't have to be a big place."

"Cattle?"

"A few, but horses are what I want. Horses like that one of yours, I think."

"Good idea. It takes less land for horses, and there's always a market for good stock." He studied the beauty of her mouth, the quietness and humor of her eyes. "Somehow I'm glad to think you're staying. It wouldn't be the same without you. Not now."

She looked at him quickly, her eyes dancing with laughter, but with the hint of a question in their depths. "Why, Tom! That sounds almost like gallantry. Like you were trying to make love to me, like all the cowboys."

"No, Connie," he said quietly, "when I make love to you there won't be any doubt about it. You'll know and I won't be fooling."

"Somehow I think you're right. You wouldn't be fooling."

"Over west of here," he said, "west and south there's a great rim that stretches for miles across the country, and a splendid pine forest atop it. There's trees, water, game, and some of the finest mountain meadows a man ever saw. I know a place over there where I camped once, a good spring, some tall trees, graceful in the wind, and a long sweep of land clear to the rim's edge, and beyond it miles upon miles of rolling, sweeping range and forest."

"It sounds fascinating, like what I've been wanting ever since I came West."

He pushed back his chair. "Maybe when this is over, you'd ride over that way with me? I'd like to show it to you."

She looked up at him. "All right, Tom. We'll look at it together."

He paused, hat in hand, staring out the door. "Together . . . " he mused. Then he glanced down at her. "You know, Connie, that's the most beautiful word in the language—together."

He walked away then, pausing to pay his check and hers, then stepping outside into the warmth of the street. A buckboard had stopped and a man was getting out of it, a man who moved warily and looked half frightened. He glanced around swiftly, then ducked through the door into the store.

CHAPTER EIGHT

TWO MEN CROSSED the street suddenly. One of them was a man Kedrick had never seen before, the other was the sly-looking loafer he had seen hanging around the back door in the saloon at Yellow Butte. The loafer, a sour-faced man called Singer, was talking. They stopped, and he indicated the buckboard to the man with him. "That's him, Abe," Singer was saying. "He's one of that crowd from across the way. He's brother-in-law to McLennon."

"This is a good place to start," Abe replied shortly, low voiced. "Let's go!"

Tom Kedrick turned on his heel and followed them. As they stepped into the door, he moved forward and caught it before it slammed shut. Neither man seemed to be aware of his presence, for they were intent on the figure at the counter.

"Hello, Sloan," Singer said softly. "Meet Abe Mixus!"

The name must have meant something to Sloan, for he turned, his face gray. He held a baby's bottle, which he was in the act of buying, in his right hand. His eyes, quick and terror stricken, went from one to the other. He was frightened, but puzzled, and he seemed to be fighting for self-control. "You in this squabble, Singer? I figured you to be outside of it."

Singer chuckled. "That's what I aim for folks to think."

Mixus, a lean, stooped man with yellow eyeballs and a thin-cheeked face drew a paper from his pocket. "That's a quit claim deed, Sloan," he said. "You can sign it an' save yourself trouble."

Sloan's face was gray. His eyes went to the deed and seemed to hold there. Then slowly, they lifted. "I can't do that. My wife's havin' a child in the next couple of days. I worked too hard on that place to give it up. I reckon I can't sign."

"I say you better." Mixus' voice was cold, level. The storekeeper had vanished, and the room was empty save for the three, and for Tom Kedrick, standing in the shadows near some hanging jeans and slickers. "I say you better sign because you don't own that prop'ty anyhow. Want to call me a liar?"

Sloan's face was gray and yet resolution seemed to have overcome his immediate fear. He was a brave man, and Kedrick knew that whatever he said now, he would die. Tom Kedrick spoke first.

"No, Abe," he said softly, "I'll call you a liar!"

Mixus stiffened as if struck. He was a killer, and dangerous, but he was a smart, sure-thing killer, and he had believed himself alone but for Singer. Now somebody was behind him. He stood stock still, then started to turn. Singer had fallen back against the wall, his eyes staring to locate Kedrick.

"It's Kedrick!" he said. "The boss gunman!"

Mixus scowled. "What's the matter?" he said irritably. "What yuh buttin' in for?"

"There's to be no more killing, Abe." Kedrick held his ground. "We're havin' a peace conference tomorrow. This killing is over."

"Got my orders," Mixus persisted. "You talk to Burwick."

There was a movement from Sloan, and Mixus whirled on him. "You stand still!" he barked.

"You can go, Sloan," Kedrick said. "Get in your outfit an' head back an' tell McLennon my word is good. You'd better stop thinking about him, Abe. You're in trouble, and I'm the trouble."

Mixus was confused. He knew Kedrick was ramrodding the gunmen for the company, and he was puzzled. Had he been about to do the wrong thing? But no, he had—"You fool!" His confusion burst into fury. "Keith tol' me to git him!"

"Shut up!" Singer yelled. "Dang it! You—"

Abe Mixus was a cold-blooded killer and no heavy-weight mentally. Orders and counter orders had come to him, and worked up to a killing pitch he had been suddenly stopped in the middle of a job and switched off into this back trail where he floundered hopelessly. Now Singer seemed to be turning on him, and he swung toward him, his teeth bared, his face vicious.

"Don't you tell me, you white-livered coyote!" he snarled.

One hand hung over a gun, and Singer, frightened, grabbed for his own gun. Instantly Mixus whipped out his .44 and flame stabbed at Singer. The renegade turned on his heel. His knees slowly buckled and he slid to the floor, his head against a sack of flour, blood welling from his mouth.

Mixus stared down at him, and then slowly, he blinked, then blinked again. Awareness seemed to return to him, and his jittery nerves calmed. He stared down at Singer almost unbelieving.

"Why, I—I—kilt Singer," he said.

"That's right." Kedrick was watching him, knowing now upon what a slender thread of irritation this man's muscles were poised. "What will Keith say to that?"

Cunning came over Abe's horselike face. "Keith? What give you the idee he had anythin' to do with this?" he demanded.

Slowly, attracted by the shooting and made confident by its end, people were gathering in front of the door. The storekeeper had come into the room and stood watching, his face drawn and frightened.

Tom Kedrick took a slow step back as Abe's eyes turned toward the front of the store. Putting the hanging slickers between them, he moved on cat feet to the opening between the counters and slid through into the living quarters and out into the alley behind the store.

Crossing the street below the crowd, he wound up in front of the St. James, pausing there. Laredo Shad materialized beside him. "What happened?" he asked swiftly.

Kedrick explained. "I don't get it," he said. "Keith may be moving on his own. Burwick was to hold off until we had our talk, and I know Keith didn't like that. He spoke right up about it."

"Ain't Singer s'posed to be a settler?" Shad asked. "Won't this serve to get 'em all riled up? Who knew that Singer was with Keith an' the company?"

"You've a point there," Kedrick said thoughtfully. "This may be the very thing that will blow the lid off!

"Both of them were mighty jumpy. It looked like they had Sloan marked because he was McLennon's relative. I sprung a surprise on them, an' Mixus just couldn't get himself located."

The crowd separated, then gathered in knots along the street to discuss the new event. Shad loitered beside Kedrick, and was standing there when Loren Keith came up. He glanced sharply at Shad, then at Kedrick. "What's happened over there?"

He kept his eyes on Kedrick as he spoke, and Kedrick shrugged. "Shooting, I guess. Not unusual for Mustang from what I hear."

"Mixus was in there," Shad commented. "Wonder if he had a hand in it?"

Keith turned and looked at Laredo, suspicion in his eyes. "Who was shot?" he inquired, his eyes going from one to the other.

"Singer, they tell me," Shad said casually. "I reckon Mixus killed him."

"Mixus? Kill Singer?" Keith shook his head. "That's preposterous!"

"Don't know why," Laredo drawled. "Mixus come heah to fight, didn't he? An' ain't Singer one o' them settlers?"

Colonel Keith hesitated, his sharp, hard features a picture of doubt and uncertainty. Watching him, Kedrick was amused and pleased. The storekeeper had not seen him, and it was doubtful if anyone had but Mixus, the dead man, and the now missing Sloan.

What Abe Mixus would offer as an explanation for shooting Singer, Tom couldn't conceive, but a traitor had died, and the enemy was confounded. Little as it might mean in the long run, it was for the moment a good thing. The only fly in the ointment was the fact that Singer had been a squatter, and that few, if any, knew of his tie-up with Keith and the company.

Watching the crowds in the street, Tom Kedrick began to perceive a new element shaping itself. Public opinion was a force Burwick had not reckoned with, and the faces of the men talking in the streets were hard and bitter.

These were mostly poor men who had made their own way or were engaged in making their way, and they resented the action of the company. Few had known Singer well, and those few had little use for the man. But to them, it wasn't important who was gunned down. To them, it was a fight between a bunch of hard-working men against the company, made up largely of outsiders, seeking to profit from the work of local people. Furthermore, whatever Singer was, he was not a gunman and he was a local man. Abe Mixus was a known killer, a gunman whose gun was for hire.

Tom Kedrick nodded toward the street. "Well, Colonel," he said, "you'd better start thinking about that unless you want to stretch hemp. That bunch is sore."

Keith stared at them nervously, then nodded and hurried away toward headquarters. Shad watched him go and turned toward Kedrick. "You know, we're sort of tied in with the company, an' I don't aim to hang for 'em. Let's light a shuck out of here an' stick in the hills a few days."

"Can't. I've got to make that meeting with Burwick. But you might get out of town, anyway. Scout around and see what you can find of Goff and the others—if they really left the country or not. Meet me at Chimney Rock about sundown tomorrow."

Leaving Shad, Kedrick hurried to his room in the St. James and bundled his gear together. He carried it down to the livery stable and saddled the palouse. When that was done, staying off the main street, he headed for headquarters. It was Connie Duane he wanted to see, and not Burwick or Keith.

There was no sign of any of them. Gunter was not around, and Burwick and Keith seemed to have vanished. Idling in the office, Tom heard a slight movement upstairs. He called out. Feet hurried along the floor above him and then Connie was at the stair head. "Yes?" Recognizing him, she hurried down. "Is something wrong?"

Swiftly he explained, holding nothing back. "Nothing may come of it. But it wouldn't take much to start something. They all know that the company's gunmen are mostly out of town. Burwick, Keith and your uncle must have lit out."

"Uncle John hasn't been around all day. I saw him at breakfast, and then he disappeared."

"I'll look around. Do you have a gun?" He shook his head

then. "Don't much think you'll need it. Most of them like you around here, and you've been pretty outspoken. But stay close to your room. The lid's going to blow off."

Before he could reach the door she called to him and he faced her again. "Tom?" He saw the pleading in her eyes. "Be careful, Tom."

Their eyes held for a long moment, and then he nodded. "I will—if I can."

He went out and paused on the steps. Burwick and Keith might get out of the way. But whatever else Gunter might be, he was scarcely the man to leave his niece behind at a time of danger. Puzzled about Gunter's disappearance, Kedrick paused and looked around him. The back street was bare and empty. The white powdery dust lay thickly and had sifted into the foliage of the trees and shrubs.

Kedrick hitched his guns into place and walked slowly around the house. The stable was usually filled with horses. Now it seemed empty. He strode back, his spurs jingling a little, and tiny puffs of dust rising from his boots as he walked.

Once, nearly to the stable, he paused by a water trough and listened for noise from the town. It was quiet, altogether too quiet. He hesitated, worrying about Connie again, but then went on and into the wide door that gave entrance to the shadowed coolness of the stable.

The stalls were empty, all save one. He walked back, then paused. The chestnut was Gunter's horse, and a saddle lay nearby. Could Gunter be somewhere around town? Kedrick considered that, then dismissed it. He removed his hat and wiped the band with his kerchief, then replaced it. His face was usually thoughtful as he examined every stall.

Nothing.

Puzzled, he stepped out into the bright glare of the sun and heard no sound anywhere. He squinted his eyes around, then saw the ramshackle old building that had done duty for a stable before the present large one was built. He stared at it and then turned in that direction. He had taken scarcely a step when he heard a rattle of hoofs, and swung swiftly around, half-crouched, his hands wide.

Then he straightened. Sue Laine slid from her horse and ran to him. "Oh, I've found you, Tom!" she cried, catching him by the arms. "Tom, don't go to that meeting tomorrow. There's going to be trouble!"

"You mean, McLennon's framed something?"

"McLennon?" For an instant she was startled. "Oh, no! Not Mac!" Her expression changed. "Come home with me, Tom. Please do! Let them have this out and get it over with! Come home with me!"

"Why all this sudden worry about me?" He was sincerely puzzled. "We've only met once, and we seem to have different ideas about things."

"Don't stand here and argue! Tom, I mustn't be seen talking to you—not by either side. Come with me and get away from here until this is all over. I've seen Dornie, and he hates you, Tom. He hates you."

"He does, does he?" He patted her arm. "Run along home now. I've things to do here."

"Oh?" Her eyes hardened a little. "Is it that woman? That Duane girl? I've heard all about her, how beautiful she is, how—how she—what kind of girl is she?"

"She's a lovely person," he said gravely. "You'd like her, Sue."

Sue stiffened. "Would I? I wonder how much you know about women, Tom? Or do you know anything about them? I could never like Connie Duane." She shook his arm. "Come, if you're coming. I just heard this last night, and I can't—I won't see this happen."

"What? What's going to happen?"

She stamped her foot with impatience. "Oh, you fool, you! They plan to kill you, Tom. Now, come on."

"Not now," he said quietly. "I've got to get this fight settled first, then maybe I'll ride your way. Now run along, I've got to look around."

Impatiently, she turned and walked to her horse. In the saddle she glanced back at him. "If you change your mind . . ."

"Not now," he repeated.

"Then be careful. Be careful, Tom."

He watched her go, then happened to glance toward the house. Connie Duane stood in the window, looking down at him. As he looked up, she turned sharply away. He started for the house, then hesitated. There was nothing he could say now, nothing that would have any effect or do any good at all.

He started toward the front of the house again, then stopped. On an impulse he turned and walked swiftly back to the little old building and caught the latch. The door was weathered and gray.

It creaked on rusty hinges and opened slowly. Inside there was the musty odor of decay. Kedrick stood there for a minute watching the sunlight filter through the cobwebbed window and fall in a faint square upon the ancient straw that littered the earthen floor. Stepping forward, he peered around the corner of the nearest stall.

John Gunter lay sprawled upon his face, his head pillowed upon one forearm, the back of his shirt covered with a dark, wide stain. Kedrick knelt beside him.

Connie's uncle had been stabbed in the back. Three powerful blows, from the look of the wounds, had been struck downward—evidently while he sat at a desk or table.

He had been dead for several hours.

CHAPTER NINE

ALTON BURWICK, for all his weight, sat his saddle easily and rode well. His horse was a blood bay, tall and long limbed. He walked it alongside Tom Kedrick's palouse. From time to time he spurred it to a trot, then eased down. On this morning Burwick wore an ancient gray felt hat, torn at the flat crown, and a soiled neckerchief that concealed the greasy shirt collar.

His shirt bulged over his belt, and he wore one gun, too high on his hip for easy use. His whiskers seemed neither to have grown nor been clipped. They were still a rough stubble of dirty mixed gray. Yet he seemed unusually genial this morning.

"Great country, Kedrick. Country for a man to live in. If this deal goes through you should get yourself a ranch. I aim to."

"Not a bad idea." Kerrick rode with his right hand dangling. "I was talking about that yesterday with Connie Duane."

The smile vanished from Burwick's face. "You talked to her yesterday? What time?"

"Afternoon." Kedrick let his voice become casual, yet he was alert to the change in Burwick's voice. Had Burwick murdered Gunter? Or had it been one of the squatters? With things as they were either would be difficult or impossible to prove. "We had a long talk. She's a fine girl."

Burwick said nothing, but his lips tightened. The red canyon walls lifted high above them. Along here they were nearly five hundred feet above the bottom of Salt Creek. There was but little left to go, and Tom became puzzled by Burwick's increased watchfulness. The man might suspect treachery, but he had said nothing to imply anything of the kind.

Tom's mind reverted to Sue's warning of the previous day—they intended to kill him—but who were "they"? She had not been specific in her warning, except to say that he should not keep this rendezvous today. Kedrick turned the idea over in his mind, wondering if she were deliberately trying to prevent a settlement, or if she knew something and was genuinely worried.

Pit Laine, her gun-slinging brother, was one element in the situation he could not estimate. Laine had not been mentioned in any of the discussions. Although he seemed always just beyond reach, he was definitely in the background as was the mysterious rider of the mouse-colored horse. The whole story of the disappearing seemed fantastic, but Kedrick did not think Sue was inclined to fall for tall stories.

The canyon of Salt Creek widened out and several branch canyons opened into it. They left the creek bed and rode closer together to the towering cliffs, now all of seven hundred feet above the trail. They were heading south, and Burwick, mopping his sweaty face from time to time with a dirty handkerchief, was no longer talking.

Kedrick pushed back his hat and rolled a smoke. He had never seen Burwick so jittery before, and he was puzzled. Deliberately, he had said nothing to any of the company about Gunter, although he had arranged with some of the townspeople to have the body moved. Tom was afraid it might precipitate the very trouble he was trying to end, and bring the fight into open battle. Moreover, he was not at all sure of why Gunter had been killed, or who had done it. That it could be retaliation for Singer's death was an answer to be considered, but it might have been done by either Keith or Burwick.

Suddenly he drew up. A horse coming in alone from the northwest had left recent tracks. Burwick saw them, too. "I've seen those tracks before," Tom Kedrick said. "Now whose horse is that?"

"We better step it up," Burwick said, impatiently. "They'll be there before us."

They pushed on into the bright, still morning. The sky

overhead was a vast blue dome scattered with fleecy puff-balls of clouds, like balls of cotton on the surface of a lake of pure blue. The red cliffs towered high on their left, and the valley on their right swept away in a vast, gently rolling panorama. Glancing off over this sagebrush-dotted valley, Tom knew that lost in the blue haze, some seven or eight miles away, was Malpais Arroyo and Sue Laine.

Was she there this morning? Or was she riding somewhere else? She was strangely attractive, that slim, dark-haired, dark-eyed girl with her lovely skin, soft despite the desert sun and desert wind. She had come to him, riding all that distance to bring him a warning of danger. Why? Was it simply that she feared for him? Was she in love with him? He dismissed that idea instantly, but continued to wonder. She was, despite her beauty, a hard, calculating little girl, hating the country around, and wanting only to be free of it.

Heat waves danced out over the bottom land, and shadows gathered under the red wall. A dust devil lifted and danced weirdly across the desert, then lost itself among the thick antelope brush and the cat claw. Tom Kedrick mopped his brow and swung his horse farther east. The tall spire of Chimney Rock lifted in the distance, its heavier shouldered companion looming beside and beyond it.

"Look!" Burwick's voice held a note of triumph. "There they come."

To the south, and still three or four miles off, they could see two riders heading toward Chimney Rock. At this distance they could not be distinguished, but their destination was obvious.

"Now that's fine." Burwick beamed. "They'll be here right on time. Say—" he glanced at his heavy gold watch—"tell you what. You'll be there a shade before them, so what say you wait for them while I have me a look at a ledge up in the canyon?"

Minutes later, Kedrick swung down in the shadow of the rock. There was a small pool of water there. He let the palouse drink and ground-hitched him deeper in the shade, near some grass. Then he walked back and dropping to the ground lit a smoke. He could see the two riders nearing now. One was on a fast-stepping chestnut, the other a dappled gray.

They rode up and swung down. The first man was Pete Slagle, the second a stranger whom Kedrick had not seen before. "Where's McLennon?" he asked.

"He'll be along. He hadn't come in from the ranch, so I came on with Steelman here. He's a good man, an' anything he says goes with all of us. Bob'll be along later, though, if you have to have his word."

"Burwick came. He's over lookin' at a ledge he saw in the canyon over there."

The three men bunched and Steelman studied Kedrick. "Dai Reid tells me you're a good man, trustworthy, he says."

"I aim to be." He drew a last drag on his cigarette and lifted his head to snap it out into the sand.

For an instant, he stood poised, his face blank, then realization hit him. "Look out!" he yelled. "Hit the dirt!"

His voice was drowned in a roar of guns and something smashed him in the body even as he fell. Then something else slugged him atop the head and a vast wave of blackness folded over him, pushing him down, down, down, deeper and deeper into a swirling darkness that closed in tightly around his body, around his throat. And then there was nothing, nothing at all.

Alton Burwick smiled and threw down his cigar. Calmly, he swung into the saddle and rode toward the four men who were riding from behind a low parapet of rocks near the Chimney. As he rode up they were standing, rifles in hand, staring toward the cluster of bloody figures sprawled on the ground in the shade. "Got 'em!" Shaw said. His eyes were hard. "That cleans it up, an' good!"

Fessenden, Clauson and Poinsett stared at the bodies, saying nothing. Lee Goff walked toward them from his vantage point where he had awaited anyone who might have had a chance to escape. He stooped over the three.

Slagle was literally riddled with bullets, his body smashed and bloody. Off to one side lay Steelman, half the top of his head blown off. Captain Kedrick lay sprawled deeper in the shadow, his head bloody, and a dark stain on his body.

"Want I should finish 'em off for sure?" Poinsett asked.

"Finish what off?" Clauson sneered. "Look at 'em—shot to doll rags."

"What about Kedrick?" Fessenden asked. "He dead for sure?"

"Deader'n Columbus," Goff said.

"Hey!" Shaw interrupted. "This ain't McLennon! This here's that Steelman!"

They gathered around. "Sure is!" Burwick swore viciously. "Now we're in trouble. If we don't get McLennon, we're—" His voice trailed away as he looked up at Dornie Shaw. The soft brown eyes were bright and boyish.

"Why, boss," he said softly, dropping his cigarette and rubbing it out with his toe. "I reckon that's where I come in. Leave McLennon to me. I'll hunt him down before sun sets tomorrow."

"Want company?" Pointsett asked.

"Don't need it," Shaw said, "but come along. I hear this Bob McLennon used to be a frontier marshal. I never liked marshals noway."

They drifted to their horses, then moved slowly away. Dornie Shaw, Poinsett and Goff toward the west and Bob McLennon. Alton Burwick, his eyes thoughtful, headed toward the east and Mustang. With him rode the others. Only Fessenden turned nervously and looked back. "We should have made sure they were dead."

"Ride back if you want," Clauson said. "They are dead all right. That Kedrick! I had no use for him. I aimed my shot right for his smart skull."

Afternoon drew on. The sun lowered, and after the sun came coolness. Somewhere a coyote lifted his howl of anguish to the wide white moon and the desert lay still and quiet beneath the sky.

In the deeper shadow of the towering Chimney and its bulkier neighbor there was no movement. A coyote, moving nearer, scented the blood, but with it there was the dreaded man smell. He whined anxiously and drew back, then trotted slowly off, turning only once to look back. The palouse, still ground hitched, walked along the grass toward the pool, then stopped, nostrils wide at the smell of blood.

Well down behind some rocks and brush, the shooting had only made it lift its head, then return to cropping the thick green grass that grew in the tiny sub-irrigated area around the Chimney. Nothing more moved. The coolness of the night stiffened the dried blood and stiffened the bodies of the men who lay sprawled there.

Ten miles north Laredo Shad, late for his meeting with Kedrick, limped along the trail leading a badly lamed horse. Two hours before, the trail along an arroyo bank had given way and the horse had fallen. The animal's leg was not broken, but was badly injured. Shad swore bitterly and walked on, debating as he had for the past two hours on the advisability of camping for the night. But remembering that Kedrick would be expecting him, he pushed on.

An hour later, still plodding and on blistered feet, he heard horse's hoofs and drew up, slipping his rifle into his hands. Then the rider materialized from the night, and he drew up also. For a long minute no word was said, then Shad spoke. ''Name yourself, pardner.''

The other rider also held a gun. ''Bob McLennon,'' he said. ''Who are you?''

''Laredo Shad. My horse lamed hisself. I'm headed for Chimney Rock. S'pose to meet Kedrick there.'' He stared at the rider. ''Thought you was to be at the meetin'? What happened?''

''I didn't make it. Steelman an' Slagle went. I'm ridin' up here because they never come in.''

''What?'' Shad's exclamation was sharp. ''McLennon, I was right afeared o' that. My bet is there's been dirty work. Nevah trusted that there Burwick, not no way.''

McLennon studied the Texan, liking the man, but hesitant. ''What's your brand read, Laredo? You a company man?''

Shad shook his head. ''Well, now, it's like this. I come in here drawin' warrior pay to do some gun slingin', but I'm a right uppity sort of a gent about some things. This here didn't size up right to me, nor to Kedrick, so we been figurin' on gettin' shut of the company. Kedrick only stayed on hopin' he could make peace. I stayed along with him.''

''Get up behind me,'' McLennon said. ''My horse will carry double an' it ain't far.''

CHAPTER TEN

HIS EYES WERE open a long time before realization came, and he was lying in a clean, orderly place with which he was totally unfamiliar. For a long time he lay there searching his memory for clues to tie all this together. He, himself. He was Captain Tom Kedrick . . . he had gone west from New Orleans . . . he had taken on a job . . . then he remembered.

There had been a meeting at Chimney Rock and Steelman had come in place of McLennon. He had thrown his cigarette away and had seen those men behind the rocks, seen the sunlight flashing on their rifle barrels. He had yelled and then dropped, but not fast enough. He had been hit in the head, and he had been hit in the body at least once.

How long ago was that? He turned his head and found himself in a square stone room. One side of the room was native rock, and so was part of another side. The rest had been built up from loose stones gathered and shaped to fit. Besides the wide bed on which he lay there was a table and a chair. He turned slightly and the bed creaked. The door opened, and he looked up into the eyes of Connie Duane.

"Connie?" He was surprised. "Where am I? What's happened?"

"You've been unconscious for days," she told him, coming to the bedside. "You have had a bad concussion and you lost a lot of blood before Laredo and Bob McLennon found you."

"What about the others?"

"Both of them were dead. By all rights, you should have been."

"But where are we?"

"It's a cliff dwelling, a lonely one, and very ancient. It is high up in the side of the mountain called Thieving Rock. McLennon knew where it was, and he knew that if word got out that you were alive they would be out to complete the job at once. So McLennon and Shad brought you here."

"Are they still here?"

"Shad is. He hunts and goes to Yellow Butte for supplies, but he has to be very careful because it begins to look like they are beginning to get suspicious."

"McLennon?"

"He's dead, Tom. Dornie Shaw killed him. He went to Mustang to find a doctor for you. He encountered Dornie on the street. Bob was very fast, you know, but Dornie is incredible. He killed Bob before he could get a shot off."

"How did you get here?"

"Bob McLennon and Shad had talked about it, and they knew I was against the company, and also that Uncle John had been killed—so they came to me. I came out here right away. I knew a little about nursing, but not much. Laredo has been wonderful, Tom. He's a true friend."

Kedrick nodded. "Who did the shooting? I thought I saw Poinsett."

"He was one of them. I heard them talking about it but was not sure until later. Poinsett was there, Goff, Fessenden, Clauson and Shaw."

"Anything else happen?"

"Too much. They burned Yellow Butte's saloon and livery stable, and they have driven almost half the people off. Their surveyors are on the land now, checking the survey they made previously. A handful of the squatters have drawn back into the mountains somewhere under Pit Laine and that friend of yours, Dai Reid. They are trying to make a stand there."

"What about Sue?"

She looked at him quickly. "You liked her, didn't you? Well, Sue has taken up with Keith. They are together all the time. He's a big man, now. They've brought in some more gunmen, and the Mixus boys are still here. Right now Alton Burwick and Loren Keith have this country right under their thumbs. In fact, they even called an election."

"An election?"

"Yes, and they counted the ballots themselves. Keith was elected mayor, and Fessenden is sheriff. Burwick stayed out of it, of course, and Dornie Shaw wouldn't take the sheriff's job."

"Looks like they've got everything their own way, doesn't it?" he mused. "So they don't know I'm alive?"

"No. Shad went back there and dug three graves. He buried the other two, and then filled in the third grave and put a marker over it with your name on it."

"Good!" Kedrick was satisfied. He looked up at the girl. "And how do you get out here and back without them becoming curious?"

She flushed slightly. "I haven't been back, Tom. I stayed here with you. There was no chance of going back and forth. I just left everything and came away."

"How long before I can be up?"

"Not long, if you rest. And you've talked enough now."

Kedrick turned over the whole situation in his mind. There could be no more than a few days before the sale of the land would come off, and if there was one thing that mattered it was that the company not be permitted to profit from their crookedness. As he lay there resting, a plan began to form in his mind, and the details supplied themselves one by one.

His guns hung on a nail driven into the wall close to his hand. His duffle, which he had brought away from the St. James, lay in the corner. It was almost dark before he completed his planning, and when Laredo came in he was ready for him.

''Cimarron?'' Shad nodded a little later. ''Bloomfield would be nearer. How's that?''

''Good.'' Kedrick agreed. ''Make it fast.''

''That ain't worryin' me,'' Laredo said, rolling his tobacco in his jaws. ''They've been mighty suspicious lately. Suppose they trail this place down while I'm gone?''

''We'll have to chance that. Here's the message. Hurry it up!''

The sun was bright in the room when Connie came through the door with his breakfast. She turned and her face went white. ''Oh, you're up!''

He grinned shakily. ''That's right. I've laid abed long enough. How long has it been?''

''Almost two weeks,'' she told him. ''But you mustn't stand up. Sit down and rest.''

There was a place by a window where he had a good view of the trail below. At his request Connie brought the Winchester and her own rifle to him. He cleaned them both, oiled them carefully, and placed them beside his window. Then he checked his guns and returned them to their holsters, digging the two Walch Navy pistols from his duffle and checking them also.

He realized that it was too late to do anything now, but it was a wonder he had not thought of Ransome before. No more able legislator existed in Washington than Frederic Ransome, and the two had been brother officers in the War Between the States, as well as friends in France during the Franco-Prussian War when Ransome had been there as an observer. If anybody could block the sale to the company, he could, even on such short notice.

His telegram would be followed by a letter supplying all the details, and with that to go on, Ransome might get something done. He was a popular and able young senator with good connections and an affable manner. Moreover, he was an excellent strategist. It would make all the difference in this situation.

The cliff dwelling was built well back from the face of the cliff, and built evidently with an eye toward concealment as well as defense. They had called this, Connie told him, Thieving Rock, long before the white man appeared, and the Indians who lived here had been notorious thieves. There was a spring, so water was not a worry, and there were supplies enough for immediate purposes.

Two days dragged slowly by, and on the morning of the third Kedrick was resuming his station by the window when he saw a rider coming into the narrow canyon below.

The man was moving slowly and studying the ground as he came. From time to time he paused and searched the area with careful eyes. Kedrick pushed himself up from his chair. Taking the Winchester, he worked his way along the wall to the next room.

"Connie?" he called softly. There was no reply. After a minute, he called a second time. Still there came no answer.

Worried now, he remembered she had said something about going down below to gather some squaw cabbage to add greens to their diet.

Back at the window, he studied the terrain carefully, and then his heart gave a leap. Connie Duane was gathering squaw cabbage from a niche in the canyon wall, not fifty yards from the unknown rider.

Lifting his rifle, Kedrick checked the range. It was all of four hundred yards and a downhill shot. Carefully, he sighted on the rider, then lowered the gun. The stranger was nearer the girl now, and a miss might ricochet and hit her. The canyon wall would throw any bullet he fired back into the canyon itself and it might even ricochet several times in the close confines.

Yet somehow, she had to be warned. If the rider saw her tracks he would find both Connie and the hideout. Suddenly, the ears of the horse came up sharply, and the rider stiffened warily and looked all around. Carefully, Kedrick drew a bead on the man again. He hated to kill an unwarned man, but if necessary he would not hesitate.

Connie was standing straight now and appeared to be listening. Tense in every fiber, Tom Kedrick watched and waited. The two were now within fifty feet of each other, although each was concealed by a corner of rock and some desert growth including a tall cottonwood and some cedars.

Still listening, they both stood rigid. Kedrick touched his lips with the tip of his tongue. His eyes blurred from strain, and he brushed his hand across them.

The rider was swinging to the ground now, and he had drawn a gun. Warily, he stepped away from his ground-hitched horse. Shifting his eyes to Connie, Tom saw the girl wave. Lifting his hand, he waved back. Then he lifted the rifle. She shook a vigorous negation with her arm, and he relaxed, waiting.

Now the man was studying tracks in the sandy bottom of the wash, and as he knelt, his eyes riveted upon the ground, a new element entered the picture. A flicker of movement caught the tail of Kedrick's eye. Turning his head, he saw Laredo Shad riding into the scene. Glancing swiftly at the window, Laredo waved his hand. Then he moved forward and swung to the ground.

From his vantage point Kedrick could hear nothing, but he saw Laredo approach, making heavy going of it in the thick sand. Not a dozen yards from the man, he stopped.

He must have spoken, for the strange rider stiffened as if shot. Slowly he stood erect. As he turned, Tom saw his face full in the sunlight. It was Clauson!

What happened then was too fast for the eye to follow. Somebody must have spoken—who, did not matter. Laredo Shad, in a gunman's crouch, flashed his right-hand gun. It sprang clear, froze for a long instant, and then just as Clauson pulled the trigger, Shad fired—but a split second sooner.

Clauson staggered a step back, and Shad fired again. The outlaw went down slowly, and Laredo walked forward and stripped his gun belts from him. Then from his horse he took his saddlebags, rifle and ammunition. Gathering up the dead man and working with Connie's help, together they tied him to the saddle, and then turned the horse loose with a slap on the hip.

Connie Duane's face was white when she came into the room. "You saw that?"

He nodded. "We didn't dare to let him go. If we had we would all have been dead before noon tomorrow. Now," he said with grim satisfaction, "they'll have something to think about."

Shad grinned at him when he came in. "I didn't see that gun he had drawed," he said ruefully. "Had it laying along his leg as he was crouched there. Might've got me."

He dropped the saddlebags. "Mite of grub," he said, "an' some shells. I reckon we can use 'em even though I brought some. The message got off, an' so did the letter. Feller over to the telegraph office was askin' a powerful lot of questions. Seems like they've been hearin' about this scrap."

"Good. The more the better. We can stand it, but the company can't. Hear anything?"

"Uh huh. Somebody from outside the state is startin' a row about Gunter's death. I hear they have you marked for that. That is, the company is sayin' you did it."

Kedrick nodded. "They would try that. Well, in a couple of days I'll be out of here and then we'll see what can be done."

"You take some time," Shad said dubiously. "That passel o' thieves ain't goin' to find us. Although," he said suddenly, "I saw the tracks of that grulla day afore yestiddy, an' not far off."

The grulla again!

Two more days drifted by. With Laredo, Tom Kedrick ventured down the trail and the ladders to the canyon below. They visited their horses concealed in a tiny glade not far away. The palouse nickered and trotted toward him, and Kedrick grinned and scratched his chest. "How's it, boy? Ready to go places?"

"He's achin' for it," Shad said. He lighted a smoke and squinted his eyes at Kedrick. "What you aim to do when you do move?"

"Ride around a little. I aim to see Pit Laine, an' then I'm goin' to start huntin' up every mother's son that was in that dry-gulching. Especially," he added, "Dornie Shaw."

"He's bad," Laredo said quickly. "I nevah seen it, but you ask Connie. Shaw's chain lightnin'. She seen him kill Bob."

"So one of us dies." Kedrick said quietly. "I'd go willing enough to take him with me, an' a few others."

"That's it. He's a killer, but the old bull o' that woods is Alton Burwick, believe me, he is. Keith is just right-hand man for him, an' the fall guy if they need one. Burwick's the pizen mean one."

With Connie they made their start three days later, and rode back trails beyond the Rim to the hideout Laine had established. It was Dai Reid himself who stopped them, and his eyes lighted up when he saw Kedrick.

"Ah, Tom!" His broad face beamed. "Like my own son, you are. We'd heard you were kilt dead."

Pit Laine was standing by the fire, and around him on the ground were a dozen men, most of whom Kedrick recognized. They sat up slowly as the three walked into the open space, and Pit turned. It was the first time Kedrick had seen him, and he was surprised.

He was scarcely taller than his sister, but wide in the shoulders and slim in the hips. When he turned, he faced them squarely, and his eyes were sharp and bitter. This was a killing man, Kedrick decided, as dangerous in his own way as that pocket-sized devil, Dornie Shaw.

"I'm Kedrick," he said, "and this is Connie Duane. I believe you know Shad."

"We know all of you," Laine said, watching them, his eyes alert and curious.

Quietly and concisely, Kedrick explained his plan. He ended by saying, "So there it is. I've asked this friend of mine to start an investigation into the whole mess and to block the sale until the truth is clear. Once the sale is halted and that investigation started, they won't be with us long. They could get away with this only if they could keep it covered up, and they had a fair chance of doing that."

"So we wait and let them run off?" Laine demanded.

"No," Tom Kedrick shook his head decidedly. "We ride into Mustang—all of us.

"They have the mayor and the sheriff, but public opinion is largely on our side. Furthermore," he said quietly, "we ride in the minute they get the news the sale is blocked. Once that news is around town they will have no friends. The band-wagon riders will get off, and fast."

"There'll be shootin'," one old-timer opined.

"Some," Kedrick admitted, "but if I have my way there'll be more of hanging. There's killers in that town, the bunch that dry-gulched Steelman and Slagle. The man who killed Bob McLennon is the man I want."

Pit Laine turned. "I want him."

"Sorry, Laine. He killed Bob, an' Bob was only in town to get a doc for me. You may," he added, "get your chance, anyway."

"I'd like a shot at him my own self," Laredo said quietly, "but somethin' else bothers me. Who's this grulla rider? Is he one of you?"

Laine shook his head. "No, he's got us wonderin' too."

"Gets aroun' plenty," the old-timer said, "but nobody ever sees him. I reckon he knows this here country better'n any of us. He must've been aroun' here for a long time."

"What's he want?" Shad wondered. "That don't figure."

Kedrick shrugged. "I'd like to know." He turned to Dai. "It's good to see you. I was afraid you'd had trouble."

"Trouble?" Dai smiled his wide smile. "It's trouble, you say? All my life there's been trouble, and where man is there will be trouble to the end of time, if not of one kind, then another. But I take my trouble as it comes, bye."

He drew deeply on his short-stemmed pipe and glanced at the scar against Kedrick's skull. "Looks like you'd a bit of it yourself. If you'd a less hard skull you'd now be dead."

"I'd not have given a plugged peso for him when I saw him," Laredo said dryly. "The three of them lyin' there, bloody an' shot up. We thought for sure they was all dead. This one, he'd a hole through him, low down an' mean, an' that head of his looked like it had been smashed until we moved him. He was lucky as well as thick skulled."

Morning found Laredo and Kedrick once more in the saddle. Connie Duane had stayed behind with some of the squatters' women. Pushing on toward Mustang, Laredo and Kedrick took their time. They had no desire to be seen or approached by any of the company riders.

"There's nothing much we can do," Kedrick agreed, "but I want to know the lay of the land in town. It's mighty important to be able to figure just what will happen when the news hits the place. Right now, everything is right for them. Alton Burwick and Loren Keith are better off than they ever were.

"Just size it up. They came in here with the land partly held by squatters with a good claim on the land. They managed to get that land surveyed and put in their claim to the best of it, posted the notices and waited them out. If somebody hadn't seen one of those notices and read it, the whole sale might have gone through and nobody the wiser. Somebody did see it, and trouble started. They had two mighty able men to contend with, Slagle and McLennon.

"Well, both of them are dead now. And Steelman, another possible leader is dead, too. So far as they are aware, nobody knows much about the deaths of those men or who caused them. I was the one man they had learned they couldn't depend on, and they think I'm dead. John Gunter brought money into the deal, and he's dead and out of the picture completely.

"A few days more and the sale goes through, the land becomes theirs and there isn't any organized opposition now. Pit Laine and his group will be named as outlaws, and hunted as such, and believe me, once the land sale goes through, Keith will be hunting them with a posse of killers."

"Yeah," Laredo drawled, "they sure got it sewed up, looks like. But you're forgettin' one thing. You're forgettin' the girl. Connie Duane."

"What about her?"

"Look," Shad said, speaking around his cigarette, "she sloped out of town right after McLennon was killed. They thought she had been talking to you before, and she told 'em off in the office, said she was gettin' her money out of it. All right, so suppose she asks for it, and they can't pay? Suppose," he added, "she begins to talk and tells what she knows, and they must figure it's plenty. She was Gunter's niece, and for all they know he told her more than he did tell her."

"You mean they'll try to get hold of her?"

"What do you think? They'll try to get hold of her, or kill her."

Tom Kedrick's eyes narrowed. "She'll be safe with Laine," he said, but an element of doubt was in his voice. "That's a good crowd."

Shad shrugged. "Maybe. Don't forget that Singer was one of them, but he didn't hesitate to try to kill Sloan, or to point him out for Abe Mixus. He was bought off by the company, so maybe there are others."

At that very moment, in the office of the gray stone building, such a man sat opposite Alton Burwick, while Keith sat in a chair against the wall. The man's name was Hirst. His face was sallow, but determined. "I ain't lyin'!" he said flatly. "I rode all night to git here, slippin' out o' camp on the quiet. She rode in with that gunman, Laredo Shad, and this Kedrick hombre."

"Kedrick! Alive?" Keith sat forward, his face tense.

"Alive as you or me! Had him most of the hair clipped on one side of his head, an' a bad scar there. He sort of favored his side, too. Oh, he'd been shot all right. But he's ridin' now, believe me!"

The renegade had saved the worst until last. He smiled grimly at Burwick. "I can use some money, Mr. Burwick," he said, "an' there's more I could tell you."

Burwick stared at him, his eyes glassy hard, then reached into a drawer and threw two gold eagles on the desk. "All right! What can you tell me?"

"Kedrick sent a message to some hombre in Washington name of Ransome. He's to block the sale of the land until there's a complete investigation."

"What?"

Keith came to his feet, his face ashen. This was beyond his calculations. When the idea of the land grab had first been brought to his attention, it had seemed a very simple, easy way to turn a fast profit. He had excellent connections in Washington through his military career, and with Burwick managing things on the other end and Gunter bringing on the money, it seemed impossible to beat it. He was sure to net a handsome profit, clear his business with Gunter and Burwick, then return East and live quietly on the profits. That it was a crooked deal did not disturb him. But that his friends in the East might learn of it . . .

"Ransome!" His voice was shocked. "Of all people!"

Frederic Ransome had served with him in the war, and their mutual relationship had been something less than friendly. There had been that episode by the bridge. He flushed at the thought of it, but Ransome knew, and Ransome would use it as a basis for judgment. Kedrick had no way of knowing just how fortunate his choice of Ransome had been.

"That does it!" He got to his feet. "Ransome will bust this wide open and love it."

He was frightened, and Burwick could see it. He sat there, his gross body filling the chair, wearing the same soiled shirt. His eyes followed Keith with irritation and contempt. Was Keith going bad on him now?

"Get back there," Burwick said to Hirst, "and keep me informed of the movements. Watch everything closely now, and don't miss a trick. You will be paid."

When Hirst had gone, Burwick turned to Keith and his fat lips twisted into a smile. "So does it matter if they slow it up a little? Let them have their investigation. It will come too late."

"Too late?" Keith was incredulous. "With such witnesses against us as Kedrick, Shad, Connie and the rest of them?"

"When the time comes," Burwick said quietly, "there will be no witnesses. Believe me, there won't be."

CHAPTER ELEVEN

KEITH TURNED ON Burwick, puzzled by the sound of his voice. "What do you mean?" he asked.

Burwick chuckled and rolled his fat lips on his cigar. There was malice and some contempt in the look he gave Keith. How much better, he thought, if Kedrick had not been so namby-pamby. He was twice the man Keith was, for all the latter's commanding presence.

"Why," he said, "if there's no witnesses, there'll be no case. What can these people in town tell them? What they suspect? Suspicions won't stand in a court of law, nor with that committee. By the time they get here this country will be peaceful and quiet, believe me."

"What do you mean to do?" Keith demanded.

"Do? What is there to do? Get rid of Kedrick, Laredo Shad, and that girl. Then you'll take a posse and clean out that rat's nest back of the Rim. Then who will they talk to? Gunter might have weakened, but he's dead. With the rest of them out of it—"

"Not Connie!" Keith protested. "Not her! For heaven's sake, man!"

Burwick snorted and his lips twisted in an angry sneer as he heaved his bulk from the chair. "Yes, Connie!" he said. "Are you a complete fool, Keith? Or have you gone soft? That girl knows more than all of them. Suppose Gunter talked to her, and he most likely did? She'll know everything—everything, I tell you!"

He paced back across the room, measuring Keith. The fool! He was irritated and angry. The sort of men they made these days, a weak and sniveling crowd. Keith had played out his time. If he finished this job alive—Dornie didn't like Keith. Burwick chuckled suddenly. Dornie! Now there was a man! The way he had killed that Bob McLennon!

"Now get this. Get the boys together. Get Fessenden, Goff, Clauson, Poinsett and the Mixus boys and send them out with Dornie. I want those three killed, you hear me? I want them dead before the week is out—and no bodies, understand?"

Keith touched his dry lips, his eyes haunted. He had bargained for nothing like this. It had all seemed such an easy profit, and only a few poverty-stricken squatters to prevent them from acquiring wealth in a matter of a few months. And everything had started off just as Burwick had suggested, everything had gone so well. Gunter had provided the money, and he had fronted for them in Washington.

Uneasily, now, Keith realized that if trouble was to come it would be he himself upon whom the blame would rest. Burwick, somehow, had remained in the background in the transactions back East as much as he, Keith, had been kept in the background here. Yet it would be Keith's guilt if anything went wrong. And with Ransome investigating everything was sure to go wrong.

Of course, he sighed deeply, Burwick was right. There was only one thing to do now. At least Dornie and the others would not hesitate. Suddenly, he remembered something.

"You mentioned Clauson. He's out of it, Burwick. Clauson came in last night, tied to his horse. He had been dead for hours."

"What?" Burwick stopped his pacing and walked up to Keith. "You just remembered?" He held his face inches away from Keith's and glared. "Is anybody backtracking that horse? You blithering idiot; Clauson was dynamite with a gun. If he's dead, shot, it had to be by one of three men, and you know it!"

Burwick's face was dark with passion and he wheeled and walked the length of the room, swearing in a low, violent voice that shocked Keith with its deep, underlying passion. When he turned again, Burwick's eyes were ugly with fury. "Can't you realize," he demanded hoarsely, "those men are dangerous?

"Every second they are alive means we are in danger! You have seen Dornie in action. Well, believe me, I'd sooner have him after me than Kedrick. I know Kedrick. He's a former Army officer—that's what you're thinking all the time—an officer and a gentleman!

"But he's something more, do you hear? He's more. He's a gentleman—that's true enough. But the man's a fighter, he loves to fight! Under all that calmness and restraint there's a drive and power that Dornie Shaw could never equal. Dornie may be faster, and I think he is, but don't you forget for one instant that Kedrick won't be through until he's down, down and dead!"

Loren Keith was shocked. In his year's association with Burwick he had never seen the man in a passion, and had never heard him speak with such obvious respect, and even—yes, even fear, of any man. What had Alton Burwick seen that he himself had not seen?

He stared at Burwick, puzzled and annoyed, but some of the man's feeling began to transmit itself to him, and he became distinctly uneasy. He bit his lips and watched Burwick pacing angrily.

"It's not only him, but it's Shad. That cool, thin-faced Texan. As for Laine"—Burwick's eyes darkened—"he may be the worst of the lot. He thinks he has a personal stake in this."

"Personal?" Keith looked inquiringly at the older man. "What do you mean?"

Burwick dismissed the question with a gesture. "No matter. They must go, all of them, and right now." He turned and his eyes were cold. "Keith, you fronted for us in Washington. If this thing goes wrong, you're the one who will pay. Now go out there and get busy. You've a little time, and you've the men. Get busy!''

When he had gone, Burwick dropped into his chair and stared blindly before him. Things had gone too far for him to draw back now even if he was so inclined, and he was not. The pity of it was that there had been no better men to be had than Keith and Gunter.

Yet, everything could still go all right, for he would know how to meet any investigating committee, how to soft pedal the trouble, turn it off into a mere cow-country quarrel of no moment and much exaggerated. The absence of any complaining witness would leave the investigators helpless to proceed, and he could make the difficulty seem a mere teapot tempest. Keith was obviously afraid of Ransome. Well, he was not.

Burwick was still sitting there when the little cavalcade of horsemen streamed by, riding out of town on their blood trail. The number had been augmented, he noticed, by four new arrivals, all hard, desperate men. Even without Keith, they might do the job. He heaved himself to his feet and paced across the room, staring out the window. It went badly with him to see Connie Duane die, for he had plans for Connie. Maybe . . . His eyes narrowed.

Out on the desert the wind stirred restlessly, and in the brassy sky above a lone buzzard circled as if aware of the creeping tension that was slowly gripping the country beneath it.

Far to the north, toward Durango, a cattle buyer pulled his team to a halt and studied the sky. There was no hint of storm, yet he had felt uneasy ever since leaving town on his buying trip down to Yellow Butte and Mustang. There had been rumors of trouble down that way. But then, there had been intermittent trouble there for some time, and he was not alarmed. Yet he was somehow uneasy, as though the very air carried a warning.

South of him, and below the Rim, Laredo Shad and Kedrick turned aside from the Mustang trail and headed toward Yellow Butte. It was only a little way out of their line of travel, but both men wanted to see what had happened there. Yet when they approached the town, aside from the blackened ruins of the destroyed buildings, everything seemed peaceful and still. Eight or ten families had moved back into the town and a few had never left. They looked up warily as the two riders drew near, then nodded a greeting.

They knew now that these two were siding with them against the company, but hardship and struggle had wearied them. They watched the two enter the settlement without excitement. The saloon had opened its door in the large, roomy office of the livery stable, and Kedrick and Laredo entered it. A couple of men leaned on the bar, and both turned as they entered, greeted them, and returned to their conversation.

It was growing cool outside and the warmth of the room felt good. Both men stepped to the bar, and Kedrick ordered and paid. Toying with his drink, Shad seemed uneasy. Finally he turned to Tom. "I don't like it," he said, low voiced. "Somehow or other Burwick is goin' to know about Ransome, an' he'll be in a sweat to get Connie out of the way, an' you an' me with her."

Kedrick agreed, for his own mind had been reading signs along the same trail. Now the only way out for the company was to face the committee, if Ransome managed one, with a plausible tale and an accomplished fact, and then let the investigating body make the most of it.

"Burwick's a snake," Shad commented. "He'll never quit wigglin' until the sun goes down for the last time. Not that one. He's in this deep, an' he ain't the man to lose without a fight."

Horses' hoofs sounded on the road outside and when they turned, Pit Laine and Dai Reid were dismounting before the door. They walked in, and Laine looked at Kedrick, then moved on to the bar. Dai appeared worried, but said nothing. After a minute, Laine turned suddenly and went outside. "What's the matter?" Kedrick asked.

"It be worry, bye, and some of it shame, an' all for that sister o' his. Who would think it o' her? To go over to the other side? He's that shy about it, you would scarce believe. When a man looks at him, he thinks it's his sister they are thinkin' on, and how she sold out to that traitor to mankind, that rascal, Keith."

Kedrick shrugged. "Ambition and money do strange things. She has the makings of a woman, too."

Laine opened the door. "Better come out," he said, "we've got trouble."

They crowded outside. Men were hurrying toward the houses, their faces grave. "What is it?" Kedrick asked quickly.

"Burt Williams signaled from the top of the butte. There's

riders coming from Mustang, a bunch of them.''

As they looked, the small dark figure of a man appeared on the edge of the mesa once more. This time they saw his arm wave: one . . . two . . . three times, and continue until he had waved it six times. When he had completed, he gestured to the southeast. Then he signaled four more times from the southwest.

''Ten riders,'' Laine spat. ''Well, we've got more than that here, but they aren't as salty as that crowd.''

Burt Williams, favoring his broken arm, knelt behind a clump of brush on top of Yellow Butte and studied the approaching horsemen through the glass. He knew all in this group by sight but not by favor. One by one he named them off to himself, ''Keith, Dornie Shaw, Fessenden an' Goff—Poinsett.'' He scowled. ''No, that ain't Poinsett. That's one o' the Mixus boys. Yep, an' there's the other.''

He swung his glass. The four riders, spaced well apart, were approaching at a steady pace. None of their faces was familiar. He stared at them awhile, but finally placed only one of them, a bad man from Durango who ran with Port Stockton and the Ketchum outfit. His name was Brokow.

Stirred, he searched the country all around the town for other movement, then turned back to the larger cavalcade of riders. Had he held on a certain high flat a minute longer he would have seen two unmounted men cross it at a stooping run and drop into the wide arroyo northeast of town.

As it was, he had been studying the approaching group for several minutes before he realized that Poinsett was not among them. He was with neither group.

Worried, Williams squinted his eyes against the sun, wondering how he could apprise them of the danger down below, for the absence of Poinsett disturbed him. The man was without doubt one of the most vicious of the company killers. He was a bitter man, made malignant by some dark happening in his past, but filled now with a special sort of venom all his own. Williams would have worried even more had he seen Poinsett at that moment.

The attack had been planned carefully and with all of Keith's skill. He surmised who they would be looking for, and hoped their watcher would overlook the absence of Poinsett. It was Poinsett whom Keith wanted in the right position, for he was unquestionably the best of the lot with a rifle.

At that moment, not two hundred yards from town, Poinsett

and his companion, Alf Starrett, were hunkered down in a cluster of brush and boulders at one side of the arroyo. Poinsett had his Spencer .56 and was settling into position for his first shot. Starrett, with a fifteen-shot Henry .44 was a half dozen yards away.

Poinsett pulled out a huge silver watch and consulted it. "At half after two, he says. All right, that's when he'll get it." With utmost composure he began to roll a smoke, and Alf Starrett, a hard-faced and wizened little man, noticed that his fingers were steady as he sifted tobacco into the paper.

Bob McLennon had planned the defense of Yellow Butte, if such a defense became necessary. Bob had been something of a hand with a gun, but he definitely had not been a soldier nor even an Indian fighter. Moreover, he had not expected an all-out battle for the town. Whatever the reason, he had committed a fatal error. That pile of boulders and brush offered perfect concealment and almost perfect cover while affording complete range of the town, its one street, and the back as well as front of most of the buildings.

Keith had been quick to see the vantage point on his earlier visits to the town. He had carefully planned to have Poinsett and Starrett approach the place some time before the main force moved in. So far, no hitch in the plan had developed.

Poinsett finished his cigarette and took up his rifle, then settled down to a careful watching and checking of the time. He had his orders and they were explicit. He was to fire on the first target offered after half past two. His first shot must kill.

Shad and Kedrick had returned to the saloon while Pit Laine loitered out front. Dai had gone across the street. Although Laine was out of Poinsett's sight, Dai made a perfect target. The Welshman, however, offered only a fleeting target and Poinsett did not get a chance to fire. In the next instant, however, the opportunity came.

The door of one of the nearest shacks opened and a man came out. He wore a broad-brimmed gray hat, torn at the crown, and a large checked shirt tucked into jeans supported by suspenders. He turned at the door and kissed his wife. Poinsett took careful aim with his .56, choosing as his aiming point the man's left suspender buckle. Taking a good deep breath he held it and squeezed off his shot.

The big bullet struck with a heavy thump. The man took a heavy lurch sidewise, tried to straighten and then went down. His wife ran from the door, screaming. Up the street a door banged and two men ran into the street, staring. Starrett's first shot knocked the rifle from the hand of one, splintering the stock. Poinsett dropped his man, but the fellow began to drag himself, favoring one leg which even from a distance they could see covered with a dark blotch at the knee.

Poinsett was a man without mercy. Coolly and carefully, he squeezed off his second shot. The man stiffened, jerked spasmodically and lay still.

"Missed my man," Alf said, apologetically, "but I ruint his shootin' iron."

Poinsett spat, his eyes cold. "Could happen to anybody," he said philosophically, "but I figured you burnt him anyways."

Within the saloon Kedrick had a glass half to his mouth when the shot boomed. It was followed almost at once by two more, the reports sounding almost as one.

"Blazes!" Shad whirled. "They ain't here yet?"

"They've been here," Kedrick said with quick realization. He swung to the door, glancing up the street. He saw the body of the last man to fall. Leaning out a bit, he glimpsed the other. His lips tightened, for neither man was moving.

"Somebody is up the draw," he explained quickly. "He's got the street covered. Is there a back way?"

Kedrick dove for the door followed by the others as the bartender indicated the exit. Catching up his shotgun, his pockets were already stuffed with shells. At the door Kedrick halted. Flattening against the wall, he stared up the draw. From here he could see the edge of the bunch of boulders and guessed the fire came from there. "Pinned down," he said. "They are up the draw."

Nobody moved. Kedrick's memory for terrain served him to good purpose now. Recalling the draw he remembered that it was below the level of the town beyond that point. But right there the boulders offered a perfect firing point.

Scattered shots came from down the draw, and nobody spoke. All knew that they could not long withstand the attack.

CHAPTER TWELVE

KEITH MADE UP his mind quickly. Defense of the town was now impossible. They would be either wiped out or burned alive if they attempted to remain. "Shad," he said quickly, "get across the street to Dai and Pit. Yell out to the others and get them to fall back, regardless of risk, to the canyon at the foot of Yellow Butte."

He took a step back and glanced at the trap door to the roof. The bartender saw the intent and shook his head. "You can't do it, boy. They'd git you from down the crick."

"I'm going to chance it. I think they are still too far off. If I can give you folks covering fire you may make it."

"What about you?" Shad demanded.

"I'll make it. Get moving!"

Laredo wheeled and darted to the door, paused an instant and lunged across the street. The bartender hesitated, swore softly, then followed. Kedrick picked up a bottle of the liquor and shoved it into his shirt, then jumped for the edge of the trap door, caught it and pulled himself through into the small attic. Carefully, he studied the situation.

Hot firing came from down stream, and evidently the killers were momentarily stopped there. He hoisted himself through, swung to the side of the roof, and carefully studied the boulders. Suddenly, he caught a movement, and knew that what he had first believed to be a gray rock was actually a shirt. He took careful aim with his Winchester, then fired.

The gray shirt jumped, and a hand flew up, then fell loose. Instantly a Spencer boomed and a bullet tore a chunk from the ridge near his face and splattered him with splinters. Kedrick moved down roof a bit. Then catching the signal from the window across the street, he deliberately shoved his rifle and head up, fired four fast shots, then two more.

Ducking his head, he reloaded the Winchester. Another bullet smashed the ridgepole. Then a searching fire began, the heavy slugs tearing through the roof about three to four inches below the top.

Kedrick slid down the roof. He hesitated at the edge of the trap door, and seeing a distant figure circling to get behind the men in the wash, he took careful aim and squeezed off his shot. It was all of five hundred yards, and he had only a small bit of darkness at which to aim.

The shot kicked up sand short of the mark by a foot or more as nearly as he could judge. He knew he had missed, but the would-be sniper lost his taste for his circling movement and slid out of sight. Kedrick went down the trap and dropped again into the saloon. Regretfully, he glanced at the stock of whisky, then picked up two more bottles and stuffed them into his pockets.

Hesitating only a second, he lunged across the street for the shelter of the opposite building. The Spencer boomed, and he knew that the hidden marksman had been awaiting this effort. He felt the shock of the bullet, staggered but kept going.

Reaching the opposite side, he felt the coldness of something on his stomach and glanced down. The bottle in his shirt had been broken by the bullet and he smelled to high heaven of good whisky. Picking the glass out of his shirt, he dove for the livery stable and swung into the saddle on the palouse.

The Spencer boomed again and again as he hit the road riding hard, but he made it. The others cheered as he rode pell mell through the canyon mouth and swung to the ground.

"This is no good," Laine said. "They can get behind us on the ridge."

Two men limped in from the draw, having withdrawn from boulder to boulder. Kedrick glanced around. There were fourteen men and women here who were on their feet. One man, the one who had the rifle knocked from his hand, had a shattered arm. The others were slightly wounded. Of them all, he had only seven men able to fight.

Quickly, he gave directions for their retreat. Then with Dai and Shad to hold the canyon mouth and cover them, they started back up the canyon.

Tom Kedrick measured his group thoughtfully. Of Laredo, Dai and Laine, he had no doubts at all. Of these others, he could not be sure. Good men, some of them, and one or two were obviously frightened. Nobody complained, however, and one of the men, whose face was pale, took a wounded man's rifle and gave him a shoulder on which to lean. Kedrick led them to the crevasse and down into it.

Amazed, they stared around. "What d'you know?" The bartender spat. "Been here nigh seven year an' never knowed o' this place!"

There were four horses in the group, but they brought them all into the cave. One of the men complained, but Kedrick turned on him. "There's water, but we may be glad to eat horse meat." The man swallowed and stared.

Laine pointed at Kedrick's shirt. "Man, you're bleedin'!"

Kedrick grinned. "That isn't blood, it's whisky. They busted one of the bottles I brought away."

Pit chuckled. "I'd most as soon it was blood," he said, "seems a waste of good likker."

The able men gathered near the escape end of the crevasse, and one of them grinned at Kedrick. "I wondered how you got away so slick. Is there another way out down there?"

He shook his head. "If there is, I don't know it. I waited and got out through the canyon when it wasn't watched."

Laine's face was serious. "They could hold us in here," he said, anxiously. "We'd be stuck for sure."

Kedrick nodded. "I'm taking an extra canteen and some grub, then I'm going atop the butte to join Burt Williams. I'd like one man with me. From up there we can hold them off, I think."

"I'm your man," Laredo said quietly. "Wait'll I get my gear."

A rifle boomed, and then Dai Reid joined them. "They are comin' up," he said. He glanced at Kedrick. "One man dead in the boulders. I got the look of him by my glass. It was Alf Starrett. Poinsett was the other."

"Starrett was a skunk," Burnett, one of the settlers said, " a low-down skunk. He kilt a man up Kansas way, an' a man disappeared from his outfit oncet that occasioned considerable doubt if he didn't git hisself another."

Kedrick turned to Pit Laine. "Looks like your show down here," he said. "Don't open fire until you have to, and don't fire even one shot unless it's needed. We'll be on top."

He led the way out of the crevasse and into the boulders and brush behind it. There was no sign of the attackers, and he surmised they were holed up awaiting the arrival of some supporting fire from the rim back of the canyon.

Tom glanced up at the towering butte. It reared itself all of a hundred and fifty feet above him and most of it was totally without cover. As they waited, a rifle boomed high above them and there was a puff of dust in the canyon mouth. Burt Williams had opened up.

Their first move toward the butte brought fire, and Laredo drew back. "No chance. We'll have to wait until dark. You reckon they'll hit us before then?"

"If they do, they won't get far." Tom Kedrick hunkered well down among the slabs of rock at the foot of the butte. "We've got us a good firing point right here." He rolled a smoke and lit up. "What are you planning when this is over, Shad? Do you plan to stay here?"

The tall Texan shrugged. "Ain't pondered it much. Reckon that will take care of itself. What you aimin' to do?"

"You know the Mogollons southwest of here? I figured I'd go down there and lay out a ranch for myself." He smoked thoughtfully. "Down in East Texas, before I came west, a fellow arrived there named Ikard. Had some white-faced cattle with him, and you should see 'em! Why, they have more beef on one sorry critter than three longhorns. I figured a man could get himself a few Hereford bulls and start a herd. Might even buy fifty or sixty head for a beginning, and let 'em mix with the longhorns if they like."

"I might go for somethin' like that," Laredo said quietly. "I always wanted to own a ranch. Fact is, I started one once, but had to git shut of it."

He stared down the canyon toward the mouth, his rifle across his knees. He did not look at Kedrick, but he commented casually, "We need luck, Cap'n, plenty of luck."

"Uh huh," Kedrick's face was sober. "I wonder who was on watch up the canyon? Or supposed to be?"

"Somebody said his name was Hirst. Sallow-faced hombre."

"We'll have to talk to him. Was he down below?"

"Come to think of it, he wasn't. He must have hid out back there."

"Or sold out. Remember Singer? He wouldn't have been the only one."

Laredo rubbed out the last of his cigarette. "They'll be makin' their play soon. You know, Kedrick, I'd as soon make a break for it, get a couple of horses an' head for Mustang. When we go we might as well take Keith an' that dirty Burwick with us."

Kedrick nodded agreement, but he was thinking of the men below. There were at least four good men aside from Shad, Laine and Dai Reid. That left the numbers not too unevenly balanced.

The fighting skill and numbers were slightly on the enemy's side, as they had at least twelve men when the battle opened, and they had lost Starrett. That made the odds eleven to eight unless they had moved up extra men, which was highly probable. Still, they were expecting defense. But an attack might . . .

He studied the situation. Suddenly, a dark shape loomed on the rim of the canyon some hundred and fifty yards off and much higher. The figure lifted his rifle and fired even as both Shad and Kedrick threw down on him with rifles, firing instantly. The man vanished, but whether hit or not they could not tell.

Desultory firing began, and from time to time, they caught glimpses of men advancing from the canyon mouth—never in sight long enough to offer a target, and usually rising from the ground some distance from where they dropped. The afternoon was drawing on, however, and the sun was setting almost in the faces of the attackers, which made their aim uncertain and their movements hesitant. Several times Shad or Kedrick dusted the oncoming party, but they got in no good shots. Twice a rifle boomed from the top of the butte, and once they heard a man cry out as though hit.

"You know, Laredo," Kedrick said suddenly, "it goes against the grain to back up those coyotes. I'm taking this grub up to Burt. When I come back down, we're going to move down that canyon and see how much stomach they've got for a good scrap."

Shad grinned, his eyes flickering with humor. "That's ace high with me, pardner," he said dryly. "I never was no hand for a hole, an' the women are safe."

"All but one," Kedrick said, "that Missus Taggart who lives in that first house. Her husband got killed and she wouldn't leave."

"Yeah, heard one o' the women folks speak on it. That Taggart never had a chance. Good folks, those two."

Colonel Loren Keith stared gloomily at the towering mass of Yellow Butte. That man atop the butte had them pinned down. Now if they could just get up there. He thought of the men he had commanded in years past, and compared them with these attacking the town. A pack of murderers. How had he got into this, anyway? Why couldn't a man know when he took a turning where it would lead him? It seemed so simple in the beginning to run off a bunch of one-gallused farmers and squatters.

Wealth—he had always wanted wealth, the money to pay his

way in the circles where he wanted to travel. But somehow it had always eluded him, and this had seemed a wonderful chance. Bitterly, he stared at the butte and remembered the greasy edge of Burwick's shirt collar, and the malice in his eyes—Burwick who used men as he saw fit, and disposed of them when he was through.

In the beginning it hadn't seemed that way. His own commanding presence, his soldier's stride, his cold clarity of thought, all these had led him to despise Gunter as a mere business man and Burwick as a conniving weakling. But then suddenly Burwick began to show his true self, and all ideas of controlling the whole show left Keith while he stared in shocked horror as the man unmasked. Alton Burwick was no dirty weakling, no mere ugly fat man, but a monster of evil, a man with a brain like a steel trap, stopping at nothing. By his very depth of wickedness he had startled Keith into obedience.

Gunter had wanted to pull out. Only now would Keith admit even to himself the cause of Gunter's death, and he knew he would die as quickly. How many times had he not seen the malevolence in the eyes of Dornie Shaw, and well he knew how close Shaw stood to Burwick. In a sense, they were of a kind.

His feeling of helplessness shocked and horrified Keith. He had always imagined himself a strong man, and had gone his way, domineering and supercilious. Now he saw himself as only a tool in the hands of a man he despised. Yet he was unable to escape. However, deep within him there was the hope that they still would pull their chestnuts from the fire and take the enormous profit the deal promised.

One man stood large in his mind, one man drew all his anger, his hate and bitterness. That man was Tom Kedrick.

From that first day, Kedrick had made him seem a fool. He, Keith, had endeavored to put Kedrick firmly in his place, speaking of his rank and his twelve years of service, and then Kedrick had calmly paraded such an array of military experience that few men could equal, and right before them all. He had not doubted Kedrick, for vaguely now, he remembered some of the stories he had heard of the man. That the story was the truth, and that Kedrick was a friend of Ransome's infuriated him still more.

He stepped into the makeshift saloon and poured a drink, staring at it gloomily. Fessenden came in, Goff with him.

"We goin' to roust them out o' there, Colonel?" Goff asked. "It will be dark, soon."

Keith tossed all his drink. "Yes, right away. Are the rest of them out there?"

"All but Poinsett. He'll be along."

Keith poured another stiff shot and tossed it off as quickly, then followed them into the street of Yellow Butte.

They were all gathered there—all but the Mixus boys, who had followed along toward the canyon, and a couple of the newcomers who had circled to get on the cliff above and beyond the boulders and brush where the squatters had taken refuge.

Poinsett was walking down the road in long strides. He was abreast of the first house when a woman stepped from the door. She was a square-built woman in a faded blue cotton dress and man's shoes, run down at the heel. She held a double-barreled shotgun in her hands. As Poinsett drew abreast of her, she turned on him and fired.

She shot both barrels, at point-blank range, and Poinsett took them right through the middle. Almost torn in two, he hit the ground, gasping once, his blood staining the gray gravel before the shocked eyes of the clustered men.

The woman turned on them, and they saw she was not young. Her square face was red and a few strands of graying hair blew about her face. As she looked at them, her work-roughened hands still clutching the empty shotgun, she motioned at the fallen man in the faded check shirt.

In that moment, the fact that she was fat, growing old, and that her thick legs ended in the grotesque shoes seemed to vanish—and in the blue eyes were no tears. Her chin trembled a little as she said, "He was my man. Taggart never give me much, an' he never had it to give, but in his own way, he loved me. You killed him—all of you. I wish I had more shells."

She turned her back on them. Without another glance, she went into the house and closed the door behind her.

They stood in a grim half circle, each man faced suddenly with the enormity of what they were doing and had done.

Lee Goff was the first to speak. He stood straddle legged, his thick hard body bulging all his clothes, his blond hair bristling. "Anybody bothers that woman," he said, "I'll kill him."

CHAPTER THIRTEEN

KEITH LED HIS attack just before dusk and lost two men before the company men withdrew. But the attack had paid off—they had learned of the hole. Dornie Shaw squatted behind the abutment formed by the end wall of the canyon where it opened on the plain near the arroyo. "That makes it easy," he said. "We still got dynamite."

Keith's head came up and he saw Shaw staring at him, his eyes queerly alight. "Or does that go against the grain, Colonel? About ten sticks of dynamite dropped into that crevasse an' Burwick will get what he wants—no bodies."

"If there's a cave back there," Keith objected, "they'd be buried alive!"

Nobody replied. Keith's eyes wandered around to the other men, but their eyes were on the ground. They were shunning responsibility for the act, and only Shaw enjoyed the prospect. Keith shuddered. What a fool he had been to get mixed up in this.

A horse's hoof struck stone, and as one man they looked up. Although they could not see the horse they heard the creak of saddle leather. A spur jingled, and Alton Burwick stood among them.

Loren Keith straightened to his feet and briefly explained the situation. Burwick nodded from time to time, then added, "Use the dynamite. First thing in the morning. That should end it, once and for all."

He drew a cigar from his pocket and bit off the end. "Had a wire. That committee is comin' out, all right. Take them a couple of weeks to get here, an' by that time folks should be over this an' talkin' about somethin' else. I'm figurin' a bonus for you all."

He turned back toward his horse, then stopped and catching Dornie Shaw's eye, jerked his head.

Shaw got up from the fire and followed him, and Keith stared after them, his eyes bitter. Now what? Was he being left out of something else?

Beyond the edge of the firelight and beyond the reach of their ears, Burwick paused and let Shaw come up to him. "Nice work, Dornie," he said. "We make a pair, you an' me."

"Yeah," Dornie nodded. "An' sometimes I think a pair's enough."

"Well," Burwick puffed on his cigar, "I need a good man to side me, an' Gunter's gone—at least."

"That company o' yours," Dornie was almost whispering, "had too many partners, anyway."

"Uh huh," Burwick said quietly, "it still has."

"All right, then." Dornie hitched his guns into a firmer seating on his thighs. "I'll be in to see you in a couple of days at most."

Burwick turned and walked away, and Dornie saw him swing easily to the saddle. He stayed where he was, looking into the darkness and listening to the slow steps of the horse. They had a funny sound—a very funny sound.

When he walked back to the campfire, he was whistling *Green Grow the Lilacs, O.*

The attack came again at daybreak. The company had mustered twenty men, of whom two carried packages of dynamite. This was to be the final blow. The squatters were to be wiped out, once and for all.

Shortly before the arrival of Burwick, Keith and Dornie Shaw, with Fessenden accompanying them, made a careful reconnaissance of the canyon from the rim. What they found pleased them enormously. It was obvious, once the crevasse had been located, that not more than two men could fire from it at once, and the attackers could find plenty of cover from the scattered boulders. In fact, they could get within throwing distance without emerging in the open for more than a few seconds at a time. Much of the squatters' field of fire would be ruined by their proximity to the ground and the rising of the boulders before them.

The attack started well, with all the men moving out. They made twenty yards into the canyon, moving fast. Here, the great slabs fallen from the slope of Yellow Butte crowded them together. And there the attack stopped.

It stopped abruptly, meeting a withering wall of rifle fire—at point-blank range!

Tom Kedrick knew a thing or two about fighting, and he knew full well that the hideout in the crevasse would in the long run become a death-trap. He put himself in Keith's place and decided what that man would do. Then he had his eight men, carrying fourteen rifles, slip like Indians through the darkness to carefully selected firing positions far down the canyon from where Keith would be expecting to find them.

Five of the attackers died in that first burst of fire. As the gunhands broke for cover, two more went down. One dragged himself to the camp of the previous night with a shattered knee cap. He found himself alone.

The wife of Taggart had begun it—the mighty blast of rifle fire completed it.

The company fighters got out of the canyon's mouth, and as one man they moved for their horses. Keith was among them and glad to be going. Dornie Shaw watched him mount up, and swung alongside him. Behind them, moving carefully as if they were perfectly disciplined troops, the defenders of the canyon moved down, firing as they came. A horse dropped, and a man crawled into the rocks, then jumped up and ran. Dai Reid swung wide of the group and started after him.

Another went down before they got away, and Kedrick turned to his group. "Get your horses, men. The women will be all right. This is a job that needs finishing now."

A quarter of a mile away, Brokow spotted a horse, standing alone, and started for it. As he arose from the rocks, a voice called out from behind. "A minute!"

Brokow turned. He saw only one man approaching him, the Welshman, Dai Reid. He stared at the man's Spencer, remembering his own gun was empty. He backed up slowly, his eyes haunted.

"My rifle's empty," he said, "an' I've lost my Colt."

"Drop the rifle then," Dai said quietly. "This I've been wanting, for guns be not my way."

Brokow did not understand, but he dropped his rifle. He was a big man, hulking and considered powerful. He watched in amazement as Reid placed his Spencer carefully on the ground, and then his gun belt. With bowlegged strides, the shorter man started for Brokow.

The outlaw stared, then started forward to meet Dai. As they drew near, he swung. His rocklike fist smashed Dai Reid flush on the chin. But Reid only blinked, then lunged. Twice more Brokow swung, blows filled with smashing panic born of the lack of effect of that first punch. Dai was unable to avoid the blows, and both connected solidly. But then Dai's huge, big-knuckled hand grasped Brokow's arm and jerked him near.

The hand slipped to the back of his head and jerked Brokow's face down to meet the rising of the Welshman's head. Stars burst before Brokow's eyes, and he felt the bone go in his nose. He swung wildly, and then those big hands gripped his throat and squeezed till Brokow was dead. Then Dai Reid dropped the outlaw to the sand. Turning, he walked away. He did not notice the horse that stood walking. It was a grulla.

In the headlong flight that followed the debacle in the canyon's mouth, only Lee Goff had purpose. The hard-bitten Montana gunman had stared reality in the face when Taggart's wife turned on him. It was only coincidence that she so resembled his own mother, long since dead of overwork in rearing seven boys and five girls on a bleak Montana ranch.

He headed directly for Yellow Butte and the Taggart home. He did not dismount, but stopped by the door and knocked gently. It opened and he faced Mrs. Taggart, her eyes red from weeping. "Ma'am," he said, "I guess I ain't much account, but this here's been too much. I'm driftin'. Will you take this here—as a favor to me?"

He shoved a thick roll of bills at her, his face flushing deep red. For an instant, she hesitated, and then she accepted the money with dignity. "Thanks, son. You're a good boy."

Goff put spurs to his horse and swung it around. The bald-faced sorrel disappeared into the darkness of the night. Lee Goff had had his belly full. He was heading for Colorado, or Utah—anywhere . . . but away.

Elsewhere, Tom Kedrick was riding to Mustang. With him were Laredo Shad, Pit Laine, Dai Reid, Burt Williams, and the others. They made a tight, grim-faced little cavalcade, and they rode with their rifles across their saddle forks.

Due west of them, however, another little drama was taking place. The riders they followed did not include all the men who had abandoned the fight in the canyon. Two of them, Dornie Shaw and Colonel Loren Keith, had headed due west on their own. Both of them had their own thoughts and their own ideas of what to do. Among other things, Keith had decided that he had had enough. Whether the others knew it or not, they were through, and he was getting out of the country.

There was some money back there in Mustang, and once he had that, he was going to mount up and head for California. Then let Ransome investigate. After a few years he would return to the East.

If the subject ever came up, he would swear he had nothing to do with it, that he only represented the company legally in the first steps of the venture.

What Dornie Shaw was thinking nobody ever guessed. At this moment, however, he had no thought at all in his mind. For his mind was not overly given to thought. He liked a few things, although he rarely drank, and seemed never to eat much. He liked a good horse and a woman with about an equal degree of affection, and he had liked Sue Laine a good bit. However, the woman who really fascinated him was Connie Duane, and she seemed unaware that he was alive.

Most of all he liked a gun. When cornered or braced into a fight, he killed as naturally and simply as most men eat. He was a creature of destruction, pure and simple. Never in his life had he been faced with a man who made him doubt his skill, and never had he fought with anything but guns—and he vowed he never would.

The two rode rapidly and both were mounted well. By the time Kedrick was leaving Yellow Butte with his men and lining out for town, Shaw and Keith reached the bank of Salt Creek Wash. Here Keith swung down to tighten his saddle cinch while his horse was drinking. After a moment, Dornie got down, too.

Absently Keith asked, "Well, Dornie, this breaks it, so where do you think you'll go now?"

"Why, Colonel," Shaw said softly, in his gentle boy's voice. "I don't know exactly where I'm goin', but this here's as far as you go."

It took a minute for the remark to sink in, and then Keith turned, his puzzled expression stiffening into black horror, then fear. Dornie Shaw stood negligently watching him, his lips smiling a little, his eyes opaque and empty.

The realization left Loren Keith icy cold. Dornie Shaw was going to kill him.

He had been an utter fool ever to allow this to happen. Why had he left the others and come off with Shaw? Why hadn't he killed him long since, from behind if need be, for the man was like a mad dog. He was insane, completely insane.

"What's on your mind, Shaw?" Without realizing it he spoke as he might to a subordinate. Shaw was not conscious of the tone. He was looking at Keith's belt line. The Colonel, he reflected, had been taking on a little weight lately.

"Why, just what I say. You've come as far as your trail takes you, Colonel. I can't say I'm sorry."

"Burwick won't like this. We're two of the men on whom he relies."

"Uh huh, that's the way it was. It ain't now. Back yonder," he jerked his head toward the butte, "he sort of implied he'd got hisself one too many partners." He shoved his hat back a little. "You want to try for your gun? It won't help you none, but you can try."

Keith was frightened. Every muscle within him seemed to have tightened until he could not move, yet he knew he was going to. But at the last, he had something to say, and it came from some deep inner conviction. "Kedrick will kill you, Dornie. He's going to win. He'll beat Burwick, too."

Suddenly, he remembered something: it had been only a fleeting expression on Dornie Shaw's face, but something. "Dornie!" he shot the word out with the force of desperation. "There behind you! The grulla!"

Shaw whirled, his face white, an almost animal-like fury on it. As he turned, Keith, gasping hoarsely and triumphantly, grabbed for his gun. He got it, and the gun swung up. But he had never coped with a fighter like Shaw. In the flashing instant that he whirled and found nothing behind him, Dornie hurled himself backward. The shot split wide the air where he had stood an instant before, and then Dornie himself fired from the ground. He fired once, then a second time.

Keith caught the bullet through the midsection, right where that extra weight had been gathering, and took the second one in the same place.

He fell, half in the trickle of water that comprised Salt Creek. Feeding shells into his gun, Dornie Shaw stared down at the glazing eyes. "How did you know?" he asked sullenly. "How did you know?"

CHAPTER FOURTEEN

FESSENDEN RODE WELL forward in the saddle, his great bulk carried easily with the movement of the horse. His wide face was somber with thought and distaste. Like the others, the wife of Taggart had affected him as nothing else could have. He was a hard man who had done more than his share of killing. But he had killed men ruthlessly, thoughtlessly, killed men in mortal combat where he himself might die as easily.

Several times before he had hired his gun, but each time in cattle or sheep wars or struggles with equals, men as gun-wise as he himself. Never before had he actually joined in a move to rob men of their homes. Without conscience in the usual sense, he had it in this case. For the men who moved West, regardless of their brand, were largely men in search of homes. Before, he had thought little of their fight. Several times he had helped to drive nesters from cattle range, and to him that was just and logical. Cows needed grass and people lived on beef, and most of the range country wasn't suited to farming anyway.

But now there was a difference, he realized, thinking of it for the first time. Now men were not being driven off for cattle, but only for profit. To many, the line was a fine one to draw; to Fessenden and his like, once the matter was seen in its true light, that line became a gap, an enormous one.

Actually, he rode in a state of shock. The victory Keith had wanted seemed so near. The taking of the few left in the canyon had seemed simple. His qualms against the use of dynamite he had shrugged off, if uncomfortably. He had gone into the canyon with the others to get the thing over with, to get his money and get out. And then, long before they expected it, came that smashing thunderous volley. It had been made more crashing by the close canyon walls, more destructive by the way the attackers were channeled by the boulders.

Shock started the panic, and distaste for the whole affair kept some of them, at least, on the move. Yet it was hard to believe that Clauson and Poinsett were dead, that Brokow had vanished, that Lee Goff was gone. For alone of the group, Goff had told Fessenden he was leaving. He had not needed to tell him why.

Behind him rode the Mixus boys, somber with disappointment at the failure of the attack. They had no qualms about killing, and no lines to draw even at the killing of women. They were in no true sense fighting men; they were butchers. Yet even they realized the change that had come over the group. What had become of Brokow or Goff they did not know. But they did know that disintegration had set in. In turn, these men had turned into a snarling pack of wolves venting their fury and their hatred on each other.

Mustang lay quiet when they rode into town. It was the quiet before the storm. The town, like that cattle buyer who had turned back to Durango, sensed the coming fury of battle. No women were on the street, and only a few hardy souls loitered at the bars or card tables. The chairs before the St. James were deserted, and Clay Allison had ridden back to his home ranch, drunk and ugly.

An almost Sunday peace lay over the sun-swept town when Fessenden drew up before the Mustang Saloon and swung down from his weary horse. Slapping his hat against his leg to beat off the dust, Fessenden stood like a great shaggy bull and surveyed the quiet of the street. He was too knowing a Western man not to recognize the symptoms of disaster. Clapping his hat all awry upon his shaggy head, he shoved his bulk through the doors and moved to the bar.

"Rye," he said, his voice booming in the cavernous interior. His eyes glinted around the room, then back to the bartender.

That worthy could no longer restrain his curiosity. "What's happened?" he asked, swallowing.

A glint of irony came into the hard eyes of the gunman. "Them squatters squatted there for keeps," he said wryly, "an' they showed us they aim to stay put." He tossed off his drink. "All Hades busted loose." Briefly he explained. "You'd a figured there was a thousand men in that neck of the rocks when they opened up. The thing that did it was the unexpectedness of it, like steppin' on a step in the dark when it ain't there."

He poured another drink. "It was that Kedrick," he said grimly. "When I seen him shift to the other side I should've lit a shuck."

"What about Keith?"

"He won't be back."

They turned at the new voice, and saw Dornie Shaw standing in the doorway, smiling. Still smiling, he walked on in and leaned against the bar. "Keith won't be back," he said. "He went for his gun out on Salt Creek."

The news fell into a silent room. A man at a table shifted his feet and his chair creaked. Fessenden wet his lips and downed his second drink. He was getting out of town, but fast.

"Seen that girl come in, short time back," the bartender said suddenly, "that Duane girl. Thought she'd gone over to the other side?"

Dornie's head lifted and his eyes brightened, then shadowed. He downed his own drink and walked jauntily to the door. "Stick around, Fess. I'll be back." He grinned. "I'll collect for both of us from the Old Man."

The bartender looked at Fessenden. "Reckon he'll bring it if he does?"

The big gunman nodded absently. "Sure. He's no thief. Why, that kid never stole a thing in his life. He don't believe in it. An' he won't lie or swear—but he'll shoot the heart out of you an' smile right in your face while he's doing it."

The show had folded. The roundup was over. There was nothing to do now but light out. Fessenden knew he should go, but a queer apathy had settled over him, He ordered another drink, letting the bartender pour it. The liquor he drank seemed now to fall into a cavern without bottom and had no effect.

On the outskirts of town, Tom Kedrick reined in. "We'll keep together," he said quietly. "We want Keith, Shaw, Burwick, the Mixus boys and Fessenden. There are about four others that you will recognize whom I don't know by name. Let's work fast and make no mistakes.

"Pit, you take Dai and two men and go up the left side of the street. Take no chances. Arrest them if you can. We'll try them, and"—his face was grim—"if we find them guilty they'll have just two sentences: leave the country or hang. They've done murder."

He turned in his saddle and glanced at the tall Texan. "Come on, Shad," he said quietly, "we'll take two men and the right side of the street, which means the livery stable, the St. James and the Mustang."

Kedrick glanced over at Laine. "Pit," he said, "if you run into Allison or Ketchum, better leave 'em alone. We don't want 'em."

Laine's face was grave. "I ain't huntin' 'em," he said grimly, "but if they want it, they can have it."

The parties rode into town and swung down on their respective sides of the street. Laredo grinned at Kedrick, but his eyes were sober. "Nobody wants to cross Laine today," he said quietly. "The man's in a killin' mood. It's his sister."

"Wonder what will happen when they meet?"

"I hope they don't," Shad said. "She's a right purty sort of gal, only money crazy."

The two men stood hesitant, waiting for orders. Both were farmers. One carried a Spencer .56, the other a shotgun. Shad glanced at them. "Let these hombres cover the street, Tom," he suggested. "You take the St. James, an' I'll take the stable."

Kedrick hesitated, "All right," he agreed finally. "But take no chances, boy."

Laredo grinned and waved a negligent hand and walked through the wide door of the stable. Inside, he paused, cold and seemingless careless, actually as poised and deadly as a coiled rattler. He had already seen Abe Mixus' sorrel pony and guessed the two dry-gulchers were in town. He walked on a step and saw the barrel of a rifle push through the hay.

He lunged right and dove into a stall, drawing his gun as he went. He ran full tilt into the other Mixus. Their bodies smashed together, and Mixus, caught off balance, went down and rolled over. He came up, clawing for a gun. Laredo kicked the gun from under his hand and sent it spinning into the wide open space between the rows of stalls.

With a kind of whining cry, Bean Mixus sprang after it, slid to his knees and got up, turning. Laredo Shad stood tall and dark just within the stall. As Mixus turned like a rat cornered and swung his gun around, Laredo Shad fired. His two shots slammed loud in the stillness of the huge barn. Bean Mixus fell dead.

The rifle bellowed and a shot ripped the stall stanchion near Laredo's head. He lunged into the open, firing twice more at the stack of straw. The rifle jerked, then thundered again, but the shot went wild. Laredo dove under the loft where Abe Mixus was concealed, and fired two more shots through the roof over his head where he guessed the killer would be lying.

Switching his guns, he holstered the empty one and waited. The roof creaked some distance away. Laredo began to stalk the escaping Mixus, slipping from stall to stall. Suddenly, a back door creaked and a broad path of light shot into the darkness of the stable. Laredo lunged to follow—too late.

The farmer outside with the shotgun was the man Sloan. As Abe Mixus lunged through the door to escape, they came face to face, at no more than twenty feet of distance. Abe had his rifle at his hip and he fired. The shot ripped through the water trough beside Sloan, and the farmer squeezed off the left-hand barrel of his shotgun.

The solid core of shot hit Mixus in the shoulder and neck, knocking him back against the side of the door. His long face was drawn and terror stricken, his neck and shoulder a mass of blood that seemed to well from a huge wound. He fought to get his gun up, Sloan stepped forward, remembering Bob McLennon's death and the deaths of Steelman and Slagle. The other barrel thundered and a sharp blast of flame stabbed at Abe Mixus.

Smashed and dead, the killer sagged against the doorjamb, his old hat falling free, his face pillowed in the gray, blood-mixed dust.

Silence hung heavy in the wake of the shots. Into that silence Laredo Shad spoke. "Hold it, Sloan!" He stepped through the door, taking no glance at the fallen man. "The other one won't hang, either," he said. "They were both inside."

The two men drew aside, Sloan's face gray and sick. He had never killed a man before, and wanted never to again. He tried to roll a smoke but his fingers trembled. Shad took the paper and tobacco from him and rolled it. The farmer looked up, shamefaced. "Guess I'm yaller," he said. "That sort of got me."

The Texan looked at him gloomily. "Let's hope it always does," he said. He handed him the cigarette. "Try this," he told him. "It will make you feel better. Wonder how Kedrick's comin'?"

"Ain't heard nothin'!"

Pit Laine stood in a door across the street. "Everythin' all right?" he called.

"Yeah," the other farmer called back, "on'y you don't hafta look for the Mixus boys no more. They ain't gonna be around."

Captain Tom Kedrick had walked up the street and turned into the door of the St. James Hotel. The wide lobby was still, a hollow shell, smelling faintly of old tobacco fumes and leather. The wrinkled clerk looked up and shook his head. "Quiet today," he said. "Nobody around. Ain't been no shootin' in days."

Guns thundered from down the street, then again and again. Then there was silence followed by the two solid blasts of the shotgun.

Both men listened, and no further sound came. A moment later

Pit Laine called out and the farmer answered. The clerk nodded. "Same town," he said. "Last couple of days I been wonderin' if I wasn't back in Ohio. Awful quiet lately," he said, "awful quiet."

Tom Kedrick walked down the hall and out the back door. He went down the weathered steps and stopped on the grass behind the building. There was an old, rusty pump there, and the sun was hot on the backs of the buildings.

He walked over to the pump and worked the handle. It protested, whining and groaning at the unaccustomed work and finally, despairing of rest, threw up a thick core of water that splashed in the wooden tub. When he had pumped for several minutes, Kedrick held the gourd dipper under the pump and let it fill. The water was clear and very cold. He drank greedily, rested, then drank again.

Far up the backs of the buildings, at the opposite end of town, a man was swinging an ax. Kedrick could see the flash of light on the blade, and see the ax strike home. A moment later, the sound would come to him. He watched, then wiped the back of his hand across his mouth and started along in back of the buildings toward the Mustang.

He moved with extreme care, going steadily, yet with every sense alert. He wore his .44 Russians, and liked the feel of them, ready to his hands. The back door of the Mustang Saloon was long unpainted and blistered by many hot suns. He glanced at the hinges and saw they were rusty. The door would squeak. Then he saw the outside stair leading to the second floor. Turning, he mounted the stairs on tiptoe, easing through the door, and walked down the hall.

In the saloon below, Fessenden had eliminated half a bottle of whisky without destroying the deadening sense of futility that had come over him. He picked up a stack of cards and riffled them skillfully through his fingers. He had not lost his deftness. Whatever effect the whisky had had, it was not on his hands.

Irritated, he slammed the cards down and stared at the bartender. "Wish Dornie'd get back," he said for the tenth time. "I want to leave this town. She don't feel right today."

He had heard the shots down the street, but had not moved from the bar. "Some drunk cowhand," he said irritably.

"You better look," the bartender suggested, hoping for no fights in the saloon. "It might be some of your outfit."

"I got no outfit," Fess replied shortly. "I'm fed up. That stunt out there to Yeller Butte drove me off that range. I'll have no more of it."

He heard the footsteps coming down the hall from upstairs and listened to their even cadence. He glanced up, grinning, "Sounds like an army man. Listen!"

Realization of what he had said came over him, and the grin left his face. He straightened, resting his palms on the bar. For a long moment, he stared into the bartender's eyes. "I knew it! I knew that hombre would—" He tossed off his drink. "Aw, I didn't want to leave town, anyway!"

He turned, moving back from the bar. He stood straddle legged like a huge grizzly, his big hands swinging at his hips, his eyes glinting upward at the balcony and the hall that gave onto it. The steps ceased, and Tom Kedrick stood there, staring down at him.

Neither man spoke for a full minute, while suspense gripped the watchers, and then it was Fessenden who broke the silence. "You lookin' for me, Kedrick?"

"For any of your crowd. Where's Shaw? And Keith?"

"Keith's dead. Shaw killed him back up on the Salt after you whipped us in the canyon. I dunno where he is now."

Silence fell once more and the two men studied each other. "You were among them at Chimney Rock, Fessenden," Kedrick said. "That was an ambush—dry-gulcher's stunt, Fess." Kedrick took another step forward, then side-stepped down the first step of the stairs which ran along the back wall until about six steps from the bottom, then after a landing, came down facing the room.

Fessenden stood there, swaying slightly on his thick, muscular legs, his brutal jaw and head thrust forward. "Aw, hell!" he said and grabbed iron.

His guns fairly leaped from their holsters spouting flame. A bullet smashed the top of the newel post at the head of the stairs, then ricocheted into the wall. Another punctured a hole just behind Kedrick's shoulder. Tom Kedrick stepped down another step, then fired. His bullet turned Fessenden, and Kedrick ran lightly down four steps while Fessenden smashed two shots at him.

Kedrick dove headlong for the landing, brought up hard against the wall, and smashed another shot at the big man. It knocked a leg from under him and Fessenden rolled over on his feet, colliding with the bar.

He had been hit twice, but he was cold sober and deadly. He braced himself and with his left hand clinging to the bar, lifted his right and thumbed back the hammer. Kedrick fired two quick shots with his left gun. One ripped a furrow down the bar and hit Fessenden below the breastbone—a jagged tearing piece of metal when it struck.

Fessenden fired again, but the bullet went wild. His sixth shot was fired in desperation as he swung up his left-hand gun, dropping the right into his holster. Taking his time, feeling his life's blood running out of him, he braced himself there and took the gun over into his right hand. He was deliberate and calm. "Pour me a drink," he said.

The bartender, lying flat on his face behind the bar, made no move. Tom Kedrick stood on the edge of the landing now, staring at Fessenden. The big gunman had been hit three times, through the shoulder, the leg and the chest, and he still stood there, gun in hand, ponderous and invulnerable.

The gun came up and Fessenden seemed to lean forward with it. "I wish you was Dornie," he said.

Kedrick triggered. The shot nailed Fessenden through the chest again. The big man took a fast step back, then another. His gun slipped from his hand, and he grabbed a glass from the bar. "Gimme a drink!" he demanded. Blood bubbled at his lips.

Tom Kedrick came down the steps, his gun ready in his hand and walked toward Fessenden. Holding his gun level and low down with his right hand, Kedrick picked up the bottle with his left and filled the empty glass. Then he pulled over another glass and poured one for himself.

Fessenden stared at him. "You're a good man, Kedrick," he said, shaping the words patiently. "I'm a good man, too—on the wrong side."

"I'll drink to that." Kedrick lifted his glass, they clicked them, and Fessenden grinned crookedly over his.

"You watch that Dornie," he advised, "he's rattler—mean." The words stumbled from his mouth and he frowned, lifting the glass. He downed his drink, choked on it, and started to hold out his big hand to Kedrick, then fell flat on his face. Holstering his gun, Tom Kedrick leaned over and gripped the big right hand. Fessenden grinned and died.

CHAPTER FIFTEEN

CONNIE DUANE HAD reached Mustang only a short time before the survivors of the fight at Yellow Butte began to arrive. Restless, after the men left to return to the squatters' town, she had begun to think of what lay ahead, of Fred Ransome, and of the impending investigation and of her uncle's part in it.

All his papers as well as many of her own remained under lock in the gray stone house in Mustang. If she was to get her own money back from Burwick, or was to clear any part of the blame from her uncle, she knew those papers would be essential. Mounting her horse she left the camp beyond the rim. Striking the Old Mormon Trail, she headed south. She was on that trail when the sun lifted, and she heard the distant sound of shots.

Turning from the trail she reined her horse into the bed of Salt Creek and rode south, passing the point where only a short time later Loren Keith was to meet his death at the hands of Dornie Shaw. Once in town she believed she would be safe. She doubted if anyone would be left in the gray house unless it was Burwick, and she knew that he rarely left his chair.

Arriving in Mustang, she rode quickly up the street, then cut over behind through the back door and went very quietly. Actually, she need not have bothered, for Alton Burwick was not there. Making her way up the old stairs, she unlocked the door to the apartment she had shared with her uncle, and closed the door behind her.

Nothing seemed to have been disturbed. The blinds were drawn as she had left them and the room was still. A little dust had collected, and the light filtering in around the blinds showed it to her. Going to her trunk, she opened it and got out the iron-bound box in which she carried her own papers. It was intact and showed no evidence of having been tampered with. From the bottom of the trunk she took an old purse in which there were two dozen gold eagles. These she put into the purse she was now carrying.

Among other things she found an old pistol, a huge, cumbersome old thing. This she got out and laid on the table beside her. Then she found a derringer seven-shot .22 caliber pistol her father had given her several years before he died, and she put it in the pocket of her dress.

Quickly she went into the next room and began to go through her uncle's desk, working swiftly and surely. Most of his papers were readily available. Apparently nobody had made any effort to go through them, probably believing they contained nothing of consequence or that there would be plenty of time later. She was busy at this when she heard a horse walk by the house and stop near the back steps.

Instantly she stopped what she was doing and stood erect. The window here was partly open and she could hear the saddle creak very gently as whoever it was swung down. Then a spur jingled, and there was a step below, then silence.

"So? It's you."

Startled by the voice, Connie turned. Sue Laine stood behind her, staring with wide eyes. "Yes," Connie replied. "I came for some things of mine. You're Sue, aren't you?"

Without replying to the question, the girl nodded her head toward the window. "Who was that? Did you see?"

"No. It was a man."

"Maybe Loren has come back." Sue studied her, unsmiling. "How are they out there? Are they all right? I mean—did you see Pit?"

"Yes. He's unhappy about you."

Sue Laine flushed, but her chin lifted proudly. "I suppose he is, but what did he expect? That I was going to live all my life out there in that awful desert? I'm sick of it! Sick of it, I tell you!"

Connie smiled. "That's strange. I love it. I love it, and every minute I'm there, I love it more. I'd like to spend my life here, and I believe I will."

"With Tom Kedrick?"

Sue's jealousy flashed in her eyes, yet there was curiosity, too. Connie noticed how the other girl studied her clothes, her face.

"Why—I—where did you ever get that idea?"

"From looking at him. What girl wouldn't want him? Anyway, he's the best of the lot."

"I thought you liked Colonel Keith?"

Sue's face flushed again. "I—I thought I did, too. Only part of it was because Tom Kedrick wouldn't notice me. And because I wanted to get away from here, from the desert. But since then—I guess Pit hates me."

"No brother really hates his sister, I think. He'd be glad to see you back with him."

"You don't know him. If it had been anybody but someone associated with Alton Burwick, why—"

"You mean, you knew Burwick before?"

"Knew him?" Sue stared at her. "Didn't you know? Didn't he tell you? He was our stepfather."

"Alton Burwick?" Connie stared in amazement.

"Yes, and we always suspected that he killed my father. We never knew, but my mother suspected later, too, for she took us and ran away from him. He came after us. We never knew what happened to mother. She went off one night for something and never came back, and we were reared by a family who took us in."

A board creaked in the hall, and both girls were suddenly still, listening.

Guns thundered from the street of the town, and both girls stared at each other, holding their breath. There was a brief silence, then a further spattering of shots. Then the door opened very gently and Dornie Shaw stood there facing the two girls.

He seemed startled at finding the girls together and looked from one to the other, his brown eyes bright, but now confused.

Then he centered his eyes on Sue Laine. "You better get out," he said. "Keith's dead."

"Dead?" Sue gasped, horrified. "They—they killed him?"

"No, I did. Up on the Salt. He drew on me."

"Keith—dead." Sue was shocked.

"What about the others? Where are they?" Connie asked quickly.

Dornie turned his head sharply around and looked hard at her, a curious, prying gaze as if he did not quite know what to make of her. "Some of 'em dead," he said matter of factly. "They whupped us. It was that Kedrick," he spoke without emotion or shadow of prejudice as though he were completely indifferent. "He had 'em set for us an' they mowed us down." He jerked his head toward the street. "I guess they are finishin' up now. The Mixus boys an' Fessenden are down there."

"They'll be coming here." Connie said, with conviction. "This is the next place."

"I reckon." He seemed indifferent to that, too. "Kedrick'll be the first one. Maybe," he smiled, "the last one."

He dug out the makings, glancing around the room, then back at Sue. "You git out. I want to talk to Connie."

Sue did not move. "You can talk to us both. I like it here."

As he touched his tongue to the paper his eyes lifted and met hers. They were flat, expressionless. "You heard me," he said. "I'd hate to treat you rough."

"You haven't the nerve!" Sue flashed back. "You know what would happen to you if you laid hands on a woman in this country! You can get away with killing me. But this country won't stand for having their women bothered—even by a ratty little killer like you!"

Connie Duane was remembering the derringer in her pocket. She lowered her hand to her hip within easy grasp of the gun.

A sudden cannonade sounded, then a scattering of more shots. At that moment Kedrick was finally shooting it out with Fessenden. Dornie Shaw cocked an inquisitive ear toward the sound. "Gettin' closer," he said. "I ain't really in no hurry until Kedrick gets here."

"You'd better be gone before he does come." Connie was surprised at the confidence in her voice. "He's too much for you, and he's not half frightened like these others are. He'll kill you, Dornie."

He stared at her, then chuckled without humor. "Him? Bah! The man doesn't live who can outdraw Dornie Shaw. I've tried 'em all. Fess? He's supposed to be good, but he don't fool with Dornie. I'd shoot his ears off."

Calmly, Connie dropped her right hand into her pocket and clutched the derringer. The feel of it gave her confidence. "You had better go," she said quietly. "You were not invited here, and we don't want you."

He did not move. "Still playin' it high an' mighty, are you? You've got to get over that. Come on, you're coming with me."

"Are you leaving?" Connie's eyes flashed. "I'll not ask you again!"

Shaw started to speak, but whatever it was he planned to say never formed into words, for Connie had her hand on the derringer, and she fired from her pocket. Ordinarily, she was a good shot, but had never fired the gun from that position. The first bullet burned a furrow along Dornie Shaw's ear, notching it at the top. The second shot stung him along the ribs and the third plowed into the table beside him.

With a grunt of surprise, he dove through the door into the hall. Sue was staring at Connie. "Well, I never!" Her eyes dropped to the tiny gun that Connie had now drawn from her pocket.

"Dornie Shaw! And with that! Oh, just wait until this gets around!" Her laughter rang out merrily, and despite herself, Connie was laughing, too.

Downstairs near the door, Dornie Shaw clutched his bloody ear. He panted as though he had been running, his face twisting as he stared at his blood. Amazed, he scarcely noticed when Kedrick came up the steps. But as the door pushed open, he saw him. For a fatal instant, he froze. Then he grabbed for his gun, but he had lost his chance. In that split second of hesitation, Kedrick jumped. His right hand grasped Dornie's gun wrist, and Kedrick swung the gunman bodily around, hurling him into the wall. Shaw's body hit with a crash and he rebounded into a wicked right to the wind.

Shaw was no fighter with his hands, and the power of that blow would have wrecked many a bigger man. As it was, it knocked every bit of wind from the gunman's body. Kedrick shoved him back against the wall. "You asked me what I'd do, once, with a faster man. Watch this, Dornie!"

Kedrick lifted his right hand and slapped the gunman across the mouth. Crying with fury, Shaw fought against the bigger man's grip. Kedrick held him flat against the wall, gripping him by the shirt collar, and slapped him over and back. "Just a cheap killer!" Kedrick said calmly. "Somebody has already bled you a little. I'll do it for good."

He dropped a hand to Dornie's shirt and ripped it wide. "I'm going to ruin you in this country, Dornie. I'm going to show them what you are—a cheap, yellow-bellied killer who terrorizes men better than himself." He slapped Dornie again, then shoved him into the wall once more and stepped back.

"All right, Shaw! You got your guns! Reach!"

Almost crying with fury, Dornie Shaw grabbed for his guns. As he whipped them free, all his timing wrecked by the events of the past few minutes, Kedrick's gun crashed and Shaw's right-hand gun was smashed from his hand. Shaw fired the left-hand gun, but the shot went wild. Kedrick lunged, chopping down with his pistol barrel. The blow smashed Dornie Shaw's wrist and he dropped the gun with a yelp.

He fell back against the wall, trembling, and staring at his hands. His left wrist was broken; his right thumb was gone. Where it had been, blood was welling.

Roughly, Kedrick grabbed him and shoved him out of the door.

He stumbled and fell, but Kedrick jerked him to his feet, unmindful of the gasps of the onlookers, attracted by the sounds of fighting. In the forefront of the crowd were Pit Laine, Dai Reid and Laredo Shad, blinking with astonishment at the sight of the most feared gunman in the country treated like a whipped child.

Shaw's horse stood nearby, and Kedrick motioned to him. "Get on him—backwards!"

Shaw started to turn and Kedrick lifted his hand and the gunman ducked instinctively. "Get up there! Dai, when he's up tie his ankles together."

Dornie Shaw, befuddled by the whipping he had taken, scarcely aware of what was happening, lifted his eyes. Then he saw the grulla tied near the stone house. It was the last straw, his demoralization was complete.

Feared because of his deadly skill with guns and his love of killing for the sake of killing, he had walked a path alone, either avoided by all, or catered to by them. Never in his life had he been manhandled as he had by Tom Kedrick. His belief in himself was shattered.

"Take him through the town," Kedrick's voice was harsh. "Show them what a killer looks like. Then fix up that thumb and wrist and turn him loose."

"Turn him loose?" Shad demanded. "Are you crazy?"

"No, turn him loose. He'll leave this country so far behind nobody will ever see him again. This is worse than death for him, believe me." He shrugged. "I've seen them before. All they need, that kind, is for somebody to face them once who isn't afraid. He was fast and accurate with his guns so he developed the idea he was tough.

"Other folks thought the same thing. He wasn't tough. A tough man has to win and lose. He has to come up after being knocked down, he has to have taken a few beatings, and know what it means to win the hard way.

"Anybody," he said dryly, "can knock a man down. When you've been knocked down at least three times yourself, and then got up and floored the other man, then you can figure you're a tough hombre. Those smoke poles of Shaw's greased his path for him. Now he knows what he's worth."

The crowd drifted away and Connie Duane was standing in the doorway. Tom Kedrick looked up at her, and suddenly, he smiled. To see her now, standing like this in the doorway, was like life-giving rain upon the desert, coming in the wake of many heat-filled days.

She came down the step to him, then looked past him at Pit. "Your sister's upstairs, Pit. You'd better talk to her."

Laine hesitated; then he said stiffly, "I don't reckon I want to."

Laredo Shad drew deep on his cigarette and squinted through the smoke at Laine. "Mind if I do?" he asked. "I like her."

Pit Laine was astonished. "After this?"

Shad looked at the fire end of his cigarette. "Well," he said, speaking seriously, "the best cuttin' horse I ever rode was the hardest to break. Them with lots of git up an' go to 'em often makes the best stock."

"Then go ahead." Pit stared after him. Then he said, "Tell her I'll be along later."

CHAPTER SIXTEEN

FOR THREE WEEKS there was no sign of Alton Burwick. He seemed to have vanished into the earth, and riders around the country reported no sign of him.

At the end of that time three men got down from the afternoon stage and were shown to rooms in the St. James. An hour later, while they were at dinner, Captain Tom Kedrick pushed open the door and walked into the dining room. Instantly, one of the men, a tall, immaculate young man whose hair was turning gray at the temples, rose to meet him, hand outstretched. "Tom! Say, this is wonderful! Gentlemen, this is Tom Kedrick, the man I was telling you about. We served together in the War Between the States! Tom—Mr. Edgerton and Mr. Cummings."

The two men, one a pudgy man with a round, cheerful face, the other as tall as Frederic Ransome and with gray muttonchop whiskers, acknowledged the introduction. When Kedrick had seated himself, they began demanding details. Quietly, and as concisely as possible, he told them his own story, beginning with his joining the company in New Orleans.

"And Burwick's gone?" Edgerton asked. He was the older man with the muttonchop whiskers. "Was he killed?"

"I doubt it, sir," Kedrick replied. "He simply vanished. The man had a faculty for being out of the way when trouble came. Since he left, with the aid of Miss Duane and her uncle's papers, we managed to put together most of the facts. However, Burwick's papers have disappeared, or most of them."

"Disappeared?" Edgerton asked. "How did that happen?"

"'Miss Duane tells me that when she entered the house before the final trouble with Shaw, she passed the office door and the place was undisturbed and the desk all in order. After the crowd had gone and when we returned, somebody had been rifling the desk and the safe."

"You imply that Burwick returned? That he was there then?"

"He must have been. Connie—Miss Duane—tells me that only he had the combination, and that he kept all the loose ends of the business in his hands."

Cummings stared hard at Kedrick. "You say this, this Shaw fellow killed Keith? How do we know that you didn't? You admit to killing Fessenden."

"I did kill him. In a fair fight before witnesses. I never even saw Keith's body after he was killed."

"Who do you think killed John Gunter?" Cummings demanded.

"My guess would be Burwick."

"I'm glad you're not accusing Keith of that," Cummings replied dryly.

"Keith wouldn't have used a knife," Kedrick replied quietly, "nor he wouldn't have attacked him from behind as was obviously the case."

"This land deal, Kedrick," Ransome asked. "Where do you stand in it?"

"I? I don't stand at all. I'm simply not in it."

Cummings looked up sharply. "You don't stand to profit from it at all? Not in any way?"

"How could I? I own nothing. I have no holdings, nor claim to any."

"You said Burwick promised you fifteen per cent?"

"That's right. But I know now that it was merely to appease me long enough to get me on the spot at Chimney Butte where I was to be killed along with the others. Burwick got me there, then rode off on the pretext that he wanted to look at a mineral ledge."

"How about this girl? The Duane girl?" Cummings asked sharply. "Does she stand to profit?"

"She will be fortunate to get back her money that her uncle invested."

"See, Cummings?" Ransome said. "I told you Kedrick was honest. I know the man."

"I'll give my opinion on that later, after this investigation is completed. Not now. I want to go over the ground and look into this matter thoroughly. I want to investigate this matter of the disappearance of Alton Burwick, too. I'm not at all satisfied with this situation."

He glanced down at the notes in his hand, then looked up. "As to that, Kedrick, wasn't Fessenden a duly elected officer of the law when you shot him? Wasn't he the sheriff?"

"Elected by a kangaroo election," Kedrick replied, "where the votes were counted by the two officials who won. If that is a legal election, then he was sheriff."

"I see. But you do not deny that he had authority?"

"I do deny it."

Connie Duane was awaiting him when he walked back to his table. She smiled as he sat down and listened to his explanation. She frowned thoughtfully. "Cummings? I think there is something in Uncle John's papers about him. I believe he was acting for them in Washington."

"That explains a lot then." Kedrick picked up his coffee cup, then put it down abruptly, for Laredo Shad had come into the room, his face sharp and serious. He glanced around, and sighting Kedrick, hurried toward him, spurs jingling. Kedrick got to his feet. "What's wrong? What's happened?"

"Plenty! Sloan was wounded last night and Yellow Butte burned!"

"What?" Kedrick stared.

Shad nodded grimly. "You shouldn't have turned that rat loose. That Dornie Shaw."

Kedrick shook his head irritably. "I don't believe it. He was thoroughly whipped when he left here. I think he ran like a scared rabbit when he left. If he did want revenge, it would be after a few months, not so soon. No, this is somebody else."

"Who could it be?"

His eyes met Connie's and she nodded, her eyes frightened. "You know who it could be, Tom. It could be Burwick."

Of course, that was what he had been thinking. Burwick had

bothered him, getting away scot free, dropping off the end of the world into oblivion as he had. Remembering the malignant look in the man's eyes, Kedrick was even more positive. Burwick had counted on this land deal; he had worked on it longer than any one of them, and it meant more to him.

"Shad," he said suddenly, "where does that grulla tie in? It keeps turning up, again and again. There's something more about all this than we've ever known, something that goes a lot deeper. Who rides the grulla? Why is it he has never been seen? Why was Dornie so afraid of it?"

"Was he afraid of the grulla?" Shad asked, frowning. "That doesn't figure."

"Why doesn't it? That's the question now. You know, that last day when I had Shaw thoroughly whipped, he looked up and saw something that scared him, yet something that I think he more than half expected. After he was gone down the street, I looked around, and there was nothing there. Later, I stumbled across the tracks of the grulla mustang. That horse was in front of the house during all the excitement!"

Frederic Ransome came into the room again and walked to their table. "Cummings is going to stir up trouble," he said, dropping into a chair. "He's out to get you, Kedrick, and if he can pin the killing of Keith on you, or that of Burwick . . . He claims your story is an elaborate build-up to cover the murder of all three of the company partners. He can make so much trouble that none of the squatters will get anything out of the land, and nothing for all their work. We've got to find Burwick."

Laredo lit a cigarette. "That's a tough one," he said, "but maybe I've got a hunch."

"What?" Kedrick looked up.

"Ever hear Burwick talk about the grulla?"

"No, I can't say that I did. It was mentioned before him once that I recall, and he didn't seem interested."

"Maybe he wasn't interested because he knowed all about it," Shad suggested. "That Burwick has me puzzled."

Connie looked up at him. "You may be right, Laredo, but Pit and Sue Laine were Burwick's stepchildren and they knew nothing about the horse. The only one who seemed to know anything was Dornie Shaw."

Tom Kedrick got up. "Well, there's one thing we can do," he said. "Laredo, we can scout out the tracks of that horse and trail it down. Pick up an old trail, anything. Then just see where it takes us."

On the third day it began to rain. All week the wind had been chill and cold and clouds had hung low and flat across the sky from horizon to horizon. Hunched in his slicker, Laredo slapped his gloved hands together and swore. "This finishes it!" he said with disgust. "It will wipe out all the trails for us!"

"All old anyway," Kedrick agreed. "We've followed a dozen here lately, and none of them took us anywhere. All disappeared on rock or were swept away by wind."

"Escavada's cabin isn't far up this canyon," Shad suggested. "Let's hit him up for chow. It will be a chance to get warm, anyway."

"Know him?"

"Stopped in there once. He's half Spanish, half Ute. Tough old blister, an' been in this country since before the grass came. He might be able to tell us something."

The trail into the canyon was slippery and the dull red of the rocks had turned black under the downpour. The rain slanted across the sky in drenching sheets. By the time they reached the stone cabin in the corner of the hills both men and horses were cold, wet and hungry.

Escavada opened the door for them and waved them in. He grinned at them. "Glad to have company," he said. "Ain't seen a man for three weeks."

When they had stripped off their slickers and peeled down to shirts, pants and boots, he put coffee before them and laced it with a strong shot of whisky. "Warm you up," he said. "Trust you ain't goin' out again soon. Whisky's mighty fine when a body comes in from the cold, but not if he's goin' out again. It flushes the skin up, fetches all the heat to the surface, then gives it off into the air. Man freezes mighty quick, drinkin' whisky."

"You ever see a grulla mustang around, Escavada?" Laredo asked suddenly, looking up at the old man.

He turned on them, his eyes bright with malicious humor. "You ain't some of them superstitious kind, be you? Skeered o' the dark like? An' ghosts?"

"No," Kedrick said, "but what's the tie-up?"

"That grulla. Old story in this here country. Dates back thirty, forty years. Maybe further'n that. Sign of death or misfortune, folks say."

Laredo looked inquiringly at Kedrick, and Kedrick asked, "You know anything about it? That horse is real enough. We've both seen the grulla."

"So've I," the old man said. He dropped into a chair and grinned at them. His gray hair was sparse, but his eyes were alive and young. "I seen it many times, an' no misfortune come my way. Not unless you call losin' my shovel a misfortune."

He hitched his chair nearer the woodpile and tossed a couple of sticks on the fire. "First I heerd of it was long ago. Old folks used to tell of a Spanish man in armor ridin' a mouse-colored horse. He used to come an' go about the hills, but the story back of it seems to be that a long time back some such feller was mighty cruel to the Injuns. That story sort of hung around an' a body heerd it ever' now and again until about fifteen, sixteen years back. Since then she's been mighty lively."

"You mean, you heard the story more since then?" Kedrick asked.

"Uh huh. Started with a wagon train wiped out by Injuns up on the Salt. Ever' man jack o' them kilt dead—women folks, too, the story was. There was a youngster come off scot free, boy about five or six years old. He crawled off into the brush, an' after, he swore them Injuns was led by a white man on a grulla horse, a white man in armor!"

"Wild yarn," Shad said, "but you can't blame the kid, imaginin' things after what he must've seen."

"He said that hombre in the armor went around with a long knife, an' he skewered ever' one of the bodies to make sure they was real dead. He said once that hombre looked right square at him, layin' in the brush. He was skeered like all git out, but must've been he wasn't seen, 'cause he wasn't bothered."

"An' this grulla has been seen since?" Shad asked. "Reg'lar?"

"Uh huh, but never no rider clost enough to say who or what. Sometimes off at a distance, sometimes just the horse, standin'. Most folks git clear off when they see that horse."

He got up and brought back the coffee pot. "Right odd you should ast me about him now," he commented. "Right odd."

Both men looked at him, and sensing their acute interest, he continued. "Been huntin' here lately. Some days back I ketched me a few bees off the cactus an' mesquite, figurin' to start a bee line. Well, I got her started, all right, an' I trailed them bees to a place far south o' here.

"South an' west, actually. Most o' this country hereabouts is worked out of bees. I been at it too long, so I was workin' a good ways off. Well, my bee line took me over toward the Hogback. You know that place?

"She's a high curvin' ridge maybe five or six hundred feet at the crest, but she rises mighty close to straight up for four hundred feet. Crawlin' up there to locate the cave them bees was workin' out of, I come on a cave like a cliff dwellin', on'y it wasn't. She was man-made, an' most likely in the past twenty years or so.

"What started me really lookin' was my shovel—the one I lost. She was right there on that ledge, so I knowed it hadn't been lost, but stole off me. I began huntin' around. I found back inside this place it was all fixed up for livin'. Some grub there, blankets, a couple of guns, an' under some duffle in the corner, an old-time breastplate an' helmet."

"You're serious?" Kedrick demanded incredulously.

"Sure as I'm alive! But," Escavada chuckled, "that ain't the best of it. Lyin' there on the floor, deader'n last year's hopes, was a young feller. He had a knife, old-time Spanish knife that a feller in armor might have carried, an' it was skewered right th'ough him!"

"A young man—dead?" Kedrick suddenly leaned forward. "Anything odd about him? I mean, was he missing a thumb?"

Escavada stared. "Well now, if that don't beat all! He was missin' a thumb, an' he was crippled up mighty bad in the other arm. Carried her in a sling."

"Dornie Shaw!" Laredo leaped to his feet. "Dornie Shaw, by all that's holy!"

"Shaw?" Escavada puckered his brows, his old eyes gleaming. "Now that's most odd, most odd. Shaw was the name o' that boy, the one who didn't git killed with the wagon train!"

Kedrick's face was a study. Dornie Shaw—dead! But if Dornie had been the boy from the wagon train, that would account for his superstitious fear of the grulla mustang. But to suppose that after all these years Dornie had been killed by the same man, or ghost if one believed in ghosts, that killed the rest of them so many years before was too ridiculous. It was, he thought suddenly, unless you look at it just one way.

"Man can't escape his fate," Escavada said gloomily. "That boy hid out from that knife, but in the end it got him."

Kedrick got up. "Could you take us to that place, Escavada? Down there on the Hogback?"

"I reckon," He glanced outside. "But not in this rain. Rheumatiz gits me."

"Then tell me where it is," Kedrick said, "because I'm going now!"

They were crossing the head of Coal Mine Creek when Laredo saw the tracks. He drew up suddenly, pointing. The tracks of a horse, well shod. "The grulla!" Kedrick said grimly. "I'd know those tracks anywhere!"

They pushed on. It was very late, and the pelting rain still poured down upon their heads and shoulders. The trails were slippery, and dusk was near. "We'd better find us a hole to crawl into," Shad suggested. "We'll never find that horse in this weather!"

"By morning the tracks will be gone, and I've a hunch we'll find our man right in that cliff dwelling where Escavada saw Dornie's body!"

"Wonder how Dornie found the place?"

"If what I think is right," Kedrick replied, wiping the rain from his face, "he must have run into an old friend and been taken there to hide out. That old friend was the same rider of the grulla that killed his family and friends with the wagon train, and when he saw that armor, he knew it."

"But what's it all about?" Shad grumbled. "It don't make sense! An' no horse lives that long."

"Sure not. There may have been a half-dozen grullas in that length of time. This man probably tried to capitalize on the fears of the Indians and Mexicans who live up that way to keep them off his trail. We'll probably find the answer when we reach the end of our ride."

The Hogback loomed black and ominous before them. The trail, partly switchback and part sheer climb, led over the sharp, knifelike ridge. They mounted, their horses laboring heavily at the steep and slippery climb. Twice Tom Kedrick saw the tracks of the grulla on the trail, and in neither case could those tracks have been more than an hour old.

Kedrick glanced down when they saw the opposite side, then dismounted. "This one is tricky," he said grimly. "We'd better walk it."

Halfway down, lightning flashed, and in the momentary brightness, Laredo called out, "Watch it, Tom! High, right!"

Kedrick's head jerked around just as the rifle boomed. The

bullet smacked viciously against the rock beside him, spattering his face with splinters. He grabbed for his gun, but it was under his slicker. The gun boomed again, five fast shots, as fast as the marksman could work the lever of his rifle.

Behind Tom Kedrick the anguished scream of a wounded horse cut the night, and Shad's warning yell was drowned in the boom of the gun again. Then he flattened against the rock barely in time to avoid the plunging, screaming horse.

His own appaloosa, frightened, darted down the trail with the agility of a mountain goat. The rifle boomed again and Kedrick dropped flat.

"Shad? You all right?"

There was a moment before the reply, then it was hoarse, but calm. "Winged me, but not bad."

"I'm going after him. You all right?"

"Yeah. You might help me wrap this leg up."

Sheltered by the glistening, rain-wet rock, with gray mist swirling past them on the high ridge of the Hogback, Kedrick knelt in the rain. Shielding the bandage from the rain with a slicker, he bound the leg. The bullet had torn through the flesh, but the bone was not broken.

CHAPTER SEVENTEEN

WHEN THE WOUND was bandaged, Kedrick drew back into the shelter of the slight overhang and stared about. Ahead and below them was a sea of inky blackness. Somewhere down that mountain would be their horses, one probably dead or dying, the other possibly crippled.

Around them all was night and the high, windy, rain-wet rocks. And out there in the darkness a killer stalked them—a killer, who could at all of three hundred yards, spot his shots so well as to score two hits on a target seen only by a brief flash of lightning. Next time those shots could kill. And there was no doubt about it. Now the situation was clear. It was kill or be killed.

"Sure," Laredo said dryly, "you got to get him, man. But you watch it. He's no slouch with that Spencer!"

"You've got to get off this ridge," Kedrick insisted, "the cold and rain up here will kill you!"

"You leave that to me," Shad replied shortly. "I'll drag myself down the trail an' find a hole to crawl into down on the flat below this Hogback. Might even find your palouse down there. You got grub an coffee in those saddle bags?"

"Yeah, but you'd better not try a fire until I come back."

Shad chuckled. "Make sure you come back. I never did like to eat alone."

Slipping his hands under his slicker, through the pockets, Tom gripped his guns. His rifle, of course, was in his saddle scabbard. He was going to have to stalk a skilled killer—a fine marksman who was on his own ground—in absolute darkness with a hand gun. And the killer had a Spencer .56!

Lightning flashed, but there was no more shooting. Somewhere out there the killer was stalking them. He would not give up now, nor retreat. This, for him, was a last stand unless he killed them both. His hideout now was known, and if they escaped he would no longer be safe. That he did not intend to be driven from the country was already obvious by the fact that he had stayed this long.

Kedrick crawled out, using a bush to cover his movement. Working along the windy top of the ridge, he moved toward a nest of boulders he had seen ahead of him by the lightning flash. The wind whipped at his hat and flapped the skirt of his slicker. His right-hand gun was drawn, but under the slicker.

He crawled on. Lightning flashed and he flattened out on the rocks. But the Spencer bellowed, the bullet smashing his eyes and mouth full of gravel. Rolling over, he held his fire, spitting and pawing desperately at his blinded eyes.

There was no sound but the wind and rain, Then in the distance, thunder roared and rumbled off among the peaks. When the lightning flashed again, he looked out along the high ridge of the Hogback. Lashed by the driving rain, its rocks glistened like steel under clouds that seemed a scarce arm's length above Kedrick's head. Mist drifted by him, touching his wet face with a ghostly hand, and the weird white skeletons of long dead pines pointed their sharp and bony fingers toward the sky.

Rain pelted against his face, and he cowered, fearing the strike of a bullet at each flash of lightning, smelling the brimstone as the lightning scarred the high ridge with darting flame. He touched his lips with his tongue and stared until his eyes ached with strain.

His mouth was dry and his stomach empty, and something mounted within him. Fear? Panic? He could stay still no longer. With infinite patience, he edged forward, working his way a little over the edge of the ridge toward the hulking black clumps of some juniper, ragged trees, whipped to agonized shapes by generations of wind.

There was no sound but the storm, no sight of anything. He moved on, trying to estimate how far away the cliff house would be, to guess if he could reach it first or get between it and the killer out there. Flame stabbed the night and something burned sharply along his shoulders. He let go everything and rolled, went crashing down a dozen feet before he brought up in a tangle of dead limbs.

But the killer was not waiting. Suddenly he loomed dark on the crest. Crouching like a hunted animal, every instinct alert, Kedrick fired.

The dark figure jerked hard, and then the Spencer bellowed. The bullet plastered a branch near Kedrick, and he knew that only his own shot had saved his life. He fired again, and then deliberately hurled himself backward into the night, falling, landing, crawling. He got to his feet and plunged into the absolute darkness, risking a broken limb or a bad fall—anything to get the distance he needed. Then lightning flashed, and as if by magic the Spencer boomed. How the man had followed his plunging career he could not know, but he felt the stab and slam of the bullets as they smashed about him. This man was shooting too close. He couldn't miss long!

His shoulders burned, but whether that shot had been a real wound or a mere graze he did not know. Something fluid trickled down his spine. But whether it was rain water through the slit coat or his own blood, he could not guess.

He moved back, circling. Another shot, but this slightly to his left. Quickly he moved left and a shot smacked right near where he had been standing. The killer was using searching fire now, and he was getting closer.

Kedrick moved back, tripped and fell, and bullets laced the air over him. Evidently the man had a belt full of ammunition, or his pockets were stuffed.

Kedrick started to rise. This time his fingers found the hard smoothness not of rock, but of earth and gravel. Carefully, he felt about in the darkness.

The path! He was on a path, and no doubt the path to the cliff house.

He began to move along it, feeling his way carefully. Once, off to his left, he heard a rock roll. He took a chance and fired blind, then rolled over three times and felt the air split apart as the shots slammed the ground where he had been. He fired again, then again, always moving.

Lightning flashed, and he saw a hulking thing back on the trail the way he had come, a huge, glistening thing, black and shining. Flame sprang from it, and he felt the shock of the bullet, then steadied himself and fired again.

Deliberately then, he turned and worked his way down the path. Suddenly, he felt space before him, and found the path here took a sharp turn. Another step and he might have plunged off! How near was his escape he knew in another instant when lightning flashed and he saw far below him the gray-white figure of the appaloosa standing in the rain.

He worked his way down the cliff, then found a ledge and in a moment, his hands found the crude stone bricks of the cliff house. Feeling his way along it, he felt for the door, and then pushing it open he crawled into the inner darkness and pushed the door shut behind him.

After the lashing of wind and rain the peace seemed a miracle. Jerking off his soaking hat he tossed it aside, and threw off the slicker. There was a chance the killer would not guess that he knew of this place. Undoubtedly had Kedrick not known of it he would have passed it by in the darkness and storm.

Working his way along the floor he found a curtain dividing the first chamber from an inner room. He stepped through it and sat down hard on the bunk. Feeling for his left-hand gun he found the holster empty, and he had fired five shots with his right gun. Suddenly, the curtain stirred and there was a breath of wind. Then it vanished. The killer was in the other room. He had come in.

Kedrick dared not rise for fear the bed would creak. He heard a match strike, and then a candle was lighted. Feet shuffled in the other room. Then a voice. "I know you're in there, Kedrick. There's water on the floor in here. I'm behind a piece of old stone wall that I use for a sort of table. I'm safe from your fire. I know there's no protection where you are. Throw your guns out and come with your hands up! If you don't, I'm going to open fire an' search every inch of that room!''

Over the top of the blanket curtain which was suspended from a pole across the door, Tom Kedrick could see the roof in the other room. The cave house was actually much higher than need be. Evidently the killer had walled up an overhang or cave. Kedrick could see several heavy cedar beams that had served to support a ceiling now mostly gone. If that was true in the other room, it might be true in his also.

He straightened to his feet. He heard a sudden move and then fired.

From the other room came a chuckle. ''Figured that would draw fire! Well, one gun's empty. Now toss out the other an' come out. You haven't a chance!''

Kedrick did not reply. He was reaching up into the darkness over his head, feeling for the beams. He touched one, barely touched it, then reached up with both hands. He judged the distance he had to jump by the width of the beams in the other room.

What if it were old and would not support his weight? He had to chance that.

He jumped, his fingers hooked well over the edge and, soundlessly, he drew himself up. Now, Kedrick could see into the lighted room, but he could not locate the killer. The voice spoke again. ''I'm giving you no more time, Kedrick. Come out or I start to shoot! Toss that other gun first!''

Silence lay in the room, a silence broken by the sudden bellow of a gun. The killer fired, emptied a six-gun, then emptied another. Tom Kedrick waited, having no idea how many guns the man had, or what he might have planned for. Then six more carefully spaced shots were fired. One of them ricocheting dangerously close to Kedrick's head.

A long pause, and then a sound of movement. ''All right, if you're alive in there now, you got a shot comin' but if you want to give up, you can. I sort of want you alive.''

Suddenly the blanket was jerked from its moorings and Alton Burwick stood in the opening, a gun gripped in his fist, ready to fire.

Kedrick made no sound, and the man stared, then rushed into the room. Almost whining with fury, he jerked Kedrick's hat from the bed, then the slicker. As the latter fell to the floor, with it fell

Kedrick's other pistol, which falling from the holster had hooked into some tear in the slicker. He stared at it furiously, and then jerked the bed aside. Almost insane with anger, he searched, unbelieving and whining like an angry hound on a trail.

He stopped, his pent-up fury worn away and stood there, his chest heaving with his exertions, his fist gripping the pistol. "Gone! Gone!" he cried, as if bereft. "When I had him right here!"

Kedrick's fingers had found a tiny sliver of wood, and, deliberately, he snapped it against Burwick's cheek. The fat man jerked as if stung, then looked up. Their eyes met, and slowly he backed away, but now he was smiling. "Oh, you're a smart one, Kedrick. Very smart! Too bad it couldn't have been you with me instead of that weakling Keith. All front and show, but no bottom to him, no staying quality!

"But," he sighed, "I've got you anyway, and you'll suffer for what you've done." He scooped Kedrick's other pistol from the floor and backed away. "All right, get down!"

Kedrick dropped to the floor, and the fat man waved irritably at the gun he clutched. "No use to bluff. That's empty. Throw it down!"

"What's it all about, Burwick?" Tom asked suddenly. "Why this place? The armor? What about Dornie Shaw?"

"Ah? How did you know about that? But no matter, no matter." He backed to the wall, watching Kedrick and holding the gun. "Why, it was gold, boy! Gold, and lots of it! It was I who stirred those Indians up to attacking that caravan! I wanted the gold they carried, and most of it belonging to Dornie's pa!

"I knew about it! Followed them from Dodge. Knew when they drew it from the bank there, and how much!

"They fooled me though. When the Indians hit, they'd buried it somewhere. It could have been a lot of places, that was the trouble. They might have buried it sooner, but somewhere along the trail. I've dug and I've hunted, but I've never found it. Maybe I will someday—but nobody else is going to!

"Wondered why I wanted the land? Profit, sure! But I wanted this piece, a couple of sections in here, all for myself. Figured on that, working it out somehow. The gold's somewhere between here and Thieving Rock. Has to be."

Kedrick nodded. "That clears up a lot of things. Now you drop that gun, Burwick, and come as my prisoner."

Burwick chuckled fatly. "Try to bluff me? I'd of expected that from you! Nervy one, huh? Bet you got that Connie Duane, too! By the Lord Harry, there's a woman! No scare to her. Not one bit! Drop your gun, boy, or I'll put my first bullet through your knee cap!''

He was going to shoot, and Tom Kedrick knew it. Coolly, he squeezed off his own shot, an instant faster. He shot for the gun hand, but the bullet only skinned the thumb knuckle and hit Burwick in the side.

The fat man jerked and his face twisted, and he stared at the gun, lifting his own. Coolly, Kedrick fired again, then again. The bullets struck with an ugly smack, and Burwick wilted, the gun going from his limp fingers to the floor. Kedrick stepped in and caught him, easing him down. The flabby cheeks were suddenly sagging and old. Bitterly, the man stared upward at him. ''What happened? That—that—?''

''The gun was a Walch twelve-shot Navy pistol,'' Tom explained. ''I started carrying them a few days ago, replacing the .44 Russians.''

Burwick stared at him, no hatred in his eyes. ''Smart!'' he said. ''Smart! Always one trick better than me, or anybody! You'll—do, boy!''

On the streets of Mustang the sun was warm after the rain. Tom Kedrick, wounded again but walking, stood beside Connie Duane. Shad was grinning at them. ''Look mighty fine in that tailored suit, Tom. You goin' to be gone long?''

''Not us! We'll be married in Santa Fe, and then we're headin' for the Mogollons and that ranch.''

''Seems a shame not to hunt for that gold,'' Laredo complained. ''But anyway, the real treasure was that box full of Burwick's papers. Sure made Cummings hunt his hole. But I do regret that gold.''

''I don't,'' Connie replied, ''it's caused too much trouble. Alton Burwick spent his life and a good many other lives after it. Let it stay where it is. Maybe a better man will find it, one who needs it more than we do.''

''Gosh!'' Laredo said suddenly. ''I got to light a shuck! I'm late to meet Sue! So long, then!'' They watched him go, waiting for the stage.

Everything was quiet in Mustang—three whole days without a killing.